Bernard Cornwell was born in London and raised in South Essex. Having graduated from London University, he worked for BBC TV for seven years, mostly as a producer on the *Nationwide* programme, before taking charge of the Current Affairs department for the BBC in Northern Ireland. In 1978 he became editor of Thames Television's *Thames at Six*. He is married to an American and now lives in the USA.

By Bernard Cornwell

The Sharpe novels
(in chronological order)

The Starbuck Chronicles

BERNARD CORNWELL

Battle Flag

The Bloody Ground

Grafton

HarperCollins*Publishers*
77-85 Fulham Palace Road
Hammersmith, London W6 8JB

www.harpercollins.co.uk

This omnibus edition published in 2004
by HarperCollins*Publishers*

Battle Flag
Copyright © Bernard Cornwell 1995

The Bloody Ground
Copyright © Bernard Cornwell 1996

The author asserts the moral right
to be identified as the author of these works

ISBN 0 007 71206 5

Set in Goudy

Printed and bound in Great Britain by
Mackays of Chatham plc, Chatham, Kent

Battle Flag

Battle Flag
is for my father, with love

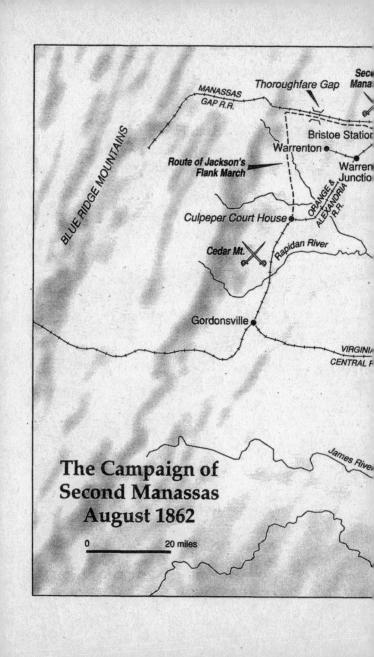

MANASSAS GAP R.R.

Thoroughfare Gap

Sec[..]
Mana[..]

Bristoe Station

Warrenton

Warren[..]
Junctio[..]

BLUE RIDGE MOUNTAINS

**Route of Jackson's
Flank March**

ORANGE &
ALEXANDRIA
R.R.

Culpeper Court House

Cedar Mt.

Rapidan River

Gordonsville

VIRGINIA
CENTRAL R[..]

James River

The Campaign of
Second Manassas
August 1862

0   20 miles

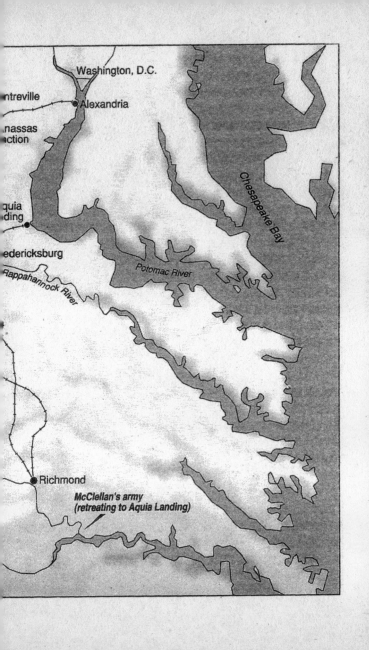

PART ONE

CAPTAIN NATHANIEL STARBUCK first saw his new commanding general when the Faulconer Legion forded the Rapidan. Thomas Jackson was on the river's northern bank, where he appeared to be in a trance, for he was motionless in his saddle with his left hand held high in the air while his eyes, blue and resentful, stared into the river's vacant and murky depths. His glum stillness was so uncanny that the marching column edged to the far margin of the ford rather than pass near a man whose stance so presaged death. The General's physical appearance was equally disturbing. Jackson had a ragged beard, a plain coat, and a dirty cap, while his horse looked as if it should have been taken to a slaughterhouse long before. It was hard to credit that this was the South's most controversial general, the man who gave the North sleepless nights and nervous days, but Lieutenant Franklin Coffman, sixteen years old and newly arrived in the Faulconer Legion, asserted that the odd-looking figure was indeed the famous Stonewall Jackson. Coffman had once been taught by Professor Thomas Jackson. "Mind you," Lieutenant Coffman confided in Starbuck, "I don't believe generals make any real difference to battles."

"Such wisdom in one so young," said Starbuck, who was twenty-two years old.

"It's the men who win battles, not generals," Coffman said, ignoring his Captain's sarcasm. Lieutenant

Coffman had received one year's schooling at the Virginia Military Institute, where Thomas Jackson had ineffectively lectured him in artillery drill and Natural Philosophy. Now Coffman looked at the rigid figure sitting motionless in the shabby saddle. "I can't imagine old Square Box as a general," Coffman said scornfully. "He couldn't keep a schoolroom in order, let alone an army."

"Square Box?" Starbuck asked. General Jackson had many nicknames. The newspapers called him Stonewall, his soldiers called him Old Jack or even Old Mad Jack, while many of Old Jack's former students liked to refer to him as Tom Fool Jack, but Square Box was a name new to Starbuck.

"He's got the biggest feet in the world," Coffman explained. "Really huge! And the only shoes that ever fitted him were like boxes."

"What a fount of useful information you are, Lieutenant," Starbuck said casually. The Legion was still too far from the river for Starbuck to see the General's feet, but he made a mental note to look at these prodigies when he did finally reach the Rapidan. The Legion was presently not moving at all, its progress halted by the reluctance of the men ahead to march straight through the ford without first removing their tattered boots. Mad Jack Stonewall Square Box Jackson was reputed to detest such delays, but he seemed oblivious to this holdup. Instead he just sat, hand in the air and eyes on the river, while right in front of him the column bunched and halted. The men behind the obstruction were grateful for the enforced halt, for the day was blistering hot, the air motionless, and the heat as damp as steam. "You were remarking, Coffman, on the ineffectiveness of generals?" Starbuck prompted his new junior officer.

"If you think about it, sir," Coffman said with a youthful passion, "we haven't got any real generals, not like the

4

Yankees, but we still win battles. I reckon that's because the Southerner is unbeatable."

"What about Robert Lee?" Starbuck asked. "Isn't he a real general?"

"Lee's old! He's antediluvian!" Coffman said, shocked that Starbuck should even have suggested the name of the new commander of the Army of Northern Virginia. "He must be fifty-five, at least!"

"Jackson's not old," Starbuck pointed out. "He isn't even forty yet."

"But he's mad, sir. Honest! We used to call him Tom Fool."

"He must be mad then," Starbuck teased Coffman. "So why do we win battles despite having mad generals, ancient generals, or no generals at all?"

"Because fighting is in the Southern blood, sir. It really is." Coffman was an eager young man who was determined to be a hero. His father had died of consumption, leaving his mother with four young sons and two small daughters. His father's death had forced Coffman to leave the Virginia Military Institute after his first year, but that one year's military schooling had equipped him with a wealth of martial theories. "Northerners," he now explained to Starbuck, "have diluted blood. There are too many immigrants in the North, sir. But the South has pure blood, sir. Real American blood."

"You mean the Yankees are an inferior race?"

"It's an acknowledged fact, sir. They've lost the thoroughbred strain, sir."

"You do know I'm a Yankee, Coffman, don't you?" Starbuck asked.

Coffman immediately looked confused, though before he could frame any response he was interrupted by Colonel Thaddeus Bird, the Faulconer Legion's commanding officer,

5

who came striding long-legged from the rear of the stalled column. "Is that really Jackson?" Bird asked, gazing across the river.

"Lieutenant Coffman informs me that the General's real name is Old Mad Tom Fool Square Box Jackson, and that is indeed the man himself," Starbuck answered.

"Ah, Coffman," Bird said, peering down at the small Lieutenant as though Coffman was some curious specimen of scientific interest, "I remember when you were nothing but a chirruping infant imbibing the lesser jewels of my glittering wisdom." Bird, before he became a soldier, had been the schoolmaster in Faulconer Court House, where Coffman's family lived.

"Lieutenant Coffman has not ceased to imbibe wisdom," Starbuck solemnly informed Colonel Bird, "nor indeed to impart it, for he has just informed me that we Yankees are an inferior breed, our blood being soured, tainted, and thinned by the immigrant strain."

"Quite right, too!" Bird said energetically; then the Colonel draped a thin arm around the diminutive Coffman's shoulders. "I could a tale unfold, young Coffman, whose lightest word would harrow up thy soul, freeze thy young blood, and make thy two eyes, like stars, start from their spheres." He spoke even more closely into the ear of the astonished Lieutenant. "Did you know, Coffman, that the very moment an immigrant boat docks in Boston all the Beacon Hill families send their wives down to the harbor to be impregnated? Is that not the undeniable truth, Starbuck?"

"Indeed it is, sir, and they send their daughters as well if the boat arrives on the Sabbath."

"Boston is a libidinous town, Coffman," Bird said very sternly as he stepped away from the wide-eyed Lieutenant, "and if I am to give you just one piece of advice in this sad

6

bad world, then let it be to avoid the place. Shun it, Coffman! Regard Boston as you might regard Sodom or Gomorrah. Remove it from your catalog of destinations. Do you understand me, Coffman?"

"Yes, sir," Coffman said very seriously.

Starbuck laughed at the look on his Lieutenant's face. Coffman had arrived the day before with a draft of conscripted men to replace the casualties of Gaines' Mill and Malvern Hill. The conscripts had mostly been culled from the alleys of Richmond and, to Starbuck, appeared to be a scrawny, unhealthy, and shifty-looking crew of dubious reliability, but Franklin Coffman, like the original members of the Legion, was a volunteer from Faulconer County and full of enthusiasm for the Southern cause.

Colonel Bird now abandoned his teasing of the Lieutenant and plucked at Starbuck's sleeve. "Nate," he said, "a word." The two men walked away from the road, crossing a shallow ditch into a meadow that was wan and brown from the summer's heat wave. Starbuck limped, not because he was wounded, but because the sole of his right boot was becoming detached from its uppers. "Is it me?" Bird asked as the two men paced across the dry grass. "Am I getting wiser or is it that the young are becoming progressively more stupid? And young Coffman, believe it if you will, was brighter than most of the infants it was my misfortune to teach. I remember he mastered the theory of gerunds in a single morning!"

"I'm not sure I ever mastered gerunds," Starbuck said.

"Hardly difficult," Bird said, "so long as you remember that they are nouns which provide—"

"And I'm not sure I ever want to master the damn things," Starbuck interrupted.

"Wallow in your ignorance, then," Bird said grandly. "But you're also to look after young Coffman. I couldn't bear to write to his mother and tell her he's dead, and I have a horrid feeling that he's likely to prove stupidly brave. He's like a puppy. Tail up, nose wet, and can't wait to play battles with Yankees."

"I'll look after him, Pecker."

"But you're also to look after yourself," Bird said meaningfully. He stopped and looked into Starbuck's eyes. "There's a rumor, only a rumor, and God knows I do not like passing on rumors, but this one has an unpleasant ring to it. Swynyard was heard to say that you won't survive the next battle."

Starbuck dismissed the prediction with a grin. "Swynyard's a drunk, not a prophet." Nevertheless he felt a shudder of fear. He had been a soldier long enough to become inordinately superstitious, and no man liked to hear a presentiment of his own death.

"Suppose," Bird said, taking two cigars from inside his hatband, "that Swynyard has decided to arrange it?"

Starbuck stared incredulously at his Colonel. "Arrange my death?" he finally asked.

Bird scratched a lucifer match alight and stooped over its flame. "Colonel Swynyard," he announced dramatically when his cigar was drawing properly, "is a drunken swine, a beast, a cream-faced loon, a slave of nature, and a son of hell, but he is also, Nate, a most cunning rogue, and when he is not in his cups he must realize that he is losing the confidence of our great and revered leader. Which is why he must now try to do something which will please our esteemed lord and master. Get rid of you." The last four words were delivered brutally.

Starbuck laughed them off. "You think Swynyard will shoot me in the back?"

Bird gave Starbuck the lit cigar. "I don't know how he'll kill you. All I know is that he'd like to kill you, and that

8

Faulconer would like him to kill you, and for all I know our esteemed General is prepared to award Swynyard a healthy cash bonus if he succeeds in killing you. So be careful, Nate, or else join another regiment."

"No," Starbuck said immediately. The Faulconer Legion was his home. He was a Bostonian, a Northerner, a stranger in a strange land who had found in the Legion a refuge from his exile. The Legion provided Starbuck with casual kindnesses and a hive of friends, and those bonds of affection were far stronger than the distant enmity of Washington Faulconer. That enmity had grown worse when Faulconer's son Adam had deserted from the Southern army to fight for the Yankees, a defection for which Brigadier General Faulconer blamed Captain Starbuck, but not even the disparity in their ranks could persuade Starbuck to abandon his fight against the man who had founded the Legion and who now commanded the five regiments, including the Legion, that made up the Faulconer Brigade. "I've got no need to run away," he now told Bird. "Faulconer won't last any longer than Swynyard. Faulconer's a coward and Swynyard's a drunk, and before this summer's out, Pecker, you'll be Brigade commander and I'll be in command of the Legion."

Bird hooted with delight. "You are incorrigibly conceited, Nate. You! Commanding the Legion? I imagine Major Hinton and the dozen other men senior to you might have a different opinion."

"They might be senior, but I'm the best."

"Ah, you still suffer from the delusion that merit is rewarded in this world? I suppose you contracted that opinion with all the other nonsense they crammed into you when Yale was failing to give you mastery of the gerund?" Bird, achieving this lick at Starbuck's *alma mater*, laughed gleefully. His head jerked back and forth as he laughed, the odd jerking motion explaining his nickname: Pecker.

9

Starbuck joined in the laughter, for he, like just about everyone else in the Legion, liked Bird enormously. The schoolmaster was eccentric, opinionated, contrary, and one of the kindest men alive. He had also proved to possess an unexpected talent for soldiering. "We move at last," Bird now said, gesturing at the stalled column that had begun edging toward the ford where the solitary, strange figure of Jackson waited motionless on his mangy horse. "You owe me two dollars," Bird suddenly remarked as he led Starbuck back to the road.

"Two dollars!"

"Major Hinton's fiftieth birthday approaches. Lieutenant Pine assures me he can procure a ham, and I shall prevail on our beloved leader for some wine. We are paying for a feast."

"Is Hinton really that old?" Starbuck asked.

"He is indeed, and if you live that long we shall doubtless give you a drunken dinner as a reward. Have you got two bucks?"

"I haven't got two cents," Starbuck said. He had some money in Richmond, but that money represented his cushion against disaster and was not for frittering away on ham and wine.

"I shall lend you the money," Bird said with a rather despairing sigh. Most of the Legion's officers had private means, but Colonel Bird, like Starbuck, was forced to live on the small wages of a Confederate officer.

The men of Company H stood as Starbuck and Bird approached the road, though one of the newly arrived conscripts stayed prone on the grass verge and complained he could not march another step. His reward was a kick in the ribs from Sergeant Truslow. "You can't do that to me!" the man protested, scrabbling sideways to escape the Sergeant.

Truslow grabbed the man's jacket and pulled his face close in to his own. "Listen, you son of a poxed bitch, I can

10

slit your slumbelly guts wide open and sell them to the Yankees for hog food if I want, and not because I'm a sergeant and you're a private, but because I'm a mean son of a bitch and you're a lily-livered louse. Now get the hell up and march."

"What comfortable words the good Sergeant speaks," Bird said as he jumped back across the dry ditch. He drew on his cigar. "So I can't persuade you to join another regiment, Nate?"

"No, sir."

Pecker Bird shook his head ruefully. "I think you're a fool, Nate, but for God's sake be a careful fool. For some odd reason I'd be sorry to lose you."

"Fall in!" Truslow shouted.

"I'll take care," Starbuck promised as he rejoined his company. His thirty-six veterans were lean, tanned, and ragged. Their boots were falling to pieces, their gray jackets were patched with common brown cloth, and their worldly possessions reduced to what a man could carry suspended from his rope belt or sling in a rolled blanket across his shoulder. The twenty conscripts made an awkward contrast in their new uniforms, clumsy leather brogans, and stiff knapsacks. Their faces were pale and their rifle muzzles unblackened by firing. They knew this northward march through the central counties of Virginia probably meant an imminent battle, but what that battle would bring was a mystery, while the veterans knew only too well that a fight would mean screaming and blood and hurt and pain and thirst, but maybe, too, a cache of plundered Yankee dollars or a bag of real coffee taken from a festering, maggot-riddled Northern corpse. "March on!" Starbuck shouted, and fell in beside Lieutenant Franklin Coffman at the head of the company.

"You see if I'm not right, sir," Coffman said. "Old Mad Jack's got feet bigger than a plowhorse."

11

As Starbuck marched into the ford, he looked at the General's feet. They were indeed enormous. So were Jackson's hands. But what was most extraordinary of all was why the General still held his left hand in midair like a child begging permission to leave a schoolroom. Starbuck was about to ask Coffman for an explanation when, astonishingly, the General stirred. He looked up from the water, and his gaze focused on Starbuck's company. "Coffman!" he called in an abrupt, high-pitched voice. "Come here, boy."

Coffman stumbled out of the ford and half ran to the General's side. "Sir?"

The ragged-bearded Jackson frowned down from his saddle. "Do you remember me, Coffman?"

"Yes, sir, of course I do, sir."

Jackson lowered his left hand very gently, as though he feared he might damage the arm if he moved it fast. "I was sorry you had to leave the Institute early, Coffman. It was after your plebe year, was it not?"

"Yes, sir. It was, sir."

"Because your father died?"

"Yes, sir."

"And your mother, Coffman? She's well?"

"Indeed, sir. Yes, sir, thank you, sir."

"Bereavement is a terrible affliction, Coffman," the General observed, then slowly unbent his rigid posture to lean toward the slim, fair-haired Lieutenant, "especially for those who are not in a state of grace. Are you in a state of grace, Coffman?"

Coffman blushed, frowned, then managed to nod. "Yes, sir. I think I am, sir."

Jackson straightened again into his poker-backed stance and, as slowly as he had lowered his left hand, raised it once more into midair. He lifted his eyes from Coffman to stare into the heat-hazed distance. "You will find it a very hard thing to meet your Maker if you are unsure of His grace," the General said in a kindly voice, "so study your scriptures and recite your prayers, boy."

"Yes, sir, I will, sir," Coffman said. He stood awkward and uncertain, waiting for the General to speak further, but Jackson seemed in his trance once again, and so the Lieutenant turned and walked back to Starbuck's side. The Legion marched on, and the Lieutenant remained silent as the road climbed between small pastures and straggling woods and beside modest farms. It was a good two miles before Coffman at last broke his silence. "He's a great man," the Lieutenant said, "isn't he, sir? Isn't he a great man?"

"Tom Fool?" Starbuck teased Coffman.

"A great man, sir," Coffman chided Starbuck.

"If you say so," Starbuck said, though all he knew about Jackson was that Old Mad Jack had a great reputation for marching, and that when Old Mad Jack went marching, men died. And they were marching now, marching north, and going north meant one thing only: Yankees ahead. Which meant there would be a battle soon, and a field of graves after the battle, and this time, if Pecker was right, Starbuck's enemies would not just be in front of him but behind as well. Starbuck marched on. A fool going to battle.

The midday train stopped at Manassas Junction amidst a clash of cars, the hissing of steam, and the clangor of the locomotive's bell. Sergeants' voices rose over the mechanical din, urging troops out of the cars and onto the strip of dirt that lay between the rails and the warehouses. The soldiers jumped down, glad to be free of the cramped cars and excited to be in Virginia. Manassas Junction might not be the fighting front, but it was still a part of a rebel state, and so they peered about themselves as though the landscape

13

was as wondrous and strange as the misty hills of mysterious Japan or far Cathay.

The arriving troops were mostly seventeen- and eighteen-year-old boys come from New Jersey and Wisconsin, from Maine and Illinois, from Rhode Island and Vermont. They were volunteers, newly uniformed and eager to join this latest assault on the Confederacy. They boasted of hanging Jeff Davis from an apple tree, and bragged of how they would march through Richmond and roust the rebels out of their nests like rats from a granary. They were young and indestructible, full of confidence, but also awed by the savagery of this strange destination.

For Manassas Junction was not an inviting place. It had been sacked once by Northern troops, destroyed again by retreating Confederates, then hastily rebuilt by Northern contractors, so that now there were acres of gaunt, raw-timbered warehouses standing between rail sidings and weed-filled meadows that were crammed with guns and limbers and caissons and portable forges and ambulances and wagons. More stores and weapons arrived every hour, for this was the supply depot that would fuel the summer campaign of 1862 that would end the rebellion and so restore a United States of America. The great spread of buildings was shadowed by an ever-present pall of greasy smoke that came from blacksmiths' shops and locomotive repair sheds and the fireboxes of the locomotives that dragged in their goods wagons and passenger cars.

Two cavalry officers waited at the depot. They had clearly gone to some considerable effort to make themselves presentable, for their uniform coats were brushed spotless, their spurred boots were shining, and their leather belts polished. The older man was middle-aged and balding, with a pleasant face and thick muttonchop whiskers. His name was Major Joseph Galloway, and he clutched a plumed hat in his

14

nervous hands. His companion was a much younger man, handsome and fair-haired, with a square beard and wide shoulders and an open face that inspired trust. His coat showed a captain's bars.

Both men were Virginians, yet both fought for the North. Joseph Galloway owned property just outside Manassas itself, and that farm was now the depot for a regiment of Northern cavalry exclusively recruited from Southerners loyal to the government in Washington. Most of the troopers for Galloway's Horse were volunteers from the border states, the disputed lands of Maryland, and the western counties of Virginia, but a good number were refugees from the Confederate States themselves. Galloway had no doubt that some of his men were fugitives from Southern justice, but the majority were idealists who fought to preserve the Union, and it had been Major Galloway's notion to recruit such men for reconnaissance work deep behind the rebel lines. Northern horsemen were solid and brave, but they rode the Virginian countryside as strangers, and in consequence they were timid compared to the rakehell Southerners who knew that every Virginian village and hamlet contained sympathizers prepared to hide and feed them. It had been Galloway's inspiration to raise a regiment that could ride the rebel states like native Southerners, yet the idea had received only lukewarm support from Washington. Raise the regiment, the government's bureaucrats had told Major Galloway, and we might deign to employ it, but only if it came properly equipped with weapons, horses, and uniforms.

Which was why Major Galloway and Captain Adam Faulconer now waited for a passenger who was supposed to have arrived on the midday train that had just steamed into Manassas. The two cavalry officers worked their way against the flood of excited soldiers toward the train's last car, which had been reserved for passengers more exalted than mere cannon fodder. A porter lowered the carriage steps, and two ladies, their hooped skirts scarce able to squeeze through the car's narrow doorway, were handed down. After the ladies came a group of senior officers, their mustaches trimmed, their uniforms brushed, and their faces flush from the day's heat and from their consumption of the railroad's whiskey. One officer, younger than the rest, broke away and shouted at some orderlies to bring horses. "Chop, chop now! Horses for the General!" the aide shouted. The ladies' twin parasols bobbed white and lacy through the mist of tobacco smoke and the crush of dark military hats.

The last man to alight from the passenger car was a thin, tall, and elderly civilian with white hair and beard, fierce eyes, and a gaunt, stern face. He had sunken cheeks, a Roman nose as imperious as his gaze, a black frock coat, a top hat, and despite the heat, a high-buttoned vest over which a pair of starched Geneva bands hung white. He carried a dark maroon carpetbag and an ebony stick that he used to push aside a black servant who was lifting the ladies' cabin trunks onto a handcart. The gesture was peremptory and unthinking, the act of a man accustomed to authority.

"That's him," Adam said, recognizing the minister whom he had heard preach in Boston just before the war began.

Major Galloway pushed through the crowd toward the white-haired man. "Sir?" he called to the newly arrived preacher. "Doctor Starbuck, sir?"

The Reverend Elial Joseph Starbuck, Doctor of Divinity, pamphleteer, and the most famous of all the North's abolitionist preachers, scowled at his welcomers. "You must be Galloway. And you're Faulconer? Good! My bag." He thrust the carpetbag into Adam's hand, which had been stretched out for a handshake.

16

"You had a pleasant journey, I trust, sir?" Major Galloway inquired as he ushered his guest toward the roadway.

"It became successively less pleasant, Galloway, as I journeyed south. I am forced to conclude that engineering has reached its apotheosis in New England and that the further one journeys from Boston the less comfortable the conveyance." The Reverend Starbuck delivered these judgments in a voice trained to reach the deepest recesses of the largest churches and lecture halls in America. "The Southern rails, I must say, are distinctly lumpy. The degraded product, no doubt, of a Slavocracy. Am I expected to walk to my destination?" the Reverend Starbuck demanded, suddenly stopping dead in his tracks.

"No, sir. I have a buggy." Galloway was about to request that Adam go fetch the carriage, then realized Adam was too encumbered with the preacher's heavy carpetbag. "I'll fetch it directly, sir. It isn't far."

The Reverend Starbuck waved Galloway on his way, then peered with a fierce inquisitiveness at a group of civilians waiting for the mail to be unloaded from the newly arrived caboose. "Have you read Spurzheim on phrenology?" he demanded of Adam.

"No, sir," Adam responded, surprised by the fiercely abrupt question.

"Science has much to teach us," the Reverend Doctor Starbuck declaimed, "so long as we remember that its conclusions are ever subject to the approval and emendations of Almighty God, but I am interested to observe these proofs of Spurzheim's treatise." He waved his stick toward the waiting civilians. "The New Englander generally possesses a noble brow shape. He displays cranial contours that denote intelligence, benevolence, wisdom, and adhesiveness, but even in these upper regions of the South I notice how the shape of men's skulls betrays depravity, combativeness,

17

destructiveness, and a distinct tendency toward cretinism."

Adam's torturing conscience, like his ingrained patriotism, might have driven him to fight against his father's land, yet he was still a native son of Virginia, and the Northern preacher's criticism made him bridle. "Was not George Washington a Southerner, sir?" he demanded stiffly.

But the Reverend Starbuck was too old a controversialist to be trapped into recantation. "George Washington, young man, like yourself, was a product of the gentry. My observations are confined solely to the common ruck of people. The general there, you see him?" The peremptory stick, narrowly missing an artillery sergeant, pointed at a plump officer who had shared the passenger car with the Reverend Starbuck.

"I see him, sir," Adam said, wondering what characteristics the general's skull shape revealed.

But the Reverend Starbuck had abandoned the subject of phrenology. "That is Pope," the preacher announced. "He was good enough to pay me his respects during the journey. A fine-looking man, indeed."

Adam looked with interest at this new commander of the North's Army of Virginia. General John Pope was a high-colored and confident-looking man with intelligent eyes and a bushy beard. If phrenology did provide an accurate guide to a man's character, then Pope's broad forehead and solid, square appearance suggested that he might indeed be the savior that the North had been seeking ever since the war's sad beginning. John Pope had distinguished himself in the fighting on the Mississippi and had now been brought east to work his magic in the intransigent Virginian countryside where Northern general after Northern general had first been bamboozled and then beaten by the ragged rebel armies.

"Pope has the right ideas," the Reverend Starbuck went on enthusiastically. "It's no good being kind to rebels.

18

Disobedience calls for punishment, and defiance demands retribution. The Slavocracy must be smitten, Faulconer, and its lands laid waste. Pope won't stay his hand, he assures me of that. He is a man for the Lord's work." And indeed, General Pope, almost as soon as he had been appointed commander of the Army of Virginia, had declared that the old policy of treating Southern civilians with respect was finished. Northern soldiers would henceforth take what they needed from the Southern population, and any Southerner who resisted such depredations would be punished. The Reverend Elial Starbuck applauded Pope's zeal. "The Southerner," the preacher now lectured Adam, "understands only one language. Brute force. It is the language he has used to oppress the Negro, and it is the language that must now be used to oppress him. You agree?"

"I think, sir," Adam said tactfully, "that the North must gain victory very soon."

"Quite so, quite so," the Reverend Starbuck said, not certain whether he had received agreement or not. He certainly deserved agreement, for it was upon the Reverend Starbuck's generosity that both the future of Adam and of Galloway's Horse depended. Adam had been penniless when he deserted the South, but it had been his good fortune to know Major James Starbuck, the preacher's eldest son, and it had been James who had informed Adam about Galloway's Horse and who had suggested that his famous father might be able to provide Adam with the necessary funds to join the regiment.

The Reverend Doctor Starbuck had proved more than willing to advance the money. Too old to fight, yet too passionate to abstain from fighting, he had watched, impotent, as the North suffered defeat after defeat in Virginia. The defeats had stirred the Reverend Starbuck into contributing his own and his church's money to the raising and equipping

19

of Massachusetts regiments, only to see those regiments led to disaster. Other men, lesser men, might have abandoned their efforts, but the disasters only fed the preacher's zeal, which was why, given the chance to contribute to the establishment of Galloway's Horse, the Reverend Starbuck had been quick to agree. He was not only supporting Adam but donating fifteen thousand dollars' worth of weaponry and ammunition to Galloway's regiment. The money was not the Reverend Starbuck's own but had been raised by God-fearing New England abolitionists. "In the past," he told Galloway and Adam as they journeyed westward from Manassas in the buggy, "we used such charitable donations for our work in the South: distributing tracts, establishing Sabbath schools for blacks, and, of course, conducting investigations into the evils of the Slavocracy, but now, cut off from those activities, our charities need other outlets for their expenditure."

"There's surely much to be spent on the welfare of escaped slaves?" Adam asked, hoping at the same time that he was not talking Galloway and himself out of their funding.

"The contrabands are amply provided for. Amply!" The Reverend Starbuck's disapproving tone suggested that those slaves who had managed to escape to the North were living in pampered luxury rather than struggling for insanitary survival in makeshift camps. "We need to strike a blow at the root of slavery, not pluck a few diseased leaves from its topmost branches." Adam, hearing the anger behind the preacher's words, suspected that the Reverend Elial Starbuck was much keener to punish the slaveholders than actually free the slaves.

The buggy climbed the shallow hill from New Market, passed between deep woods, then plunged downhill toward the Warrenton Turnpike. As Major Galloway drove, he pointed out landmarks made famous in the battle that had been fought the previous summer across this same ground. There were the ruins of the house where Surgeon Henry's widow had died in the shell fire, and there the Matthews house, which had been used as a hospital. As the buggy rattled down the Sudley road north of the turnpike, Galloway pointed to where the Northern flank attack had come from the river's far side, but as he talked he became aware that the Boston preacher was hardly enthusiastic in his responses. The Reverend Doctor Starbuck did not want a guided tour of the place where the North had met its first defeat; he only wanted to hear promises of victory, and so the conversation died away as Galloway steered the buggy onto the track leading to the farm he had inherited from his father.

Major Galloway, a kindly man, was nervous around the famous abolitionist and relieved when the Reverend Starbuck announced that he had no intention of staying overnight at the comfortable farm, but instead intended to take the evening train south to Culpeper Court House. "My friend Banks did the courtesy of inviting me," the preacher said, referring to General Nathaniel Banks, who had once been Governor of Massachusetts and was now a Union general who believed that a visit from his old friend would serve to encourage his troops' flagging spirits. The invitation had certainly done wonders for the preacher's spirits. He had been chafing in Boston, taking his war news from newspapers and letters, but now he could learn for himself exactly what was happening in Virginia, to which end he had arranged to be absent from his pulpit for the whole month of August. He was fervently praying that a month would be long enough to allow him to be the first Northern minister to preach the gospel from a Richmond pulpit.

But before joining Banks the preacher had agreed to this meeting with Major Galloway and his men. He spoke to Galloway's regiment in the meadow behind the house, where he encouraged them to fight the good fight, but his brusque manner made it plain that he was in a hurry to conclude the day's business and continue his journey. Major Galloway tactfully abandoned the planned display of saber fighting and instead conducted his guest toward the farmhouse, which was an impressive building shaded by great oaks and lapped by wide lawns. "My father prospered in the law," Galloway said, explaining the luxurious house.

"A slave owner, too?" the preacher demanded fiercely, pointing with his ebony cane at the small cabins that lay to the north of the house.

"I freed all the people," Galloway said hastily. "If I'd sold them, sir," he went on, "I wouldn't be needing to beg money for the regiment. I mortgaged the farm to raise funds, sir, and used all the money to buy the horses and weapons you've just seen, but frankly, sir, I've no resources left. I've made myself penniless in the cause of liberty."

"In which cause we must all be prepared to suffer, Galloway," the Reverend Starbuck exclaimed as he followed the Major up the veranda steps and into the hallway. The house echoed like an empty building, which it very nearly was, for with the exception of a few essential pieces of furniture Galloway had sent all his books and pictures and drapes and ornaments north into storage so that his rebellious neighbors could not take revenge on his allegiance by stealing his valuables. And if his neighbors did not steal the goods, he explained, his own brother would. "My brother fights for the South, alas," Major Galloway told the preacher, "and he'd like nothing more than to take the house and its contents from me." He paused for an instant. "There's nothing sadder, sir, is there, than family members fighting on opposite sides?" The Reverend Starbuck offered a belligerent grunt as answer, and that ill-tempered noise should have warned Major Galloway against proceeding further with the conversation, but the Major was a guileless man. "Am I right, sir," Galloway asked, "in believing you have a son who fights with the rebels?"

"I know of no such person," the preacher said, stiffening perceptibly.

"But Nate, surely—" Adam began, only to be fiercely interrupted.

"I have no son called Nathaniel," the preacher snapped. "I recognize no person called Nathaniel Starbuck. He is doomed, he is cast out, not only from my family, but also from the loving congregation of Christ! He is a reprobate!" This last condemnation was trumpeted in a voice that might have carried a half-mile into a mighty wind.

Galloway realized he had been tactless and so hurried on, talking inconsequentially about the house and its amenities until he reached the doors of the library, where a tall, heavyset Captain waited. The Captain had a ready smile and a quick, friendly manner. "May I introduce my second-in-command?" Galloway said to the preacher. "Captain William Blythe."

"Sure glad to meet you, Reverend." Blythe extended a hand.

"Captain Blythe was a horse trader before the war," Galloway said.

"You should never have told the minister that, Joe!" Blythe said with a smile. "Everyone knows that us horse traders are the crookedest folks this side of tarnation, but God bless me, sir"—he had turned back to the preacher—"I tried to be as honest a trader as a Christian man could."

"I'm glad to hear it," the Reverend Starbuck said stiffly.

"A hundred cents to an honest dollar, sir, that was always my way," Blythe said cheerfully, "and if I ever rooked a man, sir, why it was never on purpose. And I'll tell you another thing, sir." Blythe dropped his voice confidingly. "If ever a man of the cloth wanted a horse, why sir, I swallowed the profit and sometimes a good bit more besides. I confess I was never a churchgoing man myself, sir, to my regret, but my pa always contended that a bucketful of prayer never hurt no one and my dear ma, God bless her dear soul, fair wore out her knees on the church planking. And she sure would have liked to hear you speaking, sir, for they all say you do a mighty sermon!"

The Reverend Starbuck seemed pleased by Blythe's forthright and friendly manner, so pleased that he did not even show a sign of distaste when the tall Captain draped an arm around his shoulders to conduct him into the bare-shelved library. "You say you're not a churchgoing man," the preacher inquired, "but I trust you are saved, Captain?"

Blythe released his grip so that he could turn an astonished face to the Reverend Starbuck. "Washed white in the blood of the lamb, Reverend," Blythe said in a voice that suggested shock that anyone might have taken him for a heathen. "In fact I'm fair swilled in that precious blood, sir. My dear ma made sure of that before she died, praise the Lord and God rest her dear soul."

"And your mother, Captain, would approve of your allegiance in this war?" the Reverend Starbuck asked.

Captain William Blythe frowned to show his sincerity. "My dear mother, God bless her simple soul, sir, always said that in the eyes of God a nigra's soul was the same as any white man's. So long as that nigra's a Christian, of course. Then come heaven time, she said, we'd all be white as snow, even the blackest nigra, praise the Lord for His goodness." Blythe raised his eyes to the ceiling, then, over the unsuspecting preacher's head, offered Major Galloway an outrageous wink.

24

Galloway cut short his second-in-command's blarney by seating his guest at the library's large table, which was heaped with account books. Galloway, Adam, and Blythe sat opposite the preacher, and the Major described his ambitions for his regiment of cavalry; how they would ride the Southern paths with a confidence and local knowledge that no Northern horseman could hope to match. The Major spoke modestly, stressing the army's need for good reconnaissance and his own ambitions for a tightly disciplined regiment of horsemen, yet his words were plainly disappointing the Boston preacher. The Reverend Starbuck wanted swift results and dramatic victories, and it was the bombastic William Blythe who first sensed that desire. Blythe intervened with a chuckle. "You have to forgive the Major, Reverend," he said, "for not talking us up overmuch, but the real truth is we're going to twist Jeff Davis's tail, then we're going to scald the skin straight off that tail, and dang me if we won't then cut the thing clean off! I promise you, Reverend, that we're going to make the rebels squeal, and you'll hear that squeal all the way to Boston Common. Ain't that so, Major?"

Galloway merely looked surprised, while Adam stared at the table's scarred top, but the Reverend Starbuck was delighted by the implications of Blythe's promise. "You have specific plans?" he asked eagerly.

Blythe looked momentarily shocked. "We couldn't say a danged thing about specifics, sir, it would be downright unsoldierlike of us, but I do promise you, Reverend, that in the weeks to come it won't be Jeb Stuart you'll be reading about in the Boston newspapers, no sir, it'll be Major Joseph Galloway and his gallant regiment of troopers! Ain't that a fact, Joe?"

Galloway, taken aback, nodded. "We shall do our best, certainly."

"But there ain't nothing we can do, sir"—Blythe leaned forward with an earnest expression—"if we don't have the guns, the sabers, and the horses. As my sainted mother always said, sir, promises fill no bellies. You have to add a lick of hard work and a peck of money if you want to fill a Southern boy's belly, and sir, believe me, sir, it hurts me, it hurts me hard, to see these fine Southern patriots standing idle for want of a dollar or two."

"But what will you do with the money?" the Reverend Starbuck asked.

"What can't we do?" Blythe demanded. "With God on our side, Reverend, we can turn the South upside down and inside out. Why, sir, I shouldn't say it to you, but I guess you're a closemouthed man so I'll take the risk, but there's a map of Richmond up in my sleeping room, and why would a man like me need a map of Richmond? Well, I ain't going to tell you, sir, only because it would be downright unsoldierly of me to tell you, but I guess a clever man like you can work out which end of a snake has the bite."

Adam looked up astonished at this implication that the regiment was planning to raid the rebel capital, and Galloway seemed about to make a firm demurral, but the Reverend Starbuck was gripped by Blythe's promised coup. "You'll go to Richmond?" he asked Blythe.

"The very city, sir. That den of evil and lair of the serpent. I wish I could tell you how I loathe the place, sir, but with God's help we'll scour it and burn it and cleanse it anew!"

The horse trader was now speaking a language the Reverend Starbuck longed to hear. The Boston preacher wanted promises of rebel humiliation and of dazzling Union victories, of exploits to rival the insolent achievements of the rebel Jeb Stuart. He did not want to hear of patient reconnaissance duties faithfully performed, but wild promises of Northern victories, and no amount of caution from Major Galloway would convince the preacher that Blythe's promises were exaggerated. The Reverend Starbuck heard what he longed to hear, and to make it a reality he drew from his frock coat's inner pocket a check. He borrowed a pen and an inkwell from the Major and then signed the check with a due solemnity.

"Praise the Lord," William Blythe said when the check was signed.

"Praise Him indeed," the preacher echoed piously, thrusting the check across the table toward Galloway. "That money comes, Major, from a consortium of New England abolitionist churches. It represents the hard-earned dollars of simple honest working folk, given gladly in a sacred cause. Use it well."

"We shall do our utmost, sir," Galloway said, then fell momentarily silent as he saw the check was not for the fifteen thousand dollars he had expected, but for twenty thousand. Blythe's oratory had worked a small miracle. "And thank you, sir," Galloway managed to say.

"And I ask only one thing in return," the preacher said.

"Anything, sir!" Blythe said, spreading his big hands as though to encompass the whole wide world. "Anything at all!"

The preacher glanced at the wall over the wide garden doors, where a polished staff tipped with a lance head and a faded cavalry guidon was the room's sole remaining decoration. "A flag," the preacher said, "is important to a soldier, is it not?"

"It is, sir," Galloway answered. The small guidon over the door had been the banner he had carried in the Mexican war.

"Sacred, you might say," Blythe added.

"Then I should esteem it an honor if you would provide

me with a rebel banner," the preacher said, "that I can display in Boston as proof that our donations are doing God's work."

"You shall have your flag, sir!" Blythe promised swiftly. "I'll make it my business to see you have one. When are you returning to Boston, sir?"

"At month's end, Captain."

"You'll not go empty-handed, sir, not if my name's Billy Blythe. I promise you, on my dear mother's grave, sir, that you'll have your rebel battle flag."

Galloway shook his head, but the preacher did not see the gesture. He only saw a hated enemy battle flag hanging in the chancel of his church as an object of derision. The Reverend Starbuck pushed back his chair and consulted his fob watch. "I must be returning to the depot," he said.

"Adam will drive you, sir," Major Galloway said. The Major waited until the preacher was gone, then shook his head sadly. "You made a deal of promises, Billy."

"And there was a deal of money at stake," Blythe said carelessly, "and hell, I never did mind making promises."

Galloway crossed to the open garden door, where he stared out at the sun-bleached lawn. "I don't mind a man making promises, Billy, but I sure mind that he keeps them."

"I always keep my promises, sure I do. I keep 'em in mind while I'm working out how to break them." Blythe laughed. "Now are you going to give me aggravation for having fetched you your money? Hell, Joe, I get enough piety from young Faulconer."

"Adam's a good man."

"I never said he weren't a good man. I just said he's a pious son of a righteous bitch and God only knows why you appointed him Captain."

"Because he's a good man," Galloway said firmly, "and because his family is famous in Virginia, and because I like him. And I like you too, Billy, but not if you're going to argue with Adam all the time. Now why don't you go and get busy? You've got a flag to capture."

Blythe scorned such a duty. "Have I? Hell! There's plenty enough red, white, and blue cloth about, so we'll just have your house niggers run up a quick rebel flag."

Galloway sighed. "They're my servants, Billy, servants."

"Still niggers, ain't they? And the girl can use a needle, can't she? And the Reverend'll never know the difference. She can make us a flag and I'll tear it and dirty it a bit and that old fool will think we snatched it clean out of Jeff Davis's own hands." Blythe grinned at the idea, then picked up the check. He whistled appreciatively. "Reckon I talked us into a tidy profit, Joe."

"I reckon you did too. So now you'll go and spend it, Billy." Galloway needed to equip Adam's troop with horses and most of his men with sabers and firearms, but now, thanks to the generosity of the Reverend Starbuck's abolitionists, the Galloway Horse would be as well equipped and mounted as any other cavalry regiment in the Northern army. "Spend half on horses and half on weapons and saddlery," Galloway suggested.

"Horses are expensive, Joe," Blythe warned. "The war's made them scarce."

"You're a horse dealer, Billy, so go and work some horse-dealing magic. Unless you'd rather I let Adam go? He wants to buy his own horses."

"Never let a boy do a man's work, Joe," Blythe said. He touched the preacher's check to his lips and gave it an exaggerated kiss. "Praise the Lord," Billy Blythe said, "just praise His holy name, amen."

The Faulconer Legion made camp just a few miles north of the river where they had first glimpsed the baleful figure of their new commanding general. No one in the Legion knew where they were or where they were going or why they were marching there, but a passing artillery major who was a veteran of Jackson's campaigns said that was the usual way of Old Jack. "You'll know you've arrived just as soon as the enemy does and no sooner," the Major said, then begged a bucket of water for his horse.

The Brigade headquarters erected tents, but none of the regiments bothered with such luxuries. The Faulconer Legion had started the war with three wagonloads of tents but now had only two tents left, both reserved for Doctor Danson. The men had become adept at manufacturing shelters from branches and sod, though on this warm evening no one needed protection from the weather. Work parties fetched wood for campfires while others carried water from a stream a mile away. Some of the men sat with their bare feet dangling in the stream, trying to wash away the blisters and blood of the day's march. The four men on the Legion's punishment detail watered the draft horses that hauled the ammunition wagons, then paraded round the campsite with newly felled logs on their shoulders. The men staggered under the weight as they made the ten circuits of the Legion's lines that constituted their nightly punishment. "What have they done?" Lieutenant Coffman asked Starbuck.

Starbuck glanced up at the miserable procession. "Lem Pierce got drunk. Matthews sold cartridges for a pint of whiskey, and Evans threatened to hit Captain Medlicott."

"Pity he didn't," Sergeant Truslow interjected. Daniel Medlicott had been the miller at Faulconer Court House, where he had earned a reputation as a hard man with money, though in the spring elections for field officers he had distributed enough promises and whiskey to have himself promoted from sergeant to captain.

"And I don't know what Trent did," Starbuck finished.

"Abram Trent's just a poxed son of a whore," Truslow said to Coffman. "He stole some food from Sergeant Major Tolliver, but that ain't why he's being punished. He's being punished, lad, because he got caught."

"You are listening to the gospel according to Sergeant Thomas Truslow," Starbuck told the Lieutenant. "Thou shalt steal all thou can, but thou shalt not get caught." Starbuck grinned, then hissed with pain as he jabbed his thumb with a needle. He was struggling to sew the sole of his right boot back onto its uppers, for which task he had borrowed one of the three precious needles possessed by the company.

Sergeant Truslow, sitting on the far side of the fire from the two officers, mocked his Captain's efforts. "You're a lousy cobbler."

"I never pretended to be otherwise."

"You'll break the goddamn needle, pushing like that."

"You want to do it?" Starbuck asked, offering the half-finished work to the Sergeant.

"Hell no, I ain't paid to patch your boots."

"Then shut the hell up," Starbuck said, trying to work the needle through one of the old stitching holes in the sole.

"It'll only break first thing in the morning," Truslow said after a moment's silence.

"Not if I do it properly."

"No chance of that," Truslow said. He broke off a piece of tobacco and put it in his cheek. "You've got to protect the thread, see? So it don't chafe on the road."

"That's what I'm doing."

"No, you ain't. You're just lashing the boot together. There are blind men without fingers who could make a better job than you."

31

Lieutenant Coffman listened nervously to the conversation. He had been told that the Captain and Sergeant were friends—indeed, that they had been friends ever since the Yankee Starbuck had been sent to persuade the Yankee-hating Truslow to leave his high-mountain farm and join Faulconer's Legion—but to Coffman it seemed an odd sort of friendship if it was expressed with such mutual scorn. Now the intimidating Sergeant turned to the nervous Lieutenant. "A proper officer," Truslow confided to Coffman, "would have a darkie to do his sewing."

"A proper officer," Starbuck said, "would kick your rotten teeth down your gullet."

"Anytime, Captain," Truslow said, laughing.

Starbuck tied off the thread and peered critically at his handiwork. "It ain't perfect," he allowed, "but it'll do."

"It'll do," Truslow agreed, "so long as you don't walk on it."

Starbuck laughed. "Hell, we'll be fighting a battle in a day or two, then I'll get myself a pair of brand-new Yankee boots." He gingerly pulled the repaired boot onto his foot and was pleasantly surprised that the sole did not immediately peel away. "Good as new," he said, then flinched, not because of the boot, but because a sudden scream sounded across the campsite. The scream was cut abruptly short; there was a pause, then a sad wailing sound sobbed briefly.

Coffman looked aghast, for the noise had sounded like it came from a creature being tortured, which indeed it had. "Colonel Swynyard," Sergeant Truslow explained to the new Lieutenant, "is beating one of his niggers."

"The Colonel drinks," Starbuck added.

"The Colonel is a drunk," Truslow amended.

"And it's anyone's guess whether the liquor will kill him before one of his slaves does," Starbuck said, "or one of us, for that matter." He spat into the fire. "I'd kill the bastard willingly enough."

"Welcome to the Faulconer Brigade," Truslow said to Coffman.

The Lieutenant did not know how to respond to such cynicism, so he just sat looking troubled and nervous, then flinched as a thought crossed his mind. "Will we really be fighting in a day or two?" he asked.

"Probably tomorrow." Truslow jerked his head toward the northern sky, which was being reddened by the reflected glow of an army's fires. "It's what you're paid to do, son," Truslow added when he saw Coffman's nervousness.

"I'm not paid," Coffman said and immediately blushed for the admission.

Truslow and Starbuck were both silent for a few seconds; then Starbuck frowned. "What the hell do you mean?" he asked.

"Well, I do get paid," Coffman said, "but I don't get the money, see?"

"No, I don't see."

The Lieutenant was embarrassed. "It's my mother."

"She gets the money, you mean?" Starbuck asked.

"She owes General Faulconer money," Coffman explained, "because we rent one of his houses on the Rosskill road and Mother fell behind with the rent, so Faulconer keeps my salary."

There was another long pause. "Christ on his cross." Truslow's blasphemy broke the silence. "You mean that miserable rich bastard is taking your three lousy bucks a week for his own?"

"It's only fair, isn't it?" Coffman asked.

"No, it damn well ain't," Starbuck said. "If you want to send your mother the money, that's fair, but it ain't fair for you to fight for nothing! Shit!" He swore angrily.

33

"I don't really need any money." Coffman nervously defended the arrangement.

"'Course you do, boy," Truslow said. "How else are you going to buy whores and whiskey?"

"Have you talked to Pecker about this?" Starbuck demanded.

Coffman shook his head. "No."

"Hell, then I will," Starbuck said. "Ain't going to have you being shot at for free." He climbed to his feet. "I'll be back in a half hour. Oh, shit!" This last imprecation was not in anger for Washington Faulconer's greed but because his right sole had come loose on his first proper step. "Goddamn shit!" he said angrily, then stalked off to find Colonel Bird.

Truslow grinned at Starbuck's inept cobbling, then spat tobacco juice into the fire's margin. "He'll get your cash, son," he said.

"He will?"

"Faulconer's scared of Starbuck."

"Scared? The General's scared of the Captain?" Coffman found that hard to believe.

"Starbuck's a proper soldier. He's a fighter while Faulconer's just a pretty uniform on an expensive horse. In the long run, son, the fighter will always win." Truslow picked a shred of tobacco from between his teeth. "Unless he's killed, of course."

"Killed?"

"You're going to meet the Yankees tomorrow, son," Truslow said, "and some of us are going to get killed, but I'll do my best to keep you from getting slaughtered. Starting now." He leaned over and ripped the bars off the Lieutenant's collar, then tossed the cloth scraps into the fire. "Sharpshooters put telescopes on their rifles, son, just looking for officers to kill, and the Yankees don't care that you're not full-grown. See a pair of bars like that, they shoot, and you're two feet underground with a shovelful of dirt in your eyes." Truslow spat more tobacco juice. "Or worse," he added darkly.

"Worse?" Coffman asked nervously.

"You could be wounded, boy, and screaming like a stuck pig while a half-drunken doctor rummages through your innards. Or sobbing like a baby while you lie out in the field with your guts being eaten by rodents and no one knowing where the hell you are. It ain't pretty, and there's only one way to keep it from being even uglier and that's to hurt the bastards before they hurt you." He looked at Coffman, recognizing how the boy was trying to hide his fear. "You'll be all right," Truslow said. "The worst bit is the waiting. Now sleep, boy. You've got a man's job to do tomorrow."

High overhead a shooting star whipped white fire across the darkening sky. Somewhere a man sang of a love left behind while another played a sad tune on a violin. Colonel Swynyard's flogged slave tried to keep from whimpering, Truslow snored, and Coffman shivered, thinking of the morrow.

THE YANKEE CAVALRY PATROL reached General Banks's headquarters late at night. The patrol had come under fire at the Rapidan River, and the loss of one of their horses had slowed their journey back to Culpeper Court House, as had the necessity to look after two wounded men. A New Hampshire corporal had been struck by a bullet in his lower belly and would surely die, while the patrol's commander, a captain, had suffered a glancing hit on the ribs. The Captain's wound was hardly serious, but he had scratched and prodded at the graze until a satisfactory amount of blood heroically stained his shirt.

Major General Nathaniel Banks, commander of General Pope's Second Corps, was smoking a last cigar on the veranda of his commandeered house when he heard that the patrol had returned with ominous news of enemy forces crossing the Rapidan. "Let's have the man here! Let's hear him. Lively now!" Banks was a fussy man who, despite all the contrary evidence, was convinced of his own military genius. He certainly looked the part of a successful soldier, for there were few men who wore the uniform of the United States with more assurance. He was trim, brusque, and confident, yet until the war began he had never been a soldier, merely a politician. He had risen to be Speaker of the House of Representatives, though it had taken 133 ballots to achieve that honor, and afterward Governor of Massachusetts, a state so rich in men willing to be taxed that the federal government had deemed it necessary to offer its governor the chance of immortal martial glory as a token of its thanks. Governor Banks, who was as passionate in his love for his country as in his hatred of the slave trade, had leaped at the chance.

Now he waited, ramrod straight, as the cavalry Captain, wearing his jacket like a cloak so that his bloody shirt showed clearly, climbed the veranda steps and offered a salute, which he dramatically cut short with a wince as though the pain in his chest had suddenly struck hard.

"Your name?" Banks demanded peremptorily.

"Thompson, General. John Hannibal Thompson. From Ithaca, New York. Reckon you might have met my uncle, Michael Fane Thompson, when you were a congressman. He sat for New York back in—"

"You found the enemy, Thompson?" Banks asked in a very icy voice.

Thompson, offended at being so rudely cut off, shrugged. "We sure found someone hostile, General."

"Who?"

"Damned if I know. We got shot at." Thompson touched the crusted blood on his shirt, which looked brown rather than red in the lamplight.

"You shot back?" Banks asked.

"Hell, General, no one shoots at me without getting retaliation, and I reckon me and my boys laid a few of the bastards low."

"Where was this?" the aide accompanying General Banks asked.

Captain Thompson crossed to a wicker table on which the aide had spread a map of northern Virginia illuminated by two flickering candle-lanterns. Moths beat frantically around the three men's heads as they leaned over the map. Thompson used one of the lanterns to light himself a cigar, then tapped a finger on the map. "It was a ford just around there, General." He had tapped the map well west of the main road that led due south from Culpeper Court House to Gordonsville.

"You crossed to the south bank of the river?" Banks asked.

"Couldn't rightly do that, General, on account of there being a pack of rebs already occupying the ford."

"There's no ford marked there," the aide interjected. Sweat dripped from his face to stain the Blue Ridge Mountains, which lay well to the west of the rivers. The night had brought no relief from the sweltering heat.

"A local nigger guided us," Thompson explained. "He said the ford weren't well known, being nothing but a summer back road to a gristmill, and some of us reckoned he just might be lying to us, but there sure was a ford after all. Seems the nigger was truthful."

"The word, Thompson, is Negro," Banks said very coldly, then looked down at the map again. Other patrols had spoken of rebel infantry marching north on the Gordonsville road, and this new report suggested that the Confederates were advancing on a broad front and in considerable strength. What were they doing? A reconnaissance in force, or a full-scale attack aimed at destroying his corps?

"So how many men fired at you?" Banks resumed his questioning of the flippant Thompson.

"Wasn't exactly counting the minny balls, General, on account of being too busy firing back. But I reckon there was at least one regiment north of the river and more of the devils coming on."

Banks stared at the cavalryman, wondering just why responsibility always seemed to devolve onto fools. "Did you try to take a prisoner?"

"I guess I was too busy making sure I didn't end up six feet underground, General." Thompson laughed. "Hell, there were only a dozen of us and more than a thousand of them. Maybe two thousand."

"Did you ascertain the identity of the regiment which fired on you?" Banks asked with an icy pedantry.

"I sure ascertained that it was a rebel regiment, General," Thompson answered. "They were carrying that new flag, the one with the cross on it."

Banks shuddered at the man's obtuse stupidity and wondered why the North's horsemen were so inept at gathering intelligence. Probably, he thought, because they had none themselves. So who were these rebels marching north? There was a rumor that Stonewall Jackson had come to Gordonsville, and Banks winced at the thought of that bearded, ragged man whose troops marched at the speed of wildfire and fought like fiends.

Banks dismissed the cavalryman. "Useless," he said as the man paced off down Culpeper Court House's main street, where sentries stood guard on the taverns. In the town's small wooden houses yellow lights burned behind the muslin curtains used as insect screens. An undertaker's wagon, its shafts tilted up to the sky, stood outside a church where, Banks remembered, the famous Boston preacher Elial Starbuck was due to speak on Sunday morning. The town's population was not anticipating the abolitionist's sermon with any pleasure, but Banks, an old friend of the preacher, was looking forward to Starbuck's peroration and had demanded that as many of his officers as possible should be present. Nathaniel Banks had a noble vision of God and country marching hand in hand to victory.

Now, with a frown on his face, Banks looked back to the map, on which his sweat dripped monotonously. Suppose the enemy move was a bluff? Suppose that a handful of rebels were merely trying to frighten him? The rebels had surely guessed that he had his eyes on Gordonsville, because if he captured that town, then he would cut the railroad that connected Richmond with the rich farmland in the Shenandoah Valley. Sever those rails, and the enemy's armies would starve, and that thought reignited the glimmer of promised martial glory in Nathaniel Banks's mind. He saw a statue in Boston, envisaged streets and towns all across New England named after him, and even dreamed that a whole new state might be fashioned from the savage western territories and given his name. Banks Street, Banksville, the state of Banks.

Those inspired visions were fed by more than mere ambition. They were fed by a burning need for revenge. Earlier in the year Nathaniel Banks had led a fine army down the Shenandoah Valley, where he had been tricked and trounced by Thomas Jackson. Even the Northern newspapers had admitted that Jackson had cut Banks to pieces—indeed, the rebels had taken so many guns and supplies from Banks that they had nicknamed him "Commissary Banks." They had mocked him, ridiculed him, and their scorn still hurt Nathaniel Banks. He wanted revenge.

"The prudent course, sir, would be a withdrawal behind the Rappahannock," the aide murmured. The aide was a graduate of West Point and supposed to provide the politician-general with sound military advice.

"It may be nothing but a reconnaissance," Banks said, thinking of vengeance.

"Maybe so, sir," the aide said suavely, "but what do we gain by fighting? Why hold ground we can easily retake in a week's time? Why not just let the enemy wear himself out by marching?"

Banks brushed cigar ash off the map. Retreat now? In a week when Boston's most famous preacher was coming to visit the army? What would Massachusetts say if they heard that Commissary Banks had run away from a few rebels?

"We stay," Banks said. He stabbed his finger down at the contours of a ridge that barred the road just south of Culpeper Court House. If Jackson was marching north in the hope of resupplying his army at the expense of Commissary Banks, then he would have to cross that ridge that lay behind the small protection of a stream. The stream was called Cedar Run, and it lay at the foot of Cedar Mountain. "We'll meet him there," Banks said, "and beat him there."

The aide said nothing. He was a handsome, clever young man who thought he deserved better than to be harnessed to this stubborn bantam-cock. The aide was trying to frame a response, some persuasive words that would deflect Banks from rashness, but the words would not come. Instead, from the lamplit street, there sounded men's voices singing about loved ones left behind, of sweethearts waiting, of home.

"We'll meet him there," Banks said again, ramming his finger onto the sweat-stained map, "and beat him there."

At Cedar Mountain.

The Legion did not march far on the day they crossed the Rapidan. There was a curious lack of urgency about the expedition, almost as though they were merely changing base rather than advancing on the Northerners who had invaded Virginia. And next morning, though they were woken long before dawn and were ready to march even before the sun had risen above the tall eastern trees, they still waited three hours while a succession of other regiments trailed slowly by on the dusty road. A battery of small six-pounders and short-barreled howitzers was dragged past, followed by a column of Virginia infantry, who good-naturedly jeered the Faulconer Legion for its pretentious name. The day was hot and promised to get hotter still, yet still they waited as the sun climbed higher. More troops passed until, just short of midday, the Legion at last led the Faulconer Brigade out onto the dusty road.

Just moments later the guns started to sound. The noise came from far ahead, a grumble that could have been mistaken for thunder if the sky had not been cloudless. The air was sullen, moist, and windless, and the faces of Starbuck's men were pale with road dust through which their sweat ran in dark lines. Soon, Starbuck thought, some of those rivulets would be blood red, fly-coated, and twitching, and that premonition of battle turned his belly sour and caused the muscles in his right thigh to tremble. He tried to anticipate the sound of bullets as he coached himself to display courage and not the fear that was liquefying his bowels, and all the while the distant cannons hammered their flat, soulless noise across the land. "Goddamned artillery," Truslow said in a sour tone. "Some poor bastards are catching hell."

Lieutenant Coffman seemed about to say something, then decided to keep quiet. One of the conscripts broke ranks to pull down his pants and squat beside the road. Normally he would have been good-naturedly jeered, but the muffled thump of the guns made every man nervous.

In the early afternoon the Legion halted in a shallow valley. The road ahead was blocked by a Georgia battalion beyond which lay a ridgeline crested by dark trees beneath a sky whitened by gunsmoke. Some of the Georgians lay asleep on the road, looking like corpses. Others were penciling their names and hometowns on scraps of paper that they either pinned to their coats or stuck into buttonholes so that, should they die, their bodies would be recognized and their families informed. Some of Starbuck's men began to take the same gloomy precaution, using the blank end pages of Bibles as their labels.

"Culpeper Court House," George Finney announced suddenly.

Starbuck, sitting beside the road, glanced at him, waiting.

"Billy Sutton says this is the road to Culpeper Court House," George Finney explained. "Says his daddy brought him on this road two years back."

"We came to bury my grandmother, Captain," Billy Sutton intervened. Sutton was a corporal in G Company. He had once been in J Company, but a year of battles had shrunk the Faulconer Legion from ten to eight companies, and even those companies were now understrength. At the war's beginning the Legion had marched to battle as one of the biggest regiments in the rebel army, but after a year of battle it would scarcely have filled the pews of a backcountry church.

Three horsemen galloped southward through the brittle stubble of a harvested cornfield, their horses' hooves kicking up puffs of dust from the parched dirt. Starbuck guessed they were staff officers bringing orders. Truslow glanced at the three men, then shook his head. "Goddam Yankees in Culpeper Court House," Truslow said, affronted. "Got no damned business in Culpeper Court House."

"If it is Culpeper Court House," Starbuck said dubiously. Culpeper County had to be at least sixty miles from the Legion's home in Faulconer County, and few of the men in the Legion had traveled more than twenty miles from home in all their lives. Or not until this war had marched them up to Manassas and across to Richmond to kill Yankees. They had become good at that. They had become good at dying, too.

The gunfire suddenly swelled into one of those frenetic passages when, for no apparent reason, every cannon on a battlefield spoke at once. Starbuck cocked an ear, listening for the slighter crackle of musketry, but he could hear nothing except the unending thunder of artillery. "Poor bastards," he said.

"Our turn soon," Truslow answered unhelpfully.

"This rate they'll run out of ammunition," Starbuck said hopefully.

Truslow spat in comment on his Captain's optimism, then turned as hoofbeats sounded. "God damn Swynyard," he said tonelessly.

Every man in the company now either feigned sleep or kept his eyes fixed on the dusty road. Colonel Griffin Swynyard was a professional soldier whose talents had long been dissolved by alcohol but whose career had been rescued by General Washington Faulconer. Swynyard's cousin edited Richmond's most influential newspaper, and Washington Faulconer, well aware that reputation was more easily bought than won, was paying for the support of the *Richmond Examiner* by employing Swynyard. For a second Starbuck wondered if Swynyard was coming to see him, but the Colonel, closely followed by Captain Moxey, galloped past H Company and on up the slope toward the sound of battle. Starbuck's heart gave an acid beat as he guessed Swynyard was going to mark the place where the Legion would deploy, which meant that at any second the orders would come to advance into the guns.

Ahead, where the road vanished across the shallow ridge, the Georgian troops were already struggling to their feet and pulling on bedrolls and weapons. The cannon fire had momentarily abated, but the snapping sound of rifle cartridges now crackled across the dry landscape. The sound increased Starbuck's nervousness. It had been a month since the Legion last fought, but a single month was not nearly long enough to allay the terrors of the battlefield. Starbuck had been secretly hoping that the Legion might sit this skirmish out, but the Georgia battalion was already trudging north to leave a haze of dust over the road.

"Up, Nate!" Captain Murphy relayed Bird's orders to Starbuck.

Truslow bellowed at H Company to stand up. The men hitched their bedrolls over their shoulders and dusted off their rifles. Behind H Company the men of Captain Medlicott's G Company stood slowly, their lapels and belt loops dotted with the scraps of white paper on which they had written their names.

"Look for Swynyard on the road," Captain Murphy told Starbuck.

Starbuck wondered where Washington Faulconer was, then assumed the General would be leading his Brigade from behind. Swynyard, whatever his other faults, was no coward. "Forward!" Starbuck shouted; then, rifle and bedroll slung, he took his place at the head of the column. Dust thrown up by the boots of the Georgians stung his throat and eyes. The road was daubed with dark stains of tobacco juice that looked uncannily like blood spattered from wounds. The sound of rifle fire was more intense.

That sound swelled even further as Starbuck led the Legion through the woods at the crest of the ridge that had served to disguise and diminish the sound of fighting, which now spread across Starbuck's front in a furious cacophony. For a mile beyond the trees there was nothing but gunsmoke, flame, and chaos. The fields to the left of the road were filled with wounded men and surgeons hacking at broken flesh, to the right was a hill rimmed with artillery smoke, while ahead lay a second belt of woodland that concealed the actual fighting but could not hide the pall of smoke that boiled up either side of the road nor disguise the sound of the guns.

"By golly," Coffman said. He was excited and nervous.

"Stay near Truslow," Starbuck warned the young Lieutenant.

"I'll be all right, sir."

"Every damned man who's died in this war said that, Coffman," Starbuck reacted angrily, "and I want you to shave before you're shot. So stay close to Truslow."

"Yes, sir," Coffman said meekly.

An artillery bolt smacked through pine tops to the right of the road, leaving the branches whipping back and forth above the spray of needles that sifted down to the dust. Wounded men, all rebels, were lying on both verges. Some had already died. A man staggered back from the fighting. He was barechested and his suspenders were hanging loose beside his legs. He was clutching his belly, trying to keep his guts from spilling into the dust. His forearms were soaked in blood. "Oh, golly," Coffman said again and went pale. The blood on the dusty road looked blacker than the tobacco stains. The sound of rifle fire was splintering the afternoon that smelt of pine resin, sulfur, and blood. The shadows were long, long enough to give Starbuck an instant's wild hope that night might fall before he needed to fight.

Starbuck led the company on across the open land and into the cover of the second belt of timber. The leaves here flicked with the strike of bullets, and fresh scars of yellow wood showed where artillery bolts had sheared limbs off trees. An ammunition wagon with one wheel smashed was canted at the side of the road. A black teamster with a bloody scalp sat leaning against the abandoned wagon and watched Starbuck's men pass.

The trees ended not far ahead, and beyond, in the smoky open, Starbuck knew the battle was waiting for him. Common sense told him to slow down and thus delay his entry onto that bullet-riven stage, but pride made him hurry. He could see the gunsmoke sifting through the last green branches like a spring fog blowing out of Boston Harbor. He could smell the smoke's foul stench, and he knew it was almost time for the Legion to deploy. His mouth was powder dry, his heart erratic, and his bladder full. He passed a man whose body lay splayed open from the strike of an artillery shell. He heard Coffman retch dryly. Flies buzzed in the close air. One of his men laughed at the eviscerated corpse. Starbuck unslung his rifle and felt with a finger to check that the percussion cap was in place. He was a captain, but he bore no signs of rank and carried a rifle just like his men, and now, like them, he pulled his cartridge box around to the front of his rope belt, where it would be handy for reloading. His broken right boot almost tripped him as he left the shadow of the trees to see ahead a shallow valley scarred and littered by battle. The low land was rifted with smoke and loud with gunfire. Beside the road a horse lay dead in a dry ditch. Coffman was white-faced but trying hard to look unconcerned and not to duck whenever a missile howled or whipped overhead. Bullets were whickering through the humid air. There was no sign of any enemy—indeed, hardly any men were in view except for some rebel gunners and Colonel Swynyard, who, with Moxey beside him, was sitting his horse in a field to the left of the road.

"Starbuck!" Colonel Swynyard shouted. "Over here!" Starbuck led the company across the brittle corn stubble. "Form there!" Swynyard called, pointing to a spot close behind his horse; then he turned in his saddle to stare northward through a pair of binoculars. Captain Moxey was fussily ordering H Company to align themselves on his marker, so Starbuck left him to it and walked forward to join Swynyard. The Colonel lowered his glasses to watch the battery of rebel six-pounders that was deployed just a hundred yards ahead. The smoke from the small guns was obscuring the fighting beyond, but every now and then a Yankee shell would explode near the battery, making Swynyard grin in appreciation. "Oh, well done! Good shooting!" Swynyard called aloud when an enemy shell eviscerated a team horse picketed fifty paces behind the guns. The horse screamed as it flailed bloodily on the ground, panicking the other tethered horses, which reared frantically as they tried to drag their iron picket stakes out of the ground. "Chaos!" Swynyard said happily, then glanced down at Starbuck. "Yankees are damned lively this afternoon."

"Guess they were waiting for us," Starbuck said. "Knew we were coming."

"Guess someone told on us. A traitor, eh?" Swynyard offered the suggestion slyly. The Colonel was a man of startling ugliness, much of it the result of wounds honorably taken in the service of the old United States, but some of it caused by the whiskey that generally left him comatose by early evening. He had a coarse black beard streaked with gray and crusted with dried tobacco juice, sunken eyes, and a tic in his scarred right cheek. His left hand was missing three fingers, and his mouth was filled with rotting, stinking teeth. "Maybe the traitor was a Northerner, eh?" Swynyard hinted clumsily.

Starbuck smiled. "More likely to be some poor drunken son of a bitch needing cash for his whiskey . . ."—he paused—"Colonel."

Swynyard's only response was his cackling laugh, which hinted at madness. Remarkably, despite the lateness of the day, he was still sober, either because Washington Faulconer had hidden his whiskey or else because Swynyard's small remaining shred of self-protection had convinced him that he had to function efficiently on a day of battle or else lose his job altogether. Swynyard glanced up at the gunsmoke, then looked back to the notebook in which he was writing. On his right sleeve he wore a square patch of white cloth embroidered with a red crescent. The symbol was from Washington Faulconer's coat of arms, and the General had dreamed up the happy idea of issuing the badges to every man in his Brigade, though the idea had not been wholly successful. Some men refused to wear the patch, and generally it was possible to tell Faulconer's supporters from his detractors by the badge's presence or absence. Starbuck, naturally, had never worn the crescent badge, though some of his men had patched their pants' seats with the convenient square of cloth.

Swynyard tore the page out of his notebook, put the book itself away, and then drew out his revolver. He began slipping percussion caps over the firing nipples of the loaded chambers. The barrel of the gun was pointed directly at Starbuck's chest. "I could have an accident," Swynyard said slyly. "No one could blame me. I'm three fingers short of a hand so no wonder I fumble sometimes. One shot, Starbuck, and you'd be buzzard meat on the grass. I reckon General Faulconer would like that." Swynyard began to thumb the hammer back.

Then a click sounded behind Starbuck, and the Colonel's thumb relaxed. Sergeant Truslow lowered the hammer of his rifle. "I can have an accident, too," Truslow said.

Swynyard said nothing but just grinned and turned away. The nearby battery had ceased firing, and the gunners were hitching their weapons to limbers. The smoke of the battery dissipated slowly in the still air. The rebel guns had been fighting a duel with a Northern battery, a duel that the Northerners had won. "The Yankees will be raising their sights," Swynyard remarked, staring through his glasses. "They've got four-and-a-half-inch rifles. Can't fight four-and-a-half-inch rifles with six-pounder guns. We might as well throw rocks at the bastards."

Starbuck watched the Southern guns wheel fast away to the rear and wondered if he was now supposed to fight four-and-a-half-inch rifled cannon with rifles. His heart seemed to be beating too loudly, filling his chest with its drumbeats. He tried to lick his lips, but his mouth was too dry.

The sound of musketry slackened, to be replaced by Northern cheers. Yankee cheering was much deeper in tone than the blood-chilling yelp of attacking rebels. The cannon smoke had thinned sufficiently to let Starbuck see a belt of woodland a half-mile ahead, and then to see a sight he had never dreamed of witnessing on one of Thomas Jackson's battlefields.

He saw panic.

Ahead and to the left of Starbuck a horde of Southern soldiers were pouring out of the woodland and fleeing southward across the shallow valley. All discipline was gone. Shells exploded among the gray-jacketed soldiers, adding to their desperation. A rebel flag went down, was snatched up again, then disappeared in another flame-filled burst of shell smoke. Horsemen were galloping through the fleeing mass in an attempt to turn the men around, and here and there among the panic a few men did try to form a line, but such small groups stood no chance against the flood of fear that swept the majority away.

Swynyard might be a drunkard and a foul-tempered brute, but he had been a professional soldier long enough to recognize disaster. He turned to see that Captain Medlicott's G Company had formed alongside Starbuck's men. "Medlicott!" Swynyard shouted. "Take these two companies forward! You're in charge!" Medlicott, though much older than Starbuck, had less seniority as a captain, but Swynyard had given him the command of the two companies as a way of insulting Starbuck. "See that broken limber?" The Colonel pointed toward a shattered vehicle that lay two hundred paces ahead, where a strip of grass marked a divide between a patch of harvested corn and a wider field of wheat. "Form your skirmish line there! I'll bring the Legion up in support." Swynyard turned back to Starbuck. "Take this," he said and leaned down from the saddle to hold out a folded scrap of paper.

Starbuck snatched the piece of paper, then shouted at his men to advance alongside G Company. A shell screamed overhead. It was odd, Starbuck thought, how the debilitating nervousness that afflicted a man before battle could be banished by the proximity of danger. Even the day's stifling heat seemed bearable now that he was under fire. He licked his lips, then unfolded the scrap of paper that Swynyard had given him. He had supposed it would be written orders, but instead he saw it was a label for a dead man. *Starbuck*, the paper read, *Boston, Massachusetts*. Starbuck threw it angrily away. Behind, where the rest of the Legion hurried into ranks, Swynyard saw the gesture and cackled.

"This is madness!" Truslow protested to Starbuck. Two companies of skirmishers could not stand against the tide of fear that was retreating from the Yankee guns.

"The rest of the Legion will help," Starbuck said.

"They'd better," Truslow said, "or we're vulture meat."

Company G was advancing to Starbuck's right. Medlicott seemed unworried by the odds, but just stumped ahead of his men with a rifle in his hands. Or maybe, Starbuck thought, the miller just did not display his fear. "Keep the ranks straight!" Starbuck called to Coffman. "I want them steady." He felt in his pocket and found the stub of a cigar he had been saving for battle. He borrowed a lit cigar from a man in the ranks, lit his own, and drew the bitter smoke deep into his lungs.

Lieutenant Coffman had drawn ahead of H Company and was holding a brass-handled bayonet like a sword.

"Get back, Mr. Coffman!" Starbuck called.

"But, sir—"

"Your place is behind the company, Lieutenant! Go there! And throw away that toy sword!"

51

The first Northern soldiers suddenly appeared at the tree line on the valley's far crest, which blossomed with the small puffs of white rifle smoke. A shell exploded ahead of Starbuck, and pieces of its casing whipped past him. To his left the field had been partly harvested, so that some of the wheat was standing but most was drying in stooks. Small fires flickered where the shell fire had set the dry crops alight. There were patches of corn stubble among the wheat and two rows of standing corn, where a group of rebel soldiers had taken cover. The tasseled corn shivered whenever a bullet or shell whipped through the stalks. A Northern flag appeared at the far trees. The standard-bearer was waving it to and fro, making the stripes flutter brightly. A bugle was sounding, and off to the west the rebel infantry was still running. Rebel officers still galloped among the fugitives, trying to stem their flight and turn them round. General Jackson was among them, flailing with his scabbarded saber at the panicked men. More Northerners were at the tree line, some of them directly ahead of Starbuck now.

Another shell landed close to Company H, and Starbuck wondered why Medlicott did not order the two companies into skirmish order. Then he decided to hell with military etiquette and shouted the order himself. Medlicott echoed the order, thus shaking the two companies into a loose and scattered formation. Their job now was to fight the enemy skirmishers who would be advancing ahead of the main Yankee attack. "Make sure you're loaded!" Starbuck called. The Northern line had halted momentarily, perhaps to align itself after advancing through the trees. The Southern fugitives had disappeared behind Starbuck's left flank, and it suddenly seemed very quiet and lonely on the battlefield.

It also seemed very dangerous. Captain Medlicott crossed to Starbuck. "Is this right, do you think?" he asked, gesturing at the scatter of isolated skirmishers who were alone in the wide field. Medlicott had never liked Starbuck, and the red crescent patch on the shoulder of his uniform coat marked him for a loyal supporter of General Faulconer, but nervousness now made Medlicott seek reassurance from Faulconer's bitterest enemy. Close to, Starbuck could see that Medlicott was not hiding his fear at all; one cheek was quivering uncontrollably, and the sweat was pouring off his face and dripping from his beard. He took off his brimmed hat to fan his face, and Starbuck saw that even the miller's smooth, bald, chalk white pate was beaded with sweat. "We shouldn't be here!" Medlicott exclaimed petulantly.

"God knows what's happening," Starbuck said. A Northern battery had appeared where the road vanished among the farther trees. Starbuck saw the guns slew round in a shower of dirt. In a moment, he thought, that artillery will have us in their open sights. Dear God, he thought, but let it be a clean death, quick as a thought, with no agonized lingering under a surgeon's knife or dying of the sweated fever in some rat-infested hospital. He turned to look behind and saw the Faulconer Brigade streaming off the road and forming into ranks. "Swynyard's coming soon," he tried to reassure Medlicott.

The Northern infantry started forward again. A half-dozen flags showed above the dark ranks. Three of the flags were Old Glories, the others were regimental flags carrying state badges or martial insignias. Six flags translated into three regiments that were now attacking two light companies. Captain Medlicott went back to his own men, and Sergeant Truslow joined Starbuck. "Just us and them?" he asked, nodding at the Yankees.

"Swynyard's bringing the rest of the Brigade forward," Starbuck said. Shells from the newly deployed battery screeched overhead, aimed at the Faulconer Brigade. "Better them than us, eh?" Starbuck said with the callous

53

indifference of a man spared the gunners' attentions. He saw George Finney aim his rifle. "Hold your fire, George! Wait till the bastards are in range."

The Northern skirmishers ran ahead of the attacking line. Their job was to brush Starbuck's men aside, but soon, Starbuck thought, the rest of the Faulconer Brigade's skirmishers would advance to reinforce him. Another salvo of shells thundered above him, the cracks of their explosions sounding a second after the percussive thump of the guns themselves. Starbuck began looking for enemy officers among the approaching skirmishers. Yankee officers seemed more reluctant than Southerners to abandon their swords and glinting rank badges and bright epaulettes.

A second Northern battery on the crest opened fire. A shell screamed just inches over Starbuck's head. *For what we are about to receive*, he thought, *may the Lord make us truly thankful*. He could hear the beat of drums sounding from the Yankee infantry. Was this to be the breakthrough battle for the North? Were they at last to batter the Confederacy into surrender? Most of the rebel forces in Virginia were seventy miles away on the far side of Richmond with Robert Lee, but it was here that the Northerners were attacking, and if they broke through here, then what was to stop them marching south, ever south, until Richmond was cut off and the whole upper South split from the Confederacy? "Hold still now!" Starbuck called to his men as he walked slowly along his scattered skirmish line. Another minute, he thought, and the Yankee skirmishers would be in range. "You see that red-haired son of a bitch with the hooked sword, Will?" Starbuck called to Tolby, one of the Legion's finest marksmen. "He's yours. Kill the bastard."

"I'll take care of him, Captain!" Tolby eased back the hammer of his rifle.

Starbuck saw the enemy cannons disappear behind a

blossom of gray-white smoke, and he anticipated another flight of shells overhead, but instead the missiles slammed into the field all around Starbuck's men. One of Medlicott's sergeants was flung backward, his blood momentarily misting the hot air. A shell splinter whipped into the broken limber, which carried a stenciled legend announcing that the vehicle belonged to the 4th U.S. Artillery, evidence that the rebels had pushed the Yankees back across the valley before being routed in the far woods. Or perhaps, Starbuck thought, the limber had been captured earlier in the war, for it seemed that at least half of the rebels' equipment was of Northern origin. A solid shot landed close beside Starbuck, then ricocheted up and back. The nearness of the shot made him wonder why the Yankee gunners were aiming at a scattered skirmish line when they could be firing at the massed ranks of the Faulconer Brigade, and that curiosity made him turn to look for Swynyard's promised reinforcements.

But Swynyard had vanished, and with him the whole Faulconer Brigade, leaving Starbuck and Medlicott alone in the field. Starbuck turned back. The Northern skirmishers were close now, close enough for Starbuck to see that their uniforms were smart, not patched brown and gray like the rebels'. The Northerners were advancing in good style, the sun reflecting off their belt buckles and brass buttons. Behind the skirmish line a battalion trampled down a row of standing corn. There were a half-dozen mounted officers at the rear of the Yankee formation, evidence that at least one of the attacking regiments was new to the war. Experienced officers did not invite the attention of sharpshooters by riding high in saddles. But nor did two companies of skirmishers stand to fight against a whole Yankee brigade.

"Fire!" Truslow shouted, and the Legion's skirmishers began their battle. The men were in pairs. One man would fire, then reload while his companion looked for danger. The red-haired Yankee was already down, clutching his chest.

Truslow ran across to Starbuck. "I was never a religious man," the Sergeant said as he rammed a bullet down his rifle's barrel, "but ain't there a story in the Bible about some son of a bitch king sending a man to die in battle just so he could riddle the man's wife?"

Starbuck peered through the veil of rifle smoke, saw a Yankee go onto one knee to take aim, and fired at the man. A Northern bullet whipsawed the air a few inches to his left. Behind their skirmish line the Northern brigade advanced stolidly beneath their bright flags. He could hear their boots crushing cornstalks, and he knew that as soon as the marching line reached the further edge of the wheat field, they would stop to take aim, and then a killing volley would scream over the field, with every bullet aimed at the two stranded companies of the Legion. There was nothing to check the Yankees out here in the open. No rebel guns were firing, there were no bursting shells or clawing sprays of canister to fleck the wheat field red. Tom Petty, an eighteen-year-old in Starbuck's company, turned round with his mouth open and his eyes wide. He shook his head in disbelief, then sank to his knees. He saw Starbuck's eyes on him and forced a brave smile. "I'm all right, sir! Just bruised!" He managed to stand and face the enemy.

"King David," Starbuck said aloud. King David had sent Uriah the Hittite into the front line of the battle so that Bathsheba would become a widow. "Set ye Uriah in the forefront of the hottest battle"—the verse came back to Starbuck—"and retire ye from him, that he may be smitten, and die." Well, damn Faulconer, who had made Swynyard set Starbuck in the forefront of the hottest battle that he might be smitten and die. "We're getting out of here!" Starbuck shouted across to Captain Medlicott.

Medlicott, though officially in command, was grateful for

the younger man's leadership. "Back!" he shouted at G Company.

The Yankees cheered and jeered as they saw the handful of skirmishers retreat. "Enjoying your licking, boys!" one Northerner shouted. "Keep on running! We'll be right after you!" called another, while a third shouted to give his respects to Stonewall Jackson, "And tell him we'll hang him real gentle now!"

"Steady now!" Starbuck called to his men. He kept his back to the enemy, concentrating on his company. "Back to the trees! Steady, don't run!" No one else from the Brigade was in sight. Swynyard or Faulconer must have taken the whole Brigade back into the woods, abandoning Starbuck and Medlicott to the enemy. But why had Bird not protested? A shell landed just behind Starbuck, buffeting him with its hot punch of air. He turned and saw the Yankee skirmishers running toward him. "Double back to the woods!" he shouted, so releasing his men from their slow, steady withdrawal. "Muster them by the road, Sergeant!" he called to Truslow.

More Northern jeers and a handful of bullets followed the skirmishers' hurried retreat. The Yankees were in high spirits. They had waited a long time to give Stonewall Jackson a whipping, and now they were laying the lash on thick and hard. Back among the trees beside the turnpike Starbuck's men panted as they crouched and looked nervously at their officer, who, in turn, was watching the shadows lengthen across the wheat field. He was also watching the far tree line, where still more guns and infantry had appeared. The Yankees were triumphant and the rebels beaten. "If we stay here"—Medlicott had joined Starbuck again—"we'll like as not be prisoners."

"Swynyard put you in command," Starbuck said pointedly.

57

Medlicott hesitated, unhappy to take responsibility, then diffidently suggested that the two companies should retreat further through the trees. To the east of the turnpike a furious artillery battle was deafening the evening air. Smoke poured off the hillside where rebel guns were emplaced, but those cannon were of no use to the beaten men west of the turnpike, where the Yankee line had crushed the standing corn to drive Jackson's infantry back into the timber on the valley's southern crest. The Northern guns had the range of those trees now, and the green summer woods were filled with the whistling menace of shrapnel. Starbuck wondered where the Georgia regiment had gone and where the rest of the Brigade was hidden.

"I can't see the Brigade!" Medlicott said despairingly. A salvo of shells cracked ahead of the skirmishers, filling the trees with whistling shards of hot metal. The men leading the retreat had followed the twisting path into a small hollow, and now they instinctively crouched rather than leave their scanty cover to walk into that zone of fire. The perplexed and frightened Captain Medlicott seemed content to let them rest. "Maybe we should send a patrol to look for the Brigade?" he suggested to Starbuck.

"While the rest of us wait here to be captured?" Starbuck asked sarcastically.

"I don't know," Medlicott said. The miller was suddenly bereft of confidence and initiative. His doughy face looked hurt, like that of a child struck for an offense it had not committed.

"Yankees!" Truslow called warningly, pointing west to where blue uniforms had appeared in the woods.

"Stay still!" Medlicott shouted in sudden panic. "Get down!"

Starbuck would have gone on retreating, hoping to join up with the rebel reserve, but Medlicott had been panicked into making a decision, and the men crouched gratefully in the shadows. Two of Starbuck's company lowered a body they had been carrying. "Shall we bury him?" one of the two men asked Starbuck.

"Who is it?" It was dark under the trees, and the evening was drawing in.

"Tom Petty."

"Oh, dear God," Starbuck said. He had seen Petty wounded but had thought he would live, and surely Petty had deserved to live, for he had been a boy, not a man. He had used to shave each morning, but the blade had made no difference to his cheeks. He had only used the razor to explain his lack of beard, but he had been a good soldier, cheerful and willing. Starbuck had planned to make him up to corporal, but now it would have to be Mellors, who was not nearly so quick on the uptake. "Scratch him a grave," he said, "and get Corporal Waggoner to say a prayer for him."

All around them the shouts of the Yankees grew louder. The woodland was filled with screaming shells, so many that at times the torn leaves looked like a green snow drifting through the warm evening air. The trees echoed with the pathetic cries of dying men. Lieutenant Coffman hunkered down beside Starbuck, his small face showing bewilderment because his beloved Southerners were being whipped, because the North was winning, and because nothing in his world made sense.

The Reverend Elial Starbuck shared in the joy as the realization of victory dawned on the Yankee headquarters. And what a victory it was proving! Prisoners had confirmed that the enemy commander was indeed the notorious Stonewall Jackson. "The wretch won't be fetching his supper from my supply wagons tonight!" General Banks exulted. It was true that the enemy was still holding firm on the slopes of Cedar

Mountain, but Banks's staff brought message after message that told how the Federal right wing under General Crawford was driving the rebels clean across the valley and into the woods beyond. "Now we'll turn their flank!" Banks exclaimed, gesturing extravagantly to show how he meant to hook the right wing of his army around the backside of Cedar Mountain and thus surround the remnants of the Confederate army. "Maybe we'll have Jackson as our supper guest tonight!"

"I doubt he'll have much appetite after this drubbing," an artillery major observed.

"Fellow's reputed to eat damned strangely anyway," an aide responded, then blushed for having sworn in front of the Reverend Starbuck. "Nothing but stale bread and chopped cabbage, I hear."

"You and I could chop the rogue some cabbage, eh, Starbuck?" General Banks thus drew his distinguished guest into the jubilant conversation.

"I would make him eat what the slaves eat!" the Reverend Starbuck said.

"I think he eats worse than any slave!" Banks jested. "Force a slave to eat what Jackson dines on and the whole world would revile our inhumanity. Maybe we should punish the man by giving him a proper meal? Oysters and pheasant, you think?"

Banks's aides laughed, and their master turned his gaze back to the battle smoke that was already touched with a faint pink tinge of evening sunlight. In the slanting light Banks looked quite superb: straight-backed, stern-faced, the very image of a soldier, and suddenly, after months of disappointment, the politician did at last feel like a soldier. He had, Banks modestly admitted to himself, grown into the job and was now ready for the battles to come. For despite this day's splendid victory, there would be more battles. With

Stonewall Jackson defeated, General Robert Lee, who was protecting Richmond from McClellan's army, would be forced north even if such a move did open the rebel capital to McClellan's forces. McClellan would dutifully overwhelm the Richmond defenses, Pope would crush Lee, and then, bar some mopping up on the Mississippi and skull-breaking in the deep South, the war would be over. Better, it would be won. All that remained was a few battles, a rebel surrender, a Federal victory parade, and most important of all, the absolute necessity for President Lincoln and the dunderheads in the United States Congress to realize that it had been Nathaniel Prentiss Banks who had precipitated the whole process. My God, Banks thought, but others would try to steal his glory now! John Pope would doubtless make the attempt, and George McClellan would certainly write to every newspaper editor in creation, which made it all the more important for this night's victory dispatch to be written firmly and clearly. Tonight's dispatch, Banks knew, would fashion history books for years to come, but more important, the words he wrote tonight would garner votes for the remainder of his career.

Federal officers gathered round to offer the General their congratulations. The commander of Banks's bodyguard, a tall Pennsylvanian *Zouave*, handed the General a silver stirrup cup of brandy. "A toast to your triumph, sir," the *Zouave* proclaimed. A ragged line of disconsolate prisoners trudged past the group of horsemen. One or two of the captured seceshers glanced sullenly at the Northern General, and one rogue spat in his direction, but tonight, Banks thought, he would have the most valuable prisoner as his dinner guest. He would treat General Jackson with courtesy, as a gallant soldier should, and the world would wonder at the victor's modesty. Then Banks imagined himself at another dinner table, a much grander table in Washington that would gleam with massive presidential silver, and in his mind's eye he saw the foreign diplomats and their admiring bejeweled wives bend forward to catch his words. President Banks! And why not? George Washington might have made this country, but it had needed Nathaniel Prentiss Banks to save it.

A mile south of Banks, in a belt of woodland where fires started by shell fire tortured the wounded, men screamed and fought and died. The Yankee counterattack was being slowed by the undergrowth and by the stubborn defiance of Southern riflemen, whose muzzle flames stabbed bright in the smoky shadows. Shells slashed through the treetops, thrashing the branches and hammering the sky with their explosions. Blood and smoke reeked, a man called for his mother in the voice of a child, another cursed God, but still the North pushed on, yard by hard yard, going through hell in search of peace.

"Nothing is served," General Washington Faulconer said icily, "by breaking the Brigade into small detachments. We shall go into battle united."

"If there's any battle left," Swynyard said with a manic glee. He seemed to be enjoying the panic that had infected the western side of Jackson's battle.

"Watch your tongue, Colonel," Faulconer snapped. He was more than usually displeased with his second-in-command, who had already lost a quarter of the Legion instead of just Starbuck's company, and what was left of the Brigade must be husbanded, not frittered away by being committed to the battle in dribs and drabs. Faulconer edged his horse away from Swynyard and gazed at the woods, which were filled with smoke and thrashing from the passage of Northern shells and bolts. God only knew what had happened in the wide valley beyond those woods, but even here, far behind where the fighting had taken place, the evidence of impending disaster was awesome and obvious. Wounded men staggered back from the trees; some of the injured were being helped by friends, others crawled or limped painfully back to where the surgeons hacked and sawed and probed. Many of the fugitives were not wounded at all but were merely frightened men who were trying to escape the Yankee advance.

Faulconer had no intention of allowing that advance to enmesh his Brigade. "I want the 65th on the right," Faulconer called to Swynyard, referring to the 65th Virginia, which was the second largest regiment after the Legion in Faulconer's Brigade, "the Arkansas men in the center, and the 12th Florida on the left. Everyone else in reserve two hundred paces behind." That meant that the remaining six companies of the Legion, who were presently the foremost battalion in the Brigade, would now become Faulconer's rearmost line. The redeployment was hardly necessary, but moving the front line to the rear killed some precious moments while Faulconer tried to determine just what disasters were happening beyond the woods. "And, Colonel!" Faulconer called after Swynyard, "send Bird to reconnoiter the ground. Tell him to report to me within a half hour!"

"Colonel Bird's already gone," Swynyard said. "Went to fetch his skirmishers back."

"Without orders?" Faulconer asked angrily. "Then tell him to explain himself to me the instant he returns. Now go!"

"Sir?" Captain Thomas Pryor, one of Washington Faulconer's new aides, interjected nervously.

"Captain?" Faulconer acknowledged.

"General Jackson's orders were explicit, sir. We should advance quick, sir, with whatever units are available. Into the trees, sir." Pryor gestured nervously toward the woods.

But Faulconer had no wish to advance quick. The woods seemed to be alive with smoke and flame, almost as though the earth itself was heaving in the throes of some mythic struggle. Rifle fire cracked, men screamed, and cannons pumped their percussive explosions through the humid air, and Faulconer had no desire to plunge into that maelstrom. He wanted order and sense, and a measure of safety. "General Jackson," he told Pryor, "is panicking. We serve no purpose by committing ourselves piecemeal. We shall advance in good order or not at all." He turned away from the battle and rode back to where his second line would be formed. That reserve line consisted of the six remaining companies of the Legion and the whole of the 13th Florida, two regiments that Faulconer had every intention of holding back until his first line was fully committed to the fight. Only if the first line broke and ran would the second line fight, and then merely to serve as a rear guard for the fugitive first line. Washington Faulconer told himself he was being prudent, and that such prudence might well save a defeat from being a rout.

He wondered where Starbuck was and felt the familiar flare of hatred. Faulconer blamed Starbuck for all his ills. It was Starbuck who had humiliated him at Manassas, Starbuck who had suborned Adam, and Starbuck who had defied him by remaining in the Legion. Faulconer was convinced that if he could just rid himself of Starbuck, then he could make the Brigade into the most efficient unit of the Confederate army, which was why he had ordered Swynyard to place a company of skirmishers far ahead of the Brigade's position. He had trusted Swynyard to know precisely which company of skirmishers was to be thus sacrificed, but he had hardly expected the drunken fool to throw away both companies. Yet even that loss might be worthwhile, Faulconer reflected, if Starbuck was among the casualties.

On Faulconer's left a column of rebel troops advanced at the double, while another, marching just as quickly, headed for the woods to the right of his Brigade. Reinforcements were clearly reaching the fighting, which meant, Faulconer decided, that he had no need to hurl his own men forward in a desperate panic. Slow and steady would win this fight, and that natural caution was reinforced by the sight of a riderless horse, its flank a sheet of crimson, limping southward down the turnpike with its reins trailing in the dust and its stirrups dripping with blood.

The Faulconer Brigade laboriously formed its new battle lines. In the first rank were the 65th Virginia, Haxall's men from Arkansas, and the 12th Florida. The three regiments raised their dusty flags, the banners' bright colors already faded from too much sun and shredded by too many bullets. The standards hung limp in the windless air. Colonel Swynyard gave his horse to one of his two cowed slaves, then took his place at the center of the forward line, where lust at last overcame caution and made him take a flask from a pouch on his belt. "I see our gallant Colonel is inoculating himself against the risks of battle," General Faulconer remarked sardonically to Captain Pryor.

"By drinking water, sir?" Pryor asked in puzzlement. Thomas Pryor was new to the Brigade. He was the younger son of a Richmond banker who did much business with Washington Faulconer, and the banker had pleaded with Faulconer to take on his son. "Thomas is a good-natured fellow," the banker had written, "too good, probably, so maybe a season of war will teach him that mankind is not inherently honest?"

A second's silence greeted Pryor's naive assumption that Swynyard was drinking water, then a gale of laughter swept the Brigade headquarters. "Swynyard's water," Faulconer informed Pryor, "is the kind that provides the Dutch with

courage, puts men to sleep, and wakes them sore-headed."
The General smiled at his own wit, then turned indignantly
as a mounted man galloped toward him from the turnpike.

"You're to advance, sir!" the officer shouted. The man
had a drawn sword in his right hand.

Faulconer did not move. Instead he waited as the officer
curbed his horse. The beast tossed its head and stamped nervously. It was flecked with sweat and rolling its eyes white.
"You have orders for me?" Faulconer asked the excited
officer.

"From General Jackson, sir. You're to advance with the
other brigades, sir." The aide gestured toward the woods, but
Faulconer still made no move other than to hold out a hand.
The aide gaped at him. No one else on this field had
demanded written orders, for surely no one could doubt the
urgency of the cause. If the Yankees won here, then there
was nothing to stop them crossing the Rapidan and breaking
Richmond's rail links with the Shenandoah Valley, and
nothing, indeed, to stop them advancing on the rebel capital. This was not a time for written orders but for Southern
men to fight like heroes to protect their country. "General
Jackson's compliments, sir," the aide said in a tone that
barely managed to stay on the civil side of insolence, "and
his regrets that he has no time to put his orders into writing,
but he would be most obliged if you were to advance your
Brigade into the trees and help dislodge the enemy."

Faulconer looked at the woods. Fugitives still emerged
from the shadows, but most were now men wounded by the
fighting rather than frightened men seeking safety. Nearer to
the Brigade two small guns were being unlimbered by the
road, but the cannons looked a pitiable force to withstand
the noisy Northern onslaught that churned among the shadowed woods. Those shadows were long, cast by a sun that
reddened in the west. Flames started by shell fire flickered

deep among the trees where rifles snapped angrily. "Am I to tell General Jackson that you won't advance, sir?" the mounted officer asked in a voice cracked with near despair. He had not given his name nor announced his authority, but the urgency in his tone and the drawn sword in his hand were all the authority he needed.

Faulconer drew his sword. He did not want to advance, but he knew there was no choice now. Reputation and honor depended on going into the awful woods. "Colonel Swynyard!" he called, and the words were hardly more than a croak. "Colonel!" he shouted again, louder this time.

"Sir!" Swynyard pushed the flask of whiskey back into his pouch.

"Advance the Brigade!" Faulconer called.

Swynyard drew his own sword, the blade scraping into the day's dying light. Ahead of him fires burned in the wood, their flames bright in the dark shadows where men fought and died. "Forward!" Swynyard shouted.

Forward into the maelstrom where the woods burned.

Into battle.

"IT'S GOD'S WILL, BANKS! God's will!" The Reverend Elial Starbuck was beside himself with joy. The smell of battle was in his nostrils and inflaming him like an infusion of the Holy Spirit. The preacher was fifty-two years old and had never known an exultation quite like this thrill of victory. He was witnessing God's hand at work and seeing the triumph of righteousness over the Slavocracy. "On, on!" he shouted encouragingly to a fresh battery of Northern artillery that traveled toward the smoke of battle. The Reverend Starbuck had come to Culpeper Court House to preach to the troops, but instead found himself cheering them on to glory.

The Reverend Elial Starbuck's jubilation matched General Banks's excitement. The politician turned general was realizing he had won! He was actually trouncing the wretched and infamous Jackson who had given him such misery earlier in the year. The bells of Boston would ring for this success of a native son, and suddenly the realization of the Governor's most daring ambitions seemed so dazzlingly close. Nathaniel Prentiss Banks, seventeenth President of the United States of America. He said the phrase under his breath, relishing it, but then the glory of that triumph dizzied Banks in his saddle, and to steady himself he turned back to the Reverend Starbuck. "How's that son of yours, Starbuck?" Banks asked, trying to give the impression of a man humble and confident enough to make small talk at the moment of glory.

"James is well, thank you, Governor," the preacher responded. "He's with McClellan's forces in front of Richmond. He suffered a touch of fever a month ago, but writes to say he is fully recovered."

"I meant the young man you named after me," Banks said. "How is he?"

"Nathaniel's well, so far as I know," the Reverend Starbuck said curtly, then was saved from any further queries about his traitor son by the arrival of an aide on a horse that had a mane paled by dust and flanks foaming with sweat. The aide gave Banks a swift salute and a note from Brigadier General Crawford. The note had been hastily scribbled in the saddle, and Banks found it hard to decipher the penciled letters.

"News of victory, I hope?" Banks suggested to the newly arrived aide.

"The General's requesting reinforcements, sir," the aide said respectfully. His horse trembled as a rebel shell wailed overhead.

"Reinforcements?" Banks asked. In the pause after his question the rebel shell exploded harmlessly behind, scattering dirt across the road. "Reinforcements?" Banks said again, frowning as though he found the word incomprehensible. Then he straightened his already immaculate uniform. "Reinforcements?" he asked a third time. "But I thought he was driving the enemy from the field?"

"We need to break them, sir." The aide sounded enthusiastic. "One more brigade will rout them utterly."

"I hoped they were finished already," Banks said, crumpling Crawford's message in his hand.

"They're skulking in some woods, sir. Our fellows are pressing hard, but they'll need help."

"There isn't any help!" Banks said indignantly, as though

69

the aide were spoiling his moment of glory. "I sent him Gordon's brigade; isn't that enough?"

The aide glanced at the gaudily uniformed Pennsylvania *Zouaves* who formed General Banks's personal bodyguard. "Maybe we should send every man available, sir, to destroy them before they're saved by nightfall?" He spoke very respectfully, as befitted a captain offering tactical advice to a major general.

"We have no reserves, Captain," Banks said in a peevish voice. "We are fully committed! So press on. Press hard. Tell Crawford it's his responsibility now. I won't have men calling for help, not when we're on the verge of victory. Go back and tell him to push on hard, you hear me? Push on hard and no stopping till nightfall." The long speech had restored Banks's confidence. He was winning; it was God's will that the vaunted Stonewall Jackson should be humbled. "It's nervousness, plain nervousness," Banks explained General Crawford's request to the men who surrounded him. "A fellow finds himself on the winning side and can't believe his luck so he asks for help at the last moment!"

"I hope you'll be kind to Crawford in your memoirs, sir," the *Zouave* commander observed.

"To be sure, to be sure," Banks said, who had not considered his memoirs till this moment, but now found himself dreaming of a three-volume work, provisionally entitled *Banks's War*. He decided he would depict his early defeats as necessary deceptions that had lured the cabbage-eating Jackson on to destruction at Cedar Mountain. "I might have been reviled"—the General rehearsed a sentence in his head—"but I was playing a longer hand than my critics knew, especially those journalistic curs who dared to offer me advice even though not one of them could tell a Parrott gun from a bird's beak."

The Reverend Elial Starbuck broke this pleasant reverie

by begging Banks's permission to ride forward so he could observe the pursuit and final humiliation of the enemy. "Your triumph is an answer to my prayers, Governor," the preacher said, "and I would dearly like to witness its full fruits."

"My dear Starbuck, of course you must ride forward. Captain Hetherington?" Banks summoned one of his junior aides to accompany the preacher, though he also cautioned the aide not to expose the Reverend Starbuck to any danger. The caution was given to make certain that the Reverend Starbuck survived to preach Banks's fame from his influential pulpit. "A wounded cur can still bite," Banks warned the preacher, "so you must stay well clear of the dying beast's jaws."

"God will preserve me, Governor," the Reverend Starbuck averred. "He is my strong shield and protector."

Thus guarded, the Reverend Starbuck set off across the fields with Hetherington, first threading a path between rows of army wagons with white canvas hoods, then passing a field hospital where the Reverend Starbuck paused to inspect the faces of the wounded Southern prisoners who lay after surgery on the grass outside the tents. Some were still comatose from the effects of chloroform, a few slept from sheer weariness, but the majority lay pale and frightened. A few crudely bandaged casualties lay waiting for the surgeons' knives, and to anyone unaccustomed to battle the sight of such grievously hurt men might have proved more than the strongest stomach could abide, but the Reverend Starbuck seemed positively enlivened by the horrid spectacle. Indeed, he leaned out of his saddle for a closer look at one man's mangled limbs and bloodied scalp. "You note the low cranial gap and the pronounced teeth?" he observed to Hetherington.

"Sir?" Hetherington asked in puzzlement.

"Look at his face, man! Look at any of their faces! Can't

you see the pronounced difference between them and the Northern visage?"

Captain Hetherington thought that the Southerners did not look very much different from Northerners, except that they were generally thinner and a good deal more raggedly uniformed, but he did not want to contradict the eminent preacher, and so he agreed that the captured rebels did indeed display low foreheads and feral teeth.

"Such features are the classic symptoms of feeblemindedness and moral degradation," the Reverend Starbuck announced happily, then remembered the Christian duty that was owed even to such fallen souls as these rebel prisoners. "Though your sins be as scarlet," he called down to them, "yet you may be washed whiter than snow. You must repent! You must repent!" He had come equipped with copies of his tract, *Freeing the Oppressed*, which explained why Christian men should be prepared to die for the sacred cause of abolishing slavery, and now the Reverend Starbuck dropped a few copies among the wounded men. "Something to read during your imprisonment," he told them, "something to explain your errors." He spurred on, cheered by this chance to have spread the good word. "We have been remiss, Captain," the preacher declared to Hetherington as the two men left the hospital behind, "in restricting our mission work to heathen lands and Southern slaves. We should have sent more good men into the rebellious states to tussle with the demons that dwell in the white man's soul."

"There are plenty of churches, are there not, in the secessionist states?" Captain Hetherington inquired respectfully after leading the preacher around a tangle of telegraph wire that had been dumped beside a ditch.

"There are indeed churches in the South," the Reverend Starbuck said in a tone of distaste, "and pastors, too, I dare say, yet their existence should not deceive us. The scriptures

72

warn us against those false prophets who shall inhabit the latter days. And such prophets have no difficulty in persuading the feebleminded to adopt the devil's ways. But the Second Epistle of Peter promises us that the false prophets shall bring upon themselves a swift destruction. I think we are witnessing the beginnings of that providence. For this is the Lord's doing," the Reverend Doctor Starbuck declaimed happily, gesturing toward two dogs that fought over a dead man's intestines close to a smoking shell crater, "and we should rejoice and be glad in it!" A less pious impulse made the Reverend wonder whether the money he had just expended on Galloway's Horse was going to be wasted. Maybe the war would be won without Galloway's men? Then he thrust that concern away and let this day's good news fill him with joy instead.

Captain Hetherington wanted to drive the two dogs away from their offal, but the Reverend Starbuck was spurring ahead, and the aide's duty was to stay with the preacher, so he galloped to catch up. "Are you saying, sir," Hetherington asked respectfully, "that none of the rebels are Christians?"

"How can they be?" the Boston preacher responded. "Our faith has never preached rebellion against the lawful and godly authority of the state, so at best the South is in grievous error and thus in desperate need of repentance and forgiveness. And at worst?" The Reverend Starbuck shook his head rather than even consider such a question, yet the very asking of it made him think of his second son and how Nate was even now irretrievably committed to the fires of hell. Nate would burn in everlasting flames, tormented through all eternity by agonies unimaginable. "And he deserves it!" the Reverend Starbuck protested aloud.

"I'm sorry, sir?" Hetherington asked, thinking he had misheard a comment addressed to him.

"Nothing, Captain, nothing. You are saved yourself?"

"Indeed, sir. I came to Christ three years ago, and have praised God for His mercies ever since."

"Praise Him indeed," the Reverend Starbuck responded, though in truth he was secretly disappointed that his escort should thus prove to be a born-again Christian, for there were few things Elial Starbuck enjoyed so much as having what he called a tussle with a sinner. He could boast of having left many a strong man in tears after an hour's good argument.

The two men arrived at a Northern battery of twelve-pounder Napoleons. The four guns were silent, their shirt-sleeved gunners leaning on their weapons' wheels and staring across the valley to where a long-shadowed stand of trees was crowned with gunsmoke. "No targets, sir," the battery commander answered when the Reverend Starbuck asked why he was not firing. "Our fellows are inside those woods, sir, or maybe a half-mile beyond, which means our job's done for the day." He took a pull of his flask, which contained brandy. "Those shell bursts are rebel guns firing long, sir," he added, gesturing at the white explosions that blossomed intermittently on the far crest. The sound of each explosion followed a few seconds later like a small rumble of thunder. "Just their rear guard," the artilleryman said confidently, "and we can leave the peasantry to look after them."

"The peasantry?" the Reverend Starbuck inquired.

"The infantry, sir. Lowest of the low, see what I mean, sir?"

The Reverend Starbuck did not see at all, but decided not to make an issue of his puzzlement. "And the rebels?" he asked instead. "Where are they?"

The gunner Major took note of the older man's Geneva bands and straightened himself respectfully. "You can see some of the dead ones, sir, excuse my callousness, and the rest are probably halfway to Richmond by now. I've waited over a year to see the rascals skedaddle, sir, and it's a fine sight. Our young ladies saw them off in fine style." The Major slapped the still warm barrel of the closest gun, which, like the rest of the Napoleons in the battery, had a girl's name painted on its trail. This gun was Maud, while its companions were named Eliza, Louise, and Anna.

"It is the Lord's doing, the Lord's doing!" the Reverend Starbuck murmured happily.

"The seceshers are still lively over there." Captain Hetherington gestured to far-off Cedar Mountain, where gunsmoke still jetted from the rebel batteries.

"But not for long." The artillery Major spoke confidently. "We'll hook behind their rear and take every man jack of them prisoner. As long as nightfall doesn't come first," he added. The sun was very low and the light reddening.

The Reverend Starbuck took a small telescope from his pocket and trained it on the woods ahead. He could see very little except for smoke, leaves, and burning shell craters, though in the nearer open land he could make out the humped shapes of the dead lying in the remnants of the wheat field. "We shall go to the woods," he announced to his companion.

"I'm not sure we should, sir," Captain Hetherington demurred politely. "There are still shells falling."

"We shall come to no harm, Captain. Though we walk through the valley of the shadow of death we shall fear no evil. Come!" In truth the Reverend Starbuck wanted to ride closer to those bursting shells. He had decided that his exhilaration was symptomatic of a natural taste for battle, that maybe he was discovering a God-given talent for warfare, and it was suddenly no wonder to him that the Lord of Hosts had so frequently exhorted Israel to the fight. This blood and slaughter was the way to see God's work accomplished! Sermonizing and mission work were all very well, and doubtless God listened to the prayers of all those wilting women with faded silk bookmarks in their well-thumbed Bibles, but this hammer of battle was a more certain method of bringing about His kingdom. The sinners were being scourged by the holy flail of sword, steel, and gunpowder, and the Reverend Doctor Starbuck exulted in the process. "Onwards, Captain," he encouraged Hetherington. "The enemy is beaten, there's nothing to fear!"

Hetherington paused, but the artillery Major was in full agreement with the preacher. "They're well beaten, sir, and amen," the Major declared, and that encouragement was enough to make the Reverend Starbuck hand down some copies of *Freeing the Oppressed* for the weary gunners. Then, spirits soaring, he spurred his horse past the quartet of fan-shaped swathes of scorched stubble that marked where Eliza, Louise, Maud, and Anna had belched flame and smoke at the enemy.

Captain Hetherington followed unhappily. "We don't know that the rebels are yet cleared from the woods, sir."

"Then we shall find out, Captain!" the Reverend Starbuck said happily. He trotted past the remains of a Northerner who had been blown apart by the direct hit of a rebel shell, and who was now nothing but a fly-crawling mess of jagged-ended bones, blue guts, torn flesh, and uniform scraps. The Reverend felt no anguish at the sight, merely the satisfaction that the dead man was a hero who had gone to his Maker by virtue of having died for a cause as noble as any that had ever driven man onto the battlefield. A few paces beyond the dead Federal was the corpse of a Southerner, his throat cut to the bone by a fragment of shell casing. The wretch was dressed in gaping shoes, torn pants, and a threadbare coat of pale gray patched with brown, but the corpse's most repellent aspect was the grasping look on his face. The preacher reckoned he saw that same depraved physiognomy on most of the rebel dead and on the faces of the rebel wounded who cried for help as the two horsemen rode by. These rebels, the Reverend Starbuck decided, were demonstrably feebleminded and doubtless morally infantile. The doctors in Boston were convinced that such mental weaknesses were inherited traits, and the more the Reverend Elial Starbuck saw of these Southerners, the more persuaded he was of that medical truth. Had there been miscegenation? Had the white race so disgraced itself with its own slaves that it was now paying the hereditary price? That thought so disgusted the Reverend that he flinched, but then an even more terrible thought occurred to him. Was his son Nathaniel's moral degradation inherited? The Reverend Starbuck cast that suspicion out. Nathaniel was a backslider and so doubly guilty. Nathaniel's sins could not be laid at his parents' door, but only at his own wicked feet.

The Reverend Elial Starbuck thus ruminated about heredity, slavery, and feeblemindedness as he rode across the hot battlefield, yet he did not entirely ignore the cries that came from the parched, hurting men left helpless by the fighting. The wounded rebels were pleading for water, for a doctor, or for help in reaching the field hospitals, and the Reverend Starbuck offered them what comfort was in his power by assuring them that salvation could be theirs after a true repentance. One dark-bearded man, sheltering under a bullet-scarred tree and with his leg half severed and a rifle sling serving as a tourniquet about his thigh, cursed the preacher and demanded brandy instead of a sermon, but the Reverend Starbuck merely let a tract fall toward the man and then spurred sadly on. "Once this rebellion is ended, Captain," he observed, "we shall be faced with a mighty task

77

in the South. We shall needs preach the pure gospel to a people led into error by false teachers."

Hetherington was about to agree with that pious observation but was checked from speaking by a sudden sound coming from the west. To the Reverend Starbuck, unused to the noise of battle, the sound was exactly like gigantic sheets of stiff canvas being ripped across, or perhaps like the noise caused by the wretched urchins who liked to run down Beacon Hill dragging sticks along the iron palings. The noise was so sudden and intrusive that he instinctively checked his horse, but then, assuming that the weird sound presaged the end of rebellion, he urged the beast on again and muttered a prayer of thanks for God's providence in giving the North victory. Captain Hetherington, less sanguine, checked the preacher's horse. "I didn't think the rebs were that far west," he said, apparently speaking to himself.

"West?" the preacher asked, confused.

"Rifle volleys, sir," Hetherington answered, explaining the strange noise. The Captain stared toward the dying sun, where a trembling veil of smoke was starting to show above the trees.

"That noise!" the Reverend Starbuck exclaimed. "Listen! You hear that noise? What is it?" His excitement was caused by a new sound that was suddenly added to the rifle volleys. It was a high-pitched noise infused with a yelping triumph and thrilled through with a ululating and gleeful quality that suggested that the creatures who made such a sound were come willingly and even gladly to this field of slaughter. "You know what you're hearing?" The Reverend Starbuck asked the question with enthusiasm. "It's the *paean*! I never thought I should live to hear it!"

Hetherington glanced at the preacher. "The *peon*, sir?" he asked, puzzled.

"You've read Aristophanes, surely?" the preacher

demanded impatiently. "You remember how he describes the war cry of the Greek infantry? The *paean*?" Maybe, the preacher thought, some classically minded officer from Yale or Harvard had fostered the pleasant fancy of teaching his Northern soldiers that ancient war cry. "Listen, man," he said excitedly, "it's the sound of the phalanx! The sound of the Spartans! The sound of Homer's heroes!"

Captain Hetherington could hear the sound only too clearly. "That's not the *paean*, sir. It's the rebel yell."

"You mean . . ." the Reverend Starbuck began, then fell abruptly silent. He had read about the rebel yell in the Boston newspapers, but now he was hearing it for himself, and the sound of it suddenly seemed anything but classical. Instead it was infused with the purest evil; a noise to chill the blood like a scrabble of wild beasts howling or like the baying of a horde of demons begging to be released from the smoking gates of hell. "Why are they yelling?" the preacher asked.

"Because they're not beaten, sir, that's why," Hetherington said, and he reached for the preacher's reins and pulled his horse around. The Reverend Starbuck protested the about turn, for he was already very close to the woods and he wanted to see what lay beyond the trees, but the Captain could not be persuaded to continue. "The battle's not won, sir," he said quietly, "it might even be lost."

For a rebel yell meant only one thing: a rebel attack.

Because the wretches weren't beaten at all.

Captain Nathaniel Starbuck, crouched in the woods close by the turnpike, heard the screaming of a rebel counter-attack. "About goddamned time," he murmured to no one in particular. The gunfire in the trees had been sporadic for the last few minutes, and Starbuck had begun to fear that the Legion's stranded skirmishers would be trapped far behind a victorious Northern army. So far the only resistance to the Northern attack had seemed haphazard and futile, but now the rifle fire swelled into the full intensity of battle, to which the screams of the attacking Southerners added an unearthly descant. The battle was all sound to Starbuck, for he could see nothing through the smoky, deep-shadowed undergrowth, but the sounds indicated that the attacking Northerners were being checked and even counterattacked. "I reckon we should join in," Starbuck said to Captain Medlicott.

"No," Medlicott said. "Absolutely not!" The reply was too vehement, betraying Medlicott's fear. The miller turned soldier was as white-faced as though he had just come from a hard shift at his old grindstones. Sweat dripped and glistened in his beard, while his eyes flicked nervously around the sanctuary his men had fortuitously discovered among the trees. The sanctuary was a shallow scrape that would have been flooded by the smallest fall of rain, yet was so surrounded by undergrowth that an army could have marched on the road behind and not seen the men hidden just paces away. "We'll just wait here till things calm down," Medlicott insisted.

Starbuck did not like the thought of skulking in the shadows. So far the two companies had avoided any Northerners, but that luck might not last, yet Medlicott would not listen to the younger man's ideas. Medlicott had been happy enough to accept Starbuck's guidance when they were exposed to the enemy's fire, but now that he was in a seemingly safe refuge, Medlicott was rediscovering the authority that Colonel Swynyard had conferred on him. "We stay here," he insisted again, "and that's an order, Starbuck."

Starbuck went back to his company. He stretched himself at the edge of the shallow hollow and stared through the foliage toward the sounds of battle. The branches of the wood made a dark lacework against an evening sky that was layered with red-tinted bands of gunsmoke. The rebel yell swelled and faded, hinting at surges as regiments advanced and went to ground before advancing again. Volleys crashed among the trees, then footsteps trampled the undergrowth close by, but the leaves grew so thick that Starbuck could see no one. Nevertheless he feared the sudden irruption of a company of nervous Yankees, and so he twisted around and hissed at his men to fix their bayonets. If the Yankees did come, then Starbuck would be ready for them.

He pulled out his own blade and slotted it into place. Squirrels chattered unhappily in the branches overhead, and a flash of red feathers showed where a cardinal flew among the trunks. Behind Starbuck, beyond the deserted turnpike, gunsmoke lay like layers of mist above a patchwork of wheat and cornfields. There was no infantry visible there. It was almost as if the road divided the battlefield into two discrete halves, the one filled with cannon smoke and the other with struggling men.

Truslow, his rifle tipped with steel, dropped beside Starbuck. "What's wrong with Medlicott?"

"Frightened."

"Never was any damned good. His father was the same." Truslow spat a viscous gob of tobacco juice into the leaf mould. "I once saw old John Medlicott run from a pair of horse thieves who weren't a day over fifteen."

"Were you one of them?" Starbuck asked shrewdly.

Truslow grinned, but before he could answer there was a sudden panicked rush of feet, and a single Northern soldier burst through the bushes ahead. The Yankee was oblivious of the two rebel companies until he was just paces away, then his eyes widened and he slid to a panicked halt. His mouth dropped open. He turned, seemingly to shout a warning to his comrades, but Starbuck had climbed to his feet

81

and now hammered the side of the Northerner's skull with the brass butt of his rifle just a split second before Truslow pulled the man's feet out from beneath him. The Yankee fell like a poleaxed steer. Truslow and Starbuck dragged him back to the company and disarmed him. "Shut your goddamned mouth," Starbuck hissed at the man, who had begun to stir.

"I'm not . . ."

"The officer told you to shut the hell up, you son of a whore, so shut the hell up or I'll rip your damned tongue out," Truslow growled, and the Northerner went utterly quiet. The buckle on his leather belt showed he was a Pennsylvanian. A trickle of blood showed among the roots of his fair hair above his ear. "You'll have a peach of a bruise there, you bastard," Truslow said happily. He was rifling the man's pockets and pouches. He tossed the Pennsylvanian's rifle cartridges back among the company, then found a pale brown package marked with the trademark of John Anderson's Honeydew Fine-Cut Tobacco of New York. "It ain't Virginia, but someone will smoke it," Truslow said, pushing it into his pouch.

"Leave me some," the Pennsylvanian pleaded. "I ain't had a smoke in hours."

"Then you should have stayed in Pennsylvania, you son of a whore, instead of trampling our corn. You're not wanted here. If you got what you deserved you'd be breathing through a hole in your ribs by now." Truslow eased a wad of folded Northern dollar bills from the man's top pocket. "Lucky at cards, are you?"

"And with women." The Pennsylvanian had a snub-nosed and cheeky charm.

"Lie still and be quiet, boy, or your luck will end here." Truslow unlooped the boy's canteen and found it still held a half-inch of water, which he offered to Starbuck. Starbuck, despite his thirst, refused, so Truslow drained the canteen himself.

Starbuck stood to give himself a view over the surrounding brush. Captain Medlicott hissed at him to get his head down, but Starbuck ignored the miller. Another burst of screaming announced a renewed rebel charge, and this time a group of some two dozen Yankees appeared just twenty paces beyond Starbuck's hiding place. A handful of the Northerners knelt and fired into the trees before retreating again. Two of the Yankees fell as they went back, driven down by rebel bullets, and the rest of the men would doubtless have kept on running had not the color party come through the trees to rally them. A tall, white-haired officer waved a sword toward the rebels. "*Vorwärts! Vorwärts!*" the officer cried, and the retreating men turned, cheered, and delivered a splintering volley toward their pursuers. The two flags were bright squares of silk in the smoke-riven shadows. One was Old Glory, battle-torn and stained, while the second was a purple flag embroidered with an eagle and a legend Starbuck could not decipher. "*Vorwärts!*" the white-haired officer called again.

"Are they goddamned Germans?" Truslow asked. The Sergeant had an irrational dislike of German immigrants, blaming them for many of the rules and regulations that had begun to infest his former country. "Americans used to be free men," he often declared. "Then the damned Prussians came to organize us."

"We're Pennsylvania *Deutsch*," the prisoner answered.

"Then you're godforsaken son of a bitch bastards," Truslow said. Starbuck could read the Gothic-lettered legend on the second flag now: "*Gott und die Vereinigten Staaten*," it said, and it struck Starbuck that such a flag would make a handsome trophy.

"*Feuer!*" the white-haired officer shouted, and another

83

Northern volley ripped into the attacking rebels. The Germans cheered, sensing that their sudden resistance had taken the attackers by surprise.

"We can take those bastards," Starbuck said to Truslow.

The Sergeant glanced toward Captain Medlicott. "Not with that yellow bastard's help."

"Then we'll do it without the yellow bastard's help," Starbuck said. He felt the elation of a soldier given the inestimable advantage of surprise; this was a fight he could not lose, and so he cocked his rifle and twisted around to look at his company. "We're going to put one volley into those German sons of bitches and then run them off our land. Hard and fast, boys, scare the daylights out of the sumbitches. Ready?" The men grinned at him, letting him know that they were good and ready. Starbuck grinned back. There were times when he wondered if anything ever again in all eternity would ever taste as good as these moments in battle. The nervousness of anticipation was utterly gone, replaced by a feral excitement. He glanced at the prisoner. "You stay here, Yankee."

"I won't move an inch!" the prisoner promised, though in truth he intended to run just as soon as he was left unattended.

"Stand!" Starbuck shouted. The heady mix of fear and excitement swirled through him. He understood the temptation of following Medlicott's lead and staying hidden and safe, yet he also wanted to humiliate Medlicott. Starbuck wanted to show that he was the best man on a battlefield, and no one demonstrated such arrogance by cowering in the bushes. "Take aim!" he called, and a handful of the rallying Yankees heard the shouted order and looked around fearfully, but they were already too late. Starbuck's men were on their feet, rifles at their shoulders.

Then it began to go wrong.

"Stop!" Medlicott shouted. "Get down! I order you! Down!" The miller had panicked. He was running up the shallow scrape and shouting at Starbuck's men, even thrusting some of them back down to the ground. Other men crouched, and all were confused.

"Fire!" Starbuck shouted, and a puny scatter of rifle flames studded the shadows.

"Down!" Medlicott waved a hand frantically.

"Get up and fire!" Starbuck's yell was ferocious. "Up! Fire!" The men stood again and pulled their triggers, so that a stuttering mistimed volley flamed in the dusk. "Charge!" Starbuck shouted, drawing the word out like a war cry.

The white-haired officer had turned the Pennsylvanians to face the unexpected threat to their flank. Medlicott's interference had bought the Yankees a few seconds of precious time, long enough for a half-company to form a ragged firing line at right angles to the rest of their battalion. That half-company now faced Starbuck's confused assault, and as he watched the Yankees lift their rifles to their shoulders, he sensed the disaster that was about to strike. Even a half-company volley at such short distance would tear the heart from his assault. Panic whipped through him. He felt the temptation to break right and dive into the underbrush for cover, indeed a temptation to just run away, but then salvation arrived as the rebel regiment that was assaulting the Pennsylvanians from the south fired an overwhelming volley. The hastily formed Northern line crumpled. The fusillade that should have destroyed Starbuck was never fired. Instead the two Union flags faltered and fell as the overpowered Yankees began to retreat.

Sheer relief made Starbuck's war cry into a chilling and incoherent screech as he led his men into the clearing. A blue-coated soldier swung a rifle butt at him, but Starbuck easily parried the wild blow and used his own rifle's stock to hammer the man down to the leaf mould. A rifle shot half deafened him; the Northerner who had fired it was retreating backward and tripped on a fallen branch. Robert Decker jumped on the man, screaming as loudly as his terrified victim. Truslow alone advanced without screaming; instead, he was watching for places where the enemy might recover the initiative. He saw one of the Legion's new conscripts, Isaiah Clarke, being beaten to the ground by a huge Pennsylvanian. Truslow had his bowie knife drawn. He slashed it twice, then kicked the dying Pennsylvanian so that his body would not fall across Clarke. "Get up, boy," he told Clarke. "You ain't hurt bad. Nothing that a swallow of whiskey won't cure."

The Pennsylvanians were running now. The stripes of Old Glory had disappeared northward to safety, but the blue eagle flag with its ornate German legend was being carried by a limping sergeant. Starbuck ran for the man, shouting at him to surrender. A Yankee corporal saw Starbuck and leveled a revolver that he had plucked from the body of a fallen rebel officer, but the chambers were not primed, and the revolver just clicked in his hand. The corporal swore in German and tried to duck aside, but Starbuck's bayonet took him in the belly; then Esau Washbrook's rifle butt slammed onto his skull and the man went down. A great tide of screaming rebels was coming from the south. The white-haired officer snatched the blue eagle flag from the limping sergeant and swung its staff like a clumsy poleax. The sergeant fell and covered his head with his hands, and the officer, shouting defiance in German, tripped over the man's prostrate body. The fallen officer fumbled at his waist for a holstered revolver, but Starbuck was astride him now and ramming his bayonet down into the man's ribs. Starbuck screamed, and his scream, half relief and half visceral, drowned the cry of the dying Pennsylvanian. Starbuck forced the blade down until the steel would go no farther, then rested on the gun's stock as Truslow pulled the eagle flag away from the hooked, scrabbling, and suddenly enfeebled hands of the dying man whose long white hair was now blood red in the day's last light.

Starbuck, his instincts as primitive as any savage, took the flag from Truslow and shook it in the air, spraying drops of blood from its fringe. "We did it!" he said to Truslow. "We did it!"

"Just us," Truslow said meaningfully, turning to where Medlicott was still hidden.

"I'm going to kick the belly out of that bastard," Starbuck said. He rolled the bloodied flag around its varnished pole. "Coffman!" he shouted, wanting the Lieutenant to take charge of the captured flag. "Coffman! Where the hell are you, Coffman?"

"Here, sir." The Lieutenant's voice sounded weakly from behind a fallen tree.

"Oh, Christ!" Starbuck blasphemed. Coffman's voice had been feeble, like that of a man clinging to consciousness. Starbuck ran over the clearing, jumped the tree, and found the young Lieutenant kneeling wide-eyed and pale-faced, but it was not Coffman who was wounded. Coffman was fine, just shocked. Instead it was Thaddeus Bird, kind Colonel Bird, who lay death white and bleeding beside the fallen trunk.

"Oh God, Nate, it hurts." Bird spoke with difficulty. "I came to fetch you home, but they shot me. Took my revolver, too." He tried to smile. "Wasn't even loaded, Nate. I keep forgetting to load it."

"Not you, sir, not you!" Starbuck dropped to his knees, the captured flag and Medlicott's cowardice both forgotten as his eyes suddenly blurred. "Not you, Pecker, not you!"

Because the best man in the Brigade was down.

*

87

All across the field, from the slopes of Cedar Mountain to the ragged corn patches west of the turnpike, the rebels were advancing by the light of a sinking sun that was now a swollen ball of fading red fire suspended in a skein of shifting cannon smoke. A small evening wind had at last sprung up to drift the gunsmoke above the wounded and the dead.

The four guns named Eliza, Louise, Maud, and Anna suddenly found employment again as gray infantry appeared like wolf packs at the timberline. The gunners fired over the heads of their own retreating infantry, lobbing shells that cracked pale smoke against the dark-shadowed woods. "Bring up the limbers! Jump to it!" The Major, who a moment before had been tilting the pages of the battery's much-thumbed copy of *Reveries of a Bachelor* to the last rays of sunlight, saw that he would have to move his guns smartly northward if the battery were not to be captured. "Bring my horse!" he shouted.

The four guns went on firing while the teams were fetched. A lieutenant, fresh from West Point, noticed a group of mounted rebel officers at the wood's margin. "Slew left!" he called, and his team levered with a handspike to turn Eliza's white-oak trail. "Hold there! Elevate her a turn. Load shell!" The powder bag was thrust down the swabbed-out barrel, and the gunner sergeant rammed a spike down the touchhole to pierce the canvas bag.

"No shell left, sir!" one of the artillerymen called from the pile of ready ammunition.

"Load solid shot. Load anything, but for Christ's sake, hurry!" The Lieutenant still watched the tempting target.

A round of solid shot was rammed down onto the canvas bag. The Sergeant pushed his friction primer into the touchhole, then stood aside with the lanyard in his hand. "Gun ready," he shouted.

88

Eliza's limber, drawn by six horses, galloped up behind to take the gun away. "Fire!" the Lieutenant shouted.

The Sergeant whipped the lanyard toward him, thus scraping the friction rod across the primer-filled tube. The fire leaped down to the canvas bag, the powder exploded, and the four-and-a-half-inch iron ball screamed away across the smoke-layered field. The gun itself recoiled with the force of a runaway locomotive, jarring backward a full ten paces to mangle the legs of the two leading horses of the limber team. Those lead horses went down, screaming. The other horses reared and kicked in terror. One horse shattered a splinter bar, another broke a leg on the limber, and suddenly the battery's well-ordered retreat had turned into a horror of screaming, panicked horses.

A gunner tried to cut the unwounded horses free, but could not get close because the injured horses were thrashing in agony. "Shoot them, for Christ's sake!" the Major shouted from his saddle. A rifle bullet whistled overhead. The rebel yell sounded unearthly in the lurid evening light. The gunner trying to disentangle the horses was kicked in the thigh. He screamed and fell, his leg broken. Then a rebel artillery shell thumped into the dirt a few paces away, and the broken fragments of its casing whistled into the screaming, terror-stricken mass of men and horses. The other three guns had already been attached to their limbers.

"Go!" the Major said, "go, go, go!" and the black-muzzled Louise, Maud, and Anna were dragged quickly away, their crews hanging for dear life to the metal handles of the limbers while the drivers cracked whips over the frightened horses. The gun called Eliza stood smoking and abandoned as a second rebel shell landed plum in the mess of blood, broken harness, and struggling horses. Eliza's lieutenant vomited at the sudden eruption of blood that gushed outward, then began limping north.

Captain Hetherington led the Reverend Doctor Starbuck past the abandoned gun and the bloody twitching mess that remained of its team. The preacher had lost his top hat and was constantly turning in the saddle to watch the dark gray line of men who advanced beneath their foul banners. One of the advancing rebels was wearing the Bostonian's top hat, but it was not that insult that caused the preacher to frown but rather the conundrum of why God had allowed this latest defeat. Why was a righteous cause, fought by God's chosen nation, attended by such constant disaster? Surely, if God favored the United States, then the country must prosper, yet it was palpably not prospering, which could only mean that the country's cause, however good, was not good enough. The nation's leaders might be committed to the political cause of preserving the Union, but they were lukewarm about emancipating the slaves, and until that step was taken, God would surely punish the nation. The cause of abolition was thus made more explicit and urgent than ever. Thus reassured about the nobility of his mission, the Reverend Starbuck, his white hair streaming, galloped to safety.

A mile behind the Reverend Elial Starbuck, at the wooded ridge where the North's attack had surged, crested, and then been repulsed, General Washington Faulconer and his staff sat on their horses and surveyed the battlefield. Two brigades of Yankee infantry were retreating across the wide wheat field, their progress hastened by some newly arrived rebel cannon that fired shell and shot into the hurrying ranks. Only one Northern battery was replying to the gunfire. "No point in making ourselves targets," Faulconer announced to his aides, then trotted back into the trees to hide from the gunners.

Swynyard alone remained in the open. He was on foot, ready to lead the Brigade's first line down the long slope. Other rebel troops were already a quarter-mile beyond the woods, but the Faulconer Brigade had started its advance late and had yet to clear the trees. Swynyard saw that Faulconer had disappeared into the trees, so he pulled out his flask of whiskey and tipped it to his mouth. He finished the flask, then turned to shout at the advancing line to hurry up, but just as he turned so a blow like the beat of a mighty rushing wind bellowed about him. The air was sucked clean from his chest. He tried to call out, but he could not speak, let alone cry. The whiskey was suddenly sour in his throat as his legs gave way. He collapsed a second before something cracked like the awesome clangor of the gates of hell behind him, and then it seemed to Swynyard that a bright light, brighter than a dozen noonday suns, was filling and suffusing and drowning his vision. He lay on his back, unable to move, scarce able to breathe, and the brilliant light flickered around his vision for a few golden seconds before, blessedly, his drink-befuddled brain gave up its attempts to understand what had happened.

He fell into insensibility, and his sword slipped from his nerveless hand. The solid shot that had been fired from the doomed Eliza had missed his skull by inches and cracked into a live oak growing just behind. The tree's trunk had been riven by the cannonball, splaying outward like a letter Y with its inner faces cut as clean and bright as fresh-minted gold.

The Faulconer Brigade advanced past the prostrate Colonel. No one paused to help him, no one even stooped to see if the Colonel lived or was dead. A few men spat at him, and some would have tried to rifle his pockets, but the officers kept the lines moving, and so the Brigade marched on through the wheat field in laggard pursuit of the retreating enemy.

It was Captain Starbuck and Sergeant Truslow who eventually found Colonel Swynyard. They had carried

Colonel Bird to Doctor Danson's aid post, where they had pretended to believe Doc Billy's reassurance that the Colonel's chest wound might not prove fatal. "I've seen others live with worse," Danson said, bending in his blood-stiffened apron over the pale, shallow-breathing Bird. "And Pecker's a tough old fowl," Danson insisted, "so he stands a good chance." For a time Starbuck and Truslow had waited while Danson probed the wound, but then, realizing there was no help they could offer and that waiting only made their suspense worse, they had walked away to follow the footsteps of the advancing Brigade. Thus they came upon the prostrate Swynyard. The sun had gone down, and the whole battlefield was suffused by a pearly evening light dissipated by the smoke that was still sun-tinged on its upper edges. Carrion birds, ragged-winged and stark black, flapped down to the dirt, where they ripped at the dead with sharp-hooked beaks.

"The bastard's dead," Truslow said, looking down at Swynyard.

"Or drunk," Starbuck said. "I think he's drunk."

"Someone sure gave the bastard a hell of a good kicking," Truslow observed, pointing to a bruise that swelled yellow and brown across the side of the Colonel's skull. "Are you sure he ain't dead?"

Starbuck crouched. "Bastard's breathing."

Truslow stared out across the field, which was pitted with shell craters and littered with the black-humped shapes of the dead. "So what are you going to do with him?" he asked. "The son of a bitch tried to have us all killed," he added, just in case Starbuck might be moved toward a gesture of mercy.

Starbuck straightened. Swynyard lay helpless, his head back and his beard jutting skyward. The beard was crusted with dried tobacco juice and streams of spittle. The Colonel was breathing slow, a slight rattle sounding in his throat with every indrawn sigh. Starbuck picked up Swynyard's fallen sword and held its slender tip beneath Swynyard's beard as though he was about to plunge the steel into the Colonel's scrawny throat. Swynyard did not stir at the steel's touch. Starbuck felt the temptation to thrust home; then he flicked the sword blade aside. "He's not worth killing," he said, and then he rammed the sword down to skewer a pamphlet that had been blown by the small new wind to lodge against the Colonel's bruised skull. "Let the bastard suffer his headache," he said, and the two men walked away.

Back on the turnpike the Federals made one final effort to save the lost day. The retreating infantry were trading volleys with the advancing rebels, who were also under the fire of one last stubborn Yankee artillery battery that had stayed to cover the North's retreat. Now it seemed that the guns of that last battery must be captured, for the gunners were almost in range of the Southern rifles that threatened to kill the team horses before they could be harnessed to the cannons.

So, to save the guns, the 1st Pennsylvania Cavalry was ordered forward. The men rode fresh corn-fed horses in three lines, fifty troopers to a line. A bugle sounded the advance, and the horses dipped their heads so that their manes tossed in the evening light as the first rank of horsemen trotted out past the guns.

The second line advanced, then the third, each leaving a sufficient space between themselves and the line ahead so that the troopers could swerve around a dead or dying horse. Sabers scraped out of scabbards and glittered in the blood red light of dying day. Some men left their sabers sheathed and carried revolvers instead. A swallow-tailed guidon, blue and white, was carried on a lance head in the front rank.

The cannon were hitched to limbers, and the gunners' paraphernalia was stowed in boxes or hung from the trail hooks. The gunners hurried, knowing that the cavalry was buying them a few precious moments in which to escape. The cavalry horses were going at a fast trot now, leaving tiny spurts of dust behind their hooves. The three lines stretched onto the fields either side of the turnpike, which here ran between open fields that had been harvested of wheat and corn. Curb chains and scabbard links jingled as the horsemen advanced.

Ahead of the horsemen the Confederate infantry halted. There was a metallic rattle as ramrods thrust bullets hard down onto powder charges. Fingers stained black with gunpowder pushed brass percussion caps onto fire-darkened cones. "Wait till they're close, boys! Wait! Wait!" an officer shouted.

"Aim for the horses, lads!" a sergeant called.

"Wait!" the officer shouted. Men shuffled into line, and more men ran to join the rebel ranks.

The Northern bugle called again, this time raggedly, and the horses were spurred into a canter. The guidon was lowered so that the lance point was aimed straight at the waiting infantry, who looked like a ragged gray-black line stretched across the turnpike. Fires burned on the far ridge, their smoke rising slow to make grim palls in the darkening sky, where the evening star was already a cold and brilliant point of light above the smoke-clad slopes of Cedar Mountain. A waxing moon, bright and sharp as a blade, rose beyond those smoky southern woods. More infantry hurried toward the turnpike to add their fire to the volley that threatened the approaching horsemen.

The bugle called a last defiant time. "Charge!" an officer shouted, and the troopers screamed their challenge and slashed back their spurs to drive their big horses into a full gallop. They were farm boys, come from the good lands of Pennsylvania. Their ancestors had ridden horses in the wars of old Europe and in the wars to free America, and now their descendants lowered their sabers so that the blade points would rip like spears into the ribcages of the rebel line. The dry fields on either flank of the turnpike shuddered to the thunder of the pounding hooves.. "Charge!" the cavalry officer shouted again, drawing out the word like a war cry into the night.

"Fire!" the rebel cry answered.

Five hundred rifles slashed flame in the dusk. Horses screamed, fell, died.

"Reload!"

Ramrods rattled and scraped in hot rifle barrels. Unhorsed men staggered away from the carnage on the turnpike. Not one single trooper in the front rank had stayed in his saddle, and not one horse was still on its legs. The second line had been hit hard, too, but enough men survived to gallop on, mouths open and sabers bright as they galloped toward the remnants of the first rank, where horses screamed, hooves thrashed, and viscous blood sprayed from the twitching, dying beasts. A horseman of the second line leaped a bloody mound of writhing bodies only to be hit by two bullets. The rebels were screaming their own challenge now as they edged forward, loading and firing. An unhorsed cavalryman ran back a few paces, then doubled over to vomit blood. Horses screamed pathetically, their blood trickling in black rivulets to make thick puddles on the dusty road.

The third line checked behind the milling remnants of the second line. Some cavalrymen fired revolvers over the gory barricade, which was all that remained of their leading ranks, but then another volley flamed and smoked from the advancing rebel ranks, and the surviving horsemen pulled their reins hard around and so turned away. Their retreat brought jeers from their enemy. More rifles cracked and more saddles were emptied. A horse limped away, another fell among the wheat stooks, while a third raced riderless toward the west. The surviving troopers galloped north in the wake of the rescued guns that were being whipped back toward Culpeper Court House.

A hundred and sixty-four troopers had charged an army. Seventy returned.

And now, at last, under a warm wind reeking of blood, night fell.

In the fields at the foot of Cedar Mountain the battleground lay dark beneath the banded layers of smoke that shrouded the sky. High clouds had spread to hide the moon, though still a great wash of eye-bright stars arced across the northern portion of the sky.

The wounded cried and called for water. Some of the battle's survivors searched the woods and cornfields for injured men and gave them what help they could while other men looted the dead and robbed the wounded. Raccoons foraged among the bodies, and a skunk, disturbed by a wounded horse blundering through the woods, released its stench to add to the already reeking battlefield.

The new rebel front line was where the Yankees had started the day, while the Yankees themselves had withdrawn northward and made a new defensive line across the road to Culpeper Court House. Messengers brought General Banks news of more Northern troops hurrying south from Manassas in case the rebel attack presaged a full-scale thrust northward. Culpeper Court House must be held, General Pope ordered, though that command did not stop some panicked Yankees loading wagons with plunder taken from abandoned houses and starting northward in case the feared rebel cavalry was already sweeping east and west of the town to cut off General Banks's army.

Other wagons brought the first wounded from the battle-field. The town's courthouse, a fine arcaded building with a belfry and steeple, was turned into a hospital, where the surgeons worked all night by the smoky light of candles and oil lamps. They knew the morning light would bring them far more broken bodies, and maybe it would bring vengeful rebels, too. The sound of bone saws rasped in the darkness, where men gasped and sobbed and prayed.

General Banks wrote his dispatch in a commandeered farmhouse that had been looted by Northern soldiers who had taken General Pope's orders to live off the land as permission to plunder all Southern homes. Banks sat on an empty powder barrel and used two more such barrels as his table. He dipped his steel nib into ink and wrote that he had won a victory. It was not, he allowed privately, the great victory that he had hoped for, but it was a victory nonetheless, and his words described how his small force had faced and fought and checked a mighty rebel thrust northward. Like a good politician he wrote with one eye on history, making of his battle a tale of stubborn defiance fit to stand alongside the Spartans who had defended Greece against the Persian hordes.

Six miles to the south his opponent also claimed victory. The battle had decided nothing, but Jackson had been left master of the field, and so the General knelt in prayer to give thanks to Almighty God for this new evidence of His mercies. When the General's prayers were finished, he gave curt orders for the morning: The wounded must be collected, the dead buried, and the battleground searched for weapons that would help the Confederate cause. And then, wrapped in a threadbare blanket, Jackson slept on the ground beneath the thinning smoke.

Nervous sentries disturbed the sleep of both armies with sporadic outbreaks of rifle fire, while every now and then an apprehensive Northern gunner sent a shell spinning south toward the smear of fires that marked where the Southerners tried to rest amidst the horrors of a field after battle. Campfires flickered red, dying as the night wore on until at last an uneasy peace fell across the wounded fields.

And in that fretful dark a patrol of soldiers moved quietly.

The patrol was composed of four men, each wearing a white cloth patch embroidered with a red crescent. The patrol's leader was Captain Moxey, Faulconer's favorite aide, while the men themselves came from Captain Medlicott's company, the one most loyal to Faulconer. Medlicott had gladly loaned the three men, though he had not sought the permission of Major Paul Hinton, who had taken command of the Legion from the wounded Thaddeus Bird. Hinton, like Moxey and Medlicott, wore the red crescent badge, but he was so ambivalent about his loyalty that he had deliberately dirtied and frayed his patch until it could hardly be recognized as the Faulconer crest, and had Hinton known of Moxey's mission, he would undoubtedly have stopped the nonsense before it began.

The four men carried rifles, none of them loaded. The three privates had each been promised a reward of five dollars, in coins rather than bills, if their mission was successful. "You might have to break a few heads," Faulconer had warned Moxey, "but I don't want any bloodshed. I don't want any courts-martial, you understand?"

"Of course, sir."

Yet, as it turned out, the whole mission was ridiculously easy. The patrol crept through the Legion's lines well inside the ring of sentries whose job was to look outward, not inward. Moxey led the way between sleeping bodies, skirting the dying fires, going to where Starbuck's Company H slept beneath the stars. Coming close, and wary lest one of the company's dogs should wake and start barking, Moxey held up his hand.

The problem that had made this mission necessary had begun earlier in the evening when the men of Faulconer's Brigade were making what supper they could from the scraps of food they had either plundered or discovered in their knapsacks. Captain Pryor, General Washington Faulconer's new aide, had come to Starbuck and requested that the captured Pennsylvanian flag be handed over.

"Why?" Starbuck had asked.

"The General wants it," Pryor answered innocently. Thomas Pryor was far too new to the Brigade to comprehend the full enmity that existed between Starbuck and Faulconer. "I'm to take it to him."

"You mean Faulconer wants to claim that he captured it?" Starbuck demanded.

Pryor colored at such an ignoble accusation. "I'm sure the General would do no such thing," he said.

Starbuck laughed at the aide's naïveté. "Go and tell General Faulconer, with my compliments, that he can come here and ask for the flag himself."

Pryor had wanted to insist, but he found Nathaniel Starbuck a somewhat daunting figure, even a frightening figure, and so he had carried the unhelpful message back to the General who, surprisingly, showed no indignation at Starbuck's insolence. Pryor ascribed the General's reaction to magnanimity, but in truth Washington Faulconer was furious and merely hiding that fury. He wanted the flag, and even felt entitled to the flag, for had it not been captured by men under his command? He thus considered the flag to be his property, and he planned to hang the trophy in the hall-way of his house just outside Faulconer Court House, which was why, at quarter past three in the morning, Captain

Moxey and three men were poised just outside the area where Starbuck's men slept.

"There," one of Moxey's men whispered and pointed to where Lieutenant Coffman lay curled under a blanket.

"Are you sure he's got it?" Moxey whispered back.

"Certain."

"Stay here," Moxey said, then tiptoed across the dry grass until he reached the sleeping Lieutenant and could see the rolled-up flag lying half concealed beneath Coffman's blanket. Moxey stooped and put a hand on Coffman's throat. The grip woke the boy. "One word," Moxey hissed, "and I'll cut your damned throat."

Coffman started up, but was thrust hard down by Moxey's left hand. Moxey seized the flag in his other hand and started to edge it free. "Keep quiet," he hissed at Coffman, "or I'll have your sisters given the pox."

"Moxey?" Coffman had grown up in the same town as Moxey. "Is that you?"

"Shut up, boy," Moxey said. The flag was at last free, and he backed away, half regretting his failure to give a sleeping Starbuck a beating, but also relieved that he would not have to risk waking the Northerner. Starbuck had a belligerent reputation, just like his company, which was considered the most reckless in the Legion, but the men of Company H had all slept through Moxey's raid. "Let's go!" Moxey told his own men, and so they slipped safely away, the trophy captured.

Coffman shivered in the dark. He wondered if he should wake Starbuck or Truslow, but he was scared. He did not understand why Moxey should need to steal the flag, and he could not bear the thought of having let Starbuck down. It had been Captain Starbuck who had shamed General Washington Faulconer into paying his salary, and Coffman was terrified that Starbuck would now be angry with him, and so he just lay motionless and frightened as he listened to the far-off whimpers and cries that came from the taper-lit tents where the tired doctors sawed at limbs and prised misshapen bullets from bruised and bloodied flesh. Thaddeus Bird was in one of Doctor Danson's tents, still breathing, but with a face as pale as the canvas under which he slept.

The plight of the men still on the battlefield was far worse. They drifted in and out of their painful sleep, sometimes waking to the voices of other men calling feebly for help or to the sound of wounded horses spending a long night dying. The night's small wind blew north to where the frightened Yankees waited for another rebel attack. Every now and then a nervous artilleryman fired a shell from the Yankee lines, and the round would thump into the trampled corn and explode. Clods of earth would patter down, and a small thick cloud of bitter smoke would drift north as a chorus of frightened voices momentarily sounded loud before fading again. Here and there a lantern showed where men looked for friends or tried to rescue the wounded, but there were too many men lying in blood and not enough men to help, and so the abandoned men suffered and died in the small wicked hours.

Colonel Griffin Swynyard neither died nor called for help. Instead the Colonel lay sleeping, and in the dawn, when the sun's first rays lanced over the crest of Cedar Mountain to gild the field where the dead lay rotting and the wounded lay whimpering, he opened his eyes to brightness.

Thirty miles north, where train after train steamed into Manassas Junction to fill the night with the clash of cars, the hiss of valves, and the stench of smoke, Adam Faulconer watched the horses purchased with the Reverend Elial Starbuck's money come down from the boxcars. The beasts were frightened by the noises and the pungent smells of this strange place, and so they pricked their ears, rolled their eyes white, and whinnied pitifully as they were driven between two lines of men into a makeshift corral formed from empty army wagons. Captain Billy Blythe, who had purchased the horses and shipped them to Manassas, sat long-legged on a wagon driver's high box and watched to see how Adam liked his animals. "Real special horses, Faulconer," Blythe called. "Picked 'em myself. I know they don't look much, but there ain't nothing wrong that a few days in a feedlot won't set straight." Blythe lit a cigar and waited for Adam's judgment.

Adam hardly dared say a word in case that word provoked a fight with Blythe. The horses were dreadful beasts. Adam had seen better animals penned at slaughter yards.

Tom Huxtable was Adam's troop sergeant. He came from Louisiana but had chosen to fight for the North rather than strain the loyalty of his New York wife. Huxtable spat in derision of the newly arrived horses. "These ain't horses, sir," he said to Adam. "Hell, these ain't no horses. Broken-down mules is all they is." He spat again. "Swaybacked, spavined, and wormy. I reckon Blythe just pocketed half the money."

"You say something, Tom Huxtable?" a grinning Billy Blythe called from his perch.

For answer Sergeant Huxtable just spat again. Adam curbed his own anger as he inspected the twenty frightened horses and tried to find some redeeming feature among them, but in the lanterns' meager light the animals did indeed look a sorry bunch. They had capped hocks and sloping pasterns, swaybacks and, most troubling of all, too many running noses. A horse with bad lungs was a horse that needed to be butchered, yet these were the horses being given to the men under Adam's command. Adam cursed himself for not buying the horses himself, but Major

Galloway had insisted that Blythe's experience in horse dealing was one of the regiment's valuable assets.

"So what do you think, Faulconer?" Blythe asked mockingly.

"What did you pay for them?"

Blythe waved the cigar insouciantly. "I paid plenty, boy, just plenty."

"Then you were cheated." Adam could not hide his bitterness.

"There just ain't that many horses available, boy." Blythe deliberately taunted Adam with the word "boy" in hopes of provoking a show of temper. Blythe had been content to be Galloway's second-in-command and saw no need for the Major to have fetched a third officer into the regiment. "The army's already bought all the decent horses, so we late-comers have to make do with the leavings. Are you telling me you can't manage with those there horses?"

"I reckon this gray has distemper," Corporal Kemp said. Harlan Kemp, like Adam, was a Virginian who could not shake his loyalty to the United States. He and his whole family had abandoned their farm to come north.

"Better shoot the beast, then," Blythe said happily.

"Not with one of your guns," Adam snapped back. "Not if they're as good as your horses."

Blythe laughed, pleased at having goaded the display of temper out of Adam. "I got you some right proper guns, Faulconer. Colt repeaters, brand-new, still in their Connecticut packing cases." The Colt repeater was little more than a revolver elongated into a long-arm, but its revolving cylinder gave a man the chance to fire six shots in the same time an enemy rifleman needed to fire just one. The weapon was not famed for its accuracy, but Major Galloway reckoned a small group of horsemen needed volume of fire rather than accuracy and claimed that forty horsemen firing six shots were worth over two hundred men with single-shot rifles.

"It ain't a reliable gun," Sergeant Huxtable murmured to Adam. "I've seen the whole cylinder explode and take off a man's hand."

"And it's too long in the barrel," Harlan Kemp added. "Real hard to carry on horseback."

"You spoke, Harlan Kemp?" Blythe challenged.

"I'm saying the Colt ain't a horse soldier's weapon," Kemp responded. "We should have carbines."

Blythe chuckled. "You're lucky to have any guns at all. So far as guns and horses go, we're on the hindmost teat. So you'll just have to clamp down and suck hard."

Huxtable ignored Blythe's crudity. "What do you reckon, sir?" he asked Adam. "These horses can't be ridden. They ain't nothing but worm meat." Adam did not answer, and Tom Huxtable shook his head. "Major Galloway won't let us ride on nags like these, sir."

"I guess not," Adam said. Tonight Major Galloway was fetching orders from General Pope, and those orders were supposed to initiate the first offensive patrols of Galloway's Horse, but Adam knew he could do nothing on these broken-backed animals.

"So what will we do?" Harlan Kemp asked, and the other men of Adam's troop gathered round to hear their Captain's answer.

Adam looked at the sorry, shivering, diseased horses. Their ribs showed and their pelts were mangy. For a moment he felt a temptation to give way to despair, and he wondered why every human endeavor had to be soured by jealousy and spite, but then he glanced up into Billy Blythe's grinning face, and Adam's incipient despair was overtaken by a surge of resolution. "We'll exchange the horses," Adam told his anxious men. "We'll take these nags south and we'll exchange them for the best horses in Virginia. We'll change them for horses swift as the wind and strong as the hills." He laughed as he saw the incomprehension on Blythe's face. Adam would not be beaten, for he knew just where to find those horses, the best horses, and once he had found his horses, he would sow havoc among his enemies. Billy Blythe or no, Adam Faulconer would fight.

SATURDAY MORNING, the day after battle, again dawned hot and humid. Leaden clouds covered the sky and added to the air's oppression, which was made even fouler by a miasmic smell that clung to the folds of the battlefield like the morning mist. At first light, when the troops were stirring reluctantly from their makeshift beds, Major Hinton sought out Starbuck. "I'm sorry about last night, Nate," Hinton said.

Starbuck offered the Legion's new commanding officer a curt and dismissive judgment of Washington Faulconer's raid to snatch the captured flag. The Bostonian was stripped to the waist and had his chin and cheeks lathered with shaving soap plundered from a captured artillery limber. Starbuck stropped his razor on his belt, leaned close to his scrap of mirror, then stroked the long blade down his cheek.

"So what will you do?" Hinton asked, plainly nervous that Starbuck would be provoked into some rash act.

"The bastard can keep the rag," Starbuck said. He had not really known what to do with the captured standard; he had thought that perhaps he might give it to Thaddeus Bird or else send it to Sally Truslow in Richmond. "What I really wanted was the Stars and Stripes," he confessed to Hinton, "and that eagle flag was only ever second-best, so I reckon that son of a bitch Faulconer can keep it."

"It was a stupid thing for Moxey to do, all the same," Hinton said, unable to conceal his relief that Starbuck did

106

not intend to inflate the night's stupidity into an excuse for revenge. He watched as Starbuck squinted into a broken fragment of shaving mirror. "Why don't you grow a beard?" he asked.

"Because everyone else does," Starbuck said, although in truth it was because a girl had once told him he looked better clean-shaven. He scraped at his upper lip. "I'm going to murder goddamn Medlicott."

"No, you're not."

"Slowly. So it hurts."

Major Hinton sighed. "He panicked, Nate. It can happen to anyone. Next time it might be me."

"Son of a bitch damn nearly had me killed by panicking."

Major Hinton picked up the plundered jar of Roussel's Shaving Cream, fidgeted with its lid, then watched Starbuck clean the razor blade. "For my sake," he finally pleaded, "will you just forget about it? The boys are unhappy enough because of Pecker and they don't need their captains fighting among themselves. Please, Nate? For me?"

Starbuck mopped his face clean on a strip of sacking. "Give me a cigar, Paul, and I'll forget that bald-headed lily-livered gutless shadbelly bastard even exists."

Hinton surrendered the cigar. "Pecker's doing well," he said, his tone brightening as he changed the subject, "or as well as can be expected. Doc Billy even reckons he might survive a wagon ride to the rail depot." Hinton was deeply worried about replacing the popular Colonel even though he was a popular enough officer himself. He was an easygoing, heavyset man who had been a farmer by trade, a churchman by conviction, and a soldier by accident of history. Hinton had hoped to live out his years in the easy, rich countryside of Faulconer County, enjoying his family, his acres, and his foxhunting, but the war had threatened Virginia, and so Paul Hinton had shouldered his weapons out of patriotic duty. Yet he did not much enjoy soldiering and reckoned his main duty was to bring safely home as many of the Faulconer Legion as he possibly could, and the men in the Legion recognized that ambition and liked Hinton for it. "We're to stay where we are today," Hinton now told Starbuck. "I've got to detach a company to collect small arms off the battlefield and another to bring in the wounded. And talking of the wounded," he added after a second's hesitation, "did you see Swynyard yesterday? He's missing."

Starbuck also hesitated, then told the truth. "Truslow and I saw him last night." He gestured with the cigar toward the woods where his company had fought against the Pennsylvanians. "He was lying just this side of the trees. Truslow and I didn't reckon there was anything to be done for him, so we just left him."

Hinton was shrewd enough to guess that Starbuck had abandoned Swynyard to die. "I'll send someone to look for him," he said. "He ought to be given a burial."

"Why?" Starbuck demanded belligerently.

"To cheer the Brigade up, of course," Hinton said, then blushed for having uttered such a thing. He turned to look at the great smear of smoke that rose from the Northern cooking fires beyond the woods. "Keep a good eye on the Yankees, Nate. They ain't beaten yet."

But the Yankees made little hostile movement that morning. Their pickets probed forward but stopped obediently when the rebel outposts opened fire, and so the two armies settled into an uneasy proximity. Then it began to rain, slowly at first, but with an increasing vehemence after midday. Starbuck's company made shelters at the edge of the woods with frameworks of branches covered in sod. Then they lay under cover and just watched the gray, rain-lashed landscape.

In midafternoon, when the rain eased to a drizzle, Corporal Waggoner sought Hinton's permission for a prayer meeting. There had been no chance for such a service since the battle's ending, and many soldiers in the Legion wanted to give thanks. Hinton gladly gave his permission, and fifty or more Legionnaires gathered beneath some gun-battered cedars. Other men from the Brigade soon joined them, so that by the time the drizzle stopped, there were almost a hundred men sitting beneath the trees and listening as Corporal Waggoner read from the Book of Job. Waggoner's twin brother had died in the battles on the far side of Richmond, and ever since that death Peter Waggoner had become more and more fatalist. Starbuck was not sure that Waggoner's gloomy piety was good for the Legion's morale, but many of the men seemed to like the Corporal's spontaneous sessions of prayer and Bible study. Starbuck did not join the circle, but rested nearby, watching northward to where the Yankee defense line showed between the distant woodlands as a newly dug strip of earthworks broken by hastily erected cannon emplacements. Starbuck would have been hard put to admit it, but the familiar sounds of prayer and Bible reading were oddly comforting.

That comfort was broken by a blasphemous oath from Sergeant Truslow. "Christ Almighty!" the Sergeant swore.

"What is it?" Starbuck asked. He had been half dozing but now sat up fully awake. Then he saw what had provoked Truslow to blasphemy. "Oh, Jesus," he said, and spat.

For Colonel Swynyard was not dead. Indeed, the Colonel hardly appeared to be wounded. His face was bruised, but the bruise was covered and shadowed by a wide-brimmed hat that Swynyard must have plucked from among the battle-field litter, and now the Colonel was walking through the Brigade's lines with his familiar wolfish smile. "He's drunk," Truslow said. "We should have shot the bastard yesterday."

Peter Waggoner's voice faltered as the Colonel walked up to the makeshift prayer meeting. Swynyard stopped at the edge of the meeting, saying nothing, just staring at the men with their open Bibles and bare heads, and every single man seemed cowed by the baleful eyes. The Colonel had always been a mocker of these homespun devotions, though until now he had kept his scorn at a distance. Now his malevolence killed the prayerful atmosphere stone dead. Waggoner made one or two brave efforts to keep reading, but then stopped altogether.

"Go on," Swynyard said in his hoarse voice.

Waggoner closed his Bible instead. Sergeant Phillips, who was one of Major Haxall's shrinking Arkansas battalion, stood to head off any trouble. "Maybe you'd like to join us at prayer, Colonel?" the Sergeant suggested nervously.

The tic in Swynyard's cheek twitched as he considered his answer. Sergeant Phillips licked his lips while others of the men closed their eyes in silent prayer. Then, to the amazement of everyone who watched, Colonel Swynyard pulled off his hat and nodded to Phillips. "I would like that, Sergeant, I would indeed." Sergeant Phillips was so taken aback by the Colonel's agreement that he said nothing. A murmur went through the Bible study group, but no one spoke aloud. Swynyard, the bruise on his face visible now, was embarrassed by the silence. "If you'll have me, that is," he added in an unnaturally humble voice.

"Anyone is welcome," Sergeant Phillips managed to say. One or two of the officers in the group muttered their agreement, but no one looked happy at welcoming Swynyard. Everyone in the prayer group believed the Colonel was playing a subtle game of mockery, but they did not understand his game, nor did anyone know how to stop it, and so they offered him a reluctant welcome instead.

"Maybe you'll let me say a word or two?" Swynyard suggested to Phillips, who seemed to have assumed leadership of the prayer meeting. Phillips nodded, and the Colonel fidgeted with the hat in his hands as he looked around the frightened gathering. The Colonel tried to speak, but the words would not come. He cleared his throat, took a deep breath, and tried again. "I have seen the light," he explained.

Another murmur went through the circle of seated men. "Amen," Phillips said.

Swynyard twisted the hat in his nervous hands. "I have been a great sinner, Sergeant," he said, then stopped. He still wore the same hated smile, but some of the men nearer to Swynyard could sense that it was now a smile of embarrassment rather than sarcasm. The same men could even see tears in the Colonel's eyes.

"Drunk as a bitch on the Fourth of July," Truslow said in a tone of wonder.

"I'm not sure," Starbuck said. "I think he might be sober."

"Then he's lost his damn wits," Truslow opined.

Sergeant Phillips was more generous. "We have all been sinners, Colonel," the Sergeant said, "and fallen short of the glory of God."

"I more than most." Swynyard, it seemed, was determined to make a public confession of his sins and of his rediscovered faith. He was blinking back tears and fidgeting with the hat so frenetically that it fell from his hands. He let it lie. "I was raised a Christian by my dear mother," he said, "and I received the Lord into my heart at a camp meeting when I was a youth, but I have been a sinner ever since. A great sinner."

"We've all sinned," Sergeant Phillips averred again.

"But yesterday," Swynyard said, "I came to my senses. I was near killed, and I felt the very wings of the angel of death beat about me. I could smell the sulfur of the bottomless pit and I could feel the heat of its flames, and I knew, as I lay on the field, that I deserved nothing less than that terrible punishment." He paused, almost overcome by the memory. "But then, praise Him, I was pulled back from the pit and drawn into the light."

A chorus of amens and hallelujahs sounded among the circle of men. They were all sincere Christians, and though they might have hated this man with an intense hatred, the more honest among them had also prayed for the Colonel's soul, and now that their prayers were being answered, they were willing to give thanks to God for His mercies to a sinner.

Swynyard had tears on his cheeks now. "I also know, Sergeant, that in the past I have been unfair in my dealings with many men here. To those men I offer my regrets and seek their forgiveness." The apology was handsomely spoken, and the men in the group took it just as handsomely. Then Swynyard turned away from the circle and looked among the shelters for Starbuck. "I owe another man an even greater apology," the Colonel said.

"Oh, Jesus," Starbuck swore and wriggled back into the shadow of his shelter.

"Bastard's touched in the head," Truslow said. "He'll be foaming at the mouth next and pissing himself. We'll have to take him away and put him out of his misery."

"We should have shot the bastard when we had the chance," Starbuck said, then fell silent because Swynyard had left the Bible circle and was walking toward his shelter.

"Captain Starbuck?" Swynyard said.

Starbuck looked up into his enemy's face. "I can hear you, Colonel," Starbuck said flatly. He could see now that the Colonel had made an attempt to improve his appearance. His beard was washed, his hair combed, and his uniform brushed. The tic in his cheek still quivered, and his hands shook, but he was plainly making a great effort to hold himself straight and steady.

"Can I talk with you, Starbuck," the Colonel asked, then, after a moment's silence, "please?"

"Are you drunk?" Starbuck asked brutally.

Swynyard offered his rotting, yellow-toothed smile. "Only on God's grace, Starbuck, only on His divine grace. And with His help I shall never touch ardent spirits again."

Truslow spat to show his disbelief. Swynyard ignored the insult, gesturing instead to indicate that he would like to take a walk with Starbuck.

Starbuck climbed reluctantly out of his turf shelter, shouldered his rifle, and followed the Colonel. Starbuck was wearing new boots that he had taken from a dead Pennsylvanian. The boots were new and stiff, but Starbuck was convinced they would wear in well enough after a day or two. Now, though, he felt the makings of a blister as he walked self-consciously beside Swynyard. News of the Colonel's conversion had spread through the Brigade, and men were drifting toward the picket line to see the proof for themselves. Some evidently believed that the Colonel's religious experience was just another inebriated escapade, and they grinned in anticipation of a display of drunken idiocy, but Swynyard seemed oblivious to the attention he was receiving. "You know why I sent your company forward yesterday?" he asked Starbuck.

"Uriah the Hittite," Starbuck said shortly.

Swynyard thought for a second; then the story of David and Bathsheba came back from his dusty memories of childhood Sunday schools. "Yes," he said. "And I intended for you to be killed. I am sorry, truly."

Starbuck wondered how long Swynyard's manifestation of honesty would last and reckoned that it would be only until the Colonel's thirst overcame his piety, but he kept that skepticism to himself. "I guess you were just obeying someone else's orders," he said instead.

"It was still a sinful action," Swynyard said very earnestly, thus obliquely confirming that it had indeed been Washington Faulconer who had ordered Starbuck's company into the place of danger, "and I ask your forgiveness." Swynyard concluded his confession by holding out his hand.

Starbuck, excruciated with embarrassment, shook the offered hand. "Say no more about it, Colonel," he said.

"You're a good soldier, Starbuck, a good soldier, and I haven't made life easy for you. Not for anyone, really." Swynyard made the admission in a gruff voice. The Colonel had been weeping when he gave his halting testimony at the prayer meeting, but now he seemed in a more rueful mood. He turned and gazed north to where groups of Yankees could be seen in the far fields beyond the nearer stands of trees. No man on either side seemed inclined to belligerence this day; even the sharpshooters who delighted to kill at long range were keeping their rifle barrels cold. "Do you have a Bible?" Swynyard asked Starbuck suddenly.

"Sure I do." Starbuck felt in his breast pocket where he kept the small Bible that his brother had sent him. James had intended the Bible to spark Starbuck into a repentance like the one that was transforming Swynyard, but Starbuck had kept the scriptures out of habit rather than need. "You want it?" he asked, offering the book to the Colonel.

"I shall find another," Swynyard said. "I just wanted to be certain you have a Bible because I'm sure you're going to need one." Swynyard smiled at the suspicious look on Starbuck's face. The Colonel doubtless intended the smile to be friendly, but the resulting foul-toothed leer uncomfortably recalled the Colonel's usual malevolence. "I wish I could describe what happened to me last night and this morning," he now told Starbuck. "It was as though I was struck by a great light. There was no pain. There's still no pain." He touched the livid bruise on his right temple. "I remember lying on the earth and hearing voices. I couldn't move, couldn't speak. The voices were debating my death, and I knew I had come to the judgment seat and I felt a fear, a most terrible fear, that I was being consigned to hell. I wanted to weep, Starbuck, and in my terror I called out to the Lord. I remembered my mother's teaching, my childhood lessons, and I called on the Lord and He heard me."

Starbuck had heard too many testimonies of repentant sinners to be either moved or even convinced by the Colonel's change of heart. Doubtless Swynyard had received a shock, and doubtless he intended to reform his life, but Starbuck was equally convinced that Swynyard's conversion would prove soluble in alcohol before the sun went down. "I wish you well," he muttered grudgingly.

"No, no, you don't understand." Swynyard spoke with some of his old savage force and laid his maimed left hand on Starbuck's elbow to prevent the younger man from turning away. "When I recovered my senses, Starbuck, I found my sword stuck into the turf beside my head and there was a message impaled on the sword. This message." The Colonel took from his pocket a crumpled and torn pamphlet, which he pushed into Starbuck's hand.

Starbuck smoothed the tract to see that it was called *Freeing the Oppressed* and had been printed in Anne Street, Boston. The cover showed a picture of a half-naked black man springing free from broken manacles toward a cross that was infused with a heavenly light. The shattered manacles were attached to great iron weights labeled "Slavocracy," "Ignorance," and "Wickedness," and beneath those iron weights was written the name of the pamphlet's author: the Reverend Doctor Elial Starbuck. Starbuck felt his usual tremor of distaste at any reminder of his father's existence, then handed the tract back to the Colonel. "So what was your message?" he asked sourly. "That slavery is a sin against God? That America's blacks have to be returned to Africa? Is that what you're going to do with your pair? Set them free?" And never, Starbuck reflected, had two slaves more deserved freedom.

Swynyard shook his head to show that Starbuck was still misunderstanding him. "I don't know what to believe about slavery. Dear God, Starbuck, but everything in my life has to be changed, can't you understand that? Slavery, too, but that wasn't the reason God left the tract beside me last night. Don't you see? He left it there to give me a task!"

"No," Starbuck said, "I don't see."

"My dear Starbuck," Swynyard said very earnestly. "I have been brought back from the path of sin at the very last moment. At that very instant when I was poised on the edge of hell's fire, I was saved. The road to hell is a terrible path, Starbuck, yet at its beginning the journey was enjoyable. Do you understand now what I'm saying?"

"No," Starbuck said, who feared that he understood exactly what the Colonel was saying.

"I think you do," Swynyard said fervently. "Because I think that you are on the first easy steps of that downward path. I look at you, Starbuck, and I see myself thirty years ago, which is why God sent me a pamphlet with your name on it. It's a sign telling me to save you from sin and from the agonies of eternal punishment. I'm going to do that, Starbuck. Instead of killing you as Faulconer wanted I am going to bring you to eternal life."

Starbuck paused to light a cigar he had plundered from the white-haired Pennsylvanian officer who had tried so hard to protect his flags. Then he sighed as he blew smoke past Swynyard's bruised face. "You know, Colonel? I think I really preferred you as a sinner."

Swynyard grimaced. "How long have I known you?"

Starbuck shrugged. "Six months."

"And in all that time, Captain Starbuck, have you ever called me 'sir'?"

Starbuck looked into the Colonel's eyes. "No, and I don't intend to either."

Swynyard smiled. "You will, Starbuck, you will. We're going to be friends, you and I, and I shall draw you back from the paths of sin."

Starbuck blew another plume of smoke into the damp wind. "I never did understand, Colonel, just why some son of a bitch can have a lifetime of sin and then, the moment he gets scared, turn around and try to stop other folks from enjoying themselves."

"Are you telling me the path of righteousness is not enjoyable?"

"I'm telling you I've got to get back to my company," Starbuck said. "I'll see you, Colonel." He touched his hat with a deliberate air of insolence, then walked back to his men.

"So?" Sergeant Truslow greeted Starbuck, the inflection of the word inviting news of the Colonel.

"You were right," Starbuck said. "He's gibbering mad."

"So what's changed?"

"He's got drunk on God," Starbuck said, "that's what's changed." He was trying to sound dismissive of Swynyard, but a part of him was sensing the same fires of hell that had brought the Colonel to God. "But I'll give him till sundown," he went on. "Then he'll be tight on whiskey instead."

"Whiskey works faster than God," Truslow said, but he heard something wistful in his Captain's voice, and so he thrust a pewter flask at him. "Drink some of this," the Sergeant ordered.

117

"What is it?"

"The best spill-skull. Five cents a quart. Tom Canby made it two weeks back."

Starbuck took the flask. "Don't you know it's against army regulations to drink homemade whiskey?"

"It's probably against army regulations to go caterwauling with the wives of serving officers," Truslow said, "but that ain't ever stopped you yet."

"Too true, Sergeant, too true," Starbuck said. He drank, and the fierce liquor momentarily doused the fear of hellfire, and then, beneath a lowering sky, he slept.

The federal government's bureaucrats might have been reluctant to fund Major Galloway's Horse, but General Pope immediately saw the value of having Southern horsemen scouting behind Southern lines, and so he gave the Major such a slew of tasks that a cavalry force ten times larger would have been hard-pressed to fulfill them inside a month, let alone the one week that General Pope offered Galloway.

The chief task was to determine whether General Robert Lee was moving his troops from Richmond. The Northern headquarters in Washington had ordered Lee's opponent, McClellan, to withdraw his army from its camps close to the rebel capital, and Pope feared that Lee, hearing of that order, might already be marching north to reinforce Jackson. He also feared that the rebels could be building up troops in the Shenandoah Valley and had asked Galloway to make a reconnaissance across the Blue Ridge Mountains. And, as if those two tasks were not sufficient, Pope also wanted to know more about Jackson's dispositions, and so Galloway found himself under pressure to send horsemen south, east, and west. He compromised as best he could, taking his own troop south toward Richmond while Billy Blythe was ordered to cross the Blue Ridge Mountains and sniff out the rebel dispositions in the valley of the Shenandoah.

Adam, meanwhile, needed to replace the horses Blythe had wished on him. Major Galloway tried to reassure Adam that Blythe had meant no harm in buying such spavined hacks. "I'm sure he did his best," the Major said, trying to knit the unity of his squadron.

"I'm sure he did, too," Adam agreed, "and that's what worries me." But Adam at least knew where his troop could acquire more horses, and Galloway had given Adam permission to make his raid on condition that on Adam's way back he reconnoitred the western flank of Jackson's army. Adam left to perform both tasks three days after the far-off sound of the battle at Cedar Mountain had bruised the summer's heavy air.

Two miles beyond the Manassas farmhouse that was Galloway's headquarters Adam found Billy Blythe's troop waiting. "Thought we'd ride with you, Faulconer," Blythe said, "seeing as how you and I are going in the same direction."

"Are we?" Adam asked coldly.

"Hell, why not?" Blythe said.

"The Shenandoah Valley's that way," Adam said, pointing west, "while we're going south."

"Well now," Blythe said with his lazy smile, "where I come from a gentleman doesn't go around teaching other gentlemen how to suck a tit. I'll choose my own route to the valley, if that's all right with you."

Adam had little choice but to accept Blythe's company. Sergeant Huxtable whispered his suspicion that Blythe merely wanted to follow Adam and take whatever horses Adam found for his own profit, but Adam could hardly stop his fellow cavalry officer from riding in convoy. Nor, on his dreadful horses, could Adam outrun Blythe, and so, for two days, the forty cavalrymen crept slowly southward. Blythe showed no sense of urgency and no desire to turn toward one of the high passes that led through the Blue Ridge Mountains. He ignored the Chester Gap, then Thornton's Gap, and finally Powell's Gap, hinting all the while that he knew of a better route across the mountains further south. "You're a fool if you use Rockfish Gap," Adam said. "I know for a fact the rebels will guard that pass."

Blythe smiled. "Maybe I won't use any gap at all."

"You won't get horses over the mountains otherwise."

"Maybe I don't need to cross the mountains."

"You'd disobey Galloway's orders?" Adam asked.

Blythe frowned as though he was disappointed in Adam's obtuseness. "I reckon our first duty, Faulconer, is to look after our men, specially when you reckon that the Southern army ain't going to take too kindly to Southern boys riding in Yankee blue, so it ain't my aim to take any real bad risks. That's why Abe Lincoln's got all those boys from Massachusetts and Pennsylvania; if anyone's going to beat ten types of hell out of the Confederates, it'll be them, not us. The important thing for us to do, Faulconer, is just survive the war intact." Blythe paused in this long peroration to light a cigar. Ahead of the cavalrymen was a gentle valley crossed by snake fences and with a prosperous-looking farm at the southern end. "What Joe Galloway ordered me to do, Faulconer," Blythe went on, "is discover how many rebels are skulking in the Shenandoah Valley, and I reckon I can do that well enough without crossing any damned mountain. I can do it by stopping a train coming out of the Rockfish Gap and questioning the passengers. Ain't that right?"

"Suppose the passengers lie?" Adam asked.

"Hell, there ain't a woman alive who'd tell me lies," Blythe said with a smile. He chuckled, then turned in his saddle. "Seth?"

"Billy?" Sergeant Seth Kelley answered.

"Reckon we should make sure no rebel vermin are hanging around that farmhouse. Take a couple of men. Go look."

Seth Kelley shouted at two Marylanders to follow him, then led them south through the trees that bordered the valley. "Reckon we'll just wait here," Blythe said to the other men. "Make yourselves at home now."

"You say our most important duty is to survive the war?" Adam asked Blythe when the troopers had made themselves comfortable in the shade of the broad-leaved trees.

"Because I reckon that the war's ending is when our proper work begins, Faulconer," Blythe said happily. "I even reckon that surviving the war is our Christian duty. The North's going to win. That's plain as the nose on a pelican's face. Hell, the North's got the men, the guns, the ships, the factories, the railroads, and the money, while all the South's got is a heap of cotton, a pile of rice, a stack of tobacco, and more damn lazy niggers than half Africa. The North's got a whole heap of stuff and the South ain't got a besotted hope! So sooner or later, Faulconer, we're going to have an ass-whipped South and a mighty pleased North, and when that day comes we want to make sure that we loyal Southerners get our just rewards. We are going to be the good Southerners, Faulconer, and we'll be the ones who take over down south. We are going to be hogs in clover. Rolling in milk and honey, and getting the pick of the girls and making dollars like a dog makes spit." Blythe turned to stare at the farm. "Now you don't want to risk all that by getting a bullet in your belly, do you?"

Adam heard the chuckles of those men who agreed with Blythe. Others looked grim, and Adam decided he would speak for those idealists. "We've got a job to do. That's what we volunteered for."

Blythe nodded as though Adam had made a wonderfully

121

cogent point. "Hell now, Faulconer, no one agrees with you more than me! Hell, if I could reconnoitre clean down to the Rappahannock, then no one would be as happy as Billy Blythe. Hell, I'd reconnoitre down to the Pee Dee if I could, down as far as the Swanee! Hell, I'd reconnoitre to the last gol-darned river on earth for my country, so I would, but I can't do it! Just plumb can't do it, Faulconer, and you know why?" And here Blythe laid a confiding hand on Adam's elbow and leaned so close that his cigar smell wreathed Adam's head. "We can't do nothing, Faulconer, and that's the plain sad truth of it. We can't even ride to the brothel and back on account of our horses being razor-backed pieces of four-legged hogshit. What's the first duty of a cavalryman?"

"To look after his horse, Billy," one of his men answered.

"Ain't that God's blessed truth?" Blythe responded. "So I reckon that for the horses' sake we just has to go gentle and keep ourselves unpunctured for the rest of the war. Hell now, what in tarnation was that?" The question was Blythe's response to a pair of gunshots that had sounded from somewhere near the farmhouse. For a man who had just preached a gospel of staying well clear of trouble, he seemed remarkably untroubled by the gunfire. "Reckon we'd best ride to see if old Seth's in one piece, boys," he called, and the men of his troop slowly pulled themselves into their saddles and loosened the Colt repeating rifles in their holsters.

"Reckon your troop should stay and keep watch," Blythe told Adam. "I ain't saying we expects any trouble, but you can never tell. These woods are full of bushwhackers and every man jack of them is as mean as a snake and twice as treacherous. So you watch out for partisans while the rest of us make certain old Seth ain't gone to meet his Maker."

Adam watched from the trees as Blythe took his troop down to the farmhouse, which was typical of so many homesteads in the Virginia Piedmont. Adam had often dreamed of settling in just such a farm, miles away from his father's pretensions and wealth. The two-story house was weatherboarded with white-painted planks and handsomely surrounded by a deep veranda, which, in turn, was circled by a straggling but colorful flower garden. A wide vegetable garden stretched between the house and the largest of a pair of barns that formed two sides of a yard that was completed by a rail fence. Orchards ran downhill from the house to where a stream glinted in the distance. The sight of the homestead gave Adam a pang of remorse and nostalgia. It seemed wicked that war should inflict itself on such a place.

At the farm itself Sergeant Seth Kelley waited on the veranda for Captain Blythe. Kelley was a long thin man with a narrow black beard and dark eyes, who now lounged in a wicker chair with his spurred boots propped on the veranda's rail and a cigar in his mouth. His two men were leaning against the posts that flanked the short flight of veranda steps. Kelley took the cigar from his mouth as Captain Blythe dismounted on the parched lawn. "We was fired on, Billy," Kelley said with a grin. "Two shots that came from the top floor. Came damn close to killing me, so they did."

Blythe shook his head and tutted. "But you're all right, Seth? You ain't wounded now?"

"They missed, Billy, they missed. But the rascals had this piece of bunting flying from the house, so they did." Kelley held up a small rebel flag.

"Bad business, Seth, bad business," Blythe said, grinning as broadly as his Sergeant.

"Sure is, Billy. 'Bout as bad as it can be." Kelley put the cigar back in his mouth.

Blythe led his horse across the flower bed and tied its reins to a rail of the porch. His men dismounted as Blythe climbed the veranda steps and used Kelley's cigar to light one of his own. "Any folks inside?" Blythe asked the Sergeant.

"Two women and a passel of brats," Sergeant Kelley said.

Blythe pushed into the house. The hall floor was made of dark wood on which lay a pair of hooked rugs. A long case clock stood by the staircase, its face proclaiming that it had been made in Baltimore. There was a pair of antlers serving as a coatrack, a portrait of George Washington, another of Andrew Jackson, and a pokerwork plaque proclaiming that God was The Unseen Listener to Every Conversation in This House. Blythe gave the clock an appreciative pat as Seth Kelley and two men followed him through the hall and into the kitchen, where three children clung to the skirts of two women. One woman was white-haired, the other young and defiant.

"Well now, well," Blythe said, pausing in the kitchen doorway. "What do we have here?"

"You ain't got no business here," the younger woman said. She was in her thirties and evidently the mother of the three small children. She was carrying a heavy cleaver, which she hefted nervously as Blythe walked into the kitchen.

"The business we got here, ma'am, is the business of the United States of America," Billy Blythe said happily. He strolled past an ancient dresser and picked an apple from a china bowl. He bit a chunk from the apple, then smiled at the younger woman. "Real sweet, ma'am. Just like yourself." The woman was dark-haired with good features and challenging eyes. "I like a woman with spirit," Blythe said, "ain't that so, Seth?"

"You always did have a right taste for such women, Billy." Kelley leaned his lanky form against the kitchen doorpost.

"You leave us alone!" the older woman said, scenting trouble.

"Nothing in this world I'd rather do, ma'am," Blythe said.

He took another bite from the apple. Two of the children had started to cry, prompting Blythe to slam the remnants of the apple hard onto the scrubbed kitchen table. Scraps of the shattered fruit skittered across the kitchen. "I would be obliged if you kept your sniveling infants silent, ma'am!" Blythe snapped. "I cannot abide a sniveling child, no sir! Sniveling children should be whipped. Whipped!" The last word was bellowed so loud that both children stopped crying in sheer fright. Blythe smiled at their mother, displaying scraps of apple between his teeth. "So where's the man of the house, ma'am?"

"He ain't here," the younger woman said defiantly.

"Is that because he's carrying arms against his lawful government?" Blythe asked in a teasing voice.

"He ain't here," the woman said again, and then, after a pause, "There's only us women and children here. You ain't got no quarrel with women and children."

"My quarrels are my business," Blythe said, "and my business is to discover just why one of you two ladies fired a couple of shots at my nice Sergeant here."

"No one fired at him!" the older woman said scornfully. "He fired his own revolver. I saw him do it!"

Blythe shook his head disbelievingly. "That's not what Mr. Kelley says, ma'am, and he wouldn't tell me a lie. Hell, he's a sergeant in the army of the United States of America! Are you telling me that a sergeant of the army of the United States of America would tell a lie?" Blythe asked the question with feigned horror. "Are you really trying to suggest such a thing?"

"No one fired!" the younger woman insisted. The children were almost buried in her skirts. Blythe took a step closer to the woman, who raised the cleaver threateningly.

"You use that, ma'am," Blythe said equably, "and you'll be hanged for murder. What's your name?"

"My name's none of your business."

"So I'll tell you what is my business, ma'am," Blythe said, and he reached out for the cleaver and plucked it from the woman's unresisting grasp. He raised it, then slashed it hard down to bury its blade tip in the table. He smiled at the younger woman, then blew cigar smoke toward the bunches of herbs hanging from a beam. "My business, ma'am," he said, "is with General Order Number Five, issued by Major General John Pope of the United States Army, which General Order gives me the legal right and solemn duty to feed and equip my men with any food or goods we find in this house that might be necessary to our well-being. That is an order, given me by the General in command of my army, and like a good Christian soldier, ma'am, I am duty-bound to obey it." Blythe turned and jabbed a finger toward Sergeant Kelley. "Start searching, Seth! Outhouses, upstairs, cellars, barns. Give the place a good shaking now! You stay here, Corporal," he added to one of the other men who had come into the kitchen.

"We ain't got nothing!" the old woman protested.

"We'll be the judge of that, ma'am," Blythe said. "Start searching, Seth! Do it thorough now!"

"You damned thieves," the younger woman said.

"On the contrary, ma'am, on the contrary." Blythe smiled at her, then sat at the head of the kitchen table and took a preprinted form from a leather pouch at his belt. He found a pencil stub in a pocket. The pencil was blunt, but he tried its lead on the tabletop and was satisfied with the mark it made. "No, ma'am," he went on, "we ain't thieves. We are just trying to put God's own country back into one piece, and we need your help to do it. But it ain't thieving, ma'am, because our Uncle Sam is a kind uncle, a good uncle, and he'll pay you folks real well for everything you give us today." He smoothed out the form, licked the pencil, and looked up expectantly at the younger woman. "Your name, honey?"

"I ain't telling you."

Blythe looked at the older woman. "Can't pay the family without a name, Grandma. So tell us your name."

"Don't tell him, Mother!" the younger woman cried.

The older woman hesitated, then decided that giving the family's name would not cause much harm. "Rothwell," she said reluctantly.

"A mighty fine name," Blythe said as he wrote it on the form. "I knew a family of Rothwells down home in Blytheville. Fine Baptists, they were, and fine neighbors too. Now, ma'am, you happen to know what today's date is?" The house echoed with men's laughter and the heavy sound of boots thumping up the staircase; then a burst of cheering erupted as some treasure was discovered in one of the front rooms. More feet clattered on the stairs. The young woman looked at the ceiling, and a frown of distress crossed her face. "Today's date, ma'am?" Blythe insisted.

The older woman thought for a second. "Yesterday was the Lord's Day," she said, "so today must be the eleventh."

"My, how this summer is just flying by! August the eleventh already." Blythe wrote the date as he spoke, "in the year of Our Lord, eighteen hundred and sixty-two. This danged pencil is scratchy as hell." He finished the date, then leaned back in the chair. Sweat was pouring down his plump face and staining the collar of his uniform coat. "Well now, ladies, this here piece of paper confirms that me and my men are about to commandeer just about any gol-darned thing we take a fancy to in this property. Anything at all! And when we've got it, you're going to tell me the value of all that food and all those chattels, and I'm going to write that value down on this piece of paper and then I'm going to sign it with my God-given name. And what you're going to do, ladies, is keep ahold of this piece of paper like it was the sacred word in the good Lord's own handwriting, and at the end of the war, when the rebels are well beaten and kind Uncle Sam is welcoming you all back into the bosom of his family, you're going to present this piece of paper to the government and the government, in its mercy and goodness, is going to give you all the money. Every red cent. There's just one small thing you ought to know first, though." He paused to draw on his cigar, then smiled at the frightened women. "When you present this piece of paper you'll have to prove that you've stayed loyal to the United States of America from the date on this form until the day the war ends. Just one little piece of evidence that anyone in the Rothwell family might have borne arms or, God help us, even a grudge against the United States of America will make this piece of paper worthless. And that means you'll get no money, honey!" He laughed.

"You damned thief," the younger woman said.

"If you're a good girl," Blythe said mockingly, "then you'll get the money. That's what General Order Number Five says, and we shall obey General Order Number Five, so help us God." He stood. He was a tall man, and the feather in his hat brushed the kitchen's beams as he walked toward the frightened family. "But there's also General Order Number Seven. Have you folks ever heard of General Order Number Seven? No? Well General Order Number Seven decrees what punishment must be given to any household that fires on troops of the United States of America, and a shot was fired at my men from this house!"

"That's a lie!" the older woman insisted, and her vehemence made the three children start to cry again.

"Quiet!" Blythe shouted. The children whimpered and shivered but managed to keep silent. Blythe smiled. "By orders of Major General Pope, who is duly authorized by the

President and by the Congress of the United States of America, it is my duty to burn this house down so that no more shots can be fired from it."

"No!" the younger woman protested.

"Yes," Blythe said, still smiling.

"We didn't fire any shots!" the young woman said.

"But I say you did, and when it comes right down to the scratch, ma'am, whose word do you think the President and the Congress will believe? My word, which is the word of a commissioned officer of the United States Army, or your word, which is the caviling whine of a secessionist bitch? Now which of us, ma'am, is going to be believed?" He took a silver case from his pocket and clicked open the lid to reveal the white phosphorus heads of lucifer matches.

"No!" The younger woman had started to cry.

"Corporal Kemble!" Blythe snapped, and Kemble pushed himself off the kitchen wall. "Take her to the barn," Blythe ordered, pointing to the younger woman.

The woman lunged for the cleaver that was still stuck in the table, but Blythe was much too fast for her. He knocked the cleaver out of her reach, then drew his revolver and pointed it at the woman's head. "I'm not a hard-hearted man, ma'am, just a simple horse trader turned soldier, and like any good horse trader I do sure appreciate a bargain. So why don't you and I go and discuss matters in the barn, ma'am, and see if we can't work out an accommodation?"

"You're worse than a thief," the woman said, "you're a traitor."

"Sir?" Kemble was worried by Blythe's order.

"Take her, Kemble," Blythe insisted. "But no liberties! She's mine to deal with, not yours." Blythe smiled at the woman and her children. "I do so love war, ma'am. I do so love the pursuit of war. I reckon war is in my blood, my hot blood."

Kemble took the woman away, leaving her children crying while Billy Blythe went to reserve the pick of the house's plunder before snatching the real pleasure of his day.

On the Saturday after the battle Captain Anthony Murphy opened a book on how long it would take for Colonel Swynyard to begin drinking again. It had been a miracle, the whole Legion agreed, that the Colonel had lasted two nights, even if he had been concussed for much of the first, but no one believed he could last another two nights without the succor of raw spirits. Ever since his alleged conversion the Colonel had been shaking visibly, such was the strain he endured, and on the Friday night he was heard moaning inside his tent, yet he endured that night, and the next, so that on Sunday he appeared at the Brigade's church parade with his once-ragged beard trimmed and clean, his boots polished, and a determined smile on his haggard face. His was the most earnest voice in prayer, the most enthusiastic to shout amen, and the loudest in singing hymns. Indeed, when the Reverend Moss led the Legion in singing "Depth of mercy, can there be mercy still reserved for me? Can my God His wrath forbear? Me the chief of sinners spare?" Swynyard looked directly at Starbuck and smiled confidingly as he sang.

General Washington Faulconer took his second-in-command to one side after the open-air service. "You're making a damned fool of yourself, Swynyard. Stop it."

"The Lord is making a fool of me, sir, and I praise Him for it."

"I'll cashier you," Faulconer threatened.

"I'm sure General Jackson would like to hear of an officer being cashiered for loving the Lord, sir," Swynyard said with a touch of his old cunning.

130

"Just stop making a fool of yourself," Faulconer growled, then walked away.

Swynyard himself sought out Captain Murphy. "I hear you have a book on me, Murphy?"

The Irishman reddened but confessed it was so. "But I'm not sure I can let you have a wager yourself, Colonel, if that's what you'll be wanting," Murphy said, "seeing as how you might be considered partial in the matter, sir, if you follow my meaning?"

"I wouldn't have a wager," Swynyard said. "Wagering is a sin, Murphy."

"Is it now, sir?" Murphy asked innocently. "Then it must be a Protestant sin, sir, and more's the pity for you."

"But you should be warned that God is on my side, so not a drop of ardent spirits will pass my lips ever again."

"I'm overjoyed to hear that, sir. A living saint, you are." The Irishman smiled and backed away.

That night, after the Colonel had testified at the Legion's voluntary prayer meeting, he was heard praying aloud in his tent. The man was in plain agony. He was lusting after drink, fighting it, and calling on God to help him in the fight. Starbuck and Truslow listened to the pathetic struggle, then went to Murphy's shelter. "One more day, Murph'." Starbuck proffered the last two dollars of his recent salary. "Two bucks says he'll be sodden tight by this time tomorrow night," Starbuck offered.

"I'll take two bucks for tomorrow night as well," Truslow added, offering his money.

"You and a score of others are saying the exact same thing," Murphy said dubiously, then showed the two men a valise stuffed with Confederate banknotes. "Half of that money is saying he won't last this night, and the other half is only giving him till tomorrow sundown. I can't give you decent odds, Nate. I'll be hurting myself if I offered you anything better than two to one against. It's hardly worth risking your money at those odds."

"Listen," Starbuck said. In the silence the three men could hear the Colonel sobbing. There was a light in Swynyard's tent, and the Colonel's monstrous shadow was rocking back and forth as he prayed for help. His two slaves, who had been utterly taken aback by the change in their master's demeanor, crouched helplessly outside.

"The poor bastard," Murphy said. "It's almost enough to stop you from drinking in the first place."

"Two to one on?" Starbuck asked. "For tomorrow night?"

"Are you sure you don't want to put your money on tonight?" Murphy asked.

"He's survived this far," Truslow said. "He'll be asleep soon."

"For tomorrow night, then," Murphy said and took Starbuck's two dollars and then the two dollars that Sergeant Truslow had offered. When the wagers were recorded in Murphy's book, Starbuck walked back past the Colonel's tent and saw Lieutenant Davies on his knees beside the entrance.

"What the . . ." Starbuck began, but Davies turned with his finger to his lips. Starbuck peered closer and saw that the Lieutenant was pushing a half-full bottle of whiskey under the flap.

Davies backed away. "I've got thirty bucks riding on tonight, Nate," he whispered as he climbed to his feet, "so I thought I'd help the money."

"Thirty bucks?"

"Even odds," Davies said, then dusted the dirt off his pants. "Reckon I'm onto a sure thing. Listen to the bastard!"

"It's not fair to do that to a man," Starbuck said sternly. "You should be ashamed of yourself!" He strode to the tent, reached under the flap, and took out the whiskey.

"Put it back!" Davies insisted.

"Lieutenant Davies," Starbuck said, "I will personally pull your belly out of your goddamned throat and shove it up your stinking backside if I ever find you or anyone else trying to sabotage that man's repentance. Do you understand me?" He took a step closer to the tall, pale, and bespectacled Lieutenant. "I'm not goddamn joking, Davies. That man's trying to redeem himself, and all you can do is mock him! Christ Almighty, but that makes me angry!"

"All right! All right!" Davies said, frightened by Starbuck's vehemence.

"I'm serious, Davies," Starbuck said, although the Lieutenant had never actually doubted Starbuck's sincerity. "I'll goddamn kill you if you try this again," Starbuck said. "Now go away." Starbuck watched the Lieutenant vanish into the night, then let out a long sigh of relief. "We'll keep this for tomorrow night, Sergeant," he told Truslow, flourishing the whiskey that Davies had abandoned.

"Then put it into Swynyard's tent?"

"Exactly. God damn Davies's thirty bucks. I need money far more than he does."

Truslow walked on beside his Captain. "What that suffering bastard Swynyard really likes is good brandy."

"Then maybe we can find some on the battlefield tomorrow," Starbuck said, and that discovery seemed a distinct possibility, for although three days had passed since the battle, there were still wounded men lying in the woods or hidden in the broken stands of corn. Indeed, there were so many dead and wounded that the rebels alone could not retrieve all the casualties, and so a truce had been arranged and troops from General Banks's army had been invited to rescue their own men.

The day of the truce dawned hot and sultry. Most of the Legion had been ordered to help search the undergrowth in the belt of trees where the Yankee attack had stalled, but Starbuck's company was set to tree-felling and the construction of a massive pyre on which the dead horses of the Pennsylvanian cavalry were to be burned. On the turnpike behind the pyre a succession of light-sprung Northern ambulances carried away the Yankee wounded. The Northern vehicles, specially constructed for their purpose, were in stark contrast to the farm carts and captured army wagons that the rebels used as ambulances, just as the uniformed and well-equipped Northern soldiers looked so much smarter than the rebel troops. A Pennsylvanian captain in charge of the detail loading the ambulances sauntered down to Starbuck's men and had to ask which of the ragamuffins was their officer. "Dick Levergood," he introduced himself to Starbuck.

"Nate Starbuck."

Levergood companionably offered Starbuck a cigar and a drink of lemonade. "It's crystallized essence," he said, apologizing for the lemonade that was reconstituted from a powder mix, "but it doesn't taste bad. My mother sends it."

"You'd rather have whiskey?" Starbuck offered Levergood a bottle. "It's good Northern liquor," Starbuck added mischievously.

Other Pennsylvanians joined the Legionnaires. Newspapers were exchanged and twists of tobacco swapped for coffee, though the briskest trade was in Confederate dollars. Every Northerner wanted to buy Southern scrip to send home as a souvenir, and the price of the ill-printed Southern money was rising by the minute. The men made their trades beside the great pyre that was a sixty-foot-long mound of newly cut pine logs on which a company of Confederate gunners was now piling the horses. The artillerymen were using a sling-cart that had a lifting frame bolted to its bed. The wagon's real purpose was rescuing dismounted cannon

134

barrels, but now its crane jib hoisted the rotting horse carcasses six feet in the air, then swung them onto the logs, where a team of men with their mouths and nostrils scarfed against the stink levered the swollen corpses into place with handspikes. Another two masked men splashed kerosene on the pyre.

Captain Levergood peered at the sling-cart. "That's one of ours."

"Captured." Starbuck confirmed the cart's Northern origins; indeed the sling-cart still had the letters USA stenciled on its backboard.

"No, no," Levergood said. "One of my family's carts. We manufacture them in Pittsburgh. We used to make sulkies, buggies, Deerborns, and horsecars, now we mostly make army wagons. A hundred wagons a month and the government pays whatever we ask. I tell you, Starbuck, if you want to make a fortune, then work for the government. They pay more for a seven-ton wagon than we ever dared charge for an eight-horse coach with leather seats, stove, silk drapes, turkey carpets, and silver-gilt lamps."

Starbuck drew on his cigar. "So why are you being shot at here instead of building carts in Pittsburgh?"

Levergood shrugged. "Wanted to fight for my country." He sounded embarrassed at making the confession. "Mind you, I never dreamed the war would last more than a summer."

"Nor did we," Starbuck said. "We reckoned one good battle to teach you a lesson and that would be the sum of it."

"Reckon we must be slow learners," Levergood said affably. "Mind you, it won't be long now."

"It won't?" Starbuck asked, amused.

"McClellan's leaving the peninsula, that's what we hear. His men are sailing north and in another couple of weeks his army will be alongside ours and then we'll be down on you

135

like a pack of wolves. Pope's army and McClellan's combined. You'll be crushed like a soft grape. I just hope there are enough beds in Richmond to take care of us all."

"There are plenty of prison beds there," Starbuck said, "but their mattresses ain't too soft."

Levergood laughed, then turned as a voice boomed from the road. "Read it! Read it! Let the word of God work its grace on your sinful souls. Here! Take and read, take and read." An older man dressed in preacher's garb was distributing tracts from horseback, scattering the leaflets down to the rebel soldiers beside the road.

"Jesus!" Starbuck said in astonishment.

"The Reverend Elial Starbuck," Levergood said with evident pride that such a famous man was present. "He preached to us yesterday. My, but he's got a rare tongue in him. It seems he's close to our high command and they've promised him the honor of preaching the very first sermon in liberated Richmond." Levergood paused, then frowned. "You're called Starbuck, too. Are you related?"

"Just a coincidence," Starbuck said. He edged around the end of the pyre. He had faced battle with evident courage, but he could not face his father. He went to where Esau Washbrook was mounting a solitary guard over the company's stacked weapons. "Give me your rifle, Washbrook," he said.

Washbrook, the company's best marksman, had equipped himself with a European-made sniper's rifle: a heavy long-range killing machine with a telescopic sight running alongside the barrel. "You're not going to kill the man, are you?" Levergood asked. The Pennsylvanian had followed Starbuck from the road.

"No." Starbuck aimed the rifle at his father, inspecting him through the telescopic sight. The gunners had set fire to the horses' funeral pyre, and the smoke was beginning to

136

whip across Starbuck's vision while the heat of the fire was quivering the image held in the gun's crosshairs. His father, astonishingly, looked happier than Starbuck had ever seen him. He was evidently exulting in the stench of death and the remnants of battle.

"The flames of hell will burn brighter than these fires!" the preacher called to the rebels. "They will burn for all eternity and lap you with insufferable pain! That is your certain fate unless you repent now! God is reaching His hand out for you! Repent and you will be saved!"

Starbuck lightly touched the trigger, then felt ashamed of the impulse and immediately lowered the gun. For a second it seemed that his father had stared straight at him, but doubtless the preacher's own vision had been smeared by the shimmer of smoky heat, for he had looked away without recognition before riding back toward the Federal lines.

The flames of the pyre leaped higher as fat from the carcasses ran down to sizzle among the logs. The last ambulances were gone north and with them the final wagons carrying the Yankee dead. Bugles now called the Yankee living back to their own lines, and Captain Levergood held out his hand. "Guess we'll meet again, Nate."

"I'd like that." Starbuck shook the Northerner's hand.

"Kind of crazy, really," Levergood said in half-articulated regret at meeting an enemy he so liked; then he shrugged. "But watch out next time we meet. McClellan will be leading us, and McClellan's a regular tiger. He'll have you beat soon enough."

Starbuck had met the tiger once and had watched him being beaten, too, but he said nothing of that meeting nor of the beating. "Be safe," he told Levergood.

"You too, friend."

The Northerners marched away pursued by the evil-smelling smoke of the burning carcasses. "Did you know your father was here?" Colonel Swynyard's harsh voice suddenly sounded behind Starbuck.

Starbuck turned. "I saw him, yes."

"I spoke with him," Swynyard said. "I told him I had the honor to command his son. You know what he said?" Swynyard paused to dramatize the moment, then grinned. "He said he had no son called Nathaniel. You do not exist, he said. You have been written out from his life; expunged, condemned, disinherited. I said I would pray that you would be reconciled."

Starbuck shrugged. "My father ain't the reconciling kind, Colonel."

"Then you will have to forgive him instead," Swynyard said. "But first get your fellows ready to march. We're pulling back over the Rapidan."

"Tonight?"

"Before first light tomorrow. It'll be a fast march, so tell your boys not to carry unnecessary baggage. Can't have them laden down with things like this, eh, Starbuck?" Swynyard took a bottle of brandy from his pocket. "Found this in my tent, Starbuck. Just after you took that whiskey away. I heard you reprove Davies, and I'm grateful that you did, but a dozen other people brought me liquor anyway."

Starbuck felt a twinge of shame at having planned to place Davies's whiskey back in Swynyard's tent this very night. "Were you tempted?" he asked the Colonel.

"Of course I was tempted. The devil has not relinquished me yet, Starbuck, but I shall beat him." Swynyard gauged the distance to the funeral pyre, then heaved the brandy at the flames. The bottle scored a direct hit, breaking to splash a pale blue light in the heart of the fire. "I'm saved, Starbuck," Swynyard said, "so tell Murphy's friends to keep their liquor to themselves."

"Yes, Colonel. I'll do that," Starbuck said, then walked back to Sergeant Truslow. "He's saved and we're poor, Sergeant," Starbuck said. "I reckon we've just lost our damned money."

Truslow spat in the dust. "Bugger may not last the night," he said.

"Two bucks says he will."

Truslow thought about it for a second. "What two bucks?" he finally asked.

"The two bucks I'll win from you tomorrow morning if Swynyard lasts the night."

"Forget it."

The smoke blew north, there to meld with dark clouds that heaped in the summer sky. Somewhere beneath those clouds the armies of the United States were gathering to march south, and Jackson's men, outnumbered, could only retreat.

Adam waited with his troop at a place where he had a view toward the distant Blue Ridge Mountains. He was watching for partisans, but Sergeant Tom Huxtable kept glancing back toward the farmhouse. "Tidy place," he finally commented.

"Kind of house a man could live in forever," Adam agreed.

"But not after Billy Blythe's finished searching it." Huxtable could no longer keep his concern silent. "Our job's to hunt down rebels," he said, "not persecute womenfolk."

Adam was acutely uncomfortable with this direct criticism of his fellow officer. He suspected the criticism might be justified, but Adam always tried to give all men the benefit of the doubt, and now he tried to find some saving grace in Blythe's character. "The Captain's simply investigating gunfire, Sergeant. I didn't hear anything said of womenfolk."

"Gunfire that Seth Kelley shot," Huxtable said, "like as not."

Adam kept silent while he examined the woods and fields to the south. The trees lay still in the windless air as he turned the field glasses back to the mountains.

"A man should have beliefs, you see," Sergeant Huxtable said. "A man without beliefs, Captain, is a man without purpose. Like a ship without a compass."

Adam still said nothing. He turned the glasses northward. He watched an empty track, then slid the lenses across a wooded ridge.

Huxtable shifted his lump of chewing tobacco from one cheek to the other. He had been a cooper in his native Louisiana and then apprenticed to a cabinetmaker in his wife's village in upstate New York. When the war had broken out, Tom Huxtable had visited the white-spired village church, knelt in prayer for twenty minutes, then gone home and taken his rifle from its hooks over the fireplace, a Bible from the drawer in the kitchen table, and a knife from his workshop. Then he had told his wife to keep the squash well watered and gone to join the Northern army. His grandfather had been killed by the British to establish the United States of America, and Tom Huxtable was not minded to let that sacrifice go for nothing.

"It mayn't be my place to say it," Huxtable now went remorselessly on, "but Captain Blythe don't have a belief in his body, sir. He'd fight for the devil if the pay was right." Adam's men were of a like mind with their Sergeant and murmured agreement. "Mr. Blythe's not in the North by choice, Captain," Huxtable continued doggedly. "He says he's fighting for the Union, but we hear he left his home-town a pace ahead of a lynching party. There's talk of a girl, Captain. A white girl of good family. She says Mr. Blythe wrestled her down and—"

140

"I don't want to know!" Adam said abruptly. Then, thinking he had spoken too fiercely, he turned apologetically to his Sergeant. "I'm sure Major Galloway has considered all this."

"Major Galloway's like yourself, sir. A decent man who doesn't believe in evil."

"And you do?" Adam asked.

"You've seen the plantations in the deep South, sir?" Huxtable asked. "Yes, sir, I believe in evil."

"Sir!" The conversation was interrupted by one of Adam's men, who pointed northward. Adam turned and raised the field glasses. For a second his view was of nothing but blurred leaves; then he focused the lenses to see mounted men on a crestline. He counted a dozen riders, but guessed there were more. They were not in uniform but carried rifles slung from their shoulders or thrust into saddle holsters. A second group of horsemen came into view. They had to be partisans: the Southern horsemen who rode Virginia's secret paths to harass the Northern armies.

Huxtable stared at the distant horsemen. "Captain Blythe will run away," he said disgustedly.

"He needs to be warned. Come on." Adam led his troop down from the hilltop. They spurred east, and Adam wished their horses were not so decrepit.

The parched lawn in front of the farmhouse was now a bizarre array of furniture and household goods, which Blythe's men were picking through in search of plunder. There were buckets, spittoons, pictures, lamps, and rush-bottom chairs. There was a sewing machine, a long case clock, two butter churns, a chamber pot, and meal sifters. Some men were trying on suits of clothes while two more were swathed in women's scarves. A man threw a bolt of cloth from an upstairs window, and the bright cloth cascaded across the veranda roof and down to where the horses were picketed in the flower beds. "Where's Captain Blythe?" Adam demanded of one of the scarfed men.

"In the barn, Cap'n, but he won't thank you for finding him there," the man answered. Children screamed in the house. Adam threw his reins to Sergeant Huxtable, then ran to the barn, where Corporal Kemble was standing guard. "You can't go in, sir," the Corporal said unhappily.

Adam just pushed past the Corporal, unlatched the door, and pushed into the barn. Two empty horse stalls were on the right, an oat cutter stood in the floor's center, while a mound of hay filled the barn's farther end. Blythe was in the hay, struggling with a crying woman.

"Bitch!" Blythe said, slapping her. "Goddamned bitch!" There was the sound of cloth ripping; then Blythe realized the door had been thrown open, and he turned angrily around. "What the hell do you want?" He could not recognize the intruder who was silhouetted against the light outside.

"Leave her alone, Blythe!" Adam said.

"Faulconer? You son of a bitch!" Blythe scrambled to his feet and brushed scraps of hay from his hands. "I'm just questioning this lady, and what I do here is none of your damned business."

The woman clutched the remnants of her dress to her breasts and pushed herself across the floor. "He was attacking me, mister!" she called to Adam. "He was going to —"

"Get out!" Blythe shouted at Adam.

But Adam knew the time had come to make his stand. He drew his revolver, cocked it, then aimed the weapon at Blythe's head. "Just leave her alone."

Blythe smiled and shook his head. "You're a boy, Faulconer. I ain't attacking her! She's a rebel! She fired on us!"

"I never!" the woman called.

"Step away from her!" Adam said. He could sense his

heart pounding and recognized his own fear, but he knew Blythe had to be confronted.

"Shoot the interfering son of a bitch, Kemble!" Blythe shouted past Adam to the Corporal.

"Touch the trigger, Corporal, and I'll kill you." Sergeant Huxtable spoke from beyond the door.

Blythe seemed to find the impasse amusing, for he still grinned as he brushed scraps of hay from his uniform. "She's a traitor, Faulconer. A damned rebel. You know what the penalty is for firing on a Northern soldier? You've read General Order Number Seven, ain't you?" He had taken the silver case of lucifers from his pocket.

"Just step away from her!" Adam repeated.

"I never wanted to be near her!" Blythe said. "But the bitch kept trying to stop me from doing my job. And my job, Faulconer, is to burn this property down like Major General John Pope ordered." He began to strike the lucifers, then to drop the burning matches into the hay. He laughed as the woman tried to beat the flames out with her bare hands. Her torn dress dropped open and Blythe gestured at her. "Nice titties, Faulconer. Or can't you make a comparison on account of never having seen none?" Blythe chuckled as he dropped more matches and started more fires. "So why don't you shoot me, Faulconer? Lost your nerve."

"Because I don't want to tell the partisans we're here. There's a group of them a mile north of here. And coming this way."

Blythe stared at Adam for a heartbeat, then smiled. "Nice try, boy."

"Maybe two dozen of them," Sergeant Huxtable said flatly from the barn door.

Behind Blythe the hay had started to burn fiercely. The woman retreated from the heat, crying. Her hair had come

143

loose to hang either side of her face. She clasped her bodice, then spat at Blythe before running out of the barn. "Thank you, mister," she said as she passed Adam.

Blythe watched her go, then looked back to Adam. "Are you lying to me, Faulconer?" he asked.

"You want to stay here and find out?" Adam asked. "You want to run the risk of meeting that woman's husband?"

"Goddamn partisans!" Sergeant Seth Kelley shouted his sudden warning from the sunlight outside. "'Bout a mile away, Billy!"

"Jesus hollering Christ!" Blythe swore, then ran past Adam and shouted for his horse. "Come on, boys! Get out of here! Take what you can, leave the rest! Hurry now! Hurry!"

The hay was well alight, the smoke churning out the barn door. "Where to?" Sergeant Kelley asked.

"South! Come on!" Blythe was desperate to escape the farm before the partisans arrived. He snatched a bag of plunder, rammed his spurs back, and galloped south toward the woods.

His men followed in ragged order. Adam and his troop were the last to go. They found Blythe a half-mile inside the woods, hesitating over a track leading west and another going south. There were men's voices in the distant air, and that was enough to make Blythe choose the southward track that promised a faster escape because it went downhill. Adam's horses were tired, their lungs wheezing asthmatically and their flanks wet with white sweat, yet still Blythe pressed the pace, not stopping until they had ridden a good six or seven miles from the farmhouse. There was no evidence of any pursuit. "Bastards probably stopped to put out that fire, Billy," Seth Kelley opined.

"Can't tell with partisans," Blythe said. "Cunning as serpents. Could be anywhere." He looked nervously around the green woods.

The horsemen had stopped beside a stream that flowed eastward through sunlit woodlands. The horses were all winded, and a couple of the beasts were lamed. If the partisans had followed, Adam knew, then every man in Blythe's command would either be killed or captured. "What do we do now?" one of the men asked Blythe.

"We find out where the hell we are," Blythe snapped irritably.

"I know where we are," Adam said, "and I know where we're going."

Blythe, panting hard and with his red face covered in sweat, looked at his fellow officer. "Where?" he asked curtly.

"We're going to get some decent horses," Adam said, "and then we're going to fight like we're supposed to."

"Amen," Sergeant Huxtable said.

Blythe straightened up in his saddle. "Are you saying I don't want to fight, Faulconer?"

For a second Adam was tempted to accept the challenge and make Blythe either fight him or back down in front of his men. Then he remembered the partisans and knew he could not afford the luxury of fighting a duel so deep behind the enemy's lines.

Blythe saw Adam's hesitation and translated it as cowardice. He grinned. "Lost your tongue?"

"I'm going south, Blythe, and I don't care if you come or stay."

"I'll let you go, boy," Blythe said, then pulled his horse around and spurred westward. He planned to take his men to the foothills of the Blue Ridge, then follow the mountains north until he came to the Federal lines.

Adam watched Blythe go and knew he had merely postponed their confrontation. Then, after dusk, when his horses and men were rested, Adam led the troop south to where he planned a victory.

PART TWO

JACKSON, LIKE A SNAKE THAT HAD STRUCK, hurt, but not killed its prey, retreated sullenly back across the Rapidan River, thus abandoning the battlefield at the foot of Cedar Mountain with its blackened swathes of scorched turf and long raw mounds of newly turned graves where turkey vultures gorged on bodies uncovered by dogs.

The Yankees were left in possession of Culpeper County and counted its possession as a victory, though no one really believed Jackson was defeated. The snake still had fangs, which meant that the Northern generals must try to scotch it again. Yankee troops poured southward and spread their camps along the Rapidan's northern bank while, south of the river in Gordonsville, the railcars brought fresh rebel troops from Richmond.

On both banks of the river there was a nervous sense of great events waiting to happen, and inevitably rumors fed that apprehension. The rebels feared that McClellan's Army of the Potomac had joined forces with Pope's Army of Virginia, and if that prospect was not frightening enough, a Northern newspaper hinted that the Yankees had emptied every jail between Washington and the Canadian border and put the convicts in uniform, handed them guns, and sent them to lay Virginia waste. Another tale insisted that the North was recruiting mercenaries in Europe, Germans mostly, and that each foreigner had been promised an acre of Indian territory for every rebel killed. "I knew we'd end up fighting Hessians," Truslow remarked, "but we beat the sumbitches in '76 so we'll beat the sumbitches in '62 as well." Yet the most persistent rumor of all was that Abe Lincoln was enlisting freed slaves into his army. "Because he can't find anyone else willing to fight against us," Lieutenant Coffman averred patriotically.

Most men dismissed the rumor of armed slaves as unthinkable, but a week after the Legion retreated from Cedar Mountain, Captain Murphy found confirmation of the story in a two-week-old copy of the *Hartford Evening Press* that had somehow found its way into the rebel lines. "See!" Murphy exclaimed to the officers sharing a jug of whiskey around a fire. "It is true!" He tilted the newspaper toward the campfire. "'Congress has extended permission for the President to enrol colored men into the army,'" Murphy read aloud. "'Congressman Matteson of New Jersey claims that the sable brethren of America are fervent in their desire to contribute their blood toward the great crusade and that, so long as their childlike and excitable nature proves tractable to military discipline, there is no reason why they should not fight at least as well as any treasonable rebel.'" A chorus of jeers greeted the last two words. Afterward there was much discussion of the newspaper's report, and Starbuck sensed a nervousness among the officers. There was something very nightmarish in the thought of black troops coming to take vengeance on their old masters.

"Though how many of us ever owned a slave?" Lieutenant Davies asked resentfully.

"I own some," Murphy said mildly and then, after a pause, "Mind you, I pay the buggers well enough. I don't think we Irish are very good at slaveholding."

"Major Hinton owns a dozen," Lieutenant Pine of Murphy's D Company added.

"And Swynyard's owned plenty enough in his lifetime," Starbuck said.

"Though not any longer," Lieutenant Davies observed in wonderment, and indeed, to everyone's astonishment, the Colonel had manumitted his two slaves when Jackson pulled the army back across the river. The Colonel, despite coming from one of Virginia's most prominent slave-trading families, had set free at least a thousand dollars' worth of prime Negroes by sending the two men north to the Federal lines. Somehow it was that sacrifice, even more than the Colonel's astonishing achievement of staying away from liquor, that had impressed on the whole Brigade that their second-in-command truly was a converted man. "He's even given up cigars," Davies added.

Murphy took the stone jug from Starbuck. "God knows why you Protestants have such an unpleasant religion."

"Because it's the true religion," Lieutenant Ezra Pine averred, "and our reward will be in heaven."

"And heaven," Murphy insisted to his Lieutenant, "is a place of all pleasures, is it not? Which means that there'll be rivers running brimful with the tastiest of whiskeys and boxes of the choicest cigars waiting ready lit at every corner, and if those pleasures are good enough for the angels they're good enough for me. God's blessing on you, Pine," Murphy added and lifted the stone jug to his lips.

Ezra Pine wanted to start a theological argument about the nature of heaven, but he was shouted down. Out in the darkness a man sang a love ballad, and the sound of it made the officers silent. Starbuck guessed they were all thinking about that horde of convicts, Hessian mercenaries, and vengeful freed slaves that was supposedly massing on the Rapidan's far bank.

"If Lee was here," Murphy broke the silence, "he'd have us all digging trenches. It'd be sore hands, so it would."

151

Everyone agreed that Robert Lee would have fought a defensive battle, but no one understood what Thomas Jackson might do. "I wish Lee would come," Murphy said wistfully, "for there's nothing on God's earth so good for stopping a bullet as a yard or two of good clean dirt."

The next day Starbuck heard the first rumor that confirmed that Lee was indeed coming to take command of the rebel forces on the Rapidan. Starbuck heard the rumor from an old friend who rode into the Legion's encampment brandishing two bottles of fine French wine. "We took ten cases off the Yankees three miles beyond the Rappahannock!" The jubilant speaker was a Frenchman, Colonel Lassan, who was ostensibly a foreign military observer, but who actually rode with the rebel cavalry for the sheer delight of fighting. He had just come back from a raid deep behind the Yankee lines and brought news of the enemy's preparations. "There are lines of wagons as far as the eye can see, Nate! Mile after mile of them, and every one crammed full with food, powder, and shot."

"Is that McClellan's army?" Starbuck asked.

Lassan shook his head. "That's Pope's army, but McClellan's coming." The Frenchman sounded happy at such a gathering of armies with its implicit promise of fighting.

"And if McClellan comes," Starbuck said, "Lee will come, and that'll mean digging mile after mile of trenches."

The Frenchman gave Starbuck a look of surprise. "Dear Lord, no. Lee can't afford to wait. He dug trenches to protect Richmond, but trenches won't help here"—he waved at the open country—"and Lee has to break the Yankees before they join their armies together. Lee's no fool, Nate. He knows which end of a pig makes the mess."

Starbuck laughed at the quaint phrase. Lassan spoke perfect English, the legacy of a British father, but at times he transposed a Norman peasant's language into his father's tongue. Lassan himself was no peasant but a professional soldier who had fought in Italy, the Crimea, and North Africa, and who bore the scars of those wars across his eye-patched face. They were terrible scars, scars to terrify a child to nightmare, yet Lassan himself was an easygoing man whose besetting sins were warfare and women. "Both dangerous pursuits," he liked to tell Starbuck, "but why settle for dullness in this sad, bad world?"

Now, with his horse picketed, the Frenchman strolled with Starbuck through the Legion's camp lines. The weather was such that none of the men had bothered to make turf shelters, preferring instead to sleep on the open ground, and so the lines were little more than piles of belongings interrupted by the remnants of cooking fires. The Legion's new draftees were being drilled by Sergeant Major Tolliver while the veterans not on picket duty were either sleeping, playing cards, or reading.

Lassan, who seemed to have taken it on himself to educate Starbuck in matters military, was explaining why Lee could not afford a defensive strategy. "Dig trenches and gun emplacements behind this river, my friend, and how are you to stop the Yankees simply strolling round the end of your earthworks? You don't have enough men to guard a trench dug from the Chesapeake Bay to the Blue Ridge Mountains, so instead of digging you will have to march and tip the enemy off balance. It will be a war of maneuver, a cavalry-man's war! Naturally you infantrymen will have to do the real fighting and dying, that's why God made infantrymen, but we cavalrymen will do your scouting for you." Lassan scratched beneath his mildewed eye patch. "You'll know things are getting warm, Nate, when Lee arrives."

"Or when the Yankees attack," Starbuck said.

"They won't. They're too sluggish. The North is like a

man who has grown so fat he is unable to move fast. He just wants to roll over you and so crush you to death, while you have to slice him up into little pieces."

Starbuck walked a few paces in silence. The two men had left the Brigade lines behind and were now walking toward a stand of trees that screened the south bank of the Rapidan. "Can we win this war?" Starbuck finally asked the Frenchman.

"Oh, yes," Lassan said without hesitation, "but it will be expensive. If you kill enough Yankees, then they may think the game isn't worth the candle. You'll also need luck." The Frenchman had sounded confident, but it nevertheless struck Starbuck as a gloomy prescription. "Of course," Lassan went on, "if you could get European support, then everything changes."

"Can we?" Starbuck asked, as if the question had not been debated endlessly in the Confederacy.

Lassan shook his head. "France won't do anything unless Britain leads the way, and Britain has been burned too badly by its past American adventures, so Britain won't intervene unless the South looks capable of winning the war by itself, in which case you wouldn't need their help anyway, which all means, *mon ami*, that it is up to the South to fight and win its own war." They had reached the edge of the trees now, a place made ragged by the axes of men seeking firewood, and Starbuck hesitated to go further, but Lassan gestured him on. "I wanted to talk to you in private," the Frenchman said, and so he led Starbuck down a vague path that zigzagged erratically through the underbrush. Pigeons clattered through the upper leaves while a woodpecker's staccato rattle sounded sudden and close. "I have to tell you"—Lassan half turned to Starbuck as he spoke—"that I have set myself up in an establishment in Richmond."

It seemed an oddly unnecessary confession to Starbuck,

perhaps because he was not entirely sure what the Frenchman meant by an "establishment." "A business, you mean?" he asked.

"Dear Lord God, no!" Lassan laughed at the very thought. "I've no head for commerce, none! No, I mean I have established a household. It's on Grace Street. You know it?"

"Very well." Starbuck was amused by the thought of Lassan fussing with domestic arrangements.

"It's an apartment," Lassan said. "We have five rooms above a tailor's shop on the corner of Fourth Street. Then we have slave quarters downstairs at the back where there's a kitchen, a small garden for herbs, a peach tree, and a wooden stable. It's rented, of course, and the kitchen chimney smokes when the wind's in the west, but otherwise it's really very comfortable." The middle-aged Lassan had never counted comfort as one of life's priorities, and he gave the word an ironic twist.

"You've got slaves?" Starbuck asked, surprised.

Lassan shrugged. "When in Rome, *mon ami.*" He took a cigar from his pouch, lit it, and handed it to Starbuck before lighting one for himself. "I can't say that I'm comfortable with the arrangement," he went on, "but I convince myself that the slaves are better off with me than with anyone else. I have a stable boy, there are two kitchen girls who clean as well, and of course an upstairs girl who looks after clothes and all the rest of the flummery."

He sounded embarrassed again. The two men had reached an old cart track that was much overgrown but was wide enough to let them walk side by side. "You sound as if you've taken a wife," Starbuck said lightly.

Lassan stopped and faced his friend. "I have taken a companion," he said very seriously. "We are not married, nor shall we marry, but for the moment, at least, we suit each other." Lassan paused. "You introduced me to her."

"Oh," Starbuck said, coloring slightly and remembering how, when Lassan had first crossed the lines to attach himself to the rebel forces, he had asked Starbuck for an introduction to a house of pleasure in Richmond. Starbuck had sent Lassan to the best of all such houses, the most exclusive house, the house where Sally Truslow worked. "It's Sally?" Starbuck asked.

"Indeed," Lassan said. His one eye examined Starbuck anxiously.

Starbuck was quiet for a moment. Sally was the rebellious daughter of Sergeant Truslow and a girl with whom Starbuck sometimes thought he was in love himself. He had asked Sally to marry him earlier in the year, and at times Starbuck was still convinced that they could have made such a marriage work. He had been delighted when she had abandoned the brothel for the more lucrative job of being a spiritual medium, and Sally's séances were now famous in Richmond, a town obsessed with supernatural phenomena, but there was no doubt that her success had more than a little to do with the fact that the darkened shrine of Madame Royall, as Sally now called herself, was attached to Richmond's most notorious house of assignation, a proximity that added the spice of wickedness to her clients' visits. Starbuck had half dared to hope that Sally might want to complete her conversion to respectability by taking a husband, but instead she had taken a lover, and Starbuck understood that, in the gentlest possible way, he was now being warned away from Sally's bed. "Good for you," he told Lassan.

"She wanted to tell you herself," Lassan said, "but I insisted."

"Thank you," Starbuck said, wondering why he was suddenly so damned jealous. He had no call for jealousy. Indeed, if he was so in love with Sally, why did he sneak out of the

Brigade's lines at night to visit the crude tavern just south of the camp? McComb's Tavern had been put out of bounds, but there was a red-haired girl working one of the upstairs rooms, and Starbuck was happy to risk Washington Faulconer's punishment to visit her. He had no call for jealousy, he told himself again, then began walking north along the cart track. "You're a lucky man, Lassan."

"Yes, I am."

"And Sally's lucky, too," Starbuck said gallantly, even though he could not help feeling betrayed.

"I think so," the Frenchman said lightly. "I am teaching her French."

Starbuck forced a smile at the thought of Sally Truslow, a girl from a hardscrabble farm in the Blue Ridge Mountains, learning to speak French, except it was not so strange, for Sally had journeyed a long way from her father's comfortless house. She had learned society's manners, and how to dress and how to talk, and yet again Starbuck felt a pang of jealousy at the memory of Sally's exquisite beauty; then he again thought how unfair it was for him to be envious, for as often as he thought of Sally he also thought of Julia Gordon, Adam Faulconer's abandoned fiancée, and he did not know which girl he preferred, or whether, in truth, he was simply a fool for any woman, even for a red-haired whore in a country tavern. "I am glad for you, Lassan," he said with forced generosity, "truly."

"Thank you," Lassan said simply, and then stopped beside Starbuck where the cart track left the trees to run down to the river. A house had once stood on the nearer bank, but all that was left of the house now was a stub of broken brick chimney and the outlines of a stone foundation within which grew a thick and entangling clump of bushes. The farther bank of the river was a forest of shade trees that hung over the swirling water, though immediately opposite the house a cart track led between two willows into the far woods. Lassan stared at that distant cart track, then frowned. "Do you see what I see, Nate?"

Starbuck had been thinking of Sally's startling beauty and of Julia Gordon's graver face, but now, sensing that he was being tested, he stared at the landscape and tried to see whatever was significant in it. A ruined house, a river, a far bank of thick trees, and then he saw the anomaly just as clearly as Lassan's trained eye had seen it.

The track that he and Lassan had followed to this spot did not end at the river but rather continued on the farther bank. Which meant there was a ford here. Which was strange because every crossing of the Rapidan was supposedly guarded to prevent a surprise Northern attack, yet here was a ford standing empty and unwatched. "Because no one knows the ford's here," Starbuck said. "Or maybe the roadbed is washed away?" he added.

"There's an easy way to find out," Lassan said. He had the instinctive caution of any soldier coming to a river, especially a river that divided two armies, but he had stared hard at the further bank through a small glass and was satisfied that no Yankees waited in ambush, and so he now walked into the sunlight, where he took off his spurred boots and hitched up his saber. Starbuck followed the Frenchman, wading into the river, which flowed fast, clear, and shallow across a bed of fine gravel. Long weeds trailed upstream, and a few fish darted in the shadows downstream, but nothing obstructed Lassan and Starbuck's progress; indeed, the water scarce reached either man's knees. At the far bank the road reared steeply up from the water, but not so steeply that a horse team could not have pulled a heavy gun and limber out of the river. "If the Yankees knew about this ford," Lassan said, "they could be round your backside in a trice."

"I thought you said they weren't going to attack us,"

Starbuck commented as he pulled himself up onto the northern bank.

"And I've also told you a hundred times that you must always expect the unexpected from your enemy," Lassan said as he sat in the shade of a willow and stared back across the river. He gestured upstream with the cigar. "What units are that way?"

"None," Starbuck said. "We're the westernmost brigade of the army."

"So the Yankees really could hook round your backside," Lassan said softly. He smoked in silence for a few seconds, then abruptly changed the subject back to his new household. "Sally hopes you'll visit us when you're in Richmond. I hope so, too."

"Thank you," Starbuck said awkwardly.

Lassan grinned. "I am becoming domesticated. My mother would be most amused. Poor Mama. I am an adventurer, while my sister lives in England, so Mama is rather alone these days."

"You've a sister?"

"The Countess of Benfleet." Lassan gave a half-mocking grimace at the grand-sounding title. "Dominique married an English nobleman, so now she has a castle, five grown children, and probably twice as many lovers. I hope she does, anyway." He tossed the stub of his cigar into the water. "One of Dominique's sons wants to join this war and she asked me which side he should fight for. I said the North if he wants to be respectable and the South if he wants adventure." Lassan shrugged as if to suggest he did not much care either way. "I wonder if this ford's got a name," he said idly.

"Dead Mary's Ford." A man spoke suddenly from the far side of the track, and the voice so startled Starbuck that he reached for his revolver. "It's all right, massa! Silas is just plain harmless." The unseen speaker chuckled; then the bushes stirred and Starbuck saw that an old Negro had been hiding in the trees just a few feet away. The old man must have been watching them for a long time. "Silas is a free man!" the Negro said as he sidled onto the track and drew from his filthy clothes a scrap of paper that had long lost any legibility. "Free! Massa Kemp gave Silas freedom." He waved the disintegrating scrap of greasy paper. "God bless Massa Kemp."

"You're Silas?" Lassan asked.

"Silas." The old man confirmed his identity with a nod. "Mad Silas," he added as though the qualification might prove useful. He was staring keenly at the stub of Starbuck's cigar.

Lassan took out a new cigar, lit it, and gave it to the old man, who was now squatting in the road. "Do you live here, Silas?"

"Over there, massa." Silas pointed to the ruined house. "Silas has a lair in there." He chuckled, then found the internal rhyme even funnier and almost rolled backward as he laughed at himself.

"How old are you, Silas?" Lassan asked.

"Silas is older than you, massa!" Silas laughed again. "But Silas's daddy now, he saw the redcoats!"

"Why Dead Mary's Ford, Silas?" Lassan asked.

The old man shuffled a few inches nearer. His clothes looked as old as himself, and his hair was white and matted with dirt, while his face was deep lined. Lassan's question had swept the humor from that face, replacing it with suspicion. "'Cos Mary died," he said at last.

"Here?" Starbuck asked gently.

"The white folks came. Looking for Silas, but Silas wasn't here. Mistress Pearce's baby gone, see? They thought Silas took it, so they came and burned Silas's house. And burned Silas's wife." The old man looked very

160

close to tears as he stared at the house, where, Starbuck now saw, a kind of hollowed den was scooped in the bushes under the brick chimney. "But the baby was never gone after all." Silas sighed as he finished the story. "She grown up now. But Silas's Mary, she's still here too."

Lassan lit himself another cigar and smoked in companionable silence for a few moments before giving the old man a smile. "Listen, Silas. More white folk are coming here. They're going to dig trenches along the edge of the trees over there, at the top of your meadow. They don't mean you any harm, but if there's anything in your house that's valuable to you, take it away and hide it. You understand me?"

"Silas understands you, massa," Silas said very intensely.

Lassan gave the old man two more cigars, then clapped Starbuck on the shoulder. "Time to get back, Nate." The two men waded the ford, pulled on their boots, then walked back through the woods. Starbuck wanted to find Major Hinton, but the Major was out of the lines, and so, accompanied by Lassan, Starbuck went to the big farmhouse that Washington Faulconer had commandeered for his headquarters.

Washington Faulconer had gone to Gordonsville, leaving Colonel Swynyard in command of the Brigade. The Colonel was in the farmhouse parlor, sitting beneath the crossed flags of the Faulconer Legion that Faulconer kept unfurled and draped across the parlor wall. One of the two flags was the Faulconer Legion's own banner derived from the Faulconer family's coat of arms. It showed three red crescents on a white field and had the family's motto, "Forever Ardent," wreathed around the lower crescent. The flag measured thirty-six square feet and had a yellow fringe, just as did its companion flag, which was the new battle flag of the Confederate States of America.

The original flag of the Confederacy had carried three

stripes, two red and one white, with a star-spangled blue field in its upper corner, but when the wind dropped and the flag hung limp, it had resembled the Stars and Stripes, and so a new flag had been designed, a scarlet banner blazoned with a blue cross of Saint Andrew, and on that diagonal, white-edged cross were thirteen white stars. The old flag with its stars and three stripes was still the official flag of the Confederacy, but when the Confederacy's soldiers marched into battle, they now marched under their new battle flag.

The Confederate War Department had decreed that infantry regiments should carry a battle flag four feet square, but such a flag was not nearly grand enough for Brigadier General Washington Faulconer, who had insisted on having a banner six feet by six feet made of the finest silk and edged with a tasseled fringe of golden threads. The General had intended that his Legion's two flags should be the finest war banners in all the Confederacy, and so he had commissioned them from the same expensive French factory that had manufactured his ill-fated crescent-badged shoulder patches.

"Which means," Colonel Griffin Swynyard said when he saw the Frenchman admiring the lavish flags, "that every marksman in the Northern army will be aiming for them."

"Maybe you could persuade Faulconer to stand beneath them?" Starbuck suggested sweetly.

"Now, Nate. Let us be charitable," Swynyard said. The Colonel had been busily trying to reconcile the Brigade's accounts and seemed glad to be interrupted by visitors. He stood and shook hands with Colonel Lassan, apologized that General Faulconer was away from the headquarters, and insisted on hearing what circumstances had brought the scarred French cavalry officer to the Confederate army. "You're welcome to a lemonade, Colonel," Swynyard said when the story was told, indicating a jug of pale yellow liquid that was protected from wasps by a beaded cover of fine muslin.

"I have wine, Colonel." Lassan produced one of his captured bottles.

Swynyard grimaced. "Captain Starbuck will tell you that I have forsworn all ardent liquor, Colonel. For over two weeks now!" he added proudly, and it was astonishing what a change the abstinence had wrought in the Colonel. The sallow cast of his skin had vanished, his sweating fits had faded, and the twitch in his cheek that had once convulsed his face into a grotesque rictus had subsided to a faint tic. His eyes were clear and alert, he stood straighter, and he was dressed each day in clean linen. "I am a new man," he boasted, "though alas, my rebirth has not given me a facility for mathematics." He gestured at the Brigade's ledgers. "I need someone who can understand accounts, someone with an education; someone like you, Starbuck."

"Not me, Colonel," Starbuck said, "I was at Yale."

"That must make you good for something," Swynyard insisted.

"Not one whole hell of a lot," Starbuck said, "except maybe discovering unmapped fords." He crossed to a hand-drawn map of the area that lay on a claw-footed table. "Just here," he said, "not a long rifle shot away from the lines."

For a moment Swynyard thought Starbuck was being jocular; then he crossed to the map table. "Truly?" he asked.

"Truly," Lassan confirmed.

"Right there." Starbuck pointed on the pencil-drawn map. "It's called Dead Mary's Ford."

"We waded across it, Colonel," Lassan said, picking up the tale, "knee deep, passable by artillery, and as wide open as a barrack-town whorehouse on a Saturday night."

Swynyard shouted for his horse. Now that he had released his slaves, he was using Hiram Ketley, Colonel

Bird's half-witted orderly, as his servant. Bird himself was on his way home to Faulconer Court House and was expected to survive so long as his wound stayed clean. "You don't have a horse, Starbuck?" Swynyard asked as his own mare was brought to the front of the house.

"No, Colonel. Can't afford one."

Swynyard ordered another horse saddled, and then the three men rode north through the woods to where the ruined house stood beside the river. Swynyard rode across the ford, then back again. "Our lord and master," he said to Starbuck, "ordered me not to change the Brigade's dispositions without his permission, but even Faulconer, I suspect, would agree that we have to put a guard here." He stopped talking, distracted by the stooped, ragged figure of Mad Silas, who had suddenly appeared out of the bushes in his ruined house like a beast scuttling out of a burrow. "Who's that?" Swynyard asked.

"Some poor, old, mad black," Lassan said. "He lives there."

"Is that a skull he's carrying?" Swynyard asked in a tone of horror.

Starbuck stared and felt a sudden shock as he realized that the object in Silas's hands was indeed an old yellow skull. "Jesus," he said faintly.

"It's more likely to belong to Dead Mary," Lassan said dryly.

"I suppose he knows what he's doing," Swynyard said as Silas crossed the river and disappeared into the far woods, "which is more than we do." He returned his attention to the ford. "If we've not heard of this crossing, then I can't believe the Yankees know about it, but even so we can't take a chance. Why don't you bring your company here, Starbuck, with B and E as well? I'll make you a separate command, which means you'll bivouac here. You'll have to dig in, of course, and I'll inspect your earthworks at sunset tonight."

For a second Starbuck did not quite understand the implications of the Colonel's words. "Does that mean I'll be in command?" he asked.

"Who else? The tooth fairy?" Swynyard's conversion had not entirely robbed him of savagery. "Of course you're in command. B and E Companies are commanded by lieutenants, in case you hadn't noticed. But, of course," he added, "if you don't feel equal to the responsibility of command?" He left the question dangling.

"I'm up to it, sir, and thank you," Starbuck said, and then he saw Swynyard's triumphant grin and realized that he had actually called the Colonel "sir." But then this was a special occasion, the first time that Captain Nathaniel Starbuck had been given the responsibility of an independent command.

"I suspect the ford is in safe hands now," Swynyard said, pleased with himself. "So, Colonel"—he turned to Lassan—"you've plainly seen more adventure than most. Like me!" He held up his left hand with its missing fingers. "So let us exchange stories of scars. Off you go, Starbuck! Fetch your men. Leave the horse with Ketley."

"Yes, sir," Starbuck said and felt his spirits soar. He had a ford to guard.

Priscilla Bird had taken over her husband's responsibilities in the small schoolroom of Faulconer Court House where, day by day, she taught fifty-three children whose ages ranged from five to sixteen. She was a good teacher, patient with the slow, demanding of the quick, and firm in her discipline, yet since the war had begun, there were two sounds that were guaranteed to erode all order in her schoolroom. One was the noise of marching feet, and the other the clatter of massed hoofbeats on the road outside, and despite all Priscilla's strictures the older children would always respond to those sounds by first sidling along their benches to see out of the windows, and if they saw soldiers passing, they would then ignore her protests and insist on hanging over the sills to cheer their passing heroes.

Yet as the August temperatures rose to record levels, Priscilla became as sensitive to the sound of horses as any of the children. She expected her wounded husband's return, and that expectation was shot through with apprehension, love, relief, and fear, which was why she no longer protested when the children crowded at the windows, for she was as keen as they to investigate every odd sound in the street. Not that troops passed very often, for, since the Faulconer Legion had marched away a year before, the town had seen precious few soldiers in its streets. The townsfolk read about the battles in the *Faulconer County Gazette*, but the tides of war had ebbed and flowed far from the streets of Faulconer Court House. Indeed, in the summer of 1862, hardly a uniform was seen in the town at all until, on an August day as hot as any in memory, the sound of cavalry drew the children to the schoolroom windows. Priscilla joined them, scanning the street for the sight of a wagon that might be carrying her husband, but all she saw was a tired group of horsemen with weapons on their shoulders. The schoolchildren cheered while Priscilla, her heart aching, felt sorry for the weary-looking men and their poor swaybacked horses.

One or two of the troopers smiled at the cheering children, but most stayed grim-faced as they passed the school. There were only twenty of the horse soldiers, but their arrival was stirring the town with excitement and the expectation of news. "Are you with Jeb Stuart?" one boy called repeatedly from the schoolhouse. The Confederacy still buzzed with the remembered pleasure of Stuart's mocking ride clean around the whole of George McClellan's army. "Are you Jeb Stuart's men, mister?" the boy called again.

"Damn Stuart, you black-assed bastard," one of the dusty troopers called back.

Priscilla frowned, stared, and hardly dared to believe the suspicion that suddenly crossed her thoughts. These men wore blue coats, not gray or brown, and the leader of the troop was suddenly familiar beneath the mask of dust on his suntanned face. The man had a square, golden beard and blue eyes that looked up to meet Priscilla's gaze. He half smiled, then courteously touched the brim of his hat. It was Adam Faulconer.

"Get back!" Priscilla shouted at the children, and such was the fear and anger in her voice that all but the most rebellious of her pupils obeyed.

For there were Yankees in Faulconer Court House.

Adam had known it was imprudent to take his men through the very center of his hometown, but once he had thought of the notion, he could not shake it free. He wanted to flaunt his new allegiance in front of his father's neighbors, and the very hurtfulness of that disloyal act made it all the more appealing. He suddenly felt free of both his father and of his father's money, and that liberation had made him cast all caution to the wind and bring his blue troopers into the heart of his hometown. "Sergeant Huxtable!" he shouted when he saw Priscilla Bird pull back from the open schoolroom window.

"Sir?" Huxtable called.

"Let the banner fly, Huxtable. Let's not be coy!"

"Yes, sir." Huxtable grinned, then ordered Corporal Kemp to pull the cloth cover off the Stars and Stripes. Kemp unrolled the banner, then raised it high on its lance shaft-pole. A last child had been cheering from the schoolroom but fell abruptly silent as the old flag unfurled to the bright Virginia sun. Adam, looking at that flag, felt the familiar catch in his throat.

It was a sweet moment for Adam as he rode through Faulconer Court House beneath his proper flag. He rode proud in a strange uniform, and he enjoyed the astonishment on the townspeople's faces. "Good morning, Mrs. Cobb!" he called happily. "Your husband's well? You'll doubtless be hoping for some rain for your vegetables." He waved to Grandmother Mallory, who was on the steps of the bank, then greeted the blacksmith, Matthew Tunney, who was one of a group of drinkers who had crowded out of Greeley's Tavern to watch the strange horsemen pass. "Keep your hand off your gun, Southerly!" Adam warned an elderly man whose face displayed a livid outrage. Adam's own men had unslung their Colt rifles.

"Traitor!" Southerly called, but kept his hands in clear sight as the dusty, hard-faced horsemen passed by. The horses, some of the townsfolk noted, were mangy and ill-kept. "Should be ashamed of himself, a Faulconer, riding nags like that," Matthew Tunney observed.

Adam led the nags past Sparrow's Dry Goods Store, then by the Episcopal church and the Baptist church, the courthouse and the livery stable. Sleeping dogs were startled awake and slunk out of the road as the horses clattered by. Adam paused by the livery stable to touch his hat to a wan, thin woman. "I was so sorry to hear about Joseph, Mrs. May," he said, "sincerely sorry." Mrs. May just stared in apparent shock. Some townsfolk followed the horsemen, but once Adam had passed Medlicott's watermill, which marked the eastern extremity of Faulconer Court House, he quickened his troop's pace and so left the curious townspeople behind. "They'll be sending for help," Sergeant Huxtable warned Adam.

"There's no help nearer than Rosskill," Adam reassured the Sergeant, "and we'll be well gone before anyone can get there and back. And no one in Rosskill will hear that noise!" he added as someone in the town began to tug the rope of the courthouse bell. The bell was still tolling its alarm as Adam turned his troop into a white-gated entrance that opened into an avenue edged by mature live oaks. Beyond the oaks were deep, well-watered pastures, where cows stood to their bellies in cool ponds, while at the end of the avenue was a wide, comfortable house clad in creepers that smothered the house's weatherboards and encroached on its steep-gabled roofs. A weathervane shaped like a galloping horse surmounted a clock tower above the stable entrance. The only warlike aspect of the house was a pair of bronze six-pounder cannons that flanked the main entrance. The twin guns had been purchased by Washington Faulconer at the war's beginning in the expectation that the Faulconer Legion needed to have its own artillery, yet in the rush to reach the first battle the weapons had been left behind and Faulconer had found it simpler to appropriate the two cannons as garden ornaments.

Adam pointed Huxtable toward the stable. "You'll probably find a half-dozen decent horses in there," he said, "and the rest will be in the bottom fields. I'll take you there when I've finished in the house."

Huxtable paused before swerving away. "A nice place," he said, staring up at the house.

"Home," Adam said with a grin, "sweet home."

Home was Seven Springs, Adam's father's country house where Washington Faulconer kept the Faulconer stud that was reputed to breed the finest horses in all Virginia. It was here that Adam would find the remounts for his cavalrymen, and not just any remounts, but horses sprung from the best Arab blood crossed and strengthened with sturdier

169

American strains to breed a fast, willing, and enduring horse that could hunt a long cold winter's day among the short hills and wooded valleys of Virginia, or else be spurred into a winning gallop in the last furlongs of a lung-breaking, sweat-streaked steeplechase. Adam had risked coming this far south to equip his men with the best horses in America—horses that could outrun and outlast the best of the South's famed cavalry. Indeed, they were horses that should have belonged to the Southern cavalry, for the Richmond government had ordered that all saddle horses should be surrendered to the army, but Adam knew his father had chosen to ignore the command. Faulconer horses, according to Washington Faulconer, were too valuable to be wasted on war, and so the stud still existed.

Adam let himself into the house. He did not know whether or not his mother would want to see him, but he intended to pay his respects anyway, though as he walked into the front hall with its four portraits of Washington, Jefferson, Madison, and Washington Faulconer, the first person he met was Nelson, his father's personal servant. Adam stopped in surprise. "Is my father here?" He asked the question with some trepidation, for though he felt he was making a fine and defiant gesture in stealing a score of horses from Seven Springs, he did not particularly want to meet his father while he made it.

Nelson shook his head, then put a finger to his lips and gave a glance upstairs as though warning Adam of some danger. Then Nelson beckoned Adam along the corridor that led to Washington Faulconer's study. Adam followed the black man. "The mistress sent John to Rockville, Mr. Adam," Nelson said when he was certain that no one in the household could overhear him. "Young Master Finney ran here from the town, saying how you'd arrived with the soldiers, so Mistress sent young John to fetch help."

Adam smiled. "Then no one will be here for at least an hour and a half."

"Maybe," Nelson agreed, "but the mistress says you're to be held here. She says you're mind-sick, Mr. Adam. She says you're to be locked up till the doctors can see you." The two men had reached the study, and Nelson now closed the door to give them privacy. "They say you've clear gone plumb mad crazy, Mr. Adam," the servant said.

"They would say that," Adam admitted sadly. He knew his parents could not stomach his betrayal of Virginia, nor would they ever accept Adam's conviction that Virginia was best served by adherence to the Union. He looked out of a window and saw some of the stable boys running in panic from Sergeant Huxtable's men. "What are you doing here, Nelson?" he asked the servant.

"The General sent me to deliver something," Nelson said evasively. He was a trusted servant, much older than his master, and in charge of three younger black men who served the General as valets and cooks. Nelson, like all Washington Faulconer's servants, was a free man, though freedom, in Adam's experience, rarely lifted a Negro out of poverty or released him from the need to show an obsequious respect to all white men, and Adam suspected that the outwardly servile Nelson still harbored the secret resentments of most slaves. Washington Faulconer, on the other hand, believed utterly in Nelson's loyalty and had provided him with a pass enabling him to travel freely throughout Confederate-held Virginia.

Adam crossed to the giant map of Virginia that hung on a wall of the study. "Do you think I'm mad, Nelson?"

"You know I don't, Mr. Adam."

"Do you think I'm wrong?"

Nelson paused, then shrugged. Somewhere deep in the house a woman's voice called in sharp reproof and a bell rang. "The mistress will be wanting me," Nelson said.

"Where is my father?" Adam asked. "Here?" He stabbed a finger at the peninsula east of Richmond, where he had last seen the Legion.

Again Nelson paused, then seemed to cross whatever Rubicon of loyalty had been restraining him and walked to Adam's side. "The General's here," he said, placing a finger on the banks of the Rapidan River to the west of the road going north from Gordonsville to Culpeper Court House. "They fought against General Banks up here"—Nelson's finger moved up the Culpeper road—"then they went back again. I guess they're just waiting."

"For what? For the North to attack?"

"Don't know, sir. But on my way here, sir, I saw ever so many troops marching north. I reckon there'll be fighting soon."

Adam stared at the map. "How's my friend Starbuck?" he asked, half ironically, yet also interested in the fate of the man who had once been his closest friend.

"That's why the General sent me here, sir," Nelson said mysteriously, and then, when Adam frowned in puzzlement, the servant gestured across the study to where a flag lay draped across the General's desk. "Mr. Starbuck captured that flag, sir, from the Yankees. The General took it from Mr. Starbuck and made me bring it back here to be kept safe. It's a Pennsylvania flag, sir."

Adam crossed the study and picked up the powder-stained, scorched, bullet-torn flag of purple cloth. He smoothed out the embroidered eagle with its long talons above the German motto: *Gott und die Vereinigten Staaten*. "God and the United States," Adam murmured aloud, and the sight of the captured Northern banner gave him a sudden and exciting idea. He went back to the map and asked Nelson to describe the Faulconer Brigade's deployment, and as he listened Adam found his idea becoming ever more practicable. He was remembering the Reverend Elial Starbuck's fervent wish to be presented with a rebel battle flag, and Adam suddenly saw how he might be able to fulfill that desire.

For the moment, however, he contented himself with confiscating the Pennsylvanian banner. "I'll return it to its rightful owners," he told Nelson, "but first I should visit Mother."

"And your sister," Nelson said, "she's upstairs, too. But don't be long, master. Young John can ride fast."

"I won't be long." Outside the study window Sergeant Huxtable's men were busy saddling their wonderful new horses. Adam smiled at the sight, then crossed to the study door. God willing, he thought, those horses would carry him to a coup that would make the North ring with triumph and the South cringe with shame.

Then, his mother's bell clanging loud, he climbed the stairs and nerved himself for combat.

By sunset Dead Mary's Ford was properly protected. At the edge of the woodland Starbuck had dug a line of fifteen rifle pits that were invisible from the river's far bank. The red excavated earth had all been thrown back into the undergrowth, and the pits' parapets disguised with brush and dead logs so that if an enemy did try to cross the river, they would be met with a blast of rifle fire from an apparently deserted tree line. The advance picket was hidden inside Silas's ruined house, where four men could keep a close watch on the far woods, but the majority of Starbuck's 130 men were bivouacked two hundred yards behind the rifle pits. There they had made their encampment, and there they would wait in case they were needed to reinforce the men serving their turn of duty in the ruins or in the rifle pits.

Colonel Swynyard approved all he saw. "Have you sent anyone over the river?" he asked.

"Sergeant Truslow!" Starbuck called, and Truslow came and told the Colonel what he had found on the far bank.

"Nothing," Truslow said. He spat tobacco juice, hitched his pants higher, then told how he had led a dozen men up the far track until the trees ended. "That's a fair ways, 'bout a long mile. Beyond that's a farm. Family called Kemp lived there, but they're gone." He spat again. "Yankee lovers," he explained both his expectoration and the absence of the Kemp family. "Saw a neighbor at the farm. She lives another half-mile north and says she ain't seen a live Yankee in weeks."

"So you're probably in for a restful time, Captain," Swynyard said. "Did you consider putting pickets on the far bank?"

"I'd rather not," Starbuck said. "I don't want anyone shooting one of our own men by mistake."

"I told the woman at the Kemp farm to stay away from the river," Truslow said. "And the Captain said the same to the old nigger."

"But a sentry post a hundred yards up that track would give you more time to rouse your reserves," Swynyard pointed out.

Truslow answered for his Captain. "I laid a dozen felled trees over the track, Colonel. There ain't a Yankee born who can come down that road without waking the dead."

Swynyard nodded his approval, then turned and gazed westward, where another track followed the riverbank. "Where does that lead?" he asked.

"To Lieutenant Davies and twelve men," Starbuck answered. "There's a ruined barn just out of sight. That's our western picket."

"You seem to have thought of everything!" Swynyard said

approvingly. "Including, I hope, the need to provide me with supper? And after that, Captain, you'll doubtless allow me to lead a small prayer group for those men who care about their souls?"

Starbuck shrugged. "We're pretty short of food, Colonel. Not that you ain't welcome, but supper's nothing but rough rice, stewed squirrel, and pea coffee if you're lucky. But I'm staying here." He wanted to see the night fall across the river so he would know what to expect when he took the late sentry watch.

"Don't get too tired," Swynyard advised; then he strode back to where the cooking fires sifted their smoke into the leaves. Starbuck stayed at the tree line and watched as darkness fell and as the moon climbed above the far trees to silver the shallow water hurrying across its gravel bed. He walked along the rifle pits and was filled with pride because this was his first independent command. If a Yankee cavalry patrol should come south and prove foolish enough to force its way past the felled trees, then Starbuck would fight his very own battle, and if he recognized the truth, he wanted to fight that battle because he knew he would win. He would turn the silver ford bloody and add a pack of Yankee ghosts to join the unquiet spirit of poor Dead Mary.

The river ran quick, the moon threw black shadows, and Starbuck prayed that God would send him his own, his very own, small battle.

THERE WERE TIMES WHEN General Washington Faulconer needed to leave the problems of the Brigade behind him. Such times, he said, gave him an opportunity to assess his Brigade from what he called the distant perspective, though most of his officers suspected that the distant perspective merely served to relieve the General's distaste for the discomforts of campaigning. Washington Faulconer had been raised to luxury and had never lost his taste for cosseted living, and a month of bivouacs and army food inevitably drove him to discover a hotel where clean sheets were smoothed onto a properly stuffed mattress, where hot water was available at the pull of a bell rope, and where the food was not hardtack, worm-ridden, or rancid. The General even believed he deserved such trifling luxuries, for had he not raised the Legion with his own money? Other men had marched enthusiastically to war, but Washington Faulconer had added an open wallet to mere enthusiasm. Indeed, few men in all the Confederacy had spent as much on a regiment as Washington Faulconer, so why should he not reward himself with a few civilized trappings from time to time?

Thus, when his Brigade was properly settled into its bivouac on the western flank of Jackson's army, General Faulconer soon found reason to visit Gordonsville for a night of comfort. He was not supposed to leave his Brigade without General Jackson's permission, but in the certain knowledge that such permission would not be forthcoming, Faulconer found his own justification. "I need spectacles," he told Swynyard airily. "Can't see the fine detail on maps these days," and upon that medical excuse he mounted his horse and, with Captain Moxey in attendance, rode eastward. The town was barely three hours' ride away, so the dereliction was hardly serious, and Swynyard had been left with the strictest instructions that nothing was to be done without Faulconer's permission and that, if any emergency did arise, a messenger must be sent to Gordonsville immediately. The General considered that even a fool could understand those simple commands, and Swynyard, in the General's opinion, was a fool. The man had made an idiot of himself with the bottle but was now making himself an even more conspicuous idiot with his ludicrous addiction to the Holy Spirit.

The General's own spirits began to soar the moment he rode away from the encampment. He always felt such an elation when he could leave behind the small-minded irritations of the Brigade, where nothing was ever straightforward and where the simplest order provoked a flurry of queries, obstructions, misunderstandings, and even downright disobedience, and the more he pondered those frustrations, the more convinced he became that the root cause of all his problems lay in the hostility of men like Thaddeus Bird, Colonel Swynyard, and Nathaniel Starbuck. Especially Captain Nathaniel Starbuck. Take the simple matter of the crescent patches. It had been no small achievement to have the cloth badges made, for such furbelows were a luxury in the war-straitened Confederacy, yet Faulconer had succeeded in having the insignia manufactured in France and then smuggled into Wilmington on a swift blockade-runner. The cost of the badges alone demanded respect! And certainly the proposed function of the badges was admirable, for the

177

red crescent had been intended both to foster pride in the Faulconer Brigade and to serve as an identification mark in the smoky chaos of battle.

Yet what had happened? Grinning soldiers had employed the patches for gambling counters or given them to girl-friends. Others had cleaned their rifles with the badges or else used them to patch the seat of their pants, an insult that had driven the General to decree severe punishment for any man not displaying the red crescent insignia on his uniform jacket, whereupon there had been a religious outcry against the wearing of a Mohammedan symbol in a Christian country! Letters had been written to hometown newspapers, prayer meetings were held to intercede for Washington Faulconer's heathen soul, and seven army chaplains had carried their protests to the War Department itself, forcing Faulconer to explain that the crescent moon was not intended to be a religious symbol but was merely a part of his family's escutcheon, yet that explanation had only prompted new complaints about the restoration of aristocratic privileges in America. The campaign against the insignia had been an outrageous farrago of lies, and now the cause was utterly lost because any man who objected to wearing the red crescent could plausibly claim to have lost the badge in battle. Which all meant that Washington Faulconer had little choice but to accept defeat—a defeat made all the more odious because he was convinced it had been Nathaniel Starbuck who had orchestrated the whole controversy. Only Starbuck could have dreamed up the religious objection or have invented the fantastic claim that wearing the patch reduced the Brigade to the level of European serfs.

Yet even the memory of that humiliation receded as Washington Faulconer rode the summer roads toward Gordonsville. He was contemplating the pleasures of a long bath, a clean bed, and a full table, and the anticipation was more than rewarded when he entered the public parlor of the Rapidan House Hotel to be surprised by the presence of four old friends from Richmond whose visit to the town happily coincided with his own. Two of the men were Confederate congressmen and the other two, like Faulconer himself, were directors of the Orange and Alexandria Railroad. The four men formed a commission that was supposed to be reporting to the War Department on how the army's supply system could be improved, but so far not one of the four commissioners had ventured further than the house of assignation that lay next door to the hotel. Happily all four men had read and admired the account in the *Richmond Examiner* that had described how the Faulconer Brigade had captured an enemy color at the recent battle, and now they insisted that the General and his aide join them and recount their version of the triumph.

Faulconer told the story modestly, claiming to have been momentarily unsighted when the enemy standard fell, though the modesty was beautifully calculated to encourage his listeners to draw the very opposite conclusion. "The standard-bearer was a great brute of a German, ain't that so, Mox'?" The General appealed for his aide's confirmation.

"He was indeed, sir," Moxey said, "and I was damned glad you were there to deal with the fellow and not me."

"The fellow took a half-dozen bullets"—the General lightly touched the ivory handle of his revolver—"and still he kept on coming. Some of these Northern fellows are remarkably brave, but of course there's not one of the rogues who can compare with our fine boys," and here the General paid a moving tribute to the Southern soldier, describing him as the salt of the earth, a rough diamond, and an honest warrior, each compliment being accompanied by a toast, so that it was soon necessary to order another bottle of whiskey.

"Not that it's very good whiskey," one of the congressman said, "but even the worst is better than water."

"Like the *nymphs du monde* next door," his fellow politician opined. "Gordonsville's whores are hardly enticing, but even the worst is preferable to a wife."

All six men laughed. "If you've nothing more pressing," one of the railroad men said to Faulconer, "maybe you'd like to saddle one or two of the ladies yourself?"

"I should be delighted," Faulconer said.

"It shall be our pleasure to pay," the other director said, then courteously included Captain Moxey in the invitation.

"Myself, I fancy the mulatto girl tonight," the fatter of the two congressmen said as he poured himself another glass of whiskey. "And we'd better enjoy ourselves this evening, because tomorrow we'll all have to look busy. Can't have Bobby Lee thinking we're idle."

"Lee?" Faulconer asked, hiding his consternation. "Is Lee here?"

"Arrives tomorrow," one of the railroad men said. "Train was ordered this morning."

"Not that any of us are supposed to know who the train's for," the other railroad man said, yawning, "but it's true. Lee's coming to take command."

"What do you make of Lee, Faulconer?" one of the congressmen asked casually.

"Hardly know the man," the General said, which was a transparent evasion, for the Faulconer family was as prominent in Virginian society as the Lees, and Washington Faulconer had been acquainted with Robert Lee almost all his life, yet even so Faulconer found himself puzzled by Lee's present eminence. Lee had started the war with a considerable reputation, but nothing he had achieved since had justified that good standing, yet, with an apparent effortlessness that Faulconer could only admire, Lee had risen to command the Army of Northern Virginia. Faulconer's only explanation for this phenomenon was that the leaders of the Confederacy were deceived by Lee's grave demeanor into believing that deep thoughts were being pondered behind the General's calm and trustworthy eyes, but he could hardly confess as much to two of those leaders. "I worry he's too cautious," Faulconer said instead, "though, of course, caution may be the right tactic to follow at the moment."

"Let the enemy come to us, you mean?" the fatter congressman suggested.

"For the moment, yes," Faulconer said, "because there's little point in maneuvering ourselves into trouble. Let them break themselves on our bastions, eh?" He smiled, sounding confident, but inside he was worrying that if Lee was arriving in Gordonsville next day, then the town would surely be filled with high-ranking Confederate officers who would look askance when they discovered Faulconer was absent from his Brigade without permission, and the very last thing Washington Faulconer needed was the enmity of Stonewall Jackson. Jackson was already suspicious of Faulconer because of his tardiness in joining the counterattack at Cedar Mountain, though happily the capture of the enemy color had gone a long way toward preserving Faulconer's reputation, but even so Jackson could prove a powerful enemy, especially as the *Richmond Examiner* was as supportive of Stonewall as it was of Washington Faulconer. All in all, Faulconer decided, this was a moment for a tactical withdrawal. "I think this news means that we should get back to camp tonight, Mox'," Faulconer said as he turned to his aide. "If Lee's coming there'll doubtless be orders for us and we need to be ready."

Captain Moxey concealed his surprise at so sudden a departure and his disappointment at being denied the pleasures of the house of assignation next door. "I'll order the horses, sir," Moxey said, and when the tired beasts were saddled, the two officers, without so much as taking a bath let alone partaking of the town's more exquisite recreations, retraced their steps west into the twilight. Back at the hotel one of the congressmen remarked that the country was fortunate indeed in having men as devoted and disciplined as Washington Faulconer at its service, and his three colleagues solemnly agreed before heaving themselves out of their chairs and ushering each other into the house next door.

It was black dark by the time Washington Faulconer reached the farm that was his Brigade's headquarters. Colonel Swynyard was still awake, sitting in candlelight beneath the crossed banners of the Faulconer Legion as he struggled to reconcile the Brigade's muddled accounts. He stood as Faulconer came in, hid his surprise at the General's sudden return, and offered a report on the day's happenings. Two men had been arrested for drunkenness at McComb's Tavern and were waiting for punishment in the morning. "I thought I put the tavern out of bounds," Faulconer said, stretching out his right leg so Moxey could tug off a riding boot.

"So you did, sir," Swynyard confirmed.

"But you can't keep a rogue away from his liquor, is that what you were going to say, Colonel?" Faulconer asked nastily.

"I was going to say, sir, that McComb keeps a pair of whores, and plenty of men will risk punishment for that."

"McComb keeps women?" Faulconer growled. "Then have the filthy creatures arrested! Goddamn it. I don't want half the Brigade felled by pox." He lit a cigar and half listened as Swynyard went on with his report, but while appearing to pay attention Faulconer was really thinking just how much he disliked this new manifestation of Swynyard's idiocy. The old, drunken Swynyard had been largely invisible, an embarrassment to be sure, but a predictable embarrassment and a small price to pay for the support of his cousin, the editor of the *Richmond Examiner*. Yet the new Swynyard was a man who flaunted his morality with an assiduity that Faulconer found grating. Where Swynyard had once been oblivious of the Brigade's affairs, he was now endlessly busy, and endless, too, in bringing complaints and suggestions to Faulconer's attention. Tonight there was a problem with a consignment of percussion caps from the Richmond Arsenal. At least half of the caps had proved defective. "Then send the damn things back!" Faulconer snapped.

"I need your signature," Swynyard pointed out.

"Can't you forge it?"

"I can, but would rather not."

"Damn your scruples, give it to me then," Faulconer said.

"And sadly there were three more desertions, sir," Swynyard said, placing the deserters' report sheets beside the document needing the General's signature. Swynyard's hand shook, not from nerves, but because sobriety had still not wholly calmed his alcohol-ravaged body.

"Who ran?" Faulconer asked in a dangerous voice. He hated desertions, translating the crime as a criticism of his leadership.

"Two are Haxall's men," Swynyard said, referring to the Arkansas battalion, "and Haxall suspects they're making for home, and the third is one of the new men from Richmond who reckons his wife is cheating on him. He's the same fellow who ran two weeks ago."

"So catch the bastard again and this time shoot him," Faulconer said, slapping at a moth that annoyed him. "And how the hell did they run? Aren't the pickets awake?"

"All three were part of a work party carrying ammunition to Starbuck's position, sir," Swynyard said.

Faulconer pulled his left boot back from Moxey's grasp, then looked up at the scarred, bearded Colonel. "Explain," Faulconer said in a very menacing voice.

Swynyard was well aware that the mention of Starbuck's name put him in a risky position, but the Colonel possessed both the courage of his military convictions and the strength of his newfound faith, and so he confidently explained the discovery of the unsuspected ford and told how Starbuck had suggested garrisoning the river crossing. "I gave him three companies, sir, and inspected him at dusk. He's well entrenched and can't be outflanked."

"Goddamn it!" Faulconer shouted, thumping the table beside his chair. "What orders did I give you?" He paused, but he was not waiting for any answer. Indeed the General could not have listened to any answer, for all the frustrations of his last few months had swollen into an abrupt explosion that was now unstoppable. Like a volcano's molten core that had been cribbed too long by a cap of cold, hard rock, Faulconer's temper erupted into an incandescent rage that had nothing whatever to do with the point at issue. Indeed, had Swynyard merely told Faulconer that an unguarded ford had been discovered on the Brigade's open flank, then the General would doubtless have ordered two or three companies of riflemen to watch the crossing, but the mention of Starbuck's name had tipped Washington Faulconer into instant fury.

For a few seconds it was a fury so profound that Faulconer was incapable of speaking, but then the words flowed and soldiers fifty yards from the farmhouse listened in awe, while men bivouacked further away hurried closer to hear the diatribe. Swynyard, Faulconer said, was a shadbellied weakling who if he was not sucking at his goddamned bottle was clasped to the tit of his new religion. "For Christ's sake, you fool, stand on your own goddamned feet!" This was unfair, for the apparent point of Faulconer's rage was that Swynyard had dared to take responsibility for moving part of the Brigade without Faulconer's express permission, but for these first few moments the flow of white-hot anger was not directed but simply went wherever Faulconer's frustrations let it fly, and so the General's anger encompassed Swynyard's breeding, his ugly appearance, and his family's involvement in the slave trade. Then Washington Faulconer raked over Swynyard's apparent conversion, scorning the Colonel's piety as fraudulent and his newfound efficiency as a pose.

It was a spectacular explosion. Washington Faulconer was already feeling cheated because his stay in Gordonsville had been cut short, but now all the bitterness over his traitor son and his resentments over Starbuck and the mulish manner in which the Brigade reacted to his simplest orders fed the bitter torrent. Two decades of being despised by his wife and scorned by his wife's damned schoolmaster brother poured in an ugly spew from Faulconer's mouth as he screamed his insults at Swynyard, and finally, when breathlessness alone made him drop his voice from a half scream into mere loudness, he suspended Swynyard from his duties. "You will consider yourself under arrest!" the General finished.

There was silence in the room. Moxey, his face white with fear, stood backed against the flags on the wall, while not a sound came from the astonished audience outside. The tic in Swynyard's cheek had begun to quiver, and he was clenching and unclenching his maimed left hand, but when at last he spoke, he used the mildest tone. "I have to protest, sir," he began.

"You can protest all you like, damn you, but it'll do no

good! I've endured too much! Too much! You're either drunk or praying, either flat on your back or down on your knees, and in either position you're no more damned good to me than a spavined bitch. You're under arrest, Swynyard, so get the hell out of my sight. Go!" Faulconer shouted the order, unable to bear the sight of the man for one instant longer. Then he stumped one-booted onto the veranda. "Major Hinton!" he shouted into the dark, confident that the summons would be passed on and obeyed swiftly. "Major Hinton! Come here!"

The General, at last, was taking command.

Starbuck took his supper in the bivouac, sitting beside a small fire with Truslow and Coffman. The night was warm and humid, darkening every moment as clouds heaped higher and higher above the Blue Ridge Mountains. For a time the moon silvered the trees; then the clouds misted and finally shrouded its light. Supper was a piece of corn bread and fat bacon. The corn had been badly milled, and Starbuck broke a tooth on a scrap of cob embedded in the grain. He swore. "Dentists' favorite bread," Truslow said as Starbuck spat out the cob and tooth fragment together; then the Sergeant offered a ghastly grin to show how many of his own teeth were missing. "Pulled half of them myself, the rest old McIlvanney yanked. He was a well-digger who doubled up as a dentist."

Starbuck flinched with pain when he took his next bite. "I don't know why God invented teeth," he said.

"I don't know why God invented Yankees," Truslow added.

"Because otherwise there'd only be Indians and Mexicans for Christians to shoot," Lieutenant Coffman unexpectedly observed.

"I know why God invented junior lieutenants," Truslow

observed. "For target practice." He climbed to his feet, stretched his arms, and picked up his rifle in readiness to relieve the pickets in the rifle pits above the river. "I wish it would rain," he said.

Starbuck led the relief party through the trees to where the river flickered white in the night. The far bank was utterly black and impenetrable, its only lights the tiny white and evanescent sparks of fireflies. Then, to the west, where the clouds were building, a spike of lightning shattered the dark above the mountains and shed a sudden blue-white light that silhouetted the half-ruined barn where the outlying picket guarded the riverside track. Sergeant Mallory was now in charge of that picket, and he sent Edward Hunt back along the riverbank to find Starbuck. "Captain! Captain!" Hunt called.

"What is it?"

"Bob reckons there's some son of a bitch on the track, Captain."

Starbuck climbed to his feet. "Truslow!" he called. "I'm down at the barn."

A grunt acknowledged the information; then Starbuck followed Hunt along the river. "It was that lightning," Hunt explained.

"You saw the man?"

"Man and a horse," Hunt said cheerfully. "Plain as a pair of planks."

Starbuck was skeptical. He had learned in the last year just how deceptive the night could be. A bush that would not attract a second glance in daylight could be transformed by darkness into a monstrous threat. A herd of cows could be changed into a rampaging troop of enemy cavalry while, just as easily, a whole battalion of enemy troops could resemble a field of standing corn. Night fed the imagination, and the imagination feared enemies or craved security and made the dark fit its desires. Now Starbuck groped his way to where the picket was positioned behind the barn's broken wall. Sergeant Mallory was nervous. "There's someone out there, sir," he said. "We all saw him."

Starbuck could see nothing except the darkness and the slight quivering sheen of the river. "Did you challenge?" he asked.

"No, sir," Mallory answered.

Starbuck placed his rifle on the makeshift parapet, then cupped his hands. "Who goes there?" he shouted as loud as he could.

Nothing answered except the small stir of the wind and the sound of the river running.

"We saw something, sir," Mallory insisted.

"We did, sir, truly," one of the men put in.

"Are you sure it isn't the old black fellow?" Starbuck asked.

"This was a man and a horse, sir," Mallory said.

Starbuck challenged again and again received no reply. "Maybe they got the hell out of here?" Starbuck suggested, and just as he spoke the far mountain range was raked with another stab of forked lightning, the streaks slashing down to silhouette the tree-lined crests with fire, but closer, much closer, the splinter of light touched a figure standing beside a horse not fifty paces away—or so it seemed to Starbuck, who had but a second to focus his eyes and make sense of the sudden stark contrasts of white night-fire and pitch-black dark. "Who are you?" he shouted as the light faded, leaving nothing behind but an imprinted image on his retinas that seemed to suggest that the man was wearing a saber scabbard and carrying a carbine.

No one answered. Starbuck cocked his rifle, taking satisfaction from the solid heft of the spring-loaded hammer. He felt with a finger to make certain a percussion cap was in

188

place, then pointed the gun just above where he thought the man was standing. He pulled the trigger.

The explosion rebounded across the river valley, echoing back from the trees on the far bank, then fading like the crackle of the thunder in the distant mountains. The muzzle flash lit a few square yards of ground beyond the barn but could not reach as far as the solitary, silent, unmoving man whom Starbuck was now certain he had glimpsed in the lightning's glare.

"Hoofbeats, sir!" Mallory said excitedly. "Hear them?" And sure enough the sound of horses' hooves and the jingling of curb chains sounded above the endless river noise.

"Cavalry coming!" Starbuck shouted to warn the men in the rifle pits behind. He began to reload his rifle as Mallory's picket slid their guns across the wall. "We'll give the bastards a volley," Starbuck said, then checked his words because the hoofbeats were not coming from the west but from behind him, from the direction of the Brigade's lines. He turned to see a light moving among the trees above the ford, and after a few seconds he saw that the light was a lantern being carried by a horseman.

"Starbuck!" the horseman shouted. It was Major Hinton. "Starbuck!"

"Stand down," Starbuck told the picket. "Major?"

A second horseman appeared from the trees. "Starbuck!" the newcomer shouted, and in the lantern's light Starbuck saw it was General Washington Faulconer who had shouted. Moxey's ratlike face appeared next; then the three horsemen cantered down into the open ground beside the ruins of Mad Silas's cabin. "Starbuck!" Faulconer shouted again.

"Sir?" Starbuck shouldered his half-loaded rifle and walked to meet his Brigade commander.

Faulconer's horse was nervous of the distant storm and edged sideways as a volley of thunder roared in the mountains. Faulconer gave the beast a hard cut with his riding crop. "I gave orders, Mr. Starbuck, that no changes of disposition were to be made without my express permission. You disobeyed those orders!"

"Sir!" Major Hinton protested, wanting to point out that Starbuck had only been obeying Swynyard's instructions. Hinton himself had been busy at a neighboring brigade's court-martial all day, else he would have reinforced Colonel Swynyard's instructions himself. "Captain Starbuck received orders, sir," Hinton began.

"Quiet!" Faulconer rounded on Hinton. "There is a conspiracy, Major Hinton, to subvert authority in this Brigade. That conspiracy is now at an end. Major Hinton, you will take these three companies back to the Legion's lines immediately. Captain Moxey, you will escort Starbuck to headquarters. You are under arrest, Mr. Starbuck."

"Sir—" Starbuck began his own protest.

"Quiet!" Faulconer shouted. His horse pricked its ears back and tossed its head.

"There's a horseman down the path—" Starbuck tried again.

"I said quiet!" Faulconer shouted. "I do not give a damn, Mr. Starbuck, if the archangel Gabriel is on the goddamned path. You have disobeyed my orders and you are now under arrest. Give that rifle to Major Hinton and follow Captain Moxey." Faulconer waited for Starbuck to obey, but the Northerner remained stubbornly motionless. "Or do you intend to disobey those orders, too?" Faulconer asked, and underscored his implied threat by unbuttoning the flap of his revolver's holster. Truslow and Coffman, their faces dim in the lantern's small light, watched from the tree line.

Starbuck felt an insane urge to fight Faulconer, but then Paul Hinton leaned down from his saddle and took

Starbuck's rifle away. "It's all right, Nate," he murmured soothingly.

"It is not all right!" Faulconer was exultant. His evening, which had begun so ill with his precipitate flight from Gordonsville, had turned into a triumph. "Discipline is the first requisite of a soldier, Major," Faulconer went on, "and Starbuck's insolence has corrupted this regiment. There'll be no more of it, by God, none! There are going to be changes!" Lightning ripped the west, shattering the night over the mountains, and its sudden light betrayed the blissful happiness on Washington Faulconer's face. He had confronted his enemies and he had routed them both, and the General, for the first time since he had donned his country's uniform, felt like a soldier triumphant.

And Starbuck was under arrest.

Starbuck was put into Colonel Swynyard's tent. An embarrassed private from A Company stood guard outside, while inside the tent Starbuck discovered Swynyard sitting slumped on his camp bed and cradling what Starbuck supposed was a Bible. A wax taper burned on a folding table to shed a sickly and wan light. The Colonel's head was bowed, so that his hair fell lank across his bony face. Starbuck sat at the other end of the bed and announced his presence with an oath.

"A contagion," Swynyard responded mysteriously, without offering any more formal greeting to his fellow prisoner, "that's what I am, Starbuck, a contagion. A contamination. An infection. A plague. Unclean. Out of step. Do you ever feel out of step with all mankind?" The Colonel raised his head as he asked the question. His eyes were red. "I tell you, Starbuck, that the world would be a better place without me."

Starbuck, alarmed at the wild words, looked more closely

191

at the object in the Colonel's hands. He had presumed it was a Bible and now feared to see a revolver, but instead he saw it was an uncorked bottle. "Oh, no," Starbuck said, astonished at his own disappointment. "Are you getting drunk?"

Swynyard did not answer. He just stared at the bottle, turning it in his hands as though he had never seen such an object before. "What did Faulconer say to you?" the Colonel asked finally.

"Nothing much," Starbuck said, using a tone of indifference to show defiance. "He said I'd disobeyed orders."

"You obeyed my orders, but that won't make any difference with Faulconer. He hates you. He hates me, too, but he hates you more. He thinks you took his son away." The Colonel went on staring at the bottle, then shook his head wearily. "I'm not drinking. I took a sip and spat it out. But I was going to drink it. Then you came in." He held the bottle close to the dripping, spluttering taper, so that the feeble light refracted through the green glass and amber liquid. "Faulconer gave it to me. He says I deserve it. It's the best whiskey in America, he says, from Bourbon County, Kentucky. None of your bust-head tonight, Starbuck. No rotgut or pop-skull, no red-line special, no brain-buster, no skull-splitter, no tanglefoot tonight." The mention of tanglefoot whiskey evidently prompted some memory that made the Colonel close his eyes in sudden pain. "No, sir," he went on sadly, "only the best of Bourbon County whiskey for Griffin Swynyard. Clear as a dewdrop, do you see?" He again held the bottle to the taper's light. "Isn't that beautiful?"

"You don't need it, Colonel," Starbuck said softly.

"But I do, Starbuck. I need either God or whiskey, and whiskey, I have to tell you, is a great deal more convenient than God. It is more available than God and it is more predictable than God. Whiskey, Starbuck, does not make demands like God, and the salvation it offers is every bit as certain as God's, and even if that salvation is not as long in duration as God's salvation it is still a true and tried remedy for the miseries of life. Whiskey is a consolation, Starbuck, and a very present help in times of trouble, and never more so than when it comes from Bourbon County, Kentucky." He swirled the bottle slowly, gazing reverently at its contents. "Are you going to preach to me, Starbuck?"

"No, sir. I've been preached at all my damned life and it didn't do neither me nor the preacher one damned bit of good."

Swynyard lifted the bottle to his nose and sniffed. He closed his eyes at the smell of the liquor, then touched the bottle's rim to his lips. For a second Starbuck was sure that the Colonel was going to tip the whiskey down his throat; then Swynyard lowered the bottle again. "I guess preaching didn't do you any good, Starbuck, because you're a preacher's son. Probably hurt you rather than helped. If a man tells you all your born days to keep away from the women and the whiskey, then what else will you look for when they let go of the leash?"

"Is that why you looked for them?" Starbuck asked.

The Colonel shook his head. "My father was no preacher. He went to church, sure, but he was no preacher. He was a dealer in slaves, Starbuck. That's what it said on our housefront. Said it in scarlet letters three feet high: 'Jos Swynyard, Dealer in Slaves.'" The Colonel shrugged at the memory. "Respectable people didn't come near us, Starbuck, not near a dealer in slaves. They sent their overseers and managers to buy the human flesh. Not that my father minded; he reckoned he was as respectable as any man in Charles City County. He kept a respectable household, I'll say that for him. None of us dared cross him. He was a flogger, you see. He flogged his slaves, his women, and his children." Swynyard went silent, staring down at the bottle. The sentry shifted his feet outside the tent, and pots clattered in the farmhouse kitchen as the servants cleaned up after Washington Faulconer's late supper. Swynyard shook his head sadly. "I treated my slaves bad."

"Yes, you did," Starbuck said.

"But he never flogged his dogs." Swynyard was thinking of his father again. "Never once, not in all his years." He smiled ruefully, then lifted the bottle to his nose and smelt it again. "It really ain't a bad kind of whiskey, judging by its smell," he said. "Have you ever drunk Scottish whiskey?"

"Once or twice."

"Me, too." Swynyard was silent for a few heartbeats. "I reckon I drunk just about everything a man can pour down his throat, but I once knew a man who called himself a connoisseur of whiskeys. A real connoisseur"—Swynyard rolled the word round his tongue—"and this connoisseur told me there wasn't nothing in the whole wide world he didn't know about whiskeys, and do you know which whiskey he reckoned was the best?"

"Tanglefoot?" Starbuck guessed.

Swynyard laughed. "Tanglefoot! Well, it works, I'll say that for tanglefoot. It works like a mule kick to the head, tanglefoot does, but it ain't the best liquor in the world, not if you want your mule kick to taste better than horse liniment. No, this man reckoned he'd drunk every kind of whiskey that this vale of tears has to offer us, and the best, the very best, the absolute real stuff, Starbuck, was whiskey from Ireland. Ain't that the strangest thing?"

"Maybe he was drunk when he tasted it?" Starbuck suggested.

Swynyard thought about that for a second, then shook his head. "No, I reckon he knew what he was saying. He was a rich man and rich folks don't get rich by being fools. At least they might, but they sure don't stay rich by being fools, and this man stayed rich. And he didn't drink much either. He just liked the taste, you see. He liked his whiskey, and he'd pay a rich man's price for Irish whiskey, but the guzzle he liked most of all was the widow's champagne. *Clicquot!*" He raised the whiskey bottle in a tribute to Madame Clicquot's champagne. "Have you ever drunk *Veuve Clicquot?*"

"Yes."

"Good for you. Be a sad thing to die without tasting the widow's champagne. But sadder still to die without salvation, eh?" Swynyard asked, but he seemed confused by the question. He stared at the bottle and again seemed about to drink from it, then, at the very last second, relented. "There was a time, Starbuck, when I could afford the widow's champagne morning, noon, and night. Could have watered my horse in it! Could have watered all my horses in it! I was rich."

Starbuck smiled but said nothing.

"You don't believe me, do you?" Swynyard said. "But there was a time, Starbuck, when I could have purchased Faulconer."

"Truly?"

"Truly," Swynyard said, gently mocking Starbuck's accent with the repetition. "I wasn't always a soldier. I left West Point, class of '29, forty-sixth in my class. You want to guess how many there were in West Point's class of '29?"

"Forty-six?"

Swynyard extended a pistollike finger at Starbuck and made a clicking noise of affirmation. "Forty-sixth out of forty-six. I didn't exactly distinguish myself. Fact is, twenty years later I was still no more than a captain, and I knew I wasn't going to rise any higher than a captain, and I wasn't ever going to kill anything more dangerous to the Republic than a Comanche or a Mexican. I always reckoned I might be a good soldier, but the whiskey made sure I never was. Then one night in '50 I got drunk and offered my resignation and that was the end of my career."

"What did you do?"

"I did what every sensible soldier wanted to do. I went to the Feather River. Ever heard of the Feather?"

"No."

"California," Swynyard said. "The gold fields. Feather River and Goodyear's Bar and Three Snake Run. That's where I struck it rich. I found a lump of gold the size of a dog. Gold," the Colonel said, staring into the heart of the whiskey, "real thick gold, soft as butter, pure as love, and big as a coon dog. In just one day, Starbuck, I made thirty thousand bucks, and all of it before breakfast. That was before they made gold-digging mechanical. Nowadays, Starbuck, they sluice that gold out of the gravels with water jets. That water flies so hard you could kill a regiment of Yankees with that hose, except it takes a regiment to build all the flumes and dams, and not even the Yankees are stupid enough to stand still while you construct it. But I was lucky. I got there early when all a man had to do was climb high and start rolling the rocks aside." He fell silent.

"And you lost it all?"

Swynyard nodded. "Every last cent of it. It all went down the gullet or across the barrelhead. Poker. Women. Whiskey. Stupidity. I lost these fingers, too." He held up his left hand with its three missing fingers.

"I thought those went to a Mexican saber cut," Starbuck said.

"That's what I tell people," Swynyard said, "or what I did tell them before I met the Lord Jesus Christ, but it ain't true. The truth is, Starbuck, that I had them blown away when me and a German miner were using black powder up above Shirt Tail Creek. Otto, his name was, and he was mad as a snake. He reckoned there was a load of nuggets at the top of Shirt Tail and it took us a week to carry all our gear up there, and then we blew the thing wide open and there wasn't nothing up there but dirt and quartz. Only Otto blew it early, see, thinking he'd blow me to hell and get to keep all the gold to himself."

"And what happened to Otto?" Starbuck asked gently.

Swynyard blinked rapidly. His hands were gripping the whiskey bottle so hard that Starbuck feared he might break the glass. "I have many sins on my conscience," Swynyard said after a while, "many. I killed Otto. Took a long time a-dying and I mocked him all that while. God forgive me."

Starbuck waited a few seconds, praying desperately that the Colonel would not suck on the bottle. "And when the war started?" Starbuck finally asked.

"I came back east. Reckoned I could have a new beginning. I kind of persuaded myself I could do without the whiskey so long as I could be a proper soldier again. I wanted to redeem myself, you see? A new country, a new army, a new beginning. But I was wrong."

"No," Starbuck said, "you weren't. You've been off the whiskey for days now."

Swynyard did not answer but just stared into the golden depths of the expensive Kentucky whiskey.

"You don't want it, Colonel," Starbuck said.

"But I do, Starbuck, and that's the plain hard truth of it. I want a drink so bad that it hurts."

"Put the bottle down," Starbuck said.

Swynyard ignored him. "I never thought I could give up the drink, never, and then God helps me to do it at last and just as things are starting to be all right again, Faulconer does this to us. What was I supposed to do? Leave the ford unguarded?"

"Colonel," Starbuck said, reaching for the whiskey bottle.

"You did the right thing. You know that. And do you know why Faulconer gave you that bottle tonight?"

Swynyard would not relinquish the whiskey, but instead held the bottle just beyond Starbuck's reach. "He gave it to me," the Colonel said, "because he wants to humiliate me. That's why."

"No," Starbuck said. "He did it so you won't be in a fit state to testify at a court-martial. He wants you drunk, Colonel, because the son of a bitch knows he's in the wrong, but he also knows that no court will exonerate a staggering drunkard. But if you stay sober, Colonel, he's going to back down and there won't be any court-martial."

Swynyard thought about Starbuck's words, then shook his head. "But I did disobey his orders. Not that it matters, because Faulconer don't care one way or another about Dead Mary's Ford. He just wants to be rid of me. Don't you understand? It isn't what I did or didn't do, it's because I made an enemy. You too. We're being purse-whipped by a rich man, Starbuck, and there ain't nothing we can do about it."

"Goddamn it, there is!" Starbuck insisted. "Faulconer doesn't run this damned army, Jackson does, and if Jackson says you're right and Faulconer's wrong then it won't matter if you and I disobeyed George Washington's orders. Not all of Faulconer's money can change that, but I tell you one thing: If you go in front of Old Mad Jack with a hangover, or with whiskey on your breath, or looking like you used to look before you let Christ into your heart, then Old Mad Jack will have you out of this army faster than you can spit." Starbuck paused and held out his hand. "Now goddamn it, Colonel, give me the whiskey."

Swynyard frowned. "Why would Jackson care what happens to us?"

"Because we'll make him care. We'll tell him the truth.

So give me the bottle." He still held his hand outstretched. "Come on! I'm thirsty!"

Swynyard held the bottle out, but instead of handing it to Starbuck he tipped it upside down so that the liquor gurgled and slurped onto the tent's pine floorboards and there trickled between the cracks into the dirt. When the bottle was empty, Swynyard let it fall. "We've got a battle to fight, Starbuck," the Colonel said, "so let's both be sober."

"Son of a bitch," Starbuck said. The smell of the whiskey was tantalizing in the tent. "I was thirsty."

"And tomorrow you'll be sober," Swynyard said. Far in the distance the thunder grumbled. The sentry sneezed, and the Colonel closed his eyes in prayer. He had resisted temptation and endured despair. And now, like the soldier he knew he could be, he would fight.

Mad Silas began pulling the felled trees off the road that led north through the woods. It was hard work, especially as he had his darling Mary's skull in a sack hanging from his neck and he did not like to bump the skull too hard in case it hurt her. He talked to her as he worked, saying how he was keeping the road clear because the man in the blue coat had asked him to, and the man in the blue coat had said as how all the black folk would be better off if the blue ones beat the gray ones, and even though the white men in the gray coats had been polite to Mad Silas and had even given him some cigars, he still believed the blue horse soldier because the blue man had been young Master Harlan Kemp, the son of old Master Kemp who had given Silas his freedom.

By first light Silas had cleared the whole path. Then, very cautiously, he crept down to the riverbank and saw to his surprise that the gray soldiers were all gone. Their fires had cooled to ashes and their rifle pits were empty. He clutched the scorched skull in his arms and debated with it what the soldiers' absence might mean, but he could not really make any sense of it. Yet their absence made him feel safe again, and so he put his Mary back in the hole in the ruined chimney breast where she now lived. Then, glad to be home with her, he walked down beside the river, past the ruined barn, to the tree and bush that, at night, looked so like a man and a horse. He had a snare here, set to trap rabbits going down to the river.

Then, just as he was parting the leaves of the bush, he heard the hoofbeats. He rolled down the bank into the long grass and lay very still. The sun was not yet up, so the light was gray and flat and the river water had no sparkle, yet Silas could clearly see the far bank, and, after a time, he saw the men appear there. They were white men in blue coats. There were three of them, each on foot and each carrying a long rifle, a saber, and a revolver. They spent a long time staring across the river; then one of them ran through the ford, splashing the water high with his long boots and bright spurs. Silas lost sight of that man, but after a minute or two the man called back over the river. "The bastards were here, right enough, Major, but they've gone."

Then a whole column of blue horse soldiers appeared at the ford. Their spurs, scabbards, and curb chains jingled as they urged their horses through the river. The three men who had scouted the ford seized their reins and heaved themselves up into their saddles. Silas watched them go out of sight, then listened as their hoofbeats faded away to the south, and then he went on listening until there was nothing more to hear but the run of the river and the song of the birds.

Then, with a dead rabbit in his hand, he went back to tell his Mary just what excitements were happening at her ford this morning, while far to the south, unsuspected and unseen, the Yankee raiders went to ground and waited.

THE YANKEES' SPRING OFFENSIVE might have failed, stranding McClellan's Army of the Potomac on the muddy shore of the James River below Richmond, but now John Pope's Army of Virginia gathered its strength in Virginia's northern counties. More and more supplies crossed the Potomac's bridges to be piled high in the gaunt warehouses at Manassas Junction while, on the sun-ruffled water of Virginia's tidal rivers, boat after boat carried McClellan's veterans north from the James River to Aquia Creek on the Potomac. The two Northern armies were joining forces, and though that process of union was excruciatingly slow, once the Army of Virginia and the Army of the Potomac were united, then they would far outnumber Robert Lee's rebel Army of Northern Virginia.

"So we have to strike first," Lee said in a murmur that was intended only for his own ears. The General was staring northward in the dawn, scrying his enemies from the high vantage point of Clark Mountain, which lay on the southern bank of the Rapidan River. Lee's own veterans, who had first stopped and then chased McClellan away from Richmond, had all now come north to face Pope's threatened attack. Stonewall Jackson had served to deter Pope's belligerence for the best part of a month, but now the rebel army was once again united with Robert Lee at its head, and so the time had come to drive Pope back in utter defeat.

To which purpose Lee had come to Clark Mountain. He

was surrounded by mounted aides, but Lee himself was on foot and using the back of his placid gray horse, Traveller, as a rest for his telescope. The morning light was pearly soft. Great swathes of rain smoked across the western countryside, but it was dry to the north, where Lee could see folds of hills, small fields, white-painted farms, long dark woods, and, everywhere he looked, Yankees. The enemy's white-hooded wagons filled the meadows, their guns were parked on every road and farm track, and their tents dotted the fields, while above it all, like strands of tenuous mist, the smoke of their cooking fires mingled to make a blue-gray haze. In another ten days, two weeks at the most, that army would be doubled in size, and Lee knew there would be small chance of ever beating it out of his native Virginia.

But now, while McClellan's men still thumped north in their requisitioned river steamers and sleek transatlantic packets, there was a chance of victory. That chance arose because John Pope had placed himself in a trap. He had brought the bulk of his army close to the Rapidan so that it was ready to strike south, but behind Pope's new position ran the Rapidan's wide tributary, the Rappahannock, and if Lee could turn Pope's right flank, he stood a chance of driving the Northern army hard toward the rivers' junction, where Pope would be trapped between a horde of screaming rebels and the deep, fast-running confluence of the two rivers. But to make that maneuver Lee needed cavalry to screen his march and still more cavalry to mislead the enemy and more cavalry still to ride into the enemy's rear and capture the Rappahannock bridges and thus give the Yankees no way out from their water-bound slaughter yard.

"General Stuart says he's real sorry, sir, but the horses just ain't ready," an aide now told Lee in the dawn on Clark Mountain.

Lee nodded abruptly to show he had heard the gloomy report, but otherwise he showed no reaction. Instead he stared for a long last moment at the encamped enemy. Lee was not a vengeful man—indeed, he had long learned to school his emotions to prevent passion from misleading common sense—but in the last few weeks he had contracted a deep desire to humiliate Major General John Pope. The Northern general had come to Virginia and ordered his men to live off the land and to burn the houses of loyal Virginians, and Lee despised such barbarism. He more than despised it, he hated it. Carrying war to civilians was the way of savages and heathens, not of professional soldiers, but if John Pope chose to fight against women and children, Robert Lee would fight against John Pope, and if God permitted it, Lee would ruin his enemy's career. But the spring to snap the trap's lid shut was not quite ready, and Lee resisted the temptation to close that lid without the help of his horsemen. "How long before the cavalry will be ready?" Lee asked the aide as he collapsed the telescope.

"One day, sir." Most of the rebel cavalry had only just come north from its duty of screening McClellan's army beyond Richmond, and the horses were bone tired after the long march on dry, hard roads.

"By tomorrow's dawn?" Lee sought the clarification.

The aide nodded. "General Stuart says for certain, sir."

Lee showed no evident disappointment at the enforced delay but just stared at the long strands of smoke that laced the far woods and fields. He felt a twinge of regret that he could not attack this morning, but he knew it would take him the best part of a day to move his cumbersome guns and long lines of infantry over the Rapidan, and Jeb Stuart's horsemen would have to entertain and deceive the Yankees while those men and cannon moved into position. So he must wait one full day and hope that John Pope did not wake to his danger. "We'll attack tomorrow," Lee said as he climbed onto Traveller's back.

And prayed that the Yankees went on sleeping.

Major Galloway arrived just after dawn, guided by Corporal Harlan Kemp to where Adam's men waited in a stand of thick trees two miles south of the Rapidan. Galloway's troop was accompanied by Captain Billy Blythe and his men, who had returned from their frustrating reconnaissance. Blythe claimed the enemy held all the high passes through the Blue Ridge Mountains and had thus prevented him from crossing into the Shenandoah Valley, but Galloway's own foray beyond the Rapidan had convinced him that the rebels were not using the Shenandoah Valley to threaten Pope's army. Instead their regiments were bivouacking all along the Rapidan's southern bank, and it was there, in the heart of Virginia, that the threat existed, and it was there, thanks to Adam's timely message, that Galloway could both strike at the enemy and establish a rakish, hell-raising reputation for his fledgling regiment of cavalry. Which was why all Galloway's sixty-eight troopers were now concealed in a thicket just three miles from the western flank of Lee's army. Sixty-eight men against an army sounded like long odds, even to an optimist like Galloway, but he had surprise and the weather both on his side.

The weather had turned that same morning when, just one hour after dawn, a rainstorm had come from the mountains to hammer at the western rebel encampments. The roads had been turned into instant red mud. The rain poured off roofs and streamed down gutters and flooded gullies and overflowed ditches and spread along the plowed furrows of low-lying fields. Thunder bellowed overhead, and sometimes, way off in the rain-silvered distance, a slash of lightning sliced groundward. "Perfect," Galloway said as he stood at the edge of the trees and watched the rain claw and beat at the empty fields. "Just perfect. There's nothing like a good hard rain to keep a sentry's head down." He crouched under his cloak to light a cigar, then, because his own horse needed rest, asked to borrow one of Adam's newly acquired mares. "Let's look at your father's rebels," he told Adam.

Galloway left Blythe in charge of the concealed horsemen while he and Adam rode east. Adam was concerned about the danger of Major Galloway making the reconnaissance in person, but Galloway dismissed the risks of capture. "If something goes amiss tonight, then I don't want to think it was because of something I left undone," the Major said, then rode in silence for a few moments before giving Adam a shrewd look. "What happened between you and Blythe?" Adam, taken aback by the question, stammered an inadequate answer about incompatible personalities, but Major Galloway was in no mood for evasions. "You accused him of attempted rape?"

Adam wondered how Galloway knew, then decided that either Sergeant Huxtable or Corporal Kemp must have complained about Blythe. "I didn't accuse Blythe of anything," Adam said. "I just stopped him from mistreating a woman, if that's what you mean."

Galloway sucked on what was left of his rain-soaked cigar. He ducked under a low branch, then checked his horse so he could search the rain-soaked land ahead. "Billy tells me the woman was merely offering herself because she wanted Northern dollars," the Major said when he was satisfied that no rebel picket waited in the far trees, "and because she wanted to save her house. Sergeant Kelley told me the same thing."

"They're lying!" Adam said indignantly.

Galloway shrugged. "Billy's a good enough fellow, Adam. I ain't saying he's the straightest man as was ever born, I mean he sure isn't no George Washington, but we're a troop of soldiers, not a passel of churchmen."

"Does that justify rape?" Adam asked.

"Hell, that's your tale, Adam, not his," Galloway said tiredly, "and when it comes to telling tales, then you should know that Billy's telling a few on you too." The Major was riding ahead of Adam on a waterlogged path that ran beside a wood. The rain had finally extinguished his cigar, which he tossed into a puddle. "Blythe claims you're a Southern sympathizer, a gray wolf in blue clothing. In fact he says you're a spy." Galloway held up a hand. "Don't protest, Adam. I don't believe a word of it, but what else do you expect him to say about a man accusing him of rape?"

"Maybe he could tell the truth," Adam proclaimed indignantly.

"The truth!" Galloway barked a laugh at the very thought of such a notion. "The truth in war, Adam, is whatever the winner decides it is, and the best way for you to prove that Blythe is a liar is to make some rebel heads bleed tonight."

"Major," Adam said firmly, "all my men saw that woman. She didn't tear her own clothes, Blythe did, and—"

"Adam! Adam!" There was a note of pleading in Galloway's voice. The Major was a decent and honest man who had a vision of how his irregular regiment of horse could shorten this war, and now that vision was being threatened by rancorous dissension within his ranks. Nor did Galloway really want to believe Adam's accusations, for the Major liked Blythe. Blythe made him laugh and enlivened his dull evenings, and for those reasons, as well as a desire to avoid confrontation, Galloway tried to find extenuating circumstances. "Who's to say the woman didn't attack Billy when he tried to burn the barn? We don't know what happened, but I do know that we've got a battle to fight and a war to win and we're better employed fighting the enemy than each other. Now trust me. I'll keep an eye on Billy, that much I promise, but I want you to leave him to me. His behavior isn't your responsibility, Adam, but mine. You agree?"

Adam could hardly disagree with such a reasoned and earnest promise, and so he nodded. "Yes, sir."

"Good man," Galloway said enthusiastically, then slowed his horse as the two men approached the crest of a shallow rise. Their blue uniforms were smothered by black oilcloth cloaks that hung down to their boots, but each knew their disguise would serve small purpose if they were intercepted by a rebel patrol.

Yet the weather seemed to have damped down all rebel watchfulness, for Galloway and Adam were able to spy out the positions of the Faulconer Brigade without any sentry or picket challenging their presence. They mapped the Legion's turf-covered bivouacs, which were studded with pyramids of stacked arms and sifted with the smoke of the few campfires that still struggled against the windblown rain, then noted the substantial farmhouse standing among the tents that Adam knew belonged to the Faulconer Brigade's head-quarters. From time to time a soldier would run between the shelters or slouch dejectedly away from the farmhouse, but otherwise the encampment appeared deserted. Further south still was a meadow where the Brigade's supply wagons were parked and where picketed horses stood in disconsolate rows. Adam showed Galloway the white-painted ammunition carts, then trained his binoculars on some unfamiliar vehicles and saw that they belonged to an artillery battery that had camped alongside his father's Brigade. "How many sentries would you expect on the wagons?" Galloway asked, peering through his own binoculars.

"There's usually a dozen men," Adam said, "but I can only see one."

"There must be more."

"Sheltering in the wagons?" Adam suggested.

"I guess so, which means the sumbitches won't see us coming." Galloway sounded enthused at the prospect of fighting. He knew he could not seriously hurt Jackson's army—indeed, this night's attack would be but the feeblest of pinpricks—but Galloway was not trying to cause grievous damage. Instead he was hoping to inflict on the South the same kind of insult that Jeb Stuart had thrust on the North when he had led his cavalry clean about McClellan's army. Few men had died in that ride, but it had nevertheless made the North into the laughingstock of the whole world. Galloway now hoped to provide proof that Northern horsemen could ride as defiantly and effectively as any Southern cavalier.

Adam was fighting a different battle: a battle with his own conscience. He had obeyed that stern conscience when he had abandoned the South to fight for the North, but the logic of that choice meant not just fighting against fellow Southerners but against his own father, and a lifetime of love and filial obedience struggled against the inevitability of that logic. Yet, he asked himself as he followed Galloway further south along the woodland tracks, what else had he expected when he crossed the lines and pledged his allegiance to the United States? Adam had agonized for months about the war's moral choices, and at the end of all that worry and self-doubt he had reached a certainty that was weakened only by the duty he owed to his father. But this night, under a rain-lashed sky, Adam would cut that filial duty out of his life and so free himself to the higher duty of the nation's union.

Galloway stopped, dismounted, and again stared southward through his field glasses. Adam joined him and saw the Major was examining a half-dozen cabins, a plank-wall church, and a ramshackle two-story house that all stood around a small crossroads. "'McComb's Tavern,'" Galloway said, reading the sign that was painted in tar on the house wall. "'Good Licker, Clean Beds and Plenty Food.' But bad spelling. Do you see any troops there?"

"Not one."

"Off limits, I'd guess," Galloway said. He wiped the lenses of his field glasses, stared a few seconds longer at the tavern, then came back to where his horse was tethered and hauled himself into the saddle. "Let's go."

By early afternoon the wind had died and the rain had settled into a persistent and dispiriting drizzle. Galloway's men sat or lay under what small shelter they could find while their horses stood motionless between the trees. The pickets watched from the edges of the wood but saw no movement. In the late afternoon, when the light was fading to a sullen, leaden gloom, Galloway gave his last briefing, describing what the troopers would find when they attacked and stressing that their main target was the park of supply wagons. "The rebels are always short of ammunition," he said, "and of rifles, so burn everything you can find."

Galloway divided his force into three. Adam's troop would serve as a screen between the raiders and the bulk of the Faulconer Brigade while Galloway's troop, reinforced with half of Blythe's men, would attack the supply wagons. Billy Blythe would wait with the other half of his troop near McComb's Tavern, where they would serve as a rear guard to cover the raiders' withdrawal. "It'll all be over quickly," Galloway warned his men, "only as long as it takes the sumbitches to get over their surprise." He had his bugler imitate the sound of the call that would order the retreat. "When you hear that played on a bugle, boys, you get the living hell out of there. Straight down the road to the crossroads where Captain Blythe will be waiting for us."

"With a jigger of rebel whiskey for every last man jack of you," Blythe added, and the nervous men laughed.

Galloway opened his watch. "Be another two hours before we leave, boys, so just be patient."

The day darkened toward evening. The troopers' clothes were clammy with a greasy, sweaty dampness. Galloway had forbidden fires so that the smoke would not betray their presence, and thus they simply had to endure the cloying dank as the minutes ticked by. Men prepared themselves obsessively for battle, believing that every small degree of painstaking care counted toward survival. They used cloaks and saddlecloths to keep the rain from their repeating rifles and revolvers as they loaded the weapons' chambers with powder, wadding, and minié bullets. On top of each bullet they put a plug of grease that was intended to prevent the flame in the firing chamber communicating with the neighboring charges and so exploding the whole cylinder. They sharpened their sabers, the sound of the stones harsh on the curved steel. Those men whose blades rattled in their metal sheaths dented the scabbards so that the weapons were held tight and silent by the compressed metal. Corporal Harlan Kemp then led a score of men in prayer. He put one knee on the wet ground, one hand on the hilt of his sword, and raised his free hand toward God as he prayed that the Lord would bless this evening's work with a mighty success and keep His servants free from all harm from the enemy.

Adam joined the circle of prayer. He felt very close to his men as he knelt with them, and the very act of praying imbued the night's action with a sacred quality that lifted it above mere adventure into the realm of duty. "I do not want to be here," Adam prayed silently, "but as I am here, Lord, then be here with me and let me help this war to a quick and just ending." When Harlan Kemp's blessing was finished,

Adam climbed to his feet and saw Billy Blythe standing beside the mare Adam had taken from the Faulconer stud. Blythe ran his hand down the mare's legs, then slapped her rump. "You got yourself some good horses, Faulconer," Blythe said as Adam approached.

"You're in my way," Adam said brusquely, then pushed the tall Blythe aside so he could throw a saddlecloth over the mare's back.

"Real nice piece of horseflesh." Blythe peeled back the mare's lips to examine her teeth, then stood a pace away to give the horse an admiring look. "Bet she runs like a bitch in heat. Specially with a touch of the whip. Don't you find the whip tickles a female up real nice, Faulconer?" Blythe chuckled when Adam made no answer. "Reckon a horse like this would suit me real well," he went on.

"She's not for sale," Adam said coldly. He heaved the saddle onto the mare's back, then stooped to gather the girth strap.

"Wasn't reckoning on buying her from you," Blythe said, then spat a stream of tobacco spittle close to Adam's face, "because there ain't no point in buying things in war, not when they have a habit of dropping into a man's lap. That's what I like about war, Faulconer, the way things come without payment. That's real convenient to my way of thinking. I figure it takes the sweat out of a man's life." He smiled at the thought, then touched a finger to the dripping brim of his hat. "You sure mind yourself now," he said, then ambled away, grinning at his intimates and leaving Adam feeling tawdry.

Major Galloway was the first to mount up. He settled his feet in his stirrups, pushed his repeating rifle into its saddle holster, eased his saber an inch or two from its scabbard, then made sure his two revolvers were in easy reach. "Smoke your last cigars and pipes now, boys," the Major said,

211

"because once we're out of this wood there'll be no more lit tobacco till we wake the sumbitches." His incendiarists checked their supplies: lucifers, flints, steels, tinder, and fuses. Their job was to burn the ammunition, while others of his men carried axes to splinter wheel spokes and hammers and nails to spike the rebels' cannon.

One by one the men pulled themselves into their saddles. A horse whinnied softly while another skittered nervously sideways. Water dripped from the leaves, but Adam sensed that above the darkening canopy of trees the rain had stopped. The evening was young, but the clouds made the sky seem like night.

"For the Union, boys," Galloway said, and the more idealistic of the men repeated the phrase and added God's blessing. They were fighting for their beloved country, for God's country, for the best of all countries.

"Forward, boys," Galloway said, and the column lurched on its way.

To battle.

Captain Medlicott and Captain Moxey sat on the veranda of the farmhouse that served as General Washington Faulconer's headquarters and stared at the evening rain. On the western horizon, Medlicott noted, where it should have been darkest at this time of day, the sky was showing a pale strip of lighter cloud where the rainstorm had stalled, but that evidence of dry weather showed no sign of wanting to move east. "But it'll be a fine day tomorrow," Medlicott grunted. The sweat dripped off his beard. "I know these summer storms." He twisted in his chair and looked through the open parlor door to where the General was sitting at the claw-footed table. "It'll be a fine day tomorrow, General!"

Faulconer did not respond to Medlicott's optimism. The

evening was sweltering, and the General was in his shirt-sleeves. His uniform coat with its heavy epaulets and expensive braid trimming was hanging in the farmhouse hall along with his fine English revolver and the elegant saber that General Lafayette had presented to his grandfather. The General was staring at some papers on the table. He had been contemplating these papers for much of the day, and now, instead of signing them, he pushed them to one side. "I must be sure to do the right thing," Faulconer said, by which he meant that he must be sure not to make a mistake that could recoil onto his own career. "Goddamn it, but they should be court-martialed!"

Captain Moxey spat tobacco juice over the veranda's railing. "They should be in prison for disobeying orders, sir," Moxey said, emboldened by the privilege of being asked to give advice about the fate of Colonel Swynyard and Captain Starbuck.

"But they'll plead they were merely doing their duty," Faulconer said, worrying at the problem like a dog at a bone. "Our orders are to guard the river crossings, aren't they? And what were they doing? Just guarding a ford. How do we persuade a court otherwise?"

Captain Medlicott waved the objection away. "It ain't a proper ford, sir, not really. Not on the maps, anyway. It's just that the river's running uncommon shallow this year." He sounded very unconvincing, even to himself.

"But if I just dismiss them"—Faulconer now contemplated the alternative to a court-martial—"what's to stop them appealing? My God, you know their facilities for telling lies!"

"Who'd believe them?" Moxey asked. "One pious drunk and a Yankee troublemaker?"

Too many people would believe them, Faulconer thought, that was the trouble. Swynyard's cousin was influential, and Starbuck had friends, and consequently Faulconer felt as trapped as a man who has made a wonderful attack deep into enemy lines only to find that he cannot extricate his forces. Last night he had been triumphant, but a single day's reflection on the night's achievements had thrown up a score of obstacles to the completion of that triumph, not the least of which was that Swynyard had obstinately refused to get drunk. A drunken colonel would have been much easier to court-martial than a sober and repentant colonel, and it was Faulconer's deepest wish to see both Swynyard and Starbuck dragged in front of a court-martial, then marched at rifle point to the Confederate army prison in Richmond, but he did not see how he could make the prosecution case irrefutable. "The trouble is," he said, changing his argument yet again, "that there are too many people in this Brigade who'll give evidence on Starbuck's side."

Medlicott sipped brandy. "Popularity comes and goes," he said vaguely. "Get rid of the sons of bitches and everyone'll forget what they looked like in a couple of weeks." In truth Medlicott was wondering why Faulconer did not simply march the two men down to the river and put a pair of bullets into their heads.

"Rain's slackening," Moxey said.

Medlicott turned to look at the General. He was even more aware than Moxey of the privileges of being one of the General's advisers. Moxey, after all, had pretensions of gentility; his family kept horses and hunted with Faulconer's hounds, but Medlicott had never been anything except a hired man, albeit a skilled one, and he liked being in the General's confidence and wanted to keep the privilege by making sure the General did indeed rid himself of the troublemakers. "Why don't you just return the two sons of bitches to Richmond," he suggested, "with a report saying

214

they're unfit for field duty? Then recommend that they're sent to the coast defenses in South Carolina?"

Faulconer smoothed the papers on his table. "South Carolina?"

"Because by this time next year," Medlicott said grimly, "they'll both be dead of malaria."

Faulconer unscrewed the silver cap of his traveling inkwell. "Unfit for field duty?" he asked tentatively.

"One's a drunk, the other's a Northerner! Hell, I'd say they were unfit." Medlicott had been emboldened by the General's fine brandy and now, somewhat obliquely, offered his preferred solution. "But why be formal at all, sir? Why not just get rid of the bastards? Shoot them."

Moxey frowned at the suggestion while Faulconer chose to ignore it, not because he disapproved, but because he could not imagine getting away with murder. "You don't think I need to give a reason for their dismissal?" the General asked.

"What reason do you need beyond general unfitness for duty? Hell, add indiscipline and dereliction." Medlicott waved each word into the night with a careless gesture. "The War Department must be desperate to find men for the swamp stations in the Carolinas."

Faulconer dipped his pen into the ink, then carefully drained the surplus off the nib onto the inkwell's rim. He hesitated for a second, still worried whether his action might have unforeseen repercussions, then summoned his courage and signed the two papers that simply dismissed Swynyard and Starbuck from the Brigade. He regretted not recommending them for courts-martial, but expedience and good sense dictated the lesser punishment. The weather had made everything clammy, so that the ink ran thick in the paper's fibers as Faulconer scratched his name. He noted his rank beneath his name, then laid down the pen, capped the inkwell, and blew on the wet signatures to dry them. "Fetch Hinton," he ordered Moxey.

Moxey grimaced at the thought of walking a quarter-mile through the mud, but then pulled himself out of his chair and set off through the dusk toward the Legion's lines. The rain had stopped, and campfires pricked the gloom as men emerged from their shelters and blew kindling into life.

Faulconer admired the two dismissal orders. "And I give them passes for Richmond?"

"Good for tomorrow only," Medlicott suggested slyly. "That way if the bastards linger you can have them arrested again."

Faulconer filled in the two passes, then, his work done, walked across the veranda and down to the stretch of muddy grass that lay between the house and a peach orchard. He stretched his cramped arms. The clouds had made the dusk premature, casting night's pall over what should have been a sweet summer evening. "You'd have thought the rain would have broken this humidity," Medlicott said as he followed Faulconer down the steps.

"Another storm might do it," Faulconer said. He offered Medlicott a cigar, and for a few moments the two men smoked in silence. It was hardly a companionable silence, but Medlicott had nothing to say, and the General was evidently thinking hard. Faulconer finally cleared his throat. "You know, of course, that I've friends in Richmond?"

"Of course," Medlicott said gruffly.

Faulconer was silent for a few seconds more. "I've been thinking, you see," he eventually said, "and it occurs to me that we've done more than our fair share of fighting since the war began. Wouldn't you agree?"

"Hell, yes," Medlicott said fervently.

"So I was hoping we could have the Brigade assigned to

Richmond," Faulconer said. "Maybe we could become the experts on the city's defenses?"

Medlicott nodded gravely. He was not sure just how expert a brigade needed to be in order to garrison the star forts and trenches that ringed Richmond, but anything that took a man away from the slaughterfields of open battle and closer to hot baths, decent food, and regular hours seemed pretty inviting. "Experts," Medlicott said, "indeed."

"And some of my friends in the capital are convinced it's a good idea," Faulconer said. "You think the men will like it?" He added the question disingenuously.

"I'm sure, I'm sure," Medlicott said.

Faulconer examined the glowing tip of his cigar. "Politically, of course, we mustn't look too eager. We can't have people saying we shirked the burden, which means I'll probably have to make a show of refusing the job, but it would help me if my regimental commanders pressed me to accept."

"Of course, of course," Medlicott said. The miller did not really understand the prevarication but was quite happy to agree to anything that might get the Brigade back to the comparative comforts of the Richmond defenses.

"And I was thinking that I might make Paul Hinton my second-in-command," Faulconer went on, "which means that the Legion will need a new commanding officer."

Medlicott's heart gave a leap of anticipation, but he had the sense to show neither surprise nor delight. "Surely your brother-in-law will be back soon?" he said instead.

"Pecker might not want to return," Faulconer said, meaning that he hoped he could persuade Bird not to return, "but even if he does it won't be for a long time and the Legion can't manage without a new commanding officer, can it?"

"Indeed not, sir," Medlicott said.

"Some people, of course, would say the job ought to go to

217

a professional soldier," Faulconer said, teasing the eager Medlicott, "but I think this war needs fresh eyes and ideas."

"Very true, sir, very true."

"And you managed a fair number of men at the mill, didn't you?"

Medlicott's gristmill had never employed more than two free men at any one time, and one of those was usually a half-wit, but the miller now nodded sagely as though he was accustomed to giving orders to hundreds of employees. "A good few," he said cautiously, then frowned because Captain Moxey, muddied to his knees, was returning. Just a few seconds more, Medlicott thought, and he would have been the Legion's new commanding officer, but now an excited Moxey was demanding Faulconer's attention.

"Moxey?" Faulconer turned to greet his aide.

"Major Hinton's not here, sir. Not in the lines," Moxey said eagerly.

"What do you mean, not in the lines?"

Moxey was clearly enjoying making his revelations. "He's gone to McComb's Tavern, sir," he said. "It seems it's his fiftieth birthday, sir, and most of the Legion's officers went with him."

"God damn them!" Faulconer said. They were plotting. That was what they were doing, plotting! He did not believe the story about a birthday for one moment; they were conspiring behind his back! "Don't they know the tavern's off limits?"

"They know it's off limits," Captain Medlicott intervened. "Of course they know. It's downright disobedience, sir," he added to Faulconer, wondering whether he might not end up second-in-command to the whole Brigade after all.

"Fetch them, Captain," Faulconer ordered Moxey. Goddamn it, Faulconer thought, but Major Hinton would have to learn that there was a new tight discipline in the Faulconer Brigade. "Tell them to come here immediately," Faulconer said, then paused because Captain Medlicott had raised a warning hand, and the General turned to see a horseman approaching. The General recognized the rider as Captain Talliser, one of Stonewall Jackson's aides.

Talliser saluted Faulconer by touching a gloved hand to his hat brim, then fetched a packet of papers from his saddlebag. "Marching orders, General. Reckon you'll be busy packing up tonight."

"Marching orders?" Faulconer repeated the words as though he did not understand their meaning.

Talliser held on to the orders, offering a scrap of paper and a pencil instead. "I need your signature first, General. Or someone's signature."

Faulconer took the proffered paper and scribbled his name to confirm that General Jackson's orders had indeed been received. "Where are we going?" he asked as he took the orders.

"North, sir, over the river," Talliser said, tucking the receipt into a pouch on his belt.

"You'll eat with us, Talliser?" Faulconer asked, gesturing toward the farmhouse, where his cooks were busy preparing supper.

"Real kind of you, General," Talliser said, "but I should be getting back."

"You'll surely take a glass of something before you go?"

"A glass of water would be real kind." Talliser was not one of Jackson's favorite aides for nothing. He swung himself out of his saddle and winced at the soreness in his legs. "Been a long day, sir, a real long day."

Faulconer turned and was about to shout for Nelson, his servant, then remembered that the wretched man had not yet returned from his errand to Faulconer Court House.

219

"Moxey," he said instead, "before you go to McComb's Tavern, be kind enough to fetch a glass of water for Captain Talliser."

But Moxey was no longer paying attention. Moxey was instead staring slack-jawed and wide-eyed past the farmhouse. Slowly Moxey's hand began to point; then he tried to speak, but the only sound he could make was an incoherent stammer.

"What the hell?" Medlicott frowned at Moxey's pathetic display; then he, too, turned and looked south. "Oh, dear Christ!" he blasphemed; then he began to run away.

Just as the Yankees opened fire.

It all started so much more easily than Major Galloway had dared to hope. The raiders, riding in column of pairs, stole through the dank twilight to the empty road that stretched between the rebel encampment and the crossroads, where dim candlelights gleamed behind the tavern's windows. No one saw the cavalrymen move through the half-light, and no one challenged them as they urged their horses up the small embankment that edged the road. Galloway chuckled as he heard singing coming from the tavern. "Someone's sure having a good time," the Major said, then turned to Captain Blythe. "Billy? Take your men south a little. Just make sure no one from the tavern interferes with us. And listen for our bugle."

Blythe touched his hat and turned his horse southward. "You take care now, Major," he called softly as he led his men away.

The rest of Galloway's Horse rode north. The horses' hooves sank into the mud, but the going was not nearly as difficult as Galloway had feared. In winter, once the snow and ice had thawed, Virginia's unmacadamed roads could become impassable strips of filthy mud while in summer they could be baked hard enough to lame a well-shod horse, but this day's rain had merely served to turn the top few inches glutinous. A small and smoky fire burned under some trees fifty yards ahead, and Galloway guessed it marked the southernmost picket of the Faulconer Brigade. The Major eased his saber in its scabbard, licked his lips, and noted how the clouds were already reflecting the great swath of campfires that burned to the east and north. Those to the east were rebel fires, while the ones across the river were the lights of Pope's army. Only a few hours more, Galloway thought, and his men would be safe back in those Northern lines.

"Who the hell's there?" a voice challenged from the shadows some yards short of the fire.

Galloway, his heart thumping, reined in his horse. "Can't see a damned thing," he answered as unconventionally as the picket had challenged him. "Who in tarnation are you?"

There was the unmistakable sound of a rifle being cocked; then a man in rebel gray stepped out from the cover of the trees. "Who are you, mister?" the man returned Galloway's question. The sentry looked scarce a day over sixteen. His coat hung loose on his shoulders, his trousers were held up by a frayed length of rope, and the soles of his boots had separated from their uppers.

"Name's Major Hearn, Second Georgia Horse," Galloway said, plucking a regiment's name from his imagination, "and I'm sure glad you boys are Southerners else we'd have been in something wicked close to trouble." He chuckled. "You got a light, son? My cigar's plumb cold."

"You got business here, sir?" the nervous sentry asked.

"Forgive me, son, but I should have told you. We're carrying dispatches for General Faulconer. Is he anywhere about?"

"Another man just came with dispatches," the sentry said suspiciously.

Galloway laughed. "You know the army, son. Never send one man to do a job properly when twenty men can do it worse. Hell, wouldn't surprise me if our orders countermanded his orders. We'll have you boys marching in circles all week long. Now, how do I find the General, son?"

"He's just up the road, sir." The sentry's suspicions had been entirely allayed by Galloway's friendliness. There was a pause while he made his rifle safe and slung the weapon on his shoulder. "Did you ride with Jeb Stuart, sir?" The picket's voice was touched with awe.

"I just guess we did, son," Galloway said, "clean round the Yankees. Now have you got that light for my cigar?"

"Sure have, sir." The picket ran back to the fire and snatched a piece of wood out of the flames. The fire flared up, revealing two other men huddled in the shadows beyond.

"Sergeant Darrow?" Galloway called softly.

"Sir?"

"Take care of them when we're past. No noise now."

"Yes, sir."

The picket brought the flame back to Galloway, who bent toward it to light his cigar. Like all his men Galloway had a cloak drawn tight around his uniform. "Thank you, son," he said when the cigar was drawing. "Straight on up the road, you say?"

"Yes, sir. There's a farmhouse there."

"You keep dry tonight, son, you hear me?" Galloway said, then rode on. He did not look back as Darrow and his men disabled the picket. There was no gunfire, just a sickening series of thumps followed by silence. To Galloway's right was the wagon park where the Faulconer Brigade's ammunition was stored, while ahead, beyond a stand of dripping trees, he could see the farmhouse and tents that marked the Faulconer Brigade's headquarters. Galloway curbed his horse

222

to let Adam's troop catch up with him. "You go on now," he told Adam, "and burn the farmhouse."

"Must I?" Adam asked.

Galloway sighed. "If it's being used by the enemy, Adam, yes. If it's full of women and children, no. Hell, man, we're at war!"

"Yes, sir," Adam said and rode on.

Galloway drew on his cigar and walked his horse in among the supply wagons, where a dozen black teamsters sat beneath a crude shelter made from a tarpaulin stretched between two pairs of wagon shafts. A small fire flickered in the shelter's opening. "How are you in there, boys?" Galloway asked as he peered past the fire's smoke, "and where do I find the ammunition?"

"The white carts, master, over there." The man who answered was whittling a piece of wood into the shape of a woman's head. "You got an order from the quartermaster, sir?"

"Fine carving that, real fine. Me, I never could whittle. Guess I don't keep the blade sharp enough. Sure I got orders, boy, all the orders you'll ever want. My sergeant will give 'em to you." Galloway waved at the teamsters, then walked his horse on toward the nearest ammunition cart that was painted white and had a hooped cover of dirty canvas. As Galloway rode he took a length of fuse from his saddlebag and a linen bag of gunpowder from a pouch. He pushed one end of the fuse into the gunpowder, then drew aside the wet canvas flap at the back of the cart to reveal a pile of ammunition boxes. He rammed the bag between two of the wooden boxes, then touched the glowing tip of his cigar to the fuse's end. He waited a second to make sure the fuse was burning, then let the canvas curtain drop.

The fire sputtered down the fuse's powder-packed tube to leave a small trickle of gray-white smoke. Galloway was already assembling another small charge to place in the next wagon while more of his men were heading toward the artillery park, which was guarded by a handful of unsuspecting gunners armed with carbines. Galloway placed his second charge, then pulled his cloak back to reveal his blue uniform. He tugged his saber free and turned back to the sheltering teamsters. "Make yourselves scarce, boys," he told them. "Go on, now. Run! We're Yankees!"

The first bag of powder exploded. It was not a loud explosion, merely a dull thump that momentarily lit up the interior of the wagon's hooped canvas cover with a lurid red glow. The canvas swelled for a second or two; then a fire began to flicker deep inside the stacked boxes. The teamsters were running. One of Galloway's men leaned from his saddle and plucked a burning brand from the remains of their fire and tossed the burning wood into a third ammunition cart. The first load of ammunition began to explode in a series of short sharp cracks that sounded as close together as the snaps of a Fourth of July firecracker string, and then the whole wagon seemed to evaporate in sudden flame. The wet canvas cover flew into the air, flapping like a monstrous bat with wings dripping sparks. One of Galloway's men whooped in delight and tossed a firebrand into a stack of muskets.

"Keep 'em burning, boys!" Galloway shouted at those of his men who had been detailed as incendiarists; then he led the rest of his troop in a charge toward the startled gunners. The Major's saber reflected the flamelight. An artillery sergeant was still trying to prime his carbine as the saber sliced across his face. The man screamed, but all Galloway knew of the blow was a slight jar up his right arm and the juddering friction of steel scraping on bone; then the saber was free and he swung it forward to spear its tip into the neck of a running man. Two of Galloway's troopers were

224

already dismounted and starting to hammer soft nails into the cannons' touchholes, others were setting fire to limbers crammed with ammunition, while still more were cutting loose picketed team horses and stampeding them into the night. Saddle horses were being captured and led back to the road. A powder charge exploded, shooting sparks high into the night air. Men were shouting in the dark. A bullet screamed high over Galloway's head. "Bugler!" the Major shouted.

"Here, sir!" The man put his instrument to his lips.

"Not yet!" Galloway said. He only wanted to make sure the bugler was staying close, for he knew he must sound the retreat very soon. He sheathed his saber and drew out the repeating rifle, which he fired toward the shadows of men beyond the guns. The wagon park was an inferno, the sky above it bright with flame and writhing plumes of firelit smoke. A dog barked and a wounded horse screamed. In the light of the fires Galloway could see rebel gunners gathering in the darkness, and he knew that at any moment a counterattack would swarm across the artillery park. He turned to his bugler. "Now!" Galloway called, "now!" and the bugler's call rang clear in the night's fiery chaos. The Major backed his horse through the gunline, where the cannons were all spiked and the limbers burning.

"Back, lads! Back!" Galloway called his men. "Back!"

Adam was inside the farmhouse when he heard the bugle call. He had found the house empty except for two of his father's cooks, whom he had ordered to run away. Sergeant Huxtable had meanwhile chased away a group of officers standing on the lawn, killing a captain dressed in riding boots and spurs, and Huxtable now had Adam's troop lining the ditch at the end of the farm's garden from where they were blazing rifle fire into the shadowy lines of the Brigade. The repeater rifles made it seem as if a whole

225

company of infantry was attacking across the ditch.

Corporal Kemp joined Adam in the farmhouse. "Burn the place, sir?" he asked.

"Not yet," Adam said. He has found his father's precious revolver and priceless saber hanging in the hall. Explosions sounded outside, then the ripping noise of gunfire.

"Sir!" Sergeant Huxtable shouted. "We can't hold here much longer, sir!" The Faulconer Brigade had begun to fight back, and the rifle bullets were whipping thick above the farm's yard and orchard. Adam seized his father's sword and revolver, then turned as Kemp called him from the parlor.

"Look here! Look at this!" Kemp had discovered the twin standards of the Faulconer Legion on the parlor wall.

Huxtable called again from the dark outside. "Hurry, sir! For God's sake, hurry!" The bugle sounded again from the artillery park, its call sweet and pure in the night's angry fusillades.

Adam and Kemp pulled the two crossed flagstaffs off their nails. "Come on!" Adam ordered.

"We're to burn the house, sir, you heard the Major," Kemp insisted. He saw Adam's reluctance. "Belongs to a family called Pearce, sir," Kemp went on, "rebels through and through."

Adam had forgotten that Corporal Kemp was a local man. A bullet smacked into the upper floor, splintering wood. "Go! Take the flags!" Adam told him, then snatched up some papers that lay on a claw-footed table and held their corners into a flickering candle flame. He held the papers there, letting the fire take a good hold, then dropped the burning documents among the slew of other papers. There was a brandy bottle open on the table, and Adam spilt it across the floor's rush matting, then threw a burning paper onto the floor. Flames leaped up.

Adam ran outside. A bullet whipped past his head to shatter a window. He jumped the veranda's rail. The pair of captured rebel flags trailed huge and bright across the flanks of Corporal Kemp's horse. Sergeant Huxtable had the bridle of Adam's mare. "Here, sir!"

"Back!" Adam shouted as he pulled himself into the saddle.

The horsemen retreated past the farmhouse, where a fiery glow was already suffusing the parlor windows. Kemp had managed to furl the captured flags and now handed them to one of the troopers, then drew his saber to slash at the guy ropes of the nearest tents. A voice was shouting for water. Another voice shouted Adam's name, but Adam ignored the summons as he galloped toward the wagon park that now looked like a corner of hell. Flames were searing sixty feet high while the exploding ammunition spat trails of vivid smoke in every direction. The bugle sounded again, and Adam and his men spurred down the road toward Major Galloway's party. "Count!" Adam shouted.

"One!" That was Sergeant Huxtable.

"Two!" Corporal Kemp.

"Three!" the next man called, and so on through the whole troop. Every man was present.

"Anyone hurt?" Adam asked. Not one man was hurt, and Adam felt his heart leap with exultation.

"Well done, Adam!" Galloway greeted him just beyond the small stand of trees. "All well?"

"Everyone's present, sir! No one's hurt."

"And us!" Galloway sounded triumphant. Another limber of ammunition exploded, punching red fire across the wounded camp. Then, from the southern darkness, there sounded a crash of rifle fire so sudden and furious that Galloway looked momentarily alarmed. He feared his men were being cut off, then realized the noise was coming from the tavern at the crossroads, which meant that Billy Blythe and his men were in a fight. "Come on!" he shouted, dug in his spurs, and galloped to the rescue.

"I don't feel fifty," Major Hinton told Captain Murphy. "I don't even feel like forty. But I'm fifty! An old man!"

"Nonsense!" Murphy said. "Fifty's not old."

"Ancient," Hinton lamented. "I can't believe I'm fifty."

"You will tomorrow morning, God willing," Murphy answered. "Have another drink."

A dozen officers had walked to McComb's Tavern to celebrate the Major's half-century. It was not much of a tavern, merely a cavernous house where ale and home-distilled whiskey were sold and where two whores worked upstairs and two kitchen slaves served huge plates of dumplings, bacon, and corn bread downstairs. Major Hinton's private supper party was held in a back room, where the day's menu, such as it was, was crudely chalked on the plank wall. Not that the Major needed to read the bill of fare, for his officers had generously subscribed to buy a rare and expensive ham that Liam McComb's cooks had boiled especially for the dinner. Captain Murphy asked for Irish potatoes to accompany the ham, but McComb had refused the request by saying that he would be happy if he never saw another damned potato in all his born days. "Unless it's been liquidated, if you follow my meaning, Captain," he said. McComb was a giant man, more than sixty years old and with a belly on him like one of his own beer barrels.

"You mean *poteen*?" Murphy asked. "Christ, and I haven't tasted *poteen* in seven years."

"You'll find it will have been worth the wait, Captain," McComb said, and when the supper was finished and the shirtsleeved officers were sharing a bottle of fine French brandy taken at Cedar Mountain, the tavern keeper brought a gallon stone jug downstairs. "A few sips of that,

228

Captain," he told Murphy, "and you'll swear you're back in Ballinalea."

"If only I was," Murphy said wistfully.

"The wife made it," McComb said as he placed the stone jug on the table, "before she was taken bad."

"Not fatally, I trust?" Hinton asked politely.

"God bless you, no, Major. She's lying upstairs with a fever, so she is. It's the heat that does it to her. They're not natural, these summers, not natural at all."

"We'll pay for the *poteen*, sure we will," Murphy said, sounding more Irish than he had for many a long year.

"You'll not pay me a ha'penny, Captain," McComb said. "Roisin and I have two boys serving in the 6th Virginia, and they'd want you to be having a taste of it for nothing. So enjoy it now! But not too much now, not if you want to enjoy the upstairs pleasures later!" A cheer greeted this remark, for part of the night's entertainment would doubtless be afforded by the two rooms upstairs.

"But not me!" Hinton said when McComb had gone. "I'm a married man. I can't afford the pox."

"Starbuck hasn't got the pox," Murphy said, "and he must have sneaked down here at least a dozen times."

"He never did!" Hinton said, shocked at the news.

"Starbuck and women?" Murphy asked. "My God, Major, it's like whiskey and priests, you couldn't keep the two apart with a pry bar. God knows what they fed him up in Boston to give him the energy, but I wouldn't mind a bottle or two of it myself. Now try the *poteen*."

The *poteen* was passed around the table. Every captain from the Legion was there except for Daniel Medlicott, who had been summoned to Faulconer's headquarters, and Starbuck, who was under guard in Colonel Swynyard's tent. No one, not even Major Hinton, was entirely sure what fate the General planned for Starbuck, but Lieutenant Davies was certain Faulconer wanted a court-martial. Hinton averred that a court-martial was impossible. "Maybe Swynyard disobeyed Faulconer, but Nate only did what Swynyard ordered him to do." Hinton lifted the *poteen* jug to his nose and smelt it suspiciously. "It'll all blow over," he said, speaking of Starbuck's predicament rather than the liquor. "Faulconer will sleep on it, then forget all about it. He's not a man for confrontation, not like his father was. Do I drink this stuff or use it as a liniment?"

"Drink that," Murphy said, "and you'll feel fifteen instead of fifty."

"What in God's name is it?" Hinton asked as he poured a few drops of the spirit into a tin mug.

"Potato whiskey," Murphy told him, "from Ireland. If you get the recipe right, Major, it's a drink from heaven, but get it wrong and it'll blind you for life and tear your guts into tatters for good measure."

Hinton shrugged, hesitated, then decided that at fifty years old he had nothing to lose and so downed the colorless liquor in one gulp. He took a deep breath, shook his head, then let out a hoarse sound that seemed to indicate approval. He poured himself some more.

"What was that?" Captain Pirie, the Legion's quartermaster, was seated beside a window.

"That was amazing," Hinton said. "It takes your breath clean away!"

"Gunfire," Pirie said and pulled aside the gauze curtain that kept the insects away from the candlelight.

The sound of an explosion thumped across the damp landscape, followed by the splintering noise of rifles firing. A great red suffusion of light blossomed to the north, silhouetting the trees that lay between the crossroads and the Brigade's lines. "Jesus," Murphy said softly, then pulled his revolver from the holster that he had hung from a nail on the wall and went through into the tavern's main room, which, in turn, opened onto a rickety porch. The other officers followed him, joining McComb and three of his customers under the porch's wooden roof from which hung two lanterns. A second explosion spread its sheet of light across the northern sky, and this time the great flame outlined a group of cloaked horsemen on the road. "Who's there?" Hinton called.

"Fourth Louisiana Horse!" a Southern voice called back. The skyline was red with flame, and more rifle shots cracked in the camp.

"It's a raid!" Hinton called as he ran down the porch steps, revolver in hand.

"Fire!" the Southern voice shouted, and a volley of rifles slammed at the tavern from the reddened dark. Hinton was thrown to the ground by a monstrous blow to his shoulder. He rolled in the mud toward the shadows under the porch as a bullet shattered one of the lanterns and rained glass fragments down onto the startled officers. Captain Murphy fired his revolver twice, but the sheer volume of return fire made him duck into the tavern for cover. Lieutenant Davies had followed Hinton down the steps and somehow made it safe across the road to the protection of the small church, but none of the other officers succeeded in leaving the tavern's veranda. Pirie was draped over the railings, blood dripping from his dangling hands. More blood was seeping between the planks onto Major Hinton, who was gasping with pain. Liam McComb had a shotgun that he fired up the road; then a bullet smacked into the tavern keeper's great belly, and he folded onto the porch with an astonished look on his face. His breath came in huge shuddering gasps as blood spread across his shirt and pants.

Murphy ran to a side window, but a second before he reached his objective a bullet slapped the gauze curtain aside, then a second bullet ripped clean through the wall to strike a splinter out of the tavern's counter. The slaves were wailing in the kitchen, while McComb's bedridden wife was calling pathetically for her husband. The other women upstairs were screaming in terror. Murphy cupped his hands. "There are women in here! Stop your firing! Stop firing!"

Another voice took up the cry from the porch. "Cease fire! Cease fire! There are women here!"

"Keep firing!" a man shouted from the fire-rent dark. "Bastards are lying! Keep firing!"

Murphy ducked as more bullets riddled the wall. The heaviness of the rifle fire suggested there had to be scores of enemy outside. John Torrance, C Company's Captain, was lying in the porch doorway, apparently dead. One of the Legion's lieutenants was crawling across the floor, his beard dripping with blood; then he collapsed onto a full spittoon and spilt its rancid contents across the floor. A fire had started in the kitchen, and its flames roared hungrily as they fed on the old building's dry wood. Two of McComb's customers ran upstairs to try and take the women to safety as Murphy hurried into the back room, where the remains of the celebratory supper lay on the table. He snatched his coat from the nail, grabbed his cartridge pouch, and leaped straight through a gauze curtain into the night. The curtain wrapped itself round him, tripping him so that he rolled helplessly in the mud for a few seconds. He had an idea he might be able to drive the horsemen away from the front of the tavern if he could just fire at them from the darkness at the building's rear, but as he struggled to extricate himself from the muslin curtain, he heard the click of a gun being cocked and looked up to see the dark shape of a horseman. Murphy tried to raise his revolver, but the horseman fired first, then fired again. Murphy felt something hit him with a blow like the kick of a horse; then a terrible pain whipped

232

up from his thigh. He heard himself scream, then lost consciousness as the rider fired again.

The fire spread from the kitchen. Mrs. McComb screamed as the flames licked up the stairs and the bedrooms filled with a thick smoke. The two men who had tried to rescue the women abandoned their attempt, instead stepping out of a bedroom window onto the porch roof in an effort to save themselves from the flames. "Shoot them down!" Billy Blythe ordered excitedly. "Shoot the bastards down!" A half-dozen bullets struck the two men, who collapsed, rolled twitching down the shingled roof, then dropped to the ground. Blythe whooped with victory while his men kept pouring their withering fire into the burning building.

A bugle called to the north, summoning the raiders to their retreat, but Blythe had his enemy trapped like rats in a burning barrel, and like rats, he decided, they would die. He fired again and again while the flames spread through the tavern, leaping up the gauze curtains, devouring the ancient wooden floors, exploding barrels of liquor, and hissing where it met the blood that was spilt so thick across the planks.

A man with burning clothes crawled across the porch, then fell shuddering as bullets ripped at him. A roof beam collapsed, showering sparks into the night, and Billy Blythe, his mouth open and eyes bright, watched enthralled.

Major Galloway arrived at the head of his raiders. "Come on, Billy! Didn't you hear the bugle?"

"Too busy," Blythe said, his eyes wide and fixed on the glorious destruction. Flames writhed out of collapsing liquor barrels and flared fierce and brief when they caught a dead man's hair. Ammunition crackled in the flames, each cartridge flashing white like a miniature firecracker.

"What happened?" Galloway stared in awe at the burning house.

233

"Sons of bitches fired on us," Blythe said, still gazing enraptured at the horror he had engendered, "so we taught the sons of bitches a lesson."

"Let's go, Billy," Galloway said, then seized Blythe's bridle and dragged his second-in-command away from the fire. "Come on, Billy!"

A figure stirred under the porch, and two horsemen emptied their rifles' revolving cylinders into the man. A woman screamed at the tavern's rear; then the kitchen roof collapsed and the scream was cut sharply off. "It was a horse," Blythe assured Galloway, who had frowned when he heard the woman's distress, "just a dying horse, Joe, and dying horses can sound uncommon like women."

"Let's go," Galloway said. There was a smell of roasting meat from the tavern, and horrid things twitching in the furnace heat, and Galloway turned away, not wanting to know what horrors he abandoned.

The horsemen rode west, leaving the sparks whirling cloudward and a whole brigade whipped.

Starbuck had wanted to challenge the raiders, but Swynyard stopped him from leaving the tent. "They'll slash you down like a dog. Ever been chased by a cavalryman?"

"No."

"You'll end up saber-cut to ribbons. Keep quiet."

"We must do something!"

"Sometimes it's best to do nothing. They won't stay long."

Yet the wait seemed forever to Starbuck as he crouched in the tent; then at last he heard a bugle call and voices shouting orders to retreat. Hooves thumped close by the tent, which suddenly twitched and half collapsed as its guy ropes were cut. Starbuck squirmed out of the sagging wet canvas and saw Adam on horseback not five paces away.

"Adam!" Starbuck shouted, not really believing his own eyes.

But Adam was already spurring south, his horse's hooves throwing up great gobs of mud and water as he went. Starbuck saw the headquarters house burning and more fires flaring skyward among the supply wagons. The sentry guarding Swynyard's tent had vanished.

"So how did they cross the river?" Colonel Swynyard asked as he crawled out from the tent's wreckage.

"The same way they'll go back," Starbuck said. The horsemen might have withdrawn southward, but he had no doubt they would be riding a half-circle to get back to the unguarded ford, which meant a man on foot might just be able to cut them off. General Faulconer was shouting for water, but Starbuck ignored the orders. He leaped over the ditch that separated the headquarters from the bivouac lines and shouted for Sergeant Truslow. "Turn out! Fast now!"

H Company fell into ranks. "Load!" Starbuck ordered.

Truslow had rescued Starbuck's rifle and now threw it to him with an ammunition pouch. "The General says we're not to take orders from you," the Sergeant said.

"The General can go to hell." Starbuck bit a cartridge and poured powder down the barrel.

"That's what I reckoned too," Truslow said.

Swynyard arrived, panting. "Where are you going?"

Starbuck spat the bullet into the muzzle. "We're going to Dead Mary's Ford," he said, then rammed the bullet hard down, slotted the ramrod back into place, and slung the rifle from his shoulder.

"Why Dead Mary's Ford?" Swynyard asked, puzzled.

"Because, damn it, we saw one of the bastards there last night. Ain't that right, Mallory?"

"Saw him plain as daylight," Sergeant Mallory confirmed.

"Besides," Starbuck went on, "where else would they cross the river? Every other ford's guarded. Follow me!" Starbuck shouted, and the men ran through a darkness made livid by the great fires that burned uncontrollably in the Brigade lines. The farmhouse roof collapsed to spew a gout of flames skyward, but that inflagration was dwarfed by the huge fires in the ammunition park. Every few seconds another powder cask would explode to send a ball of fire soaring up into the low clouds. Shells cracked apart, rifle ammunition stuttered, and dogs howled in terror. The inferno lit Starbuck's path across the waterlogged meadow and into the trees, but the deeper he ran into the woods the darker it became and the harder it was to find the path. He had to slow down and feel his way forward.

Sergeant Truslow wanted to know just what had happened at headquarters. Colonel Swynyard told him about the Northern raiders, and Starbuck added that he had seen Adam Faulconer among the enemy horsemen. "Are you sure?" Colonel Swynyard asked.

"Pretty damn sure, yes."

Truslow spat into the dark. "I said we should have shot the bastard when he crossed the lines. This way."

They stumbled on through the woods; then, when they were still a quarter-mile short of the river, Starbuck heard hoofbeats and saw a glimmer of flamelight showing through the black tangled silhouette of the trees. "Run!" he shouted. He feared his company would arrive too late and that the Northern horsemen would escape before he could reach the line of rifle pits at the wood's edge.

Then he saw the riders milling at the river's nearer bank. Someone had made a torch by strapping dead twigs to a length of timber, and the torch lit the horsemen's passage through a ford made dangerously deep by storm water. Starbuck guessed most of the riders had long crossed the river, but a dozen cavalrymen were still waiting on the southern bank as he slipped and skidded into a flooded rifle pit. He held his weapon up high to keep it dry and saw the nearest horsemen turn in alarm as they heard the splash of his fall. "Spread out!" Starbuck shouted to his men, "and open fire!" Three horses were in the middle of the ford with the river up past their bellies. One of the cavalrymen cut with a whip to urge his horse on. "Fire!" Starbuck shouted again, then aimed his own rifle at the nearest enemy. He pulled the trigger and felt a surge of relief that at last they were fighting back.

Someone fired from Starbuck's right. The woods were full of trampling feet, and the edge of the meadow was suddenly black with rebel infantry. The ruined house where Mad Silas lived was a dark shadow in the meadow's center, beyond which the Yankee carried his flaming torch high; then the man suddenly realized that he was illuminating the target, and so he hurled the brand into the river to plunge the night into instant and utter blackness. A horse was screaming in the dark. More rifles cracked, their flames stabbing the sudden dark.

The Yankees returned the fire. Rifles flared on the far bank. Men were shouting in panic, calling on each other to get the hell across the water. Northern bullets whipped through the leaves over Starbuck's head. He was up to his thighs in the flooded rifle pit. He rammed a new bullet down the rifle's barrel, then fired again. He could not see his targets because the muzzle flashes were dazzling him. The night was a chaos of gun flames, screams, and splashes. Something or someone floundered in the water, and Starbuck could hear desperate shouts as the horsemen tried to rescue their comrade. "Cease fire!" he shouted, not because he wanted to help the rescuers, but because it was time to take prisoners. "Cease fire!" he shouted again and heard Sergeant Truslow take up the call. "H Company!" Starbuck called when the rifles had fallen silent. "Forward!"

The company advanced out of the trees and ran down the grassy slope. A few Yankee shots came over the river, but in the dark the enemy's aim was much too high, and the bullets simply ripped their way through the black canopy of leaves. Starbuck ran past the ruined house, where Mad Silas was cradling his dead Mary. The company began screaming the rebel yell, wanting to scare the men who were still trying to rescue their wounded comrade from the river. Starbuck reached the ford first, dropped his rifle, and threw himself into the water. He gasped at the storm-given strength of the current, then grabbed at the shadows in front and found himself clasping a wet handful of uniform. A gun exploded a foot from his face, but the bullet went wide; then a man screamed as Starbuck dragged him back toward the southern bank. More rebels splashed into the river to help Starbuck. One of them fired at the Yankees, and the flash of his rifle's muzzle showed a group of Northerners wading to the far bank and a horse and rider being swept downstream.

Starbuck's prisoner gasped for breath while the drowning horse smashed the river's surface with its flailing hooves. "Give them a goodbye shot, boys!" Colonel Swynyard called, and a handful of Starbuck's men fired across the water.

"Come on, you bastard," Starbuck grunted. His prisoner was struggling like a fiend and throwing wild fists at Starbuck's face. Starbuck hammered the man hard with his right hand, kicked him, and finally dragged him back to the southern bank, where a rush of men overpowered the Yankee.

"Rest of the bastards got away," Truslow panted ruefully as the hoofbeats receded across the river.

"We got all we needed," Starbuck said. He was soaked through, bruised, and winded, but he had won the victory he wanted. He had proof that the ford had needed guarding, and it had been Washington Faulconer who had removed the guard and so let the Northern raiders cross the river. "Just let that son of a bitch put us on trial now," he told Swynyard, "just let that son of a goddamned bitch try."

GENERAL STUART'S AIDE reached Lee's headquarters before dawn and found the army's commander standing outside his tent in contemplation of a crude map scratched in the dirt. The map showed the rivers Rapidan and Rappahannock, while the fords across the further river were marked by scraps of twig. It was those fords that the cavalry needed to capture if Pope was to be trapped at the rivers' confluence, but it seemed there was to be no chance of success this day, for the aide brought only a repetition of the previous day's bad news. "The cavalry just aren't ready, sir. General Stuart's real sorry, sir." The aide was very sheepish, half expecting a tirade from an angry Lee. "It's the horses, sir," he went on lamely, "they ain't recovered. The roads are wicked hard, sir, and General Stuart was expecting to find more forage up here, and . . ." The aide let his hopeless explanations trail away.

Lee's grave face scarce registered his disappointment; indeed, he seemed much more disappointed in the taste of the coffee than in the failure of his cavalry. "Is this really the best coffee we have, Hudson?" he asked one of his younger staff officers.

"Until we can capture more from the Yankees, sir, yes."

"Which we can't do without our cavalry. Upon my soul, we can't." He sipped the coffee again, grimaced, then laid the tin mug on a washstand that was set with his aides' shaving tackle. On the General's own washstand, inside his tent, there lay a dispatch that reported that 108 Federal ships had steamed up the Potomac River in the previous twenty-four hours, and what that figure meant, Lee knew, was that McClellan's forces were well on their way to reinforcing Pope's army. The ships' sidewheels and screws were churning the Potomac white in their efforts to combine the enemy armies, and meanwhile the Confederate cavalry was not ready. Which meant Pope's army would be safe for one more day. The frustration rose in Lee, only to be instantly suppressed. There was no profit in displaying temperament, none at all, and so the General looked placidly back at the crude map scratched in the dirt. There was still time, he told himself, still time. It was one thing for the Northern generals to move an army by boat, but quite another to land the troops and reunite them with their wagons and guns and tents and ammunition. And McClellan was a cautious man, much too cautious, which would give the rebels even more time to teach John Pope a lesson in civilized warfare. Lee ruefully obliterated the map with the toe of a riding boot and gave orders that the army would not, after all, be marching that morning. He retrieved his coffee. "What exactly do they do to this coffee?" he asked.

"Mix it with ground goober peas, sir," Captain Hudson answered.

"Mashed peanuts!" Lee sipped again. "Good Lord."

"It makes the coffee go farther, sir."

"It surely does, it surely does."

"Of course, sir, we can always get some real beans from Richmond," Hudson said. "If we say they're for you, I'm sure they'll find some."

"No, no. We must drink what the soldiers drink. At least when it comes to coffee we must." The General forced himself to swallow more of the sour liquid. "The horses will be ready tomorrow, you think?" he asked Stuart's messenger very courteously, almost as though he regretted pressing the cavalryman for a decision.

"General Stuart's confident of that, sir. Very confident."

Lee forbore to remark that twenty-four hours earlier Stuart had been equally confident that the cavalry would be ready in this dawn, but nothing would be achieved by recrimination, and so Lee offered the discomfited aide a grave smile. "My respects to General Stuart," he said, "and I look forward to marching tomorrow instead."

Later that morning Lee returned to Clark's Mountain to examine the enemy on the river's far bank. As he climbed the wooded slope, he saw a pyre of dirty smoke smearing the western sky, but no one on his staff knew what the smoke meant. It came from Jackson's lines, and doubtless Jackson would deal with whatever had caused the fire. Lee was more concerned with what was happening across the river, and so, once at the summit, he dismounted and rested his telescope on Traveller's patient back.

And once again the Yankee presence in the Virginia hills was denoted by a myriad of smoking fires that hazed the green land like a winter mist, but then Lee saw that something was missing beneath that mist. There were fires aplenty, but no tents. He moved the glass. No wagons, no horses, and no guns. There was nothing but the remains of campfires that the Yankees had lit in the night, stacked high with wood, then left to burn as they crept away. "They've gone," Lee said.

"Sir?" One of his aides stepped forward to hear better.

"They've gone." Lee collapsed his telescope but still stared northward. "They've gone," he said again, almost as if he did not believe his own eyes.

Pope had taken his men out of the trap. He had retreated across the Rappahannock. He had seen his danger and abandoned the land between the rivers, which meant, Lee thought, that in a week's time Pope would have been re-inforced by McClellan and then it would all be finished. Blue-coated Yankees would be rampaging all across Virginia, and John Pope, the wretched John Pope who so passionately hated Southerners, would be the tyrant of all he surveyed.

Unless, that is, the Confederacy risked everything on a daring and desperate chance. Not a maneuver from the rule book, but something from the devil's box of tricks instead. Lee sensed the idea like a temptation. He suddenly saw how he could tip John Pope off balance and then savage him, and the idea burgeoned in his mind even as the well-schooled and conventional part of his training attempted to reject the notion as too risky. But another part of Lee was tantalized by the beauty and symmetry of the outrageous idea. It was a maneuver that would humiliate John Pope and drive the Yankees clean out of Virginia, and as Lee considered the rewards and risks of his maneuver, he felt the excitement of a gambler staking everything on a single run of cards. The thing could be done! Yet his face betrayed no hint of that excitement as he climbed into his saddle and settled his boots into his stirrups. "My compliments to General Jackson," he said calmly, pushing his telescope back into its case and gathering Traveller's reins into his hands, "and I would be much obliged if he would call on me at his earliest convenience."

And then, Lee thought, he would let Old Mad Jack off his leash.

And God help John Pope then.

It was not convenient for Major General Thomas Jackson to call on General Robert Lee. It would be convenient soon, but not yet, for General Jackson had two urgent duties to perform. They were not pleasant duties—indeed, lesser men might have shrunk from them altogether—but Thomas

Jackson considered them simple responsibilities, and so he performed them with his customary dogged diligence.

Men had to be shot. Southern men. Except to the General they were not men, but curs and trash who had deserted their duties and thus placed themselves beneath contempt. Their commanding officers had pleaded for the condemned men's lives, but Jackson had answered that men who desert their comrades deserve to be shot and officers who pleaded for such men deserved to be hung, and after that curt response there had been no more pleas for clemency. Now, beneath a clearing sky and on a meadow still damp from the previous day's rains, Jackson had assembled his whole corps. Three divisions of soldiers, twenty-four thousand men, were paraded in rank after shabby gray rank to form three sides of an open square. The morning was hot and the air stifling.

Drums beat slow as a band played a ragged funeral dirge. The band was paraded a few paces behind Jackson, who sat on his small, rawboned horse and stared morosely at three wooden stakes that had been plunged into the dirt beside three rough-sawn pine coffins and three freshly dug graves. Behind him his staff sat silent in their saddles, some of them more nervous of this morning's killings than they had ever been of battle. Captain Hudson, Lee's aide, who was waiting to escort General Jackson back to meet the army's commander in Gordonsville, watched the gaunt, famous figure and wondered if ever, in all the history of warfare, any commander had appeared so unprepossessing. The General's beard was unkempt, and his clothes looked in worse condition than any of his soldiers' uniforms. He had an old blue coat that was vaguely military in cut but threadbare and faded, while for a hat Jackson favored a shabby cadet's cap with a creased brim that was pulled low over his eyes. His horse was a big-headed, knock-kneed, clumsy beast with a patchy chestnut pelt, while the General's enormous boots were thrust into rusted stirrups that hung from mended leather straps. The most impressive military aspect of the General, apart from his reputation, was his rigid pose, for he sat his horse straight-backed and with his head held high, but then, as if to spoil that martial stance, he slowly and inexplicably raised his left hand until it was poised higher than his scruffy, creased cap. He then held the hand motionless, as though he was beseeching the Almighty for blessing.

The three doomed men were marched onto the field, each man escorted by his own company. The General had insisted that the criminals must be shot by their own comrades, for those comrades were the men most immediately betrayed by each deserter. An army chaplain waited for the condemned men, who, on reaching the stakes, were ordered onto their knees. The chaplain stepped forward and began to pray.

A small wind stirred the sullen air. To the west a sifting plume of smoke showed where the Yankee raiders had struck in the night, and Jackson, reminded of that impudent raid, looked toward the Faulconer Brigade to see the regiment that paraded without its colors. They had lost their colors, just as they had lost most of their officers, and Jackson, brooding on the Yankee coup, felt a spasm of anger.

The prayer seemed unending. The chaplain's eyes were screwed tight shut, and his hands clenched hard about a battered Bible as he commended the three sinners' souls to the God they were about to meet. The chaplain reminded God of the two thieves who had shared His Son's death on Calvary and implored the Almighty to look as charitably upon these three sinners as Christ had looked upon the repentant thief. One of the three men was unable to check his tears. He was a beardless youth who had deserted because his sixteen-year-old wife had run away with his uncle, and now he was to die in a green field because he had loved her so much. He looked up at his Captain and tried to make a last-minute plea, but the chaplain simply raised his voice so that the useless request could not be heard. The other two men showed no emotion, not even when the band finished its funereal music and went suddenly silent after a last uneven flurry on the drums.

The chaplain also finished. He stumbled as he stepped backward from the victims. A staff officer took the chaplain's place and in a loud, slow voice that almost carried to the rearmost ranks of the twenty-four thousand witnesses, read aloud the charges against the three men and the verdicts of their courts-martial. The bleak sentences finished, he stepped back and looked at the three company officers. "Carry on."

"No, for the love of God, no! Please, no!" The young man tried to resist, but two of his comrades dragged him to the stake and there pinioned him with rope. The three men wore shirts, pants, and ragged boots. A sergeant blindfolded the weeping youth and told him to stop his noise and die like a man. The other two deserters refused their blindfolds.

"Ready!" the staff officer shouted, and over a hundred rifles were raised to the firing position. Some men aimed wide, some blatantly had their rifles uncocked, but most of the men obeyed the order.

"Aim!" the staff officer called, and two nervous men pulled their triggers instead. Both bullets flew wide.

"Wait for it!" a sergeant snarled. A company officer had his eyes closed, and his lips were moving in silent prayer as he waited for the order to fire. One of the doomed men spat onto the grass. To Lee's aide, who had not expected to witness death this morning, it seemed as though three whole divisions of troops were holding their collective breath, while Jackson, his left hand held high, seemed carved from stone.

"No, please! No!" the young man called. His blindfolded head was thrashing from side to side. "Nancy!" he shouted desperately, "my Nancy!"

The staff officer took a deep breath. "Fire!"

The smoke jetted suddenly. The volley's huge sound rolled across the fields to explode birds from far-off trees.

The three men jerked in sudden spasms as their shirts erupted with blood. The companies' commanding officers walked to the three stakes with their revolvers drawn, but only one of the men was still alive. The man's breath bubbled in the wreckage of his ribs, and his bearded head twitched. His company officer cocked his revolver, held his breath, and tried to stop his hand shaking. For a second or two it looked as though he would be unable to give the *coup de grace*; then he managed to pull the trigger, and the living man's head was shattered by the bullet. The Captain turned away and vomited into the open grave as the band jerked into the tune of "Old Dan Tucker." Lee's aide let out a long slow breath.

"Put 'em in their boxes!" a sergeant called, and men ran forward to cut the dead men away from their stakes and lift them into the open-topped coffins, which were then ramped up on the red earth mounds so that a passer-by could see the corpses clearly. "Take the wrap off the young lad," the sergeant ordered and waited as the cuckolded youth's blindfold was removed.

Then, one by one the regiments were marched past the dead. Men from Virginia and Georgia, from the Carolinas and Tennessee, from Alabama and Louisiana, were all shown the three corpses, and after the infantry came the artillery and the engineers, all made to look into the eyes of the fly-infested dead, so that they would understand what fate awaited a deserter. General Jackson had been the first man to inspect the three corpses, and he had stared intently

247

into the faces as though trying to understand the impulse that could drive a man to the unforgivable sin of desertion. As a Christian the General had to believe that such sinners could be redeemed, but as a soldier he could not imagine any of the three men knowing a moment's peace throughout eternity, and his face showed nothing but disgust as he twitched his horse's reins and headed toward the farm that served as his headquarters.

It was there, in a parlor that was hung with an ancient portrait of President George Washington and a newer one of President Jefferson Davis, that the General undertook his second unpleasant duty of the day. He stood with his ramrod-straight back to the portrait of Washington and, flanked by three senior staff officers, summoned General Washington Faulconer into his presence.

The parlor was a small room made even smaller by a map table that almost filled the space between its lime-washed walls. Washington Faulconer entered the room to find himself cribbed in a narrow space and faced by four men behind the map table, all standing and all looking uncomfortably like judges. He had half expected to be seated opposite the General, but instead this meeting was evidently to be conducted formally, and Washington Faulconer felt even more uncomfortable at that daunting prospect. He was wearing a borrowed sword and a borrowed jacket that was at least one size too big for him. Sweat was trickling into his golden beard. The small parlor stank of unwashed bodies and dirty clothes. "General," Faulconer said in cautious greeting as he stood opposite his commanding general.

Jackson said nothing at first but just stared at the fair-haired Faulconer. The General's face showed the exact same expression as when he had stared down at the three slack-jawed, chest-shattered deserters in their cheap pine coffins, and Faulconer, unable to meet the intensity of that blue-eyed gaze, looked guiltily away. "I gave orders," Jackson spoke at last in his clipped, high voice, "that all the crossings of the Rapidan were to be guarded."

"I—" Faulconer began, but was instantly silenced.

"Quiet!" Even Jackson's three staff officers felt a frisson of terror at the intensity of that command, while Washington Faulconer visibly shook. "I gave orders," Jackson began again, "that all the crossings of the Rapidan were to be guarded. Men of your brigade, General, discovered an unmapped ford and were intelligent enough to obey my orders. While you"—and here the General paused just long enough for a rictus to shiver his body—"countermanded them."

"I—" Faulconer began, and this time was stopped not by a word of command but simply by the look in the General's blue eyes.

"The damage?" Jackson turned abruptly to one of his most trusted aides, Major Hotchkiss, a scholarly and painstaking man who had been deputed to discover the truth about the night's incursion. Hotchkiss had arrived at the remnants of the Faulconer Brigade's headquarters at dawn and had spent the next two hours questioning survivors, and now, in a dry, neutral voice, he offered his horrid list.

"Fourteen dead, sir," Hotchkiss said, "and twenty-four seriously hurt. Those are soldiers, but there were at least six civilians killed, and three of those, maybe more, were women. We won't know for sure till the tavern ruins are cool enough to be searched." Hotchkiss's news was all the more damning for being announced in a placid voice. Major Hinton was among the dead, while Captain Murphy was wounded so grievously that no one was certain that his name would not soon be added to the grim tally.

"And among the dead is Captain Talliser, my aide," Jackson added in a dangerous voice.

No one responded.

"Captain Talliser was the son of a good friend," Jackson delivered his aide's obituary, "and was himself a loyal servant of Christ. He deserved better than to be mauled to death by night raiders."

In the back of the house a man's voice suddenly began singing "How sweet the name of Jesus sounds." Pots clattered in that distant room; then the hymn was interrupted by laughter. The sound of the pots woke a tabby cat that had been sleeping on the parlor's windowsill. The cat arched its back, yawned, delicately stretched out each front paw, then began to wash its face. Major Hotchkiss looked back to his list. "Of material losses, sir," he said, "my preliminary estimate is that sixteen thousand rifle cartridges were lost in the fire, plus eighty-six charges of powder and thirty-eight rounds of common shell. Two limbers, four caissons, and three wagons were burned out and at least six horses taken." Hotchkiss folded the list, then raised scornful eyes to Washington Faulconer. "Two battle flags were also carried away by the enemy."

Another pained silence ensued. It seemed to stretch forever before, at last, Jackson spoke again. "And how did the raiders cross the river?"

"At a place called Dead Mary's Ford," Hotchkiss answered, "which had been properly guarded until the previous night. The raiders were intercepted during their withdrawal and a prisoner taken. The raiders also lost one horse." Hotchkiss, a dry, stern man who had once taught school, added the fact of the horse's death in a sarcastic voice. Faulconer colored.

"And it was by your orders, General," Jackson said, ignoring Hotchkiss's sarcasm, "that the ford was uncovered "

This time Faulconer tried no defense. He looked up briefly, but he still could not meet Jackson's gaze, and so he looked down again. He wanted to say that he had only been trying to instill discipline into his Brigade and that he had lost his precious saber in the night and, worst of all, that the whole humiliation had been at the hands of his own son. And not just one humiliation, for his servant Nelson had returned that same morning with the dreadful tale of Adam's raid on Seven Springs, which meant that Adam had attacked both his mother and his father, and the realization of those two awful betrayals filled Faulconer's eyes with tears.

"You must have something to say, Faulconer," Jackson said.

Faulconer cleared his throat. "Accidents happen," he suggested feebly. "The ford," he shrugged, "it wasn't on the map, sir, merely a shallow spot. Lack of rain, really." He knew he was stammering like a fool and tried to pull himself together. Goddamn it! Was he not one of Virginia's wealthiest men? A landowner who could buy this Tom Fool general a million times over? And Faulconer tried to remember all the risible stories about Jackson: how the General taught in a Negro Sunday school and how he gave a tenth of his income to the church and how he took a cold bath at six o'clock every morning, summer and winter alike, and how he held his left hand in the air so the blood would not collect and turn an old wound rancid, but somehow the catalog of Jackson's eccentricities and imbecilities did not make Faulconer feel any more confident. "I deemed that the ford was not important," he managed to say.

"And what did you deem my orders to be?"

Faulconer frowned, not understanding the question.

"I ordered all fords, regardless of their importance, to be guarded," Jackson said. "You thought I was amusing myself by delivering such a command?"

Faulconer, defeated, could only shrug.

Jackson paused a second, then delivered his verdict. "You are dismissed from your command, General." Jackson's voice was harsher than ever, prompted not just by Faulconer's dereliction of duty but also by the tears he saw in Faulconer's eyes. General Jackson did not mind tears in their proper place: at a deathbed, say, or in contemplation of Christ's miraculous atonement, but not here where men spoke of duty. "You will leave this army forthwith," Jackson continued, "and report to the War Department in Richmond for further orders. If there are any further orders for you, which it is my fervent hope there are not. Dismissed!"

Faulconer looked up. He blinked back his tears. For a second it seemed he might try and protest the hard sentence, but then he turned without any acknowledgment and left the room.

Jackson waited for the door to close. "Political generals," he said bitterly, "are as fit for soldiering as lapdogs for hunting." He reached for Major Hotchkiss's list and read its depressing statistics without showing any sign of regret or surprise. "Make the arrangements for Faulconer's replacement," he said as he handed the paper back to the staff officer. Then he picked up his shabby hat in readiness for his visit to Lee's headquarters. A final thought struck him as he reached the door and he paused there, frowning. "The enemy did well," Jackson said, apparently to himself, "so we shall just have to do better."

It was midday before the ruins of McComb's Tavern were cool enough to let a work party retrieve the bodies from the heart of the wreckage, and even then the salvage work had to be done by men wearing protective strips of water-soaked sacking around their boots and hands. The corpses had been shrunk by the fierce heat into black, brittle manikins that smelt disturbingly of roasted pork. Starbuck supervised the work. He was still officially under arrest, but no one else seemed willing to take charge of the salvage, and so, while the Brigade marched off to witness the executions and while General Washington Faulconer waited at General Jackson's headquarters, Starbuck took a dozen men from his own company and set them to work.

"So what's happening?" Truslow had asked Starbuck at dawn when the early light revealed the blackened and smoking wreckage.

"Don't know."

"Are you under arrest?"

"Don't know."

"Who's commanding the Legion?"

"Medlicott," Starbuck said. Faulconer had made the appointment during the night.

"Dan Medlicott!" Truslow said disgustedly. "Why in hell's name appoint him?"

Starbuck did not answer. He felt slighted by the appointment, for he had been a captain long before Daniel Medlicott had bribed his way to the rank in the spring election, but Starbuck also understood that Washington Faulconer would never have appointed him to command the Legion. "I've got a job for you," Starbuck told Truslow instead. "The prisoner's being unhelpful." The man they had captured was called Sparrow and came from Virginia's Pendleton County, one of the fractious western counties that had declared themselves to be a new state loyal to the Union.

"I'll make the sumbitch squeal," Truslow said happily.

The morning wore on. Most of the Legion witnessed the three executions, but even when they returned to their encampment, they still seemed dazed and stupefied by the night's disasters. Of the Legion's captains only Medlicott, Moxey, and Starbuck remained alive and unwounded, and of

253

the officers who had attended Major Hinton's birthday supper only Lieutenant Davies had survived serious harm. Davies had received a bullet slash on his left forearm but had escaped the worst of the massacre by taking cover behind the small church. "I could have done more," he kept telling Starbuck.

"And died? Don't be a fool. If you'd have opened fire they'd have hunted you down and killed you like a dog."

Davies shook at the memory. He was a tall, thin, bespectacled man, three years older than Starbuck and with a perpetually worried expression. He had been reading law in his uncle's office before the war began and had often confided in Starbuck his fears that he might never master the intricacies of that profession. "They knew there were women in the house," he now said to Starbuck.

"I know. You've told me." Starbuck's tone was callous and peremptory. In his view there was little point in endlessly discussing the night's tragedy in the vain hope of finding some consolation. The mess had to be cleaned up, avenged, and forgotten, which was why he was employing his company in retrieving the bodies from the burned-out tavern. Davies had come to watch the salvage, perhaps to remind himself how narrowly he had escaped being one of the shrunken, charred bodies.

"Murphy told them there were women inside," Davies said indignantly. "I heard him!"

"It doesn't matter," Starbuck said. He was watching the Cobb twins, who were rummaging among the ashes in the center of the burned building. Izard Cobb had found some coins and an ivory cribbage board that had somehow survived the fire undamaged. "Those go to Sergeant Waggoner!" Starbuck called across the ruins. The newly promoted Waggoner had been charged with collecting what few pitiable valuables might be rescued from the burned tavern.

"But it does matter!" Davies protested. "They killed women!"

"For Christ's sake"—Starbuck turned on the pale, bespectacled Davies—"you're about to get a captaincy, which means your men don't want to hear what went wrong last night. They want to hear how you intend to find the son of a damned bitch who did it to us and how you're going to kill him."

Davies looked shocked. "Captaincy?"

"I guess," Starbuck said. The night's disasters had virtually beheaded the Faulconer Legion, which meant there would either have to be wholesale promotions or else new people drafted in from other regiments.

"Maybe Pecker will come back?" Davies said wistfully, as though Colonel Bird could make everything in the Legion better.

"Pecker'll be back when he's mended," Starbuck said, "and that won't be for a few weeks yet." He suddenly whipped around to look at the wreckage again. "Cobb! If you've pocketed that silver I'll hang you!"

"I ain't pocketed nothing! You want to search me?"

"I'll search your brother," Starbuck said, and saw his suspicion that Izard Cobb would palm the coins to his brother Ethan had been plumb right. "Give the money to Sergeant Waggoner," he told Ethan Cobb, then watched as his orders were obeyed. "Now pick up that body." He pointed to the blackened figure of one of McComb's cooks.

Izard Cobb made a great display of horror. "She's a nigger, Captain!" he protested.

"If she was alive you'd have been happy enough to bed her, so now you can carry her to the grave. And do it respectfully!" Starbuck waited until the Cobb brothers had stooped to their work, then turned back to Davies. "They're lazy sons of bitches."

"All the Cobbs are lazy," Davies said, "always were. The family ruined some prime bottom land off Hankey's Run, just let it go to rack and ruin. A shame." His knowledge of such matters was a reminder that the Legion was still largely composed of men who came from within a day's walk of the town of Faulconer Court House; men who knew each other and each other's families and each other's business. Men like Starbuck, an outsider, were the exception. It was that close-knit family feeling that had added to the regiment's pain; when Major Hinton was killed, the Legion lost not just a commanding officer but a friend, a sidesman of the church, a brother-in-law, a creditor, a hunting companion, and above all, a neighbor, and if Murphy died they would lose another. "Still," Davies said, "Dan Medlicott is a decent man."

Starbuck believed Daniel Medlicott was a sly, ponderous, and cowardly fool, but he also knew better than to criticize one local man to another. Instead he turned away to watch as Izard and Ethan Cobb carried the distorted body free of the ashes. Truslow's inquisition of the captured cavalryman had revealed that it was not Adam who had been responsible for this massacre but a man called Blythe, yet Starbuck still felt an extraordinary bitterness toward his erstwhile friend. Adam had ridden the high moral horse for so long, preaching about the sanctity of the North's cause, and now he rode with men who slaughtered women.

"Starbuck!" Colonel Swynyard called from the road beside the burned wagon park.

Starbuck shouted at Truslow to take charge, then went to join Swynyard. "Five dead women." Starbuck delivered the final tally in a harsh voice. "Two cooks, McComb's wife, and the upstairs girls."

"The whores?"

"They were decent enough girls," Starbuck said. "One of them, anyway."

"I thought the tavern was out of bounds?"

"It was," Starbuck said.

"And I didn't think you had any money?"

"I don't, but she was a sweet girl."

"Sweet on you, you mean," Swynyard said tartly, then sighed. "I do pray for you, Starbuck, I do indeed."

"Fitzgerald, her name was," Starbuck said, "from Ireland. Her husband ran off and left her with a pile of debts, and she was just trying to pay them off." He stopped, suddenly overwhelmed with the misery of such a life and death. "Poor Kath," he said. He had been hoping Sally Truslow might help the girl, maybe by finding her a more lucrative job in Richmond, but now Kath Fitzgerald was a shrunken corpse waiting for a shallow grave. "I need a goddamned drink," Starbuck said bitterly.

"No, you don't," Swynyard said, "because you and I are summoned to headquarters. To see Jackson, and he's not a man to visit if you're stinking with whiskey."

"Oh, Christ," Starbuck blasphemed. He had hoped that the night's raid would have finished his troubles, but now it seemed Jackson himself had taken an interest in his derelictions. "What does Mad Jack want?"

"How would I know?" Swynyard said. He scuffed a foot in the road, which was still imprinted with the hoofmarks of the night's raiders. "He's seeing Faulconer now."

"Who'll be bitching about us."

"But we were right about Dead Mary's Ford," Swynyard said in a hopeful voice. "Maybe Jackson will acknowledge that?"

"Maybe," Starbuck said, but without any real hope that justice might be done. General Washington Faulconer would doubtless have his wrist slapped, but colonels and captains, especially poverty-stricken colonels and captains, made far more convenient scapegoats for disasters. Last night, when he had captured the prisoner at the ford, Starbuck had been sure that he could defeat Faulconer's malevolence, but in his interview with Major Hotchkiss, Jackson's aide, Starbuck had not felt a flicker of understanding or sympathy, just a dry disapproval. Justice, he reckoned, was a rare commodity. He swore at life's unfairness, then changed the subject by fishing a scrap of paper from his pocket. "Did you ever hear of a fellow named Joe Galloway?" he asked the Colonel.

Swynyard thought for a second, then nodded. "Cavalryman. Regular army. Never met him, but I've heard the name. Why?"

"He led last night's raid." Starbuck described what he had learned about Galloway's Horse; how it was composed of renegade Southerners who could ride the paths of Dixie with the same familiarity as rebel horsemen, and how a Captain Billy Blythe had led the detachment that had surrounded and savaged the tavern with their repeating rifles.

"How did you find all this out?" Swynyard asked.

"Prisoner talked," Starbuck said.

"I'm surprised he told you so much," Swynyard said, staring disconsolate at the scorched field where the remnants of the burned-out ammunition wagons stood.

"He struck up a kind of rapport with Truslow," Starbuck said. "It seems Galloway has a farm near Manassas that he's using as his depot, and I was kind of hoping we might get back there one day."

"To do what?"

"That," Starbuck said, pointing to the ruins of the tavern.

Swynyard shrugged. "I doubt we'll get the chance. Young Moxey says we're both to be posted to coastal defenses in the Carolinas."

"Moxey's a poxed piece of ratshit," Starbuck said.

258

"No doubt you once said that about me," the Colonel said.

"Oh no, sir," Starbuck grinned, "I was never that complimentary about you."

Swynyard smiled, then shook his head ruefully. "Be ready to leave in an hour, Starbuck. I'll arrange a horse for you. And stay sober, you hear me? That's an order."

"I'll stay sober, sir, I promise," for he had a whore to bury and a general to see.

Major Galloway's raiders did not survive entirely unscathed. The unfortunate Sparrow was captured, a Marylander was missing, while Corporal Harlan Kemp, the Virginian whose local knowledge had led the raiders to Dead Mary's Ford, had been shot in the belly. All those casualties had been caused during the brief and unexpected fight at the river, which had left Kemp in terrible pain. He spent the homeward journey drifting in and out of consciousness, and every few minutes he would beg one of the men supporting him in his saddle to do him the same favor they would render to a badly wounded horse. "Just shoot me, for the love of Christ, please shoot me."

Adam carried Kemp's rifle and one of the captured flags. He was continually looking for any sign of pursuit, but no rebel pursuers appeared as the raiders crossed the Robertson River, then the Hazel and the Aestham, each waterway more swollen with storm water than the last, until just after midday they came to the flooded Rappahannock and were forced to ride six miles upstream to find a passable ford. Then, safe at last on the northern bank, they rode east toward the rail depot at Bealeton.

Two miles outside the town a shell screamed overhead to explode in a gout of mud and smoke just a hundred paces behind the horsemen. Galloway ordered the Stars and

Stripes unfurled. A second shell howled past to smash into a pine tree, splitting the wood with a smoky crack that startled the tired horses, so that the troopers had to struggle with their reins and slash back with spurs. They could see the roofs of Bealeton beyond the trees and see the smoke of the artillery edging one of those patches of woodland. More smoke, this time from a locomotive, plumed up from the town itself. "The rebels can't have captured the place!" Galloway said and told the standard-bearer to wave the flag more vigorously.

The field gun did not fire again. Instead an apologetic Northern artillery officer rode out to investigate the horsemen and to explain that General Pope was nervous of rebel cavalry who might be probing the Federal army's new positions on the Rappahannock's north bank. "We've seen no secesh horse," Galloway told the artilleryman, then spurred on into a town crammed with confused soldiery. Troops that had embarked in Alexandria and Manassas expecting to arrive in Culpeper Court House now waited for new orders, and meanwhile the rails south of Bealeton were being torn up and carried north for safekeeping, and the trains employed on that task were blocked by the stalled troop trains that had been heading south, so that now there were no fewer than eight trains marooned at the depot. The town's roads were equally clogged. There were men who had lost their regiments, regiments that had lost their brigades, and brigades that had lost their divisions. Staff officers sweated and shouted contradictory orders, while the townspeople, most of whom were rebel sympathizers, watched with amusement. Galloway and Adam added to the noise as they demanded a doctor for Corporal Kemp, while every few moments a nervous Northern gunner on the outskirts of the town would contribute to the chaos by loosing a shell into the steaming heat of the countryside in an attempt to see off some nonexistent Southern horsemen.

"Makes you proud to be a Yankee, don't it?" Galloway said sourly as he forced a path through the chaos. "I thought these boys were supposed to be marching down Richmond's Main Street, not running away?"

A doctor was found, and Harlan Kemp could at last be lifted from his horse. His pants were stuck to the saddle's leather by a mass of dried blood and had to be cut away before the moaning man could be carried into the Presbyterian church lecture hall that was serving as a hospital. A doctor gave the Corporal ether, then extracted the bullet from his guts, but claimed there was little more that could be done for him in Bealeton. "There's a hospital car on one of the trains," the harried doctor said, "and the sooner he's back in Washington the better." He did not sound hopeful.

Adam helped carry Kemp on a stretcher to the depot, where nurses of the Christian Sanitary Commission took the sweating and shivering Corporal under their care. The hospital car was a sleeping car requisitioned from the New York Central and still possessed its peacetime cuspidors, fringed curtains, and engraved lamp shades, though now the luxurious bunks were attended by four nurses and two army doctors, who were protected by a pair of faded red flags that hung at either end of the car's roof to proclaim that the vehicle was a hospital. Perforated zinc screens in the car's roof were supposed to provide ventilation, but there was no wind, and so the car stank of castor oil, urine, blood, and excreta. Major Galloway attached a label to Kemp's collar that gave his name, rank, and unit, put a few coins into a pocket of the Corporal's uniform coat, then he and Adam climbed down from the pustulant car to walk slowly past a heap of coffins carrying stenciled labels directing their contents homeward. There were corpses going to Pottstown, Pennsylvania; Goshen, Connecticut; Watervliet, New York; Biddeford, Maine; Three Lakes, Wisconsin; Springfield, Massachusetts; Allentown, Pennsylvania; Lima, Ohio; and Adam, reading the roll call of town names and knowing that each represented a family distraught and a town in mourning, winced.

"Faulconer! Major Galloway!" An imperious voice broke into Adam's reflections. At first neither he nor Major Galloway could see who had summoned them; then they saw a white-haired man waving vigorously from a window further up the train. "Wait there!" the man shouted. "Wait there!"

It was the Reverend Elial Starbuck, who, in deference to the oppressive heat, was wearing a linen jacket over his shirt and Geneva bands. Having attracted their attention, he worked his way out of the crowded passenger car and jumped down to the trackside, where he pulled on a ragged straw hat that had replaced his lost top hat. "You have news?" he demanded. "Good news, I trust? We need good news. You observe we are retreating again?" The preacher made this speech as he plunged toward the two cavalrymen, dividing the crowds with the aid of his ebony cane. "I fail to understand these things, I truly do. We have raised an army, the largest that God has seen fit to put upon the face of the earth, yet whenever a rebel scowls at us we scuttle backward like trespassing children fleeing a householder." The Reverend Elial Starbuck made this trenchant criticism despite the presence of a number of senior Federal officers who scowled at his words, but there was an authority in the Reverend Starbuck's presence that subdued any attempt to contradict his opinions. "No one is sure, anymore, if they can capture Richmond or whether they will simply defend the Rappahannock. There is confusion." The Reverend Starbuck made the accusation darkly. "If I administered a church the way this government runs an army, then I daresay Satan would turn Boston into an outpost of hell without so much as a bleat of opposition. It's too bad, too bad! I had hoped to return home with better news than this."

"To Boston? You're returning so soon?" Major Galloway asked politely.

"I undertook to be back in my pulpit by month's end. If I believed the capture of Richmond was imminent, then I would beg my congregation's indulgence and stay with the army, but I can no longer believe any such thing. I had hoped your horsemen might inspire the army. I recall some talk of making raids on Richmond?" This accusation was accompanied by a scowl from the preacher. "We shilly-shally, Major. We linger. We tremble at the slightest sign of the enemy. We leave the Lord's work undone, preferring timidity to boldness. It grieves me, Major, it truly grieves me. But I am making notes, and I shall report my findings to the Northern people!"

Major Galloway tried to reassure the preacher that Pope's retreat was merely a temporary precaution intended to give the North time to build its army into an irresistible force, but the Reverend Starbuck would have none of such reasoning. He had learned from one of Pope's aides that the retreat behind the Rappahannock had been calculated to take advantage of the defensive capability of the river's steep northern bank. "We have gone on the defensive!" the Reverend Starbuck exclaimed in a disgusted voice. "Would there have been an Israel if Joshua had merely defended the river Jordan? Or a United States if George Washington had done nothing but dig ditches behind the Delaware? The Lord's work, Major, is not done by digging and tarrying, but by smiting the enemy! 'And it shall be, when thou shalt hear a sound of going in the tops of the mulberry trees, then shalt thou go out to battle: for God is gone forth before thee to smite the host of the Philistines.' Does not the First Book of Chronicles promise us as much? Then why are we not hearkening to the mulberries and going forth!" The Reverend Starbuck asked the question magisterially.

"I'm certain we shall be advancing soon," Galloway said, wondering what mulberries had to do with the prosecution of war.

"Then, alas, I must read about your advance in the *Journal* rather than witness it for myself. If, indeed, I ever reach Boston again." This last sentence was uttered in savage reproof of the chaos in Bealeton's small depot. The Reverend Starbuck had been waiting a full day to leave for Manassas Junction, but his train was trapped in the town by three supply trains that were being unloaded. No one knew how long that unloading would take, nor even if the offloaded supplies might not need to be reloaded in preparation for a further retreat. "Still, we are not without our comforts," the preacher said sarcastically, "so follow me," and he led the two cavalrymen to the end of the depot, where volunteer ladies from the Christian Sanitary Commission were serving reconstituted lemonade, buckwheat bread, and ginger cakes. The Reverend Starbuck wiped the sweat from his face with an enormous handkerchief, then used his cane to force a way to the trestle table, where he demanded three servings of the refreshments. One of the ladies timidly pointed to a hand-lettered sign proclaiming that the comestibles were for the consumption of uniformed men only, but one ferocious glance from the preacher quelled her small protest.

Once the ginger cakes and lemonade were secured and a suitable spot found for their consumption, Major Galloway gave the Reverend Starbuck the splendid news. John Pope's army might be retreating, but Galloway's Horse had stung the enemy. The Major forgivably exaggerated the damage his raiders had inflicted on the rebels, multiplying the wagons and ammunition destroyed at least fourfold, and while admitting to his own casualties, he claimed his men must have killed at least two score of rebels. "We left their camp smoking with fire, sir," Galloway said, "and reeking of blood."

The Reverend Starbuck put down his mug of lemonade so he could join his hands in a prayerful clasp. "'Bless the Lord,'" he said, "'who smote great nations and slew mighty kings!'"

"The news is better still, sir," Adam said, for while Kemp had been under the doctor's knife, Adam had found paper and string and made a parcel addressed to the Reverend Elial Starbuck on Walnut Street in Boston. He had been planning to send the parcel from the depot, but now he could deliver the prize personally.

It was obvious from the consistency of the package that it contained cloth, and the Reverend Starbuck, prodding with his finger, was scarce able to believe what he suspected. "It isn't . . ." he began, then without waiting to finish his question he tore the paper and string greedily away to reveal a bundle of folded scarlet silk slashed with white and blue. The preacher sighed as he held up a golden fringe of the rebel battle flag. "God bless you, my dear boy," he told Adam, "God bless you."

Adam intended to keep the Faulconer standard for himself, just as he intended to use his father's saber and revolver, but the battle flag, the red silk flag with the eleven white stars on the blue Saint Andrew's cross, was a gift for the Reverend Elial Starbuck: a trophy dragged from the filthy heart of secession that the preacher could use to show his subscribers that their donations were not being wasted. "I'm not sure if you want to know this, sir," Adam continued diffidently as the preacher gazed entranced at the beautiful silk, "but that flag comes from Nate's battalion."

But the mention of his son's name only enhanced the preacher's pleasure. "You took Nate's tawdry rag away, did you? Well done!"

"You'll take it to Boston, sir?" Major Galloway asked.

"I surely will. We shall put it on display, Major. We shall hang it for all to see, and maybe we shall invite people to throw mud at it on payment of a small sum toward the war effort. Then we shall burn it next July fourth." He gazed at the rich red silk, and a shudder mixed of lust and loathing racked his body. "'And your altars shall be desolate,'" he said in his marvelous voice, "'and your images shall be broken: and I will cast down your slain men before your idols. He that is far off shall die of the pestilence; and he that is near shall fall by the sword, and he that remaineth and is besieged shall die by the famine: thus will I accomplish my fury upon them. Then shall ye know that I am the Lord.'" There were a few seconds of awed silence from the dozens of people who had turned to listen to the preacher, who now, to show that his peroration was done, picked up his mug of lemonade. "The prophet Ezekiel," he added helpfully.

"Amen," Major Galloway said weakly. "Amen."

"So what becomes of you now, Major?" the Reverend Starbuck asked as he bundled the flag together. He had ripped the wrapping paper into useless shreds, but he managed to salvage enough string to tie the big silk folds into an approximation of neatness.

"We'll look to do some work here, sir. Hurt the enemy again, I hope."

"It's the Lord's work you're engaged in," the preacher said, "so do it well! Lay their land waste, Major, strike them down! And God give your arm the strength of ten while you do it. You'll write a full account of your raid? So I might publish it to our subscribers?"

"Of course, sir."

"Then on to victory! On to victory!" The Reverend Doctor Starbuck thrust his empty lemonade mug into Adam's hand, and then, carrying the rebel flag as proudly as though he had captured it himself, went back to wait in his car.

Galloway sighed, shook his head in marvel at such energy, then went to find someone, anyone, who might have orders for his cavalry.

Colonel Swynyard and a nervous Captain Starbuck waited all afternoon to see General Thomas Jackson, and they were still waiting as dusk fell and as one of the General's aides brought a pair of lanterns out to the veranda of the house where Jackson had his headquarters. "Not that he sleeps in the house," the aide said, stopping to gossip. "He prefers the open air."

"Even when it's raining?" Starbuck forced himself to make conversation. He did not feel like socializing, not when he was facing an unpleasant interview, but the aide seemed friendly enough.

"Just so long as it ain't storming." The aide clearly relished retailing stories of his master's eccentricities. "And he's up every morning at six to take a cold dip. Jaybird naked and shoulders under. Out here he uses that old horse trough and on a summer morning that might be pleasant enough, but in winter I've seen Old Jack skim the ice off a tub before baptizing himself." The aide smiled, then turned as a black man appeared around the side of the house. "Jim!" he called. "Tell these gentlemen what the General likes to eat."

"He don't like to eat nothing!" the black man grumbled. "He eats worse than a heathen. It's like cooking for a fighting cock."

"Mr. Lewis is the General's servant," the aide said. "Not his slave, his servant."

"And he's a great man." Jim Lewis's admiration for the eccentric Jackson was every bit as heartfelt as the uniformed aide's. "There ain't more than a dozen men like the General in all the world, and that's a straight fact, and there ain't any man in the wide world like the General for the whippin' of Yankees, and that's a straighter fact, but he still eats worse than a goat."

"Nothing but stale bread, dirt-plain meat, egg yolk, and buttermilk," the aide said, "and fruit in the morning, but only in the morning. He reckons that fruit ingested in the afternoon is bad for the blood, you see."

"While the General's real bad for Yankee blood!" Lewis said with a laugh. "He sure is lethal for Yankee blood!" Lewis dipped a pail in the General's bathtub, then carried the water toward the kitchen at the back of the house, while the aide carried his second lantern to the far end of the porch. Voices sounded inside the house where candlelight shone at a muslin-curtained window.

"Win battles, Starbuck, and you can be whatever it pleases you to be," Swynyard said bitterly. "You can be mad, you can be eccentric, you can even be rich and privileged like Faulconer." The Colonel paused, watching the dark fall over the far woods and fields where the host of campfires glimmered. "You know what Faulconer's fault is?"

"Being alive," Starbuck said sourly.

"He wants to be liked." Swynyard ignored Starbuck's venom. "He really believes he can make the men like him by treating them leniently, but it won't ever work. Men don't like an officer for being easy. They don't mind being treated like dogs, like slaves even, so long as you give them victory. But treat them soft and give them defeats and they'll despise you forever. It don't matter what kind of man you are, what kind of rogue you are, just so long as you lead the men to

268

victory." He paused, and Starbuck guessed the Colonel was reflecting on his own career rather than Faulconer's.

"Colonel Swynyard? Captain Starbuck?" Another aide appeared in the doorway. His voice was peremptory and his manner that of a man who wants to discharge an unpleasant duty quickly. "This way."

Starbuck plucked his coat straight, then followed Swynyard through the hall and into a candlelit parlor that was much too small for the trestle table that served as a stand for the General's maps. Not that Starbuck had time to take in the room's furnishings, for as soon as he entered he felt himself come under the fierce and off-putting gaze of the extraordinary figure who glared at the two visitors from the table's far side.

Jackson said nothing as the two men were shown in. The General was flanked by Major Hotchkiss and another staff officer. Swynyard, hat in hand, gave a short, sharp nod in salute, while Starbuck just stood to attention and stared at the gaunt, rough-bearded face with its bright wild eyes and malevolent frown; a face, Starbuck suddenly realized, that was uncommonly like Colonel Swynyard's own ravaged visage. "Swynyard"—Jackson finally acknowledged his visitors— "once of the 4th U.S. Infantry. But not a good record. Accused of drunkenness, I see." He had a sheaf of papers that he glanced at continually. "You were court-martialed and acquitted."

"Wrongly," Swynyard said, causing Jackson to look up from the papers in surprise.

"Wrongly?" the General asked. Like many artillery officers he was notoriously hard of hearing, his eardrums having been hammered by too many cannon blasts. "Did you say you were wrongly acquitted?"

"Wrongly, sir!" Swynyard spoke louder. "I should have been cashiered, sir, for I truly was drunk, sir, frequently drunk, sir, helplessly drunk, sir, unforgivably drunk, sir, but thanks to the saving grace of our Lord Jesus Christ, sir, I shall be drunk no more."

Jackson, confronted with this ready admission of guilt, seemed rather taken aback. He drew another sheet of paper from the sheaf and frowned as he read it. "Brigadier General Faulconer"—he said the name with a wry tone of distaste—"talked with me this morning. Afterwards he saw fit to write me this letter. In it, Swynyard, he says that you are a drunkard, while you, young man, are described as an immoral, womanizing, and ungrateful liar." The hard blue-gray eyes looked up at Starbuck.

"He's also a fine soldier, General," Swynyard put in.

"Also?" The General pounced on the word.

Starbuck suddenly resented the inquisition. He had been trying to win a damn war, not run a Sunday school. "Also," he said flatly and then, after a very long pause, "sir."

Hotchkiss looked intently down at his feet. Two of the candles on the map table were guttering badly, sending streams of sooty smoke to the yellowed ceiling. In the back of the house a voice began singing "How Sweet the Name of Jesus Sounds." Jackson looked momentarily annoyed by the sound; then he slowly lowered himself into a straight-backed chair, or rather he perched on the edge of the cane seat with his spine held rigidly parallel to, but not touching, the back. Starbuck supposed that his stupid belligerence had just destroyed any chance of receiving lenience, but it was too late to back down now.

Jackson turned his gaze back to Swynyard. "When did you find Christ, Colonel?" he asked, and Swynyard answered with a passionate testimony of seeing the light on the battlefield of Cedar Mountain. For a moment he ceased to be a soldier talking to his superior, but became just a simple man talking to his brother in Christ. He told of his former sinfulness and of his continual drunkenness, and he contrasted that fallen condition with his newfound state of grace. It was a testimony of salvation like the thousands of others that Starbuck had heard, the same kind of transforming story that had comprised the bulk of his youthful reading, and he supposed that the General, too, must have heard a myriad of such tales, but Jackson was plainly enthralled by Swynyard's tale.

"And now, Colonel," Jackson asked when the testimony was done, "do you still crave ardent spirits?"

"Every day, sir," Swynyard said fervently, "every minute of every day, but with the help of our Lord Jesus Christ I shall abstain."

"The great danger of temptation," Jackson said in a rather puzzled voice, "is how very tempting it is." He turned his gaze on Starbuck. "And you, young man, were brought up in a Christian household, were you not?"

"Yes, sir." A tabby cat had started to wind itself around Starbuck's ankles, rubbing its flanks on his frayed trouser ends and playing with the tags of his bootlaces.

"This letter claims you're a Northerner?" Jackson said, gesturing at Faulconer's letter, which now lay on the table.

"From Boston, sir."

"So why then are you fighting for the South?" Jackson frowned.

"That was the womanizing, sir," Starbuck said defiantly. He sensed Swynyard stir beside him, and he guessed the Colonel was trying to convey the message that Starbuck should quell his combativeness, but Starbuck was annoyed by the implication that he needed to prove his loyalty to these Southerners. The cat was purring loudly.

"Go on," Jackson said in a dangerously toneless voice.

Starbuck shrugged. "I followed a woman south, sir, then stayed on here because I liked it."

Jackson stared into Starbuck's face for a few seconds. He seemed to dislike what he saw and looked down at the papers instead. "We have to decide what to do with the Brigade. It isn't in a good state, eh, Hotchkiss?"

Hotchkiss gave a very small shrug. "No reserve ammunition, no transport, and one regiment virtually officerless."

Jackson looked at Swynyard. "Well?"

"We'll just have to take the ammunition from the enemy, sir," Swynyard said.

Jackson liked that answer. He turned his gaze back to Starbuck, who was suddenly and belatedly realizing that this interview was not a disciplinary affair but something altogether different. "What is this army's greatest failing?" Jackson asked Starbuck.

Starbuck's mind whirled in panic. Its greatest failing? For a second, remembering the morning's executions, he was tempted to say desertion, but before his tongue could frame the word a previous thought blurted itself out. "Straggling, sir." Some regiments lost a quarter of their number through men falling out of the ranks during long marches, and though a good number of those stragglers reappeared within a day or two, some went missing forever. He had given the General a good answer, but even so Starbuck wished he had thought for a moment longer and given a more considered response.

Then, astonishingly, he saw he had answered correctly, for Jackson was nodding his approval. "And how have you prevented straggling in your unit, Starbuck?"

"I just tell the sons of bitches they're free to go, sir," Starbuck said.

"You do what?" Jackson barked in his high voice. Hotchkiss looked alarmed, and the other staff officer shook his head as though he pitied Starbuck's stupidity.

"I just tell them they can leave the regiment, sir, but I

also tell them that they ain't allowed to leave with any property of the Confederate government just in case they straggle all the way home or into the enemy's arms. So I tell them they're free to go, but first I strip the sons of bitches stark naked and confiscate their guns. Then I kick them out."

Jackson stared at him. "You do that? Truly?"

It was hard to tell whether the General approved or not, but Starbuck could not back out of the tale now. "I did it once, sir," he admitted, "just the once. But I only needed to do it the once, sir, because we haven't had another straggler since. Except for the sick, sir, and they're different."

Starbuck's voice tailed away as the General began to behave in the strangest fashion. First he brought up a bony knee, then he clasped the raised knee in both his huge hands, and after that he rocked his body back as far as the stiff chair would allow. Then he put his head back and opened his mouth as wide as it would go though without uttering any sound at all. Starbuck wondered if the General was suffering a seizure, but then he saw the two staff officers grinning, and he realized that this odd display was Jackson's peculiar method of displaying amusement.

The General stayed in the weird pose for a few seconds, then rocked forward again, let his knee go, and shook his head. He was silent for a few more seconds, then turned to Swynyard. "How old are you, Colonel?"

"Fifty-four, sir," Swynyard said, sounding rather ashamed. Fifty-four was old for a soldier unless, like Lee, he was the commander in chief. Jackson himself was thirty-eight, while most of the fighting was done by boys yet to see their twenty-first birthday.

But Jackson's point was not about the optimum age for a soldier, but was instead a theological comment. "I was myself of mature years before I found Christ, Colonel. I do not say one should be of ripe age before conversion, but nor should we blame the young for failing to do what we ourselves did not do. As for your womanizing"—he looked at Starbuck—"marriage will cure that if self-discipline fails. I find that daily immersion in cold water and regular exercise helps. Chop wood, young man, or swing from a branch. You can leap fences. But exercise! Exercise!" He suddenly stood and snatched up Washington Faulconer's letter, which he held into a candle flame. He held the paper in the flame until it was well alight, then moved it gently and safely into the empty fireplace, where he watched it burn into ash. "War brings change," he said as he turned back to his visitors. "It changed me, it will change you. I confirm your appointments. You, Colonel Swynyard, will take over Faulconer's Brigade and you, Major Starbuck, will take command of his Legion. In return you will fight for me, and fight harder than you have ever fought in your lives. We are not here to defeat the enemy, but with God's help to destroy him, and I look for your help in that ambition. If I receive that help I will accept it as your duty, but if you fail then I shall send you both after Faulconer. Good night to you."

Starbuck could not move. He had entered the room expecting punishment and had instead received promotion, and not just promotion, but command of his own regiment. My God! He had command of the Legion, and suddenly he felt terrified of the responsibility. He was only twenty-two, surely much too young to command a regiment; then he remembered Micah Jenkins, the Georgian who had led his whole brigade hard and deep into the Yankee army at Seven Pines, and Jenkins was not much older than Starbuck himself. There were other officers in their twenties who were leading regiments and brigades, so why should Starbuck not be ready?

"Good night, gentlemen!" Jackson said pointedly.

Starbuck and Swynyard were both startled from their

astonishment. They allowed themselves to be led outside by an aide, who offered his own congratulations on the lantern-lit porch. "Major Hotchkiss," the aide said, "recommended you both. He felt that the Brigade had suffered enough without having outsiders thrust on it."

"Give him our thanks," Swynyard said.

"And if I might give some advice, gentlemen," the aide said, "you should have your men cook as many rations as they possess and have them ready for a very early march in the morning." He smiled and walked back into the house.

"My God," Swynyard said faintly, "a brigade." The Colonel seemed moved nearer to tears than to exultation. He was silent for a few seconds, and Starbuck guessed he was praying; then Swynyard led the way to where their horses were picketed. "I wasn't altogether honest with you earlier," the Colonel said as he untied his horse. "I knew Hotchkiss was sounding me out about the Legion's new commanding officer, but I dared not raise your hopes. Or mine, I confess."

Starbuck clumsily mounted the borrowed horse. "Medlicott won't be happy."

"The object of this war," Colonel Swynyard said tartly, "is to correct Abraham Lincoln's political misconceptions, not to make Captain Medlicott happy." He waited until Starbuck had settled himself in the saddle. "I thought you were going to upset Jackson."

Starbuck grinned. "Old Jack can hardly be expected to approve of womanizing, can he?"

Swynyard looked up at the sky. The last clouds had gone, and there was a splendor of stars arching over their heads. "I suppose I shouldn't pass on rumor," the Colonel said, "but there are stories that Old Jack had a love child once. Long ago. The stories are probably untrue, but who knows? Maybe you have to know sin before you can hate it. Maybe the best of Christians are made from the worst of sinners?"

"So there's hope for me yet?" Starbuck asked teasingly.

"Only if you win battles, Starbuck, only if you win battles." The Colonel looked at the younger man. "The Legion won't be an easy job, Starbuck."

"No, sir, but I'm the best man for it." Starbuck smiled at the Colonel. "I'm an arrogant son of a bitch, but by God I can fight." And now he had a whole regiment to fight for him, and he could not wait to start.

General Thomas Jackson put the interview with Swynyard and Starbuck out of his mind the very second that they left the room, concentrating instead on the maps that Major Hotchkiss had painstakingly drawn for him. Those handmade maps, spread edge to edge on the trestle table where their corners were weighted down by candlesticks, showed the country north of the Rappahannock, the country where Robert Lee's impudent and daring idea would be put to the test. It was an idea that Jackson liked because it was challenging, and because it held immense possibilities.

Which meant it also held enormous risks.

The enemy was digging in beyond the steep northern bank of the Rappahannock, inviting the rebels to throw away their lives in vain attacks across the deep river. The enemy doubtless planned to stay behind the river while more and more of McClellan's regiments joined their ranks until, at last, their numbers were overpowering and they felt confident of sweeping Lee's ragged army clean out of history.

So Lee, in response, was proposing to break one of the fundamental rules of war. Lee was planning to split his already outnumbered army into two smaller armies, each one horribly vulnerable to attack. That vulnerability was the risk, but it was a risk predicated on the likelihood that John Pope would not attack but would instead sit tight behind his steep riverbank and wait for McClellan's regiments to swell his ranks.

So Lee planned to divert Pope's attention by making threatening movements on the Rappahannock's southern bank, and while Pope watched that diversion, Thomas Jackson would march westward with the smaller rebel army. Jackson would march with just twenty-four thousand men, who would go west, then north, and then, with God's help, eastward until they had hooked far and deep into the enemy's rear, and once behind Pope's lines that small rebel army would cut and slash and burn and destroy until John Pope would be forced to turn back to destroy it. Then the small army, the vulnerable army, would have to fight like the devil itself to give Lee time to come to its aid, but at least the rebels would be fighting on ground of their own choosing and not attacking across a blood-dyed river. Jackson's small army was the anvil, and Lee's bigger army the hammer, and by God's good grace John Pope's army would be caught between the two.

But if the hammer and anvil failed to come together, then the history books would say that Lee and Jackson had thrown away a country by breaking the basic rules of war. By mere tomfoolery.

But tomfoolery was the only weapon the rebels had left. And it might just work.

So tomorrow, in the dawn, Tom Fool Jackson would march.

THEY MARCHED

They marched like they had never marched in their lives before and like they hoped they would never have to march again.

They marched like no troops had ever marched, and they did it through a day as hot as hell and as dry as hell's bones, and through a thick dust kicked up by the men and horses who marched in front; a dust that coated their tongues and thickened their throats and stung their eyes.

They marched on broken boots or with no boots at all. They marched because Old Mad Jack had told them he expected them to march, but no one knew why they were marching or where. First they marched west into a plump country unvisited by forage parties from either army, where the folk greeted the leading regiments with crackers, cheese, and milk, but there was not enough food to serve all the men who trudged past: regiment after regiment, brigade after brigade, the long hurting line of Jackson's foot cavalry heading west into America with dust on their faces and blood in their boots and sweat in their beards. "Where are you going, boys?" an old man shouted at the troops.

"Going to lick the Yankees, Pa!" one man found the energy to call back, but no one except the General really knew their destination.

"Lick 'em good, boys! Lick the sumbitches good and hard!"

The Legion had been woken at three in the morning by bugles that had stirred weary men from a shallow sleep. The soldiers grumbled and cursed at Old Jack, then blew their fires alive to boil their foul-tasting coffee.

Starbuck issued all the ammunition the Legion possessed. Each man would carry thirty rounds, half the usual issue, but that was all the cartridges that were left him. The men would carry their thirty rounds, their weapons, their bedroll, and a haversack with as much hardtack and boiled beef as they could carry, but they could carry nothing else. All knapsacks and heavy baggage were to be left south of the Rappahannock under a corporal's guard of wounded and sick men too weak to march.

Daniel Medlicott, whose promotion to major had been Washington Faulconer's final gift to the Legion, came with Sergeant Major Tolliver to make a formal protest at Starbuck's orders. If the Legion met an enemy, they said, then the men could not fight properly with only half an issue of ammunition. Starbuck, nervous at this first challenge to his authority, had delayed the confrontation by stooping to his campfire and lighting himself a cigar. "We'll just have to fight twice as hard then," he said, trying to turn away their unhappiness with levity.

"It isn't a joke, Starbuck," Medlicott said.

"Of course it isn't a joke!" Starbuck snapped the rejoinder louder than he had intended. "It's war! You don't give up fighting just because you don't have everything you want. The Yankees do that, not us. Besides, we ain't fighting alone. All of Jackson's men are marching with us."

The Sergeant Major looked unhappy but did not press the argument. Starbuck suspected Medlicott had talked the Sergeant Major into joining a protest that arose more from Medlicott's pique than from a genuine concern, and Medlicott, Starbuck conceded, did have cause to feel misused. For one day the miller had thought himself the commander of the Faulconer Legion, and then, out of the blue, the man he most disliked in the regiment had been promoted over his head. Medlicott maintained his protest had a more noble aim than salving his hurt pride. "You don't understand," he told Starbuck, "because you're not a local man. But I am, and these are my neighbors"—he waved a hand at the Legion—"and it's my duty to get them home to their wives and little ones."

"Makes you wonder why we're fighting a war at all," Starbuck said.

Medlicott blinked at the Bostonian, unsure how to understand the remark. "I don't think we should march," he reiterated his protest heavily. "And it won't be my fault if there's disaster."

"Of course it won't be your fault," Starbuck spoke caustically. "It'll be my fault, just as it'll be my fault if there ain't a disaster." A year before, he thought, his pride in being grammatical would never have allowed him to say "ain't," but now, to his private amusement, his Boston accent was following his allegiance south. "And your duty, Major," he went on, "is not to make sure your neighbors get home, but to make damn sure the Yankees get home, and if the sumbitches don't have the sense to go of their own accord, then your duty is to send them back to their wives and little ones inside boxes. That's your duty. Good morning to you both." He turned away from the two unhappy men. "Captain Truslow!"

Truslow shambled over. "Just Truslow's good enough," he said.

"Your company's at the rear," Starbuck said, "and you know what to do if you find stragglers." He paused. "And that includes straggling officers." Truslow nodded his bleak assent. In addition to commanding Company H Truslow also had command of the regiment's eight surviving draught horses that had once pulled the ammunition wagons and supply carts. Now, without any vehicles to drag, they would serve as ambulances for the men who genuinely could not keep up the pace.

The Legion marched at dawn. The order to leave their heavy baggage behind had alerted the men to the fact that this was to be no ordinary march, no stroll through the countryside from one bivouac to another, but no one had been prepared for a march as hard as this. Thomas Jackson usually allowed his men a ten-minute rest every hour, but not today. Today they marched without any rest stops, and there were staff officers beside the road to make sure no one dawdled, and there were more staff officers waiting at the first ford to make certain no man paused to take off his boots or roll up his pants. "Just keep marching!" the staff officers shouted. "Keep going! Come on!" The troops obeyed, squelching out of the ford to leave wet footprints that dried swiftly under the hot August sun.

The sun rose still higher. It had been one of the hottest summers in living memory, yet today it seemed as though the heat would reach new heights of discomfort. Sweat drove trickles through the layers of dust that caked men's faces. Sometimes, when the road ran across the summit of a shallow crest, they would see the line of infantry stretching far ahead and far behind, and they guessed that a whole corps was on the march, but where it was going only God and Old Jack knew. They did not march in step but loped along in the gait of experienced infantrymen who knew they would have to endure this agony a whole day through. "Close up!" the sergeants shouted whenever a gap appeared in a company's files, and the call would echo up and down the long shambling line. "Close up! Close up!" They passed parched fields, dried ponds, and empty barns. Farm dogs growled from the road's verges and sometimes started fights with the soldiers' pet dogs; such fights were usually popular diversions, but today the sergeants kicked the beasts apart and beat the country dogs away with rifle butts. "Keep going! Close up!" Every hour or so one of the cavalry patrols that were screening the march from the enemy's horsemen would canter past the Legion on its way to take up new positions far ahead of the long column, and the horsemen would answer the infantrymen's questions by saying they had seen no enemy. So far, it seemed, the Yankees were oblivious to Jackson's men as they moved across the hot summer landscape.

Men hobbled as muscles first tightened and then seized with cramp. The pain began in the calves, then spread to the thighs. Some men, like Starbuck, wore boots they had taken at Cedar Mountain, and within a few miles those new boots had worn men's heels and toes to bloody blisters. Starbuck took his boots off and tied them round his neck, then marched barefoot. For a few hundred yards he left small bloody footprints in the dust; then the blisters dried but went on hurting. His feet hurt, his legs ached, there was a stitch in his side, his throat burned, his bad tooth throbbed, his lips were cracked, his eyes stung with the sweat and dust, and this was just the start of the march.

Some officers rode horses. Swynyard was mounted, as were Major Medlicott and Captain Moxey. Moxey was now back with the Legion. Starbuck had not wanted him, but nor did Swynyard want him to stay as an aide, and so Moxey was now the Captain of Company B. The newly promoted Major Medlicott had gone to Company A with the consolatory honor of commanding the Legion's four right-flank companies. Moxey had the next company, Sergeant Patterson, now Lieutenant Patterson, had command of C, while Murphy's old Lieutenant, Ezra Pine, was now the

Captain of D Company. The left four companies had Sergeant Howes, now a Lieutenant, in command of E, a Captain Leighton, who had been borrowed from Haxall's Arkansas regiment to command Company F, Captain Davies took over Medlicott's old Company G, and Truslow, whom Starbuck had insisted on promoting into a full Captain, was in charge of Company H.

It was a ramshackle list of officers, cobbled together from disaster, and the men in the Legion knew it was makeshift and did not like it. Starbuck understood the disquiet. Most men did not want to be soldiers. They did not want to be torn away from home and women and familiarity, and even the most reckless young man's sense of adventure could be quickly eroded by minié bullets and Parrott gun shells. What held these reluctant warriors to their duty were discipline, friendship, and victory. Give them those things, Starbuck knew, and the men of the Faulconer Legion would believe they were the best damn soldiers in all the damned world and that there was not a man alive or dead, in any uniform in any country of any era, who could lick them in a fight.

But the Legion had no such belief now. Its sense of comradeship had been shattered by Galloway's raid and by the disappearance of Washington Faulconer. Most of the Legion's men had known Faulconer since childhood; he had dominated their civilian lives as he had their military existence, and, whatever his faults, unkindness had never been among them. Faulconer had been an easy master because he had wanted to be liked, and his disappearance had unsettled the ranks. They were ashamed, too, because the Legion was the only regiment that marched without colors. Every other unit marched with flying banners, but the Legion, to its disgrace, had none.

So, as they marched, Starbuck spent time with each company. He did not force himself on them but instead began by ordering them to close up and march faster, and then he would just march alongside and endure the embarrassed or unfriendly looks that told him most of his men believed he was too young to be their commanding officer. He knew those looks did not mean he was unpopular, for in the spring, when the Legion had held its final election for field officers, nearly two-thirds of the men had written Starbuck's name on their ballots despite Washington Faulconer's opposition, but that springtime defiance had not meant they wanted the young Northern rebel to be their commanding officer. Not at twenty-two, and not at the expense of men from their own Virginian community. And so Starbuck marched with them and waited for someone to throw the first question. The conversation he had with Company G was typical enough. "Where are we going?" Billy Sutton, newly made up to Sergeant, wanted to know.

"Old Jack knows and he ain't saying."

"Are we going to see General Faulconer again?" That question came from a man who had once worked on Washington Faulconer's land and who doubtless wanted to know that his old job would be waiting for him at the war's end.

"Reckon you will," Starbuck answered. "He's just gone on to higher things. Can't keep a man like General Faulconer down, you should know that."

"So where's he gone?" The question was hostile.

"Richmond."

There was another silence, except for the sound of boots slapping the road, rifle stocks knocking against tin canteens, and the hoarse rasp of men breathing. Dust drifted off the road to coat the bushes a reddish gray. "Story is that Old Jack gave Faulconer the back of his hand," Sergeant Berrigan asked. "Is that what you hear, Major?"

Starbuck noted the use of his new rank and guessed that

Berrigan was a supporter. He shook his head. "Way I hear it is that Old Jack just reckoned General Faulconer could be more use in Richmond. Faulconer weren't never happy with all this marching and sleeping rough, you all know that. He wasn't reared to it and he never got a taste for it, and Old Jack just agreed with him." That was a shrewd enough reply, intimating that Faulconer was not as tough as his men. Most of the Legion did not really want to believe that their General had been dismissed, for that truth reflected on themselves, and so they were ready enough to embrace Starbuck's kinder version of Faulconer's sudden disappearance.

"What about Colonel Bird?" a man asked.

"Pecker'll be back soon," Starbuck assured them. "And he'll have his old job back."

"And Captain Murphy?" another man called.

"Last I heard he was doing real well. He'll be back, too."

The company trudged on. "Are we still the Faulconer Legion?" a corporal asked.

"I reckon," Starbuck said. "Most of us come from there." The answer was an evasion, for given time Starbuck intended to change the regiment's name, just as Swynyard planned to change the Brigade's name.

"They going to make Tony Murphy a major? Like you?" That surly question came from a tall, scowling man called Abram Trent, who sounded deliberately unfriendly. Trent's question suggested that Starbuck's promotion had come too quickly and at the expense of men who were native to Faulconer County.

Starbuck met the question head-on. "Ain't my decision, Trent, but if you reckon I shouldn't be a major then I'll be real happy to discuss it with you just as soon as we stop walking. You and me together, no one else."

The men liked an officer who was ready to use his fists,

and Starbuck's offer to fight made them respect him, while the reluctance of any man to take up the offer only increased that respect. Starbuck knew that men like Abram Trent were the centers of resistance to his new and fragile authority, and by facing them down he helped make their defiance impotent. He finished by telling Company G what little he knew about their destination. "Old Jack doesn't march us like dogs for the hell of it, boys. We're on our way to give the Yankees a whipping, so save your breath and keep marching." Battle, he thought, and specifically victory in battle, was the elixir that would restore the Legion's confidence.

But not every man was eager for battle. Late in the morning, when few men had any breath left for questions or answers, Captain Moxey caught up with Starbuck. Moxey had been riding his horse, but now he led the beast by its reins. "I can't go on," he said.

Starbuck gave the sallow Moxey an unfriendly glance. "You look fresh enough to me, Mox'."

"It ain't me, Starbuck, but the horse."

Starbuck edged the sling of his rifle away from the spot on his right shoulder that was being chafed to rawness, though he knew that within seconds the sling would work its way back to the sore spot again. "Your horse ain't in command of a company, Mox', you are."

"She's lame," Moxey insisted.

Starbuck looked at the mare, which was indeed limping slightly on her right rear leg. "So let her loose," he said.

"It ain't probably nothing more than a bad shoeing job," Moxey said, "so if you give me a pass, Starbuck, I'll find a blacksmith in a village near here and catch you up."

Starbuck shook his head. "Can't do that, Mox'. Old Jack's orders. No one's to leave the march."

"I won't be long!" Moxey insisted. "Hell, it's what we've

always done on a march." He tried to sound offhand, but only succeeded in being petulant. His family had money, but, as Pecker Bird had always maintained, not quite enough money for its pretensions, just as Moxey did not possess quite enough grace to be a gentleman. There was a perpetual air of grievance in Moxey, as though he resented a world that had inexplicably denied his family the last few thousand dollars that would have made its existence free of all financial worry, while Moxey, the eldest son, lived in terror that one day he might have to work for a living.

Starbuck grimaced as he trod on a sharp-edged stone. He was marching barefoot, and for a pace or two the pain stopped him from speaking. Then the brief agony subsided. "So what is it, Mox'?" Starbuck asked. "You don't want to fight?"

Moxey bristled. "Are you accusing me of cowardice?"

"I'm asking you a goddamned question," Starbuck snapped.

Moxey immediately backed down. "My horse is lame! That's all!"

Starbuck shifted the rifle onto his left shoulder, though immediately the sore spot on that shoulder began to chafe. "The orders are clear, Mox'. If your horse can't keep up, then you're to leave it behind. Put her in a field where some farmer can find her."

"She's a valuable mare!" Moxey protested. "From Faulconer's stud."

"I don't care if she's a goddamned unicorn from the stables of the sun," Starbuck said coldly. "If she can't keep up then she stays behind."

Moxey's anger flared raw. "She ain't a Boston coal hauler's nag, Starbuck. She's real horseflesh. Worth near a thousand bucks."

Starbuck changed his rifle back to his right shoulder. "Just keep up with us, Mox', horse or no horse."

"You can boil your son of a bitch brains," Moxey said and turned angrily away.

Starbuck felt a sudden rush of fresh energy. He turned after Moxey, took him by his elbow, and steered the smaller man forcefully into some trees that grew beside the road. Starbuck made himself smile so that the watching men would not construe the scene as a fight between two officers, but as soon as he had Moxey and his horse safe out of the column's sight, he turned the smile off. "Now listen here, you son of a goddamned bitch. You may not like it, but I'm in charge of this goddamned regiment and you're nothing but a captain in it, and you're going to do what every other man in this regiment has to do. I don't care if you ride your damned horse till she's broke, and I don't care if you leave her here to starve, but I do care that you're leading Company B when we face the damned Yankees. So what are you going to do, Mox'? March or ride?"

Moxey had gone pale. "I ain't going to leave my horse. She's too valuable."

Starbuck pulled his revolver from its holster. "I tell you, Mox'," he said as he thumbed a percussion cap onto one of the cones, "they should have drowned you at birth and saved the rest of us a heap of trouble." He spun the cylinder so that the primed chamber would be the next under the hammer, then placed the revolver at the tired mare's drooping head with the muzzle just above her eyes.

"What the hell . . ." Moxey began.

Starbuck thumbed back the hammer as the mare stared at him with her soft brown eyes. "You're a leprous piece of ratshit, Mox'," Starbuck said in a calm voice, "but it just happens that I need you despite that, and if this here mare's the obstacle to you doing your job, why then, the mare'll just have to go to heaven." He tightened his finger on the trigger.

"No!" Moxey dragged the mare away from the revolver. "She'll make it!"

Starbuck lowered the hammer. "Just be sure you make it, too, Mox'."

"Goddamn it! You're mad!"

"And I'm your commanding officer too, Mox', and I reckon it's a wise thing not to upset commanding officers, especially mad commanding officers. Next time it'll be your brains, not the mare's." Starbuck lowered the revolver's hammer, then jerked his head toward the road. "Get back to your company."

Starbuck followed Moxey back to the road. Company H was just passing, and Truslow spat toward Moxey's disconsolate figure. "What was that about?" he asked Starbuck.

"Mox' and me were just looking at his horse. Deciding whether it could make the distance."

"It could go on forever," Truslow said scathingly, "so long as he takes the damn stone out of its hoof."

"Is that all it is?"

"What the hell did you think it was?" Truslow seemed not to be affected by either the day's heat or the speed of the march. He was one of the oldest men in the Legion, but also the toughest. He did not much care for being made into an officer, because rank had always been a matter of indifference to Truslow, but he did care about Starbuck, whom he perceived as being a clever man and a cunning soldier. "You need to watch Moxey," he said.

"I guessed as much," Starbuck said.

"I mean really watch him." Truslow moved a wad of chewing tobacco from one cheek to the other. "He's Faulconer's pet, and Faulconer won't want us to succeed."

Starbuck shrugged. "What can Moxey do about that? He

doesn't even want to be here, he just wants to run away."

"He's a sly one," Truslow said. "He's like a dog. He needs a master, see? And now that Faulconer's gone he'll like as not shove his nose into Medlicott's pocket." Truslow sniffed. "You hear the rumor that Medlicott is putting around? He says that if he'd kept command of the Legion we wouldn't be fighting with Jackson, but sitting in the trenches at Richmond. Says it's a fact."

"Like hell it is," Starbuck said, wincing as the weight of the rifle dug into his shoulder.

"But it's the kind of rumor men believe if they get unhappy," Truslow said, "and it ain't any good pretending that everyone in the Legion wants you to be in charge. You forget how many men in this regiment depend on Washington Faulconer for a living. They cut his trees, fish his streams, take his wages, keep their money at his bank, and live in his houses. Look at Will Patterson." Truslow was referring to the newly promoted commander of C Company.

"Patterson's been trying to become an officer ever since the fighting began," Starbuck said. "He should be grateful to me!"

"That family ain't grateful for nothing!" Truslow said. Sergeant Patterson, the son of a stonemason in Faulconer Court House, had twice tried to win election to officer but had failed both times. Starbuck was not certain Patterson would make a good officer, but there had been no one else he could promote. "And a good half of the Patterson business comes from Washington Faulconer," Truslow went on, "so do you think Will Patterson can afford to be your supporter?"

"So long as he fights," Starbuck said, "that's all that matters."

"But Medlicott, Moxey, and Patterson," Truslow said pointedly, "are in charge of your three right-hand

290

companies. So just how hard do you think those boys will fight when matters get bloody?"

Starbuck thought about that observation and did not like what he was thinking. He kept his conclusion to himself, grinning at Truslow instead. "Some people like me," he said.

"Who?"

"Coffman."

"He's a boy, too young to know better."

"Swynyard?"

"Madder than a rabid bat."

"Pecker?"

"Madder than two rabid bats."

"Murphy."

"Murphy likes everyone. Besides, he's Irish."

"You?"

"I like you," Truslow said scornfully, "but just what kind of recommendation do you think that is?"

Starbuck laughed. "Anyway," he said after a few paces, "we're not here to be liked. We're here to win battles."

"So make sure you do," Truslow said, "make goddamn sure you do."

The tired, hot men received a respite when they came close to the Rappahannock. So far the army had marched well to the south of the river, but now they were turning north to march past the Yankees' flank. The river's northern bank was a bluff up which the road climbed steeply, and one of Jackson's eighty guns had stuck on the slippery bank. The teamsters used their whips, and the nearest infantry were summoned to put their shoulders to the gun wheels, but the delay inevitably backed the column up, and the grateful men collapsed beside the road to rest their aching legs and catch their breath. Some men slept, their faces given a corpselike look by the dust coated on their skin. Moxey surreptitiously removed the stone from his mare's hoof, then sat beside a glum-looking Major Medlicott. Most of the Legion's other officers gathered around Starbuck, hoping to glean more information than he had given to their men, but Starbuck insisted he did not know where they were going.

"It'll be the Shenandoah Valley," Captain Davies opined, and when no one contradicted him or even asked why he held the opinion, he explained it anyway. "That's Old Jack's backyard, right? He's a terror in the Shenandoah. Once the Yankees know we're in the Shenandoah, then they'll have to split their army in two."

"Not if they decide to let us rot in the Shenandoah," the newly promoted Lieutenant Howes commented.

"So we won't rot there, but cross into Maryland," Davies suggested. "Up the Shenandoah, straight across the Potomac and over to Baltimore. Once we've got Baltimore we can attack Washington. I reckon a month from now we could be running Abe Lincoln out of the White House on one of his own fence rails."

Davies's confidence was greeted with silence. Someone spat in the road, while another man tilted his canteen to his mouth and held it there in hope of finding one last trickle of tepid water. "Down the Shenandoah," Truslow finally said, "not up."

"Down?" Davies asked, puzzled by the contradiction. "Why should we march south?"

"Down's north and up's south," Truslow said, "always has been and always will be. You go to the valley and ask the way up and they'll send you south. So we'll be going down the Shenandoah, not up."

"Up or down," Davies said, offended by the correction, "who cares? We're still going north. It'll be a two-day march to the Shenandoah, another two to the Potomac, and then a week to Baltimore."

"I was in Baltimore once," Captain Pine said dreamily. Everyone waited to hear more, but it seemed Pine had nothing to add to his brief announcement.

"Up!" Starbuck saw the battalion in front being ordered to their feet. "Get your lads ready."

They crossed the river and headed north. They did not follow the road, which here tended westward, but marched over fields and through woods, across shallow streams and wide paddocks, following a shortcut that at last brought the column to a dirt road leading northward. Starbuck held a hazy map of Virginia in his head, and he sensed how they were now marching parallel to the Blue Ridge Mountains, which meant that just as soon as they reached the Manassas Gap Railroad they could turn west and follow the rails through the pass into the Shenandoah Valley. And that valley was aimed like a gun at the hinterland of Washington, so maybe the excitable Davies had it right. Starbuck tried to imagine the fall of Washington. He saw the ragged rebel legions marching through the conquered ring of forts that surrounded the Yankee capital and then, under the eyes of the silent, shocked spectators who lined the streets, parading past the captured White House. He heard the victory music and saw in his mind's vivid eye the starcrossed battle flag flying high above the white, plump, and self-satisfied buildings, and when the victory parade was finished, the soldiers would take over the captured city and celebrate their triumph. Colonel Lassan, the Frenchman, had spent a week in the North's capital and had described the city to Starbuck. It was a place, Lassan had said, devoid of hard sinews. There was no industry in Washington, no wharves, no factories, no steam-driven mills to scream their whistles and shroud the sun with their filth. It was, Lassan said, a small city with no purpose but to manufacture laws and regulations; an artificial city where slyness passed for intelligence and venality replaced industry. It was peopled by pale lawyers, plump politicians, rich whores, and faceless hordes of black servants, and when the rebels marched in, the lawyers and politicians would doubtless be long gone, which meant that only the good souls would be left behind.

That tantalizing prospect served to keep Starbuck's mind off his blistered feet and burning muscles. He dreamed of a soft city, of captured champagne, of wide beds and starched white sheets. He dreamed of fried oysters and turtle soup and roast beef and tenderloin steaks and peach tarts, all of it eaten in the company of the lawyers' rich Washington whores, and that tantalizing thought suddenly reminded him of the golden-haired woman he had glimpsed in her husband's open carriage behind the Yankee lines at the battle of Bull Run. She lived in Washington and had invited Starbuck to visit her, but now, for the life of him, he could not remember her name. Her husband had been a Northern congressman, a pompous and dim-witted man, but the wife had been golden and beautiful, a vision whose memory was lovely enough to console a weary man marching through the small Virginia towns where excited people applauded as their soldier boys went by. Year-old rebel flags, hoarded through the months when the Yankees had been the nearest troops, were hung from balconies and eaves, while small boys brought the troops buckets of tepid well water to drink.

Starbuck's pains seemed almost numb by the time the sun began to sink behind the serrated peaks of the Blue Ridge Mountains. Ahead of him he saw the soldiers taking off their hats, and he wondered why so many would make that gesture, and then a staff officer cantered back along the line of march calling out that the men were not to cheer. "We don't want any Yankee cavalry scouts to hear us," the staff officer said, "so no cheering."

Cheering? Why no cheering? Starbuck, his thoughts wrenched back from imagined Washington luxuries to his wretched, sweating reality, suddenly saw a poker-backed figure standing atop a house-sized rock beside the road. It was Jackson, hat in hand, watching his troops march by. Starbuck instinctively straightened his shoulders and tried to put some spirit into his step. He snatched the ragged, sweat-stained hat off his long black hair and stared at the hard-faced man, who, seeing Starbuck, gave the smallest nod of recognition. Behind Starbuck the Legion pulled off their hats and fell into step to march past the legendary General. No one cheered, no one said a word, but for the next mile it seemed to Starbuck that there was an extra spring in every man's pace.

They marched on into the evening. The western sky was a livid crimson streaked with gold, a blaze of color that slowly shrank and faded into a gray twilight. The marching pains came back, relieved now by the slow fall in the day's fierce temperature. The men looked for signs of bivouacs that would tell them they had arrived at their destination, but no troops were camped beside the road and no campfires drifted smoke into the evening; instead the march went on and on into the darkness. The moon rose to whiten the dust that coated the Legion's rifles and clung to the men's skin. No one sang, no one spoke, they just marched on and on, mile after damned mile under a gibbous moon. To their right, far off, a great red glow showed where the smear of Yankee cooking fires covered the northern Virginia counties, and Starbuck, trying to keep himself alert, realized that Jackson's army was already north of most of that glow, which surely meant that the enemy was outflanked, and for the first time he wondered if they were indeed planning to turn west into the Shenandoah. Maybe, he thought, they would turn east instead, to plunge like a dagger into the Yankee rear.

"In here! In here! No fires!" A voice startled Starbuck out of his reverie, and he saw a horseman gesturing toward a night-dark meadow. "Get some rest." The horseman was evidently a staff officer. "We'll be marching at dawn. No fires! There's a stream at the bottom of the hill for water. No fires!"

Starbuck acknowledged the orders, then stood in the meadow's gate to watch the Legion shamble past. "Well done!" he called out to each company. "Well done." The men scarcely acknowledged his presence, but just limped into the meadow that lay at the crest of a small hill. Moxey kept on the far side of his company so he would not even have to acknowledge Starbuck's existence.

Truslow's company went past last. "Any stragglers?" Starbuck asked.

"None that you need know of."

Starbuck walked beside Truslow into the meadow. "A hell of a march," he said tiredly.

"And tomorrow we probably do it again," Truslow said. "You want me to set a guard?"

Starbuck was tempted to accept the offer, but he knew the men of Company H would think he had picked on them because they were his old company, and so he deliberately chose Company A instead. Major Medlicott was too tired to complain.

Starbuck limped round his men's bivouac. He wanted to make certain that they had water to drink, but most had already fallen asleep. They had simply lain down on the grass and closed their eyes, so that now they lay like the dead collected for burial at battle's end. A few walked to the stream to fill their canteens, a few smoked, a few gnawed at hardtack, but most of the men just lay sprawled in the moonlight.

Starbuck stayed awake with the pickets. To the south the moon shone on yet more men tramping up the road, but one by one the regiments turned into the fields to snatch their brief rest. The regiments were still coming when Starbuck woke Medlicott to relieve him, and still marching when he lay down to sleep. He dreamed of marching, of pain, of a sun-bitten day spent sweating northward on a stone-hard road that led, not to whores on white sheets in a fattened city, but to battle.

On the morning that Jackson's army marched west Major Galloway received orders to report to General McDowell, whose troops formed the right wing of Pope's army. An odd and disquieting report had come from that western flank. One of General Banks's staff officers had been spying the enemy positions from a hill north of the Rappahannock and had spotted a distant column of mixed infantry and artillery marching westward on the river's far bank. The road the rebels were following snaked up and down through hilly country, so that the staff officer could only glimpse scattered parts of the column, but he had estimated the number of regiments by counting their flags and reported that the rebel force must have numbered at least twenty thousand men. The column had eventually disappeared in the heat haze that shimmered over the distant farmland and woods.

General Banks forwarded the report to General McDowell, who in turn sent it on to General Pope with an added comment that the column was probably aiming to cross the Blue Ridge Mountains and then advance north through the Shenandoah Valley. Maybe, McDowell surmised, the rebel force planned to attack the Federal garrison at Harpers Ferry, then cross the river and threaten Washington?

Pope added the report to all the other disquieting evidence of rebel activity. Jeb Stuart's horsemen had raided one of the army's forward supply depots at Catlett's Station. The rebel horse had swarmed out of a rainswept night like fiends from hell, and though the raid had done little real damage, it had made everyone nervous. There were more reports of rebel activity on Pope's eastward flank near Fredericksburg, while other observers saw clear signs that the rebels were planning a direct assault across the Rappahannock River. General Pope felt like a juggler given one Indian club too many, and so he sent a stream of peremptory telegrams to the War Department in Washington demanding to know when he might expect McClellan's forces to join his own, then rattled off a series of orders designed to repel all the threatened attacks at once. Union troops marched and countermarched under the hot sun, none of them knowing quite what they were doing or where the enemy was supposed to be.

It was the cavalry's job to determine the enemy's position, and so Major Galloway was ordered to report to General McDowell, who in turn instructed him to lead his men into the swathe of empty country that lay between the Northern army and the Blue Ridge Mountains. It was into that hazy spread of land that the mysterious enemy column had been seen marching, and McDowell wanted Galloway to find it, but just as Galloway was ready to leave, a new order arrived from General Pope's headquarters. It seemed a party of rebel horsemen had recently crossed Kelly's Ford, and Galloway was ordered to find out where that enemy was headed.

The Major demanded a map. It took him a long time to discover Kelly's Ford. He had somehow expected it to be near Warrenton, where McDowell's forces were anchored, but instead he found it to be fifteen miles away on the army's eastern flank. He protested the stupidity of one cavalry regiment being required to be in two places at once, but was told that most of the army's cavalry was either immobilized through lack of fodder or else was busy. Galloway stared down at the map. "Which job's the most important?" he asked.

Pope's staff officer, a Colonel, scratched in his beard. "I reckon that if the Johnnies are crossing Kelly's Ford, then they'll be planning to cut us off from McClellan's boys." He ran a nicotine-stained finger up from the ford to show how a rebel force could cut Pope's men off from Aquia Creek, where McClellan's army was coming ashore. "They'd split us up. And that'd be bad. Real bad."

"And this other column?" Galloway asked, gesturing toward the western landscape.

The Colonel squashed a louse between two nicotine-stained thumbnails. In truth he had no idea which threat was the greater, but nor did he want to consult his master, who was already in a furious mood because of the constant stream of conflicting intelligence reports that were confusing all his careful plans. "My guess," the Colonel ventured, "and it is only a guess, mark you, is that the seceshers are dragging a false trail. They probably want us to weaken ourselves by sending men to the Shenandoah Valley. But the war isn't going to be won in the Shenandoah, but here, on the river lines." He slapped the map across the band of rivers that barred the roads between Washington and Richmond. "But on the other hand, Major"—the Colonel was too canny not to qualify his judgment—"we sure would like to know just what in tarnation those twenty thousand Johnnies are doing. And everyone says your boys are the best for that kind of job. They say you can ride behind the enemy lines, isn't that right?"

So Galloway had no choice but to split his small force. If the threat at Kelly's Ford was the more dangerous, then that justified using two troops of men, and so Galloway decided to go there himself and to take Adam's troop with him, while Billy Blythe would take his men and investigate the mysterious western column. "You ain't to get in a fight, Billy," Galloway warned Blythe. "Just find out where in hell the rebs are headed and then get word back to McDowell."

Blythe seemed happy with his orders. His horses were tired and hungry, but he did not have so far to ride as Galloway, and once in the saddle, his men rode slowly. They headed into an empty countryside that was parched by an afternoon sun that burned like a furnace. Blythe led his troop a few miles west of the last Union pickets and then stopped at the summit of a small hill to stare into the empty landscape. "So just what in hell are we doing, Billy?" Sergeant Kelley asked Blythe.

"Chasin' our tails, Seth. Just chasin' our born-again tails."

Sergeant Kelley spat in disgust. "So what if the enemy are out here? Hell, Billy, our horses ain't been fed proper in three days and they ain't been rested proper neither. You reckon we can outrun Jeb Stuart's boys on these nags?" The men murmured their agreement.

Blythe waved at the serene, heat-hazed countryside. "What enemy, Sergeant? Do you see an enemy?"

Kelley frowned. There was a smear of dust way off to the northwest, but that was so far beyond the Rappahannock that it was surely being kicked up by Northern troops, while to the west, where the mysterious column had supposedly disappeared, there was nothing but trees and sun-glossed fields and gentle hills. "So what the hell are we doing here?" the Sergeant asked again.

Blythe smiled. "Like I told you, Seth, chasin' our tails. So why in hell's name don't we do something more useful instead? Like give our horses a proper feed." He tugged at his reins, turning his horse's head south. "I seem to remember a farm not so far away. A den of rebel vipers, it was, but there was fodder there and maybe it didn't all burn up to hell and I reckon you and I have got unfinished business there."

Kelley grinned. "You mean that Rothwell woman and her children?"

"I hate children," Blythe said, "I do so hate young children. But their mothers?" Blythe smiled. "Ah, I do so love a ripe young mother."

Twenty miles to the east Major Galloway found Kelly's Ford guarded by a strong rebel garrison on the southern bank. That garrison sniped ineffectually at Galloway's horsemen as they explored the northern side of the river, where they discovered no hoofprints nor any other evidence of a rebel force across the river. The local black population, always the best source of information for Northern scouts, said that no Confederates had crossed the river in two days, and those men had only come across to get fodder for their horses. Galloway dutifully searched the riverbank for five miles east and west, but neither he nor Adam found any rebels. The rumor had been false, and Galloway, knowing his day had been wasted, rode slowly home.

A dozen miles north of the ford was Warrenton Junction, where the branch rails from Warrenton joined the main Orange and Alexandria line. Confusion besieged the junction. Two trains loaded with guns and ammunition were trying to pass south to the Bealeton depot, while another was trying to haul twenty-four boxcars loaded with hardtack, uniforms, percussion caps, and artillery shells down to Warrenton. Meanwhile three empty trains and a hospital train waited in the pitiless sun for clearance northward. The sweet smell of pinewood lay over the depot, coming from the log stacks that waited to feed the locomotive furnaces.

The Reverend Elial Starbuck's passenger car was attached to the hospital train. The preacher escaped the heat in the car's stifling interior by walking up and down in the train's long shadow, where he was forced to watch as a succession of newly dead men were carried from the red-flagged cars. The men were not dying from their wounds but from heat prostration, and their fate angered the Reverend Elial Starbuck. These were good, decent young Americans who had gone to fight for their country, and their reward was to be dumped beside a rail track where their corpses crawled with flies. If the hospital train did not move soon, then every sick man in the cars would be dead, and so the Reverend Starbuck discovered an engineer colonel who appeared to possess some authority over the railroad and of whom he demanded to know when the trains would be cleared north. "In Boston," the Reverend Starbuck assured the Colonel, "we have such things as timetables. We find them useful."

"In Boston, sir," the Colonel retorted, "you don't have Jeb Stuart." The delay on the railroad was caused by the raid Stuart had made on Catlett's Station, the next depot on the line, where the rebel cavalry had taken scores of prisoners, captured a paychest, and even snaffled up General Pope's best uniform coat. A teeming rain had prevented the raiders from burning the bridge that carried the rails over Cedar Run, yet even with the bridge intact the raid had inflicted chaos on the rail schedule. "But your train will be the first one north tomorrow afternoon," the Colonel promised the Reverend Starbuck. "You'll be in Washington by Wednesday, sir."

"I had hoped to be in Richmond by then," the Reverend said caustically.

The Colonel bit back any retort, and instead arranged for the hospital cars to be moved into the shade of a warehouse and for water to be brought to the surviving wounded. Some fugitive slaves who were now employed as laborers on the railroad were ordered to dig graves for the dead.

The Reverend Starbuck wondered if he should witness for Christ to the laboring blacks but decided his mood was too bleak for effective evangelism. His opinion of the army had slipped all week but now reached fulminating bottom. In all his born days he had never witnessed any organization so chaotic, so incapable, or so sluggish. The smallest Boston grocery shop displayed more managerial acumen than these uniformed incompetents, and it was no wonder that the lumpen-skulled rebels were making such fools of the North's generals. The preacher sat on the open platform at one end of his passenger car, and as the sun sank huge in the west, he wiped the sweat from his forehead and took on the pleasurable chore of making notes in his diary for a pungent letter he planned to send to the Massachusetts congressional delegation.

Five miles away, in Warrenton itself, Major Galloway reported to the army headquarters. He found the same Colonel who had dispatched him that morning and who now seemed disappointed that no enemy had crossed Kelly's Ford. "You're sure," the Colonel asked.

"Certain. Absolutely certain."

The Colonel scratched at his beard, found a louse, and squashed it between his thumbnails. "What about the twenty thousand Johnnies in the west?" the Colonel asked.

"I sent my second-in-command that way, but he hasn't reported yet."

The Colonel yawned, then stretched his arms. "No news is good news, eh? If your fellow had found anything he'd have doubtless sent word. And no one else is squealing about twenty thousand rebels, so it's probably all moonshine, pure moonshine. Which reminds me." He turned in his chair and reached for two glasses and a whiskey bottle.

"You'll join me? Good." He poured the whiskey. "But even if there are twenty thousand Johnnies loose, what damage can they do?" He paused, thinking about his question, then laughed at the very thought of the whole United States Army being frightened of such a tiny force. "Twenty thousand men," he said disparagingly, "what harm can they do?"

Captain Davies woke Starbuck. "Reveille, sir."

Starbuck thought he had to be dreaming. No, worse, he thought he was not dreaming. His muscles were strips of pain, his bones were set solid.

"Starbuck! Up!" Davies said.

Starbuck groaned. "It's dark."

"They want us marching in twenty minutes."

"Oh, no, Jesus no," Starbuck muttered. He groaned again, then turned onto one side. The mere effort of rolling over hurt. Everything hurt. He could not bear to think of trying to stand on his blistered feet.

"Water." Davies, who had taken over picket duty from Medlicott, offered Starbuck a canteen. Starbuck drank, then felt for a cigar. He had two left, both preserved from harm by being wrapped in his hat. He borrowed Davies's cigar to light one of his own, then coughed some life into his lungs.

"Jesus," he said again, then remembered he had to set an example, and so he struggled to his feet. He blasphemed again.

"Stiff?" Davies asked.

"Why didn't I join the cavalry?" Starbuck asked, then tottered a few steps. It was night-dark still, without even a hint of dawn in the eastern sky. Stars were bright overhead, while the moon hung low above the Blue Ridge to mark its forested draws deep black and starkest white. He sat to pull on his boots. It hurt just to tug them over his raw feet.

"Awake?" Colonel Swynyard's voice asked.

"I think I died and went to hell," Starbuck said as he forced himself to stand again. "Maybe that's it, Colonel. Maybe none of this is real. We're all in hell."

"Nonsense! We're heavenbound, praise Him."

"Then I wish He'd hurry," Starbuck complained. Around him the field heaved and groaned as waking men realized the ordeal that waited for them. Starbuck scratched at a louse, transferred the one remaining cigar to his pocket, pulled the hat onto his head, slung his rolled blanket over his left shoulder and the rifle on his right, and thus was ready to start.

Breakfast was taken on the march. For Starbuck it was a slate-hard slab of hardtack that gnawed at his aching tooth. He tried to remember when he had last had a decent meal. His uniform trousers were belted with rope that gathered in at least five inches of material that had been well stretched before the war's first battle. Then the blisters on his feet began hurting again and the sore spot on his right shoulder began to chafe, and he forgot about food and just concentrated on walking through the pain.

The column still marched north. Once, when the road rose to offer a view of the moonlit western hills, Starbuck saw the notch that marked where the Manassas Gap carried the railroad through the Blue Ridge and into the fertile Shenandoah Valley. In the moonlight the gap looked a far way off, and Starbuck's spirits fell at the thought of marching all that long way. His muscles were slowly unknotting, but only to hurt even more. The Legion passed between two rows of houses, their windows dimly lit with candlelight. A tethered dog barked at the passing soldiers, and an unseen woman called from a window to offer the soldiers her blessings.

Then, abruptly, the road climbed a steep few feet, and Starbuck almost tripped on a steel rail. He recovered his

305

footing and stepped safely over the metal to realize that the Legion had at last reached the Manassas Gap Railroad. The road divided here, one branch climbing west toward the Blue Ridge and the other going east toward the Yankees. A mounted staff officer dominated the junction, and he was pointing the troops east. So they were not going to the Shenandoah Valley after all but were instead to march toward the rising sun that climbed through the vast smear of smoke marking where a waking army's cooking fires burned. They were to march east toward battle.

The sun rose like hellfire in their eyes. It dazzled them and cast their shambling shadows long on the dusty road behind. Every now and then Starbuck would see the rails of the Manassas Gap Railroad lying alongside the road like twin streaks of reflected fire, but no trains ran on those strips of molten steel. All the locomotives and stock had been taken south or else commandeered by the Yankees to shuttle their supplies from Alexandria through Manassas Junction to their forces on the Rappahannock.

And now, Starbuck realized, Stonewall Jackson was behind those forces. And maybe, Starbuck thought, the Yankees knew he was coming, for how could twenty-four thousand men hope to avoid a hostile army's scouts? Ahead of the marching column lay a low range of hills, so low that in peacetime the hills would scarcely have been noticeable, but Starbuck could see that the apparently innocuous slopes were more than steep enough to check an infantry attack. And if the Federals had put guns in the dark trees at the crest of those hills, then Jackson's long march must end in bloody defeat.

The road and the empty railroad arrowed side by side toward a pass through the low hills. Jackson's cavalry advanced either side of the rail embankment, their carbines cocked as they nervously watched every fence and wood and house. The passage through the unregarded hills was called Thoroughfare Gap, and if the Yankees had been shadowing Jackson's march, then Thoroughfare Gap was the place to put their ambush, and as the steep walls of the pass narrowed, the horsemen advanced ever more slowly and cautiously. They tried not to think of hidden gunners waiting with taut lanyards or of lines of concealed infantry poised with loaded rifles. Every creak of a saddle or rustle of wind or clatter of a horseshoe on stone startled the scouting horsemen's nerves; then suddenly they reached the pass's summit and the whole eastern countryside lay open before them, and it was empty. There were no limbers, no guns, no caissons, no Federals at all. There was nothing but low hills and thick woods stretching into the long blue distance. Stonewall Jackson had hooked his small army clean and undetected into the Yankees' unprotected belly.

Now all he had to do was twist the hook and start the killing.

"Close up!" the officers shouted. "Close up!"

The men marched in silence, too tired to talk or sing. From time to time a man would break ranks to snatch a green apple or an ear of unripe corn from the farmlands on either side of the road, while other men broke ranks to be ill behind a hedge, but always they hurried on after their comrades and pushed themselves back into line. The horses pulling the guns labored under the whips, and their guns' wheels ripped the road's surface into broken ruts that turned men's ankles, but still they marched at the same cracking pace behind a cavalry vanguard that, late in the morning, rode into a small town where a Federal band was practicing in the main street. The band belonged to a regiment that had gone on a daylong route march, leaving their musicians to entertain the sullen Virginian townspeople. Those sullen people cheered up as the band fell slowly silent. The music ended with one last astonished and froglike grunt of a sax-horn tuba as the musicians realized that the horsemen in the street were pointing guns straight at their heads. The bandsmen had been assured that they were at least twenty miles from any enemy forces, yet now they were faced by a gray-coated pack of grinning men on dusty, sweat-foamed horses. "Let's hear you play Dixie, boys," the cavalry leader ordered. Some of the bandsmen began to edge backward, but the cavalry officer cocked his rifle one-handed and the bandmaster hastily turned around, raised his hands to ready the musicians, and then led them in a ragged rendition of the rebel anthem.

In the middle of the afternoon, with the musicians now silent prisoners under guard, General Jackson's column struck southeast on a wide road that passed through harvested fields and plundered orchards. The men could guess where they were going now, for ahead of them was a great moving plume of smoke that showed where the Orange and Alexandria Railroad carried the Northern army's supplies south to the Yankee troops. Every bullet, every cartridge, every slab of hardtack, every percussion cap, every shell, every pair of boots, every bayonet, every small and large thing that an army needed to fight was being carried down that single track, and Jackson's leading infantry was now within earshot of the wailing, whippoorwill cadence of the locomotives' whistles. They could even hear the distant and rhythmic clatter of car wheels crossing the rail joints.

The trains were running out from Manassas Junction, which lay only a few miles to the north. For a time Jackson had been tempted by the thought of marching directly on the Junction, but it seemed inconceivable that the largest Federal supply base in Virginia would not be guarded by earthworks and guns and regiments of prime infantry, so instead the General planned to cut the railroad at Bristoe

Station, which lay just four miles south of the depot. Local people said that Bristoe Station was guarded by a mere handful of cavalry and only three companies of Northern infantry.

Dusk was falling as the leading rebel infantry breasted a slight rise and started down the long slope to Bristoe. Rebel cavalry had ridden ahead of the infantry, but those horsemen were nowhere in sight, and all the leading infantry could see were the twin rails gleaming empty in the day's dying light and a scatter of clapboard houses from which kitchen smoke trickled skyward. The small garrison had no idea that danger threatened. A Northern cavalryman, stripped to the waist and with his suspenders dangling, carried a canvas pail of water from a well to a horse trough. Another man played a fiddle, assiduously practicing the same phrase over and over again. Men smoked pipes in the small warm breeze or read hometown newspapers in the last light of the setting sun. A few men saw the infantry on the western road, but they assumed the approaching soldiers must be Federal troops. The infantry's flags were flying, but the sinking sun was huge and red behind the rebel column, and so the Yankees could make out no details of the approaching banners or uniforms.

The leading rebel regiment was from Louisiana. Its Colonel gave the order for his men to put percussion caps on the cones of their loaded rifles. Till now they had marched with their guns unprimed in case a stumbling man set off a cartridge and so alerted the enemy. "I guess we arrived here before the cavalry," the Colonel said to his adjutant as he scraped his sword clear of its scabbard.

The sound of the steel on its scabbard's throat seemed to release the village to hell. For just as the Colonel pulled his sword into the sun's scarlet light, so the hidden rebel horsemen launched their charge from a belt of trees north of the settlement. Bugles ripped the sky and hooves pounded the earth as a screaming line of rebel cavalry broke from cover and stormed down on the village.

The man with the pail of water stood frozen for a second. Then he dropped the pail and ran toward a house. Halfway there he changed his mind and ran back toward his tethered horse. More Northerners mounted up and, abandoning everything except their weapons, fled eastward. A few of the Yankee horsemen were too late and were trapped in the small village as the rebel cavalry thundered into the single street. A Northerner wheeled his horse and cut with his saber, but before his stroke was half completed, a Southern blade was in his belly. The Southerner rode on, dragging his saber free from the clinging flesh.

Rifles crashed and smoked from the houses where the Northern infantry had taken cover. A horse and man went down, their blood splashing together across the dusty road. The Southern cavalry fired back with revolvers until their Colonel shouted at them to forget the sheltering infantry and capture the rail depot instead.

Another volley splintered from the houses, and a horseman was snatched back from the saddle. His comrades spurred on to the depot, where scattered groups of Northern infantry gathered under the water tower and alongside the fuel bunkers where the pine logs were stacked. The largest group of Yankees rallied around the green-painted shed where a terrified telegrapher was sheltering under the table rather than sending a message. The man was still cowering with his head in his arms when the victorious Southern horsemen scattered the infantry and threw open the shed's door and ordered the telegrapher out. "I ain't done nothing!" the telegrapher called desperately. He had been too frightened to send any message, so that no Northerner yet knew that the army's vital rail line was severed.

"Come on, Billy!" The horseman pulled the telegrapher

out into the dusk, where the victorious Southern horsemen were chasing the last of the Northern garrison out into the fields.

Behind them a cheer sounded as the Louisiana infantry swept into Bristoe's single street. A volley of shots crashed and splintered into a house where a group of Yankee infantry still tried to defy the attackers, but then the village's other defenders began to call out their surrender. The Louisiana men ran from house to house, yanking blue-coated soldiers out into the street. One last stubborn Yankee fired at the attackers from a shed behind a general store and received a full company volley for his pains, and then the firing in the village died away. A few shots still sounded in the field beyond the railroad, but otherwise the fighting had ended, and Stonewall Jackson had hooked clean behind John Pope and cut his eighty thousand men off from their supplies.

It was a feat that had been achieved by just twenty-four thousand men, who, on bloodied feet and with aching muscles and dry mouths and empty bellies, now marched into Bristoe. It was a summer's evening, and the light was fading into a warm soft darkness. They had marched more than fifty miles across country to sever the Yankees' supply line, and soon, Jackson knew, the stung Northerners would turn on him like fiends. Which was exactly what Lee wanted the Northerners to do. Lee wanted Pope's army to abandon its well-dug earthworks behind the Rappahannock's steep northern bank, and Jackson's job was to lure them out. Jackson's men were now the bait: twenty-four thousand vulnerable men isolated among a sea of Northern troops.

Which all added up, Jackson reckoned, to the probability of a pretty rare fight.

To the south of the depot a train whistle offered its mournful sound to the falling night. Smoke misted the sky;

then a locomotive's lamp appeared around a bend to glimmer its shivering reflections on rails that had begun to quiver from the thunder of the approaching wheels. The train, unsuspecting, steamed north to where a rebel army and a Yankee nightmare waited.

THE LEGION MARCHED INTO BRISTOE just as the train rounded the bend south of the depot. The doors of the locomotive's firebox were open so that the flames were reflecting bright on the underside of the long, rolling plume of smoke. The train was traveling so slowly that Starbuck's first thought was that it planned to make a stop at the depot; then a fountain of sparks whirled from the tall stack as the locomotive accelerated. There was just enough light remaining in the day for the engineer to have seen troops milling about the station, and, suspecting trouble, he pulled his whistle cord in warning and threw the regulator hard across to put all the locomotive's power into the great driving wheels. The reflected glow of the furnace disappeared as the firebox doors were slammed shut. The locomotive was hauling a light load: just two sleeper cars showing red flags to denote they were carrying wounded men, a passenger car that was routed through to Alexandria, and a mixture of unladen gondolas and boxcars that would be unhitched in Manassas Junction to be loaded with guns and ammunition for the next day's southward run.

There was a disorganized flurry of activity in the depot as rebel infantry seized whatever obstacles lay close to the track and hurled them across the rails. The most substantial blockage was formed from a pile of ties and rails that had been stacked ready for repair work and that were now hurriedly thrown into the locomotive's path.

The whistle sounded again. The bell was clanging incessantly, a tocsin of alarm in the darkness, while the rails were shaking with the weight of the approaching train. "Get back! Get back!" officers shouted, and the rebel soldiers scurried away from the tracks that were now bright with the reflected light cast by the locomotive's huge kerosene lamp. The windows of the passenger car flickered washes of yellow light over the fuel bunkers and water tower. Two rebels dropped a last length of rail over the track, then scrambled for their lives as the train thundered into the depot. The gilded and scarlet-painted locomotive plowed through the smaller barricades, splintered a heap of barrels and fence rails, scattered a cord of firewood as though the pine logs were mere twigs; then the engine flashed through the lamplit depot with its pistons pounding and its tall stack churning out a torrent of spark-ridden smoke. The engineer hauled on the whistle's chain as the kerosene lamp illuminated the ominous barricade of steel rails and massive timber ties that lay just beyond the depot. The train was still accelerating. Watching rebels held their breath in anticipation of spectacular disaster, then cheered as the locomotive's wooden cowcatcher struck the barrier, but the heavy barricade simply disintegrated in the face of the speeding train. There was a cascade of sparks from the front wheels, a tumbling of wooden baulks and clanging rails, a crash as the locomotive's lantern shattered into scraps of glass and metal, then the defiant whistle sounded once again as the train buffaloed its way through the remnants of the makeshift barrier and sped on northeast toward Manassas.

Passengers had peered anxiously out of the car windows as the train swayed and rattled through the depot, but the faces vanished when a handful of rebel soldiers opened fire. A bullet clanged off the locomotive, another severed a steam line, while a dozen windows in the hospital and passenger cars were shattered. Most of the bullets were fired at the boxcars, which the rebels fondly imagined contained a fortune in plunder that was being denied them. The train, safe through the obstacles, was sounding its whistle continually as a warning to the Federal troops ahead, though to the rebels the whistle sounded more like a mocking call of victory. The locomotive rumbled over the bridge that crossed the Broad Run stream just north of the depot, then disappeared into woods, and the caboose's twin red lanterns were the last things the rebels saw as the train hurried away. Men began firing at those lamps until officers shouted at them to cease fire.

The rumble of the rails died, then, mysteriously, swelled again. A staff officer had ridden a hundred yards south to where a small hillock offered a view, and now he cupped his hands and shouted back to the station. "Another train coming!"

"Pull up the track!" a second staff officer ordered. Just north of the depot, where the rails ran on top of an embankment toward the stream, an officer had discovered the trunklike box where the repair crews kept their tools, and suddenly the embankment was swarming with men carrying sledgehammers and crowbars.

The second train was still a mile away, but its rhythmic noise swelled drumlike in the night as the first lengths of rail were lifted and thrown aside. The work became more effective as it was organized; some troops were detailed to knock aside the chairs that held the rails to the ties, while others heaved the loosened rails off the track and down the embankment's slopes. Staff officers ordered the men not employed in lifting rails to hold their fire so that the approaching train would not be warned of danger.

"You'll get a passel of them through now," an elderly

315

civilian observed to Starbuck. The Legion's help was not needed to destroy the line, so its men were standing in the village street, from where they hoped to get a prime view of the destruction. "They run 'em up empty this time of evening," the old man went on. "Then they start hauling 'em back again all night and day. One-way traffic, see? Empty this way, full that. You boys come far?"

"Far enough."

"Right glad to see you. Yankees are too high and mighty for my taste." The old man grinned as the new train sounded its whistle to warn the depot of its approach. "That first one'll be pulling into Manassas right now. Guess those Northern boys there will be pissing themselves with worry. They told us we'd never see you boys again! Leastwise not till they marched you through as prisoners."

The locomotive whistle sounded again. Men scattered away from the embankment as staff officers cleared the milling soldiers from the depot so that the engineer of the approaching train would not be alerted to his danger by the sight of a waiting crowd. The locomotive thudded into sight. It was hauling a train of boxcars that rattled and swayed under the moonlit smoke.

Starbuck looked down at the old fellow who had spoken to him. "Are you saying that first train will be in Manassas by now?" he asked.

"It's only an hour's walk that way." The old man pointed northeast. "Train does it in ten minutes!"

Ten minutes, Starbuck thought. He was that close to where Galloway's Horse had its lair? My God, he thought, but what pleasure there would be in doing to Galloway's house what Galloway's men had done to McComb's Tavern. Then he pushed that apprehension of revenge aside as the train thundered into the village. "Hold your fire!" an officer shouted from somewhere down the line. "Hold your fire!"

Starbuck saw some of his own men level their rifles. "No firing!" he shouted: "Guns down!"

But the target was irresistible. The men nearest Starbuck lowered their guns, but a score of others fired, and suddenly the whole village crackled with rifle fire. On board the locomotive the fireman's first reaction was to jump to the tender and haul on the hand brake, and for a second there was a shower of sparks from the protesting machinery, but then the engineer realized his danger and shouted for the brakes to be released as he poured more steam into the driving wheels. The train lurched forward with gouts of steam hissing from a score of bullet holes that surrounded the locomotive with a lamplit halo of vapor through which the boxcars were dragged toward the embankment.

The engineer ducked to shelter from the rifle fire and so never saw the missing track ahead of his train. His locomotive was still accelerating as it plowed off the end of the rails. For a few seconds the whole train kept going in a straight line as dirt and stones spewed in a dark wave beneath the locomotive's churning wheels, but then the boxcars began to concertina and tumble, and the locomotive rolled slowly over, spilling fire as it slid down the embankment. The boxcars piled into a heap of twisted frames and shattered planks. Jackson's men cheered as the destruction continued, and still cheered as the commotion ended. The engine had stopped a few yards short of the bridge over Broad Run, while, fifty yards behind, the last dozen boxcars still stood upright on the undamaged track. The wrecked train had no caboose; instead a pair of red-lensed oil lamps glowed at the back of the last boxcar. Some men began to tear open the undamaged cars, hoping to find Yankee luxuries to replace the stone-hard biscuit, hard green apples, and unripe scavenged corn they had eaten in the last two days. Rightly or wrongly every Southerner believed that no Yankee could go to war without a larder of delicacies on his back, and so the rebels splintered the cars open in hopes of finding a lavish supper, but the wagons were all empty.

A whistle sounded in the dark. "Another train!" The staff officer watching from the hillock to the south of the station shouted the warning.

"Get back! Back!" Officers and sergeants pushed the disappointed plunderers away from the wrecked train, while other men stamped out the fires that had been sparked when the locomotive spilt down the embankment. Cavalry helped clear the scene so that the crew of the oncoming train would suspect nothing.

"Hold your fire this time!" A bearded officer rode along the line of grinning soldiers. "Hold your fire!"

"Son of a bitch won't keep coming with those lights burning." Truslow appeared beside Starbuck and nodded toward the stalled boxcars, where the twin red lamps still glowed to reflect on the steel rails. Truslow waited for someone to realize the fact, but no one seemed to have noticed the lamps, so he took matters into his own hands by running across the strip of waste ground that separated the rail line from the nearest houses. A cavalryman saw the running figure and wheeled his horse to intercept.

"Let him be!" Starbuck shouted.

Truslow reached the train, unhitched his rifle, and swung its brass-hilted butt into the two lanterns. There was a tinkle of glass, and the twin lights vanished just seconds before the new train rocked around the western bend. A hush fell over the watching men as the train steamed past the hillock, clattered over some switchgear that led to an unused siding, vented smoke around the water tower, and then hurtled into the dim yellow light cast from the lanterns hanging in the depot. No one fired a rifle. The engineer leaned from his cab to wave a greeting to anyone who might be in the depot but saw no one and so sounded his whistle instead. The engineer was anticipating the comforts of Manassas, where he and his fireman would cook their supper by grilling two steaks on a greased shovel held in the locomotive's firebox. Afterwards they would play cards and drink some liquor in the engineer's shed before hauling a heavy train of ammunition south in the early morning. Both men were professional Pennsylvanian trainmen who had volunteered to serve in the U.S. Military Railroad, where the money was good, the liquor plentiful, the whores cheap, and the danger, they told each other constantly, pretty much minimal.

The engineer was still thinking of shovel-grilled steaks as his locomotive struck the remnants of the first train. The cowcatcher lifted up the rearmost boxcar, catapulting the vehicle high enough to scrape along the top of the boiler and shear the lamp, smokestack, steam dome, and bell clean off the locomotive. The impact of the third train collapsed the remaining cars of the second; then the deadweight of the moving boxcars piled into the crash and drove the locomotive deeper into the wreckage. The wheels finally jumped the rails, and the locomotive slid sideways to a halt. There was a passenger car behind the tender, and screams sounded from the chaos as the boxcars crashed in behind. The last boxcars stopped upright in the depot itself, while deep among the wreckage at the front of the train a fierce fire started to burn. On either side of the track, well out of danger's range, men were whooping with joy.

"Another train!" the staff officer called from the hillock, and once again a whistle sounded from the darkness.

"We'll do this all night!" Truslow was unusually animated. There was a brute joy in such freedom from all the customary and careful regulations of normal life.

A squad ran to the depot to extinguish the rear lamps of

the stalled train. Other men doused the depot's own lights so that the oncoming train would not glimpse the boxcars standing among the buildings. Deep among the burning wreckage smoke hissed from the locomotive. Men were trying to extricate the crew and passengers as well as extinguish the fires as the fourth train of the night rocked into sight with its lantern flaring yellow-white in the ever-blackening darkness.

"Come on, you son of a bitch!" Truslow growled.

But instead of a third crash there was a scream of brakes as the engineer scented trouble ahead. Maybe it was the darkened depot, or perhaps it was the unextinguished fires that still flickered in the wreckage, but something made the engineer apply his brakes. The wheels locked to skid down the rails through a fountain of flowing sparks. The locomotive stopped just short of the hillock, and the engineer rammed it into reverse gear and released the steam. Smoke poured from the stack as the machinery labored to push the great train backward. The staff officer on the hillock dragged his revolver free and spurred toward the locomotive that was now spinning its wheels. The officer's horse reared away from a jet of steam; then the wheels began to bite and the tons of steel and iron and wood began to crawl away southward. The staff officer fired at the cab and shouted at the engineer to halt, but the engineer kept the regulator fully open, and the protesting cars gathered speed and the rhythm of the locomotive became faster and faster as the train backed safely away. The staff officer fired again, but the train was now moving quicker than his horse could gallop, and so he abandoned the chase and just watched as the train disappeared into the dark with its whistle screaming shrilly.

It was clear no more trains would come this night, and so Jackson ordered his men back into the depot. There was work to do. The survivors had to be brought out of the two wrecked trains, the bridge north of the village had to be destroyed, and the prisoners had to be interrogated. The lanterns in the depot were lit once more, and the General paced up and down beneath their feeble light as he gave his orders.

The survivors of the train wrecks were brought to the depot. Confederate surgeons worked on the wounded while food and water were fetched from the houses. One Northerner, a burly and white-haired civilian dressed in an expensive suit and with a seal-hung gold watch chain stretched across his ample vest, heaved himself onto an elbow to stare across the track at the rebel officers in the depot. The civilian had a new bandage around his head and a splint on his left leg. He stared for a long time, seemingly unable to take his eyes from the skinny, bearded, unkempt, and plain-uniformed man who snapped his orders in a high-pitched voice. The Northerner finally beckoned one of the rebel soldiers to his side. "Son, who is that?"

"That's Stonewall, sir," the soldier said, and then, seeing that the civilian was weak and in pain, he knelt and supported the man's head. "That's Old Jack, sir, large as life."

The wounded man stared at the ragged figure who carried no insignia of rank and whose headgear was nothing but a cadet's shabby cap. The Northerner was a bureaucrat from Washington who was returning from a visit to discuss General Pope's supply problems. He was a man accustomed to the high, imperious style of officers like John Pope or George McClellan, which was why he found it so hard to believe that this unprepossessing figure with its tangled beard and threadbare coat and torn boots was the bogeyman who gave waking nightmares to the whole United States Army. "Are you sure that's Jackson, son?" the bureaucrat asked.

"I'm sure, sir, dead sure. That's him."

The civilian shook his head sadly. "Oh, my God," he said, "just lay me down." A gust of laughter echoed from the nearby soldiers.

Jackson, across the tracks, frowned at the laughter. The General was listening to a brigadier who was assuring him that the Yankees had tons of ammunition, a treasure-house of equipment, and a cornucopia of food stuffed into the warehouses at Manassas Junction. "But they ain't got nothing more than a corporal's guard to watch over it all," the brigadier asserted, "and by morning, General, they'll have a ton of boys out of Washington to keep us at bay. And the sons of bitches, excuse my language, General, are only four miles away. Let me take my two regiments, General, and I'll give you Manassas by dawn."

"With just two regiments?" Jackson asked skeptically.

"With my two regiments, General, I could take hell by storm, let alone a supply depot." The brigadier paused. "You want to talk to the man?" He jerked his head toward the captured engineer who had revealed just how small was the garrison and great the prize at Manassas Junction.

Jackson shook his head, then paused a second. "Go," he finally said, "go."

Because the night was still young, and the mischief merely beginning.

The Reverend Elial Starbuck had been an impatient passenger on the first train that left Warrenton Junction for the North. The rails were supposedly clear, yet even so the train made miserably slow progress. In New England, as the preacher proudly informed his traveling companions, the rails were capable of continuous high-speed travel, but he supposed army railroad management combined with Southern construction techniques had rendered the Orange and Alexandria Road incapable of matching the unsurpassed efficiency of the Boston and Albany. "Sixty miles an hour is not unusual in New England," the Reverend Starbuck declared.

A civilian engineer spat into a cuspidor and declared that a coal-burning locomotive of the Illinois Central had been timed at over seventy miles an hour. "Long way from New England, too," he added pointedly.

"Doubtless it was going downhill," the preacher responded, "or perhaps the timing watch was manufactured in Richmond!" He was pleased with that riposte and could not resist laughing aloud. Night was falling, glossing the car's windows with reflected lamplight. The preacher settled the bundled rebel flag more comfortably on his lap and tried to see some detail of the countryside, but just as he put his face to the glass, the train gave a sudden jerk and began to speed up.

The engineer pulled out his watch. "Just ten minutes to Manassas Junction," he said. The rhythm of the steam engine quickened as the car rattled faster and faster over the jointed rails to shake the brass cuspidors and vibrate the gas-jet flames behind their misted lamp globes. "I suppose you'd call this a snail's pace in New England, Reverend?" the engineer called across the car. The lanterns of a depot flashed by in the half-darkness; then, just as the Reverend Starbuck was about to respond to the engineer's taunt, the window beside him collapsed in a shower of broken glass. For a terrifying few seconds the preacher was certain the train was derailed and crashing. Eternity seemed suddenly imminent; then he heard men whooping outside, and there was the alarming sight of gray uniforms and a heart-stopping glimpse of rifle flames flashing in the dark. The train gave a violent lurch, but somehow kept going. A woman passenger screamed in fear.

"Keep down!" an artillery officer shouted from the front

of the car. Another window was smashed and a bullet ripped into the stuffing of the empty seat opposite the preacher, but then the train was running free into the welcome darkness beyond the depot. The wheels thundered over a bridge as the locomotive's whistle and bell sounded their warning.

"Is anyone hurt?" the artillery officer called as passengers' heads cautiously surfaced above the seat backs. The rush of air through the broken windows guttered the lamp flames and scattered the pages of a newspaper along the central aisle. "Anyone hurt?" the officer demanded again. "Sing out now!"

"By God's grace, no," the Reverend Starbuck answered as he shook spicules of broken glass from the folds of the flag. He was still picking the scraps from the precious silk as the wounded locomotive panted and groaned into Manassas Junction.

"All off now!" an imperious voice commanded the passengers. "Everyone off! Bring your luggage! Everyone off!" The ambushed car had been bound for the Alexandria depot, hard across the river from Washington, and the Reverend Starbuck had been looking forward to an early departure from the capital on the cars of the Baltimore and Ohio. At Baltimore he planned to take a horse-drawn tram across town to the depot of the Philadelphia, Wilmington, and Baltimore Road, where he would find a car bound for New York. Once in New York he would abandon the railroads for a cabin on one of the fast and comfortable Boston steamships, but now it seemed his journey was again to be delayed. "Take your luggage, folks!" the man ordering everyone off the train called.

The Reverend Starbuck's carpetbag was now considerably heavier than when he had first come south. It was true that he had distributed all his abolitionist tracts, but in their place he had gathered some valued souvenirs of battle. None, to be sure, was as precious as the great silken banner, but nevertheless he had discovered some objects with which he expected to excite Boston's curiosity. Packed in his carpetbag were two gray rebel caps, one with a bullet hole and the other satisfyingly stained with blood, a zinc plug from an unexploded shell, a revolver with a barrel shattered by a cannonball, the knucklebone of a dead rebel, and a rusting belt buckle with the initials CSA stamped clearly on its face. The heaviest of his souvenirs were copies of Southern newspapers: ill-printed on crudely made paper and containing editorials of an evil that even the Reverend Doctor Starbuck found breathtaking. It all added up to a considerable weight that he lugged off the train before accosting the young Captain who had so peremptorily ordered the passengers off the car. "You're preparing another train?" the preacher demanded.

"For what?" the Captain retorted, turning around from the open window of the telegraph office.

"For Washington, of course!"

"For Washington? My God, uncle, you'll be lucky! Don't suppose anything will move now till first light. If there are bushwhackers at Bristoe then God knows where else they might be."

"I have to be in Washington by morning!" the preacher protested.

"You can walk," the Captain said rudely. "It isn't a step more than twenty-five miles, but there won't be any more trains tonight, uncle. And in the morning I daresay they'll be sending troops down from Washington." He paused. "I guess you can wait for one of those trains to go back? But this train isn't moving anyplace, not till it's been in the workshops for repairs." He turned back to the telegrapher. "What do they say?"

The telegrapher eased back from his machinery, which

was still stuttering tinnily. "They want to know how many raiders, sir."

"Well?" the Captain demanded of the train's engineer, who was standing behind the telegraphers. "How many bushwhackers did you see?"

"Two or three hundred?" the engineer suggested uneasily.

The Reverend Elial Starbuck cleared his throat. "They were not bushwhackers," he said sternly, "but rebel soldiers. I saw them clearly."

The Captain gave the elderly minister a tired look. "If they were troops, uncle, they'd have cut the telegraph. But they haven't, which makes me think they're amateurs. But we've told the army what's happening, so there's no need to worry."

"They've cut the wire now, sir," the telegrapher broke in. "Just this second, sir." He jiggled his key, but nothing came back. "Line's still open to Alexandria, but everything's dead to the south of us, sir."

"So what are we to do?" one of the dispossessed travelers demanded plaintively.

The Captain grimaced. "You might get rooms at Micklewhite's Tavern here, but if Mick's full you'll have to leg it into Manassas town. It's not far up the track, or there's a road beyond the wagon park."

If the Reverend Elial had wanted rest and shelter, he would have used Major Galloway's house, which lay not far beyond the town, but he had no mind for creature comforts this night. Instead, with his ebony cane clutched firmly in his right hand, and with the flag and carpetbag clasped awkwardly in his left, he set out in search of some officer who might pay him more attention than the glib young Captain. The depot itself hardly encouraged his hopes, for it consisted of nothing but great, dark buildings hastily thrown up on the foundations of the warehouses burned by the rebels when

326

they had abandoned the depot earlier in the year, while here and there among the dark monstrosities a sentry's brazier fought the night with a small red glow. Between the huge warehouses were weed-strewn rail spurs where more materials were stored in boxcars and where long, low gondola cars carried brand-new field guns. The moon silvered the cannons' long barrels, and the Reverend Starbuck wondered why the guns were here instead of pounding the rebels into submission. The war, he decided, was being prosecuted by half-wits.

He left the warehouses behind and stumped through a wagon park toward the lights of the nearby town. A lesser man than the Reverend Elial Starbuck might have hesitated before entering the town's main street, for the place was raucous with drunks. Most of the drinkers were railmen, but there were plenty of black folk among them, and the sight of the Negroes angered the Reverend Starbuck. Where, he wondered, were the missions? And where the Christian teachers? The town had been declared an official refuge for escaped slaves, but by the evidence before his eyes it seemed that the Negroes would have been better off in servitude than being thus exposed to debauchery, uncleanness, and liquor. There would need to be changes!

He asked a soldier where the commander of the garrison might be found and was directed to a guardroom attached to the post office. A lieutenant scrambled to his feet as the Reverend Starbuck entered, then answered the preacher's query by saying that Captain Craig was absent. "He's gone to look to our defenses, sir. It seems there are bandits on the rail line south, sir."

"More than bandits, Lieutenant. The raiders are rebel troops. I saw them with my own eyes. Infantry, definitely rebel infantry. I saw the same scum at Cedar Mountain, so I know of what I speak."

"I'll make sure Captain Craig hears what you have to say, sir." The Lieutenant spoke respectfully, though he was privately dubious about the preacher's report. There had been rumors of rebel raiders near Manassas every night for the last two weeks, but none of the rumors had proved true, and the Lieutenant doubted whether a minister of the gospel could tell the difference between rebel soldiers and bushwhackers, especially as even the best-dressed rebels looked little better than cutthroat outlaws. "But not to worry, sir," the Lieutenant continued, "Captain Craig ordered our artillery and cavalry to deploy, and he put all our infantry on alert." The Lieutenant decided it might be wiser not to add that there were only eight cannon in the defenses, aided by a mere hundred cavalrymen and a single company of infantry. Manassas was supposed to be a safe posting, as safe as garrison duty in Maine or California. "I don't think our sleep will be disturbed, sir," the Lieutenant said soothingly.

The Reverend Starbuck was pleasantly surprised to discover that at least one officer seemed to have performed his proper duty this night. "Captain Craig? Is that his name?" The Reverend Starbuck had taken out his diary and was now penciling a note. "He's done well, Lieutenant, and I like to report commendable behavior when I encounter it."

"His name is Captain Samuel Craig, sir, of the 105th Pennsylvania," the Lieutenant said, wondering just how important this authoritative minister was. "You report to the government, perhaps, sir?"

"I report to the greatest government that ever ruled on this earth, Lieutenant, or on any other," the Reverend Starbuck said as he finished writing his note.

"Then maybe you'd like to add my name, sir?" the Lieutenant said eagerly. "It's Gilray, Lieutenant Ethan Gilray of the Provost Guard. Just the one L, sir, and thank you for asking." Gilray waited as the minister penciled his name. "And will you be wanting quarters for the night, sir? There's a Mrs. Moss in Main Street, a most Christian woman who keeps a very clean house. For a Virginian."

The Reverend Starbuck closed his diary. "I shall wait in the passenger depot, Lieutenant." Much as he was tempted by a clean bed, he dared not miss the chance of a northbound train, yet before he returned to the depot he still had one Christian obligation to discharge. "The Provost Guard is responsible, is it not, for discipline?" the Reverend Starbuck asked.

"Indeed it is, sir."

"Then I shall have no alternative but to report you for the grossest dereliction of duty, Lieutenant, a duty that is Christian before it is military. There are Negroes in town, Lieutenant Gilray, who have been permitted access to inebriating liquor. Would a loving parent put ardent spirits in the way of his children? Of course he would not! Yet the Negroes came to Manassas on just such a promise of protection, a promise made by our government that you, as that government's representative, have broken by allowing them to fall prey to the temptation of strong drink. It is a disgrace, sir, a shameful disgrace, and I shall make certain that our authorities in Washington are made fully aware of it. Good day to you." The Reverend Starbuck left the speechless Gilray and went back into the night. He felt better for that discharge of his duty, for he was a fervent believer that each man, every day, should leave the world a better place than he found it.

He walked back through the town, listening to the drunken songs and seeing the scarlet women who lifted their skirts in the stinking alleys. He fended a drunk off with his cane. Somewhere in the dark a dog whined, a child cried, a man vomited, and a woman screamed, and the sad sounds made the Reverend Starbuck reflect on how much sin was souring God's good world. Satan, he thought, was much abroad in these dark days, and he began to plan a sermon that likened the Christian life to a military campaign. Maybe, he thought, there was more than a sermon in that idea, but a whole book, and that pleasant thought kept him company as he strode down the moonlit road toward the depot. Such a book would be timely, he decided, and might even earn him enough to add a new scullery to the house on Walnut Street.

He had already planned his chapter headings and was beginning to anticipate the book's adulatory notices when suddenly, shockingly, the sky ahead of him flashed red as a cannon fired. The sound wave crashed past him just as a second cannon belched flame that briefly illuminated a rolling cloud of gunsmoke; then the Reverend Starbuck heard the chilling and ululating sound that he had mistaken at Cedar Mountain for Aristophanes' *paean*. He stopped, knowing now how the devil's noise denoted a rebel attack, and he watched in disgust as a scatter of blue-coated soldiers fled from the depot's shadows. Northern cavalrymen were galloping between the dark buildings, and fleeing infantrymen were running along the rail lines. The Reverend Starbuck listened as the rebels' foul *paean* turned into cheers, and then, to his chagrin, he saw gray coats in the moonlight and knew that the devil was scoring yet another terrible victory in this summer's night. A brazier was tipped over, causing fire to flare bright between two warehouses, and in the sudden flamelight the Reverend Starbuck saw the satanic banner of the Southern rebels coming toward him. He gaped in horror, then thought of the greater horror of being captured by such fiends, and so he hid the captured flag under his coat and, stick and bag in hand, turned and fled. He would seek shelter in Galloway's house, where, hidden from this rampaging and seemingly unstoppable enemy, he would pray for a miracle.

The Legion marched at dawn. They were hungry and tired, but their steps were lightened by rumors that the warehouses at Manassas had been captured and that all the hungry men in the world could be fed from their contents.

Starbuck had last seen the Manassas depot wreathed in smoke when the Confederates had destroyed the junction. The Legion, indeed, had been the very last rebel infantry regiment to abandon Manassas, leaving the warehouses nothing but ashes, yet as the depot came into view, Starbuck saw that the great spread of buildings was now more extensive than ever. The Northern government had not just replaced the burned warehouses but had added new ones and built fresh rail spurs for the hundreds of freight wagons that waited to be hauled south, but even those new facilities were not enough to hold all the Northern supplies, and so thousands of tons of food and materiel had to be stored in hooded wagons parked wheel-to-wheel in the fields beyond the warehouses.

A staff officer spurred back down the marching column. "Go get your rations, boys! It's all yours. A present from Uncle Abe. All yours!"

The men, invigorated by the thought of plunder, quickened their pace. "Slow down!" Starbuck shouted as the leading companies began to break away from the rest. "Major Medlicott!"

The commander of A Company turned in his saddle and offered Starbuck a lugubrious expression.

"We'll take the end warehouse!" Starbuck pointed to the easternmost part of the depot, which was still clear of rebel troops. He feared the chaos that would result if his regiment was scattered among a score of warehouses and mixed with revelers from a dozen other brigades. "Captain Truslow!" he shouted toward the rear of the column. "I'm relying on you to find ammunition! Lieutenant Howes! I want pickets around the warehouse! Keep our men inside! Coffman? I want you to find some local people and discover where the Galloway farm is."

Yet for the moment there was no time to consider revenge on Galloway's Horse, only to plunge into the stacks of boxes and barrels and crates that were piled in the vast, dim warehouse and inside the adjacent boxcars and wagons. It was a hoard that the hard-pressed Confederate army could only dream of possessing. There were uniforms, rifles, ammunition, haversacks, belts, blankets, tents, saddles, boots, bridles, percussion caps, gum rubber groundsheets, picket pins, telegraph wire, signal flags, and lucifer matches. There were candles, lanterns, camp furniture, drums, sheet music, Bibles, buckets, oilcloth capes, jars of quinine, bottles of camphor, folding flagpoles, bugles, replacement pay books, friction fuses, and artillery shells. There were spades, axes, augurs, saws, bayonets, cooking pots, sabers, swords, and canteens.

Then there was food. Not just army-issue hardtack in boxes and desiccated soup in canvas bags, but luxuries from the wagons of the Northern army's sutlers, who made their money by selling delicacies to the troops. There were barrels of dried oysters and casks of pickles, cakes of white sugar, boxes of loose tea, slabs of salt beef, sacks of rice, cans of fruit, sides of bacon, jars of peaches, combs of honey, bottles of catsup, and flasks of powdered lemon. Best of all there was coffee, real coffee; ready-sweetened coffee, baked, ground, mixed with sugar and packed into sacks. There were also bottles of liquor: rum and brandy, champagne and wine, cases and cases of wine and spirits packed in sawdust and all disappearing fast into thirsty men's haversacks. A few conscientious officers fired revolvers into the cases of liquor in an effort to keep their men from drunkenness, but there were simply too many bottles for the precaution to be of any effect.

"Lobster salad, sir!" Private Hunt, his dirty face smeared from ear to ear with a pink confection, offered Starbuck a knife blade loaded with the delicacy from a newly opened can. "Came from a sutler's wagon."

"You'll make yourself sick, Hunt," Starbuck said.

"I hope so, sir," Hunt said. Starbuck tried the proffered salad and found it delicious.

Starbuck wandered in a daze from one store bay to the next. The supplies seemed to have been stacked without any system, but just crammed into the warehouse in whatever order they had arrived from the North. There were cartridges from Britain, tinned food from France, and salt cod from Portugal. There was lamp oil from Nantucket, cheese from Vermont, and dried apples from New York. There was kerosene, medical sulfur, calcined magnesia, sugar of lead, and laxatives made of powdered rhubarb. There was so much material that if two armies the size of Jackson's force had plundered the depot for a month, they could not have opened every box or explored every dusty stack of crates.

"What you can't carry away, we'll have to burn," a staff officer called to Starbuck, "so search it well!" and the Legion, like small boys released to a toyshop, splintered open the crates and whooped with glee at every fresh discovery. Patrick Hogan of C Company was distributing officers' shoulder boards, while Cyrus Matthews was cramming his face with a nauseating mix of dried apple and chipped beef. One man had discovered a cabin trunk that seemed to contain nothing but chess sets, and he was now disgustedly scattering knights, rooks, and bishops as he dug down in search of greater treasures. Bandmaster Little had found a box of sheet music, while Robert Decker, one of the best men in Truslow's company, had discovered a cased match rifle, precision-made for a marksman and equipped with a barrel-length telescopic sight, a hair trigger, a separate cocking trigger, and a small pair of legs at the barrel's muzzle to support the weapon's huge weight. "It'll kill a mule at five hundred paces, sir!" Decker boasted to Starbuck.

"It'll be heavy to carry, Bob," Starbuck warned him.

"But it'll even things against the sharpshooters, sir," Decker answered. Every rebel hated the Yankee sharpshooters, who were lethally equipped with similar long-range target rifles.

Captain Truslow had commandeered two brand-new seven-ton wagons that both carried small brass plates proclaiming them to be the products of Levergood's Carriage Factory of Pittsburgh, Pennsylvania. There were boxes attached to the wagon sides that were filled with repair tools, lanterns, and cans of axle grease, and Truslow, always reluctant to concede that anything could be well made in the hated North, nevertheless admitted that the Levergood's Company built a half-decent vehicle. The two gray-painted wagons would replace the old ammunition carts burned in Galloway's raid, and Truslow had his men busy stacking the wagon beds with boxes of rifle ammunition and crates of percussion caps. The draught horses were fitted with brand-new collars, hames, and traces, then backed into the shafts.

Captain Pine's men were distributing boots, while Lieutenant Patterson's company was handing out sacks of coffee. Captain Davies's company was employed in taking down the barn doors from a warehouse; the doors were needed as ramps so that a Georgian artillery battery could maneuver some brand-new Northern cannons off their gondola cars. The Georgians were presently equipped with Napoleon twelve-pounders that were, in their commander's word, "tired," but now they would be armed with a half-dozen Parrott twenty-pound rifles so new that the packing grease from the foundry was still sticky on their barrels. The artillerymen wrecked the wheels and spiked the vents of their old guns, then dragged away their new weapons, each of which displayed a neatly stenciled legend on its trail: PROPERTY OF THE USA.

Colonel Swynyard watched the plunder from horseback. He had helped himself to a brand-new saddle and was sucking on a strip of beef jerky. "Sixteen men," he said gnomically to Starbuck.

"Sir?"

"That's all we lost to straggling. Out of the whole Brigade! And most of them will turn up, I don't doubt. Some other brigades lost hundreds." Swynyard grimaced as the strip of beef aggravated a sore tooth. "I don't suppose you came across any false teeth, did you?"

"No, sir, but I'll keep a lookout."

"I think I'll have Doc Billy take all mine out. They're nothing but trouble. I confess, Starbuck, that my new faith in Almighty God is shaken by the existence of teeth. Do your teeth hurt?"

"One does."

"You probably smoke too much," Swynyard said. "Tobacco smoke might be good for keeping the lungs open, but I've long believed that the juice of the weed rots the teeth." He frowned, not for the thought of tobacco juice, but because a train whistle had sounded in the warm morning wind. Swynyard gazed toward the northern horizon, where a billow of smoke showed above distant trees. "We've got company, I guess," Swynyard said.

The thought of Northerners reminded Starbuck that Stonewall Jackson would not have marched fifty miles in two days just to replenish his army's stock of ammunition and food. "Does anyone know what's happening?" Starbuck asked the perennial soldier's question.

"I'm told that General Jackson is not given to confiding in his inferiors," Swynyard said, "or in his superiors either, for that matter, so I can only guess, and my guess is that we've been sent here as bait."

"Bait." Starbuck repeated the word flatly. It did not sound good.

"I'm guessing that we've been sent up here to pull the Yankees out of their defenses on the Rappahannock," Swynyard said, then paused to watch a soldier shake loose yards and yards of mosquito netting, "which could mean that in a few hours we'll have every blessed Yankee in Virginia trying to kill us." He finished, then stared northward to where a brisk rattle of rifle fire had sounded. The volley was followed by the heavier sound of artillery. "Someone's getting thumped," Swynyard said with a bloodthirsty relish, then twisted in his saddle to watch a sad procession come into sight beside the warehouse. A group of rebel soldiers were escorting a long line of black men and women, some crying but most walking with a stiff dignity. "Escaped slaves," Swynyard explained curtly.

A woman tried to break away from the column but was shoved back into place by a soldier. Starbuck counted almost two hundred of the slaves, who were now ordered to form a line close beside a captured portable forge. "What they should have done," Swynyard said, "is keep running north of the Potomac."

"Why didn't they?"

"Because the Yankees declared Manassas a safe refuge for contrabands. They want to keep the darkies down here, you see, south of the Mason-Dixon line. It's one thing to preach emancipation, but quite another to have them living in your street, ain't that the case?"

"I don't know, sir." Starbuck grimaced as he saw a leather-aproned blacksmith test the heat of the forge's furnace. The portable forge was a traveling blacksmith's shop mounted on the back of a heavy wagon that could travel with the army and shoe horses or provide instant repairs to broken metal. The smith dragged a length of chain out of a barrel, and Starbuck immediately understood what was about to happen to the recaptured slaves.

"So how many blacks live in your father's street?" Swynyard demanded.

"None, except for a couple of servants."

"And has your father ever had a black at his dinner table?"

"Not that I know of," Starbuck said. A hammer clanged on the anvil. The smith was fashioning manacles out of barrel hoops, then brazing the open manacles onto the chain. Heat shimmered over the small open furnace, which was being fanned by two soldiers pumping a leather bellows. Every minute or so a recaptured slave was forced to the forge to have one of the newly made manacles closed around an ankle. A huge-bellied captain with a bristling black beard was supervising the operation, cuffing the slaves if they showed any resistance and boasting how they would suffer now they had been recaptured. "What happens to them?" Starbuck asked.

"You can never trust a black that's run away," Swynyard said, speaking with the authority of a man born into one of Virginia's oldest slave-trading families. "It don't matter how valuable he is, he's been spoilt for good if he's tasted a bit of liberty, so they'll all get sold down the river."

"Women too?"

The Colonel nodded. "Women too. And children."

"So they'll all be dead in a year?"

"Unless they're real lucky," Swynyard said, "and die sooner." Being sold down the river meant going to the sweated chain gangs on the cotton plantations of the deep South. Swynyard looked away. "I guess my two boys had the good sense to keep on running. They ain't here, anyway, I looked for them." He paused as the gunfire to the north reached a crackling crescendo. Powder smoke was whitening the sky, indicating that a skirmish of some severity was taking place, but the fact that no staff officers were demanding reinforcements from the troops rifling the depot suggested that the enemy was well in hand. "Right now," Swynyard said, "I'd guess that we've just got a few odds and ends coming to attack us. The real attack won't hit till tomorrow."

"Something to look forward to," Starbuck said dryly. The Colonel grinned and rode on, leaving Starbuck to stroll among his happy men. There was no grumbling now about missing a chance to join the Richmond garrison; instead the Legion was reveling in its chance of loot. Captain Moxey had found some frilled shirts and was pulling them on one above another to save himself the trouble of cramming them into a haversack already stuffed with tins of chicken in aspic. Sergeant Major Tolliver had unpacked a whole case of long-barreled Whitney revolvers and was attempting to stow as many as possible in his clothing, while Lieutenant Coffman had discovered a handsome black cloak edged with blue silk braid that he swirled dramatically around his body. At least two men were already blind drunk.

Starbuck dragged one of the drunken men off a case marked "Massachusetts Arms Co. Chicopee Falls." The man groaned and protested, but Starbuck snarled at him to shut up, then levered the case open to find a shipment of Adams .36-caliber revolvers. The guns, with their blued barrels and cross-hatched black-walnut grips, looked deadly and beautiful. Starbuck discarded the clumsier long-barreled Colt he had taken from a dead New Yorker at Gaines Mill and helped himself to one of the new revolvers. He was just loading the last of the Adams's five chambers when a chorus of shouts erupted from further down the warehouse. Starbuck turned to see an excited mob of his men chasing an agile black figure, who swerved around an astonished Coffman, leaped over an opened crate of canteens, and would have got clean away had not the drunk beside Starbuck reached out an oblivious hand that inadvertently tripped the fugitive. The boy—he was hardly more than a boy—sprawled in the mud, where he was pounced on by his cheering pursuers.

"Bring the bastard here!" Major Medlicott strode down the warehouse carrying a teamster's whip.

The prisoner yelped as Abram Trent cuffed him around the head. "Goddamned nigger thief!" Trent had the boy by one ear and was hitting him with his free hand. "Thieving black bastard."

"Enough!" Starbuck pushed a man aside. "Let go of him."

"He's a thieving—"

"I said let go of him!"

Trent reluctantly let go of the boy's ear, but not without giving the captured fugitive a last savage blow. The boy staggered but managed to stay on his feet. He looked around for an escape, realized he was trapped, and so adopted a defiant air. He had a thin face, long black hair, a straight nose, and high cheekbones. He was dressed in a sailor's bell-bottom pants and a billowing striped shirt that gave him an exotic look. Starbuck had once spent a few weeks with a traveling troupe of actors, and there was something in the boy's flamboyance that reminded him of those distant times. "What's your name?" Starbuck asked him.

The boy looked up at his savior, but instead of showing gratitude, he spat. "Ain't got a name."

"What's your name?" Starbuck insisted again, but only received a truculent glare for answer.

Medlicott pushed through the ring of men. "Stay out of this, Starbuck!" he said, raising the whip against the black lad.

Starbuck stepped in front of Major Medlicott. He kept a smile on his face as he put his mouth close to Medlicott's right ear, and he kept smiling as he spoke softly, so softly that only Medlicott could hear him. "Listen, you lily-livered son of a bitch, you give me orders one more time and I'll pistol-whip you down to corporal." Starbuck was still smiling as he stepped a pace backward. "Don't you agree that's the best way to proceed, Major?"

Medlicott was not certain at first that he had heard right and just blinked at Starbuck. Then he took a backward pace and flicked the whip toward the captured boy. "He stole my watch," Medlicott said. "The little black bastard lifted it out of my pocket when I laid my coat down. It was a present from my wife, too," he added indignantly, "from Edna!"

Starbuck looked at the boy. "Give the Major his watch."

"Don't have it."

Starbuck sighed and stepped forward. The boy tried to twist aside, but Starbuck was too quick for him. He grabbed a handful of long dirty hair and held the squirming boy still. "Search him, Coffman," he said.

Lieutenant Coffman nervously began searching the boy's pockets. At first he found nothing; then it became apparent that the pants pockets had been elongated into long, capacious, sausage-shaped sacks specially strengthened to hold and conceal plunder, and the men watched in amazement as the evidence of the boy's thefts was dragged into the light. Coffman produced two hunter watches, a gilt picture frame, a collapsible silver cup, a folding mirror, two razors, a brass match case, a carved pipe, a signet ring, an ivory-handled shaving brush, a comb, a pack of cards, and a handful of coins. The men stared in awe at the hoard. "Oh, my God," one of them said, "just lay me down," and a bellow of laughter swept through the crowd.

Coffman stepped away from the boy. "That's all, sir," he said.

"They're all my property!" the boy insisted, trying to retrieve one of the watches, and the ring of men laughed and cheered at his insolence. They had been baying for his blood just a minute before, but there was something irresistible about the young man's unrepentant face and impressive haul of thefts.

Medlicott retrieved his watch. "He's a goddamn thief. He should be whipped."

"But I thought we were all thieves today," Starbuck said, and he was about to kick the boy on his way when a stentorian voice shouted from outside the ring of Legionnaires.

"Hold on to that nigger!" the voice shouted, and the men slowly parted to make way for the big, bearded Captain who had been supervising the manacling of the recaptured slaves. "Another damn runaway," the man said, reaching for the boy.

"I'm a free man!" the boy insisted.

"And I'm Abraham Lincoln," the Captain said as he grabbed the boy's striped shirt. He cuffed the long black hair aside and displayed one of the boy's earlobes to Starbuck. "Took his earring out, didn't he? First thing a runaway does, take off the earring." Earrings denoted slave status. "So if you're free, lad," the Captain went on, "why don't you show us your papers?"

The boy plainly had no papers. For a second or two he looked defiant; then he was overwhelmed by despair and tried to twist out of the Captain's grip. The Captain slapped him hard around the head. "You'll be picking cotton now, lad."

"He belongs to me," Starbuck said suddenly. He had not intended to speak, and certainly he had never intended to claim ownership of the boy, but there was something appealing about the young man's spirit that reminded Starbuck of his own desperate attempts to remake himself in an image of his own devising, and he knew that if he did not speak up, then the boy would be hammered and burned into the chains and then sold down the river to the living hell of the cotton plantations.

The Captain gave Starbuck a long, hard look, then spat a viscous brown stream of tobacco juice. "Out my way, boy."

"You call me 'sir,'" Starbuck said, "or I'll have you arrested and charged for rank insubordination. Now, boy, get the hell out of my regiment."

The Captain laughed at Starbuck's presumption, then twitched the fugitive slave toward the forge. Starbuck kicked the man hard between the legs, then rammed a flat palm into the bearded face. The Captain let go of the escaped slave and staggered backward. He was in terrible pain, but he succeeded in keeping his footing and was just starting forward with his fists clenched when there was the unmistakable click of a gun being cocked. "You heard the Major," Truslow's voice said, "so git."

The Captain put a hand to his face to wipe blood away from his mustache. He looked askance at Starbuck, wondering if the youngster really was a major, then decided that anything might be true in wartime. He pointed a blood-smeared finger at the cowering boy. "He's a contraband. The law says he's got to be returned—"

"You heard the Captain," Starbuck said, "so git."

Starbuck waited till the man had gone, then turned and took hold of the boy's ear. "Come here, you son of a bitch," he said, dragging the boy away from the crowd and into the warehouse, where he threw the lad hard onto a pile of grain sacks. "Listen, you little bastard, I've just saved you from a whipping, and better still, I've just saved you from being sold down the river. So what's your name?"

The boy rubbed his ear. "You really a major?"

"No, I'm the goddamn archangel Gabriel. Who are you?"

"Whoever I want to be," the boy said defiantly. Starbuck guessed he was fourteen or fifteen, an urchin who had learned to live by his wits.

"So who do you want to be?" Starbuck asked.

The boy was surprised by the question, but he thought about it, then grinned and shrugged. "Lucifer," he said at last.

"You can't be Lucifer," Starbuck said, shocked, "that's the devil's name!"

"Only name I'm giving you, master," the boy insisted.

Starbuck guessed that was true, so he settled for the satanic name. "So listen to me, Lucifer, my name's Major Starbuck, and I need a servant real bad and you just got the job. Are you hearing me?"

"Yes, sir." There was something cheeky and mocking in the response.

"And I need a comb, a toothbrush, field glasses, a razor that'll hold an edge, and something to eat other than hardtack and shoe leather. Are you hearing me?"

"I got ears, master! See?" Lucifer insolently plucked back his long ringlets. "One on each side, see?"

"So you go and get those things, Lucifer," Starbuck said. "I don't care how, and you be back here within the hour. Can you cook?"

The boy pretended to think about the question, drawing out his silence just beyond the edge of rudeness. "Sure, I can cook."

"Good. So get whatever you need for cooking utensils." Starbuck stood aside. "And bring me as many cigars as you can carry."

The boy sauntered into the sunlit doorway, where he stopped, plucked his disarrayed clothing into shape, then turned to look at Starbuck. "Suppose I don't come back?"

"Just make sure you aren't sent down the river, Lucifer."

The boy stared at Starbuck, then nodded at the wisdom of that advice. "Are you making me into a soldier?" he asked.

"I'm making you my cook."

The boy grinned. "How much are you paying me, Major?"

"I just saved your worthless life and that's all the wages you're getting from me."

"You mean I'm your slave?" The boy sounded disgusted.

"I mean you're a goddamn servant to the best goddamn officer in this goddamn army, so get the goddamn out of here and stop wasting my goddamn time before I goddamn kick you out."

The boy grinned. "Do I get a goddamn gun?"

"You don't need a gun," Starbuck said.

"In case I have to protect myself from the Yankees who want to make me into a free man," Lucifer said, then laughed. "Can't be a soldier without a gun."

"You ain't a soldier," Starbuck said. "You're a cook."

"You said I can be whatever I want to be," the boy said, "remember?" Then he ran off.

"That's one nigger you won't see again," Truslow said from just outside the door.

"I don't really want to see him again."

"Then you shouldn't have risked a fight for him," Truslow said. "That Captain would have murdered you."

"So thank you," Starbuck said.

"I didn't run him off to save your good looks," Truslow said sarcastically, "but because it don't do the boys no good to see their Major having the shit thumped out of him. You want a pickled oyster?" He held out a jar of the delicacies;

344

then, as Starbuck helped himself, Truslow turned and watched as a disconsolate herd of blue-coated prisoners limped past. The men were smartly uniformed but looked utterly whipped. Some of their heads showed livid saber slashes, wounds that had cut so deep that the blood had soaked their tunics down to their waists. The Northerners limped past, going to their long imprisonment, and Truslow grinned. "Just ain't their day, is it?" he said. "Just ain't their goddamn day."

Colonel Patrick Lassan of His French Majesty's Imperial Guard, who was officially a foreign military observer attached to the rebel army but who preferred to do his observing from the front ranks of the rebel cavalry, took a handful of his horse's mane and slowly drew his long straight sword through the coarse hair to scrub the blade clean of blood. He needed to clean the steel three times before it was fit to slide back into the scabbard; then, lighting a cigar, he trotted slowly back along the path of the cavalry charge.

A brigade of New Jersey troops had come from the defenses of Washington to evict what they believed was a band of rebel cavalry raiders from the depot at Manassas Junction. Only instead of encountering a handful of ragged cavalrymen, they had marched straight into the depot's old defensive earthworks manned by Stonewall Jackson's veteran infantry and artillery. Whipped by rifle fire and flayed by cannons, the New Jerseymen had retreated. It was then that Jackson had unleashed the cavalry, who had turned their retreat into a rout.

Dazed Northerners still reeled blindly about the field where the horsemen had charged. The Northerners were mostly wounded in the head or shoulders, the bloody wounds of men caught in the open by cavalrymen carrying sabers. Their comrades were either lying dead where the volleys of the entrenched defenders had ambushed them, or else were struggling to safety across the rain-swollen Bull Run, where, a year before, so many of their countrymen had drowned in the defeat of the first invasion of the Confederate States of America.

Lassan watched the rebels round up the living and loot the dead. The Confederates were joking about the ease of their victory, claiming it was further proof that a half-dozen Northerners were no match for a single Southerner, but Lassan was both more experienced and more sanguine and knew that the attack of the New Jersey brigade had been a blunder by an inexperienced general. The New Jersey officers had been so new to war that they had attacked with drawn swords, oblivious that they were thus making themselves targets for Southern marksmen. The Northern officers had led their men to horror, but Lassan knew that this slaughter of the innocents was an aberration and that soon the real fighting would begin. The North had been surprised by Jackson's march, but it would not be long before the Yankee veterans arrived to snap at the bait that hung so temptingly at Manassas Junction. For the North now had Stonewall Jackson outnumbered, they had him isolated, and, so they must surely believe, they had him doomed.

ALL DAY THE YANKEES tried to make sense of the storm that had broken behind their backs. The first confused reports merely spoke of bushwhackers, then it was claimed the raiding party was a large band of Jeb Stuart's horsemen, and finally there were worrying reports of rebel infantry and artillery inside the defenses of Manassas Junction, but no one could tell John Pope precisely what was happening at his supply depot. He knew that no trains were coming from Manassas and that the telegraph to Washington had been cut, but neither of these events was uncommon, and for much of the day Pope regarded all reports from Manassas as mere alarmist rumors spread by panicking men frightened by a handful of Confederate cavalry raiders. John Pope was unwilling to abandon his conviction that Lee must do what John Pope had planned for Lee to do, which was to launch a grand yet suicidal attack across the swirling Rappahannock, but slowly, grudgingly, like a man refusing to admit that the heavy clouds above his parade had begun to rain, Pope began to understand that the commotion at Manassas amounted to a great deal more than a raid. It was the opening move of a campaign he had not planned to fight but to which he was now forced to react.

"We'll be riding north tonight, you mark my words," Major Galloway observed. "Did you hear me, Adam?" But Adam Faulconer was not listening to his commanding officer. Instead he was staring at a recent copy of the *Richmond*

Examiner that had been exchanged for a *New York Times* by one of the Northern pickets, then brought to John Pope's headquarters, where Major Galloway and Adam had been peremptorily summoned. The Major had scanned the ill-printed sheets, snorted in disgust at the editor's secessionist distortions, then relinquished the rag to Adam. Now Galloway was kicking his heels in the hallway and waiting while a succession of flustered aides carried maps into the parlor, where the General was trying to comprehend the day's events.

"Did you read this?" Adam suddenly demanded of Galloway.

Galloway did not need to be told what item in the newspaper had offended Adam. "I read it," the Major said, "but I don't necessarily believe it."

"Five women dead!" Adam protested.

"It's a rebel newspaper," Galloway pointed out.

The story was headlined "Outrage in Orange County." Yankee raiders, the newspaper reported, seeking to emulate the exploits of Jeb Stuart, had crossed the Rapidan to raid Lee's forces, but had instead burned down a country tavern and killed everyone inside. There was no mention of the raid on the Faulconer Brigade, nor of the guns and wagons that Galloway's men had destroyed, but only a pitiful description of the innocent civilians dying inside the inferno that had engulfed what the newspaper described as "McComb's Hotel," presumably because a goodly number of the *Examiner*'s readers might well approve of taverns being destroyed, even if their destroyers were the hated Yankees. Hotels, on the other hand, were not necessarily the devil's way stations, and so Liam McComb's establishment had been appropriately elevated. "The reader can only imagine the terror of the women as they beseeched their attackers to spare their lives," the *Examiner* trumpeted, and a paragraph later, "It seems Northern cavaliers can be brave enough when their foes are women and children, but they display nothing but clean heels and horses' tails when faced by Southern soldiers."

"They're beating the patriotic drum," Galloway said wearily, "by telling half-truths and outright lies. There were soldiers in that so-called hotel, Adam, even the newspaper admits as much."

"And it says here, sir, that those soldiers called on the enemy to cease fire."

"What else would it say?" Galloway asked, and then, in grudging acknowledgment of Adam's anger, he went on, "When Billy gets back we'll ask him the truth."

"And you think he'll tell you the truth?" Adam asked hotly.

Galloway sighed. "I think maybe Billy has an excess of zeal, Adam, but I don't reckon Billy murdered any woman that night. I ain't saying no woman died, but only that it was an accident. Tragedy happens in wartime, Adam. It's why we're trying to end the war quickly."

Adam threw the newspaper down in disgust. His disgust was not so much with the *Examiner* but with Galloway's refusal to face the truth that Billy Blythe was a man who used warfare as an excuse for criminality. Blythe even boasted about using the war as a means of enrichment, and the more Adam reflected on Blythe the angrier he became, so that he was forced to calm himself down by taking a deep breath. He listened to the angry voices coming from the General's parlor, and it struck him that war was a dreadful instrument that stirred a whole society into turmoil, bringing the worst to the top and driving the best down.

Galloway saw the anger on the younger man's face and wondered whether Adam was too tender for war; maybe a man needed Billy Blythe's callous carapace to be a good soldier, yet it was undeniable that it had been Adam and not Blythe who had provided Galloway with his one victory. Galloway now wondered where Blythe was, for his second-in-command had never returned from his patrol into the west. Maybe he had followed the strange column to its destination and would be waiting at Galloway's farm, or maybe, more disastrously, Blythe's troop had been ambushed and cut to pieces by the rebels. Beyond the town a train whistle hooted mournfully, while further away, where the Federal army was dug in on the Rappahannock's northern bank, the thunder of cannon fire rumbled incessantly. The Southern gunners had started an artillery duel that had been raging all day, probably, Galloway now realized, as a means of diverting John Pope from what was happening behind his back.

"When this war's over"—Adam broke his silence after a long pause—"we shall have to live in this community. We shall have to make our peace with neighbors and family, but we'll never have peace if we condone murder." The North's virtue, he wanted to add, lay in its moral rectitude, but the sentiment sounded too pompous for utterance.

Galloway privately doubted whether any Southerner who had fought for the North could ever hope to make a home south of Washington again, but he nodded anyway. "I'll make inquiries, Adam, I promise you," he said, and Adam had to be content with that promise, for suddenly the parlor door was thrown open and John Pope himself strode into the hallway.

The Northern commander checked when he saw the waiting cavalry officers. "You're Galloway, right?"

"Yes, sir."

"A Manassas man, aren't I right?"

"Yes, sir," Galloway acknowledged.

Pope snapped his fingers. "The very man! You're to take

your fellows home, Galloway. Jackson's there. One of our fellows saw the wretch in person and escaped to tell the tale. There's no doubt about it, Jackson's in Manassas, and you know what that means? It means we've got him in the bag! You understand me?" The General was suddenly exultant. He might have been reluctant to accept that his battle lay at Manassas and not across the Rappahannock, but a few hours of reflection had convinced him of the advantages of accepting Jackson's foolhardy challenge. "The damned fool has marched halfway round our army to maroon himself in Manassas, and tomorrow we're going to snap him up! My God, Jeb Stuart might make a fool of George Brinton McClellan by riding clean around his army, but no Stonewall Jackson will march clean round John Pope! No, sir! So, Galloway"—Pope jabbed a finger at the Major—"take your fellows north and find out just where the wretched man is, and report to me when you know. We're going to Bristoe tonight. If you want to put your horses on our train, then come now, hurry!" The commander strode into the street, followed by flustered aides clutching luggage and maps.

"So where's Lee?" Galloway asked faintly, but no one responded, perhaps because no one heard him or perhaps because no one thought the question important. All that mattered was that Stonewall Jackson had marched himself into a trap and that John Pope was about to destroy him once and for all. "We've got the fool in the bag!" Pope boasted as he hurried toward the train he believed would carry him northward to victory. "Right in the bag!"

Lucifer did return. He returned with a leather grip that had been put in store by a Northern officer but that now held Starbuck's new possessions. "Every damn thing you wanted," Lucifer said proudly, "and a silver hairbrush, too. See? Make you look real good. And I got you cigars. Good ones." Lucifer had also discarded his flamboyant clothes and replaced them with a Northern cavalryman's pants over which he was wearing a gray jacket, a leather belt, and a button-flapped holster, yet somehow his natural elegance imbued even that humdrum uniform with flair.

"Is there anything in that holster?" Starbuck demanded.

"I got myself a cooking implement," Lucifer said, "made by Mr. Colt of Hartford in Connecticut."

"You mean you've got a gun," Starbuck said flatly.

"It is not a gun," Lucifer protested. "It is a utensil for killing the food you want me to cook for you, and if I can't have a utensil I can't get meat, and I can't cook the meat I can't get, and you can't eat the meat I can't cook, and then you'll starve and I'll be so hungry I won't even have the strength left to bury you."

Starbuck sighed. "If you're caught with a gun, Lucifer, then someone will take the skin off your back."

"If I have got myself a Colt cooking utensil, Major, then there ain't no son of a stinking bitch alive who can take the skin off any one little part of me."

Starbuck gave in. He sent the boy to find some food but warned him to be ready to leave at any minute. The daylight was fading, its twilight obscured by the myriad of fires that burned among the wagons and boxcars, and Starbuck expected imminent orders to move away from the fiery smoke pillars that were surely serving as beacons to draw every Northern soldier within twenty miles. Not that the rebel army was in a fit state to move; some men snored in alcoholic stupors, while others, gorged with rich food, slept, oblivious of the incendiary parties who went from warehouse to warehouse burning what could not be carried away.

In the last of the light Starbuck shaved himself, using a new mirror and razor that Lucifer had found; then he feasted on pickled oysters and fresh bread and butter. Dark came and there were still no orders to move. Starbuck assumed Jackson had decided to run the risk of spending the night in the captured, burning depot, and so he made himself a bed from a pile of brand-new Northern overcoats, but the softness of the makeshift mattress was disconcertingly comfortable, and so he rolled off the pile onto the familiar dirt. And there slept well.

And woke to inferno.

He opened his eyes to see a sky lancing with red fire and to hear a thunderous roll of monstrous noise filling the night. He started up, reaching for his rifle, while all around him the men of the Legion woke to the same terrifying cacophony. A burning fragment fell from the sky to thump into the dirt beside Starbuck. "What the hell's happening?" Starbuck asked of no one in particular.

Then he realized that the North's great supply of ammunition was being destroyed. Boxcar after boxcar of cartridges, percussion caps, shells, and artillery propellant was being torched. The explosions thumped across the depot, each one flashing a bright illumination that pulsed its brilliance high into the sky. Monstrous flames boiled hundreds of feet into the air, where hissing missiles spat through churning smoke. "Oh, my God," a man said after one particularly sharp and bright explosion, "just lay me down." The phrase, which was spreading throughout Jackson's army, prompted an immediate burst of laughter.

"Major Starbuck! Major Starbuck!" Captain Pryor, now Swynyard's aide, searched among the startled men.

"I'm here!"

"We're to march now."

"What time is it?"

"Midnight, sir. A little after."

Starbuck shouted for Sergeant Major Tolliver. A warehouse crammed with shrapnel disintegrated in flame to make the night momentarily as bright and red as hell's deep at noon. The explosion was followed by a tantalizing smell as barrels of cured bacon caught the flames and fried. A loose horse galloped in terror past a gang of sweating demons who were destroying the last locomotives in the depot by stuffing their fireboxes with gunpowder and mangling the condenser tubes with bullets.

"Ready?" Colonel Swynyard shouted. He was already on horseback, and his gelding's eyes reflected the night's fires like some mythical beast. "March!"

They went north, blindly following the brigade in front and leaving behind a writhing pit of red horror. Explosion after explosion ripped through the burning depot as flames climbed yet higher into the night. The North had labored mightily to amass the supplies necessary to subdue the South, and now all that labor was evaporating into flame, smoke, and ash.

Starbuck's men trudged wearily, burdened by their plunder and hardly refreshed by the few hours of sleep they had snatched at the day's end. Some of the men's heaviest loot was abandoned early, joining the other trophies thrown aside by tired soldiers. In the flickering, unnatural light Starbuck saw a discarded snare drum beside the road, then two swords with chased gilt handles, a pair of post office scales, and a fine saddle. There were piles of food, candlesticks, greatcoats—whatever treasures a man had fancied, taken, then abandoned as his muscles cramped again.

No one knew where they were going, or why. Their progress was slow, and never slower than when it was discovered that the column was on the wrong road and local guides had to be stirred from their beds to guide the heavily laden soldiers across the country toward dark woods. The gun teams were whipped bloody as they hauled their heavy cannon through entangling hedges and across fields of growing wheat.

Lieutenant Coffman, still swathed in his handsome cloak, fell in beside Starbuck. "I found out what you wanted, sir," he said.

Starbuck could not even remember what he had asked Coffman to discover. "So?" he asked.

"It's just off the Sudley road, sir. There's a farm track near the fords and you go north a quarter-mile and there it is. There's meant to be a lime-washed pillar at the gate of the track, though the fellow I spoke to says it needs repainting."

Starbuck frowned down at the young Lieutenant. "What in hell's name are you talking about?"

"The Galloway farm, sir." Coffman sounded aggrieved.

"Yes, of course. Sorry." Yet now the information seemed very trivial. Starbuck would dearly have liked to visit the Galloway farm, but he realized the wish was quixotic in this night of fire and tumult. Jackson was withdrawing from Manassas, so the Legion's revenge on Galloway must wait. "Thank you, Coffman," he said, "and well done," he added, trying to soothe the young man's ruffled feathers.

Just before dawn the Legion stumbled across a road, climbed a hill, and so came to a stretch of deep woods. Behind the soldiers, beyond a fold of night-black land, the depot's fires roared like the stokehold of hell. The glow of the destruction was furnace fierce, and the smoke a gigantic pyre, so that to Starbuck, standing at the wood's edge and looking back, it seemed as though a great section of the earth itself was burning. The fires had been set four hours before, yet still the bright explosions pulsed the night and churned their smoke skyward. Beyond the fire, and dimmed by its brightness, the world's edge just showed the first cold silver line of dawn.

"Back now, back now." A mounted staff officer was

pushing men away from the open meadow and into the cover of the woods. "And no fires! No fires!"

"What's happening?" Starbuck asked.

"Get some rest," the man said, "and stay hidden. And no one's to light a fire unless they want to be burned alive by Old Jack himself."

"We're not marching any further?" Captain Davies asked the staff officer.

"Not for the moment. Just stay in hiding. Get some rest. And no fires!" The staff officer rode on, repeating his message.

Starbuck pulled his men back into the wood. Jackson had come to Manassas, turned the place to hell, and gone to ground.

The Reverend Elial Starbuck hardly slept that night. At times his eyes closed out of sheer weariness, and he would lean his aquiline head against the chair's high back and begin to snore gently, but almost immediately another great explosion would rattle the windows of Major Galloway's parlor, and the preacher would wake with a start to see yet another ball of fire climbing up from the incandescent glow that marked where the great depot was now a furnace. The devil was at his work, the preacher thought grimly, then tried to sleep again. He had decided against using one of the bedrooms in case he needed to make a quick escape from marauding rebels, and so he spent the night in the half-furnished library parlor with his stick, his heavy bag, and his precious flag beside him. The only weapon to hand was Major Galloway's decorative guidon on its lance-tipped staff that the preacher leaned against the chair in the fond hope that its spear point might be useful to skewer a godless rebel.

He had spent the whole of the previous day in the same parlor. His frustrations had twice driven him from the house in search of an escape from the rebel forces, but each time he had glimpsed gray-clad horsemen in the distance and so had scurried back to the dubious safety of the farm. Before the preacher's arrival there had been a guard of four cavalry troopers in residence, their job to protect Galloway's depot against the depredations of the Major's sullen Southern neighbors, but the men had fled when Jackson's troops had arrived. The farm's three black servants had stayed, and they had fed the preacher and prayed with him, but none of the servants was convinced by the Reverend Starbuck's optimism that John Pope would surely come to punish the men who had dared put Manassas to the torch.

The preacher did manage to sleep a little toward dawn. He lay slumped in the wing chair with the rebel banner clasped to his lean belly until a final massive explosion woke him to the wan light of early morning. He felt stiff and cold and tired as he climbed to his feet. From the parlor window he could see an enormous pillar of smoke climbing heavenward, but he could see no enemy cavalrymen in rat gray coats disturbing the landscape.

It seemed too early to expect breakfast, and so, leaving his luggage in the house and taking only his cane and the precious flag, he ventured timidly into the morning. There was dew on the grass and mist in the folds of land. Two white-tailed deer bounded away from him and crashed through a thicket. Just to the north he could see the glint of the Bull Run through a gap between trees, but he could still see no soldiers. He walked past the servants' cabins to the end of Galloway's yard and searched for enemies, but all that moved in the pearl gray landscape was the pillar of smoke churning from the depot. There was a sense of lonely desolation in the landscape, almost as though the preacher was the last man left on earth. He walked slowly up the farm path, ever watchful, but he saw nothing that threatened him, and when he reached the road, he turned to his left and climbed to the crest of the gentle rise so he could see across the long valley that lay to the east. There was still no enemy in sight. The fields were stripped of livestock, the farms seemed deserted, and the land lay barren.

He walked on. He kept meaning to turn back to the farm and roust the servants to their morning duties in the kitchen, yet curiosity kept him walking just a few paces more, and every few paces he would determine to go just a little bit further still, until at last he decided he would explore as far as the crest at the valley's far side, and if he had still seen no sign of the enemy, then he would return to the farm, take his breakfast, and carry his luggage northward. So resolved, he walked doggedly on, following the pillar of smoke as Moses had followed the pillar of cloud across the wilderness. He climbed the valley's eastern side, following, though he did not know it, the course of the first Northern attack in the battle that had opened the fighting in Virginia and passing, though he would not have wanted to know it, the place where his son had first stood in the rebel battle line. This was the ground where the North's first invasion of the South had been turned back, and the fields on either side of the road still showed white where fragments of bones had been unearthed from shallow graves by scavenging animals. Someone had placed a skull atop a tree stump at the entrance to a farm road, and the macabre face grinned yellow teeth at the preacher as he passed by.

He reached the wooded crest. He had now walked a mile from Galloway's farm, and in front of him he could see the Warrenton Turnpike running empty through a valley, while, on the valley's far side, at the crest of a steep green hill, the ruins of a burned-out house stood gaunt and black against the great smear of dirty smoke that hideously obscured the dawn. The house had been destroyed in the battle fought across these Manassas fields a year before, but the preacher assumed the dwelling had been burned by the rebels on the previous day. It did not occur to him that a Southern army would hardly torch a Virginia farm; he simply saw new evidence of the devil's work and knew it had to be the responsibility of the forces of Slavocracy. "Barbarians!" he said aloud into the empty country. "Barbarians!"

Something thumped on the road behind, and the preacher turned to see the grinning skull had been tipped from its tree stump and was now rolling across the road. Beyond the skull was a horseman holding a rifle that was aimed straight at the Reverend Starbuck. To his surprise the preacher discovered he was not really frightened at thus facing one of the devils who had scourged this land. "Barbarian!" the preacher shouted angrily, waving his stick at the horseman. "Heathen!"

"Doctor Starbuck?" the horseman responded politely. "Is it you, sir?"

The preacher gaped at the cavalryman. "Major Galloway?"

"You're hardly the person I expected to meet here, sir," Major Galloway said as he spurred toward the preacher. A whole troop of horsemen followed the Major from the trees as Galloway explained to the Reverend Starbuck how he and his men had taken a train north to Bristoe during the previous night and were now trying to establish the whereabouts of Stonewall Jackson's army.

"I haven't seen any rebels this morning," the preacher said, and he told how he had spent the night at Galloway's farm. He confirmed that the property was unscathed and reported that although he had seen a handful of Southern horsemen the day before, he had seen none in this dawn. "They appear to have vanished," the Reverend Starbuck said darkly, as though the rebels possessed satanic powers.

"So has Captain Blythe," Galloway said, "unless, perhaps, he's at the farm?"

"Alas, no."

"I'm sure he'll turn up in his own good time," Galloway said wanly, then turned in his saddle and called on Adam to bring one of the spare horses for the preacher's convenience. "We were on our way to the farm," Galloway told the Reverend, "and after that we're ordered to search the country north of the Bull Run."

"I was hoping to go north," the preacher announced. "I have to reach Washington."

"I'm not sure you've much hope of doing that today, sir," Galloway said respectfully. "There's some evidence that Jackson took his troops north. Maybe they're planning to attack the Centreville defenses? He might have vanished, but he's certainly not far away." The Major peered round the empty landscape as though he half expected the rebels to appear like stage villains springing from a trapdoor.

"I can't tarry here!" the preacher protested vigorously. "I have a church to administer, responsibilities I cannot escape!"

"You'll certainly be safer here, sir," Galloway suggested calmly, "seeing as how General Pope's here now and the rest of his army is on its way." He leaned out of his saddle to hold the spare horse while the preacher clambered into its saddle. The rebel flag almost fell from the Reverend Starbuck's grip, but he managed to hold on to the bundled silk as he settled himself on the horse's back. A trooper handed up the preacher's stick, then gave him the reins. "In fact if you do stay here, sir," Major Galloway went on, "I reckon you might even see a scrap of history being made."

"History! I have been promised nothing but history all month, Major! I was promised a pulpit in Richmond, but for all those fine promises I might just as well have planned on preaching God's word in Japan!"

"But the rebels have blundered now, sir," Galloway explained patiently, "leastwise, General Pope reckons they have. Jackson's stranded here, sir, miles from his own lines, and General Pope plans to cut him off and destroy him. That's why Pope's here, sir. We're going to finish Jackson once and for all."

"You really think Pope can do that, Major?" The preacher's question was caustic.

Galloway's reply was emollient. "I reckon General Pope means to try, sir, and none of us really know just what the General can do in battle. I mean he was pretty successful in the west, sir, but he ain't fought here, and that was why he was brought to Virginia, so I guess he might astonish us all yet. Yes, sir, I reckon we might see a fair battle before the day's out, and I even reckon we might win it, too."

The prospect tempted the Reverend Starbuck. He had come to Virginia with such high hopes and had seen those hopes crumble to nothing, but now it seemed there was a chance of victory after all. Besides, it was now Thursday morning, and he knew he could never reach Boston in time for Sunday worship, which meant he might just as well stay here and see the North's nemesis beaten in battle. And what a fine subject for a sermon that would make, he thought. Like Satan plunging into the abyss, Jackson would be brought low, and the Reverend Starbuck would be a witness to the demon's shattering fall. He nodded assent. He would stay and fight.

All day long Jackson's troops waited in the woods. Most slept like the dead, so that Starbuck, setting his sentries just inside the tree line, could hear the murmur of the sleeping army like a swarm of bees. Twenty-four thousand rebel soldiers were snoring not six miles from Manassas, yet the Northern army was oblivious of their presence.

Lucifer brought Starbuck an early dinner of cold pork, apples, and walnuts. "Still eating off the Yankees," he explained the luxury foodstuffs; then he squatted beside Starbuck and stared down the hill toward the empty turnpike in search of Yankees. There were none in sight. "So where are the black folks' friends?" Lucifer asked.

"God knows. Let's hope they don't find us." The sun was low in the sky, and with any luck night would fall before the enemy found Jackson's hiding place.

"You don't want to fight?" Lucifer asked sarcastically.

"I don't want to die."

"You won't die. You were born under a lucky star. Like me. I can tell."

Starbuck scoffed at the boy's confidence. "And I tell you, Lucifer, that just about every poor son of a bitch who's died in this war thought he was too lucky to get killed."

"But I really am lucky," Lucifer insisted, "and you'd better be just as lucky as me, because you know what I was hearing back there among the other humble servant folk? That there are men in this regiment who don't like you."

"I know that," Starbuck said. The pork was tender and the apples fresh. He wondered how long it would be before he was back on hardtack and salted offal.

"But did you know they've written a letter about you?" Lucifer offered a sly sideways glance, then lit himself one of the cigars he had acquired for Starbuck. "The bald fellow wrote the letter, you know? The man you made me give his watch to, Meddlesome, is that his name? And I hear some three or four officers have signed it, and at least forty or fifty soldiers, and they're sending the letter to a congressman. They say you're too young and that you should be sent down the river just as fast as the army can get itself rid of you." The boy grinned, then drew his finger across his throat. "They got nothing but trouble for you, Major."

Starbuck told Lucifer what the letter writers could do with their damned letter. "No one's sending me down the river," he added, "not if I win battles."

"But suppose they don't let you win?" Lucifer asked.

Starbuck acknowledged the question with a deprecating shrug, then stole the boy's cigar. "You know what I've learned about soldiering?"

"To take another man's smoke away?"

"That the worst enemy is never the fellow in the other uniform, that's what." He paused with the cigar halfway to his lips because a sudden fusillade had sounded in the west. The shots were from far away, but they ripped and crackled angrily in the late afternoon. "Here we go again," Starbuck said and sucked on the cigar as his heart lurched. He wondered if fear ever decreased, or whether it got worse and worse until a man could no longer make himself stand upright in battle.

Men woke among the trees and listened uneasily to the sound of firing. All but the newest conscript had learned to judge a fight's intensity from the sound of its guns, and this fight was hard and furious, and so they expected orders that would send them to join in, but no such orders came. The fight continued into the dusk, and no one knew who was fighting or who was winning, only that a skim of powder smoke showed white above the tree line in the west.

Colonel Swynyard finally brought the Legion news. It seemed that a column of Yankee troops had been marching on the turnpike and that Jackson had ordered his own Stonewall Brigade to intercept and destroy the column. "Except the Yankees are too stubborn to run," Swynyard said. "They're standing toe-to-toe and fighting like demons."

"I thought we were supposed to be hiding from the Yankees?" Starbuck said.

"I guess we've hid long enough. Maybe Old Mad Jack reckons it's time to draw the Yankees on to us," Swynyard suggested. He looked up at the darkening sky and grimaced. "Not that they'll come tonight, but tomorrow?" He glanced over at Lucifer, who was crouched beside Starbuck's few possessions. "How's your darkie?" the Colonel asked gruffly.

"He seems willing enough."

"He looks a sly one to me. He's got soft hands, Starbuck, which like as not means he's been someone's house pet. And those pants he was wearing when you found him, the long-pocket ones, they ain't the pants of an honest man. If you want a good slave get yourself a bone-brained field hand who ain't afraid of a bit of work, but your boy looks more like the dangerous type of slave to me."

"What is the dangerous type?"

"The clever type. Not all the darkies have brains like mules, you know. Some of them are real sharp, and my father always reckoned it was the clever ones who needed breaking first. Whip 'em bloody, he'd say, then work them to death because if there's trouble among the people then you can be sure it's the clever ones who started it, so get rid of the clever ones and that way you'll have no trouble. That's the first and last rule of keeping slaves, Starbuck, and you're probably breaking it. I don't suppose it's Christian to beat a darkie without cause, so I won't suggest you do it, but I'd still advise you to send the boy away."

"I won't do that. I like Lucifer," Starbuck said.

"Lucifer? Is that what he calls himself? Dear Lord," Swynyard said, shocked by the name's impiety. "Find out what he's really called, Starbuck. Don't put up with that kind of nonsense! And have him cut his hair off. You don't want a black dandy. And for the Lord's sake take that gun off him! For a start it's illegal, but more important if you encourage him to think he's a cut above the other darkies he'll soon think he's a cut above you. Give a clever slave an inch and he'll take you for everything you've got." The Colonel checked this stream of advice to listen to the firing, which had reached a new intensity, almost as if the two sides were equally desperate to reach a victory before the sun dipped beneath the horizon. "Not our business, thank God. Get some sleep tonight, Starbuck, because I daresay we'll be neck deep in Yankees tomorrow."

The long-haired, gun-toting Lucifer watched the Colonel go. "What did he say about me?" he asked Starbuck.

"He gave me good advice," Starbuck said. "He told me to whip you bloody then work you to death."

Lucifer grinned. "You don't want to do that. I'm your good luck, Major." He turned back toward Swynyard's retreating figure and made a deliberately formal gesture with his clenched right fist, which, at the last moment, he uncurled to let fall a few scraps of fragile bone and powdery white dust.

Starbuck thought he recognized the ribs of a small bird among the litter Lucifer had let drop, but he did not like to ask what the strange gesture meant. He was afraid to know, so instead he looked out from the trees and saw, at last, Yankees. Horsemen were galloping across distant fields, spurring toward the firefight that still crackled in the west. The enemy was gathering like storm clouds heaping. And tomorrow they would fight.

The Reverend Elial Starbuck's hopes, which had plunged so low during the inconveniences of the rail journey, now soared again, and once again it was the acrid smoke of battle that filled him with that fierce exaltation. He had breakfasted with Major Galloway, and afterward, leaving his luggage in the farm, the preacher had ridden to Manassas Junction to see the damage done to the depot and to introduce himself to General Pope's headquarters. The General had been affability itself and had willingly given his permission for the famous preacher to stay with the army, even inviting him to share the headquarters' potluck suppers for the next few nights. Thus honored, the Reverend Starbuck had ridden south to Bristoe to commiserate with his old friend Nathaniel Banks, who had been given the undemanding task of guarding the rail depot. Banks, who still considered his action at Cedar Mountain a victory, complained bitterly about his present duties, but the Reverend Starbuck was in no mood to encourage such backbiting. His spirits were being revived by the arrival of train after train from Warrenton Junction, each train crammed with troops fetched from the Rappahannock defenses. The damage to the rail line north of Bristoe meant that the trains had to disgorge their passengers in the open country, and soon the line of parked locomotives and cars stretched for more than two miles. The men marched in from the fields where they had alighted and boasted that they had come to knock Stonewall down once and for all. The preacher liked their spirit. His own spirits rose even higher when, late in the afternoon, he heard the sound of gunfire coming from the north.

He took his tired horse toward the sound of the guns, passing through quiet fields and deserted woods until at last he came to the valley where the Warrenton Turnpike ran and where a rill of smoke showed where men fought in the valley's bottom. He rode toward the fighting, arriving just as an enemy regiment made an attack on the Yankees' open right flank.

The gray-coated attackers advanced in a line two ranks deep. Their rifles were tipped with bayonets that reflected the dying sun's scarlet light. They came in good order, kicking down a snake fence and then advancing across a pasture. The attack was silent, suggesting that these rebels planned to save their famous yell for the last few yards of their charge. Some rebels were screaming that weird sound off to the preacher's left, but that larger battle seemed stalemated between two opposing lines of riflemen.

The Northerners had seen the threat to their right flank and hurried three regiments to meet it. Two of the regiments were from Wisconsin and the third from New York. The Northerners formed their ranks in a fold of land where they crouched behind a fence. The attackers, oblivious to the number of Yankees facing their charge, began to hurry, and their first shrill yells yipped in the dusk. The defiant sound prompted the Northern line to stand behind their fence and fire a shattering volley across the pasture. The volley's noise ripped over the valley and rolled back. Rifle flames glittered in the failing light, while the layered cloud of powder smoke drifted across the meadow to where the Confederates had been brought to a sudden, astonished halt. The Reverend Starbuck, oblivious of the bullets that whipsawed around his horse, cheered his Northerners on. Their first volley had stopped the rebel attack dead, their second turned it into a bloody mess, and their third began to drive the gray-clad regiment backward. The rebel fire became ever more feeble as the Northern fire increased. One of the rebel's banners toppled, was plucked up, and immediately fell again as the new standard-bearer was thrown back by a dozen bullets. "That's the way to deal with devils, boys!" the Reverend Starbuck shouted. A heaped line of dead and injured men showed where the tide of the Confederate attack had stalled, and now the survivors grudgingly abandoned that writhing, bloody heap as they edged backward. Earlier in the day the preacher had equipped himself with a Colt revolver from among Galloway's stores, and now he remembered the weapon and drew it from his saddle pouch. He fired at the stubborn rebels who, though their line had been broken and bloodied, still tried to return the overwhelming Northern fire.

"By the left oblique! Forward!" a stentorian voice shouted, and the New York regiment swung forward like a gate that threatened to close on the remnants of the rebel attackers.

"Halt!" the New Yorkers' commanding officer called. "Aim!"

The preacher hurried his horse after the advancing New Yorkers.

"Fire!"

The New York volley slashed into the rebels' tattered flank. It was a killing volley, a massive blow that seemed to twitch the surviving rebels bodily backward. Blood misted the evening air as the bullets smacked home. Gray coats were splattered with red, and the field littered with still more dead and dying bodies. A man reeled out of the rebel line, blood pouring from an eye socket. He collapsed to his knees, looking as if he was praying, and the Reverend Starbuck cried in triumph as he fired his revolver at the man.

"Doing God's work?" The New Yorkers' Colonel rode across to the preacher's side.

"'Think not that I am come to send peace on earth: I came not to send peace, but a sword.'" The Reverend Starbuck trumpeted the text, then fired at a rebel who seemed to be giving orders. "Our Lord's own words," he added to the Colonel.

"We're certainly doing His work well this time!" the Colonel shouted over the sound of his men's volleys.

"I pray as much!" The Reverend Starbuck fired his gun's last cylinder and hoped he had slaughtered at least one rebel with his efforts. His wrist hurt from the gun's massive kick. It was a long time since he had fired a gun, and he was not sure he could remember quite how to load a revolver.

"I suppose you wouldn't know where Pope is?" the Colonel asked the preacher.

"I last saw him in Manassas."

"Would you be going back there, sir? And if so, can you take a message?"

"Willingly."

The Colonel scribbled on a page of his notebook. "Lord knows where Jackson's main body is, but it can't be far away. We need to bring everyone here tomorrow morning to flush the mudsill out and finish him off." He tore the page out of his book and handed it to the preacher. "Just like we've finished off these rogues," the Colonel said, gesturing at the rebel regiment that had been beaten back with terrible loss. The field writhed with bodies, while a sorry handful of survivors limped back toward the far woods. "Poor fellows," the Colonel said.

"Poor fellows? The scum of creation!" the preacher averred. "Devils in cretinous shape, Colonel, as even a casual glance at their skull shapes might reveal. They are Southerners: half-witted, morally infantile, and criminal. Don't feel sorry for them. Expend your pity on the Negroes they enslaved."

"Indeed," the New Yorker muttered, taken aback by the vehemence of the preacher's words. "You'll deliver my message to Pope, sir?"

"With pleasure, Colonel, with pleasure," the Reverend Starbuck said, and then, feeling as though he was at last making a real contribution toward the destruction of the Slavocracy, he turned his tired horse and headed back across the hills.

He arrived in the day's last light at the smoking ruins of the depot, where lines of twisted, scorched boxcar frames

369

stood on blackened wheels amidst great drifts of smoking ashes. There was acre upon acre of ruin, of desolation, of destruction. Indeed, to the preacher's heightened senses, there was something biblical in the awful sight, almost as though he witnessed the results of a visitation of God's wrath upon a people who had been lax in their duty. The Reverend Starbuck did not doubt that God could use even the hated Slavocracy to scourge the North for its sins, but the time would surely come when the North would repent, and on that happy day the armies of the godly would inflict a destruction similar to this horror upon all the rebels' habitations and towns and farms. And perhaps, the Reverend Starbuck fervently prayed, that great revival and consequent victory was starting here and now.

He discovered the army's commanding general in a farm just north of the depot. A score of senior officers surrounded Pope; among them and outranked by all of them was Major Galloway, his face coated with dust and his uniform soaked with sweat. Pope snatched at the message the Reverend Starbuck carried. "It's from Wainwright," he announced. The General read the scribbled note quickly and was so pleased by what he read that he slapped the table. "We've got him! We've got him! He's on the Warrenton road, but he's been blocked there. He's trapped. He was at Centreville, now he's retreating toward Warrenton." Pope made a fine, slashing pencil mark on one of the maps that lay on the table.

"I saw no sign of him at Centreville, sir," Galloway said nervously.

"No wonder! The fellow was going backwards!" Pope laughed. "But who minds whether you saw him or not, Galloway? It doesn't matter where he was, but where he is now! And he's right here!" He made another pencil slash, forming a cross on the Warrenton Turnpike at the place

370

where the Reverend Starbuck had seen the rebel attack trounced. "So tomorrow we'll bag the whole crowd!" The General could not hide his elation. For almost a year the North had shuddered at the name of Stonewall Jackson, and tomorrow Pope would end the fear and destroy the bogeyman.

Major Galloway, though outranked by the bearded men around him, stuck to his guns. "But what about the fellows my officer saw at Salem, sir?" He was speaking of Billy Blythe, who had at last reappeared with a convoluted and not wholly convincing story of being chased by Southern horsemen and of being forced to take shelter for two days and nights in a draw of the Blue Ridge Mountains, but however false the tale rang, the final part seemed true enough. Blythe claimed he had returned to the North's lines by following the foothills of the Blue Ridge until he reached the deserted rails of the Manassas Gap Railroad, but that when he had tried to follow that rail line east, he had almost been captured by Southern cavalry pickets who had been guarding an immense column of troops hurrying toward Thoroughfare Gap. Blythe's men had confirmed that part of their Captain's story, and Galloway had brought the grim news to Pope.

"But how reliable is this fellow?" Pope asked Galloway. The Northern General did not want to believe that yet more rebels were marching toward Manassas; he preferred his own theory that Jackson's panicked retreat had been intercepted on the turnpike.

"Captain Blythe is . . ." Galloway began, then could not continue. "Billy can be wild at times, sir," he admitted truthfully, "but his men are telling the same tale."

"And so they should. Men ought to support their officers," Pope said dismissively. "So what exactly did they see?"

"Men approaching the Thoroughfare Gap, sir. Wagons, guns, and infantry."

Pope chuckled. "What your fellows saw, Galloway, was Jackson's supply train slipping off to the west. Stands to reason, Major! If Jackson's retreating this way"—he slashed the pencil from east to west—"then his wagons and guns won't be going in the opposite direction, not unless he's a good deal more stupid than we suppose. No, Major, your fellow saw the rebels retreating, not advancing, and tomorrow we'll turn that retreat into a rout!" His aides murmured agreement. Tomorrow the North would turn the war around. Tomorrow the North would begin the utter destruction of rebellion in Virginia.

Only one of Pope's senior officers demurred. He was an elderly artillery officer wearing the star of a brigadier general on his collar, and he seemed worried enough by Galloway's report to ask whether it was worth running any risks. "If we pull back behind the Centreville defenses, sir, we can wait for McClellan's troops to join us. In a week, sir, with respect, we can overwhelm every rebel in Virginia."

"You want me to retreat?" John Pope asked scathingly. "This army, sir, is far too accustomed to retreat. It has been led by men who know nothing except how to retreat! No, it's time we advanced, time we fought, and time we won."

"Hallelujah!" the Reverend Starbuck interjected.

"But where's Lee?" Galloway asked, but no one had heard the question. General Pope and his staff had gone to their potluck supper, taking the generals and the visiting preacher with them, and leaving Galloway alone.

The fighting died as darkness swamped the turnpike. The North, assuming that Jackson had tried to force his way past them, claimed victory, while Jackson, whose object had been to draw the Northerners into a full attack, kept his silence. The wounded cried in the dark, while all around them, rustling in the night, an army gathered for the kill.

372

AT MANASSAS, ON FRIDAY AUGUST 29, 1862, the first light showed a few moments after half past four. It was a gray wolfish light, at first little more than a cold thinning of the eastern darkness, yet it was sufficient to rouse Jackson's army. The men rolled their blankets and, for the first time since they had left the burning depot, were allowed to light fires. "The sons of bitches know we're here now, so we don't have to hide," Starbuck told his men, then sighed with content as he smelt the wondrous aroma of real coffee being brewed on dozens of fires.

At a quarter past five, a mug of the coffee clasped in his hands, he watched the scenery take shape across the turnpike. There were troops now where there had been none the night before. The brown smear of smoke that still rose from the depot had drawn an army to Manassas, and Starbuck could see lines of bivouacked infantry, parks of guns, and rows of tethered cavalry horses. The enemy, like his own men, were brewing coffee or shaving, while curious Yankee officers trained their field glasses and telescopes toward the silent western woods where the mingling plumes of smoke at last revealed the true extent of Jackson's position.

"We'll fight here, you reckon?" Captain Ethan Davies asked Starbuck. Davies was cleaning his spectacle lenses on the skirt of his coat. "It ain't a bad place to defend," Davies added, hooking the spectacles back onto his ears. The land fell away from the woods toward the turnpike, and Starbuck, like Davies, reckoned it was not a bad place to stand and fight, because the Yankees would have to attack uphill while the rebels would have the concealing woods at their back.

Yet, as the sun rose, Jackson abandoned the position and ordered his army to retreat westward. They did not go far, just a half-mile across untilled fields into another ragged stretch of blackjack oaks, maples, and birch trees. This new wood was interrupted by small patches of rough meadowland and cut by two streams and a railbed that had been graded but never finished with ties and rails. The railbed had been intended to carry a line that would bypass Manassas Junction and so keep the trains of the Manassas Gap Railroad from paying the exorbitant fees required to use the rails of the Orange and Alexandria Railroad, but the investors had run out of cash and abandoned the work, leaving only a smooth, wide, grassy roadway that ran through deep cuttings and along high embankments as it curved, always level, through the undulating woods. It was on the railbed that Jackson stopped with his twenty-four thousand men.

Colonel Swynyard's brigade would defend a stretch of the unfinished railroad that ran through a deep cutting. The eastward-facing bank of the cutting provided a firestep for riflemen, who could, if overwhelmed, retreat across the wide entrenchment into the woods on the western side. A hundred paces behind the cutting the ground rose steeply, though to the right of Swynyard's line, where the Faulconer Legion was posted, that hill faded away so that Starbuck's right-hand companies had no natural barrier behind them, only a flat stretch of young woodland and dense shrub. That change in topography also meant that the cutting became shallow as the railbed rose toward an embankment, while the existence of a deep spoil pit behind the line only made the defense line even more confusing. The spoil pit, only half filled, was where the railroad men had dumped the dirt and rocks they had not needed to build up their embankments.

The spoil pit marked the dividing line between Swynyard's brigade and their neighbors to the south, and Starbuck, once his men were in position, walked to meet those neighbors, a regiment from North Carolina. Their Colonel was a very tall, very thin, very fair-haired man in his early middle age with an elaborately drooping mustache, amused eyes, and a weather-beaten face. He had very long and studiedly old-fashioned hair that flowed past the faded blue collar of his gray frock coat. "Colonel Elijah Hudson," he introduced himself to Starbuck, "of Stanly County, and uncommon proud of it."

"Major Starbuck, of Boston, Massachusetts."

Colonel Hudson pushed back a lock of his curled hair to uncover one ear. "I do believe my hearing has been quite obliterated by the artillery, Major, for I could swear you said Boston."

"So I did, Colonel, so I did, but my boys are all Virginians."

"The good Lord alone knows why you came here from Massachusetts, Major, but I sure am glad to make your acquaintance. Your boys up to hum, are they?"

"I reckon."

"Mine are rogues, each and every one of them. Not a man of them's worth a wooden nickel, but Lord above, how I do love the wretches. Ain't that so, boys?" Colonel Hudson had spoken loud enough for his nearest men to hear, and those men grinned broadly at his words. "And this here Major," Hudson went on to introduce Starbuck to his men, "is a poor lost Northerner fighting for us miserable rebels, but you all be nice to him, boys, because if his lads give way then we'll all be so many dead ducks waiting for John Pope to pluck us. And I don't have a fancy to be plucked by a cleric this day."

Starbuck led Hudson past the spoil pit to the Legion and introduced him to Major Medlicott, explaining that Medlicott not only commanded the company immediately adjacent to the North Carolinians but was also responsible for the whole right wing of the Legion. "Sure pleased to meet you, Major," Hudson said, putting out a hand. "My name's Elijah Hudson and I'm from Stanly County, the best county in all the Carolinas even though my dear wife does come from Catawba County, God bless her, and how are you?"

Medlicott seemed disconcerted by the tall man's friendliness but managed to make a civil response.

"We've got ourselves a killing patch," Hudson said, gesturing across the rail cutting to where the ground ran bare to the closest stretch of woods. It was a killing patch because any Yankees attacking out of the woods would be forced to cross those fifty paces of open land under constant fire. "I can't say it was ever my burning ambition to kill Yankees," Hudson said, "but if the dear good Lord above wants me to do it, then he sure does make it easy in a place like this. Mind you, if the Northern gentlemen do manage to get past the railbed, then we're all going to be in a heap of trouble. If that happens we might as well all pack it in and go back to our jobs. What is your job, Major?" he inquired of Starbuck.

"Soldiering, I guess. I was a student before the war."

"I'm a miller," Medlicott answered to a similar inquiry.

"And what better job could a man have," Hudson asked, "than to grind the Lord's corn into our daily bread? That sure is a privilege, Major, a genuine privilege, and I'm proud to know you for it."

"And your profession, sir?" Starbuck asked the tall Hudson.

"Can't rightly say I've got any profession, Starbuck, other than a love of God and Stanly County. I guess you could say I do a little of everything and a fair heap of nothing, but if I was pushed to the scratch I'd have to confess to being a farmer. Just one of America's toil-laden farmers, but proud as heck of it." Hudson smiled broadly, then offered his hand again to both men. "I guess I should go and make sure my rogues aren't running away out of sheer boredom. I count it a real privilege to fight beside you gentlemen and I wish you much happiness of the day." With a wave of his hand the lanky Hudson strode away.

"A nice fellow," Starbuck said.

"Grasping folk, North Carolinians," Medlicott said dourly. "I never did trust a North Carolinian."

"Well, he's trusting you," Starbuck said tartly, "because if we give way here then he'll be outflanked." He stared at Medlicott's riflemen, who were making themselves comfortable in the shallow stretch of the railbed cutting, then turned to look at the remains of the construction crew's spoil pit, which was now an overgrown hollow stretching for thirty yards behind the makeshift entrenchment. The hollow's stony, overgrown bed could serve as a hidden path into the rear of the rebel defenses. "I guess we ought to barricade the pit," Starbuck said. .

"I don't need you to teach me my business," Medlicott answered.

Starbuck's temper whiplashed uncontrollably. "Listen, you son of a damned bitch," he said, "I ain't losing this damned battle because you don't like me. If the Yankees use that pit to get behind my line I'm going to use your damned skull for regimental target practice. You understanding me?"

Medlicott, unable to compete with the intensity of Starbuck's anger, backed away two paces. "I know how to fight," he said uneasily.

Starbuck resisted the temptation to remind Medlicott of his cowardice at Cedar Mountain. "Then make sure you do fight," he said instead, "and to help you, put an abatis across the pit." An abatis was a barrier of branches that would entangle an attacker and offer a breastwork to a defender. Starbuck saw the hurt in the miller's face and regretted the fierceness of his tone. "I know you don't like me, Medlicott," he said, trying to make amends, "but our quarrel ain't with each other, it's with the Yankees."

"And you're a Yankee," the miller said sullenly.

Starbuck resisted the impulse to tongue-lash the wretched man a second time. "Get your fellows to build the abatis"—he forced himself to speak calmly—"and I'll be back soon to look at it."

"Don't trust me, is that it?"

"I hear you write a good letter," Starbuck said, "but I just don't know how good an abatis you can build." With that parting shot he walked away, blowing the frustration from his lungs in a plume of cigar smoke. He wondered if he should have reversed the Legion's usual order of battle by putting Truslow's men on the right and Medlicott's on the left, but such an act would have been construed as a deep insult to the right-flank companies, and Starbuck wanted to demonstrate to the men of those companies, if not to their officers, how he trusted them. He walked on to the northern end of his line, where Truslow's company was entrenched in the deepest section of the railbed's cutting. On their left was one of the Brigade's small Florida battalions. Truslow had paced the open land in front of the cutting to make certain his men knew the exact range of the woods.

"It's seventy-five yards from here to the timberline," Truslow told Starbuck, "and even a blind son of a bitch can hit a Yankee at seventy-five yards. The bullet will hardly have started to drop." He raised his voice so that the nearest

Floridans could hear him. "Aim straight at the bastards' hearts and at worse you'll puncture their bellies. This is infant-school killing, not the hard stuff." The hard stuff was open-field fighting, where a bullet's long-range trajectory was so pronounced that a shot properly sighted at a man standing three hundred yards away would sail high over the cap of a soldier a hundred paces nearer. Starbuck had seen a full regimental volley fired at a line of skirmishers without a single bullet finding its mark.

There was a constant coming and going of staff officers probing the woods beyond the killing patch to watch for the Yankee advance. Colonel Swynyard made a similar reconnaissance and returned to give Starbuck what news he could. "They ain't advancing yet," he said.

"You think they'll come?"

"If they do what they're supposed to do, yes." He confirmed that the previous evening's action on the turnpike had indeed been designed to draw the Yankees to the attack. "I guess our job is to hold them here while Lee brings up the rest of the army."

Swynyard's mention of Lee was the first mention Starbuck had heard of the army's commander since they had arrived in Manassas. "Where is Lee?" he asked.

"Just the other side of Thoroughfare Gap," Swynyard said.

"He's that close?" Starbuck was surprised.

"I guess that's where he always intended to be," Swynyard said with undisguised admiration. "He sent us on ahead to draw the Yankees away from the river, and now he's following on behind, which means that if we can just hold the Yankees all morning, then Lee should hog-tie the lot of them this afternoon. If the good Lord wills it, that is," the Colonel added piously. The tic in his right cheek, which had slowly subsided after his abandonment of liquor, had mysteriously returned to full force. For a second Starbuck wondered if Swynyard had been at the bottle, then realized the tic must be a symptom of nervousness; this was the Colonel's first battle as a brigade commander, and he desperately wanted it to be a success. "How are your boys?" Swynyard asked.

"Good enough," Starbuck said, wondering what symptoms of nervousness he was displaying. Shortness of temper, maybe?

Swynyard turned and pointed to the hill behind the Legion's line. "I've got Haxall's Arkansas boys up there. If things get hard I'll send them down to help, but once they've gone we don't have any reserves."

"Artillery?" Starbuck asked.

"None that I've seen," Swynyard said. "None at all, I guess, but if Lee gets here fast then maybe we won't need none."

The Colonel climbed back to his command post. The sun rose higher, promising to bring another stifling day. Off to the south, muffled by distance, rifle shots sounded, but it was hard to tell whether they were being fired in anger or were merely the sound of men trying to provoke distant pickets. Some of Starbuck's men slept as they waited. A few pinned paper labels to their jackets to identify their bodies in case they died, others wrote letters or read or played cards. In the spoil pit the abatis was now breast high. "Tall enough for you?" Medlicott asked Starbuck.

"Is it tall enough for you?" Starbuck retorted. "It's your life it might save, not mine."

"If they attack at all," Medlicott said in a tone of voice suggesting that Starbuck's expectation of battle was merely alarmist.

By late morning Starbuck was himself wondering if the Northern army would ever attack.

380

Maybe the Northerners had detected Lee's approach and slipped away to fight another day, for this day had become somnolent, its peace broken by nothing more threatening than an occasional and distant rifle shot. Then, just as Starbuck had convinced himself that he was safe from battle this day, the woods to the left erupted with furious rifle fire. Startled men woke and pushed their rifles over the cutting's crude parapet. All along the line hammers clicked as men cocked their guns, but no Yankees appeared in the killing patch, only a frightened deer that ducked in and out of the sunlight before any man could squeeze off a shot.

Then a staff officer from the brigade to the north rode up the line, shouting for men to advance into the woods.

"To do what?" Starbuck shouted back.

The staff officer was excited and sweating, a drawn sword in his hand. "Yankees are over there. You can hit them in the flank."

"Do it, Starbuck!" Colonel Swynyard had arrived just in time to hear the officer. "Go for them!"

Starbuck sent Coffman to tell Colonel Hudson what was happening. He wanted to keep the North Carolinian well informed, just as Hudson had promised to keep Starbuck apprised of any threats on his southern flank. Then Starbuck scrambled up the cutting's face. "Legion!"

The men climbed from the cutting and formed in two ranks. There were no battle flags to be raised in the Legion's center, where Starbuck took his place. "Forward!" he shouted. The fighting was crackling and spitting in the woods, punctuated by rebel yells. It was hard to tell just what had provoked the fight, but plainly some rebel troops had crossed the railbed to intercept some Yankees among the trees, where Starbuck now led the Legion. He went fast, knowing that his careful battle line would be shredded by the oaks, but also knowing that any chance of finding an open Yankee flank was too compelling to be ignored.

The men panted behind him, crashing through undergrowth and splintering dry fallen branches as they ran. Starbuck was leading the Legion to his left, going slantwise across the rebels' front line. He could see gunsmoke sifting through the leaves ahead; then he glimpsed flashes of blue where a handful of Northern soldiers ran through the woods. He ran toward those enemy, but the blue coats disappeared in the trees. Somewhere a rifle fired, and Starbuck heard the bullet ripping through the leaves overhead, but he could not see the gunsmoke or tell whether it was a friend or foe who had fired. He slowed down to catch his breath. The Legion had long lost its cohesion as the companies broke apart in the woodland, so that now they were streaming through the trees like packs of hunters on a quick scent. A volley crashed to Starbuck's left, but no bullets came his way. A riderless horse foaming with sweat and with white eyes flashing plunged through the brush and galloped unchecked between two of Starbuck's companies. The wood suddenly seemed empty of enemy. Starbuck could hear shouted orders and sporadic rifle fire, but he could see no one, and he feared he had led his men far astray; then a sudden warning shout turned him to his left.

And there, suddenly, was an enemy. A huddle of Yankees were kneeling and firing, loading and aiming, but their targets were not the men of the Legion but other Southerners way off to the Legion's left, which suggested that Starbuck had indeed discovered the North's open flank. "Legion, halt! Aim!" He was giving his men precious little time. They skidded to a halt and raised their guns.

"Fire!"

The small group of Yankees were swept cruelly away. Over two hundred bullets had been fired at a score of men, and only one of them was able to stand when the volley was done, and that man was staggering and bleeding.

"Charge!" Starbuck shouted. "And let me hear you scream!"

The Legion began to sound the rebel yell. Starbuck remembered that he had not ordered the men to fix bayonets, but it was too late to remedy the lack now. The Legion had been unleashed, and nothing could stop the ragged charge that screamed through the wood to take the enemy's open flank. The trees ahead were filled with fleeing Yankees. More rebels were coming from the left, and Starbuck shouted at his men to wheel right. "This way! This way!" The breath was pounding in his lungs. Somewhere a man screamed again and again, the sound terrible and pathetic until it was blissfully cut short by a rifle shot.

Starbuck leaped a dead man, stumbled on a fallen log, pushed through a laurel screen, then saw he had blundered into an open field covered with running men. "Halt!" he shouted. "Stop here! Reload!"

The Legion made a rough line at the wood's edge and fired at the horde of retreating Yankees. The men were too breathless and too excited to shoot well, but their rifle fire did serve to hasten the Yankees' panicked retreat. Another rebel regiment appeared to the Legion's left and pursued the enemy into the open meadow, but when Company H began to follow, Captain Truslow pulled them back just a second before a Northern battery unmasked itself in a stand of trees on the meadow's far side. The first cannon whipped a barrelload of canister through the exposed rebel pursuers. A second gun fired, this gun aiming shell at Starbuck's men. The missile cracked overhead and exploded in the trees just as a ragged Northern volley whistled over the pasture.

"Back!" Colonel Swynyard had advanced with the Legion. "Back to the railbed, lads! Well done!"

"Lieutenant Howes?" Starbuck shouted. "A party to collect guns and ammunition!"

"We've got some prisoners here, sir," Howes called back.

Starbuck had not been aware of any prisoners being taken, but sure enough there was a disconsolate group of a dozen men under a corporal's guard who had to be escorted back to the Brigade headquarters. Howe's men found a score of usable rifles and several hundred cartridges that they carried back through the woods.

"A nice beginning," Colonel Swynyard said to Starbuck when the Legion was back in its cutting.

"Easy pickings." Starbuck was dismissive. He could not recall a single bullet coming near him. He knew the Legion had not needed to be involved in the fight, but he was glad that his regiment had been given such a swift and simple victory. It was, as Swynyard had told him, a good beginning.

"But your man Meddlesome didn't move." Lucifer waited till Swynyard was gone before talking to Starbuck. "I watched him. He took his men into the woods and stopped there. You went on, he stayed back."

Starbuck grunted, not wanting to encourage Lucifer's indiscretion. "How old are you?" he asked the runaway slave instead.

Lucifer blinked with surprise at the unexpected question. "Seventeen," he said after a while. "Why?"

Starbuck suspected Lucifer had added at least a year to his age. "Because you're too young to die, that's why, so take yourself back to the wagon park."

"I ain't going to die. I'm charmed!" Lucifer said.

"Charmed?" Starbuck asked. "How?" He was remembering the crushed bird bones.

"Just charmed," Lucifer said. "Like I never got caught as a thief. Till your men trapped me, and there you were!" He grinned. "See? Charmed."

"But you were a thief," Starbuck said, not with disapproval, but simply to pin down the first piece of information about his past that Lucifer had so far offered.

"You think I'd wear those pants with long pockets otherwise? Mick gave them to me."

"Mick?"

"Mr. Micklewhite," Lucifer said. "He owns the big tavern at Manassas Junction and I worked for him."

"You were his slave?"

"I was his thief," Lucifer said. "But he wanted me to do other things. Because he said I'm young and good-looking." He laughed in self-mockery, but Starbuck detected an anxiety behind the words.

"What sort of things?" Starbuck asked.

"You need to be told? You don't know about appetite?"

"Appetite?"

But before Lucifer could answer there was a loud snap of a breaking twig in the woods beyond the killing patch. The Legion went still, fingers poised on triggers, but nothing more sounded from the trees. Off to the right the firing began again, but that far-off battle belonged to someone else. Starbuck looked for his servant again, but Lucifer had vanished, taking his past with him. Ahead of Starbuck the green woods were silent. Somewhere beyond the silence eighty thousand Yankees gathered, but here, for the moment, there was peace.

Starbuck had chosen not to put skirmishers into the woods. The killing patch between the railbed's cutting and the tree line was too wide, so that by the time his own skirmishers would have returned to the Legion's lines the pursuing Yankees would already have been halfway across the open space. The North Carolinians on the Legion's right, however, were faced by an ever-narrowing strip of open land and had taken the precaution of putting a skirmish line among the trees, and it was those men who alerted Starbuck to the day's second Yankee attack, an assault much better organized than the North's first motley advance.

The battle between the skirmishers did not take long. The Yankees were advancing in too much force, and the woods were no place for scattered men to fight against a horde. Hudson's skirmishers fired a single round each, then ran for their lives, yet that scattered volley was sufficient to warn the Legion that the attack was coming.

Starbuck was in the cutting with Company C, which was now commanded by the excitable, quick-tempered William Patterson, who was a stonemason and thus the unwilling butt of too many jokes about gravestones. Patterson had pretensions of gentility and had greeted his unexpected promotion by adorning himself with a red waist sash, a plumed hat, and a sword. He had discarded the sword and plumed hat for this day's fight, but the sash still marked him as an officer. "Ready, boys, ready!" he shouted, and his men licked dry lips and watched the trees anxiously. "They're coming, boys, they're coming!" Patterson called, yet still the green woods were empty, the trees dappled by sunlight alone and the humid air unsullied by powder smoke.

Then, suddenly, the Northerners were in sight. A mass of men ran soundlessly into view. Flags and bayonets were bright. For a second, a split heartbeat, Starbuck watched the rare sight of a whole army attacking straight into his face, then bellowed the order to open fire.

"Fire!" Patterson echoed the shout, and his company's front vanished in a cloud of powder smoke.

"Fire!" Moxey screamed at the company next door. Patterson's men were spitting bullets into rifles, shoving ramrods down barrels, and scrabbling for percussion caps in the upturned hats placed conveniently beside the firestep.

"Fire!" Company D's Captain Pine shouted.

"Fire!" Lieutenant Howes called from Company E. The Yankee attack was oblique, emerging from the trees first to the south, then to the north.

And suddenly, like a great tide bursting on a beach, the sound of the attack overwhelmed Starbuck. It was the sound of a great infantry charge: the noise of cheering, screaming, swearing men, and the noise of drums and bugles behind them, and the noise of his own men's bullets whacking into rifle stocks, and the noise of minié bullets thumping into flesh, and the noise of the first wounded men screaming and gasping, and the noise of ramrods rattling metallic in rifles, and the whistling whip-quick noise of hollow-tailed minié bullets, and the noise of thousands of heavy boots, and the noise of screaming orders, and the noise of men cursing their clumsiness as they fumbled to tear open cartridges.

It was an unending crescendo of noise, a tumult of battering sound waves that obliterated senses already swamped by powder smoke. All a man could do now was fight, and fighting meant pouring lead into the gunsmoke to drive away the pounding, cursing enemy. And the enemy still came forward, rank after rank of blue-coated men beneath their high striped banners. "Fire!" a Yankee shouted.

"Fire!" Truslow's voice answered from the Legion's left flank.

"They're firing high," Private Matthews exulted just five paces from Starbuck, then Matthews was flicked backward by a bullet to the head that took away a saucer-sized piece of his skull and spattered his neighbor with blood and brains. Lieutenant Patterson stood transfixed as Matthews's body slid to a halt at his feet. The body twitched, blood pouring from the shattered cranium.

"Fire!" Starbuck shouted. He saw a boy pull the trigger; nothing happened, yet the boy started to ram another charge down a barrel probably stuffed with unfired charges. Starbuck picked up Matthews's blood-sticky rifle and ran to the boy. "Fire the damn thing before you load it!" he snapped, handing the frightened lad the new gun. Starbuck took the boy's rifle and tossed it back out of the cutting. He fired his own rifle into the gray mist of smoke, then ran along the cutting past Moxey's company to where Medlicott guarded the vulnerable right flank. The miller was fighting well enough, firing his revolver into the smoke that was now being fed by the volleys of both sides to create a single filthy-smelling leprous yellow cloudbank. The Yankee charge seemed to have stalled, though it had not been defeated. Instead the Northerners were holding their ground in the killing patch and trying to overwhelm the rebel line with volley fire.

"We're still here, Starbuck, still here!" The speaker was the genial Colonel Hudson, who had come to his own left flank on an errand not dissimilar to Starbuck's own. "Mr. Lincoln's Republican party is noisy today, is it not?" the Colonel said, gesturing toward the Yankees with a switch of hazel that was apparently his weapon of choice. A bullet slapped past Hudson's long hair. "Rotten shot," the Colonel lamented, "terrible shooting! They really should look to their musket training."

Then a second great cheer sounded from beyond the smoke, and there was a resurgence of that first terrible sound that had swollen to burst against the rebels' defenses. "Dear Lord," Hudson said, "I do believe a second line is coming. Hold hard, boys! Hold hard!" He strode back along his line.

"Oh, Christ, oh, Christ!" Major Medlicott was fumbling percussion caps onto his revolver. "Oh, Christ!" He raised the gun, only half primed, and shot blindly into the smoke. Beyond that smoke the Yankee fire had slackened as the first wave of attackers made way for the second. The rebels fired on into the gloom, seeing their targets only as dark shadows in the luminous smoke cloud; then a screaming mass of men with fixed bayonets materialized in that fogbank.

"Back!" Medlicott shouted, and his men scrambled away from the shallow cutting.

"Stay and fight, damn it!" Starbuck bellowed, but the panic was infectious, and the company streamed past him. For a second Starbuck was alone in the wide ditch; then he saw the open mouths of Yankee attackers not ten paces away, and he ran for his life. He expected a bullet in the back at any second as he scrambled up the western bank and followed Medlicott's company into the tangle of saplings and bushes.

The Yankees scented victory. They cheered as they jumped down into the cutting and as they scrambled up its further bank. Their flags streamed forward. A gap had opened between the Legion and Hudson's North Carolinians, and the Northern infantry poured into the gap, where they discovered the unguarded spoil pit. Like a wave of water released by a broken dam they swarmed into the hollow, only to surge up against the abatis. They recoiled for a second as the tangle of branches checked their headlong charge; then they flowed around the barrier's flanks to swarm up to the spoil pit's edge.

"Fire!" Colonel Swynyard had brought Haxall's Arkansas battalion down the hill to meet the Yankee charge where it tried to climb out of the spoil pit. Rifles slashed fire into the pit. The rebels could not miss, for the Yankees were crammed tighter than rats in a terrier pit. "Fire!" Major Haxall called, and a second volley whipped down and the Yankee mass seemed to quiver like a great wounded beast.

"Get your men formed, and fight!" Swynyard shouted angrily at Starbuck. "Goddamn it, fight!"

"Damn!" Starbuck was lost, confused. The attackers in the pit were being slaughtered, but more Yankees had crossed the ditch and were charging through the scrub, where handfuls of dogged rebels resisted them. Starbuck blundered through the trees, seeking men, any men, finding nothing but chaos, and then he saw Peter Waggoner, the giant, Bible-thumping Sergeant from Company D. Sweet Jesus, Starbuck thought, but if Company D had been thrown out of the railbed, then the Legion must be unraveling all along its length. "Waggoner!"

"Sir?"

"Where's your company?"

"Here, sir! Here!" And there, crouching frightened behind the big Sergeant, was most of Company D. Captain Pine was pushing men into line, screaming at them to stand and fight.

"Fix bayonets," Starbuck called, "and follow me! And scream! For God's sake, scream!"

The ululating, blood-chilling sound of the rebel yell whipsawed in the air as the company followed Starbuck back toward the railbed. Goddamn it, but he would not be beaten! A Yankee appeared in front of Starbuck, and he fired his revolver straight into the man's face, which seemed to vanish in a spray of red as the shock of the gun's recoil jarred up to Starbuck's shoulder. He half slipped in a slick of blood, then fired into a mass of blue uniforms in front. "Charge!" he screamed. "Charge!" And Waggoner's men came with him, screaming like devils released to mischief, and the disordered Yankees went backward. The desperate charge through the brush had collected more groups of scattered Legionnaires, so that Starbuck was now leading almost a third of his regiment in a blood-crazed, desperate, vicious counterattack. The Northerners had been on the brink of victory but were suddenly confused by this unexpected opposition. The Yankees retreated.

Starbuck leaped back into the railbed. A Northerner

slipped on the far bank, turned, and swung his rifle. Starbuck fired at the man, heard him scream, then jumped over the falling body to sprawl and trip at the top of the embankment. A rifle shot cracked over his head, then a wave of his own men went past him and a giant hand plucked him onto his feet. "Come on, sir!" It was Sergeant Peter Waggoner. A cannon fired somewhere, adding its new noise to the din of battle. Behind Starbuck, at the rim of the spoil pit, the rifle volleys still flailed down to turn the hollow into a charnel house. The Yankees were retreating, stunned by the violence of the rebel backlash. Starbuck ran past the heap of bodies killed in the rifle duel that had preceded the second Yankee surge forward. He knew he had lost command of his men and that now they were fighting from instinct and without proper guidance, and so he sprinted forward to try and get ahead of them and somehow bring them under control.

The Yankees had brought a small cannon forward to the edge of the trees. The gun was scarcely four feet high and had a short, wide-muzzled barrel. They had managed to fire one shot with the gun, and now its four-man crew was desperately trying to haul the weapon back through the trees to save it from being captured by the screaming, battle-maddened gray wave. In their haste the gunners rammed one of the gun-wheels into a tree and thus stalled their retreat. "The gun!" Starbuck shouted. "The gun!" If he could concentrate his men at the gun, then he had a chance of regaining control of the Legion. "Go for the gun!" he shouted and ran toward the cannon himself. Something hit him hard on the left thigh, spinning him and almost knocking him down. He limped for a pace, waiting for the delayed agony to sear through his body. He took a breath ready to scream and almost sobbed instead as he felt wetness spill down his leg, then realized the enemy bullet had merely smashed his canteen. It was not blood, but water. His hip was bruised, but he was unwounded, and his self-pitying scream turned into a defiant yelp of relief. All around him the rebel yell filled the air. One of the Yankee gunners, knowing that the trapped weapon was lost, leaned across a wheel to tug the lanyard of the cannon's primer, and Starbuck, realizing with horror that the cannon was still loaded and that a storm of canister was about to be unleashed on his men, fired the last shots of his revolver. He saw a slash of bright metal show on the cannon's barrel as a round ricocheted off the bronze; then his last bullet whipped the enemy gunner backward onto the ground.

"Legion!" Starbuck screamed. "To me!" He was among the trees now, just yards from the gun. The Yankees had fled into the broken, smoking wood, where the trunks were bitten by rifle fire. "Legion! Legion! Legion!" Starbuck shouted. He reached the cannon and put a proprietorial hand on its bullet-flecked barrel. "Legion! Form line! Form line! Fire! Legion! Legion!" He was screaming like a mad thing, as though he could impose his will on the excited men by sheer force of mind and voice. "Form!" He shouted the word desperately.

And men at last heard him and at last obeyed him. Companies were mixed together, officers were missing, sergeants and corporals were dead, but the maddened charge somehow shook itself into a crude firing line that slammed a volley into the wood. The volley was matched by one from the enemy. The Yankees, retreating into the trees, had turned and formed their own battle line. One of Starbuck's men screamed as he was hit in the leg, another staggered back into the smoky sunlight with blood seeping between fingers that were clutched to his belly. A bullet smacked hollowly into one of the captured cannon's ammunition chests. Somewhere a man gasped the name Jesus over and over.

God Almighty, Starbuck thought, but somehow they had

survived. He felt sick to his stomach. He felt ashamed, and his hands were shaking as he reloaded his revolver. He had failed. He had felt the Legion disintegrate around him like a crumbling dam, and there had been nothing he could do. There were tears on his face, tears of shame at having failed. He pressed the percussion caps onto the revolver's cones and fired it into the shadowed smoke beneath the trees.

"Sir!" Captain Pine of D Company, his lips blackened by powder and his eyes red from the smoke, appeared beside him. "Do we take the gun, sir?" He gestured at the captured cannon.

"Yes!" Starbuck said, then forced himself to calm down, to think. "Keep firing!" he shouted at the Legion's ragged line; then he looked more carefully at the gun. A dead horse lay nearby, just one horse, and there was no limber, but only wooden chests of ammunition, and Starbuck remembered Swynyard telling him about the mountain howitzers of the old U.S. Army, and he realized that this twelve-pounder cannon was one of those old rough-country guns that were transported on the backs of single packhorses. This captured howitzer was not a heavy gun, but even so it would need a half-dozen men to drag it through the trees and back to the railbed, and Starbuck knew that the absence of even a half-dozen men would weaken his line enough to let the Yankees surge back. Maybe, he thought, he should just spike the gun and abandon it; then he saw a mass of blue uniforms behind his fragile line and panic soared in him.

He was about to scream at his men to turn and drive this new enemy away, then realized that the blue coats belonged to prisoners. They were Yankees who had survived the horror in the spoil pit and who had now climbed out into the open ground. "Get some of those Yankees," Starbuck said to Pine, "and have them drag the gun back. And be careful, it's loaded!"

"Use prisoners, sir?" Pine asked, apparently shocked at the idea.

"Do it!" Starbuck turned back to the east to see that his men were doggedly firing and loading, firing and loading. Most were sheltering behind trees, just as the Yankees were, which meant that the firefight was settling into a stalemate, but soon the Legion must withdraw to its railbed trench, and Starbuck was determined that the retreat should be made in good order. He would not lose control as he had before.

Lieutenant Pine was arguing with a captured Yankee officer. Starbuck stooped to the gun's trail and picked up a length of one-inch rope with iron prolonge hooks spliced into its ends. He threw the rope to Pine. "Shoot the bastard if he won't do as he's told!" he shouted.

Pine finally organized a morose work party of a dozen prisoners, who were given the rope to hold. Pine himself attached one of the hooks to the lunette, the ring at the tip of the gun's trail, then shouted at his unwilling team to haul away. The trail swung around, and the gun eased itself away from the tree, so that its short, black-mouthed muzzle was turned to face back toward its erstwhile owners. "Stop!" Starbuck shouted.

The astonished prisoners dropped the rope. "Clear me! Clear me!" Starbuck bellowed at those of his men who were firing at the enemy from in front of the cannon. "Clear me!" Two men looked around, saw the gun facing them, and ran hastily to one side. Starbuck, when he was sure the field of fire was clear of his own men, leaned across the wheel and grasped the primer's lanyard. He waited a handful of seconds until he could see some Northerners stepping from behind trees to aim their rifles, then pulled the lanyard.

The gun cracked like the shattering hammer blow of doom. Smoke jetted thirty yards forward, while the gun itself recoiled clear out of the trees and almost ran down its blue-coated haulers. The tin canister had split apart at the muzzle to scatter its balls like giant buckshot. Starbuck's ears were ringing from the explosion. "Take it away! Hurry!" Starbuck shouted at the scared Yankee prisoners. "Whip them if they won't work," Starbuck shouted at Pine. "We slavers know how to whip!" The startled Yankee prisoners began to haul as though their lives depended on it, and the smoking gun trundled away across the rough ground so fast that it bounced two feet in the air when its wheels struck a sprawling corpse. In the trees the cannon smoke cleared to reveal a patch of woodland ripped and scarred by canister. "Keep firing!" Starbuck shouted at his men; then, as Pine's team dragged the gun back across the shallowest part of the cutting and so up to the sparse woodland beyond, Starbuck ran to his right to determine where his men's line ended.

He found Lieutenant Patterson. "Where's Medlicott?" Starbuck shouted over the rifle fire.

"Haven't seen him, sir."

"Have your men load, then go back to the railbed and be ready to fire when the rest of us come back!" Starbuck had to shout over the splintering rifle fire. Patterson nodded. He was wild-eyed and frenetic, firing a revolver again and again at the Yankees. Even when the revolver's hammer began clicking on exploded percussion caps, Patterson kept cocking and firing, cocking and firing. Starbuck slapped the unprimed gun down and made the Lieutenant repeat the orders he had been given. "Do it now!" Starbuck ordered, then ran northward to find Lieutenant Howes, Sergeant Tyndale, and Captain Leighton. He told them to pull their men back to the railbed. "One last volley to keep the Yankees busy," he ordered, "then run like hell, understand?" Starbuck was beginning to understand the Legion's ragged dispositions now. Medlicott and Moxey were missing, the four center companies were either in the trees or gone back with Lieutenant Patterson, while presumably Truslow and Davies had never moved from the railbed.

"Fire!" Captain Leighton shouted, and the rifle flames speared bright in the trees.

"Back!" Starbuck shouted. "Back!"

They ran back, leaping the tideline of blue-coated bodies and then jumping over their own dead into the railbed. The Northerners were slow to realize that the rebels were gone, and it was a long moment before their first skirmishers appeared at the tree line. "Had enough, Johnny?" one Northerner shouted.

"Go back, Billy, before we send you home in a box!" a rebel called back.

"Oh, my God," another man said, panting from the exertions of the last few minutes, "just lay me down."

Starbuck ran down the railbed until he came to Captain Davies's company, which, as he had suspected, had never moved from its position. Truslow had seen to that, barricading the railbed with a fallen tree so that the threatening disaster to the South had been given no chance of spreading as far as his company. There were dead Yankees all along the front of Truslow and Davies's men, but none of the enemy had come closer than fifteen yards from the parapet. "So what were you doing up there?" Truslow asked calmly.

"Not very well," Starbuck confessed.

"The Legion's still in place," Truslow said in a voice so grim that it was a moment or two before Starbuck realized the words were probably meant as a compliment.

"God knows if we can take another attack," he said.

"Ain't none of God's business," Truslow said, "but if the bastards do come again, then we'll just have to drive them off again. Well done!" This rare enthusiastic praise was not directed at Starbuck but at Sergeant Bailey, who had brought replacement ammunition to the railbed. Two other men were tending a fire so that Truslow's company would have boiling water to scour the powder deposits from their rifles.

Starbuck walked back along his defense line. The Yankees had settled at the tree line, from where they were directing a constant and harassing rifle fire at the railbed. Starbuck's men kept their heads down, sometimes raising themselves to fire a shot or sometimes just lifting a rifle over the makeshift parapet and squeezing the trigger blindly. "Don't waste ammunition!" Starbuck snarled at one man who had thus fired without sighting first. "If you're going to shoot, aim, and if you're not, keep low."

There were bodies in the railbed. Some were the Legion's own dead, lying on their backs, mouths open and hands curled. Starbuck recognized a few men with sadness, some without any regret, and a handful with satisfaction. One or two of the rebel dead were strangers. He should have known them, but he had not had time to learn the names and faces of every new conscript. The Yankee dead had mostly been hoisted onto the parapet to help protect the rebel living, while the Legion's white-faced wounded lay breathing shallowly against the rear slope of the cutting.

Starbuck resisted the urge to crouch as the cutting became shallower. An officer was supposed to show his men an example of fearlessness, and Starbuck kept his pace steady even as his mind screamed and his pulse raced with fear. Bullets slapped the air around him for the few seconds that he was exposed to the Yankees; then he was able to jump down into the spoil pit, which was grotesque with enemy dead. The smell of blood was thick, and the first flies already swarming on the bloodied wounds. It was the spoil pit, Starbuck reckoned, that had saved the Legion. The hollow had drawn the attackers away from the rest of the line because of its promise of a safe, covered route into the rebel rear. But once in the pit the Northerners had been trapped, first by the abatis and then by the fire of Haxall's battalion, which Swynyard had brought down from the hill.

"We're thin on the ground, sir," Lieutenant Patterson greeted Starbuck.

"Thin?"

Patterson shrugged. "Half A and B companies are missing."

"Medlicott? Moxey?" Starbuck need not have asked. Both men were absent, and no one knew where they might be. Coffman was safe, crouching under the railbed's shallow parapet with a rifle he had taken from a dead man, and Captain Pine's mountain howitzer was also safe. It had been parked at the back crest of the spoil pit, where it was attracting Yankee bullets.

Patterson saw Starbuck glance at the gun. "We forgot to bring the ammunition, sir."

Starbuck swore. Nothing was going right this day, nothing, except, as Truslow had said, the Legion was still in place. Which meant the battle was not lost. And happily, except for the one hapless mountain howitzer, the Yankees had not deployed any artillery against the Legion. The woods were too thick to let the gunners of either side deploy their weapons, though just as that thought occurred to Starbuck, some shells began to explode. They were rebel shells, and they burst in the woods over the Yankees, who, astonished by the shrapnel, crept back from the tree line. The gunfire seemed to be coming from far to the south, but it stopped abruptly as a surge of cheering and rifle fire sounded further down Jackson's line. Starbuck, listening to the sound of battle, guessed he was hearing a Yankee attack like the one the Legion had just, though barely, survived. The gunners had shortened their range to enfilade the attackers, and the Yankees close to the Legion crept back to the tree line to begin their harassing fire again.

Haxall's men had returned to the hill, from where they were now sharpshooting across the railbed, while Hudson's North Carolinians were also back in place. The tall Colonel Hudson saw Starbuck and strode toward him. "A hot place, Starbuck!" He meant the railbed hard by the spoil pit.

"I'm sorry my fellows ran."

"My dear man, mine went as well! Scattered like barnyard fowls!" Hudson decently refrained from pointing out that his men had no choice but to run once Medlicott had exposed their flank. "Have you the time?" the Colonel now asked. "A Yankee shot my watch, see?" He showed Starbuck the torn pocket where the watch had been stored. "Bullet went straight through without touching me, but it rather mangled the watch. Pity. It belonged to my grandfather. It kept terrible time, but I was fond of it and hoped to pass it on to my son."

"You've got a son?" Starbuck asked, somehow surprised by the information.

"Three altogether, and a brace of daughters. Tom's my oldest boy. He's twenty-four now and serves as one of Lee's aides."

"Lee!" Starbuck was impressed. "The Lee?"

"Bobby himself. Nice fellow. Still, pity about the watch." The Colonel picked a piece of shattered watch glass from the remnants of his pocket.

"Coffman!" Starbuck shouted. "What time is it?"

Coffman had inherited an ancient timepiece from his father, and now he fished its bulbous case from an inner pocket and clicked open the lid. "It says thirty minutes after four, sir."

"It must have stopped this morning," Starbuck said. "It can't be that late."

"But look at the sun!" Hudson said, intimating that it truly was that late in the afternoon.

"Then where's Lee?" Starbuck asked. "I thought he was coming to relieve us."

"I find it best to plan military affairs on the twin principles that whatever I am told is certain will never occur, and that whatever is proclaimed impossible is disastrously imminent. There is no good news in war," Hudson pronounced grandly, "only less bad news. Dear, oh dear." The mild oath had been caused by a resurgence of enemy rifle fire from the tree line. "I do believe, my dear Starbuck, that the Republican party claims our attention again. Ah, well, to our toil, to our toil."

And the storm broke again.

The Reverend Elial Starbuck was trying to understand what was happening. Comprehension, he thought, was not much to ask. War was as rational an activity as any other human endeavor and must, he presumed, yield to analysis, yet whenever he inquired of a general officer what exactly was occurring in the western woods, he received a different answer.

The North was attacking, one general said, yet the general's own men were sprawling in the meadows playing cards and smoking pipes. "All in good time, all in good time," the General said when the preacher asked him why his men were not supporting the attack. One of the General's staff officers, a superior young man who made clear his disapproval of a civilian intruding on a battlefield, informed the Reverend Starbuck that Jackson was retreating, the Yankees were pursuing, and that the commotion in the woods was nothing but a noisy rear guard.

Major Galloway also tried to reassure the preacher. Galloway had been ordered to wait until the attacking infantry broke through Jackson's line, after which his men would join the Northern cavalry in their pursuit of the shattered enemy. The Reverend Starbuck waited on horseback for that promised breakthrough and tried to convince himself that the Major's explanation made sense. "Jackson's attempting to retreat southward, sir," Galloway told the preacher, "and our fellows have him pinned against the woods over there," but even Galloway was unhappy with that analysis. The Major, after all, had failed to find any evidence that Jackson had ever gone to Centreville, so it did not make sense that he would now be retreating from that town, which raised the mystery of what exactly the Southern general was doing. And that mystery was made even more worrying by Billy Blythe's repeated assertions that he had seen a second rebel army marching toward Manassas from the west. Galloway was unwilling to share his anxiety with the Reverend Doctor Starbuck, but the Major had the distinct impression that perhaps General Pope had utterly misunderstood what was truly happening.

Galloway's unhappiness was compounded by the acrid mood that prevailed within his small regiment. Blythe's return had stirred Adam Faulconer's anger, an anger that had come to a head the night before when the Virginian had accused Blythe of murdering civilians at McComb's Tavern. Blythe had denied the accusation. "We was fired on by soldiers," Blythe maintained.

"And the soldiers begged you to stop firing because there were women there!" Adam insisted.

"If a man had done that," Blythe said, "I would have ceased fire instantly. Instantly! Upon my word, Faulconer, but what kind of a man do you take me for?"

"A liar," Adam had said, and before Galloway could intervene, the challenge had been made.

But the duel had not yet been fought, and perhaps, Galloway dared hope, the duel would never be fought, to which end he now enlisted the Reverend Starbuck's aid. The preacher, happy to have a purpose while the infantry battle still raged, spoke first to Captain Blythe and afterward brought a report of the conversation back to Galloway. "Blythe admits there might have been women in the tavern," the Reverend Starbuck said, "and the thought distresses him greatly, but he plainly wasn't aware of them at the time and he promises me that he heard no calls for any cease-fire." The preacher paused for a moment to watch the smoke trails of artillery shells arching across the distant woods, then frowned at the Major. "What kind of women would be in a tavern anyway?"

Galloway hoped the question was rhetorical, but the preacher's expression suggested he wanted an answer. The Major cast around for a suitable evasion and found none. "Whores, sir," he finally said, coloring with embarrassment for having used such a word to a man of God.

"Precisely," the preacher said. "Women of no virtue. So why is Faulconer making this commotion?"

"Adam has a tender conscience, sir."

"He is also in your regiment, Major, by courtesy of my money," the preacher said sharply, conveniently overlooking that the money for Galloway's Horse had actually been subscribed by hundreds of humble, well-meaning folk throughout New England, "and I will not have the Lord's work hampered by a misplaced sympathy for fallen women. Captain Faulconer must learn that he cannot afford a tender conscience, not on my money!"

"You'll talk to him, sir?" Galloway asked.

"Directly," the preacher said and immediately beckoned Adam to one side. The two men rode far enough for their conversation to be private; then the preacher demanded to know exactly what evidence Adam had for his accusation of murder.

"The evidence of a newspaper, sir," Adam said, "and my own apprehension of Captain Blythe's character."

"It was a Southern newspaper." The Reverend Starbuck easily demolished the first part of Adam's evidence.

"So it was, sir."

"And your other evidence is merely founded upon your dislike of Captain Blythe's character? You think we can afford the luxuries of such self-indulgent judgments in wartime?"

"I have grounds for that dislike, sir."

"Grounds! Grounds!" The Reverend Starbuck spat the two words out. "We are at war, young man, we cannot indulge in petty squabbles!"

Adam stiffened. "It was Captain Blythe who issued the duel challenge, sir, not me."

"You called him a liar!" the Reverend Starbuck said.

"Yes, sir, I did."

The Reverend Starbuck shook his head sadly. "I have talked with Blythe. He assures me, on his word as a gentleman, that he had no idea any women were present in the tavern, and he still maintains there were none present, but he accepts he might be mistaken, and all he asks of you is your acceptance that he would never have continued the battle had he known that his actions were risking the lives of women. I believe him." The Reverend Starbuck paused, offering Adam a chance to utter agreement, but Adam remained obstinately silent. "For the love of God, man," the preacher protested, "do you really believe that a man of honor, an officer of the United States Army, a Christian, would persecute women?"

"No, sir, I don't believe that," Adam said pointedly.

It took a few seconds for the Reverend Starbuck to

appreciate the debating point Adam had made, and the appreciation did not improve the preacher's temper. "I'll thank you not to be clever with me, young man. I have investigated this matter. I know the wickedness of mankind better than you, Faulconer. I have wrestled with iniquity all my life and my judgments are not based on Southern newspapers, but on hard experience tempered, I trust, with prayerful charity, and I am telling you now that Captain Blythe is no murderer and that his actions that night were chivalrous. It is unspeakable that a man could behave in the way you describe! Unthinkable! Manifestly impossible!"

Adam shook his head. "I could tell you of another occasion, sir," he said, and was about to tell the tale of the woman he had discovered in the barn with Blythe, but the preacher gave him no chance to tell the story.

"I will not listen to rumor!" the Reverend Starbuck insisted. "My God, I will not listen to rumor. We are engaged upon a crusade, Faulconer, a great crusade to forge God's chosen nation. We are purging that nation of sin, burning the iniquity from its heart with a fierce and righteous fire, and there is no room, no merit, no satisfaction, no justification for any man to put his personal whims ahead of that great cause. As our Lord and Savior Himself said, 'He that is not with Me is against Me,' and upon my soul, Faulconer, if you oppose Major Galloway in this matter then you will find that Christ and I are both become your enemies."

Adam began to feel a sympathy for his onetime friend, Nathaniel Starbuck. "I would have no one doubt my loyalty to the cause of the United States, sir," he said in feeble protest to the preacher.

"Then shake Blythe's hand and admit you were wrong," the Reverend Starbuck said.

"Me? That I was wrong?" Adam could not help asking the astonished question aloud.

"He admits you might be right, and that perhaps there were women there, so can you not do the same and admit that he would have behaved differently had he known?"

Adam's head was awhirl. Somehow, he was not sure how, he had been maneuvered into the wrong. He was also painfully aware that he was in the preacher's debt, and so, though it cut hard against a stubborn grain, he nodded his head. "If you insist, sir," he said unhappily.

"It's your conscience that should insist, but I am glad all the same. Come!" And the Reverend Starbuck thumped his horse's flanks to lead Adam across to where the grinning Billy Blythe waited. "Mr. Faulconer has something to say to you, Captain," the Reverend Starbuck announced.

Adam made his admission that he might have misjudged Captain Blythe, then apologized for that misjudgment. He hated himself for making the apology, but he nevertheless tried to make it sound heartfelt. He even held out his hand afterward.

Blythe shook the offered hand. "I guess we Southern gentlemen are just too hotheaded, ain't that right, Faulconer? So we'll say no more about it."

Adam felt demeaned and belittled. He put a brave face on the defeat, but it was still a defeat and it hurt. Major Galloway, though, was touchingly pleased by the apparent reconciliation. "We should be friends," Galloway said. "We have enemies enough without making them from our own side."

"Amen to that," Blythe said, "amen to that."

"Amen indeed," the Reverend Starbuck echoed, "and hallelujah."

Adam said nothing but just stared at the woods where the smoke rose from the guns.

While to the south, unseen by any Northern troops, regiment after regiment of rebel infantry was marching on a country road that led to the open flank of John Pope's army. Lee's reinforcements were arriving just as the Yankees' last great charge of the day was hurled against the railbed in the woods.

Above the Blue Ridge Mountains the sun sank slowly into a summer's evening. The Reverend Starbuck saw the imminence of nightfall and clenched his fists as he prayed that God would grant John Pope the same miracle that He had granted unto Joshua when He had made the sun stand still above Gibeon so that the armies of Israel would have the time to strike down the Amorites. The preacher prayed, bugles sounded in the woods, a loud cheer echoed among the trees, and the last great onslaught of the day charged on.

THE LAST NORTHERN ATTACK of the day was by far the strongest and most dangerous, for instead of being launched in line it came in an old-fashioned column that struck like a hammer blow at the shallowest section of the railbed. It also struck at the vulnerable junction between Starbuck's men and Elijah Hudson's North Carolinians, and Starbuck, watching from the lip of the spoil pit at the back of the rail-bed, instinctively understood that his men would never stand against this tidal wave that streamed from the woods. The attacking battalions were so close together that their flags made a bright phalanx above the dark ranks. The flags showed the crests and badges of New York and Indiana, of Pennsylvania, Maine, and of Michigan, and beneath the flags the shouts of the attackers drowned the snapping sound of the Legion's rifles.

"Ten paces back!" Starbuck shouted. He would not wait to be overrun. He heard Hudson shouting a similar command; then all sound from the rebel side was momentarily obliterated by the vast Northern cheer that greeted the retreat of the defenders. "Back," Starbuck shouted again when the Northern cheer faded. "Back! Keep in line! Keep in line!" He strode along the Legion's ranks, watching his men rather than looking at the surging enemy. "Backwards! Steady now! Steady!" He was suddenly so proud of the Legion. They were watching blue-coated death come at them in a massive rush, yet they retreated in good steady order as he took them back another ten paces into the thin woodland behind the railbed. He halted them among the saplings. "Reload!" he shouted. "Reload!"

Men bit cartridges, poured powder, and spat bullets. They rammed the charges hard down, then upended the rifles and pressed percussion caps onto fire-blackened cones.

"Aim!" Starbuck shouted. "But wait! Wait for my order!" All along the Legion's line the heavy rifle hammers clicked into place. "Wait for my order and aim low!" Starbuck called. He turned to watch the charge just as the Northerners reached the railbed's cutting. The triumphant Yankee troops poured down the trench's sloping outer wall and then, still cheering, swarmed up its rearward slope straight into the sights of the waiting Legion.

"Fire!" Starbuck shouted.

The volley exploded along the line, hurling Northerners back into the trench. At twenty paces such a volley was mere slaughter work, but it did no more than check the onrushing attack for the few seconds necessary for the unwounded attackers to push aside their encumbering dead and dying. Then, urged on by officers and inflamed with the prospect of victory, the Yankees came forward for their revenge.

But Starbuck had already taken his men back to the hill, where Haxall's Arkansas battalion waited in support. The Legion's retreat had again opened a gap in front of the spoil pit, and again that gap enticed the Yankee attackers. It was the place of least resistance, and so the attacking column poured into the inviting open space. A few of the Northerners found themselves among the stinking bodies in the spoil pit, but most ran around the pit's rim and then charged on toward the open country beyond. They left behind a litter of wounded men, a trail of crushed saplings, and Starbuck's forlorn, captured howitzer, which had been thrown off its carriage.

Haxall's men helped seal the gap by firing one blistering volley, and by the time the smoke of that volley had cleared, the Legion's rifles were loaded again. "Fire!" Starbuck shouted and heard the command echoed toward the regiment's left flank. The Northern attack was slowing, not because it was being outfought, but simply because too many Yankees were trying to push through the narrow gaps either side of the spoil pit and were meeting a stiffening resistance as Starbuck's right flank and Hudson's left closed on each other. Haxall's men extended Starbuck's line and, when at last the gap was closed, turned back to hunt down the Yankees who had broken through. The junction of Starbuck's Virginians and Hudson's North Carolinians was now some fifty paces behind the spoil pit, and it was there that the line steadied and began a murderous fight with the Yankees who had not succeeded in breaking through Jackson's line.

The fight started with the two sides just thirty paces apart; close enough for men to see their enemies' faces, close enough to hear an enemy's voice, close enough for a bullet to mangle a man's flesh with undiminished horror. This was an infantry fight, rifle against rifle, the ordeal for which both sides had trained incessantly. Starbuck had to forget those Yankees who had broken through and were now loose at his rear; his sole duty was to stand and fight and trust someone else to worry about the Yankees who had breached the line, just as someone else must worry about the possibility of more Yankees crossing the railbed to join this duel of rifles. If those enemy reinforcements arrived, Starbuck knew, then the Legion must be overwhelmed, but for the moment the Northerners were being held. They were being held by men who knew their survival depended on being able to load their rifles faster than the enemy. There was no need for any officers or sergeants to give commands. The men knew what to do. They did it.

Lieutenant Patterson was dead, killed by his red sash that had attracted too many Yankee bullets. It was a miracle to Starbuck that any man survived the maelstrom of close-range rifle fire, but the sulfurous powder smoke served as a screen, and the Yankee fire slackened as the Northerners edged back toward the railbed. No regiment, however brave, could long survive a rifle duel at close range, and the instinct for both sides was to retreat, but Starbuck's men were standing hard against the hill's base, and the slope inhibited their natural instinct to shuffle a few inches backward every time they reloaded their rifles, but the open land behind the Yankee line tempted the Northerners to yield their ground inch by bloody inch, then yard by smoldering yard.

Starbuck lost count of the bullets he fired. His rifle was now so fouled with powder that it was painful to ram each new bullet down the barrel. He fired and fired again, his shoulder bruising from the recoil, his eyes smarting from the smoke, and his voice hoarse from the day's shouting. He heard the distinctive meat-ax sound as bullets struck men around him and was dimly conscious of bodies falling backward from the line. He was also conscious that rank gave him the freedom to leave the battle line, except that the responsibility of command perversely decreed that he could not take that voluntary backward step.

And so he fought. Sometimes he shouted at the line to close up, but mostly he just rammed and fired, rammed and fired, consumed by the conviction shared by every man in the line that his were the bullets that were pushing the enemy back. He flinched each time the heavy gun slammed back into his shoulder, and he choked each time he bit open a cartridge and so tasted the acrid, salt-rich, mouth-drying

410

gunpowder. Sweat stung his eyes. Somewhere in the back of his mind was the terror of being injured, but he was too busy loading and firing to let that terror overwhelm him. An occasional bullet slicing close by left him momentarily shaking, but then he would ram another round into the recalcitrant rifle and crash another shoulder-bruising shot toward the Yankees and fish for another cartridge in his haversack as he let the rifle's heavy stock fall to the ground. Once, pouring powder into the barrel, the new charge caught fire and exploded a bright gash of flame into his face. He recoiled from the pain, his eyeballs seared raw, then angrily rammed the embers dead in the barrel with his ramrod. Minutes later another sharp pain shot hard through his right arm, and he almost dropped the rifle from the sudden agony; then he saw he had been struck not by a bullet but only by a sharp-tipped splinter of bone that had been ripped from his neighbor's ribcage by a Yankee bullet. The man was on the ground, twitching as the blood flooded from his shattered chest. He looked up at Starbuck, tried so hard to speak, then choked on blood and died.

Starbuck stooped to feel in the man's haversack for more cartridges and found just two. He was down to the bottom layer of his own rounds now. "Close up!" he shouted. "Close up!" And a momentary lull in the fighting gave him an opportunity to back out of the line, where men were asking friends and neighbors for any extra ammunition. Starbuck handed out what few rounds he had left and then climbed the steep hill in search of the Legion's spare ammunition supply. A score of wounded men had taken refuge on the hill. One of Haxall's Arkansas men, his left arm hanging bloody, tried to load his rifle one-handed. "Goddamned sons of bitches," the man muttered over and over, "Goddamned sons of Yankee bitches." A shell burst overhead to slap hot scraps of smoking metal into the hill.

"Yankees have brought up two more howitzers!" Colonel Swynyard was seated halfway up the hill, field glasses in hand. He sounded very calm.

"We need ammunition!" Starbuck said, trying to sound as collected as the Colonel but unable to keep a note of panic out of his voice.

"None left!" The Colonel shrugged helplessly. "I have to apologize to you, Starbuck."

"Me?"

"I swore at you earlier. I apologize."

"You did? Christ!" Starbuck spat out the blasphemy as another shell screamed low overhead to ricochet up from the slope and explode somewhere beyond the summit. Had Swynyard sworn at him? Starbuck did not remember, nor did he much care. He was suddenly worrying far more about what had happened to the mass of Yankees who had streamed through the gap into the army's rear and there disappeared. Suppose those men were about to counterattack? "We must have ammunition!" he shouted to Swynyard.

"Used it all. Long day's fighting." The Colonel seemed remarkably calm as he aimed his revolver at the Northern battle line and methodically pulled the trigger. "They're slackening! When they're gone we'll pillage the dead for ammunition."

Starbuck ran downhill and pulled two of Captain Davies's men out of the ranks. "You're to search the dead and wounded," he told them, "and find ammunition. Hand it out! Hurry!" He sent one man to the left, the other to the right, then took their place in the ranks and drew his revolver.

Starbuck found himself standing alongside the bespectacled Captain Ethan Davies, who was fighting with a rifle. "They're from Indiana," Davies said, as though Starbuck would be interested in the news.

412

"What? Who?" Starbuck had not been listening. Instead he had been searching the smoke-smeared enemy line for any sign of a man giving commands.

"These fellows." Davies indicated the nearest Yankees with a jerk of his chin. "They're from Indiana."

"How do you know?"

"I asked them, of course. Shouted at them." He fired, flinching from the painful impact of the rifle's heavy recoil against his bruised shoulder. "I almost married a girl from Indiana once," Davies added as he dropped the rifle's butt onto the ground and pulled out a paper-wrapped cartridge.

"What stopped you?" Starbuck was priming his revolver with percussion caps.

"She was Catholic and my parents disapproved." Davies spoke mildly. He bit off a bullet, poured the gritty powder down the hot barrel, then spat the bullet into the muzzle with powder-blackened lips. His spectacles were smeared into opaqueness with dust and sweat. "I often think of her," he said wistfully, then rammed the bullet down hard, swung the rifle up, capped it, and pulled the trigger. "She came from Terre Haute. Don't you think that's a wonderful name for a town?"

Starbuck cocked his revolver. "How did a Virginian happen to meet a Catholic girl from Terre Haute?" He had to shout the question over the splintering noise of gunfire.

"She's some kind of distant cousin. I met her when she came to Faulconer Court House for a family funeral." Davies cursed, not because of the memory of his lost love, but because the cone of his rifle had become brittle from the heat and shattered. He threw the gun down and took another from a dead man. Somewhere in the battle smoke a young man screamed horribly. The scream went on and on, punctuated by short gasps of breath. Davies shuddered at the awful sound. "Oh, my God," he said callously when the screaming ended suddenly, "just lay me down."

"I wish people would stop saying that," Starbuck said, "it's getting on my nerves."

"You'd prefer biblical quotes?" Davies asked. "Lambs to the slaughter," he offered, misquoting Isaiah.

"'The sword of the Lord is filled with blood.'" Starbuck offered another quotation from the same prophet as he fired two rounds of the revolver. "'It is made fat with fatness and with the blood of lambs.'"

Davies shuddered at the sentiment. "I keep forgetting you were a theology student."

"There's nothing like a course of Old Testament studies to make a soldier ready for battle," Starbuck said with relish. He lowered his revolver and listened to the sound of the fighting. The Yankee fire was definitely slackening. "They won't last long now," he said. His mouth was so dry that talking was difficult. He had replaced his shattered canteen with another but had long drained its tepid contents. Now he stooped and unlooped a dead man's canteen.

"Her name was Louisa," Davies said.

"Who?" Starbuck said. He tipped the canteen to his mouth and was rewarded by a trickle of lukewarm water. "Who?" he asked again.

"My distant Catholic relative from Indiana," Davies said as he primed his new rifle, "and two years ago she married a corn chandler."

"With any luck you're about to kill the bastard," Starbuck said, "and that'll make the lovely Louisa into a respectable young widow and you can marry her when the war's over." He emptied the rest of his revolver's chambers into the smoke. "Keep firing!" he shouted at the company, then slapped Davies on the shoulder as he left the company to walk back along the Legion's rear. "Bastards are giving way,

414

boys! Keep firing! Keep firing!" He reloaded his revolver as he walked, doing the job without needing to look down at the weapon. Starbuck remembered his first day of battle, not a mile or two from this very spot, when he had been unable to load his revolver because his hands had been trembling and his vision blurred, while now he did it without thinking or looking.

The Legion kept firing but were taking very little return fire except for an occasional shell lobbed by the small howitzers at the edge of the trees, and those shells were mostly fused too long and so exploded harmlessly among the shattered saplings behind the battle line. The Yankee line, splintered into groups by the steady rebel firing, was stumbling back across their own dead toward the railbed. There was a danger they might go to ground there, and Starbuck reckoned his dazed and bloodied men would have to charge with fixed bayonets to keep the Northern retreat moving, but just a second before he shouted the order, so a great backwash of attackers surged from the west.

The Northerners who had passed clean through the rebel line into the open land beyond were now streaming back. They had been harried by Haxall's Arkansas battalion, then intercepted by a brigade sent by Lee to reinforce Jackson's hard-pressed men, and now the Northerners were in full retreat. "Let 'em through!" Hudson shouted at Starbuck. The choice was either to open ranks and let the Northerners go back beyond the railbed or else to turn and fight, but Hudson's implied choice was to give the enemy a free pass home. There were simply too many Yankees for the battle-weary rebel line to take on, especially as there were still plenty of Northerners firing from the railbed. A decision to fight would have meant firing both east and west, so Starbuck gratefully shouted his assent to Hudson and then pulled the Legion's right wing clear of the retreating Yankees. The fleeing enemy surged past the spoil pit.

Starbuck watched the disorganized enemy run past; then another flicker of movement closer to the hill made him look right to see a small group of gray-clad men running parallel with the enemy but keeping well away from danger. Major Medlicott and Captain Moxey were in the lead of a score of men who now tried to rejoin the Legion's ranks without their arrival being noted. Starbuck ran toward the fugitives. "Where were you?" he asked Medlicott.

"What do you mean?" Medlicott demanded. He turned away from Starbuck and aimed his rifle at the Yankees running past fifty paces away.

Starbuck slapped the rifle down. "Where were you?"

"The Yankees pushed us back," Medlicott said, his tone daring Starbuck to contradict him. "We tried to rejoin."

Starbuck knew the man was lying. He could see from the state of Medlicott's soldiers that none of them had been fighting. Their eyes were not reddened by smoke, their lips were not blackened by powder, and their faces did not have the feral, half-scared, half-savage look of men pushed to the edge of endurance. All still wore the red crescent badge denoting their loyalty to Washington Faulconer, and all of them, Starbuck was sure, had skulked for the best part of the day. Yet he could prove nothing, and so he settled for a feeble acceptance of Medlicott's lie. "Keep fighting," he said. He knew he had handled the confrontation badly, a suspicion confirmed when Moxey laughed aloud. The laughter was drowned by a sudden ear-hurting roar as a flight of shells crashed into the killing patch beyond the railbed. The rebel artillery, which had been preoccupied these last long minutes with Yankee attackers further south, had switched their fire back to the ground opposite Swynyard's brigade, and the effect of the shrieking, bursting, smoke-riven shells was to drive the enemy's howitzers away from the tree line and the retreating Yankees into the shelter of the railbed cutting.

"You've got to get them out of there, Starbuck!" Swynyard immediately shouted from the hillside.

The Yankees had suddenly learned the value of the railbed and were using its protection to start a galling rifle fire on the Legion. The men returned the fire, but the rebels were getting by far the worst of it. Starbuck, still standing beside the recalcitrant right-hand companies, cupped his hands. "Fix bayonets!" He watched as his men crouched behind the thin cover of the fire-blasted saplings and slotted long blades onto the black, hot muzzles of their rifles. He turned and saw Moxey's resentful men doing the same. Moxey was wearing one of the frilled shirts he had looted at Manassas Junction, and somehow the finery made Starbuck hate the man even more. He pushed that hatred out of his mind as he capped the five chambers of his new Adams revolver. "Ready?" he called to Medlicott's men. One or two nodded, but most ignored him. He looked to his left and saw the strained, anxious faces of the other companies. "Charge!" he shouted. "Charge!"

The Legion rose from its crouch like men snapping from nightmare. The Yankees in the railbed responded with a volley that billowed smoke along the lip of their makeshift parapet. A shell cracked overhead to make an instant black cloud. Men were falling, bleeding, calling in pain, but most of the Legion were still running through the blackened scrub and reeking smoke. They screamed their war scream. The smoke of the Yankee volley cleared, and the Northerners, armed now with unloaded rifles, saw a glitter of bayonets fast approaching, and so they scrambled hurriedly out the railbed's far side.

Just as a salvo of rebel-fired shells crashed into the dirt and exploded shrapnel into their faces. Most of the Northerners

417

instinctively shied away from that high-explosive death just as the rebel line leaped into the trench.

"Kill them!" Truslow shouted and rammed forward with a bayonet that he abandoned in his first victim so that he could unsheath his bowie knife. Most of the Yankees decided that fleeing through the shells offered a better chance of survival than being disemboweled in a blood-sodden trench, and so a horde of Northerners scrambled out of the railbed and ran across the open ground. Others stayed and surrendered. A handful tried to fight the rebel counter-attack and were killed. Starbuck saw Peter Waggoner lead-ing a squad of men against a stubborn group of Northerners; there was a volley, a scream, then Waggoner swung his rifle by the muzzle to smash its stock against a man's head, and the other Northerners began to shout their surrender. Out in the open ground another salvo of shells ripped smoke, flame, and metal shards through the fugitives. Starbuck, a smoking revolver in his hand, saw a man's head bowling along the ground like a spent cannonball. He gaped at it, not sure that his eyes were really seeing what his brain was registering.

"No, no, no, no, please!" A Northerner was staring up at Starbuck with horror on his face. The man's hands were raised. He was shaking in terror, thinking that he was about to be executed by the tall Southern officer with the bitter eyes and smoking gun.

"You're safe," Starbuck told the man, then turned to see that neither Medlicott's men nor Moxey's company had charged with the Legion. Instead they were in the spoil pit, where they were attempting to look busy by rounding up prisoners. There was unfinished business there, and business that had to be settled soon or else there would be no Legion left to command. "Major Medlicott?" he shouted across to the spoil pit.

"Yes?" Medlicott's tone was cautious.

"I want the Legion's ammunition pooled, then redistributed. And search the dead for cartridges." He looked up at the sky. It would be dark soon. "Your men have first picket duty. And keep a careful watch."

"They always do," Medlicott said defiantly. He had been half expecting a reprimand for disobeying the order to charge the railbed, and his tone suggested the scorn in which he now held Starbuck for not daring to impose discipline.

Starbuck ignored him. He had other things to do. He had the dead to count, the wounded to rescue, and ammunition to find. So he could be ready to fight again. Tomorrow.

"A good day's work, gentlemen, an excellent day's work." John Pope was ebullient about his army's achievement as he strode into the farm that was his field headquarters. A dozen men awaited his arrival, and so infectious was the General's pleasure that they actually burst into applause as he came through the door. Most of those who had been waiting for Pope were general officers, but there was also a congressman from Washington and the Reverend Elial Starbuck from Boston carrying, inevitably, the bundled rebel flag that was his precious trophy and souvenir. The Reverend Starbuck had spent the day on the field and was as dusty, dirty, and tired as any of the soldiers, though Pope himself looked very fresh as he lifted the lid of one of the supper tureens on the long dining table. He sniffed its contents appreciatively. "Venison steak? Good! Good! I hope there's some cranberry jelly to go with it?"

"Alas, sir," one of the aides murmured.

"Never mind." Pope was in a forgiving mood. The railroad bridge at Bristoe had been repaired, so that trains could now run the length of the Orange and Alexandria, which meant that the last regiments being carried north from

Warrenton could be transported all the way into the smoking ruins of Manassas Junction, from where it was a short step to tomorrow's battlefield. Or rather to tomorrow's victory, for John Pope was now convinced that he was on the brink of a historic triumph.

General McDowell, who had lost the first battle fought at Manassas but who now led Pope's Third Corps, was similarly confident of victory, especially as more troops were arriving hourly. Those reinforcements were coming not just from Pope's own Army of Virginia but also from McClellan's Army of the Potomac. "Though I doubt we'll see the young Napoleon here tomorrow," McDowell said heavily.

"I doubt it, too," Pope said, sitting at the table and helping himself to a piece of venison. "George won't want to witness another man winning a victory. That would take far too much shine off his buttons, eh?" He laughed, inviting the table to laugh with him. "Whereas I don't mind who gets the credit so long as the U.S.A. gets the victory, ain't that a fact?" Pope threw this outrageous statement at one of his aides, who blandly confirmed its truth. "You know what George wants me to do?" Pope went on as he helped himself to buttered beans. "George wants me to pull the army back to Centreville and wait there! Here we are with Stonewall Jackson skewered to the wall, and I'm supposed to walk away to Centreville! And why? So the young Napoleon can take command!"

"He doesn't want you to win the victory he couldn't win," McDowell suggested loyally.

"And I've no doubt that if I did pull back to Centreville," Pope went on without actually disagreeing with McDowell's statement, "then the very first thing our young Napoleon would do is hold a parade. I hear George is uncommon fond of parades."

"Very fond," the visiting congressman said, "and why not? Parades are very good for the public's confidence."

"A victory might be better for their confidence," McDowell suggested. The Third Corps's commander had piled his plate with venison steaks and sweet potatoes.

"Well, damn George's parades," Pope said, wondering like everyone else about the table whether McDowell could possibly add another spoonful of supper to his heaped plate. "I shall not retreat to Centreville. I shall win a victory instead. That'll astonish Washington, isn't that so, Congressman? You're not used to generals who fight and win!" Pope laughed, and his laughter was echoed about the supper table, though the General noticed that the famous Boston preacher alone seemed unamused. "You look tired, Doctor Starbuck," the General observed genially.

"A day in the saddle, General," the preacher said. "I'm most unaccustomed to such exertions."

"No doubt I'd be weary if I spent a day in your pulpit," Pope responded gallantly, but the preacher did not even smile at the response. Instead he put a notebook on the table, pulled a candle close to its open pages, and expressed a polite puzzlement at some of the events he had witnessed that day. "Such as what?" John Pope asked.

"Men attacking, other men doing nothing to help them," the preacher said succinctly. It seemed to the Reverend Starbuck that the Federal attacks had come so close to success, yet the survivors complained that the reinforcements who might have guaranteed Northern victory had never stirred from their bivouacs.

John Pope felt an impulse of anger. He had no need to explain himself to meddlesome priests, yet Pope knew that he possessed few allies in the army's highest reaches, and fewer still in Washington. John Pope was an abolitionist, while most of his rivals, like McClellan, were fighting not for the slaves but for the Union, and John Pope knew that he needed public opinion to be on his side if he was to prevail against his many political enemies. The Reverend Starbuck was a powerful persuader of the Northern public, and so the General subdued his irritation and patiently explained his day's achievements. He spoke between mouthfuls, gesturing with a fork. What the Army of Virginia had done, he said, was to pen Stonewall Jackson up against the western hills and woods. Pope glanced at the congressman to make sure that he was listening, then went on to explain how Jackson had wanted to escape down the Warrenton Turnpike but had instead been corralled.

The preacher nodded impatiently. He understood all this. "But why do we need wait till tomorrow to kill the snake? We had him trapped today, surely?"

Pope, mindful of what the pencil in the preacher's hand could achieve, smiled. "We've pinned Jackson into some rough country, Doctor, but we haven't quite cut off all his escape routes. What you were witnessing today was a gallant fight to keep Jackson staring in this direction while our other fellows curled around his flanks." The General demonstrated the strategy by surrounding a gravy boat with cruets. "And tomorrow, Doctor, we can attack again with the absolute assurance that this time the wretches have no escape." He dropped a salt cellar into the gravy, splashing the tablecloth. "No escape at all!"

"Amen!" McDowell said through a mouthful of venison and butter beans.

"You only saw a small part of a greater design," Pope explained to the preacher. "Does not the good book have something to say about there being more things in heaven and earth than we can dream of?"

"Shakespeare said it," the preacher remarked stiffly, still penciling his notes. "'There are more things in heaven and

422

earth, Horatio, than are dreamt of in your philosophy.' *Hamlet*, Act One, Scene Five." He closed the book and slipped it into his pocket. "So tomorrow, General, we might expect a victory to rank with Cannae? Or with Yorktown?"

Pope hesitated to claim ground quite that high, especially in front of a congressman, yet he had raised the expectation himself. "So long as McClellan's men fight as they should," he answered, neatly shifting the responsibility onto his rival. No one responded. Indeed, no one liked to stir that can of worms. McClellan's men were famously loyal to their general, and many of them resented being under the orders of John Pope, and there was a fear that resentment might be translated into a reluctance to fight.

"I wonder what Lee's doing?" an artillery officer at the table's far end asked.

"Robert Lee is doing what Robert Lee always does best," Pope declared, "which is sitting on his hands and letting someone else do the scrapping. Lee's waiting south of the Rappahannock, digging in. He sent Jackson to disrupt our preparations, but he reckoned without the swiftness of our response. He underestimated us, gentlemen, and that will be his undoing. Is that a plate of pears? Might I trouble you for a serving? Thank you." An orderly brought a jug of lemonade for the teetotalers and a decanter of wine for the others. Beyond the farm windows there was a pretty sprinkling of firelight where the nearest battalions were bivouacking on a hillside. A band was playing in the distance, the music sweet and plangent in the warm summer darkness.

"Did anyone discover what those rebel troops were doing beyond Groveton?" one of McDowell's officers asked as he spooned thick cream onto his pears. There had been a handful of reports about rebel troops arriving on the open western flank of Pope's army.

"Alarmist rumors," Pope said confidently. "All they saw

were enemy cavalry scouts. The last throes of a dying army, gentlemen, are always the sight of its cavalry scouts looking for a way out. But not tomorrow, not anymore. From now on this army marches forward. To Richmond!"

"To Richmond," the assembled officers murmured, "and to victory."

"To Richmond," the congressman said, "and reelection."

"To Richmond," the Reverend Starbuck said, "and emancipation."

All in the morning.

During the night Hudson's North Carolinians made a new abatis in front of the railbed, where neither the cutting nor its adjacent embankment offered a real obstacle to the Yankee attackers. "I should have thought of it before," Hudson admitted.

"So should I," Starbuck said. He paused. "Except I thought Lee was coming. I never reckoned we'd have to fight alone all day."

"I told you," Hudson said in a kindly voice, "always to expect the worst."

"But where is Lee?" Starbuck insisted on the question despite the older man's advice.

"The Lord only knows," Hudson said softly, "and I guess we'll just have to go on fighting till the good Lord lets us into the secret."

"I guess so, too," Starbuck said bleakly. He was morose, aware that his first day in command of a fighting regiment had not been a success. The Legion had twice been driven from its position, and though it had twice regained the railbed, it had suffered cruelly in the process. Worse, two whole companies of the regiment were in virtual mutiny. Starbuck remembered Moxey's laughter, and he knew as certainly as he knew anything in all his life that the mocking laughter had been his opportunity to crush the defiant right-hand companies once and for all. Starbuck knew he should have pulled out his revolver and put a bullet smack between Moxey's eyes, but instead he had pretended not to hear, and so had given his enemies a victory.

The construction of the new abatis was harassed by Yankee sharpshooters, whose fire did not end at nightfall. In the dark the sharpshooters fired wherever they saw movement beside a distant fire, and that constant danger drove men to take cover in the railbed or else to seek the safety of the hill's rearward slope, where the Brigade's surgeons worked by candlelight. The Brigade's own sharpshooters replied to the Yankee fire, the flames of their heavy-barreled rifles spitting long and whip-thin in the darkness. The marksmen held their fire only when a shout requested that they respect the movements of a stretcher party, but whenever the stretcher bearers had finished their task and had called their thanks for the enemy's courtesy, the firing would begin again.

The only good news of the night was the arrival of a mailbag that had been brought from Gordonsville with Lee's advancing troops. Sergeant Tyndale distributed the letters and parcels, making a sad pile of mail addressed to dead men. One of the parcels had come from the Richmond Arsenal and was addressed to the officer commanding the Faulconer Legion. The big package proved to contain a standard-issue battle flag: a four-foot-square banner woven from common cloth that was intended to replace the captured silk standard. There was no flagstaff, so Starbuck sent Lucifer to cut down a straight, ten-foot sapling.

Then, in the light of a campfire at the rear of the hill, he opened his two letters. The first came from Thaddeus Bird, who reported that he was recovering remarkably well and

425

hoped to return to the Legion very soon. "Priscilla does not share this hope and constantly discovers new symptoms that might require a further period of convalescence, yet I feel my absence from the Legion keenly." The letter went on to say that Anthony Murphy had safely reached Faulconer Court House and was also recuperating, though he was not expected to be on his feet for a week or two yet. "Is it true," Bird then asked, "that Swynyard has seen the divine light? If so then it proves Christianity must be of some use in this world, but I confess I find it hard to comprehend such a conversion. Does the dragon purr? Does he pray before he beats his slaves, or after? You must write to me with all the malicious details." The letter finished with the news that Washington Faulconer had not been seen in Faulconer Court House but was rumored to be stirring up political trouble in Richmond.

Starbuck's second letter had come from the Confederate capital. To his surprise and pleasure the letter was from Julia Gordon, Adam's erstwhile fiancée, who now regarded Starbuck as her friend. She wrote with good news. "My mother has yielded to my wish and allowed me to become a nurse in Chimborazo Hospital. She did not yield graciously, but under the pressure of poverty and to the hospital's solemn undertaking to pay me a wage, though I have yet to see that promise fulfilled. I am being tutored, they say, and so must abjure all hopes of payment until I can distinguish a bandage from a bottle of calomel. I learn, I learn, and at night I weep for the poor boys here, but doubtless I shall learn not to do so." She made no mention of Adam, nor was there anything personal in the letter; it was simply the words of a friend seeking a sympathetic ear. "You would not recognize the hospital now," Julia concluded. "It daily spreads fresh buildings across the park, and each new ward is filled with wounded before the builders' sawhorses are even moved out. I pray daily that you will be spared seeing it from one of the cots."

Starbuck stared at the letter and tried to recall Julia's face, but somehow the picture would not form in his head. Dark hair and good bones, he remembered, and a quick intelligence in the eyes, but still he could not see her image in his mind's eye. "You're looking homesick," Colonel Swynyard interrupted Starbuck's thoughts.

"Letter from a friend," Starbuck explained.

"A girl?" Swynyard asked as he sat opposite Starbuck.

"Yes," Starbuck said, then, after a pause, "a Christian girl, Colonel. A good, virtuous, and Christian girl."

Swynyard laughed. "How you do yearn for respectable citizenship in the Kingdom of God, Starbuck. Maybe you should repent now? Maybe this is the hour for you to put your trust in Him?"

"You're trying to convert me, Colonel." Starbuck made the accusation sourly.

"What greater favor could I do you?"

Starbuck stared into the fire. "Maybe," he said slowly, "you could replace me as commander of the Legion?"

Swynyard chuckled. "Suppose, Starbuck, that after one day of abandoning alcohol I had told you I was finding the whole thing too hard. Would you have approved?"

Starbuck managed a rueful grin. "Back then, Colonel, I'd have told you to wait a day, then go back to the bottle. That way I might have won the bet I had on you."

Swynyard was not altogether pleased with the reply, but he managed a smile. "So I'll give you the same advice. Wait a day, see how you feel tomorrow."

Starbuck shrugged. "I didn't do well today. I panicked. I was shouting and running around like a scalded cat."

Swynyard smiled. "None of us did well today. I'm not real sure Jackson did well today, and the good Lord alone knows what happened to Lee, but the enemy didn't do well either. We're still here, Starbuck, and they ain't beat us yet. See how you feel tomorrow." The Colonel stood up. Sparks whirled past his lean face. "Maybe you should turn your companies around tomorrow?" he suggested. "Put Truslow on the right and Medlicott on the left?"

"I did think about doing just that," Starbuck admitted.

"And?"

Starbuck plucked a burning brand from the fire and used it to light a cigar. "I think I've got a better idea, Colonel." He tossed the brand back onto the flames and looked up at Swynyard. "You remember what you said about Old Mad Jack? That it didn't matter how eccentric a man was, so long as he won?"

"I remember. So?"

Starbuck grinned. "So you won't approve of what I'm going to do. Which means I won't tell you what it is, but it'll work."

Swynyard thought about that answer. "So you didn't really want to be replaced?"

"I'll let you know tomorrow, Colonel."

Starbuck spent the night in the railbed, where he slept for a few precious moments, but it seemed he was woken every time a sharpshooter let a bullet fly across the ground separating the armies. In the morning, before the mist lifted to make him into an easy target, he climbed the hill to watch the land emerge from the vapor. In the distance, beyond the trees, a swarm of smoke tendrils marked the enemy's cooking fires, while off to the left, and much closer than he had expected, a bright gleam between two stands of trees briefly showed beneath the shifting skeins of mist. He borrowed a rifle from one of Haxall's sharpshooters and used its telescopic sight to inspect the gleam. "I guess that's the Bull Run," he said to the sharpshooter.

428

The man shrugged. "Can't think there's another river that big 'round here. Sure ain't the Big Muddy though."

Nearer at hand Starbuck could see a stretch of road running between two pastures. He suspected it was the Sudley road, which meant the Legion was less than half a mile from the twin fords across the Catharpin and Bull runs. He had crossed those fords a year before on the day that Washington Faulconer had tried to eject him from the Legion, and if that far gleam was indeed the run and the road really was the highway leading from Manassas to Sudley, then it meant that the Legion was close, tantalizingly close, to the Galloway farm.

With nothing but an army between the Legion and its vengeance.

Starbuck handed the sharpshooter's rifle back, then went downhill to where the surgeons still worked on the previous day's wounded. He talked with the Legion's casualties, and then, with a dead man's rifle on his shoulder and a handful of salvaged cartridges in his haversack, he ran back to the railbed. A sharpshooter tried to kill him as he crossed the scrubland, but the Yankee's bullet whipped a foot wide to thump into a bloated corpse and startle a swarm of flies into the warm morning air. Then Starbuck leaped the parapet and slid down into the railbed's cutting to begin his new day's work.

THE FIRST ATTACK OF the Saturday morning was an advance by two companies of Northern infantry who emerged from the trees in skirmish order. They walked gingerly and with bayonets fixed, almost as if they suspected that their orders to advance on the railbed were a mistake. "Oh, my God." Captain Davies began the idiotic refrain that had the mysterious power to convulse Jackson's army.

"Don't," Starbuck growled, but he could have saved his breath.

"Just lay me down." A half-dozen of Davies's men finished the sentence and immediately began laughing.

"Imbeciles," Starbuck said, though no one could tell whether he referred to the Legionnaires or to the handful of Yankees who were crossing the open ground where hundreds had died the day before.

"Some idiot got his orders confused," Davies commented with an indecent relish. "Lambs to the slaughter, march!" He eased his rifle over the parapet.

"Hold your fire!" Starbuck called. He was waiting for the enemy's main body to appear at the edge of the trees, but it seemed the handful of Northern skirmishers was expected to capture the railbed on their own. Such suicidal behavior suggested Davies was right and that some poor Northern officer had misunderstood his orders, or perhaps the enemy believed the rebels had abandoned the railbed during the night. Starbuck disabused them of the notion. He used just two of his companies. He wanted the other companies to conserve their ammunition, but the fire of F and G Companies was sufficient to send the Northern soldiers scuttling ignominiously back to the tree line. Two skirmishers were left on the ground and another half-dozen limped as they fled. One of the wounded men repeatedly flapped an arm as though gesturing at the rebels not to fire again. None did.

"I suspect our Northern neighbors were feeling us out, Starbuck. Taking our pulse to see if any life remains in us. Good morning to you!" The speaker was the exuberant Colonel Elijah Hudson, who was ambling down the railbed as though he were merely taking a morning stroll. "I trust you slept well?"

"Half well," Starbuck said. "It was a noisy night."

"So it was, so it was. I confess I abandoned my efforts to sleep and retired into the woods to read Homer by lantern light. I was struck by the line about arrows rattling in their quivers as the archers advanced to battle. You remember it? He must have heard the noise to have described it. Those were the days, Starbuck. None of this loitering in a trench, but up with the sun, a quick sacrifice to all-seeing Zeus, and then a chariot ride to glory. Or to death, I suppose. You breakfasted?"

"Cold chicken and hot coffee," Starbuck said. Lucifer was proving adept at feeding Starbuck, though admittedly the boy still had the supplies taken from the Manassas depot as his larder. Lucifer's real test would come when all he had was weevil-ridden hardtack, rancid bacon grease, and rotting salt beef. If the boy even stayed long enough to face such a culinary test. So far the fugitive slave seemed amused at being a part of the Confederate army, but doubtless he would run whenever the whim took him.

"My son came to see me last night," Hudson now told Starbuck, who had to think for a second before remembering that Hudson's eldest son was an aide of Robert Lee. "Tom told me that Lee arrived yesterday," the Colonel went on, "but Pete Longstreet declined the order to attack. Our Mr. Longstreet is a meticulous fellow. He likes to make certain he has a sufficiency of mud and water before he makes his pies. Let us hope the Yankees stay long enough to be attacked. Or maybe I shouldn't hope that. My boys are wicked low on cartridges."

"Mine too," Starbuck said.

"Well, if all else fails," Hudson said, "we shall just have to throw rocks at them!" He smiled to show he was jesting, then prodded his stick into the cutting's bank like a farmer testing the dirt at planting season. "Did your fellows suffer badly yesterday?" He asked the question in a deceptively casual tone.

"Badly enough. Twenty-three killed and fifty-six with the doctors."

"Much the same, much the same," Hudson said, shaking his head at the news. "A bad business, Starbuck, a bad business. But can't be helped. What fools we mortals be. I have some coffee on the boil if you want to make a neighborly call." Hudson gave a wave with his stick and strode back to his own regiment.

Lieutenant Coffman had resumed his role as Starbuck's aide. He had been slightly wounded the day before by a bullet that had cut a ragged, dirty groove in the flesh of his upper left arm. Truslow had cleaned and dressed the wound, and Coffman kept touching the makeshift bandage as if to make certain that the badge of his courage was still in place. He bore no other badges; indeed, it was now impossible to tell that the ragged Coffman was an officer, for he carried a rifle, had a haversack and cap box on his belt, and had the half-starved, half-fearful, dirty face of a common soldier. "What happens now, sir?" he asked Starbuck.

"That's up to the Yankees, Coffman," Starbuck said. He was watching Sergeant Peter Waggoner lead a small prayer group and remembering how another group of men had willingly followed the big Sergeant into the railbed's cutting, where Waggoner had swung his rifle like a club to break apart a knot of Yankee resistance. It was not so much the Sergeant's bravery that now impressed Starbuck as the fact that men had so willingly followed Waggoner into the fight. "Captain Pine!" Starbuck shouted at Company D's commanding officer.

"Six cartridges apiece," Pine said, leaping to the conclusion that Starbuck needed to know the bad news of how many rounds his men had left.

"Who's your best sergeant after Waggoner?" Starbuck asked instead.

Pine thought about it for a second. "Tom Darke."

"You might have to lose Waggoner, that's why."

Pine flinched at that news, then shrugged. "To replace poor Patterson?"

"Maybe," Starbuck said vaguely. "But don't say anything to Waggoner yet." He walked back to the south, passing the remnants of Patterson's Company C, now under the command of Sergeant Malachi Williams, who offered a curt nod as Starbuck passed. None of Company C had joined Medlicott's retreat the day before, nor indeed had every man in A and B Company. The rot, Starbuck decided, was confined to a stubborn handful who doubtless assumed that Washington Faulconer still wielded more power in the Legion than Nathaniel Starbuck.

Starbuck resisted the temptation to crouch as the trench became shallower. "Keep your head down," he told Coffman.

"You're not keeping yours down," the Lieutenant replied.

"I'm a Yankee. I lack your valuable blood," Starbuck said

just as a sharpshooter in the Northern-held woods tried for him. The bullet struck a branch in the new abatis and ricocheted up into the air while the sound of the gun echoed back from the hillside. Starbuck gave a derisive wave to his unseen assailant, then jumped down into the spoil pit, where Medlicott and Moxey were standing beside a small fire over which a coffeepot was suspended. A half-dozen of their men were lounging near the fire and looked up suspiciously as Starbuck and Coffman arrived. "Is that coffee fresh?" Starbuck asked cheerfully.

"There isn't much left," Moxey said guardedly.

Starbuck peered into the pot. "Plenty enough for Lieutenant Coffman and me," he said, then gave his tin mug to Coffman. "Pour away, Lieutenant." Starbuck turned to Medlicott. "I had a letter from Pecker. You'll doubtless be pleased that he expects to be back soon."

"Good," Medlicott said forcefully.

"And Murphy's well. Thank you, Lieutenant." Starbuck took the proffered mug and blew across the steaming coffee. "Is it sweetened?" he asked Medlicott.

Medlicott said nothing but just watched as Starbuck sipped the coffee. "We heard from General Faulconer," Moxey blurted out, unable to keep the news to himself.

"Did you now?" Starbuck asked. "And how is the General?"

For a moment neither man answered. Indeed Medlicott seemed annoyed that Moxey had even mentioned the letter, but now that its existence was known the Major decided to take responsibility for its contents. "He's offered Captain Moxey and I jobs," he said with as much dignity as he could muster.

"I am glad," Starbuck said feelingly. "What sort of jobs? In his stables, perhaps? Serving at table? Kitchen hands, maybe?" Somewhere a cannon barked flat and hard. The noise of the shot rolled and faded across the countryside; then a train whistle sounded in the far-off depot. The whistle was a very homely sound, a reminder that a world existed where men did not wake to sharpshooters and bloated corpses. "The General needs a pair of boot-cleaners, maybe?" Starbuck asked. He sipped the coffee again. It was very good, but he made a disgusted face and poured the liquid onto the spoil pit's stones so that it splashed onto Medlicott's boots. "What sort of a job, Major?" Starbuck asked.

Medlicott was silent for a few seconds as he controlled his temper; then he managed a grim smile. "General Faulconer says there are vacancies in the Provost Guard at the Capitol."

Starbuck pretended to be impressed. "You'll be guarding the President and Congress! And all those Richmond politicians and their whores! Is it just the pair of you who are needed? Or can you take the rest of us with you, too?"

"We can take enough men, Starbuck," Medlicott said, "but only the right kind of men." He added the childish insult, and there was a murmur of agreement from the nearby soldiers, who had clearly been invited to share Medlicott's supposed good fortune.

"And that explains why you're avoiding all the fighting!" Starbuck said as though the idea had only just dawned on him. "Dear Lord above! And I thought you were simply being cowards! Now you tell me you're keeping yourselves safe for higher and better duties. Why didn't you tell me before?" Starbuck waited, but neither man answered. Starbuck spat at their feet. "Listen, you sons of bitches, I've served in the Richmond provosts, and General Winder runs that crew of spavined leprous bastards, not General Faulconer. General Faulconer has about as much influence in Richmond as I do. He's promising you an easy berth just to make you unhappy here, but I ain't going to let you play that game. You're here to fight, not dream, so this morning you sons of bitches are fighting with the rest of us. Is that clear?"

Moxey looked apprehensive, but Medlicott had more faith in Washington Faulconer than Moxey. "We'll do what we have to do," he said stubbornly.

"Good," Starbuck said, "because what you have to do is fight." He walked to the edge of the spoil pit and leaned with pretended nonchalance on its slope. He propped his rifle against the bank and started cleaning his fingernails with the bodkin he used for reaming out the cones of his revolver. "I forgot to shave this morning," he said to Coffman.

"You should grow a beard, sir," Coffman said nervously.

"I don't like beards," Starbuck said, "and I hate cowards." He was watching the men around Medlicott, seeing their hatred and wondering if any dared threaten him with violence. That was a risk he would have to take when the moment came, and until it came he would wait in the spoil pit that he turned into a temporary regimental headquarters. Bandmaster Little, who served as the battalion's chief clerk as well as its fussy maker of music, brought him a bagful of tedious paperwork, and Starbuck passed the time filling in the lists of dead, indenting for rations, and sending urgent pleas for ammunition.

No ammunition came, but nor did the Yankees. The sun rose to its height and still no attack came. Once in a while a rattle of gunfire would crackle across the country, but otherwise there was silence. Two armies were poised side by side, yet neither moved, and the peace of the day frustrated Starbuck. He needed a fight to bring his confrontation with Medlicott to fruition.

"Maybe the bastards have gone home," he told Lucifer

when the boy brought him a midday meal of bread, cheese, and apples.

"They're still over there. I can smell them," Lucifer said. The boy glanced at the brooding Medlicott, then looked back to the cheerful Starbuck. "You've been tugging on his chains," Lucifer said with amusement.

"It's none of your business, Lucy."

"Lucy!" The boy was offended.

Starbuck smiled. "I can't call you Lucifer, it isn't proper. So I shall call you Lucy."

The boy bridled, but before he could think of a response, there was a sudden shout from one of Colonel Hudson's pickets, and then a great rushing and trampling noise in the woods beyond the killing patch. Starbuck abandoned the bread and cheese, snatched up his rifle, and ran to the pit's forward edge, where a squad from Moxey's company was lying on their bellies with their rifles trained under the abatis. "See anything?" Starbuck asked.

"Nothing."

Yet the noise was getting louder. It was the noise, Starbuck reckoned, of hundreds if not thousands of boots trampling down the undergrowth. It was the noise of an infantry attack designed to break through Jackson's line once and for all. It was the noise that foretold battle, and all along the railbed men pushed rifles over the parapet and cocked hammers.

"Sumbitches don't give up," the man next to Starbuck said. He was one of those who had stayed and fought the day before.

"What's your name?" Starbuck asked him.

"Sam Norton."

"From Faulconer Court House?"

"Rosskill," Norton answered. Rosskill was the nearest railhead to the Legion's hometown.

"What did you do there?"

Norton grinned. "Last job I had in Rosskill was sweeping out the county jail."

Starbuck grinned back. "Unwillingly, I guess?"

"Never minded sweeping it out, Major, 'cos once you'd swept out the jail you had to sweep out the sheriff's house and Sheriff Simms had two daughters sweeter than honey on a comb. Hell, I know men who robbed stores and stood rock still just begging to be locked up for a chance at Emily and Sue."

Starbuck laughed, then went silent as the trampling of feet was translated into a sudden rush of men, hundreds of men who shouted their hoarse war cry and charged across the narrow strip of open land toward the embankment where Elijah Hudson's North Carolinians waited.

"Fire!" Hudson shouted, and the embankment was rimmed with smoke.

"Fire!" Starbuck shouted, and the Legion gave what flanking fire they could, but for most of the men the angle was too acute for their rifles to help the beleaguered Hudson.

The Yankee charge reached the embankment's foot and surged up its face. Hudson's men stood up. For a second Starbuck thought the Carolinians had merely stood to run away, but instead they advanced across the flat railbed and met the Yankee charge head-on. They swung rifles, slashed with bowie knives, and rammed forward with bayonets.

Starbuck stared into the woods directly opposite the Legion and saw no threat there. The noise of the hand-to-hand fighting to his right was terrible, an echo from the medieval days of men being butchered by steel and crushed by clubs. The bestiality of the sound was a temptation to leave well alone and stay in the railbed's cutting on the excuse that a second Yankee attack might come straight for the Legion's position, but Starbuck knew that assumption was merely an excuse for cowardice, and so he slung his rifle and jumped down to the spoil pit's floor. "Major Medlicott! We're going to help."

Major Medlicott did not move. The men with him stared sullenly at Starbuck.

"You heard me?" Starbuck asked.

"It ain't our fight, Starbuck." Medlicott summoned his courage to articulate his defiance of Starbuck. "Besides, if we leave here the Yankees could attack straight into the pit again and then where would we be?"

Starbuck did not answer. Instead he looked sideways at Coffman. "Go and send Sergeant Waggoner to me," he said softly so that only Coffman could hear, "then tell Truslow that he's got to hold the railbed with Companies G and H. He's to ignore my order to charge. Understand?"

"Yes, sir." Coffman ran off on his errand. Medlicott had not heard the orders Starbuck gave but sneered anyway. "Sending for Swynyard?"

Starbuck could feel his heart beating flabbily in his chest. "Major Medlicott," he said very slowly and distinctly, "I'm ordering you to fix bayonets and go to Colonel Hudson's assistance."

Medlicott's big red face seemed to twist in a spasm of loathing, but he managed to make his answer sound respectful. "It's my judgment we should guard our own position," he said just as formally as Starbuck.

"You're disobeying an order?" Starbuck asked.

"I'm staying here," the miller said stubbornly, and when Starbuck did not respond immediately, Medlicott grinned in anticipation of victory. "No one's to move!" he called to his men. "Our job's to stay here and—"

He stopped speaking because Starbuck had shot him.

Starbuck did not really believe he was doing it. He was aware that the act would either seal the Legion as his regiment or else condemn him to a court-martial or a lynching. He drew the heavy Adams revolver and straightened his right arm while his thumb clicked the hammer smoothly back; then his finger took the trigger's pressure so fast that the look of triumph on Medlicott's face had scarcely started to change when the bullet struck him just beneath his right eye. Blood and bone made a cloud of droplets about the Major's shattering skull as he was thrown backward. His hat went straight up in the air while his body flew back three yards, twitching as it flew, then flapping like a landed fish as it thumped heavily onto the dirt. There the body lay utterly still with its arms outstretched. "Oh, my God," Starbuck heard himself saying, "just lay me down." He began to laugh.

Medlicott's ashen-faced men watched him. None of them moved. Medlicott's dead fingers slowly curled.

Starbuck pushed the revolver into its holster. "Captain Moxey?" he said very calmly.

Moxey did not wait for the rest of the sentence. "Company!" he shouted. "Fix bayonets!"

Moxey's men ran south along the railbed to help Hudson's left-hand company. Medlicott's men still stared dumbly at the body of their officer, then up at Starbuck. This was the moment that Starbuck had half expected to turn mutinous, but none of the company made any move to avenge the dead miller. "Anyone else want to disobey my orders?" Starbuck asked them.

No one spoke. The men seemed dazed; then Peter Waggoner ran up, panting. "Sir?"

"You're a Lieutenant now, Waggoner," Starbuck said, "in charge of A Company. Take over, follow Captain Moxey, and get rid of those Yankees."

"Sir?" Waggoner was slow to understand.

"Do it!" Starbuck snapped. Then he unslung his rifle and

pushed his bayonet into place. He turned toward the rest of the regiment. "Legion! Fix bayonets!" He waited a few seconds. "Follow me!"

It was a risk, because if the Yankees were waiting to attack the Legion's positions, then Starbuck was giving them victory, but if he did not help the North Carolinians, then the Yankees would probably break through into the woods, and so he took three-quarters of the Legion down the railbed to help Hudson's men. Some of those men were out of ammunition and were hurling rocks at the Yankees, throwing so hard that the heavy stones drew blood when they struck on sweat-streaked faces.

"Follow me!" Starbuck shouted again. Moxey and Waggoner were helping Hudson's left-hand companies, but the biggest threat was in the center of the Colonel's line, and Starbuck now led his reinforcements down the back of the embankment to where that Yankee pressure was fiercest. Some of the Northerners had gained the flat summit of the embankment, where they were struggling to take Hudson's two standards, and it was there that Starbuck intervened. "Come on!" he screamed, and he heard his men begin the terrible, shrill rebel yell as they scrambled up the slope and into the fight. Starbuck pulled his rifle's trigger as he neared the mêlée, then rammed the bayonet hard into a blue jacket. He was screaming like a banshee, suddenly feeling the extraordinary release of Medlicott's death. My God, but he had cut the rot clean out of the Legion's soul!

There was a rebel on the ground trying to fight off a Northern sergeant who had his hands around the rebel's throat. Starbuck kicked the Northerner's head up, then sliced his bayonet back and upward so that the blade slit the man's throat open. The sergeant collapsed, gushing blood over his intended victim. Starbuck clambered over both men and rammed the bayonet forward again. Men

441

were grunting and cursing, tripping on the dying and slipping in blood, but the Yankees were giving ground. They had been trying to fight up the embankment's slope, and the rebels had managed to keep most of them on that forward slope and at a consequent disadvantage until the Legion's arrival tipped the balance. The Northerners retreated.

They went down the embankment, but they were not beaten yet. The woods here grew close to the railbed, so close that the Yankees could retreat to the tree line and still fire over open sights at the rebel position, and once back among the trees they poured an immense fire at the embankment. The storm of bullets drove the rebel defenders back from the crest and down into cover. The bullets whistled and hissed overhead; they thumped into the bodies of the dead or else ricocheted off the embankment to tear through the leaves behind. Every few moments a group of Yankees would charge the apparently empty parapet only to be met by a sparse rebel volley, a shower of stones, and the sight of waiting bayonets.

"They don't yield easily, do they? My God, Starbuck, but I owe you thanks. Upon my soul, I do." Colonel Hudson, his long hair matted with blood and his eyes wild, tried to shake Starbuck's hand.

Starbuck, encumbered with a rifle, ramrod, and cartridge, fumbled the handshake. "You're wounded, Colonel?"

"Dear me, no." Hudson pushed the long, blood-thick hair out of his face. "Other fellow's blood. You killed him, remember? Cut his throat. Dear me. But upon my soul, Starbuck, I'm grateful. Grateful, truly."

"Are you sure you're not hurt, sir?" Starbuck asked, for Hudson seemed unsteady on his feet.

"Just shocked, Starbuck, just shocked, and I shall be just dandy in a moment or two." The Colonel looked up at the railbed, where a rock had just landed. It seemed the Yankees were throwing the stones back now. Starbuck finished loading his rifle, wriggled up the bank, and pushed the gun between two bodies. He sighted on a blue jacket, pulled the trigger, and slid back to reload. He had five cartridges left, while most of his men were now reduced to just one or two. Elijah Hudson was similarly short of ammunition. "One more attack, Starbuck," the North Carolinian said, "and I suspect we're done for."

The attack came almost as he spoke. It was a frantic, desperate charge of tired, bloodied men who burst out of the woods to throw themselves up the embankment. For two days these Northerners had tried to break the rebel line, and for two days they had been frustrated, but now they were on the very brink of success, and they summoned their last reserves of strength as they scrambled up the scorched bank with fixed bayonets.

"Fire!" Hudson shouted, and the rebels' last guns flamed as a barrage of rocks hurtled overhead. "Now charge, my dears! Charge home!" the Colonel called, and the tired men threw themselves forward to meet the Yankee assault. Starbuck thrust with the bayonet, twisted the blade, and thrust again. Coffman was beside him, firing a revolver; then he glimpsed Lucifer, of all people, firing his Colt. Then Starbuck's bayonet stuck in a man's belly, and he tried to kick it free, then tried to twist it free, but nothing would loosen the flesh's grip on the steel. He cursed the dying man, then felt a gush of warm blood on his hands as he unslotted the blade and pulled the rifle away from the trapped blade. He reversed the rifle and swung it overhand like a club. He was keening a mad noise, half exultation, half lamentation, expecting death at any second, but determined not to give an inch against the mass of men who pushed into the rebels' blades and rifle stocks.

Then, suddenly, without any apparent reason, the pressure eased.

Suddenly the great charge was gone, and the Northerners were running back into the trees and leaving behind a tideline of bodies heaped on bodies, some of the bodies moving slow beneath their pall of blood, others lying still. And there was silence except for the panting of the wild-eyed rebels who stood on the embankment they had held against the charge.

"Back now!" Starbuck broke the silence. "Back!" There might still be sharpshooters in the woods, and so he pulled his men back down the embankment into cover.

"Don't leave me, don't leave me!" a wounded man cried aloud, and another wept because he had been blinded. The stretcher bearers went across the railbed. No one shot at them. Starbuck cleaned the blood from his rifle's stock with a handful of oak leaves. Coffman was beside him, eyes gleaming with a maniacal delight. Lucifer was reloading his revolver. "You're not supposed to kill Northerners," Starbuck told him.

"I kill who I want," the boy said resentfully.

"But thank you anyway," Starbuck said, but Lucifer's only response was a look of hurt dignity. Starbuck sighed. "Thank you, Lucifer," he said.

Lucifer immediately grinned. "So I ain't Lucy?"

"Thank you, Lucifer," Starbuck said again.

A triumphant Lucifer kissed the muzzle of his gun. "A man can be whatever a man wants to be. Maybe next year I'll decide to be a rebel killer."

Starbuck spat on the rifle's lock to help clean the blood clotted there. Somewhere in the woods behind him a bird burst into song.

"It's quiet, isn't it?" Hudson said from a few paces away.

Starbuck looked up. "Is it?"

"It's quiet," the Colonel said, "so beautifully quiet. I do believe the Yankees are gone."

The line had held.

The Reverend Doctor Starbuck beheld a nightmare.

He had spent a second day with Major Galloway's horsemen in the hope that he would have a chance to join in the pursuit of a broken rebel army. He was aware that the next day would be the Lord's Day, and he whiled away the waiting hours planning the sermon he would give to the victorious troops, but as the hours passed and there was still no sign of a rebel collapse, the prospect of the sermon receded. Then, in the afternoon, just after the firing in the woods had died suddenly away, a message came ordering Galloway's men to investigate some strange troops seen marching to the southwest.

The preacher rode with Galloway. They passed trampled cornfields and orchards looted of their fruit. They crossed the turnpike where the battle had started two days before, splashed through a stream, then rode up a bare hillside to where two gaudily uniformed regiments of New York *Zouaves* were resting on the grassy crest with their rifles stacked.

"All quiet here," the young, dapper commander of the nearer regiment, the 5th New York, proclaimed, "and we've got a picket line in the woods"—he gestured downhill to where thick woods grew—"and they're not being disturbed, so I guess it will stay quiet."

Major Galloway decided he would ride as far as the New York picket line, but the preacher elected to stay with the infantry, for a moment's small talk had elicited the astonishing information that the 5th New York's commanding officer was the son of an old colleague, and that old colleague, the Reverend Doctor Winslow, was actually the chaplain to his own son's regiment. Now the Reverend Winslow galloped across to greet his Boston friend. "I never thought to find you here, Starbuck!"

"I trust I shall always be found where the Lord's work needs doing, Winslow," the Boston preacher said, then shook hands.

Winslow looked proudly at his son, who had ridden back to his place at the head of the regiment. "Just twenty-six, Starbuck, but in charge of the finest volunteer regiment in our army. Even the regulars can't hold a candle to the New York 5th. They fought like Trojans in the peninsula. And your own sons? They're well, I pray?"

"James is with McClellan," the Reverend Starbuck said. "The others are too young to fight." Then, wanting to change the subject before Winslow remembered the existence of Nathaniel, the Boston preacher asked about the 5th New York's flamboyant uniform, which consisted of bright red baggy pantaloons, short blue collarless jackets with scarlet trim, a red waist sash, and a crimson cap rimmed with a white turban and crowned with a long golden tassel.

"It's a copy of a French uniform," Winslow explained. "*Zouaves* are reputedly the fiercest fighters in the French army, and our patron wanted us to emulate their dress as well as their *élan*."

"Patron?"

"We're paid for by a New York furniture manufacturer. He paid for everything you see here, Starbuck; paid for it lock, stock, and barrel. You're seeing the profits of mahogany and turned legs at war."

The Reverend Starbuck eyed his old friend's uniform and wished that he was able to wear such finery. He was about to inquire what arrangements Winslow had made to fill his pulpit while he served with the army but was distracted by a burst of gunfire in the woods. "Our skirmishers, I guess,"

Winslow said when the sound had faded. "They were probably attacking a regiment of wild turkey. We ate a couple last night, and very good eating they were, too." The resting regiment had stirred at the sudden fusillade, and some men retrieved their rifles from the stacks, but most just cursed for being half woken up, pulled the turbans over their eyes again, and tried to go back to sleep.

"Your son said there's been no sign of the enemy here?" the Reverend Starbuck inquired, wondering why the hairs on the back of his neck were suddenly prickling.

"None at all!" the chaplain said, staring toward the woods. "I think you might say we've drawn the short straw. Our part in the great victory is to be spectators. Or maybe not."

His last three words were prompted by the appearance of a group of *Zouaves* at the tree line on the regiment's left flank. They were evidently skirmishers returning to their parent regiment, and they were agitated. "Rebels!" one of the men shouted. "Rebels!"

"They're panicking!" the chaplain said scornfully.

More of the *Zouaves* snatched up their rifles. A captain mounted on a nervous black horse cantered past the two pastors and touched his hat respectfully. "I think they're imagining things, chaplain!" the Captain called good-naturedly to Winslow, then put his hand to his throat and started making a mewing sound as he struggled to breathe. Blood began to seep through his fingers, and while the Reverend Starbuck tried to make sense of this strange apparition, he was suddenly overwhelmed by the sound of firing that had somehow taken a second or two to register on his stunned senses. Stunned because the hilltop was being swept by a typhoon of fire, a whistling whipping terror of bullets that crashed from the tree line where, appallingly, regiment after regiment of rebels now appeared. One moment there had been a summer's peace prevailing on the warm hilltop, where bees had sucked at clover blossoms, then there was death and screaming and blood, and the transition had been too abrupt for the preacher's mind to comprehend.

The dying captain was jerked back from the saddle to be dragged along the ground by a foot trapped in a stirrup. He cried pathetically; then a great rush of blood silenced him forever. The chaplain began shouting encouragement to the dazed *Zouaves*, who seemed to shrink back from the weltering rifle fire. The Reverend Starbuck's horse bolted from the unending splintering crack of rifles that outflanked the two New York regiments. The horse ran north, fleeing the attack, and it was not till he reached the edge of the hill that the preacher was able to curb the scared animal and turn it just in time to see a line of rebel regiments appear from the far trees. These were Lee's men, who had marched one day after Stonewall Jackson and who were now being unleashed from the valleys and woods where they had hidden overnight. They all made their devilish, ululating scream as they attacked, and the preacher's blood ran chill as the terrible sound washed across the hilltop.

The Reverend Starbuck dragged his revolver out of its saddle holster but made no effort to fire it. He was faced by a nightmare. He was watching the death of two regiments.

The New Yorkers tried to fight. They stood in line and returned the rebel fire, but the gray lines overlapped and decimated the *Zouave* ranks with an overwhelming volume of rifle fire. Brightly uniformed men were plucked back from the New York ranks, and though the sergeants and corporals tried to close the gaps, the gaps kept coming faster than they could be filled. Men slipped away, running north and east. The Reverend Starbuck shouted at the fugitives to hold their ground, but they ignored his ravings and ran downhill toward the stream. The furniture maker's regiment was reduced to three groups of men who tried to hold off the overpowering assault, but three times their number could not have stopped this rebel surge.

The New Yorkers died. There was a spatter of final shots, a scream of defiance, then the flags toppled as the last stubborn defenders were overrun. The hill was suddenly swarming with rebel rat gray coats, and the preacher, startled from his shocked immobility, kicked his horse and let it run downhill among the scattered fugitives. The first rebels were already firing after the running men, and the Reverend Starbuck heard the bullets whiplash about him, but the preacher's horse kept running. It splashed through the stream and so up into the safety of the trees on the far side. The scream of the obscene rebel yell soured the preacher's ears as he slowed the sweating horse. All around him now he could hear that terrible scream, the noise of the devil on the march, and he sensed, even if he did not understand, that another Northern army was being ignominiously beaten. Tears ran down his cheeks as he tried to understand the unfathomable ways of God.

He crossed the turnpike, going back to where he had spent so long waiting to begin the pursuit of the beaten rebels, but there was no sign of Galloway's men there, nor, thank God, any rebels either. The preacher cuffed the tears from his cheeks as he rested his horse. To his right, where the smoke from the burning depot still made a brown smear in the sky, there was only a tangle of woods and steep valleys, and it was through that broken ground, he suspected, that the rebel advance was being made. To his left, across the wider fields, lay the woods where one Northern attack after another had been launched toward the railbed, but none of those attacks had succeeded, which surely meant that the rebels still lurked among those woods, while behind him the devil's troops had just made carrion out of Winslow's *Zouaves* on a Virginia hilltop, which left the preacher just one place to go.

He rode northeast, his grief turning into a rage fit to fill all heaven. What dolts led the armies of the North! What strutting turkey-cock fools! The preacher felt a duty being laid upon him, the duty to awaken the North to the poltroons who were leading its sons into one defeat after another. He would go to Galloway's house, fetch his luggage, then have one of the Major's servants show him an escape route north across the Bull Run. It was time to return to the sanity of Boston, where he would begin his campaign that would wake a nation to its sins.

Cannons fired in the hills, their sound echoing confusedly around the sky. Rifles cracked, the gunsmoke showing in rills above trees and streams. Robert Lee had brought twenty-five thousand men and placed them at right angles to Jackson's beleaguered line, and not one Yankee had known the rebels were there until the starry banners came forward above the gray lines. Now the rebels' flank attack advanced like a door swinging shut on John Pope's glory. And the Reverend Elial Starbuck carried his righteous anger back toward home.

The sun sank slow toward the western hills. Nothing stirred in the woods to the east. The noise of battle rolled like distant thunder, but what the noise meant or where the Yankees were no one knew. A patrol from Truslow's Company H was the first to cross the shell-scorched strip of land into the trees, but they found no Yankees there. The sharpshooters had gone, and the woods were empty except for the litter of the abandoned Northern bivouacs.

Ammunition arrived and was handed out among the weary men. Some troops slept, indistinguishable in their

450

exhaustion from the dead around them. Starbuck tried to compile a list of the dead and the wounded, but the work was slow.

An hour before sundown Colonel Swynyard rode his horse up to the railbed. He was leading another horse by the reins. "It belonged to Major Medlicott," he told Starbuck. "I hear he died?"

"Shot by a Yankee, I hear," Starbuck said straight-faced.

Swynyard's mouth flickered in what might have been a smile. "We're ordered to advance, and I thought you might appreciate a horse."

Starbuck's initial reaction was to refuse, for he took pride in marching like his men, but then he remembered the house with the lime-washed stone pillar at its lane gate and thanked Swynyard for bringing him the animal. He pulled himself into the saddle just as the Legion was stirred from its rest. The tired men grumbled at being disturbed but shouldered their rifles and climbed from the railbed. The wounded, the surgeons, the servants, and a sergeant's guard stayed behind while the rest of the Legion formed ranks around the color guard, where Lieutenant Coffman carried the replacement battle flag on its sapling staff. Starbuck took his place at the head of the regiment on Medlicott's horse. "Forward!" he called.

Hudson's North Carolinians advanced to the Legion's right. Colonel Hudson was mounted on an expensive black mare and was now accoutred with a sword in a gold-mounted scabbard. Hudson waved in friendly greeting as the two regiments advanced in line, but once among the trees Starbuck deliberately led the Legion to the left and so opened a gap between himself and the Carolinians.

He crossed the small pasture where they had checked their pursuit of the first Yankee attack the day before. There were still unburied dead in the field. Beyond the pasture was a strip of woods, then a wider stretch of open farmland that was bisected by a road climbing to a far crest. Starbuck rode to the left of his line. "Remember this place?" Starbuck asked Truslow.

"Should I?"

"We fought our first battle here." Starbuck pointed to his left. "The Yankees came out of those trees and we waited up there"—he pointed right to the ridge—"and I was scareder than hell and you behaved like it had all happened before."

"It had. I was in Mexico, remember?"

Starbuck let the horse walk at its own pace across the old battlefield. There were yellowing bone fragments in the furrows, and he wondered for how many years the farmers would plow up men's bones and the bullets that put them there.

"So what happened with Medlicott?" Truslow asked. The two men were thirty paces ahead of the ranks.

"What do your men say happened?"

"That you picked a fight with him, then shot the son of a bitch."

Starbuck thought about it, then nodded. "Just about. Do they mind?"

Truslow twisted a piece of tobacco from a plug and put it in his mouth. "Some of them feel sorry for Edna."

"His wife?"

"She has children to feed. But hell, no, they don't mind about the miller. He was a mean son of a bitch."

"He's a hero now," Starbuck said. "He's going to get his name on a statue in Faulconer Court House. Dan Medlicott, hero of our War of Independence." He crossed the road, remembering when he had watched a Northern army attack across these fields. They were not much changed; the snake fences were long gone, burned to boil the coffeepots of soldiers, and flecks of bone disfigured the dirt, but otherwise it was just as Starbuck remembered. He led the Legion on across the farmland, angling still more to his left until, rather than heading toward the eastern ridge with the rest of the Brigade, he was heading toward a stand of timber that topped a small ridge that lay to the north.

Swynyard galloped up to Starbuck. "Wrong way! Up there!" He pointed eastward up the road.

Starbuck reined in. "There's a place I want to visit, Colonel, just over the hill. Not more than a quarter-mile now."

Swynyard frowned. "What place?"

"The house of the man who took our flags, Colonel, and the house of the man whose troops burned women in a tavern."

Swynyard's initial reaction was to shake his head; then he had second thoughts and looked at Truslow's company before turning back to the two officers. "What can you achieve?"

"I don't know. But then we didn't know what we were going to achieve when we ran to Dead Mary's Ford in the middle of the night." Starbuck deliberately reminded Swynyard of that night and the implicit favor that the Colonel owed him as a result.

The Colonel smiled. "You've got one hour. We'll be going up the road," he said, pointing to the right, "and I guess it would only be prudent for someone to take a patrol north, just in case any of the rascals are lurking. Do you think one company will be enough?"

"Plenty, sir," Starbuck said and touched the brim of his hat to the Colonel. "Company!" he called to his old company. "Follow me!"

He borrowed a lit cigar from John Bailey and lit one of his own with its glowing tip. He walked the horse slowly, pacing the beast beside Truslow. The rest of the Legion climbed the gentle eastern slope toward the sound of battle that now seemed very far away—so far that none of the advancing battalions seemed in any hurry to join that distant fighting. Starbuck looked to his left and saw the white-painted pillar on the road at the end of the stand of trees. "Not far now," he told Truslow. "Through these woods and in the next fields."

"What happens if the place is full of Yankees?" Truslow asked.

"Then we'll go back," Starbuck said, but when the company emerged from the trees on the ridge, they saw that the place was not full of Yankees. Instead the Galloway homestead seemed deserted as the rebel soldiers walked slowly down the long slope toward the farm buildings that were set among a grove of leafy, mature trees. It looked a handsome house, Starbuck thought, a place where a man could settle and live a good life. It seemed to have good watered land, well-drained fields, and plenty of timber.

A black man met them at the yard gate. "There's no one here, massa," the man said nervously.

"Whose house is it?" Starbuck asked.

The man did not answer.

"You heard the officer!" Truslow growled.

The black man glanced at the approaching company, then licked his lips. "Belongs to a gentleman called Galloway, massa, but he's not here."

"He's with the army, is he?" Starbuck asked.

"Yes, massa." The man smiled ingratiatingly. "He's with the army."

Starbuck returned the smile. "But which army?"

The black man's smile vanished instantly. He said nothing, and Starbuck kicked his heels to ride past him. "Any slaves in the house?" he called over his shoulder to the black man.

"Three of us, massa, and we're not slaves. We're servants."

"You live in the house?"

"In the cabins, massa." The servant was running after Starbuck, while Truslow brought the company on behind.

"So the house is empty?" Starbuck asked.

The man paused, then nodded as Starbuck looked back at him. "It's empty, massa."

"What's your name?"

"Joseph, massa."

"Then listen, Joseph, if you've got any belongings in the house, get them out now, because I'm about to burn this goddamned house to the ground, and if your master wants to know why, tell him it's with the compliments of the whores he burned alive at McComb's Tavern. You got that message, Joseph?" Starbuck curbed the horse and swung himself out of the saddle. He jumped down, spurting dust from beneath his boots. "Did you hear me, Joseph?"

The black servant gazed in horror at Starbuck. "You can't burn it, sir!"

"Tell your master that he killed women. Tell him my name is Starbuck, you hear that? Let me hear you say it."

"Starbuck, sir."

"And don't you forget it, Joseph. I am Starbuck, avenger of whores!" Starbuck declaimed that final sentence as he climbed the veranda steps and threw open the house's front door.

To see his father.

Clouds heaped in the south, darkening a day already declining toward dusk. In the steep hills and valleys where the rebel flank attack surged forward, the fading light made the rifle flames stab brighter and the smoke look grayer. There was a sense that the weather must break soon, and indeed, far to the south, on the empty earthworks that the Yankees had abandoned by the Rappahannock River, the first drops of rain splashed heavy. Lightning flickered in the clouds.

At Manassas the rebel flank attack grew ragged. It had been launched across broken country, and the advancing brigades soon lost touch with each other as they detoured about thorn-choked gullies or around thick groves of trees. Some regiments forged ahead while others met Yankee troops, who put up unexpectedly stubborn resistance. Cannons cracked from hilltops, canister fire shredded woodlands, and rifle fire stuttered along a crooked three-mile front.

Behind the Yankees was the Bull Run, a stream deep and wide enough to be a river in any country other than America, and a stream deep and wide enough to drown a man encumbered with a pack, haversack, cartridge box, and boots, and if the rebels could just break the Yankees and hurl them back in panic, then eighty thousand men might be struggling to cross that killing stream, which boasted only one small bridge. The beaten army could drown in its thousands.

Except the Yankees did not panic. They streamed back across the bridge, and some men did drown as they tried to swim the run, but other men stood shoulder-to-shoulder on the hill where once a man called Thomas Jackson had earned the name of Stonewall. They stood and met the oncoming rebel troops with a cannonade that lit the hill's forward slope red with the flash of its gun flames and made the valley beyond crackle with the echo of rifle volleys; volley after killing volley, a stinging flail of lead that ripped the gray ranks apart and held the land west of the bridge long enough to let the bulk of John Pope's army escape. Only then did the stoic blue ranks yield Stonewall Jackson's hill to Stonewall Jackson's countrymen. It was a Northern defeat, but the Northerners had not been routed. Lines of blue-uniformed men trudged away from a battlefield where they had been promised victory but had been led to defeat, and where the victorious rebels began to count the captured weapons and captured men.

And at Joseph Galloway's farm, on the southern bank of the Bull Run, the Reverend Starbuck stared at his son, and his son stared back.

"Father?" Starbuck broke the silence.

For a second, a heartbeat, Starbuck thought his father would relent. For that one second he thought his father was about to hold out his arms in welcome, and there was indeed a sudden expression of pain and longing on the older man's face, and for that one second all the plans Starbuck had ever made for defying his father should they ever meet again vanished into thin air as he felt a swamping wave of guilt and love sweep through him, but then the vulnerable expression vanished from the preacher's face. "What are you doing here?" the Reverend Starbuck demanded gruffly.

"I've business here."

"What business?" The Reverend Starbuck barred the hallway. He was carrying his ebony stick, which he held out like a sword to prevent his son from stepping further into the house. "And don't you dare smoke in my presence!" he snapped, then tried to swat the cigar out of his son's hand with his ebony cane.

Starbuck easily evaded the blow. "Father," he said, trying to appeal to old ties of stern affection, but he was brusquely interrupted.

"I am not your father!"

"Then what kind of a son of a bitch are you to tell me not to smoke?" Starbuck's temper flared high and fierce. He welcomed the anger, knowing it was probably his best weapon in this confrontation, for the instant that he had seen his father's stern face a lifetime of filial obedience had made him cringe inside. At that moment when the door had swung open, he had suddenly felt eight years old again and utterly helpless in the face of his father's unforgiving certainty.

"Don't you swear at me, Nathaniel," the preacher said.

"I'll goddamn swear where I damn well want. Now move!" Starbuck's anger burned bright. He pushed past his father. "You want to pick a quarrel with me," he shouted over his shoulder, "then make up your mind whether it's a family quarrel or a fight between strangers. And get yourself out of this house, I'm burning the damn place down." Starbuck shouted these last words from the library. The shelves were empty, though a handful of account books were piled on a table.

"You propose to do what?" The Reverend Starbuck had followed his son into the big room.

"You heard me." Starbuck began tearing the account books into scraps that would burn easily. He piled the scraps at the edge of the table, where their flames would work on the empty shelving above.

The Reverend Starbuck's face showed a glimmer of pain. "You have become a whoremonger, a thief, a traitor, and now you will burn a good man's house?"

"Because he burned a tavern"—Starbuck started tearing apart another book—"and killed women. They pleaded with his soldiers to stop firing, but they wouldn't. They went on shooting and they burned the women alive."

The Reverend Starbuck swept the pile of paper scraps off the table with his cane. "They didn't know there were women in the tavern."

"They knew," Starbuck said, starting to make another pile of torn paper.

"You're a liar!" The Reverend Starbuck raised his cane and would have slashed it down on his son's hands had not a

458

shot been fired inside the room. The sound of it echoed terribly inside the four walls, while the bullet ripped a scar into the empty shelves opposite the door.

"He ain't lying, preacher. I was there." Truslow had appeared in the open garden door. "I carried one of the women out of the ruins myself. Burned to a crisp, she was. Kind of shriveled to the size of a newborn calf. There were five women burned like that." He spat tobacco juice, then tossed a tin to Starbuck. "Found these in the kitchen," he said. Starbuck saw they were lucifers.

"This is my father," Starbuck said in curt introduction.

Truslow nodded. "Preacher," he said in brief acknowledgment.

The Reverend Starbuck said nothing but just watched as his son made another pile of broken paper. "We kind of got upset," Starbuck went on, "on account of not fighting against women ourselves. So we decided to burn this son of a bitch's house down to teach him that fighting against women ain't worth the price."

"They were whores!" the Reverend Starbuck snapped.

"So they're making me a bed in hell right now," Starbuck snarled back, "and you think they won't be better company than you saints in heaven?" He struck one of the lucifers and held its flame to the heap of paper scraps.

The cane struck again, scattering the new heap of paper and instantly extinguishing the small flame. "You have broken your mother's heart," the preacher said, "and brought shame on my house. You lied to your brother, you have cheated, you have stolen!" The catalog of sins was so great that the Reverend Starbuck was momentarily overcome and he was forced to hold his breath and shake his head.

"The son of a bitch drinks whiskey, too." Truslow used the silence to add his contribution from the doorway.

459

"Yet!" The preacher shouted the word, the shout intended to govern his temper. "And yet," he said, blinking back tears, "your Lord and Savior will forgive you, Nate. All He asks is that you go to Him on bended knee with a confession of faith. All our sins can be forgiven! All!" Tears ran down the preacher's cheeks. "Please?" he said. "I cannot bear to think that in heaven we must look down on your eternal torment."

Starbuck felt another great tidal surge of emotion. He might have rejected his father's house and his father's stern religion, but he could not deny that it had been a good house and an honest religion, nor could he claim that he did not fear the flames of eternal damnation. He felt the tears pricking at his own eyes. He stopped tearing paper and tried to summon up the anger that would let him face his father again, but instead he seemed to tremble on the brink of total surrender.

"Think of your younger brothers. Think of your sisters. They love you!" The Reverend Starbuck had found his theme now and pressed it hard. He had so often sworn to disown this child, to cast Nathaniel out from the fellowship of Christ as well as from the Starbuck family, but now the preacher saw what a victory over the devil his son's repentance and return would make. He imagined Nathaniel making a confession of his sins in the church, he saw himself as the father of the prodigal son, and he anticipated the joy in heaven at the repentance of this one sinner. Yet there was more than a spiritual victory at stake. The preacher's anger had flared just like his son's, but the father was also discovering that a year of angry denial had been destroyed by a moment's proximity. This son, after all, was the one most like himself, which was why, he supposed, this was always the son with whom he had fought the hardest. Now he had to win this son back, not just for Christ, but for the Starbuck family. "Think of Martha!" he urged Starbuck, naming Starbuck's favorite sister. "Think of Frederick and how he's always admired you!"

The preacher might have won the battle had he not spread his arms as he mentioned his son Frederick. He had intended the gesture as a reminder that Frederick, five years Starbuck's junior, had been born with a withered arm, but the gesture also released the battle flag that had been clasped under the preacher's left arm. The flag fell to the floor, where it sagged out of its fraying, abused string binding. Starbuck, glad not to have to meet his father's gaze, looked at the flag.

He saw the silk, the lavish fringe, and he looked up at his father's face and for an instant all memories of Martha and Frederick vanished. He looked back to the flag.

Truslow had also noticed the richness of the flag's material. "Is that a battle flag, preacher?" he asked.

The Reverend Starbuck stooped to snatch up the flag, but the violence of the motion only destroyed what was left of the string so that the banner spilt richly into the evening light. "It's none of your business," the preacher said to Truslow defiantly.

"That's our flag, goddamn it!" Truslow said.

"It's the devil's rag!" the preacher snapped back, bundling the silk into his arms. He had dropped the cane to make the task easier.

"I'll take the flag, mister," Truslow said grimly, stepping forward with an outstretched hand.

"You want this flag," the Reverend Starbuck said, "then you'll have to strike me down!"

"Hell if I care," Truslow said and reached for the banner. The preacher kicked at him, but Elial Starbuck was no match for Thomas Truslow. The soldier hit the preacher's arm once, but hard, then took the flag from the suddenly nerveless grip.

461

"You would let your father be hit?" The preacher turned to Starbuck.

But the moment when Starbuck's surrender was just a tremble of remembered emotion away had passed. He scraped another lucifer alight and put it to a page torn from an account book. "You said you weren't my father," he said brutally, then ripped more pages and piled them onto the tiny fire. He sprinkled the flames with powder from a revolver cartridge that he tore apart, so that the small fire flared violently. His father snatched up his cane and tried to sweep the burning papers off the table again, but this time Starbuck stood in his way. For a second the two stood face-to-face; then a voice called from the yard.

"Johnnies!" It was Sergeant Decker.

Truslow ran to the door. "Yankees," he confirmed.

Starbuck joined Truslow on the veranda. A quarter-mile to the east was a ragged band of men who were watching the house. They wore blue, and some were on horseback and some on foot. They had the look, Starbuck decided, of a cavalry troop that had been put through hell. One of the men had golden hair and a short square beard. "Is that Adam?" he asked Truslow.

"I guess."

Starbuck turned to see that his father was obliterating the last vestiges of his fire. "Truslow," he said, "burn this damn house down while I go and tell those Yankees to get the hell out of Virginia. And I'll take the flag."

There was a spear-tipped lance pole in a corner of the room. Starbuck took the lance, stripped it of its spearhead and swallow-tailed cavalry guidon, then slotted the silk flag onto the staff. Then, ignoring his father's angry voice, he jumped down into the yard and called for a man to bring his horse.

He rode eastward, carrying the flag.

Adam rode to meet him, and the two erstwhile friends met in the middle of the pasture next to the farmhouse. Adam looked ruefully at the flag. "So you got it back."

"Where's the other one?"

"I'm keeping it."

"We always used to share," Starbuck said.

Adam smiled at the remark. "How are you, Nate?"

"Alive. Just," Starbuck said.

"Me too," Adam said. He looked tired and sad, like a man whose hopes have taken a beating. He gestured at the ragged band of men and horses behind. "We got ambushed in some woods. Not many of us left."

"Good." Starbuck turned in the saddle to see a wisp of smoke showing at a window of the house. "I know it wasn't your fault, Adam, but some of us took badly to women being burned alive. So we thought we'd do the same to Galloway's house."

Adam nodded dully, as though he did not really care about the destruction of the farmhouse. "The Major's dead," he said.

Starbuck grimaced, for it seemed that he was burning the house for nothing. "And the son of a bitch who killed the women? Blythe?"

"God knows," Adam said. "Billy Blythe disappeared. Billy Blythe has a way of making himself scarce when there's trouble about." Adam leaned on his saddle's pommel and stared toward Galloway's farm, where more smoke was showing at a half-dozen windows. "I can't imagine Pecker giving you permission to do this," he said with an obvious distaste for the destruction.

Adam clearly had not heard about Bird's wound, nor any of the Legion's other news. "Pecker's back home wounded," Starbuck told him, "and I'm the new colonel."

Adam stared at his friend. "You?"

"Your father was thrown out."

Adam shook his head in apparent disbelief, or maybe denial. "You have the Legion?" he asked.

Starbuck twitched the reins to turn his horse. "So the next time you want to play games with a regiment, don't choose mine, Adam. I'll goddamn kill you next time."

Adam shook his head. "What's happening to us, Nate?"

Starbuck laughed at the question. "We're at war. And your side says that houses have to be burned and goods taken from civilians. I guess we're matching you stride for stride."

Adam did not even try to argue the point. He stared at the farmhouse, which was now gushing thick smoke from several windows. Truslow had clearly set about his incendiarism with an expertise that quite outstripped Starbuck's feeble efforts. "Is that your father?" Adam had seen the black-dressed figure come from the burning house.

"Send him safe home, will you?"

"Surely."

Starbuck clumsily turned his horse away. "Look after yourself now. And don't interfere with us. We'll be gone in five minutes."

Adam nodded his agreement; then, just as Starbuck was urging his horse forward, he spoke again. "Have you heard from Julia?"

Starbuck twisted in his saddle. "She's well. She's a nurse in Chimborazo."

"Remember me to her," Adam said, but his onetime friend had already ridden away.

Starbuck rode back to the house, where his old company had gathered outside the yard fence to watch the flames. His father shouted something at Starbuck, but the words were lost in the roar of the fire. "Let's go!" Starbuck called and turned away from the burning house. He did not say farewell to his father but just rode up the hill. He thought how close he had come to a tearful reconciliation, then tried to convince himself that there were some roads that could never be revisited, no matter what lay at their ends. He stopped at the wooded ridge and looked back. A roof beam collapsed into the fire, spewing a fountain of sparks into the evening air. "Come on!" he called to the company.

They caught up with the Brigade a mile to the east. Swynyard was resting the men and waiting for orders. There were rain clouds in the south and a fresh wind gusting, but to the west, above the Blue Ridge Mountains, the sun flared bright as it dipped behind America's rim. In the North an army was in full retreat, while to the east and south, wherever a man looked, there were only rebel banners advancing in victory. And now a brighter banner joined the triumph as Starbuck kicked back his heels and let his borrowed horse run free, so that the shining colors of the recaptured flag streamed and rippled in the breeze. He rode in a curve, bringing the flag back to its Legion, and as he turned the horse toward their ranks, he raised the flag higher still, standing in the stirrups with his right arm braced aloft so that the battle flag's white stars and blue cross and crimson silk were made livid and brilliant by the last long rays of daylight. He was bringing the bright flag home, and in the sudden cheer that filled the sky Starbuck knew that he had made the Legion his. It was Starbuck's Legion.

HISTORICAL NOTE

ALL THE BATTLES AND SKIRMISHES in the novel are based on real actions that were fought in the summer of 1862, a campaign that ended Northern hopes for a swift victory in the east that year. McClellan had failed in his ambitious amphibious attack; now John Pope had been beaten back overland.

I simplified some of the events that took place in between Cedar Mountain and Jackson's epic march around the Northern flank. There was an extra week of fighting in between those two events, but it was very confused fighting, and so I took a fiction writer's liberty and simply pretended it never happened. Readers who would like to know the true story of the confrontation across the Rapidan and Rappahannock should read John Hennessy's splendid account of the campaign, *Return to Bull Run*, a book that was constantly at my elbow as I wrote *Battle Flag*.

Washington Faulconer's stupidity at Dead Mary's Ford is based on an exactly similar event at Raccoon Ford, when Robert Toombs, a Georgia politician turned soldier, stripped the ford of its guard on the grounds that he had not ordered the guard set and therefore the guard should not exist, and on that very night the ford was crossed by a force of Federal cavalry that raided the Confederate lines and very nearly succeeded in capturing Jeb Stuart. They had to settle for the famous man's hat instead. Stuart vowed to repay the insult, which he did by capturing John Pope's best uniform coat at

Catlett's Station. Stuart offered to exchange the hat for the coat, but Pope, a humorless man, refused the offer. The unfortunate Toombs, meanwhile, was placed under arrest.

Pope's notorious General Orders numbers Five and Seven were issued and, unsurprisingly, were regarded by many Northern soldiers as licenses to steal. They also offended Robert Lee grievously, which is why he was so intent on destroying Pope. He did. After the second battle of Manassas (Bull Run to Northerners) Pope was never to hold high command again.

The battle is not as well known as it deserves to be. Jackson's flank march was a fine achievement, and Lee's strategy thoroughly confused a pedantic Northern command. The train crashes at Bristoe Station and the sack of the Federal depot at Manassas all happened, and the wounded civilian's weary judgment on the improbable Jackson ("Oh, my God, lay me down") did become a catch-phrase in Jackson's army. Lee's victory might have been more complete had Longstreet attacked on the day he arrived on Pope's unguarded flank rather than waiting a full twenty-four hours, but the battle was still a notable Southern victory and marked by at least one gruesome record. The casualty rate in the 5th New York *Zouaves* was the greatest in a single regiment on a single day in the whole war: 490 men entered the fight, 223 were wounded, and 124 killed, a casualty rate of 70 percent. The Reverend Doctor Winslow and his son both survived. Lee's overall casualty rate was 17 percent, which, to a country short of manpower, was an ominous loss.

The battlefield is well preserved and a short drive from Washington, D.C. Much of the ground is shared with the field of First Manassas, and the two share an informative visitor center, where a pamphlet outlining a driving tour of the second battle is available.

One reason why Second Manassas is not as well known as it might be is that it is inevitably overshadowed by the events that followed. The North has just seen its latest invasion of the Confederate States of America trounced, and now Lee will try to exploit that victory by leading the first Confederate invasion of the United States of America. His army will march to the banks of the Antietam Creek in Maryland, and there, not three weeks after fighting each other on the Bull Run, the two armies will contest the bloodiest day in all American history. It seems that Starbuck and his men must march again.

The Bloody Ground

The Battle of Antietam
September 17, 1862

VIRGINIA
(NOW WEST VIRGINIA)

M

POTOMAC RIVER

SHEPHERDSTOWN

To
HARPER'S
FERRY

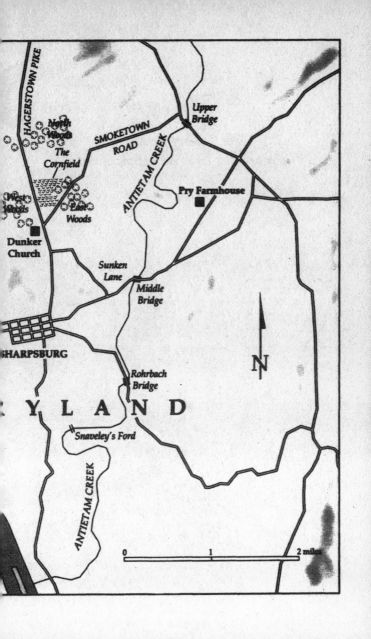

For Zachary Arnold,
may he never know the horrors of war

PART ONE

IT RAINED. It had rained all day. At first it had been a quick, warm rain gusted by fitful southern winds, but in the late afternoon the wind had turned east and the rain became malevolent. It pelted down; a stinging, slashing, heavy rain fit to float an ark. It drummed on the armies' inadequate tents; it flooded the abandoned Yankee earthworks at Centreville; and it washed the shallow dirt off the grave mounds beside the Bull Run so that an army of fish-white corpses, scarcely a day or two buried, surfaced like the dead on Judgment Day. The Virginia dirt was red, and the water that poured in ever-widening muddy streams toward the Chesapeake Bay took on the color of the soil so that it seemed as if the whole tidewater was being drenched in blood. It was the first day of September 1862. The sun would not set on Washington till thirty-four minutes after six, yet by half past three the gas mantles had been lit in the White House, Pennsylvania Avenue was a foot deep in mud, and the open sewers of Swampoodle were overflowing. In the Capitol the rain slashed through the beams and scaffolding of the half-finished dome to pour onto the newly arrived wounded from the North's defeat at Manassas, who lay in misery on the rotunda's marble floor.

Twenty miles west of Washington more fugitives from John Pope's beaten army trudged toward the safety of the capital. Rebels tried to bar their road, but rain turned the

3

confrontation into confusion. Infantrymen huddled for shelter under soaking trees, artillerymen cursed their rain-soaked powder charges, cavalrymen tried to calm horses terrified by the bolts of lightning that raked from the heavy clouds. Major Nathaniel Starbuck, commander of the Faulconer Legion of Swynyard's Brigade of Jackson's Corps of the Army of Northern Virginia, was trying to keep a cartridge dry as he poured its powder into his rifle. He tried to protect the cartridge with his hat, but the hat was drenched and the powder that he shook from the wax paper was suspiciously lumpy. He shoved the crumpled paper onto the powder, spat the bullet into the rifle's muzzle, then rammed the charge hard down. He pulled back the hammer, fished a percussion cap from the box at his belt and fitted it onto the rifle's cone, then took aim through the silver sheeting of the rain. His regiment was at the edge of a dripping wood, facing north across a rain-beaten cornfield toward another stand of trees where the Yankees sheltered. There was no target in Starbuck's sights, but he pulled the trigger anyway. The hammer thumped onto the percussion cap that exploded to puff its little wisp of smoke, but the powder in the rifle's breech obstinately refused to catch the fire. Starbuck swore. He eased back the hammer, prised the shattered percussion cap off the cone, and put another in its place. He tried again, but still the rifle would not fire. "Might as well throw rocks at the bastards," he said to no one in particular. A rifle fired from the far trees, but the bullet's passage through the leaves over Starbuck's head was drowned by the thrashing rain. Starbuck crouched with his useless rifle and wondered what the hell he was supposed to do now.

What he was supposed to do now was cross the cornfield and drive the Yankees out of the farther trees, but the Yankees had at least one regiment and a pair of field

4

guns in that far wood and Starbuck's combat-shrunken regiment had already been bloodied by those two guns. At first, as the Legion had waded into the tangle of rain-drenched cornstalks, Starbuck had thought the guns' noise was merely thunder; then he had seen that his left-hand companies were being shredded and broken and he had noticed the Yankee gunners handspiking their weapons about to take the rest of the Legion in the flank. He had ordered his men to fire on the guns, but only a handful of rifles had powder dry enough to fire, and so he had yelled at the survivors to go back before the artillery fired again and then he had listened to the northerners jeering at his defeated men. Now, twenty minutes later, he was still trying to find a way across or around the cornfield, but the ground to the left was an open space commanded by the enemy guns while the woods to the right were filled with still more Yankees.

The Legion plainly did not care if the Yankees stayed or went, for rain was their enemy now, not the North. Starbuck, as he walked toward the left-hand end of his line, noticed how the men took care not to catch his eye. They were praying he would not order another attack, for none of them wanted to stir out of the trees and go back into the waterlogged corn. All they wanted was for the rain to stop and for a chance to make fires and a time to sleep. Above all to sleep. In the last month they had marched the length and breadth of Virginia's northern counties; they had fought; they had beaten the enemy; they had marched and fought again; and now they were weary with marching and fighting. Their uniforms were rags, their boots were in tatters, their rations were moldy, and they were bone tired, and so far as Starbuck's men were concerned the Yankees could keep the rain-soaked wood beyond the cornfield. They just wanted to rest. Some of them were sleeping now, despite the rain. They lay like the dead at the wood's edge, their mouths open to the rain, and their beards and mustaches lank and dripping. Other men, truly dead, lay as though asleep in the bloodied corn.

"I thought we were winning this damned war," Captain Ethan Davies greeted Starbuck.

"If it doesn't stop raining," Starbuck said, "we'll let the damned navy come and win it for us. Can you see the guns?"

"They're still there." Davies jerked his head toward the dark wood.

"Bastards," Starbuck said. He was angry with himself for not having seen the guns before ordering the first attack. The two cannon had been concealed behind a breastwork of branches, but he still cursed himself for not having suspected the ambush. The small Yankee victory galled him and the gall was worsened by an uncertainty whether the attack had really been necessary, for no one else seemed to be fighting. An occasional gun sounded somewhere in the bleak, wet gloom, and sometimes a rattle of musketry sounded over the crashing rain, but those sounds had nothing to do with Starbuck and he had received no further orders from Colonel Swynyard since the first urgent command to cross the cornfield. Perhaps, Starbuck hoped, the whole battle had been soaked into stalemate. Perhaps no one cared anymore. The enemy had been going back to Washington anyway so why not just let them go. "How do you know the guns haven't gone?" he asked Davies.

"They tell us from time to time," Davies answered laconically.

"Maybe they have gone," Starbuck said, but no sooner had he spoken than one of the Yankee field guns fired. It had been loaded with canister, a tin cylinder crammed with musket balls that shredded apart at the gun's muzzle to scatter its missiles like a giant charge of buck-shot, and the balls ripped through the trees above Starbuck. The gun had been aimed fractionally too high and its fire wounded no one, but the blast of metal cascaded a deluge of water and leaves onto Starbuck's miserable infantrymen. Starbuck, crouching low beside Davies, shivered from the unwanted shower. "Bastards," he said again, but the useless curse was drowned by a crack of thunder that split the sky and rumbled into silence. "There was a time," Starbuck said sourly, "when I thought guns sounded like thunder. Now I think thunder sounds like guns." He considered that thought for a second. "How often did you ever hear a cannon in peacetime?"

"Never," Davies said. His spectacles were mottled with rainwater. "Except maybe on the Fourth."

"The Fourth and Evacuation Day," Starbuck said.

"Evacuation Day?" Davies asked, never having heard of it.

"March seventeenth," Starbuck said. "It's the day we kicked the English out of Boston. There are cannon and fireworks in Boston Garden." Starbuck was a Bostonian, a northerner who fought for the rebel South against his own kind. He did not fight out of political conviction, but rather because the accidents of youth had stranded him in the South when the war began and now, a year and a half later, he was a major in the Confederate army. He was barely older than most of the boys he led, and younger than many, but a year and a half of battles had put a grim maturity into his lean, dark face. By rights, he sometimes reflected wonderingly, he should still be studying for the ministry at Yale's Divinity School, but instead he was crouched in a soaking wet uniform beside a soaking

7

wet cornfield plotting how to kill some soaking wet Yankees who had managed to kill some of his men. "How many dry charges can you muster?" he asked Davies.

"A dozen," Davies answered dubiously, "maybe."

"Load 'em up and wait here. When I give the order I want you to kill those damn gunners. I'll fetch you some help." He slapped Davies's back and ran back into the trees, then worked his way further west until he reached A Company and Captain Truslow, a short, thick-set, and indefatigable man whom Starbuck had promoted from sergeant to captain just weeks before. "Any dry cartridges?" Starbuck asked as he dropped beside the Captain.

"Plenty." Truslow spat tobacco juice into a puddle. "Been holding our fire till you needed it."

"Full of tricks, aren't you?" Starbuck said, pleased.

"Full of sense," Truslow said dourly.

"I want one volley into the gunners. You and Davies kill the gunners and I'll take the rest of the Legion over the field."

Truslow nodded. He was a taciturn man, a widower, and as hard as the hill farm he had left to fight against the Northern invaders.

"Wait for my order," Starbuck added, then backed into the trees again, though there was small respite from the rain under the thick leaf cover that had long before been soaked by the downpour. It seemed impossible for rain to go on this venomously for this long, but there seemed to be no diminution to the cloudburst that beat on the trees with its sustained and demonic force. Lightning flickered to the south, then a crash of thunder sounded so loud overhead that Starbuck flinched from the noise. A slash of pain whipped across his face and he staggered back, dropped to his knees, and clapped a hand to his left cheek. When he took his hand away he saw that his palm was

8

covered in blood. For a moment he just stared helplessly at the blood being diluted and washed off his hand, then, when he tried to stand, he discovered that he was too weak. He was shaking and he thought he was going to vomit, then he feared his bowels would empty. He was making a pathetic mewing noise, like a wounded kitten. One part of his mind knew that he was not in any trouble, that the wound was slight, that he could see and think and breathe, but still he could not control the shaking, though he did manage to stop the stupid kitten noise and take in a deep breath of humid air. He took another breath, wiped more blood from his cheek, and forced himself to stand. The thunder, he realized, had not been thunder at all, but a blast of canister from the second Yankee gun, and one of the canister's musket balls had driven a splinter from a tree trunk that had razored his face to the cheekbone. An inch higher and he would have lost an eye, but instead the wound was clean and trivial, though it had still left Starbuck quivering and frightened. Alone in the trees he leaned for an instant on the scarred trunk and closed his eyes. Get me out of here alive, he prayed, do that and I'll never sin again.

He felt ashamed of himself. He had reacted to the scratch as though it had been a mortal wound, but still he felt bowel-threatening spasms of fear as he walked east toward his right-hand companies. Those companies were the least loyal, the companies that resented being commanded by a renegade Yankee, and those were the companies he would have to provoke out of their miserable shelters into the open cornfield. Their reluctance to attack was not just a question of loyalty, but also the natural instinct of wet, tired, and miserable men to crouch motionless rather than offer themselves to enemy rifles. "Bayonets!" Starbuck shouted as he passed behind the

9

line of men. "Fix bayonets!" He was warning them that they would have to advance again and he heard grumbling coming from some of the soldiers, but he ignored their sullen defiance, for he did not know if he was in a fit state to confront it. He feared his voice would crack like a child's if he turned on them. He wondered what in God's name was happening to him. One small scratch and he was reduced to shivering helplessness! He told himself it was just the rain that had soaked his tiredness into pure misery. Like his men he needed a rest, just as he needed time to reshape the Legion and to scatter the trouble-makers into different companies, but the speed of the campaign in northern Virginia was denying Lee's army the luxury of time.

The campaign had started when the North's John Pope had begun a ponderous advance on Richmond, the capital of the Confederacy. That advance had been checked, then destroyed at the second battle to be fought on the banks of the Bull Run, and now Lee's army was pushing the remaining Yankees back toward the Potomac River. With any luck, Starbuck thought, the Yankees would cross into Maryland and the Confederate army would be given the days it so desperately needed to draw breath and to find boots and coats for men who looked more like a rabble of vagabond tramps than an army. Yet the vagabonds had done all that their country had demanded of them. They had blunted and destroyed the Yankees' latest attempt to capture Richmond and now they were driving the larger Northern army out of the Confederacy altogether.

He found Lieutenant Waggoner at the right-hand end of the line. Peter Waggoner was a good man, a pious soldier who lived with rifle in one hand and a Bible in the other, and if any of his company showed cowardice they would be hit by one of those two formidable weapons.

Lieutenant Coffman, a mere boy, was crouching beside Waggoner and Starbuck sent him to fetch the captains of the other right-flank companies. Waggoner frowned at Starbuck. "Are you all right, sir?"

"A scratch, just a scratch," Starbuck said. He licked his cheek, tasting salty blood.

"You're awful pale," Waggoner said.

"This rain's the first decent wash I've had in two weeks," Starbuck said. The shaking had stopped, but he nevertheless felt like an actor as he grinned at Waggoner. He was pretending not to be frightened and pretending that all was well, but his mind was as skittish as an unbroken colt. He turned away from the Lieutenant and peered into the eastern trees, searching for the rest of Swynyard's Brigade. "Is anyone still there?" he asked Waggoner.

"Haxall's men. They ain't doing nothing."

"Keeping dry, eh?"

"Never known rain like it," Waggoner grumbled. "It never rains when you want it. Never in spring. Always rains just before harvest or when you're cutting hay." A rifle fired from the Yankee wood and the bullet thudded into a maple behind Waggoner. The big man frowned resentfully toward the Yankees almost as though he felt the bullet was a discourtesy. "You got any idea where we are?" he asked Starbuck.

"Somewhere near the Flatlick," Starbuck said, "wherever the hell that is." He only knew that the Flatlick ran somewhere in Northern Virginia. They had pitched the Yankees out of their entrenchments in Centreville and were now trying to capture a ford the northerners were using for their retreat, though Starbuck had seen neither stream nor road all day. Colonel Swynyard had told him that the stream was called the Flatlick Branch, though the Colonel had not been really sure of that. "You ever

11

heard of the Flatlick?" Starbuck now asked Waggoner.

"Never heard of it," Waggoner said. Waggoner, like most of the Legion, came from the middle part of Virginia and had no knowledge of these approaches to Washington.

It took Starbuck a half hour to arrange the attack. It should have taken only minutes, but the rain made everyone slow and Captain Moxey inevitably argued that the attack was a waste of time because it was bound to fail like the first. Moxey was a young, bitter man who resented Starbuck's promotion. He was unpopular with most of the Legion, but on this rainy afternoon he was only saying what most of the men believed. They did not want to fight. They were too wet and cold and tired to fight, and even Starbuck was tempted to give in to the lethargy, but he sensed, despite his fear, that if a man yielded to terror once then he would yield again and again until he had no courage left. Soldiering, Starbuck had learned, was not about being comfortable, and commanding a regiment was not about giving men what they wanted, but about forcing them to do what they had never believed possible. Soldiering was about winning, and no victory ever came from sheltering at a wood's edge in the slathering rain. "We're going," he told Moxey flatly. "Those are our orders, and we're damned well going." Moxey shrugged as if to suggest that Starbuck was being a fool.

It took still more time for the four right-flank companies to ready themselves. They fixed bayonets, then shuffled to the corn's edge, where a vast puddle was churning with water flooding from between the furrows. The Yankee guns had fired sporadically during the long moments when Starbuck had been preparing the Legion, each shot sending a blistering cloud of canister into the Southern-held trees as a means of dissuading the Confederates from any

12

thoughts of hostility. The cannon fire left a sulfurous cloud of gunsmoke that drifted in the rain like mist. It was getting darker and darker, an unnaturally early twilight brought on by the sodden gray clouds. Starbuck positioned himself at the left-hand side of the attackers, closest to the Yankee guns, drew his bayonet, and slotted it onto his rifle's muzzle. He wore no sword and carried no badges of rank, while his revolver, which might betray him to the Yankees as a Confederate officer, was holstered at his back where the enemy could not see it. He made sure the bayonet was firm on the rifle, then cupped his hands. "Davies! Truslow!" he shouted, wondering how any voice could cut through the pelting rain and gusting wind.

"Hear you!" Truslow called back.

Starbuck hesitated. Once he shouted the next command he committed himself to battle and he was suddenly assailed with another racking bout of shivering. The fear was sapping him, but he forced himself to draw breath and shout the order. "Fire!"

The volley sounded feeble, a mere crackle of rifles like the snapping of cornstalks, but Starbuck, to his surprise, found himself on his feet and shoving forward into the corn. "Come on!" he shouted at the men nearest him as he struggled through the stiff, tangling stalks. "Come on!" He knew he had to lead this attack and he could only hope that the Legion was following him. He heard some men crashing through the crop near him and Peter Waggoner was roaring encouragement from the right flank, but Starbuck could also hear the sergeants shouting at the laggards to get up and go forward. Those shouts told him that some men were still cowering in the shelter of the trees, but he dared not turn round to see how many were following him in case those followers should think that he was giving up the advance. The attack was ragged, but it was launched now and Starbuck forced himself blindly on, expecting a bullet at any second. One of his men raised a feeble rebel yell, but no one else took it up. They were all too tired and wet to shrill the defiant call.

A bullet flickered through the bent corn tops, shedding water from the drooping cobs as it whipped across the field. The cannon were silent and Starbuck had a terror that the two guns were being slewed round to enfilade his attack. He shouted again, urging his men on, but the attack could only go at a slow walking pace, for the field was too muddy and the corn too entangling to let the men run. Other than the one rifle shot, the Yankees were silent and Starbuck knew they must be holding their fire until the ragged gray attackers were at point-blank range. He wanted to cringe from that expected volley, he wanted to drop into the wet stalks and hug the earth and wait for the war to pass. He was too terrified to shout or think or do anything except plunge blindly on toward the dark trees that were now just thirty paces away. It seemed stupid to die for a ford across the Flatlick, but the stupidity of the endeavor did not explain his fear. Instead it was something deeper, something he tried not to admit to himself because he suspected it was pure unalloyed cowardice, but the thought of how his enemies in the Legion would laugh at him if they saw his fear kept him going forward.

He slipped in a puddle, flailed for balance, and thrust on. Waggoner was still roaring defiance to his right, but the other men were just trudging through the soaking stalks. Starbuck's uniform was as wet as if he had just waded through a river. He felt he would never be dry or warm again. The drenched heavy clothes made each pace an effort. He tried to shout a battle cry, but the challenge emerged like a strangulated sob. If it had not been raining

14

he would have suspected he was weeping, and still the Yankees did not fire and now the enemy wood was close, very close, and the terror of the last few yards gave him a maniacal energy that hurled him through the last clinging stalks, through another vast puddle and right into the trees.

Where he found that the enemy was gone. "Oh, Jesus Christ!" Starbuck exclaimed, not sure if it was a profanity or a prayer. "Jesus Christ," he said again, staring in sheer relief at the empty wood. He stopped, panting, and stared about him, but the wood really was empty. The enemy had vanished, leaving nothing behind except a few scraps of damp cartridge paper and two sets of deep wheel ruts showing where they had pushed their two guns back out of the trees.

Starbuck called his remaining companies across the cornfield, then walked gingerly through the timber until he reached the far side and could stare over a wide stretch of rainswept pastureland to where a stream was flooding its banks. There was no enemy in sight, only a big house half obscured by trees on a far rise of land. A fork of lightning whipped down to silhouette the house, then a surge of rain blotted the building like a sea fog. The house had looked like a mansion to Starbuck, a mocking reminder of the comfortable life that a man might expect if his country was not riven by war.

"What now?" Moxey asked him.

"Your men can stand picket," Starbuck said. "Coffman? Go and find the Colonel, tell him we're across the cornfield." There were the dead to bury and the wounded to patch up.

The intermittent sounds of battle died utterly, leaving the field to rain and thunder and the cold east wind. Night fell. A few feeble fires flickered in the depths of woods, but most men lacked the skill to make fires in such rain, so instead they shivered and wondered just what they had done and why and where the enemy was and whether the next day would bring them warmth, food, and rest.

Colonel Swynyard, lean, ravaged, and ragged bearded, found Starbuck after nightfall. "No trouble crossing the cornfield, Nate?" the Colonel asked.

"No, sir, no trouble. No trouble at all."

"Good man." The Colonel held his hands toward Starbuck's fire. "I'll hold prayers in a few minutes. I don't suppose you'll come?"

"No, sir," Starbuck answered, just as he had answered every other evening that the Colonel had invited him to prayers.

"Then I'll pray for you, Nate," the Colonel responded, just as he had every other time. "I surely will."

Starbuck just wanted sleep. Just sleep. Nothing but sleep. But a prayer, he thought, might help. Something had to help, for he feared, God how he feared, that he was becoming a coward.

Starbuck took off his soaking clothes, unable to bear their chafing any longer, and hung them to take what drying warmth they could from the remains of his fire, then he wrapped himself in the clammy embrace of his blanket and slept despite the rain, but the sleep was a wicked imitation of rest for it was a waking sleep in which his dreams were mingled with rain and dripping trees and thunder and the spectral figure of his father, the Reverend Elial Starbuck, who mocked his son's timidity. "Always knew you were rotten, Nathaniel," his father said in the dream, "rotten all the way through, rotten like decayed timber. No backbone, boy, that's your trouble," and then his father capered unscathed away through a gunfire that left Starbuck dreaming that he was clinging to damp soil. Sally was in his dream too, yet she was no comfort for she did not recognize him, but just walked past him into nothingness, and then he was woken as someone shook his shoulder.

At first he thought the shaking was a part of his dream, then he feared the Yankees must be attacking and rolled quickly out of his wet blanket and reached toward his rifle. "It's all right, Major, ain't the Yankees, just me. There's a man for you." It was Lucifer who had woken him. "Man for you," Lucifer said again, "a real smart man." Lucifer was a boy who had become Starbuck's servant; an escaped slave with a high opinion of himself and an impish helping of sardonic humor. He had never revealed his true name and instead insisted on being called Lucifer. "You want coffee?" he asked.

"Is there any?"

"I can steal some."

"Then get thieving," Starbuck said. He stood, every muscle aching, and picked up his rifle that he remembered was still loaded with its useless charge of damp powder. He felt his clothes and found them still damp and saw that the fire had long gone out. "What time is it?" he called after Lucifer, but the boy was gone.

"Just after half past five," a stranger answered and Starbuck stepped naked out of the trees to see a cloaked figure on horseback. The man clicked shut his watch's lid and drew back his cloak to slip the timepiece into a fob of his uniform jacket. Starbuck glimpsed a braided smart coat that had never been blackened by powder nor soaked in blood, then the scarlet lined cloak fell back into place. "Maitland," the mounted man introduced himself, "Lieutenant-Colonel Ned Maitland." He blinked a couple of times at Starbuck's nakedness, but made no comment.

"I've come from Richmond with orders for you," Maitland added.

"For me?" Starbuck asked dully. He was still not awake properly and was trying to work out why anyone in Richmond should send him orders. He did not need orders, he needed rest.

"You are Major Starbuck?" Maitland asked.

"Yes."

"Good to meet you, Major," Maitland said and leaned out of his saddle to offer Starbuck his hand. Starbuck thought the gesture inappropriate and was reluctant to take the offered hand, but it seemed churlish to refuse and so he stepped over to the horse and clasped the Colonel's hand. The Colonel withdrew his hand quickly, as though fearing that Starbuck might have soiled it, then pulled his glove back on. He was hiding his reaction to Starbuck who, Maitland thought, looked an atrocious mess. His body was white and skinny while his face and hands were burned dark by the sun. A clot of blood scarred Starbuck's cheek, and his black hair hung long and lank. Maitland was proud of his own appearance and took care to keep himself smart. He was a young man for a Lieutenant-Colonel, maybe thirty, and boasted a thick, brown beard and carefully curled mustaches that he oiled with a scented lotion. "Was that your mess boy?" He jerked his head in the direction Lucifer had disappeared.

"Yes." Starbuck had fetched his damp clothes and was pulling them on.

"Don't you know blacks ain't supposed to carry guns?" Maitland observed.

"Ain't supposed to shoot Yankees either, but he killed a couple at Bull Run," Starbuck answered ungraciously. He had already struggled with Lucifer over the Colt revolver the boy insisted on wearing and Starbuck had no energy to refight the battle with some supercilious colonel come from Richmond. "What orders?" he asked Maitland.

Colonel Maitland did not answer. Instead he was staring through the dawn's wan light toward the mansion beyond the stream. "Chantilly," he said wistfully. "I do believe it's Chantilly."

"What?" Starbuck asked, pulling on his shirt and fumbling with its remaining bone buttons.

"That house. It's called Chantilly. A real nice place. I've danced a few nights under that roof, and no doubt will again when we've seen the Yankees off. Where will I find Colonel Swynyard?"

"On his knees, probably," Starbuck answered. "Are you going to give me those orders?"

"Aren't you supposed to call me 'sir'?" Maitland enquired courteously, though with an undercurrent of impatience because of Starbuck's antagonism.

"When hell freezes over," Starbuck said curtly, surprised at the belligerence that seemed to be an ever more salient part of his character.

Maitland chose not to make an issue of the matter. "I'm to hand you the orders in the presence of Colonel Swynyard," he said, then waited while Starbuck pissed against a tree. "You look kind of young to be a major," he remarked as Starbuck buttoned his pants.

"You look kind of young to be a colonel," Starbuck responded surlily. "And my age, Colonel, only matters to me and the fellow who carves my tombstone. If I ever get a stone. Most soldiers don't, not unless they do their fighting from behind a desk in Richmond." After delivering that insult to a man who looked like a desk soldier, Starbuck stooped to tie the laces of the boots he had collected off a dead Yankee at Cedar Mountain. The rain had stopped, but the air was still heavy with moisture and the grass thick with water. Some of the Legion had drifted out of the trees to stare at the elegant Lieutenant Colonel who endured their scrutiny patiently as he waited for Starbuck to collect his coat. Lucifer had come back with a handful of beans that Starbuck told him to take to Colonel Swynyard's bivouac. He pulled his wet hat onto his unruly black hair, then gestured to Maitland. "This way," he said.

Starbuck deliberately forced the elegant Maitland to dismount by leading him through the thickest part of the timber where the leaves and brush soaked the Colonel's silk-lined cloak. Maitland made no protest, nor did Starbuck speak until the two men had reached Swynyard's tent where, as Starbuck had predicted, the Colonel was at his prayers. The tent's flaps were brailed back and the Colonel was kneeling on the tent boards with an open Bible on his cot's blanket. "He found God three weeks ago," Starbuck told Maitland in a voice loud enough to disturb the Colonel, "and he's been bending God's ears ever since." The three weeks had worked a miracle on Swynyard, turning a drink-sodden wretch into a fine soldier who now, dressed in shirt-sleeves and gray pants, turned his one good eye toward the men who had disturbed his morning prayers.

"God will forgive you for interrupting me," he said magnanimously, climbing to his feet and tugging his suspenders over his lean shoulders. Maitland gave an involuntary shudder at the sight of Swynyard, who seemed even more unkempt than Starbuck. Swynyard was a thin, scarred man with a ragged beard, yellow teeth, and three missing fingers from his left hand.

"Bites his nails," Starbuck explained, seeing Maitland staring at the three stumps.

Maitland grimaced, then stepped forward with an out-

20

stretched hand. Swynyard seemed surprised at the offered gesture, but responded willingly enough, then nodded at Starbuck, "Good morning, Nate."

Starbuck ignored the greeting, jerking his head toward Maitland instead. "Man's called Lieutenant-Colonel Maitland. Got orders for me, but says he has to see you first."

"You've seen me," Swynyard said to Maitland, "so give Nate his orders."

Instead Maitland led his horse to a nearby tree and tied its reins to a drooping branch. He unbuckled a saddlebag and took out a packet of papers. "You remember me, Colonel?" he called over his shoulder as he rebuckled the bag.

"Alas, no," Swynyard sounded suspicious, wary of someone from his old, pre-Christian life. "Should I remember you?"

"Your pa sold some slaves to my pa. Twenty years back."

Swynyard, relieved that one of his old sins was not being revisited on him, relaxed. "You must have been a boy, Colonel."

"I was, but I remember your pa telling my pa that the slaves were good workers. They weren't. They were no damn good."

"In the trade," Swynyard said, "they always say that slaves are no better than their masters." Swynyard had spoken equably, though the words made it clear he had taken as great a dislike to Maitland as Starbuck had. There was an assumption of privilege about Maitland that grated on both men, or perhaps the irritation came from the incursion into their lives of a man who so obviously spent his time far from the bullets.

"Lucifer's bringing some coffee, Colonel," Starbuck said to Swynyard.

21

The Colonel hospitably fetched a pair of camp chairs from his tent and invited Maitland to sit. He offered Starbuck an upturned crate and set another as a table. "So where are these orders, Colonel?" he asked Maitland.

"Got 'em right here," Maitland said, putting the papers on the crate and covering them with his hat to stop either Swynyard or Starbuck from plucking them up. He took off his damp cloak to reveal a uniform that was immaculately cut and decorated with a double line of brass buttons polished to a high gloss. The twin gold stars on each of his shoulders seemed bright enough to be made of gold, while the braiding on his sleeves appeared to be fashioned from gold thread. Starbuck's coat was threadbare, had no gold or brass or even cloth marks of rank, but only white salt marks where sweat had dried into the material's weave. Maitland brushed the chair seat then twitched up his pants with their elegant yellow stripes before sitting. He lifted the hat, put the sealed papers aside, and handed another single sheet to Swynyard. "I am reporting to you as ordered, Colonel," he said very formally.

Swynyard unfolded the sheet, read it, blinked, then read it again. He looked up at Maitland, then back to the paper. "You done any fighting, Colonel?" he asked in what struck Starbuck as a bitter voice.

"I was with Johnston for a time."

"That ain't what I asked you," Swynyard said flatly.

"I've seen fighting, Colonel," Maitland said stiffly.

"Done any?" Swynyard demanded fiercely. "I mean have you been in the rifle line? Have you shot your piece, then stood to reload with a line of Yankees taking a bead on you? Have you done that, Colonel?"

Maitland glanced at Starbuck before answering and Starbuck, puzzled by the conversation, caught a look of

22

guilt in Maitland's eye. "I've seen battle," Maitland insisted to Swynyard.

"From a staff officer's horse," Swynyard said caustically. "It ain't the same, Colonel." He sounded sad as he spoke, then he leaned forward and plucked the sealed papers off the crate and tossed them onto Starbuck's lap. "If I weren't a saved man," he said, "if I hadn't been washed in the redeeming blood of Christ, I'd be tempted to swear right now. And I do believe God would forgive me if I did. I'm sorry, Nate, more sorry than I can tell you."

Starbuck tore open the seal and unfolded the papers. The first sheet was a pass authorizing him to travel to Richmond. The second was an order requiring him to report to a Colonel Holborrow at Richmond's Camp Lee, where Major Starbuck was to take over the command of the 2nd Special Battalion. "Son of a bitch," Starbuck said softly.

Swynyard took Nate's orders, read them quickly, then handed them back. "They're taking you away, Nate, and giving the Legion to Mister Maitland." He pronounced the newcomer's name bitterly.

Maitland ignored Swynyard's tone. Instead he took out a silver case and selected a cigar that he lit with a lucifer before staring serenely into the wet trees where the men of Swynyard's Brigade were coaxing fires and hacking at hardtack with blunt bayonets. "I doubt we'll get more rain," he said airily.

Starbuck read the orders again. He had commanded the Legion for just a few weeks and had been given that command by Major General Thomas Jackson himself, but now he was ordered to hand his men over to this popinjay from Richmond and take over an unknown battalion instead. "Why?" he asked, but no one answered. "Jesus!" he swore.

"It ain't right!" Swynyard added his protest. "A regiment is a delicate thing, Colonel," he explained to Maitland. "It ain't just the Yankees who can tear a regiment to bits, but the regiment's own officers. The Legion's had a bad stretch, but Nate here was turning it into a decent unit again. It don't make sense to change commanders now."

Maitland just shrugged. He was a handsome man who carried his privilege with a calm self-confidence. If he felt any sympathy for Starbuck, he did not betray it, but just let the protests flow past him.

"It weakens my brigade!" Swynyard said angrily. "Why?"

Maitland offered an airy gesture with his cigar. "I'm just the messenger, Colonel, just the messenger."

For a second it looked as though Swynyard would swear at Maitland, then he conquered the impulse and shook his head instead. "Why?" he asked again. "This brigade fought magnificently! Doesn't anyone care what we did last week?"

It seemed no one did, or no one for whom Maitland spoke. Swynyard momentarily closed his eyes, then looked at Starbuck. "I'm sorry, Nate, real sorry."

"Son of a bitch," Starbuck said of no one in particular. The gall of the moment was particularly bitter, for he was a northerner who fought for the South and the Faulconer Legion was his home and his refuge. He looked down at the orders. "What's the Second Special Battalion?" he asked Maitland.

For a second it looked as though Maitland would not answer, then the elegant Colonel gave Starbuck a half smile. "I believe they're more commonly known as the Yellowlegs," he said with his irritating tone of private amusement.

Starbuck swore and raised his eyes to the clouded heavens. The Yellowlegs had gained their nickname and lost their reputation during the week of springtime battles in which Lee had finally turned McClellan's Northern army away from Richmond. Jackson's men had come from the Shenandoah Valley to help Lee and among them were the 66th Virginia, a newly raised regiment that saw its first and, so far, last action near Malvern Hill. They had run away, not from a hard fight, but from the very first shells that fell near them. Their nickname, the Yellowlegs, supposedly described the state of their pants after they pissed themselves in fright. "Pissed in unison," Truslow had told Starbuck on hearing the story, "and made a whole new swamp." Later it was determined that the regiment had been too hastily raised, too skimpily trained, and too badly officered, and so its rifles had been given to men willing to fight and its men taken away to be retrained. "So who's this Colonel Holborrow?" Swynyard asked Maitland.

"He's in charge of training the punishment battalions," Maitland answered airily. "Wasn't there one at the battle last week?"

"Hell, yes," Starbuck answered. "And it was no damn good." The punishment battalion at the previous week's battle had been a makeshift collection of defaulters, stragglers, and shirkers, and it had collapsed within minutes. "Hell!" Starbuck said. Now, it seemed, the 66th Virginia had been renamed as a punishment battalion, which suggested its morale was no higher than when it had first earned its nickname and, if the performance of the 1st Punishment Battalion was anything to go by, no better trained either.

Lucifer put two mugs of coffee on the makeshift table and then, after a glance at Starbuck's distraught face, backed far enough away so that the three officers would think he was out of earshot.

"This is madness!" Swynyard had found a new energy to protest. "Who sent the order?"

"The War Department," Maitland answered, "of course."

"Who in the War Department?" Swynyard insisted.

"You can read the signature, can't you, Colonel?"

The name on the order meant nothing to either Starbuck or to Swynyard, but Griffin Swynyard had a shrewd idea where the papers might have come from. "Is General Faulconer posted to the War Department?" he asked Maitland.

Maitland took the cigar from his mouth, spat a speck of leaf from his lips, then shrugged as if the question were irrelevant. "General Faulconer's been made Deputy Secretary of War, yes," he answered. "Can't let a good man idle away just because Tom Jackson took a dislike to him."

"And General Faulconer made you the Legion's commanding officer," Swynyard said.

"I guess the General put in a good word for me," Maitland said. "The Legion's a Virginia regiment, Colonel, and the General reckoned it ought to be led by a Virginian. So here I am." He smiled at Swynyard.

"Son of a bitch," Starbuck said. "Faulconer. I should have known." General Washington Faulconer had been the Legion's founder and the brigade's commander until Jackson had dismissed him for incompetence. Faulconer had fled the army convinced that Starbuck and Swynyard had been responsible for his disgrace, but instead of retreating to his country house and nursing his hurt, he had gone to Richmond and used his connection and wealth to gain a government appointment. Now, safe in the Confederate capital, Faulconer was reaching out to take his revenge on the two men he saw as his bitterest enemies. To Swynyard he had bequeathed a man of equal rank who would doubtless be an irritant, but Faulconer was trying to destroy Starbuck altogether.

"He'd have doubtless liked to get rid of me too," Swynyard said. He had led Starbuck away from the tent and was walking him up and down out of Maitland's hearing. "But Faulconer knows who my cousin is." Swynyard's cousin was the editor of Richmond's *Examiner*, the most powerful of the five daily papers published in the Confederate capital, and that relationship had doubtless kept Washington Faulconer from trying to take an overt revenge on Swynyard, but Starbuck was much easier meat. "But there's something else, Nate," the Colonel went on, "another reason why Maitland took your job."

"Because he's a Virginian," Starbuck said bitterly.

Swynyard shook his head. "I guess Maitland shook your hand, yes?"

"Yes. So?"

"He was trying to see if you're a Freemason, Nate. And you're not."

"What the hell difference does that make?"

"A lot," Swynyard said bluntly. "There are a lot of Masons in this army, and in the Yankee army too, and Masons look after each other. Faulconer's a Mason, so's Maitland, and so am I, for that matter. The Masons have served me well enough, but they've done for you, Nate. The Yellowlegs!" The Colonel shook his head at the awful prospect.

"I ain't good for much else, Colonel," Starbuck admitted.

"What does that mean?" Swynyard demanded.

Starbuck hesitated, ashamed to admit a truth, but

27

needing to tell someone about his fears. "I reckon I'm turning into a coward. It was all I could do to cross that cornfield yesterday and I'm not sure I could do it again. I guess I've used up what courage I ever had. Maybe a battalion of cowards deserve a coward as their commander."

Swynyard shook his head. "Courage isn't like a bottle of whiskey, Nate. You don't empty it once and for all. You're just learning your trade. The first time in battle a boy reckons he can beat anything, but after a while he learns that battle is bigger than all of us. Being brave isn't ignorance, it's overcoming knowledge, Nate. You'll be all right the next time. And remember, the enemy's in just the same funk that you are. It's only in the newspapers that we're all heroes. In truth we're most of us frightened witless." He paused and stirred the damp leaves with the toe of a boot from which the sole was gaping. "And the Yellowlegs ain't cowards," he went on. "Something went wrong with them, that's for sure, but there'll be as many brave men there as in any other battalion. I reckon they just need good leadership."

Starbuck grimaced, hoping Swynyard told the truth, but still unwilling to leave the Legion. "Maybe I should go and see Jackson?" he suggested.

"To get those orders reversed?" Swynyard asked, then shook his head in answer. "Old Jack don't take kindly to men questioning orders, Nate, not unless the orders are plumb crazy, and that order ain't plumb crazy. It's perverse, that's all. Besides," he smiled, trying to cheer Starbuck, "you'll be back. Maitland won't survive."

"If he wears all that gold into battle," Starbuck said vengefully, "the Yankees will pick him off in a second."

"He won't be that foolish," Swynyard said, "but he won't stay long. I know the Maitlands, and they were always high kind of folk. Kept carriages, big houses, and acres of good land. They breed pretty daughters, haughty men, and fine horses, that's the Maitlands. Not unlike the Faulconers. And Mister Maitland hasn't come to us because he wants to command the Legion, Nate, he's come here because he has to tuck one proper battlefield command under his belt before he can become a general. Mister Maitland has his eye on his career, and he knows he has to spend a month with muddy boots if he's ever going to rise high. He'll go soon enough and you can come back."

"Not if Faulconer has anything to do with it."

"So prove him wrong," Swynyard said energetically. "Make the Yellowlegs into a fine regiment, Nate. If anyone can do it, you can."

"I sometimes wonder why I fight for this damn country," Starbuck said bitterly.

Swynyard smiled. "Nothing to stop you going back North, Nate, nothing at all. Just keep walking north and you'll get home. Is that what you want?"

"Hell, no."

"So prove Faulconer wrong. He reckons that a punishment battalion will be the end of you, so prove him wrong."

"Damn his bastard soul," Starbuck said.

"That's God's work, Nate. Yours is to fight. So do it well. And I'll put in a request that your men are sent to my brigade."

"What chance is there of that?"

"I'm a Mason, remember," Swynyard said with a grin, "and I've still got a favor or two to call in. We'll get you back among friends."

Maitland stood up as the two ragged officers walked back to the tent. He had drunk one of the two cups of coffee and started on the second. "You'll introduce me to the Legion's officers, Starbuck?" he said.

"I'll do that for you, Colonel," Starbuck said. He might resent this man displacing him, but he would not put difficulties in Maitland's way because the Legion would have to fight the Yankees whoever commanded them and Starbuck did not want their morale hurt more than was necessary. "I'll talk you up to them," he promised grudgingly.

"But I don't think you should stay after that," Maitland suggested confidently. "No man can serve two masters, isn't that what the good book says? So the sooner you're gone, Starbuck, the better for the men."

"Better for you, you mean," Starbuck said.

"That, too," Maitland agreed calmly.

Starbuck was losing the Legion and been consigned to a battalion of the damned, which meant he was being destroyed and would somehow have to survive.

LUCIFER WAS NOT HAPPY. "Richmond," he told Starbuck soon after they had arrived in the city, "is not to my taste."

"Then go away," Starbuck retorted grumpily.

"I am considering it," Lucifer said. He was liable to pompousness when he perceived that his dignity was under assault, and that dignity was very easily offended. He was only a boy, fifteen at the very most, and he would have been small for his age even if he were two years younger, but he had crammed a lot of living into those few years and was possessed of a self-assurance that fascinated Starbuck quite as much as the mystery of the boy's past. Lucifer never spoke directly about that past, nor did Starbuck ask about it, for he had learned that every query merely prompted a different version. It was plain the boy was a contraband, an escaped slave, and Starbuck suspected Lucifer had been trying to reach the sanctuary of the North when he had been apprehended by Jackson's army at Manassas, but Lucifer's life before that moment, like his real name, remained all mystery, just as it was a mystery why he had elected to stay with Starbuck after his recapture.

"He likes you, that's why," Sally Truslow told Starbuck. "He knows you'll give him plenty of rope and he's mischievous enough to want rope. Then one day he'll grow up and you won't ever see him again."

Starbuck and Lucifer had walked from the rain-soaked battlefield to the railhead at Fredericksburg, then taken the Richmond, Fredericksburg, and Potomac Railroad to the capital. Starbuck's travel pass gave him admission to one of the passenger cars while Lucifer traveled in a boxcar with the other Negroes. The train had puffed and jerked and clanked and shuddered and thus crept south until, at dawn, Starbuck had been woken by the cry of a Richmond milkmaid. The Richmond, Fredericksburg, and Potomac depot was in the heart of the city and the rails ran right down the center of Broad Street, and Starbuck found it a strange experience to see the familiar city through the soot-smutted window of a slow-moving railcar. Newspaper boys ran alongside the train offering copies of the *Examiner* or *Sentinel*, while on the sidewalk pedestrians edged past the carts and wagons that had been herded to the street's sides by the train's slow, clangorous passage. Starbuck stared bleary-eyed through the window, noticing gloomily how many doors were hung with black, how many women were in mourning, how many cripples begged on the sidewalk, and how many men had crêpe armbands.

Starbuck had convinced himself that he would not call on Sally. He told himself that she was no longer his woman. She had found a lover, Starbuck's good friend Patrick Lassan, a French cavalryman who was ostensibly observing the war on behalf of the French army but who really rode with Jeb Stuart. Starbuck told himself that Sally was no longer his business and he was still telling himself that truth when he knocked on the blue painted door beside the tailor's shop on the corner of Fourth and Grace. Sally had been glad to see him. She was already up, already busy, and she ordered her slaves to bring Starbuck a breakfast of coffee and bread. "It's bad bread," she said, "but there ain't any good bread. Nor any good coffee, for that matter. Hell, I'm using acorns, wheat berries, and chicory for coffee. Nothing's good now except the cigars and business." Sally's business was to be Madame Royall, Richmond's most expensive medium, who offered expensive seances to reunite the living with the dead. "It's all tricks," she said scornfully, "I just tell 'em what they want to hear and the more I charge the more they believe me." She shrugged. "Dull business, Nate, but better than working nights." She meant the brothel on Marshall Street where Sally had first discovered her business acumen.

"I can imagine."

"I doubt that you can, Nate," Sally said good humoredly, then gave him a long searching look. "You're thin. Look worn out like a mule. That a bullet cut on your face?"

"Tree splinter."

"The girls will love it, Nate. Not that you ever needed help in that department, but tell them it's a bullet and they'll all want to pet you. And you got a slave too?"

"I pay him when I can," Starbuck said defensively.

"Then you're a damn fool," she said fondly. "Bad as Delaney." Belvedere Delaney was a lawyer officially attached to the War Department, but his duties left him plenty of time for running his various businesses, which included Richmond's most exclusive brothel as well as the crêpe-curtained premises where Sally manufactured conversations with the dead. Sally had first met Delaney by being one of his employees in the brothel, and not just any employee, but the most sought-after girl in Richmond. She was Captain Truslow's only child and had been raised to hard work and small reward on Truslow's hill farm, but she had fled the farm and embraced the city, a transition made easy by her striking looks. Sally had a deceptively soft face, a mass of golden hair, and a quick spirit to liven her attractiveness, but there was far more to Sally Truslow than nature's accident of beauty. She knew how to work and knew how to profit from that work, and these days she was Delaney's business partner rather than his employee. "Delaney's a fool," she said tartly. "He lets his house boy twist him round his little finger, and you're probably just as bad. So let's have a look at your boy. I want to know you're being looked after." And thus Lucifer was summoned up to the parlor where he quickly charmed Sally who recognized in the boy someone who, like herself, was working up from rock bottom. "But why are you carrying a gun, boy?" she demanded of Lucifer.

"'Cos I'm in the army, miss."

"The hell you are. You get caught with a gun in this town, boy, and they'll skin your backside and then send you down the river. You're damn lucky to have survived this long. Take it off. Now."

Lucifer, who had resisted every former effort to disarm him, meekly unbuckled the gunbelt. It was plain that Lucifer was awestruck by Sally, and he made not even the smallest complaint as she told him to hide the revolver in Starbuck's baggage and then dismissed him to the kitchen. "Tell them to feed you up," she said.

"Yes, miss."

"He's got white blood," Sally said when Lucifer had gone.

"I guess."

"Hell, it's obvious." She poured herself more of the strange-tasting coffee, then listened as Starbuck told her why he was in Richmond. She spat derisively when Washington Faulconer's name was mentioned. "The city was full of rumor about why he'd left the army," she said, "but he rode right over the rumor. Arrived here bold as brass and just claimed Jackson was jealous of him. Jealous! But your General Jackson, Nate, he makes enemies like a louse makes itches and there are plenty of men here ready to sympathize with Faulconer. He got office soon enough. I guess you're right and the Masons looked after him. Delaney will know, he's a Mason. So what do you do now?"

Starbuck shrugged. "I have to report to Camp Lee. To a Colonel Holborrow." He was not looking forward to the moment. He was unsure of his ability to lead the worst battalion in the South's army, and he already missed the companionship of the Legion.

"I know Holborrow," Sally said, "not personally," she added hastily, "but he's pretty considerable in town." Starbuck was not surprised at her knowledge, for Sally kept an ear very close to the ground to snap up every trifle of gossip that she could turn into a mystical revelation in her seances. "He's got money," she went on, "God knows how, 'cos he wasn't nothing but a penitentiary governor in Georgia before the war. A prison man, right? Now he's in charge of training and equipping the replacements at Camp Lee, but he spends most of his time down in Screamersville."

"The brothels?"

"Them and the cockpit."

"He gambles?" Starbuck asked.

Sally shook her head at Starbuck's naïveté. "He don't go there to admire the birds' feathers," she said tartly. "What the hell did they teach you at Yale?"

Starbuck laughed, then perched his muddy boots on a tapestry-covered ottoman that stood on an Oriental rug. Everything in the room was in the best of taste; understated but expensive. Napoleon's bust glowered on the mantel, leatherbound books stood ranked in glass-fronted cases, while exquisite pieces of porcelain were displayed on shelves. "You live well, Sally," Starbuck said.

"You know any merit in living badly?" she asked. "And you can get your boots off the furniture while you think about the answer."

"I was thinking of going to sleep," Starbuck said, not moving.

"Hell, Nate Starbuck," Sally said, "are you reckoning on staying here?"

He shook his head. "I thought I might let you buy me lunch at the Spotswood, then walk with me to Camp Lee."

Sally waited until he had moved the offending boots from the ottoman. "Now why," she asked, "would I want to do that?"

Starbuck smiled. "Because, Sally, if I've got to take a pack of skulking cowards to war, then they need to know I'm a lucky man. And how much luckier can a man be than to show up with someone like you on his arm?"

"Glad to see the Yankees haven't shot your glib tongue out," she said, disguising her pleasure at the compliment. "But are you reckoning on going into the Spotswood looking like that?"

"Got nothing else to wear." He frowned at his disheveled uniform. "Hell, if it's good enough for fighting battles it's good enough for the Spotswood Hotel." Six hours later a well-fed Starbuck walked with Sally and Lucifer west out of the city. Sally wore a bonnet and shawl over a simple blue dress that was nowhere near plain enough to hide her beauty. She carried a fringed parasol against the sun, which had at last appeared from the clouds and was sucking up the remnants of the rainstorm into drifting patches of mist. They walked past the State Penitentiary, crossed the head of Hollywood Cemetery where the freshly turned earth lay in grim rows like the battalions of the dead, and skirted the municipal waterworks, until at last they could see Camp Lee on its wide bluff above the river and canal. Starbuck had visited the camp earlier in the year and remembered it as a grim, makeshift place. It had once been the Richmond Central Fairgrounds, but the onset of war had turned it into a giant dumping ground for the battalions that had flocked to the defense of Richmond. Those battalions were now on Virginia's northern border and the camp was a dirty stretch of muddy ground where conscripts received a rudimentary training and where stragglers were sent to be assigned to new battalions. At the war's beginning the camp had been a favorite place for Richmonders to come and watch the troops being drilled, but that novelty had worn off and these days few people visited the dank, derelict-looking barracks where old moldering tents stood in rows and tarpaper huts flapped in the breeze. The gallows of the camp jail still topped the hill, and round the jail was clustered an array of wooden huts where most of the camp's present occupants seemed to be billeted. Two sergeants playing horseshoes confirmed to Starbuck that the huts were the Special Battalion's quarters and he walked slowly uphill toward the flat crest where a half dozen companies were being drilled. A few lackluster work parties were patching the decrepit buildings among which, like a palace among hovels, stood the house that the sergeants had said was Holborrow's headquarters. The house was a fine two-story building with a wide verandah all around and slave quarters and kitchens in its backyard. Two flagpoles stood in front of the house, one with the Confederate's stars and bars and the other flying a blue flag crested with the coat of arms of Georgia.

Starbuck paused to watch the companies being drilled.

There seemed small point to the activity, for the men were proficient enough, though every tiny fault was enough to force the sergeant in charge to a barrage of obscene abuse. The sergeant was a tall, gangling man with an unnaturally long neck and a voice that could have carried clean across the river to Manchester. The troops had no weapons, but were simply being marched, halted, turned, and marched again. Some were in gray coats, but most wore the increasingly common butternut brown that was easier to produce. At least half the men, Starbuck noted with alarm, had no boots, but were marching barefoot.

Sally put her arm into Starbuck's elbow as they walked closer to the headquarters, where a group of four officers was stretched out in camp chairs on the verandah. One of the idling officers trained a telescope toward Starbuck and Sally. "You're being admired," Starbuck said.

"That was the point of me wasting an afternoon, wasn't it?"

"Yes," Starbuck said proudly.

Sally paused again to watch the troops on the parade ground who, so far as the screaming sergeant allowed, returned her inspection.

"They're your men?" she asked.

"All mine."

"The pick of a bad bunch, eh?"

"They look all right to me," Starbuck said. He was already trying to imbue himself with a loyalty toward these despised troops.

"They can kill Yankees, can't they?" Sally said, sensing Starbuck's apprehension. She brushed at the ingrained dirt on his uniform sleeve, not because she believed the dirt could be swept off, but because she knew he needed the small consolation of touch. Then her hand paused. "What's that?" she asked.

Starbuck turned to see that Sally was gazing at a punishment horse that had been erected between two of the huts. The horse was a long beam that was mounted edgewise on a pair of tall trestles, and the punishment consisted of a man being forced to straddle the beam's edge and stay there while his own weight turned his groin into a mass of pain. A prisoner was on the horse with his hands bound and his legs tied to prevent him dismounting, while an armed guard stood beside the steps that were used to mount the instrument. "A punishment," Starbuck explained, "called a horse. Hurts like hell, I'm told."

"That's the point of punishment, ain't it?" Sally said. She had taken her share of beatings as a child and the experience had thickened her skin.

The man beneath the horse appeared to ask a question of the straddling man. The prisoner shook his head and the man yanked down on his bound ankles so that the man screamed.

"Shit," Starbuck said.

"Ain't that a part of it?" Sally demanded.

"No."

Sally looked at the distaste on Starbuck's face. "You going soft, Nate?"

"I don't mind punishing soldiers, but not torture. Besides, think of them." He nodded toward the companies on the parade ground who were mutely watching the horse. "A regiment's a fragile thing," he said, echoing Swynyard's words to Maitland. "It works best when the men are fighting the enemy, not each other." He flinched as the guard tugged on the prisoner's ankles again. "Hell," he said, reluctant to intervene, but also unwilling to watch any more brutality. He strode toward the horse.

The guard who had tugged on the prisoner's ankles was a sergeant who turned and watched Starbuck's approach.

Starbuck wore no badges of rank and had a rifle slung on his left shoulder, both of which suggested he was a private soldier, but he carried himself confidently and had a woman and servant, which suggested he might be an officer and the sergeant was consequently wary. "What's he done?" Starbuck demanded.

"Being punished," the sergeant said. He was a squat, bearded man. He was chewing tobacco and paused to spit a stream of yellowish spittle onto the grass. "Sergeant Case's orders," he added as though that should be sufficient explanation.

"I know he's being punished," Starbuck said, "but I asked what he had done."

"Being punished," the sergeant said obstinately.

Starbuck moved so he could see the drawn face of the prisoner. "What did you do?" he asked the man.

Before the prisoner could give any answer the drill sergeant abandoned the companies on the parade ground and marched toward the horse. "No one talks to prisoners under punishment!" he screamed in a terrifying voice. "You know that, Sergeant Webber! Punishment is punishment. Punishment is what will turn this lily-livered rabble of squirrel shit into soldiers." He slammed to a halt two paces from Starbuck. "You have questions," he said forcefully, "you ask them to me."

"And who are you?" Starbuck asked.

The tall sergeant looked surprised, as though his fame must have been obvious. He gave no immediate answer, but instead inspected Starbuck for clues to his status. The presence of Sally and Lucifer must have convinced him that Starbuck was an officer, though Starbuck's age suggested he was not an officer who needed to be placated. "Sergeant Case," he snapped. Case's long neck and small head would have looked risible on any other man, and his ridiculous appearance was not helped by a wispy beard and a thin broken nose, but there was a malevolence in the sergeant's dark eyes that turned amusement into fear. The eyes were flat, hard, and merciless. Starbuck noted too that Case's gangly body was deceptive; it was not a weak, thin frame, but lean and muscled. He was uniformed immaculately, every button polished, every crease hot-pressed, and every badge shining. Sergeant Case looked just as Starbuck had imagined soldiers ought to look like before he discovered that, at least in the Confederacy, they were generally ragged as hell. "Sergeant Case," Case said again, leaning closer to Starbuck, "and I," he stressed that word, "am in charge here."

"So what did the prisoner do?" Starbuck asked.

"Do?" Case asked dramatically. "Do? What he did is of no business to you. Not one scrap."

"What battalion is he?" Starbuck demanded, nodding toward the prisoner.

"He could belong to the Coldstream bloody Guards," Case shouted, "and it still ain't your business."

Starbuck looked up at the prisoner. The man's face was white with pain and rigid with the effort needed not to show that pain. "Battalion, soldier?" Starbuck snapped.

The man grimaced, then managed to say a single word. "Punishment."

"Then you are my business," Starbuck said. He took his folding knife out of a pocket, unsnapped the blade, and sawed at the rope binding the prisoner's ankles. The motion made the prisoner whimper, but it provoked Sergeant Case to leap forward threateningly.

Starbuck paused and looked up into Case's eyes. "I'm an officer, Sergeant," he said, "and if you lay a damned hand on me I'll make sure you spend the rest of today on

41

this horse. You won't walk for a goddamn week. Maybe not for a goddamn month."

Sergeant Case stepped back as Starbuck cut through the last strands of hemp and put a hand under one of the prisoner's boots. "Ready?" he called, then heaved up hard, throwing the prisoner off the beam. The man thumped onto the damp ground where he lay still as Starbuck crouched and sliced through the rope about his wrists. "So what did he do?" Starbuck asked Sergeant Case.

"Son of a bitch!" Case said, though whether of Starbuck or the prisoner it was impossible to tell, then he turned abruptly and strode away with his companion.

The prisoner groaned and tried to stand, but the pain in his crotch was too savage. He crawled to one of the horse's supporting trestles and dragged himself to a sitting position, then just clung to the timber. His eyes watered and his breath came in small, stuttering gasps. Even Sally flinched at his evident pain. "Guns," he finally said.

"Guns?" Starbuck asked him. "What about them."

"Son of a bitch is stealing guns," the freed prisoner said, then was forced to stop because of the pain. He clutched his groin, held a deep breath, then shook his head in an effort to banish the dreadful agony. "You asked why I was on the horse? Because of guns. I was on a detail to unload rifles. We got twenty boxes of them. Good ones. But Holborrow made us put them in crates marked 'CON- DEMNED' and then gave us muskets instead. Richmond muskets. Hell," he spat, then momentarily closed his eyes as a spasm of pain made him grimace. "I don't want to go shooting no Yankees with buck and ball, not if they've got minie balls. That's why I argued with that son of a bitch Sergeant Case."

"So where are the rifles now?" Starbuck asked.

"Hell knows. Sold, probably. Holborrow don't care so

long as we never go to war. We're not supposed to fight, see? Just get supplies that the son of a bitch sells." The man frowned up at Starbuck. "Who are you?" he asked.

"Potter!" A new and angry voice yelled from the headquarters building. "Potter, you son of a bitch! You bastard! You lunkheaded piece of dog shit. You black-assed fool!" The speaker was a tall, lean officer in a braided gray coat who stumped toward Starbuck with the help of a silver-tipped cane. Sergeant Case marched behind the officer, who had a neat blond goatee beard and a narrow mustache that had been carefully waxed into stiff points. He shoved the cane hard into the turf to aid each step and in between he brandished it toward the astonished Starbuck. "Where the hell have you been, Potter?" The officer demanded. "Just where the hell have you been, boy?"

"He's talking to you?" Sally asked Starbuck in bemusement.

"Hell, boy, are you drunk?" The limping officer bellowed. "Potter, you black-ass lunkhead piece of leper shit, are you drunk?"

Starbuck was about to deny being either Potter or drunk, then a mischievous impulse welled up inside him. "Don't say a word," he said quietly to Sally and Lucifer, then shook his head. "I ain't drunk," he said as the officer came close.

"Is this how you repay a kindness?" the officer demanded fiercely. He had the stars of a colonel on his shoulders. "My apologies, ma'am," the Colonel touched his free hand to the brim of his hat, "but I can't abide tardiness. Can't abide it. Are you drunk, Potter?" The Colonel stepped close to Starbuck and thrust his goatee up toward the younger man's clean-shaven chin. "Let me smell your breath, Potter, let me smell your breath.

43

Breathe, man, breathe!" He sniffed, then stepped back. "You don't smell drunk," the Colonel said dubiously, "so why the hell, forgive me, ma'am, did you throw Private Rothwell off the horse. Answer me!"

"It was upsetting the lady," Starbuck said.

The Colonel looked at Sally again and this time he registered that she was a startlingly pretty young woman. "Holborrow, ma'am," he said, snatching off his brimmed hat to reveal a head of carefully waved gold hair, "Colonel Charles Holborrow at your service." He gaped at Sally for a second. "I should have known," he said, his voice suddenly softening, "that you come from Georgia. Ain't girls anywhere in the world as pretty as Georgia girls, and that's a plain straight fact. 'Pon my precious soul, ma'am, it's a fact. The Reverend Potter did say as how his son was married and was bringing his good lady here, but he never did say just how pretty you are." Holborrow shamelessly leered down to judge Sally's figure before grasping her hand and giving it a firm kiss. "Sure pleased to meet you, Mrs. Potter," he said, still holding on to her hand.

"Pleasure's all mine, Colonel." Sally pretended to be flattered by Holborrow's admiration and left her hand in his.

Holborrow leaned his cane against his hip so he could fold his other hand over Sally's. "And you were upset by the punishment, ma'am, is that it?" he inquired solicitously, massaging Sally's hand between his.

"Reckon I was, sir," Sally said humbly, then sniffed.

"Right upsetting for a lady," Holborrow agreed. "But you have to understand, ma'am, that this lunkhead prisoner struck Sergeant Case. Struck him! A serious military offense, ma'am, and your husband here had no business interfering. None at all. Ain't that the case, Sergeant Case?"

"Sir!" Case snapped, evidently his way of articulating an affirmative to officers.

Holborrow let go of Sally's hand to step closer to Starbuck. "Sergeant Case, boy, is from North Carolina, but he spent the last fourteen years in the British army. Ain't that the case, Case?"

"Sir!" Case snapped.

"Which regiment, Case?" Holborrow asked, still staring into Starbuck's eyes.

"Seventh, sir, Royal Fusiliers, sir!"

"And while you were still sucking the milk from your mother's titties, Potter, forgive me, ma'am, Sergeant Case was fighting! Fighting, boy! Ain't that the case, Case?"

"Battle of the Alma, sir! Siege of Sevastopol," Case snapped, and Starbuck got the impression that he was listening to a much practiced dialogue.

"But Sergeant Case is a patriot, Potter!" Holborrow continued, "and when the Yankees broke the Union by attacking us, Sergeant Case left Her Majesty's service to fight for Jeff Davis and liberty. He was sent here, Potter, to turn the Yellowlegs into a proper regiment instead of a bunch of schoolgirls. Ain't that the case, Case?"

"Sir!"

"And you," Holborrow spat at Potter, "dare to countermand a man like Sergeant Case! You should be ashamed of yourself, boy. Ashamed! Sergeant Case has forgotten more about soldiering than you ever learned or ever will learn. And if Sergeant Case says a man deserves punishment, then punished he shall be!" Holborrow stepped back and took Sally's hand into his again. "But seeing as how you're a ray of Georgia sunshine, ma'am, I'll spare you from seeing any more unpleasantness this afternoon. I think your husband has learned his lesson, so thank you, Sergeant Case." Holborrow nodded to the sergeant, who scowled at Starbuck, then marched stiffly back to the parade ground. Holborrow ordered the freed prisoner to make himself scarce, and then, his grip still enfolding Sally's hand, he turned back to Starbuck. "So where have you been, boy? Your father wrote that you'd left Atlanta ten days back. Letter got here, but you didn't! Ten days! It don't take ten days from Atlanta to Richmond, boy. You been drinking again?"

"It was my fault," Sally said in a frightened little voice. "I had the fever, sir. Real bad, sir."

Lucifer giggled at Sally's invention and Holborrow's head snapped round. "You snigger once more, boy, and I'll whip the flesh clean off your black bones. Is he your nigger?" he asked Starbuck.

"Yes," Starbuck said, wondering how the hell he would back out of this deception.

"Yes, sir," Holborrow said, correcting him. "You forgetting I'm a Colonel, Potter?"

"Yes, sir. I mean no, sir."

Holborrow, still holding Sally's hand, shook his head at Starbuck's apparent confusion. "So how is your father?" he asked Starbuck.

Starbuck shrugged. "I guess," he began, then shrugged again, suddenly bereft of imagination.

"He's mending," Sally said. She was enjoying the play-acting much more than Starbuck who, though he had started it, was now regretting the deception. "Thank the Lord," Sally said as she finally extricated her fingers from Holborrow's grasp, "but he is surely mending."

"Praise the Lord," Holborrow said. "But you've been a burden to him, boy, a burden," he snarled at Starbuck, "and you'll forgive my bluntness, Mrs. Potter, but when a man's son is a burden it's right he should be told plain."

"It sure is," Sally agreed firmly.

"We was expecting you a week ago!" Holborrow snarled at Starbuck, then gave Sally a yellow-toothed smile. "Got a room all set up for you, ma'am. Bed, washstand, clothes press. The Reverend wanted you comfortable. Not to be pampered, he said, but comfortable."

"You're too kind, sir," Sally said, "but I'm sleeping with my cousin Alice in the city."

Holborrow looked disappointed, but Sally had spoken firmly and he did not contest the issue. "Your cousin's gain is our loss, ma'am," he said, "but you'll stay for a lemonade and maybe partake of a peach? I'm partial to a fine peach, as all Georgians ought to be."

"Pleasure, sir."

Holborrow glanced at Lucifer, who was carrying Starbuck's shabby bag. "Get to the kitchen, boy. Move your black ass! Go!" Holborrow turned to Starbuck again. "Hope you've got a decent uniform in that bag, boy, because the one you're wearing is a disgrace. A dis-grace. And where the hell are your lieutenant's bars?" He gestured at Starbuck's shoulders. "You sell your bars for liquor, boy?"

"Lost them," Starbuck said hopelessly.

"You are a sad man, Potter, a sad man," Holborrow said, shaking his head. "When your father wrote and asked my help he had the grace to tell me as much. He said you were a sore disappointment, a reproach to the good name of Potter, so I can't say as how I wasn't warned about you, but get drunk with me, boy, and I'll kick your son of a bitch ass blue, forgive me, ma'am."

"Forgiven, Colonel," Sally said.

"Your father now," Holborrow continued to lecture Starbuck, "he never drinks. Every day we had an execution the Reverend would come to the penitentiary to pray with the bastards, forgive me, ma'am, but he never touched a

47

drop of the ardent. Not a drop! Even after the bastards, forgive me, ma'am, were strung up and kicking away and the rest of us felt the need for a restorative libation, your father would stick to lemonade, but he often said that he feared you'd end up on that same scaffold, boy, with him saying a prayer on one side of you and me ready to push the stool out from under your feet on the other. So he's sent you here, Potter, to learn discipline!" This last word was shouted into Starbuck's face. "Now, ma'am," he turned his attention back to Sally, "give me your pretty little hand and we'll divide ourselves a peach, and after that, ma'am, if you'll permit me, I'll give you a ride back to the city in my carriage. It's not the best day for walking. A mite too hot and a pretty lady like you should be in a carriage, don't that sound good?"

"You're too kind, Colonel," Sally said. She had thrust her left hand, which was conspicuously lacking a wedding ring, into a fold of her shawl. "I ain't never ridden in a carriage," she added in a pitiful voice.

"We must accustom you to luxury," Holborrow said lasciviously, "like a pretty little Georgia girl should be." He led her to the house and put his free arm around her waist at the bottom of the steps. "I've been riding in a carriage ever since a Yankee bullet took away the use of my right leg. I must tell you the tale. But for now, ma'am, allow me to assist you up the stairs. There's a loose board or two," Holborrow half lifted Sally up the verandah's stairs, "and you just sit yourself down, ma'am, next to Captain Dennison."

The four officers, all captains, had stood to greet Sally. Captain Dennison proved to be a thin clean-shaven man whose face was horribly scarred by some skin disease that had caused his cheeks and forehead to be foul with livid sores. He pulled a wicker chair forward and brushed at its cushion with his hand. Holborrow gestured at Starbuck. "This here's Lieutenant Matthew Potter, so he ain't a rumor after all." The four captains laughed at Holborrow's witticism, while the Colonel ushered Sally forward with his right arm still firmly planted about her slender waist. "And this his wife. I'm sorry, my dear, but I don't have the advantage of your name."

"Emily," Sally said.

"And a prettier name I never did hear, upon my soul, but I never did. You sit down, ma'am. This here is Captain Dennison, Captain Cartwright, Captain Peel, and Captain Lippincott. You make yourself at home and I'll settle your husband. You don't mind if I put him to work straight off? He should have been at work a week ago."

Holborrow limped ahead of Starbuck into a gloomy hall where a tangle of gray officers' coats hung on a bentwood stand. "Why a good woman like that would marry a no-good son of a bitch like you, Potter," the Colonel grumbled, "the good Lord only knows. Come in here, boy. If your wife ain't staying then you don't need a bedroom. You can put a cot in here and sleep by your work. This here was Major Maitland's office, but then the son of a bitch got himself promoted and given a real battalion, so now we're waiting for a Yankee son of a bitch called Starbuck. And when he gets here, Potter, I don't want him pestering me about unfinished paperwork. You understand me? So get those papers straight!"

Starbuck said nothing, but just gazed at the pile of untidy papers. So Maitland had originally been assigned to the Yellowlegs? That was intriguing, but the bastard had evidently persuaded his lodge brothers to pull strings and so Maitland had been promoted and given command of the Legion and Starbuck had got the punishment battalion.

"Are you dozing, boy?" Holborrow thrust his face into Starbuck's.

"What am I to do, sir?" Starbuck asked plaintively.

"Tidy it up. Just tidy it. You're supposed to be the adjutant of the Second Special Battalion, ain't you? Now get on with it, boy, while I entertain your wife." Holborrow stumped out of the room, banging the door shut behind him. Then the door suddenly opened again and the Colonel's narrow face peered round the edge. "I'll send you some lemonade, Potter, but no liquor, you hear me?"

"Yes, sir."

"No liquor for you, Potter, not while you're under my orders."

The door slammed shut again, so hard that the whole house seemed to shudder, then Starbuck let out a long breath and sank into a leather-upholstered chair that stood at a desk littered with a mess of papers. What the hell, he wondered, had he got himself into? He was tempted to end the deception right now except that there was a possible profit in it. He was certain that if he announced himself as Major Starbuck then he would learn nothing, for Holborrow would take care to cover up any deficiencies in the training and equipment of the Special Battalion, while the despised Lieutenant Potter was clearly a man from whom nothing needed to be hidden. Besides, Starbuck thought, there was no elegant way out of the deception now. Better to play the tomfoolery through while he spied on Holborrow's work, then he would go back into the city and find Belvedere Delaney, who would make sure Starbuck had a fine time and a warm bed for the next few nights.

He began to sift through the heaps of paper. There were receipts for food, receipts for ammunition, and urgent letters asking for the receipts to be signed and returned to the relevant departments. There were pay books, lists, amendments to lists, and prison rosters from all the military jails in Richmond. Not every man in the Special Battalion was from the Yellowlegs; at least a fifth had been drafted in from the prisons, thus leavening the cowards with crooks. Under the prison rosters Starbuck found a letter addressed to Major Edward Maitland from the Richmond State Armory acknowledging that the Special Battalion was to be equipped with rifles and requesting that the twenty boxes of muskets be returned forthwith. There was a grudging tone to the letter, suggesting that Maitland had used his influence to have the despised muskets replaced with modern weapons and Starbuck, knowing he would have to fight the battle all over again, sighed. He put the letter aside to find, beneath it, yet another letter, this one addressed to Chas. Holborrow and signed by the Reverend Simeon Potter of Decatur, Georgia. Starbuck leaned back to read it.

The Reverend Potter, it seemed, had the superintendence of the prison chaplaincies in the State of Georgia and had written to his old acquaintance—he seemed no more than an acquaintance and scarcely a friend—Charles Holborrow, to beg his help in the matter of his second son, Matthew. The letter, written in deliberate strokes in a dark black ink, irresistibly reminded Starbuck of his own father's handwriting. Matthew, the letter said, had been a sore trial to his dear mother, a disgrace to his family's name, and a shame to his Christian upbringing. Though educated at the finest academies in the south and enrolled in Savannah Medical School, Matthew Potter had insisted upon the paths of iniquity. "Ardent liquor has been his downfall," the Reverend Potter wrote, "and now we hear he has taken a wife, poor girl, and,

51

furthermore, has been ejected from his regiment because of continual drunkenness. I had apprenticed him to a cousin of ours in Mississippi, hoping that hard work would prove his salvation, but instead of entering upon his duties he insisted upon engaging in Hardcastle's Battalion, but even as a soldier, it seems, he could not be trusted. It pains me to write thus, but in begging your help I owe you a duty of truthfulness, a duty thrice burdened by my faith in Christ Jesus, to Whom I daily pray for Matthew's repentance. I also recall a service I was once able to perform on your behalf, a service you will doubtless recollect clearly, and in recompense for that favor I would ask that you find employment for my son who is no longer welcome under my roof." Starbuck grinned. Lieutenant Matthew Potter, it was clear, was a ton of tribulation and Starbuck wondered what service the Reverend Simeon Potter had rendered to make it worth Holborrow's while to accept the Lieutenant. That favor had been subtly emphasized in the Reverend Potter's letter, suggesting that Holborrow's debt to the preacher was considerable. "I believe there to be good in Matthew," the letter finished, "and his commanding officer commended his behavior at Shiloh, but unless he can be weaned from liquor then I fear he is doomed to everlasting hellfire. My wife unites with me in sending our prayers for your kind aid in this sad business." A note, evidently in Holborrow's handwriting, had been penned at the bottom of the letter. "I'd be thankful if you could employ him." Maitland must have said yes, and Starbuck wondered how tangible Holborrow's thanks had been.

The door opened and a rebellious Lucifer brought in a tall glass of lemonade. "I was told to bring this, Lieutenant Potter,' he said sourly, stressing the false name with a mocking pronunciation.

"You don't like it here, Lucifer?" Starbuck asked.

"He beats his people," Lucifer said, jerking his head toward the sound of Holborrow's voice. "You ain't thinking of staying here, are you?" he asked with alarm, seeing how comfortably Starbuck's boots rested on the edge of the Major's desk.

"For a short while," Starbuck said. "I reckon I'll learn more as Lieutenant Potter than I ever could as Major Starbuck."

"And what if the real Mister Potter comes?"

Starbuck grinned. "Be one hell of a tangle, Lucifer."

Lucifer sniffed. "He ain't beating me!"

"I'll make sure he doesn't. And we won't be here long."

"You're crazy," Lucifer said. "I should have kept going north. I'd rather be preached at in a contraband camp than be living in a place like this." Lucifer sniffed his disgust and went back to the kitchens, leaving Starbuck to hunt through the rest of the papers. None of the battalion lists tallied exactly, but there seemed to be around a hundred and eighty men in the battalion. There were four captains—Dennison, Cartwright, Peel, and Lippincott—and eight sergeants, one of whom was the belligerent Case, who had joined the battalion just a month before.

Sally came to the office after a half hour. She closed the door behind her and laughed mischievously. "Hell, Nate, ain't this something?"

Starbuck stood and gestured at the mess in the room. "I'm beginning to feel sorry for Lieutenant Potter, whoever the hell Lieutenant Potter is," he said.

"You staying on here?" Sally asked.

"Maybe one night."

"In that case," Sally said, "I'm saying good-bye to my

dearest husband and then the Major's going to take me in his coach back to the city and I just know he's going to ask me to take supper with him. I'll say I'm too tired. You sure you want to stay?"

"I'd look an idiot telling him who I am now," Starbuck said. "Besides, there must be something to discover in all these papers."

"You discover how the hog's making his money," Sally said. "That'd be real useful." She stood on tiptoe and kissed his cheek. "Watch that Captain Dennison, Nate, he's a snake."

"He's the one with the pretty face, right?"

She grimaced. "I thought it had to be syphilis, but it ain't 'cos he ain't shaking or babbling like a loon. Must be nothing but a skin disease. I hope it hurts."

Starbuck grinned. "Begged you for a kiss, did he?" he guessed.

"I reckon he wants more than a kiss," she grimaced, then touched Starbuck's cheek. "Be good, Matthew Potter."

"And you, Emily Potter."

A few minutes later Starbuck heard the jingle of trace chains as the Major's carriage was brought to the front of the house. There was the sound of good-byes being said, then the carriage clattered away.

And Starbuck suddenly felt lonely.

A hundred miles north of Starbuck, in a valley where corn grew tall between stands of thick trees, a fugitive crouched in a thicket and listened for sounds of pursuit. The fugitive was a tall, fleshy young man who was now severely hungry. He had lost his horse at the battle fought near Manassas four days before and, with the beast, he had lost a saddlebag of food and so he had gone hungry

54

these four days, all but for some hardtack he had taken from a rebel corpse on the battlefield. Now, a dozen miles north of the battlefield and with his belly aching with hunger, the fugitive reluctantly gnawed at a cob of unripe corn and knew his bowels would punish him for the diet. He was tired of the war. He wanted a decent hotel, a hot bath, a soft bed, a good meal, and a bad woman. He could afford all those things for around his belly was a money belt filled with gold, and all he wanted to do was to get the hell away from this terrible countryside that the victorious rebels were scouring in search of fugitives from the Northern army. The rest of the Northern army had retreated toward Washington and the young man wanted to join them, but somehow he had got all turned about during the day of pouring rain and he guessed he had walked five miles west that day instead of north and now he was trying to work his way back northward.

He wore the blue coat of a Northern soldier, but he wore it unbuttoned and unbelted so that he could discard it at a moment's notice and pull on the gray coat that he had taken from the corpse that had yielded him the hardtack. The dead man's coat was a mite small, but the fugitive knew he could talk his way out of trouble if any rebel patrol did find and question him. He would be in more trouble if Northern soldiers found him for, though he had fought for the Yankees, he spoke with the raw accent of the Deep South, but deep in his pants pocket he had his papers that identified him as Captain William Blythe, second in command of Galloway's Horse, a unit of Northern cavalry composed of renegade Southerners. Galloway's Horse were supposed to be scouts who could ride the Southern trails with the same assurance as Jeb Stuart's confident men, but the fool Galloway had taken them right into the battle near Manassas where they had been shot to hell by a Confederate regiment. Billy Blythe knew that Galloway was dead and Blythe reckoned Galloway deserved to be dead for having got mixed up in a full battle. He also guessed that most of Galloway's men were probably dead and he did not care. He just needed to get away to the North and find himself another comfortable billet where he could stay alive until the war ended. On that day, Blythe reckoned, there would be rich pickings for Southerners who had stayed loyal to the Union and he did not intend to be denied those rewards.

But neither did he intend to land up in a Confederate prison. If capture was unavoidable he planned to discard the blue coat, don the gray, then talk his way out of trouble. Then he would find another way back North. It just took guile, planning, a little intelligence, and a helping of luck, and that should be enough to avoid the numerous folks in the Southern states who wanted nothing more than to put a rope around Billy Blythe's fleshy neck. One such rope had damn nearly done for him before the war's beginning, and it was only by the most outrageous daring that Billy had escaped the girl's family and fled north. Hell, he thought, it wasn't that he was a bad fellow. Billy Blythe had never thought of himself as a bad fellow. A bit wild, maybe, and a fellow who liked a good time, but not bad. Just faster witted than most others, and there was nothing like quick wits to provoke envy.

He scraped at the raw cob with his teeth and chewed on the tough corn. It tasted foul, and he could already feel a ferment in his belly, but he was half starving and needed strengthening if he was to keep going. Hell, he thought, but his life had gone all wrong these last few weeks! He should never have got mixed up with Major Galloway, nor with the Yankee army. He should be further north, in New York say. Somewhere the guns did not sound. Somewhere there was money to be made and girls to impress.

A twig snapped in the woodland and Blythe went very still. At least he tried to go very still, but there was an uncontrollable shaking in his legs, his belly was rumbling from the fermenting corn, and he kept blinking as sweat trickled into the corners of his eyes. A voice sounded far away. Pray God the man was a Northerner, he thought, then wondered why the hell the Yankees were losing all the battles. Billy Blythe had wagered his whole future on a Northern victory, but every time the Federals met the men in gray they got beat. It just plain was not right! Now the Northerners had got whipped again and Billy Blythe was eating raw corn and was dressed in clothes still damp from the rainstorm of two days before.

A horse whinnied. It was hard to tell what direction the sound came from, at first it seemed to come from behind him, but then Billy heard the slow thump of hooves from in front of him and so, confused, and very cautiously, he raised his head out of the leaves until he could see across the corn. The shadows were harsh among the further trees, but suddenly, in a slash of bright sunlight that cut across the dark, he saw the horsemen. Northerners! Blue coats. There were glints of reflected sunlight from saber scabbards, belt buckles, curb chains, carbine hooks, then a flash of white as a horse rolled its eye and sneezed. The ears of the other horses pricked forward. The wary cavalrymen had stopped at the corn's edge. There were a dozen or so troopers there, carbines at the ready, all watching across the crop toward Billy's left, and it was their watchfulness that kept Billy motionless. What was worrying them? He turned very slowly, but could see nothing. Were there rebels nearby? A bluebird flitted above the corn and Billy decided the bright feathers were a good omen and he was about to stand fully upright and shout toward the cavalrymen when suddenly their leader made a gesture with his hand and the troopers spurred their horses out into the corn. Billy stayed still. One of the cavalrymen had holstered his carbine and scraped his saber free of its scabbard, and that persuaded Billy that this was not a good time to attract the troopers' attention. One shout now and a volley of minie balls could be his answer and so he just watched as the horses advanced noisily through the stiff cornstalks.

A horse whinnied again, and this time the sound was definitely behind Billy and he turned softly, parted the screen of leaves, then peered hard through the dappled shadows of the woodland. He was holding his breath and wondering what the hell was going on, then suddenly he saw a movement down by the far end of the cornfield and he blinked sweat away from his eyes and saw that there was a horse there. A riderless, lonely horse. A horse all on its own. A horse that seemed to be tethered. A horse with a saddle and bridle, but no rider. A horse, he thought, for Billy Blythe and he wondered what would be the safest way to attract the attention of the nervous Yankee troopers when suddenly a blast of rifle fire ripped the warm afternoon to shreds.

Billy cried aloud with fear and dropped to his haunches. No one heard his cry, for the Yankee horses were screaming terribly. There was a great thrashing sound from the corn, then more rifles fired and suddenly the hateful rebel yell was sounding and a voice was roaring orders. It had been an ambush. One riderless horse had been the bait that had sucked the Yankees down the long narrow cornfield to where the rebels had been hidden among the trees, and now the horsemen were either dead, wounded, or desperately trying to gallop away. Two more rifles cracked and Billy saw a blue-coated trooper arch his back, let go of his reins, and fall backward off his galloping horse. Two more riderless horses galloped north while a trooper was running desperately with his scabbard held free of his legs. Two Northern horsemen seemed to have made it safely into the shelter of the far trees, but otherwise there seemed to be no survivors from the small Yankee patrol. It had taken less than a minute.

"Fetch the horses!" a voice snarled. A Yankee in the corn was calling for help, his voice desperate with pain. A horse was whinnying, then a flat, hard shot abruptly ended the pathetic sound. Rebel voices laughed, then Billy heard the scraping rattle as a rifle was reloaded. The rebels were evidently collecting the horses; valuable prizes for an army already short of good cavalry mounts, and Billy hoped they would be content with that booty, but then the officer shouted again. "Look for any survivors! Careful now, but look good."

Billy swore. He thought about running, but he guessed he was too weak to outrun a fit man and besides the noise he made would bring a slew of the bastards chasing after him, so instead he feverishly stripped off his blue coat and pulled on the threadbare gray jacket, and then he pushed the betraying blue garment deep under the bushes where he covered it with a thick layer of leaf mold. He buttoned the gray coat and buckled his belt about its waist and then he waited. Damn, he thought, damn and son of a bitch and damn again, but now he would have to play the rebel for a few weeks while he found another way to get back north.

Footsteps came nearer and Billy decided it was time to play his role. "Are you Southern boys?" he called aloud. The footsteps stopped. "The name's Billy Tumlin!" he called out, "Billy Tumlin from New Orleans." There was

59

no future in using his real name, not when so many men in the Confederacy were eager to test a rope on Billy Blythe's gullet. "Are you boys rebs?" he asked.

"Can't see you," a voice said flatly, neither friendly nor hostile, but then came the unmistakably hostile sound of a rifle being cocked.

"I'm standing up, boys," Billy said, "standing up real slow. Standing up right plumb in front of you." Billy stood and held his hands high to show he was not armed. Facing him were a pair of scruffy rebels with bayonet-tipped rifles. "Thank the good Lord above, boys," Billy said, "praise His holy name, amen."

The two faces showed only caution. "Who did you say you was?" one of the men asked.

"Captain Billy Tumlin, boys. From New Orleans, Louisiana: I've been on the run for weeks now and sure am pleased to see you. Mind if I lower my hands?" He began to lower his arms, but a twitch of a blackened rifle muzzle put them back up fast.

"On the run?" the second man asked.

"I was taken at New Orleans," Blythe explained in his broadest Southern accent, "and I've been a prisoner up north ever since. But I slipped away, see? And I'm kind of hungry, boys. Even a piece of hardtack would be welcome. Or some tobacco? Ain't seen good tobacco since the day I got captured."

An hour later Captain Billy Tumlin was introduced to Lieutenant Colonel Ned Maitland, whose men had discovered the fugitive. Maitland's regiment was bivouacking and the smoke from hundreds of small fires sifted into the early evening air. Maitland, a courtly and generous host, hospitably shared a leg of stringy chicken, some hard-boiled eggs, and a flask of cognac with the newly escaped prisoner. He seemed blessedly uninterested in

Blythe's supposed experiences as a captive of the Northerners, preferring to discuss which prominent New Orleans families might be common acquaintances. Billy Blythe had spent just long enough in New Orleans to pass that test, especially when he figured that Maitland knew less about the city's society than he did himself.

"I guess," Maitland said after a while, "that you'd better report to brigade."

"I can't stay here?" Blythe suggested. Maitland would be a considerate commander, he reckoned, and the Legion would be serving close enough to the Yankees to give Blythe an easy chance to slip across the lines.

Maitland shook his head. He would have liked to keep Billy Tumlin in the Legion, for he considered most of his present officers to be well below the proper standard, but he had no authority to appoint a new captain. "I could use you," Maitland admitted, "I surely could. It looks like we'll all be moving north soon so there'll be plenty of fighting and I'm not exactly fixed right with good officers."

"You're invading the North?" Billy Blythe asked, horrified at the thought.

"There's nothing north of here but foreign soil," Maitland observed dryly, "but sadly I can't keep you in the Legion. Things have changed since you were captured, Captain. We don't elect or appoint officers anymore. Everything goes through the War Department in Richmond and I guess you'll have to report there. At least if you want wages, you will."

"Wages would help," Blythe agreed and so, an hour later, he found himself in the altogether less prepossessing company of the brigade commander. Colonel Griffin Swynyard's queries about Blythe's captivity were brief, but much sharper than Maitland's. "Where were you held?" he asked.

"Massachusetts," Blythe said.

"Where exactly?" Swynyard demanded.

Blythe was momentarily flustered. "Union," he finally said, reckoning that every state in the United and Confederate States had a town called Union. "Just outside, anyway," he added lamely.

"We must thank God for your escape," Swynyard said, and Blythe eagerly agreed, then realized he was actually expected to fall onto his knees to offer the thanks. He got down awkwardly and closed his eyes while Swynyard thanked Almighty God for the release of His servant Billy Tumlin from captivity, and after that Swynyard told Billy he would have the brigade major issue a travel pass permitting Captain Tumlin to report to the army headquarters.

"In Richmond?" Blythe asked, not unhappy at that thought. He had no enemies in Richmond that he knew of, for his foes were all further south, so Richmond would be a fine resting place for a short while. And at least in the Confederacy's capital he would be spared the bloodletting that would surely follow if Robert Lee took this hardscrabble army of ragged-uniformed men across the Potomac into the North's plump fields.

"They may send you to Richmond," Swynyard said, "or they might post you to a battalion here. Ain't my decision, Captain."

"Just so long as I can be useful," Billy Blythe said sanctimoniously. "That's all I pray for, Colonel, to be useful." Billy Blythe was doing what Billy Blythe did best. He was surviving.

YOU DON'T SOUND like a Southerner, Potter," Captain Dennison said and the three other captains who shared the supper table stared accusingly at Starbuck.

"My ma was from Connecticut," Starbuck said.

"Sir," Dennison corrected Starbuck. Captain Dennison was more than a little drunk, indeed he had almost fallen asleep a moment before, but now he had jerked himself into wakefulness and was scowling at Starbuck down the length of the table. "I'm a captain," Dennison said, "and you're a shad-belly piece of ordure, otherwise known as a lieutenant. You call me sir."

"My ma was from Connecticut, sir," Starbuck said dutifully. He was playing his role as the hapless Potter, but he was no longer enjoying it. Impetuosity, if not downright foolishness, had trapped him in the deception and he knew that every moment he stayed in the role would make it more difficult to extricate himself with any dignity, but he still reckoned there were things to learn so long as the real Lieutenant Potter did not arrive at Camp Lee.

"So you picked up your momma's accent with her titty milk, did you, Potter?" Dennison asked.

"I reckon I must have done, sir."

Dennison leaned back in his chair. The sores on his face gleamed wetly in the flickering light of the bad candles set on the dinner table that bore the remains of a meal of fried chicken, fried rice, and beans. There were some of

Colonel Holborrow's beloved peaches to end the meal, though Holborrow himself was not present. The Colonel, having carried Sally to the city, had evidently stayed to make a night of it, leaving Starbuck to share this evening meal with the four captains. There were plenty of other officers in Camp Lee, but they ate elsewhere for no one, it seemed, wanted to be contaminated by this handful of officers who remained with the Yellowlegs.

And no wonder, Starbuck thought, for even the few hours he had spent in the camp had proved enough to confirm his worst expectations. The men of the 2nd Special Battalion were bored and dispirited, kept from desertion only by the ever-present provosts and by their fears of execution. The sergeants resented being posted to the battalion and so entertained themselves with petty acts of tyranny that the battalion officers, like Thomas Dennison and his companions, did nothing to alleviate. Sergeant Case appeared to run the battalion and those men who were in his favor prospered while the rest suffered.

Starbuck had talked with some of the men and they, thinking that he was a harmless lieutenant and, besides, the man who had dared to take Case's prisoner off the horse, were unguarded in what they said. Some, like Caton Rothwell, whom Starbuck had rescued, were keen to fight and were frustrated that Holborrow appeared to have no intention of sending the battalion north to join Lee's army. Rothwell was not one of the original Yellowlegs, but had been posted to the Special Battalion after being found guilty of deserting from his own regiment. "I went to help my family," he explained to Starbuck, "I just wanted a week's furlough," he added, "because my wife was in trouble."

"What trouble?" Starbuck had asked.

"Just trouble, Lieutenant," Rothwell said bluntly. He

was a big, strong man who reminded Starbuck of Lieutenant Waggoner. Caton Rothwell, Starbuck suspected, would be a good man to have alongside in a fight. Given fifty other such men, Starbuck knew, the battalion could be made as good as any in Lee's army, but most of the soldiers were near mutinous through boredom and the knowledge that they were the most despised unit in all the Confederate army. They were the Yellowlegs, the lowest of the low, and no one thing was more symptomatic of their status than the guns they had been issued. Those weapons were still in store, but Starbuck had found the key hanging behind the office door and had unlocked the armory shed to find it filled with crates of old smoothbore muskets. Starbuck had brushed the dust off one musket stock and lifted out the weapon. It felt clumsy, while the wooden shaft beneath the barrel had shrunk over the years so that the metal barrel hoops were loose. He peered at the lock and saw the word "Virginia" stamped there, while behind the hammer was written "Richmond, 1808." The gun must have been a flintlock originally and at some time updated by conversion to percussion cap, but despite the modernization it was still a horrible weapon. These old muskets, made for killing Redcoats, had no rifling inside the barrel, which meant that the bullet did not spin in its flight and so lacked the accuracy of a rifle. At fifty paces the big-bore 1808 musket might be as lethal as an Enfield rifle, but at any greater range it was hopelessly inaccurate. Starbuck had seen plenty of men carrying such antiquated guns into battle and had felt sorry for them, but he knew for a fact that thousands of modern rifles had been captured from the North during the summer's campaign, and it seemed perverse to arm his men with these museum pieces. Such antique weapons were a signal to the Special Battalion that they were on the army's hind teat, but that was probably a truth the men already knew. They were the soldiers no one else wanted.

Sergeant Case had seen the open armory door and come to investigate. His tall body filled the doorway and shadowed the dusty room. "You," he had said flatly when he saw Starbuck.

"Me," Starbuck agreed pleasantly enough.

"Got a habit of poking your nose where it don't belong, Lieutenant," Case said. His menacing presence loomed in the dusty shed while his flat, hard eyes stared at Starbuck like a predator sizing up its kill.

Starbuck had thrown the musket to the sergeant, thrown it hard enough to make Case step back a pace as he caught it. "You'd want to fight Yankees with one of those, Sergeant?" Starbuck asked.

Case twirled the musket in his big right hand as though it weighed no more than a cornstalk. "They won't be doing no fighting, Lieutenant. These men ain't fit to fight. And that's why you were sent to us." Case's small head jerked back and forth on the ludicrous neck as he spat his insults. "Because you ain't fit to fight. You're a bloody drunkard, Lieutenant, so don't give me any talk of fighting. You don't know what fighting is. I was a Royal Fusilier, boy, a proper soldier, boy, and I know soldiering and I know fighting, and I know you ain't up to it else you wouldn't be here." Case threw the musket hard back, stinging Starbuck's hands with the impact of the weapon. The tall sergeant stepped further inside the armory and thrust his broken-nosed face close to Starbuck. "And one other thing, boy. You pull rank on me one more time and I'll nail your hide to a tree and piss all over it. Now put that musket back where you found it, give me the armory key, and bugger off where you belong."

Not now, Starbuck had told himself, not now. This was

not the time to put Case right, and so he had merely put the musket in its box, meekly handed Case the key, and walked away.

Now, at the supper table, Starbuck was again the butt of bullies only this time it was Thomas Dennison and his cronies who had their sport with a man they believed was a weakling. Captain Lippincott rolled a peach to Starbuck. "Reckon you'd prefer a brandy, Potter," Lippincott said.

"Reckon I would," Starbuck said.

"Sir," Dennison said immediately.

"Reckon I would, sir," Starbuck said humbly. He had to play the fool so long as he decided against revealing his identity, but it went hard on him. He told himself to stay calm and to play the failure for a short while yet.

Lippincott edged his brandy glass toward Starbuck, daring him to take it, but Starbuck did not move. "Of course there's one thing to be said for being a drunk," Lippincott said, taking the glass back, "it means you'll probably sleep away the days here. Better than sitting around doing nothing. Ain't that right, Potter?"

"Right," Starbuck agreed.

"Sir," Dennison said, then hiccuped.

"Sir," Starbuck said.

"I ain't saying I'm not grateful for being here," Lippincott went on gloomily, "but, hell, they could give us some entertainment."

"Plenty in Richmond," Dennison said airily.

"If you've got the money," Lippincott acknowledged, "which I ain't."

Dennison stretched back in his chair. "You'd rather be in a fighting regiment?" he asked Lippincott. "They could always transfer you. If that's what you want, Dan, I'll tell Holborrow you're eager to go." Lippincott, a sallow man with a fringe of beard, said nothing. Most of the Yellowlegs officers had been transferred, either to garrison duty or to the provosts, but a few had been posted to fighting battalions, a fate that plainly worried these remaining captains, though not Dennison, whose skin disease was sufficient to keep him out of harm's way. He gingerly touched one of the horrid sores on his face. "If the doctors could just cure this," he said in a tone that suggested he was confident that the disease was incurable, "I'd volunteer for a transfer."

"You are taking the medicine, Tom?" Lippincott asked.

"Of course I am," Dennison snapped. "Can't you smell it?"

Starbuck could indeed smell something medicinal, and the smell was oddly familiar; a thin rank odor that disturbed him, but which he could not quite place. "What medicine is it, sir?" he asked.

Dennison paused while he considered whether the question constituted impudence, then he shrugged. "Kerosene," he answered after a while.

Starbuck frowned. "Is it ringworm?" he asked, then added, "sir."

Dennison sneered. "One year at medical college and you know it all, is that it? You mind your own damn business, Potter, and I'll mind the advice of a proper doctor."

Lippincott looked back at the glistening sores and shuddered. "It's all right for you, Tom," he said resentfully, "but what if this Starbuck wants us to fight? Holborrow can't keep us here for ever."

"Holborrow's a colonel," Dennison said, hiccuping again, "and Starbuck's a major, so Holborrow will get what he wants and Starbuck can go piss himself. And hell," he went on resentfully, "none of us should be serving under Starbuck. He's a goddamn Northerner and I ain't taking orders from any goddamn Northerner."

Cartwright, a plumpish man with a petulant face and

fair curly hair, nodded agreement. "You should have taken over from Maitland, Tom," he told Dennison.

"I know that, you know that, Holborrow knows that," Dennison agreed then clumsily extracted a cigar from his pocket and lit it at the nearest candle. "And Mister Starbuck will have to learn it," he finished when the cigar was lit.

Peel, a thin young man who seemed the best of this unprepossessing bunch, wiped peach juice from his clean-shaven chin then shook his head. "Why did they send us Starbuck?" he asked no one in particular. "They must be wanting us to fight. Otherwise why send him to us?"

"Because he's an unwanted son of a bitch," Dennison snapped, "and they want to be rid of him."

"He's got a reputation," Starbuck said, enjoying himself, "sir."

Dennison's dark eyes inspected Starbuck through the flickering light of the guttering candles. "It don't take much of a reputation to impress a drunkard," he said dismissively, "and I don't recall anyone here inviting you to speak, Lieutenant."

"Sorry, sir," Starbuck said.

Dennison went on inspecting Starbuck and finally prodded his cigar toward him. "I will say one thing for you, Potter, you've got a pretty wife."

"Reckon I have, sir," Starbuck agreed.

"Pretty, pretty, pretty," Dennison said. "Pretty enough to turn a head or two. Too pretty for a lunkhead like you, don't you agree?"

"She's sure pretty," Starbuck said, "sir."

"And you're a drunk," Dennison observed, "and drunks ain't no good where it counts with a lady. Know what I mean, Potter? Drunks ain't up to it, are they?" Dennison, half drunk himself, laughed at his own wit. Starbuck held the Captain's eyes, but said nothing and Dennison

69

mistook his silence for fear. "You know where your pretty wife is tonight, Potter?"

"With her cousin Alice, sir," Starbuck said.

"Or maybe she's dining with Colonel Holborrow?" Dennison suggested. "The Colonel sure had his hopes up. Put on his best uniform coat, shined his boots, and oiled his hair. I reckon he thought your Emily might appreciate a little entertainment. Maybe a cockfight?" The other captains laughed at this jest while Dennison sucked on his cigar. "And maybe," he went on, "your Emily's so desperate after being married to you that she'd even say yes to Holborrow. You reckon she's playing the mattress to Holborrow's quilt, Potter?" Starbuck said nothing and Dennison shook his head scornfully. "You're a weak passel of shit, Potter, you truly are. God knows what that girl sees in you, but I guess she needs her pretty little eyes fixing." He drew on his cigar again as he stared at Starbuck. "Reckon I just might call on the little lady myself. Would you object, Lieutenant Potter, if I paid my respects to your lady wife? My skin might just benefit from a lady's healing touch."

Peel looked embarrassed, but the other two captains smiled. Both were weak men and were enjoying this chance to see an apparently weaker man being mercilessly bullied. Starbuck leaned back in his chair, making it creak. "What do you reckon your chances are with her, sir?" he asked Dennison.

Dennison seemed surprised that the question had been asked, but he pretended to consider it anyway. "A good-looking girl like that? And a handsome fellow like me? Oh, pretty fair chances, I'd say, Lieutenant."

"Out of five," Starbuck insisted, "what do you reckon, sir? Two chances out of five? One chance? Three?"

Dennison frowned, not entirely sure whether the conversation was going entirely to his liking. "Pretty fair, I'd say," he repeated.

Starbuck shook his head ruefully. "Hell, sir, I know Emily, and Emily never did take overmuch to poxed sons of bitches like yourself, sir, begging your pardon, sir, and I can't reckon you've got more than one chance in five. Pretty good odds, though, seeing as how pretty she is, but how lucky are you? That's the question, sir, ain't it?" He smiled at Dennison who was not smiling back. None of the captains was smiling; instead they were watching Starbuck, who had drawn out his Adams revolver while he was talking and had used a fingernail to lever four of the five percussion caps off the gun's cones. He tipped the caps onto an empty plate then looked up at Dennison through the candle flames. "How lucky are you, sir?" Starbuck asked and leveled the revolver's blued barrel at Dennison's scared eyes as he thumbed the hammer to half cock so that the cylinder was free to turn. He spun the cylinder and not one of the captains moved as the gun sounded a series of tiny clicks that only stopped when the cylinder came to rest. Starbuck eased the cock all the way back. "One chance in five, Captain, sir," he said, "so let's see how good those odds are." He pulled the trigger and Dennison gave a tiny jump of alarm as the hammer fell onto an empty cone. "You didn't make it that time," Starbuck said, "sir."

"Potter!" Dennison shouted, then stilled his protest as Starbuck half cocked the gun and spun the cylinder a second time.

"Of course a gentleman like you wouldn't be content with a lady's first refusal, would you, sir?" Starbuck asked and eased the hammer all the way back once more. It made two tiny clicks as the pawl engaged. He could see that the cone under the hammer was empty, but none of the others around the table knew which of the chambers was primed.

71

They would be able to see the bullets nestled inside the lower chambers, but not the cones at the cylinder's rear. Starbuck smiled. "So my Emily's refused you once, Captain," he said, "but you'd surely ask her a second time, wouldn't you? I mean you don't have the manners of a goat, so you're sure to ask her a second time." He straightened his arm as though bracing himself for the gun's recoil.

Cartwright fumbled for his own revolver, but Starbuck pointed the gun momentarily at the frightened face and Cartwright immediately subsided. Starbuck shifted the gun back to Dennison. "Second chance coming up, Captain, sir. Dear Emily, please lay yourself down and play mattress for me. Let's see how lucky you are the second time of asking, Captain." He pulled the trigger and once again Dennison shuddered as the dead click echoed loud in the room. Starbuck immediately spun the chamber a third time and straightened his arm.

"You're mad, Potter," Dennison said, suddenly seeming very sober.

"I'm sober too," Starbuck said and reached out with his left hand for Cartwright's brandy, which he drank in one go. "I'll be madder still when I'm drunk," he said, "so how many chances do you reckon you've got with my wife, Captain? Are you going to ask her three times for the favor of a ride?"

Dennison considered reaching for his own revolver, but it was buttoned in its holster and he knew he would have no chance to free the weapon before a bullet slashed through the candle flames and shattered his skull. He licked his lips. "I guess I don't have any chance, Lieutenant," he said.

"I guess you don't, Captain," Starbuck said, "and I guess you owe me an apology too."

Dennison grimaced at the thought. "You can go to hell, Potter," he said defiantly.

Starbuck pulled the trigger, then immediately half cocked the gun and spun the cylinder a fourth time. When it came to rest he pulled the cock back and this time he could see the single percussion cap was waiting under the hammer. He smiled. "Three times lucky, Captain, but how good is your luck? I'm waiting for that apology."

"I apologize, Lieutenant Potter," Dennison managed to say.

Starbuck eased the hammer down, thrust the Adams into its holster, and stood up. "Never start what you can't finish, Captain," he said, then leaned forward and picked up the half full bottle of brandy. "Reckon I can finish this, though, but in privacy. You all have a nice conversation now." He walked out of the room.

It was a humid, rainy night in Washington with no wind to take away the thick stench of the garbage dump that lay at the southern end of Seventeenth Street just a few yards from the hospital tents pitched on the ellipse. The sewage in Murder Bay added its own fetid smell to the air above the northern capital that was more than usually crowded with soldiers. They were men who should have been marching in John Pope's army toward Richmond, but instead they had been whipped backward by Robert Lee from the banks of the Bull Run and now they filled the tented camps inside Washington's ring of forts and thronged the capital's taverns.

One young cavalry officer hurried along Pennsylvania Avenue to the corner of Seventeenth Street, where he took off his wide-brimmed cavalryman's hat to peer up at the street lamp. At every corner in Washington the lamps had their street's name painted in black on the glass covering the mantel, an intelligent device, and once the young man was sure he was in the right place he walked up

Seventeenth until he reached a three-story brick building that was thickly surrounded by trees. Gas lights showed where the building's narrow end abutted onto the sidewalk and where a flight of steps led to a door guarded by two blue-coated sentries, though when the young cavalryman presented himself at that door he was told to go back to the garden entrance on Pennsylvania Avenue. He retraced his steps and discovered a driveway that led through night-blackened trees to an imposing portico of six massive columns that protected and dwarfed a small doorway guarded by a quartet of blue-coated infantrymen. Gas lamps hissed yellow under the portico, lighting a carriage that waited for its owner.

A clock struck nine as the cavalryman was granted entrance into the hallway where yet another guard demanded his name. "Faulconer," the young man replied. "Captain Adam Faulconer." The guard consulted a list, ticked off Adam's name, then told him to put his scabbarded saber into an umbrella stand and afterward climb one flight of stairs, turn left at the stairhead, and walk to the very end of the corridor where he would find a door marked with the name of the man who had summoned him. The guard rattled off these directions, then went back to his copy of *The Evening Star*, which heralded Major General George McClellan's reappointment as commander of the Northern army.

Adam Faulconer mounted the stairs and walked down the long, gloomy corridor. This building was the War Department, the very center of the North's military effort, yet there was little sense of urgency in its darkened passages where Adam's footfalls echoed as forlornly as the steps of a man pacing a deserted sepulcher. Most of the fanlights above the office doors were dark, though one light showed at the corridor's far end and in its small glow

Adam saw the name "Col. Thorne" painted in white letters against one of the door's black panels. He knocked and was summoned inside.

He found himself in a surprisingly large room with two tall windows that were shut against both the rain and the moths that beat against the panes. The walls of the room were covered with maps, and one large desk stood beside one window, while two smaller clerks' tables occupied the rest of the room. All the desks were covered in papers that had flowed onto the chairs and hardwood floor. Two cast-iron gasoliers hissed beneath the high ceiling, while a longcase clock ticked hollowly between the windows. The room's only occupant was a tall uniformed man who stood with a ramrod-straight back as he stared at the scatter of lit windows showing above the trees in the White House. "Faulconer, yes?" the man asked without turning from the window.

"Yes, sir."

"My name is Thorne. Lyman Thorne. Colonel Lyman Thorne." Thorne had a coarse, almost angry voice, very deep toned, and when he abruptly turned toward Adam he revealed a face that matched the voice perfectly, for Thorne was a gaunt, white-bearded man with fierce eyes and with deep lines carved into his sun-darkened cheeks. His most prominent feature was his white hair, which grew thick, long, and wildly enough to make Thorne appear like a bearded version of Andrew Jackson. The Colonel carried himself straight and proud, though when he moved he favored his right leg, which suggested that his other might have been injured. He gazed at Adam for an instant, then turned back to the window. "There have been celebrations in Washington these last two days," he growled.

"Yes, sir."

"McClellan is back! John Pope is dismissed and the Young Napoleon has been given charge of the army again, and thus Washington celebrates." Thorne spat into a brass cuspidor, then glared at Adam. "Do you celebrate this appointment, young Faulconer?"

Adam was taken aback by the question. "I haven't considered it, sir," he eventually admitted lamely.

"I do not celebrate, young Faulconer. My God, I do not. We gave McClellan a hundred thousand men, shipped him to the Virginia peninsula, and ordered him to take Richmond. And what did he do? He took counsel of his fears. He havered, that's what he did, he havered! He dithered while the rebels scraped together a handful of rapscallion soldiers and trounced him straight back out to sea. Yet now the ditherer is to be our commanding general again, and do you know why, young Faulconer?" This question, like the rest of Thorne's words, was directed at the windowpane rather than toward Adam.

"No, sir," Adam answered.

"Because there is no one else. Because in all this great republic we cannot find one better general than little George McClellan. Not one!" Thorne spat into the cuspidor again. "I admit he can train troops, but he doesn't know how to fight them. Doesn't know how to lead. The man's a humbug!" Thorne snarled the last word, then abruptly turned and glared at Adam once more. "Somewhere in the Republic there's a man who can beat Robert Lee, but on my soul we haven't found him yet. But we will, Faulconer, we will, and when we do we shall pulverize the so-called Confederacy into bone and blood. Bone and blood. But until we do find that man then it is our duty to mollycoddle the Young Napoleon. We have to pat him and soothe him, we have to tell him not to be frightened of ghosts and not to imagine enemies where there are none. In short, we have to wean him off Pinkerton. Do you know Pinkerton?"

"I know of him, sir."

"The less you know, the better," Thorne growled. "Pinkerton isn't even a soldier! But McClellan swears by him, and even as you and I stand here talking Pinkerton is being given command of all the army's intelligence once more. He had that same command in the peninsula, and what did he do with it? He summoned rebel soldiers out of thin air. He told the Young Napoleon that there were hundreds of thousands of men where there was nothing but a huddle of hungry rogues. Pinkerton will do the same again, Faulconer, mark my words. Within one week we shall be told that Lee has two hundred thousand men and that little McClellan dare not attack for fear of being beat. We shall haver again, we shall dither, and while we piss our collective pants Robert Lee will attack. Do you wonder that Europe laughs at us?"

"Do they, sir?" Adam, confused by the tirade, asked the question feebly.

"Oh they do, Faulconer, they do. American pride is being humbled by a rebellion we seem powerless to defeat and Europe takes pleasure in that. They pretend not, but if Robert Lee destroys McClellan then I daresay we'll see European troops in the South. The French would love to join in, but they won't jump till Britain decides, and Britain won't join the game until they know which side is winning. Which is why Lee will attack us, Faulconer. Look!" Thorne strode to a map of the eastern seaboard that hung behind his desk. "We've made three efforts to capture Richmond. Three! And all have been defeated. Lee now controls all of northern Virginia, so what's to stop him coming further north? Here, Faulconer, into Maryland, and maybe farther north still, into Pennsylvania." The Colonel demonstrated these threats by sweeping his hand across the map. "He'll grab our good harvest for his starving men and beat up little McClellan and so demonstrate to the Europeans that we can't even defend our own territory. By next spring, Faulconer, there could be a hundred thousand European troops marching for the Confederacy, and what will we do then? Treat for peace, of course, and so the Republic of Washington and Jefferson will have lasted a mere eighty years and North America, Faulconer, will be fatally weakened for the next eighty years." Thorne leaned over his desk and glared at Adam. "Lee cannot be allowed to win, Faulconer. He cannot," the Colonel said in a grave voice, almost as if he were charging Adam with the personal responsibility for saving the Republic.

"No, sir," Adam said, and felt it was a weak response, but he was being swamped by the sheer force of Lyman Thorne's personality. Sweat trickled down Adam's face. The night was oppressive, and the rain had not diminished the humidity at all, while the gasoliers' flaring mantles only added to the room's stifling heat.

The Colonel waved Adam toward a chair, then sat down himself and lit a cigar from a gas flame that burned from a tabletop gas jet connected to a long rubber extension cord that snaked down from the nearest gasolier. Once the cigar was lit he pushed the gas jet and papers aside, then leaned back and rubbed his face as though he was suddenly tired. "You're a scalawag, right?" he demanded.

"Yes, sir," Adam said. A scalawag was a Southerner who fought for the North, the opposite of a Copperhead.

"And three months ago," Thorne went on, "you were a rebel on Johnston's staff, am I right?"

"Yes, sir."

"And back then, Faulconer, our Young Napoleon was marching on Richmond. No, that is the wrong verb. He was crawling toward Richmond, while Detective Pinkerton," Thorne mocked the description with his tone, "was convincing little George that the rebels had two hundred thousand troops. You sent information that would have corrected that misapprehension, only the news never got through. Some clever bastard on the other side replaced your dispatch with one of their own devising and so Richmond survived. I almost stopped that clever bastard, Faulconer, indeed I broke a leg trying, but I failed." He grimaced, then sucked on his cigar. The smoke hung in the room like the lingering skein of a rifle shot.

"Back then, Faulconer," Thorne continued, "I was working for the Inspector General's Department. I did the jobs no one else wanted. Now I am more exalted, but still no more popular with this army than I was when I inspected their damned latrines or wondered why they needed so many clerks. But now, Faulconer, I have a measure of power. It is not mine, but belongs to my master and he lives in that house there." He jerked the cigar toward the White House. "You follow me?"

"I think so, sir."

"The president, Faulconer, believes as I do that this army is largely commanded by cretins. The army, of course, believes that the country is ruled by fools, and perhaps both are right, but for the moment, Faulconer, I'd put my money on the fools rather than the cretins. Officially I am a mere liaison officer between the fools and the cretins, but in reality, Faulconer, I am the president's creature in the army. My job is to prevent the cretins from being more than usually cretinous. I want your help."

Adam said nothing, not because he was reluctant to help, but because he was astonished by Thorne and his words. He was also cheered by them. The North, for all its power, seemed to be wallowing helplessly in the face of the rebellion's energy and that made no sense to Adam, but here, at last, was a man who had a vigor to match the enemy's defiance.

"Did you know, Faulconer, that your father has become Deputy Secretary of War for the Confederacy?" Thorne asked.

"No, sir, I didn't."

"Well, he is. In time, maybe, that will be useful, but not now." Thorne pulled a sheet of paper toward him and in so doing toppled another pile that spilt close to the gas jet. A corner of paper burst into flames that Thorne slapped out with the air of a man forever extinguishing such accidental fires. "You left the Confederacy three months ago and joined Galloway's Horse?" he asked, taking the facts from the paper he had selected.

"Yes, sir."

"He was a good man, Galloway. He had some bright ideas, which is why, of course, this army starved him of men and resources. But it was still a damn fool idea for Galloway to get mixed up in battle. You were supposed to be scouts, not shock troops. Galloway died, yes?"

"I'm afraid so, sir."

"And his second in command is missing, maybe dead, maybe captured. What was his name?"

"Blythe, sir," Adam said bitterly. He had never liked, much less trusted, Billy Blythe.

"So Galloway's Horse, so far as I can see, is a dead beast," Thorne said. "No employment for you there, Faulconer. Are you married?"

The sudden question surprised Adam. He shook his head. "No, sir."

"Quite right, too. A mistake to marry early." Thorne went silent for a moment. "I'm making you a major," he said abruptly, then waved Adam's embarrassed thanks to silence. "I'm not promoting you because you deserve it, I don't know if you do, but because if you work for me you'll be constantly harassed by brainless staff officers and the higher your rank the less obnoxious that harassment will be."

"Yes, sir," Adam said.

Thorne drew on his cigar and stared at Adam. He liked what he saw. Major Adam Faulconer was a young man, fair haired and bearded, with a square, trustworthy face. He was, Thorne knew, an instinctive Unionist and an honest man, but maybe, Thorne reflected, those were the wrong qualities for this job. Maybe he needed a rogue, but the choice had not belonged to Thorne. "So what are you to do, Faulconer? I shall tell you." He stood again and began pacing up and down behind his desk. "We have hundreds of sympathizers behind the enemy lines and most of them are no damn good. They see a rebel regiment march past and they're so overawed by the column's length that they report ten thousand men where in truth they've only seen a thousand. They send their messages and Detective Pinkerton multiplies their figure by three and Little George quakes in his fighting boots and begs Halleck to send him another army corps, and that, Faulconer, is how we've been conducting this war."

"Yes, sir," Adam said.

Thorne tugged up a window sash to let some of the cigar smoke out of the room. The city's sewage stench wafted in with a flutter of moths that flew suicidally toward the yellow-blue flames of the gas jets. Thorne turned back to Adam. "But I have a handful of agents of my own, and one of them is of particular value. He's a lazy man and I doubt that his allegiance to the North is anything other than a cynical calculation as to the war's outcome, but he has the possibility of revealing the rebels' strategy to us, everything! How many? Where? Why? The same kind of thing you tried to reveal on the peninsula. But he's also a timid man. His patriotism is not so strong that he fancies a hempen rope round his neck on a rebel gallows, and for that reason he is a cautious man. He will send us dispatches, but he will not use any means except those of his own devising. He won't risk his neck trying to ride through the lines, but said I could provide a courier who could run that risk, but he insisted it would have to be someone he could trust." Thorne paused to draw on his cigar, then jabbed it toward Adam. "He named you."

Adam said nothing. Instead he was trying to think of someone who matched Thorne's description, someone he obviously knew well in his native Virginia, but he could pluck no name or face out of his tangled memories. For a few wild seconds he wondered if it was his father, then he dismissed that thought. His father would never betray Virginia as Adam had done. "Might I ask—" Adam began.

"No," Thorne interrupted. "I'm not giving you his name. You don't need his name. If a message reaches you then you'll probably realize who he is, but it won't help you to know now. To be frank, Faulconer, I don't know what will help you. All I know is that one weak man in the Confederacy has told me he'll address his dispatches to you, but beyond that all is mystery." Thorne spread his arms in a gesture that expressed his own dissatisfaction with the clumsy and imprecise arrangements he was describing. "How my man will reach you, I don't know. How you will reach him, I cannot guess. He won't take risks, so you'll have to. All I can tell you is this. Just over a week ago I sent this man a message demanding that he find an excuse, any excuse, to attach himself to Lee's headquarters and I have no reason to think he will disobey. He won't like it, but he will do as I ask. He will stay close to Lee's headquarters and you will stay close to

82

McClellan's. Little George will think you're a nuisance, but you'll have papers saying that you work for the Inspector General and are preparing a report on the efficacy of the army's signaling systems. If Little George does try to hobble you, tell me and I'll rescue you." For a moment Thorne faltered, suddenly beset by the hopelessness of what he tried to do. He had told Adam the truth, but he had not revealed how ramshackle the whole arrangement was. His man in Richmond had provided Adam's name weeks before, not in connection with this scheme, but as a messenger who could be trusted and now, in utter desperation, Thorne was recruiting Adam in the hope that somehow his reluctant Southern agent could discover Lee's strategy and communicate it to Adam. The chances of success were slender, but something had to be done to neutralize Pinkerton's defeatist intelligence and to ward off the dreadful prospect of a Southern victory that would invite the damned Europeans to come and dance on America's carcass.

"You've got a good horse?" Thorne asked Adam.

"Very good, sir."

"You'll need money. Here." He took a bag of coins from his desk drawer. "United States gold, Faulconer, enough to bribe rebels and maybe get you out of trouble. My guess, and it is only a guess, is that my man will send you a message saying where he will leave his dispatches. That place will be behind enemy lines, Faulconer, so you'll need a good horse and the ability to bribe any rebel scum who give you trouble. Tomorrow morning you go to the camp on Analostin Island to meet a Captain Bidwell. He'll tell you all you need to know about the signals system so that you can talk intelligently to Little George about telegraphs and wig-waggers. After that you follow Little George and wait for a message. Take the gold with you. That's all."

Adam, so summarily dismissed, hesitated. He had a

score of questions, but Thorne's brusqueness discouraged him from asking any of them. The Colonel had uncapped an inkwell and had begun writing, so Adam just went to the desk and lifted the heavy bag, and it was not until he had reached the hallway downstairs and was buckling on his sword belt that it occurred to him that Thorne had never once asked him whether he was willing to risk his life by riding behind the rebel lines.

But maybe Thorne had already known the answer. Adam was a patriot, and for his country that he loved so passionately, any risk was worth taking and so, at a spy's bidding, he would ride into treachery and pray for victory.

Starbuck carried the brandy back to the office, locked the door, and lay down with the fully loaded Adams beside him. He heard Holborrow return, and later he heard the four captains go to their beds upstairs, and sometime after that he slept, but he was wary of Captain Dennison's revenge and so his sleep was fitful, though he was dreaming by the time Camp Lee's bugles called a raucous reveille to startle him awake. The sight of the undrunk brandy bottle reminded him of the previous night's confrontation and he took care to strap his revolver about his waist before he went through the house to the backyard, where he pumped himself a bucket of water. A mutinous Lucifer glared at him from the kitchen door. "We'll be leaving here in an hour or so," Starbuck told him. "We're going back to the city."

"Heaven be praised."

"Bring me some coffee with the shaving water, would you? And bread?"

Back in Maitland's old office Starbuck went through the papers to glean whatever other information he could about the battalion. This, he had decided, was the day that he revealed his true identity, but not till he had bargained the knowledge he had gleaned for some advantage and to do that he needed a bargainer. He needed the lawyer, Belvedere Delaney, and so he spent the dawn hours writing Delaney a long letter. The letter enabled him to put his ideas into order. He decided he would have Lucifer deliver the letter, then he would wait at Sally's apartment. The letter took the best part of an hour, but at last it was done and he shouted for Lucifer. It was well after reveille, but no one else was stirring in the big house. It seemed that neither Holborrow nor the battalion's four captains were early risers.

The door opened behind Starbuck. "We can go," he said, without turning round.

"Sir?" A timid voice answered.

Starbuck whipped round. It was not Lucifer at the door, but instead a small anxious face surrounded by brown hair that hung in pretty long curls. Starbuck stared at the girl who stared back at him with something akin to terror in her eyes. "I was told—" she began, then faltered.

"Yes?" Starbuck said.

"I was told Lieutenant Potter was here. A sergeant told me." The girl faltered again. Starbuck could hear Holborrow shouting down the stairs for his slave to bring hot shaving water. "Come in," Starbuck said. "Please, come in. Can I take your cloak?"

"I don't want to cause no trouble," the girl said, "I truly don't."

"Give me your cloak. Sit, please. That chair will be fine. Might I have your name, ma'am?" Starbuck had almost called her miss, then saw the cheap wedding ring glinting on her left hand.

"I'm Martha Potter," she said very faintly. "I don't want to be no trouble, I really don't."

"You aren't, ma'am, you aren't," Starbuck said. He had suspected from the moment the brown curls had timidly appeared around the door that this was the real Mrs. Potter and he feared that the real Lieutenant Potter could not be far behind. That would be a nuisance, for Starbuck wanted to reveal his true identity in his own way and not have the dénouement forced on him by circumstance, but he hid his consternation as Martha timidly perched on the edge of a chair. She wore a homespun dress that had been turned so that the lower skirt had become the upper to save the material's wear and tear. The pale brown dress was neatly sewn, while her shawl, though threadbare, was scrupulously clean. "We were expecting you, ma'am," Starbuck said.

"You were?" Martha sounded surprised, as if no one had ever paid her the compliment of expectation before. "It's just—" she began, then stopped.

"Yes?" Starbuck tried to prompt her.

"He is here?" she asked eagerly. "My husband?"

"No, ma'am, he's not," Starbuck said and Martha began to cry. The tears were not demonstrative, nor loud, just a helpless silent weeping that embarrassed Starbuck. He fumbled in his coat pocket for a handkerchief, found none, and could see nothing suitable to mop up tears anywhere else in the office. "Some coffee, ma'am?" he suggested.

"I don't want to be no trouble," she said through her quiet sobs, which she tried to staunch with the tasseled edge of her shawl.

Lucifer arrived, ready to leave for Richmond. Starbuck waved him out of the room. "And bring us a pot of coffee, Lucifer," he called after the boy.

"Yes, Lieutenant Potter," Lucifer said from the hall.

The girl's head snapped up. "He . . ." she began, then stopped. "Did I?" She tried again, then sniffed back tears.

86

"Ma'am." Starbuck sat opposite her and leaned forward. "Do you know where your husband is?"

"No," she wailed the word. "No!"

He gradually eased the tale out of the waiflike girl. Lucifer brought the coffee, then squatted in the office corner, his presence a constant reminder of Starbuck's promise that they were supposed to be leaving this hateful place. Martha cuffed at her tears, sipped at the coffee, and told the sad tale of how she had been raised in Hamburg, Tennessee, a small river village a few miles north of the Mississippi border. "I'm an orphan, sir," she told Starbuck, "and was raised by my grandma, but she took queer last winter and died round Christmas." After that, Martha said, she had been put to work by a family in Corinth, Mississippi, "but I weren't never happy, sir. They treated me bad, real bad. The master, sir, he—" she faltered.

"I can guess," Starbuck said.

She sniffed, then told how, in May, the rebel forces had fallen back on the town and she had met Matthew Potter. "He spoke so nice, sir, so nice," she said, and marriage to Potter had seemed like a dream come true as well as an escape from her vile employer and so, within days of meeting him, Martha had stood in the parlor of a Baptist minister's house and married her soldier.

Then she discovered her new husband was a drunkard. "He didn't drink those first few days, sir, but that was because they locked all the liquor up. Then he found some and he didn't never look back. Not that he's a bad drunk, sir, not like some men. I mean he don't hit anyone when he's drunk, he just don't ever get sober. Colonel Hardcastle threw him out of the regiment for drunkenness, and I can't blame him, but Matthew's a good man really."

"But where is he, ma'am?" Starbuck asked.

"That's it, sir. I don't know." She began sobbing again,

but managed to tell how, after Potter had been dismissed from the 3rd Mississippean Infantry Battalion, he had used Martha's small savings to take them back home to Georgia, where his father had refused to receive either Potter or his new wife. "We stayed in Atlanta awhile, sir, then his pa told us to get ourselves up here and see Colonel Holborrow. He sent us the money to come here, sir, which was real Christian of him, I thought. Then Matthew and me got here three days since and I ain't seen him once in all those days."

"So he's drunk in Richmond?" Starbuck suggested flatly.

"I guess, sir, yes."

"But where have you been staying?" Starbuck asked.

"At a Mrs. Miller's house, sir, in Charity Street, only Mrs. Miller says her rooms ain't charity, if you follow me, and if we don't pay her the rent by this morning she'll throw me out, sir, and so I came here. But I don't want to be no trouble." She looked as if she would cry again, but instead she frowned at Starbuck. "You ain't Colonel Holborrow, are you, sir?"

"No, I'm not, ma'am," Starbuck paused, then offered Martha what he hoped was a reassuring smile. He liked her, partly because she seemed so very fragile and timid, and partly, he guiltily confessed to himself, because there was an appealing prettiness under her mask of misery. There was also, he suspected, a streak of stubborn toughness that she would probably need to survive marriage to Matthew Potter. "I'm a friend of yours, ma'am," he told her. "You have to believe that. I've been pretending to be your husband and doing his work so that he wouldn't get into trouble. Can you understand that? But now we have to go and find him."

"Hallelujah," Lucifer murmured.

"You've been doing his work, sir?" Martha asked, incredulous that anyone would perform such a kindness for her wastrel husband.

"Yes," Starbuck said. "And now we're all going to walk out of here and go find your Matthew. And if anyone speaks to us, ma'am, then I beg you to keep silent. Do you promise to do that for me?"

"Yes, sir."

"Then let's go, shall we?" Starbuck handed Martha her thin cloak, collected his papers, paused to make certain no one was outside the door, then ushered Lucifer and Martha through the hall and across the verandah. It promised to be a hot, sunlit day. Starbuck hurried toward the nearest huts, hoping to make good his escape without being seen, but then a voice shouted at him from the house. "Potter!"

Martha uttered an exclamation and Starbuck had to remind her of the promise to say nothing. "And stay here," he went on, "both of you." Then he turned and walked back toward the house.

It was Captain Dennison who had called and who now jumped down the verandah steps. The Captain looked as if he had just risen from his bed, for he was in his shirtsleeves and was pulling bright red suspenders over his shoulders as he hurried toward Starbuck. "I want you, Potter," he called.

"Looks like you found me," Starbuck said as he confronted the angry captain.

"You call me 'sir.'" Dennison was standing close to Starbuck now and the smell of the ointment the Captain had smeared on his diseased face was almost overpowering. It was a peculiarly sour smell, not kerosene, and suddenly Starbuck placed it, and the memory of his time in the Richmond prison came flooding back in a wave of nausea. "You call me 'sir'!" Dennison said again, thrusting a finger hard into Starbuck's chest.

"Yes, sir."

Dennison grimaced. "You threatened me last night, Potter."

"Did I, sir?"

"Yes you damn well did. So either you come into the house, Potter, right now and apologize in front of the other officers, or else you face the consequences."

Starbuck pretended to consider the alternatives, then shrugged. "Guess I'll take the consequences, Captain, sir."

Dennison gave a grim smile. "You are a miserable fool, Potter, a fool. Very well. Do you know Bloody Run?"

"I can find it, sir."

"You find it at six o'clock tonight, Potter, and if you have trouble just ask anyone where the Richmond dueling grounds are. They're by the Bloody Run under the Chimborazo Hill at the other end of the city. Six o'clock. Bring a second if you can find anyone stupid enough to support you. Colonel Holborrow will be my second. And one other thing, Potter."

"Sir?"

"Try and be sober. I don't relish killing a drunk."

"Six o'clock, sir, sober," Starbuck said. "I look forward to it, sir. One thing, sir?"

Potter turned back. "Yes?" he asked suspiciously.

"You issued the challenge, sir, so I get to choose weapons. Ain't that the way it's done?"

"So choose," Dennison said carelessly.

"Swords," Starbuck said instantly and with sufficient confidence to make Dennison blink with surprise. "Swords, Captain!" he called airily as he turned and walked away. The smell of the medicine had betrayed Dennison's secret and Starbuck was suddenly looking forward to the day.

LIEUTENANT COLONEL SWYNYARD stood at the river's edge and thanked his God that he had been spared to witness this moment. A small breeze rippled the water to splinter up a myriad of bright sparkles reflected from a sun that blazed in a cloudless summer sky. At least three bands were playing and in this place, on this day, there was only one tune that they would ever play, though the Colonel thought it was a pity that they did not play in unison, but instead competed merrily as they celebrated the momentous event. Swynyard's maimed left hand beat against his sword scabbard in time to the closest band, then, almost unaware of it, he began to sing. "Dear mother," the Colonel sang softly, "burst the tyrant's chain. Maryland! Virginia should not call in vain, Maryland!" His voice became louder as the emotion of the hour embraced him. "She meets her sister on the plain; *Sic semper*! 'tis the proud refrain that baffles minions back amain, Maryland, my Maryland."

A burst of clapping sounded from the nearest company of the Faulconer Legion and Swynyard, oblivious that he had raised his voice loud enough to be heard, blushed as he turned and acknowledged the ironic applause. There had been a time, and not long before either, when these men cursed the very sight of Griffin Swynyard, but they had been won over by Christ's grace, or rather by the workings of that grace inside Swynyard, and now the

Colonel knew that the men liked him and for that blessing he could have wept this day, except that he was already weeping for sheer joy at this moment.

For the Southern army of Robert Lee, which had fought again and again against the northern invaders of its country, was crossing the Potomac.

They were going north.

The Confederacy was taking the war into the United States of America. For a year now the Yankees had marched on Southern soil, had stolen from Southern farms, and boasted of sacking the Southern capital, but now the invaded had become the invaders and a great dark line of men was crossing the ford beneath the battle flags of the South. "I hear the distant thunder-hum," Swynyard sang and this time the Legion sang with him, their voices swelling beside the river in wondrous harmony. "Maryland! The old line's bugle, fife and drum, Maryland! She is not dead, nor deaf, nor dumb; Huzzah! She spurns the northern scum! She breathes, she burns, she'll come, she'll come! Maryland, my Maryland!"

"They're in good voice, Swynyard, good voice!" The speaker was Colonel Ned Maitland, the Legion's new commander, who spurred his horse to Swynyard's side. Swynyard was on foot because his horse, the one luxury he possessed, was being rested. A man like Maitland might need three saddle horses and four pack-mules loaded with belongings to ensure his comfort on a campaign, but Swynyard had forsworn all such fripperies. He owned a horse because a brigade commander could not do his job without one, and he had inherited a tent and a servant from Thaddeus Bird, but the tent belonged to the army and the servant, a half-witted soldier called Hiram Ketley, would return to Bird's service when Bird was recovered from the wound he had taken at Cedar Mountain.

"What will you do, Maitland, when Bird comes back?" Swynyard asked, needling the self-satisfied Maitland, who rode to war with two tents, four slaves, a hip bath, and a canteen of silver cutlery with which to eat his scumbled vegetables.

"I hear he won't return," Maitland said.

"I hear he will. His wife wrote to Starbuck saying he was mending well, and when he does come back I'll have to give him the Legion. He's their proper commander."

Maitland waved the problem away. "There'll be plenty of other vacancies, Swynyard."

"You think I might be killed, eh? You reckon you'll be brigade commander? You look the part, Maitland, I'll say that for you. What did that uniform cost?"

"Plenty enough." Maitland was a placid man who rarely rose to Swynyard's baiting, perhaps because he knew that his connections in Richmond would ensure his smooth rise up the army's senior ranks. The trick of that rise, Maitland reckoned, was to have just enough battle experience beneath his belt to make it plausible; just enough and no more. He took a pair of field glasses from a saddlebag and trained them on the distant Maryland shore while Swynyard watched a squadron of Stuart's cavalrymen spur into the river. The troopers reached down with their hats to scoop up water that they flung at each other like children at play. The army was in a holiday mood.

"I wish the Legion still had a band," Swynyard said as the nearest musicians launched into "My Maryland" for the umpteenth time. "We did have one," he said, "but it got lost. At least, the instruments did."

"A lot of things seem to get lost from the Legion," Maitland said airily.

"What on earth does that mean?" Swynyard asked, trying to disguise his irritation at Maitland's condescension.

93

Swynyard was not certain that Maitland intended to give the impression he did, but that impression was of a superior man who observed and disapproved of all he encountered.

"Officers, mainly," Maitland said. "Most of the officers seem to have come up from the ranks in the last few weeks."

"We were fighting," Swynyard said, "which meant officers got killed. Didn't you hear about it in Richmond?"

"A rumor of it reached us," Maitland said mildly, cleaning the lenses of his field glasses. "Even so, Swynyard, I reckon I need some better men."

"Fellows who know what knife and fork to use on their hardtack?" Swynyard guessed.

Maitland let the sarcasm sail past him. "I mean more confident fellows. Confidence is a great morale booster. Like young Moxey. Pity he's gone." Captain Moxey had gone to Richmond to serve as Washington Faulconer's aide.

"Moxey was useless," Swynyard said. "If I was going into battle, Maitland, I wouldn't want weak reeds like young Moxey, but men like Waggoner and Truslow."

"But they're hardly inspirational men," Maitland observed tartly.

"Victory's the best inspiration," Swynyard said, "and men like Truslow deliver it."

"Maybe," Maitland allowed, "but I'd have liked to have held onto Moxey. Or that Tumlin fellow."

Swynyard had to think for a second to place Tumlin, then remembered the man from Louisiana who claimed to have been a prisoner in the North since the fall of New Orleans. "You wanted him?" he asked, surprised.

"He seemed a decent fellow," Maitland said. "Eager to serve."

"You think so?" Swynyard asked. "I thought he was a

94

bit plump for a fellow who'd spent five months in a Yankee prison, but maybe our erstwhile brethren can afford to feed their captives well. And I have to say I thought young Tumlin was a bit glib."

"He had confidence, yes," Maitland said. "I suppose you sent him back to Richmond?"

"Winchester," Swynyard said. Winchester, in the Shenandoah Valley, was the campaign's supply base and all unattached men were now being sent there to be reappointed. "At least he won't get wished onto poor Nate Starbuck," Swynyard added.

"Starbuck could count himself lucky if he had been," Maitland said, raising the glasses again toward the far riverbank. That bank was heavily wooded, but beyond the trees Maitland could see enemy farmland basking in the strong sunlight.

"If Starbuck's lucky," Swynyard said, "he'll be back with this brigade. I requested that his battalion be given to us if it's ordered to the army. No one else will want them, that's for sure."

Maitland shuddered at the thought of seeing the Yellowlegs again. His appointment to its command had been the nadir of his career and only the most energetic string-pulling had rescued him. "I doubt we'll see them," he said, unable to hide his relief. "They aren't ready to march and won't be ready for months." Not ever, he reflected, if Colonel Holborrow had his way. "And why would we want them anyway?" he added.

"Because we're Christians, Maitland, and turn away no man."

"Except Tumlin," Maitland retorted tartly. "Looks as if they're ready for us, Swynyard."

A messenger was spurring toward the brigade. A horse-drawn ambulance had just splashed into the ford accompanied by a cheer from the closest troops. Robert Lee was inside the vehicle, put there by injuries to his hands when he tried to quiet his frightened horse. A wounded commander, Swynyard thought, was not a good omen, but he put that pagan thought behind him as the messenger rode to Maitland under the assumption that the elegant Lieutenant-Colonel was the brigade commander. "He's the fellow you want," Maitland said, indicating Swynyard.

The messenger brought orders for Swynyard's brigade to cross the river and Swynyard, in turn, gave the Legion the honor of leading the brigade onto Northern soil. The Colonel walked down the Legion's column of companies. "Remember, boys," he shouted again and again, "no looting! No roguery! Pay in scrip for whatever you want! Show them we're a Christian country! Go now!"

Truslow's A Company waited until a battery of South Carolinian guns had splashed into the ford, then followed onto the road and down the muddy ramp into the water. The color party followed with the Legion's single flag held aloft by young Lieutenant Coffman, who found it a struggle to hold the big battle flag high against the wind while his slight body was buffeted by the Potomac's swirling current, which rose above his waist. He pushed on gamely, almost as though the whole war's outcome depended on him keeping the fringed silk out of the water. Many of the men were limping, not through wounds but because their ill-booted feet were blistered and to those men the river's cool water was like the balm of Gilead. Some men, though, refused to cross. Swynyard paused to talk with half a dozen such men who were led by a gaunt young corporal from D Company. The corporal's name was Burridge and he was a good soldier and a regular worshipper at the Colonel's prayer meetings, but now, as respectful and stubborn as ever, Burridge insisted he must disobey Swynyard's orders. "Ain't our task to go north, Colonel," he said firmly.

"It's your task to obey a lawful order, Burridge."

"Not if it's against a man's conscience, Colonel, and you know it. And it is lawful for us to defend our homes, but not to attack other folks' homes. If a Yankee comes south then I'll kill him for you, but I won't go north to do my slaughtering," Burridge declared and his companions nodded their support.

Swynyard ordered the men back to where the provosts were collecting other soldiers whose consciences could not abide carrying the war off their home soil. It grieved Swynyard to lose the six men, for they were among the best in the brigade, but it had been a confrontation he could never win and so he bid them farewell then followed the Legion into the river. Some of the men ducked their heads into the water to give their hair a brief washing, but most just pressed on toward the Northern bank, climbed onto Maryland soil, then crossed the bridge over the Chesapeake and Ohio Canal that lay just beyond the river. And thus they entered the enemy country.

It was a fine place of comfortable farms, good wooded land, and gentle hills; no different from the landscape they had left, only these hills and farms and woods were ruled by an enemy government. Here a different flag flew and that gave a piquancy to the otherwise unremarkable countryside. Not that most of the men in the five regiments in Swynyard's Brigade considered Maryland an enemy; rather they believed it was a slave state that had been forced to stay with the Union because of geography, and there were high hopes that this incursion of a Confederate army would draw a flock of recruits to the rebels' slashed cross flags. But however sympathetic Marylanders might be to the rebellion, it was still an enemy state and here and there some farms yet flew a defiant stars and stripes to show that this was Yankee territory.

But such stars and stripes were far outnumbered by rebel flags, most of them homemade things with faint colors and uncertain design, but they were hung to welcome Lee's army and when, at midafternoon, Swynyard's men marched through Buckeystown they were greeted by a small crowd that was hoarse from cheering the arrival of the rebels. Buckets of water or lemonade were placed beside the road and women carried trays of cookies along the weary columns. One or two of Buckeystown's houses, it was true, were shuttered close, but most of the village welcomed the invasion. A Texan band played the inevitable "My Maryland" as the column passed, the tune becoming ever more ragged and the harmony more cacophonous as the bandsmen were supplied with cider, beer, and whiskey by the villagers.

The brigade trudged on, their broken boots kicking up a plume of white dust that drifted westward on the breeze. Once, a mile beyond Buckeystown, a sudden crackle of firing sounded far away to the east and some of the men touched the stocks of their worn rifles as if preparing for battle, but no more shots sounded. The countryside stretched warm away, bounteous and calm under the summer sun. God was in His heaven, all seemed well in the world, and Lee's rebel army was loose in the North.

Starbuck walked into Richmond where he left Lucifer, his small luggage, and the letter for Belvedere Delaney at Sally's house, then he led Martha Potter on a tour of Richmond's drinking dens. Alcohol was officially banned from the city, but the government might as well have tried to outlaw breathing for all the difference their high-mindedness had made.

Starbuck began with the more respectable houses close to the Byrd Street depot of the Richmond and Petersburg Railroad, where Martha had last seen her husband. Starbuck spared her the brothels, reckoning that no whore would have endured a drunk for three days. Instead they would have picked Matthew Potter clean on the first night and then pitched him into the street to be swept up by the provosts. Once sober the Lieutenant would have been sent to Camp Lee and his failure to arrive suggested that he had discovered some liquor-sodden haven, or worse.

Starbuck worked his way down the hierarchy of liquor shops. The first places he searched had some pretensions to gentility, maybe a gilded mirror or a stretch of tobacco-soaked carpet, but gradually the furnishings, like the liquor, worsened. He knocked on a half dozen doors in Locust Alley, but found no sign of the missing Lieutenant. He tried Martin Street, where the whores hung out of the upper windows and made Martha blush. "He didn't have the money to drink all these days, sir," she told Starbuck.

"He might have," Starbuck insisted.

"There weren't more than three dollars in my purse."

"Three dollars will take you a long way in this town, ma'am," Starbuck said, "and I daresay he had a coat? He had a pair of boots? A revolver?"

"All those, yes."

"Then he could sell those and be drunk for three months. Hell," he said, then apologized. "Forgive my language, ma'am, but that's where he is. The Hells. I think, ma'am, I'd better take you back to Miss Sally's."

"I'm coming with you," Martha insisted. For all her timidity she was a dogged girl and no amount of Starbuck's persuasion could convince her to abandon the search.

"Ma'am, it ain't safe in the Hells."

"But he might be injured."

He might be dead, Starbuck thought. "I must insist, ma'am."

"You can insist all you want, sir," Martha said stubbornly, "but I'm still coming. I'll just follow you if you won't escort me."

Starbuck took out his revolver and checked that all five cones were primed with percussion caps. "Ma'am," he said, "where I'm going ain't called the Hells for nothing. It's in Screamersville, down by Penitentiary Bottom. Ugly names, ma'am, ugly place. Even the provosts don't go there under company strength."

Martha frowned. "They outlaws there?" she asked.

"In a manner, ma'am. Some deserters, a lot of thieves, and a lot of slaves. Only these slaves aren't under orders, ma'am, they're out of the Tredegar Iron Works and they're tougher than the stuff they roll in the mills."

"Hell," Martha said, "I ain't afraid of niggers."

"Then you should be, ma'am."

"I'm coming with you, Major."

He led her down the hill past Johnny Worsham's barnlike establishment where gambling tables crowded close to the stage on which a troupe of girls danced in between entertaining their clients upstairs. Two black men in bowler hats guarded the door and watched Starbuck with flat, cold stares. He led Martha over a wooden bridge that spanned a creek flooded with sewage and then into an alley that ran between damp brick walls. "You know the town pretty well, sir?" Martha asked, lifting her skirts as she stepped between the fetid rubbish that lay on the cobbles.

"I served a few weeks with the provosts here," Starbuck said. They had been miserable weeks that had ended with his imprisonment on suspicion of being a Northern spy. A gutless little officer called Gillespie had made Starbuck's life a hell in that prison, and that was one prospect of revenge that Starbuck treasured.

He stepped over a pile of garbage and turned into an unnamed street. The stench of the iron works hung heavy here and the sound of the furnaces roared to rival the foaming of the nearby river where it cascaded over the rapids. A dozen slaves lay in the smoke-dimmed sunlight with stone bottles of liquor, which they raised in an ironic salute as Starbuck passed. "Why ain't they at work?" Martha demanded.

"They work hard enough," Starbuck said. "You can't whip a man into working hard, ma'am. You have to give them some rope and once the slaves are trusted in the Iron Works they can come and go pretty much as they please. Long as they stay down here and don't go into the upper town, no one minds. This is their territory, not ours."

"Matthew wouldn't come here, would he?"

"Lots of soldiers do. There aren't any rules here, and the liquor's real cheap."

A mad preacher in an ankle-length black coat stood on a corner yelling the good news of Christ to a town that was not listening. A dwarf woman, drunk to the wind, reeled down the cobbles singing, but otherwise there were not many people in the streets. Midday was the witching hour for the Hells, the time when the sun shone brightest and Screamersville's denizens slept indoors as they prepared for the night's business. Starbuck chose a random tavern and plunged inside. A few soldiers slouched on benches, but none was Potter. One offered Martha a dollar if she would go upstairs with him, while another looked up at her, sighed with lust, and then vomited. "I told you," Starbuck said as he led her back into the street, "that this is no place for a lady."

101

"Hell, Major," Martha said sturdily, "no real lady would have married Matthew Potter. Besides, I've heard worse."

She did hear worse that day, but she stayed close to Starbuck as they searched the canalside shacks where most of the Hells business was done. The smell of the place was nauseating; a mix of coal smoke, vomit, sewage, and raw liquor. They were summarily ejected from one house by four black men who had been playing cards. A thin white woman sat in the room's corner with a bruised face. She spat when Starbuck entered and one of the men picked up a shotgun and rammed it into the stranger's face. "She don't want you here, mister," the black man said.

Starbuck took the hint and backed out into the alley. "I'm looking for a friend," he explained hurriedly.

"Not me, soldier, not them," the slave gestured at his companions, "not her, not no one in here." He paused and gave Martha a long speculative look. "She can come in, though."

"Not today," Starbuck said.

"He shouldn't talk uppity like that," Martha protested when the door was slammed on them. "And why's he got a gun? That ain't allowed!"

"Ma'am," Starbuck sighed, "I told you there weren't any rules here. He'd love me to pick a fight and a minute later you'd have a dozen black folk beating me to pulp."

"It ain't right."

"The underside of Dixie, ma'am. Sweet liberty." He gently edged Martha into the entry of an alley to keep her out of the way of a furious woman who pursued a man onto the street and hurled insults after him. The row became general as neighbors joined in. "Social gravity," Starbuck said.

"What does that mean?"

"It means we all go downhill, ma'am, till we hit the bottom."

"Some of us didn't start very high up."

"But keep going up, ma'am, keep going up." Christ, Starbuck thought, but if it were not for the rebel army then he would probably be down in these same slums. He had fled New England for a woman, and for her he had become a thief, and only the outbreak of war had offered him a chance of escape. What would he have done without the war, he wondered. Become a clerk and sought the solace of cheap drink and women, probably. And what would he do when the war was over, he wondered.

"Are you married?" Martha suddenly asked him.

"No, ma'am." Starbuck pushed open a door to find a cockpit made of straw bales arranged in a circle. Three rats fled the pit's floor, which was stained with blood and feathers, as Starbuck flooded the hovel with daylight. A soldier lay asleep on the bales stacked for the spectators, but he was not the missing Lieutenant.

"Matthew's real good looking," Martha said after she had inspected the sleeper, who was missing one eye and most of his teeth.

"Is that why you married him?" Starbuck asked, going back into the street.

"Marry in haste, my grandma always said, and repent at leisure," Martha said sadly.

"I've heard the advice," Starbuck said, and crossed the road to push open another shaky door. And there they discovered Matthew Potter.

Or rather Martha recognized the man sleeping on the wooden verandah that creaked under their weight as they stepped onto its thin boards. Rats scuttled from under the planks and ran along the canal's edge. "Matthew!" Martha called and knelt beside her husband, who was dressed in nothing but gray pants.

Potter did not wake up. He groaned and stirred in his sleep, but did not open his eyes.

"I wondered when some soul would come for him," a black woman appeared at the verandah door.

"Been here long, has he?" Starbuck asked her.

"So long I thought he'd take root. Likes his liquor, don't he?"

"I hear he's fond of it."

The woman wiped her nose with a corner of her apron, then grinned. "He's a nice boy, though. Speaks nice. Kind of took pity on him. Tried to feed him, even, but he didn't want food, just his guzzle."

"Sold you his shirt, did he?"

"And his coat, and his shoes. Just about every damned thing he had."

"His revolver?" Starbuck asked.

"He wouldn't have done that, sir. 'Gainst the law, isn't it?" She grinned at Starbuck, who grinned back. "He says he's from Georgia," the woman said, peering at the prostrate Lieutenant.

"He is."

"A preacher's son, see? They're always the worst." The woman laughed. "He was dancing for a time, and he even spoke poetry. Such nice poetry, I could have listened to him all night except that he fell over. Is that his wife?"

"Yes."

"Born to trouble. I never did understand why good women marry bad men."

"Lucky for us they do, eh?"

She smiled. "You going to take him away?"

"I reckon."

"Well, he had a good time. He won't remember it, but

he did. Sad to think he'll probably go down to a Yankee bullet; a nice boy like that."

"He won't wake up!" Martha wailed.

"He will," Starbuck promised, then he pulled her away from her husband and made her go inside the shack. "Wait there," he told her, and once he had shepherded her off the verandah and closed the door he put his hands under Potter's armpits and hauled him first to a sitting position and then upright. It was not difficult, for Potter, though tall, was frailly built and as thin as a rail. Starbuck leaned the Lieutenant against the shack's wall.

Potter stirred at last. "Time is it?" he asked. He was, as Martha had said, a good-looking man with fair lank hair and a week's growth of pale beard. His face was long and thin and had a delicacy, almost a look of noble suffering that, when Potter was sober, might have suggested spirituality or some artistic sensitivity, but now, in the throes of his monumental hangover, the Lieutenant simply looked like a whipped and sick puppy. A young puppy too, Starbuck guessed; certainly not more than nineteen. The Lieutenant tried to raise his head. He blinked slackly at Starbuck. "How do ye do," he managed to say.

Starbuck thumped him in the belly. He thumped him real hard, grunting with the effort of the blow that made Potter open his eyes wide, then double over. He almost fell, but Starbuck shoved him back against the wall before stepping smartly to one side as Potter threw up. Starbuck skipped further aside to stop the stream of vomit from splashing onto his boots.

"Jesus," Potter complained and cuffed at his mouth. He groaned. "You do that?"

"Stand up, Lieutenant."

"Oh, Jesus. Sweet Jesus. Sweet Lord Jesus." Potter tried to straighten. "Oh, suffering Jesus," he moaned as a stab of pain rammed down from his head. He pushed a long hank of hair off his face. "Who are you?" he demanded. "Announce yourself."

"The best son of a bitch friend you ever had," Starbuck said. "Is anything left in your belly?"

"It hurts," Potter said, rubbing his yellow-white skin where Starbuck had hit him.

"Stand straight!" Starbuck barked.

"Soldier! Soldier!" Potter said as he made a feeble effort to stand to attention. "Jesus wants me for a soldier." He retched again. "Oh, my God."

Starbuck pushed him back onto the wall. "Stand up straight," he said.

"Discipline," Potter said as he tried to straighten up. "The cure for all that ails me."

Starbuck took a handful of Potter's long, fair hair and rammed it back against the shack's wall, thus forcing the Lieutenant to look into his eyes. "What's going to cure you, you son of a bitch," he said, "is looking after your wife."

"Martha? Is she here?" Potter immediately cheered up and looked left and right. "Don't see her."

"She's here. And she's been looking for you. Why the hell did you leave her?"

Potter frowned as he tried to remember his last few days. "I didn't precisely leave her," he finally said. "I wandered, true, and did misplace her for a time. I was in need of a drink, you understand, and met a friend. Do you notice how that happens? You go to a strange city, incur a thirst, and the very first person you meet is someone you were at school with. The workings of providence, I suppose. Would you mind, sir, very much letting go of my hair so that I can be sick again? Thank you," he managed to say the last two words before jackknifing forward and spewing up a last pathetic throatful of vomit. He moaned, closed his eyes, and slowly stood up again. "Rinsed out now," he said reassuringly as he looked at Starbuck. "Do I know you?"

"Major Starbuck."

"Ah! Starbuck! A famous name!" Potter said and Starbuck tensed himself for the usual attack on his father, a notorious enemy of the South, but Matthew Potter had a different Starbuck in mind. "First mate of the *Pequod*, aren't I right?"

"Think of me as Captain Ahab, Lieutenant," Starbuck said.

Potter gazed momentarily at Starbuck's legs. "Rather overendowed with pins, aren't you, for such a role? Or is one of those an ivory peg?" Potter giggled, then winced as another pain lashed at him. "Should I be pleased to meet you?"

"Yes, you damn well should. Now come on, you son of a bitch, we're going to fight a duel."

Potter stared with horror at Starbuck, then shook his head. "Not in my line of business, sir. Really not. Don't mind battle, but not pistols at dawn."

"It's swords at dusk. Now come on! Don't tread in that!" Too late.

Potter placed a bare foot in his puddle of vomit, grimaced, then followed Starbuck into the tavern where an emotional Martha threw herself into her husband's enfeebled arms. Starbuck thought about offering to buy back the Lieutenant's shoes and shirt, then decided against wasting his money. Potter could be equipped from the thin stores at Camp Lee, and until then he could go barefoot and barechested.

He persuaded a now-remorseful Lieutenant out into the street. Martha led Potter by the hand while he tried to explain his conduct. "Not intentional, my most darling one, not with malice aforethought, as the lawyers would say. It was merely a whim, a notion, a gesture of amity for an old friend. Thomas Snyder. That is his name and Snyder will vouch for the purity of my motives. He is an artilleryman now, he told me, and has gone partly deaf. All those loud bangs, you see? Whatever, I merely kept him company. We were at school together and together we mastered McGuffey's readers, together we added and subtracted and divided, and together we got drunk, for which I apologize. It will not happen again until the next time. Oh God, do I really have to walk?"

"Yes," Starbuck said, "you do."

"I do dislike strong, noisy men," Potter said, but stumbled obediently behind Starbuck up the hill toward Main Street. "The army is filled with strong, noisy men. The life must attract them. You didn't, I suppose, bring anything to eat, my dearest chick?" he inquired of Martha.

"No, Matthew."

"Or a mouthful to drink, perhaps?"

"No, Matthew!"

"Water, dearest love, mere water. A moment, Captain Ahab!" Potter called, then pulled away from his wife and staggered over the street to a horse trough that was already occupied by a shaggy cab horse. Potter stood beside the horse and plunged his face into the water, scooped it over his hair, and then drank greedily.

"I'm so ashamed," Martha said to Starbuck.

"I like him," Starbuck said, realizing as he spoke that it was true. "I do like him."

Potter stood and belched. He apologized to the horse, patted its neck, and walked unsteadily back to his wife. "My father," he said to Starbuck, "always maintains that self-knowledge is the harbinger of self-improvement, but

108

I'm not entirely persuaded of that truth. Do I improve myself by knowing I am eternally thirsty, overeducated, and sadly fallible? I think not. Would you both excuse me for another trifling moment?" He walked to the nearest wall, unbuttoned his pants, and pissed noisily onto the brick. "Oh, dear God," he said, raising his eyes, "in one end and out the other"

"So ashamed," Martha whispered.

"Did you say ashamed, sweet love of my benighted life?" Potter called loudly from the wall. "Ashamed? Do not the poets piss? Does not an anointed king empty his royal bladder? Did not George Washington micturate? Was our dear Lord spared the need to sprinkle?"

"Matthew!" Martha protested, shocked. "He was perfect!"

"And that, sweetest one, was a perfect piss." He turned back to them, buttoning his trousers, then waved imperiously at Starbuck. "Onward, Captain Ahab! Death to Moby Dick! God hunt us all if we do not hunt Moby Dick to his death! Onward, dear souls!"

Sally, as she had promised, was waiting outside Mitchell and Tyler's jewelry store on Main Street and with her, as Starbuck had hoped, was Belvedere Delaney. The lawyer was dressed in one of the expensive uniforms he bought from Shaffer's, but no amount of tailoring could disguise Delaney's unmilitary soul. He was a short, plump, kindly man whose talents were making money and taking amusement from other men's weaknesses. Officially he was a captain in the legal office of the Confederate War Department, an appointment that seemed to require no duties except to take the pay and to wear a uniform when it was convenient. Today he sported a major's stars. "You've been promoted?" Starbuck asked, gladly greeting his old friend.

"I deemed the rank appropriate," Delaney answered grandly. "No one else seems to have the power to promote or demote me, so I assumed the rank as one more fitting for my dignity. In time, just like a gas balloon, I shall rise to the dizziest of heights. Dear Nate, you look dreadful! Scarred, dirty, used up. Is this what soldiering does to one?"

"Yes," Starbuck said, then introduced the barechested Lieutenant Potter, who seemed rather frightened by Delaney. Martha nervously shook the lawyer's hand, then fell back to cling to her disreputable husband.

"Here," Sally said to Starbuck as they began to walk eastward along Main, "you need this," and she held out one of Patrick Lassan's sabers.

Starbuck buckled the sword belt round his waist. "Did you find anything?" he asked Delaney.

"Of course I didn't find anything," the lawyer said testily. "I am not a detective bureau, I am merely an attorney." Delaney paused to raise his peaked cap to a passing acquaintance. "But it's quite obvious," he went on, "what Holborrow is doing. He is using the Special Battalion as a milch cow. He feeds it scraps and it yields him money. He doesn't want it to go to war, because that would mean he loses the income."

"What does that mean?" Starbuck asked.

Delaney sighed. "It's obvious, isn't it? The government issues the Special Battalion boots, so Holborrow sells the boots to another regiment, then complains to the government that the boots were faulty. In time he will receive more boots that will also be sold. The same for rifles, canteens, coats, and anything else he can gouge out of the system. He's doing it quite cleverly, for the system hasn't discovered him, but I'm sure that's his game. Are you really going to fight a duel?"

"Son of a bitch challenged me," Starbuck said belligerently, then, unable to hide his disappointment, glanced back at the lawyer. "So you can't help me?" he asked. Starbuck, in the careful letter he had written to Delaney that morning, had described his suspicions that Holborrow had purloined the rifles meant for the Special Battalion and then sold them. He had hoped that somehow Delaney might discover some evidence in the War Department, but his hopes had been dashed.

"I can help you," Delaney said, "by being a lawyer."

"You mean you'll threaten Holborrow?"

Delaney sighed. "You are so blunt, Nate, so hopelessly blunt. How can I threaten him? I know nothing. I can, however, drop broad hints. I can insinuate. I can pretend to know what I do not know. I can suggest a formal investigation might be undertaken, and it is possible, just possible, that he'll come to an arrangement rather than call my bluff. How many men in the battalion?"

"A hundred and eighty nine."

"Ah, that's something. He's drawing rations and pay for two hundred and sixty." Delaney smiled, seeing an advantage. "I can tell you one other thing. Holborrow was never wounded by a Yankee bullet. That bad leg came from a fall off his horse and the damage isn't half so bad as he pretends. He doesn't want to go to war, you see? So he's playing up the wound. What he wants is a nice, safe, profitable war in plump Richmond, and I guess he'll do quite a lot to make sure he gets it. But what do you want, Nate?"

"You know what I want."

"Two hundred rifles?" Delaney shook his head. "The rifles will have been sold long ago. I doubt Holborrow can lay his hands on fifty, but I'll do my best. But do you really want to be sent to Lee's army?" That was Starbuck's main request; that Holborrow would affirm that the Special Battalion was ready for combat and so release it to the war. "Why?" Delaney asked in genuine puzzlement. "Why don't you just take the God-given rest, Nate? Haven't you fought enough?"

Starbuck was not really sure of the answer. One part of him, a great shadowed horrid part of him, feared combat like a small child feared the night-ghouls, but still he felt compelled to take his battalion to war. He doubted if he could live with the knowledge that he was skulking while other men fought, but it was more than that. All he now possessed in the world was his reputation as a soldier. He had no family, no wealth, and no position other than his Confederate commission and if he betrayed that commission by skulking then he was abandoning his pride. He did not want to go to battle, he only knew he had to go to battle. "I'm a soldier," he answered inadequately.

"I shall never understand you," Delaney said happily, "but maybe the next few weeks will give me an answer. I'm joining Lee myself."

"You?" Starbuck asked, astonished. He stopped on the sidewalk and looked at his friend. "You're going to the army?"

"My country calls!" Delaney said grandiloquently.

"To do what?"

Delaney shrugged and walked on. "My idea, really. No one ordered me to go, Nate, but it seemed like a good idea when it occurred to me. Lee's invading the North, did you know? Well, he is and there are bound to be tricky points of law involved. If a man steals from enemy property, is it theft? It might seem a trivial thing to you, even irrelevant, but when this war does end there's bound to be all sorts of legal settlements to be made between the two jurisdictions and it seems only prudent to try and anticipate the issues."

"You'll hate campaigning," Starbuck said.

"I'm sure I shall," Delaney said fervently. In truth the lawyer had absolutely no wish to join Lee's army, but the orders had come from an angry man in Washington, and Delaney, who was convinced the North would win the war and had no desire to be attached to the losing side, had weighed his future and decided that the discomforts of a brief campaign should prove a good investment. He still resented Thorne's peremptory demand that he should spy on Lee's headquarters, for Delaney had reckoned he could do all his spying from Richmond's comfortable parlors rather than from some muddy and dangerous bivouac in the countryside, and he doubted that he would be made privy to any useful information. It was all, he reckoned, a waste of time, but he dared not refuse Thorne's demand, not if he wanted the rewards that would be in Washington when the war ended, and so he had invented a reason for attaching himself to Lee's army and now, with a mixture of horror and apprehension, he planned to travel north. "Tomorrow morning!" he announced. "George has packed us some wine and tobacco, so we won't be comfortless." George was his house slave.

"You'll be a damned fool to carry expensive wine to war," Starbuck said. "It'll be stolen."

"What a suspicious mind you do have," Delaney said. He was hiding his fears, and so was pleased to have this evening's distraction at Richmond's dueling ground. Duels were supposedly illegal, but still the Richmond Anti-Dueling Society had its headquarters not two doors down from Belvedere Delaney's expensive brothel and the society kept itself busy raising funds and prosecuting men known to have fought affairs of honor. But not all the

113

pious efforts of a hundred such societies had succeeded in eliminating dueling from the Confederate states. Richmond's dueling ground lay just beyond the city's limits, beneath the Chimborazo Hill on which was built the sprawling military hospital. Starbuck led his companions up Elm Street, crossed a plank bridge that spanned the dirt and garbage through which the Bloody Run trickled down to the James, and so reached the patch of desolate land squeezed between the shoulder of the hill and the rusting rails of the York River Railroad. Scrubby, soot-darkened trees fringed the dueling ground, which was overshadowed by the tall, gaunt, and windowless facade of a sawmill.

Colonel Holborrow's carriage was standing at the end of a track that led from the sawmill, while Holborrow and Dennison were pacing up and down the worn length of turf where the fights took place.

"Potter!" Holborrow limped forward as Starbuck walked into the slanting late sunlight. "You're under arrest! You hear me, boy? You ain't fighting no duel! You're going back to Camp Lee, where I'm going to break you down to private unless you can explain yourself. Just where the hell have you been all day? Are you drunk, boy? Let me smell your breath!"

"I ain't Potter, Holborrow," Starbuck said. "That's Potter," he pointed to the half-clothed Lieutenant, who was weakly leaning against the balustrade of the wooden bridge that crossed the Bloody Run. "Sorry son of a drunken bitch, ain't he? And that's his wife with him. You want to go talk to them while I teach Dennison some manners?"

The effect of Starbuck's words was everything he could have wished. Holborrow's confused face turned between Potter and Starbuck, but no words came, only a spluttering indignation. Starbuck patted the Colonel's shoulder and walked toward Dennison. "Ready, Captain?" he called.

"Who are you?" Holborrow shouted after him.

Starbuck looked into Dennison's eyes while he answered. "Major Nathaniel Starbuck, Colonel, once of the Faulconer Legion, now commander of the Second Special Battalion. And, according to Captain Dennison, a goddamned Yankee who ain't worth fighting for. Isn't that what you said, Captain?"

Dennison blanched, but did not answer. Starbuck shrugged, unbuckled the sword belt, and took off his jacket. He drew the saber, tossed its scabbard onto the coat then gave the blade two hissing cuts through the evening air. "I kind of reckoned you'd have the Colonel arrest me, Captain," he said to Dennison, "on account of your being a coward. I knew you wouldn't want to fight me, but you ain't got any choice now." He gave another practice cut, then smiled into Dennison's scarred face. "There was a fencing society at Yale," he said in a conversational tone, "where we goddamned Yankees learned to fight." Starbuck had never joined the society, but he did not need to make that plain to his opponent. "It was larded with European rubbish, of course. *Derobement* of the *prise de fer.*" He gave the naked blade an impressive twisting cut. "Bind from *quarte* to *seconde*," he gave the sword another meaningless flourish before bringing it up into the salute. "Ready, Dennison?" he asked. "I got business to do tonight, so let's get it over with."

"That's Potter?" Colonel Holborrow had hurried back to Starbuck's side, even forgetting to limp in his haste. "Are you telling me that's Potter?"

"Don't shout so!" Starbuck said chidingly. "Lieutenant Potter is badly hung over, Holborrow. I found the sorry son of a bitch down in the Hells."

"Hell," Holborrow said, still thoroughly confused.

115

"Then what in hell's name were you doing at Camp Lee?"

Starbuck smiled. "Looking you over, Holborrow, so I could report back to the War Department. See that short, plump fellow there? That's Major Belvedere Delaney from the Legal Department. He's my second tonight, but he also wants a word with you." Starbuck looked back to Dennison. "I decided against bringing a surgeon, Captain. I know it's against the rules printed in Wilson's *Code of Honor*, but I never did think that a duel was proper unless it ends in death, don't you agree?"

"He's from the Legal Department?" Holborrow rapped Starbuck's arm with his cane and gestured toward Delaney.

"He heads the department," Starbuck said, then turned back to the aghast Dennison. "Ready, Captain?"

Holborrow again demanded Starbuck's attention with a tap of his cane. "Are you really Starbuck?" he asked.

"Yes."

"Then you're a slippery son of a bitch," Holborrow said, but not without some admiration.

"It takes one to recognize another," Starbuck said.

"Inside the carriage, Colonel?" Delaney had joined them and gestured at the vehicle. "I find our sort of business is best done in privacy. Let's leave Starbuck to his slaughter, shall we? He enjoys slaughter," Delaney smiled at Dennison, "but I find the sight of blood upsetting before supper."

Holborrow clambered inside the coach, Delaney followed, and the carriage door slammed shut. The Negro driver watched impassively from the high box as Starbuck gave his saber another practice cut. "You ready, Captain?" he asked Dennison.

"You're Starbuck?" Dennison asked in a faint voice.

Starbuck frowned, looked left and right as though for inspiration, then gazed back into Dennison's face. "Sir,"

116

he said, "I'm a major and you're a captain, so that makes you a shad-bellied piece of ordure, otherwise known as a captain. Isn't that right?"

"Sir," Dennison said miserably.

"Yes," Starbuck answered the original question, "I'm Starbuck."

"I ain't got a quarrel with you," Dennison said, then, after a pause, "sir."

"But you do, Dennison, you do. Would it matter whose wife you insulted? As it happens, that lady is not my wife," he gestured toward Sally, who watched from the ground's far end, "but she is a dear friend."

"I didn't mean to give offense, sir," Dennison said, desperate to escape the wicked curved blade in Starbuck's hand.

"The offense you gave me, Dennison," Starbuck said, hardening his voice, "was by thinking you could bully a man of lower rank. Do that again in my battalion, Captain, and I'll whip your backside bloody and break you down to private. You understand me?"

Dennison stared into Starbuck's eyes for a second, then nodded. "Yes, sir," he said.

"Now let's discuss your disease, Captain," Starbuck said.

Dennison glanced up into Starbuck's eyes again, but could find nothing to say.

"It sure ain't ringworm," Starbuck said, "and it ain't psoriasis, and I've never seen a case of eczema that bad. Just what is your proper doctor giving you?"

"Turpentine," Dennison said softly.

Starbuck laid the flat of his saber blade against one of the open, gleaming sores on Dennison's cheek. The Captain flinched from the pain, but then submitted meekly to the weapon's touch. "It ain't turpentine, is it?" Starbuck asked. Dennison said nothing. Starbuck twitched the

117

blade, making Dennison flinch. "It's croton oil, Captain, that's what it is, and no doctor gave it to you. You're rubbing it on yourself, ain't you? Every morning and every night you slap the stuff on. Must hurt like hell, but it makes damn sure no one can transfer you to a fighting battalion, ain't that it? Keeps you away from the nasty Yankee bullets, don't it?"

Dennison could not even meet Starbuck's eyes, let alone speak as Starbuck drew the blade slowly back along the sore. Starbuck remembered croton oil, the foul purgative that Lieutenant Gillespie had forced down Starbuck's throat in an effort to force an admission that he was a Northern spy. Where the oil had spilled onto Starbuck's cheeks it had formed smallpox-like pustules, and it was plain that Dennison was using the purgative as a means of fabricating an illness that would keep him safely in Richmond. "What will it be next, Captain?" Starbuck asked. "Swallowing gunpowder to make yourself vomit? I know all the tricks, you bastard, every last one of them. So what you're going to do now is throw away your croton oil, you hear me?"

"Yes, sir."

"Throw it away, wash your face in good clean water, and I guarantee you'll be as handsome as ever by the time you face the Yankees in battle."

Dennison forced himself to look up at Starbuck and the look was of utter hatred. He was a proud man and he had been utterly humbled, but he had no belly to try and retrieve his pride by fighting his new commanding officer. Starbuck picked up his scabbard and coat. "We've started badly, you and I," he told Dennison, "but no one but you and me knows what passed between us here, and I won't be telling. So you can go back to Camp Lee, Captain, repair your face, and make damn sure that your company is ready to fight. Because that's what I intend to do with the battalion, fight." He had meant his words to be conciliatory, but he saw no grateful response in Dennison's dark eyes, only bitterness. Starbuck was tempted to let Dennison go and let the bastard rot in his own self-inflicted misery, but he needed every officer he could get and besides, why should Dennison evade his duty? Dennison must fight like every other man defending his country.

The carriage door opened suddenly and Delaney jumped awkwardly down to the turf. Colonel Holborrow followed, but more slowly because he was exaggerating his limp. Delaney took Starbuck's arm and steered him out of earshot of Dennison or the Colonel. "The Colonel and I have come to an understanding," Delaney said. "He believes it his patriotic duty to spare the Confederacy an expensive inquiry into his handling of the Special Battalion, even though, of course, he avers that nothing would be discovered by such an inquiry, and he also feels that under your leadership the battalion could well acquit itself nobly in battle."

Starbuck felt a pang of terror at the news. He had got what he wanted. "We're going north then?"

"Isn't that what you wanted?" Delaney asked. He had caught a whiff of Starbuck's fear.

"Yes," Starbuck said, "it is."

"Because you're going in two days," Delaney said. "I don't think Holborrow wants you in his sight a moment longer than possible."

"Jesus!" Starbuck swore. Two days! "What about my rifles?"

"Thirty."

"Thirty!" Starbuck protested.

"Nate! Nate!" Delaney held up a cautionary hand. "I

told you I had no ammunition to force that issue. The rest of the rifles are sold, I know that and you know that, but Holborrow's never going to admit it. But he says he can find thirty good rifles, so be grateful. You'll just have to steal the others off the enemy. Aren't you supposed to be good at that?"

Starbuck swore again, but his anger ebbed as he considered the deal Delaney had struck. He had got what he wanted, a battlefield command, and somehow in the next few days he had to make the Special Battalion into a unit that could stand against the Yankees. He would make it so damned special that other Confederate battalions would wish that they too were punishment units. "Thanks, Delaney," he said grudgingly.

"I am overwhelmed by your gratitude." The lawyer smiled. "And now, I suppose, you want to spend an evening of dissipation at my expense?"

"No," Starbuck said, because if the Yellowlegs really were going north then he had work to do. He had men to train and boots to find and a battalion to shake into efficiency and only two days to work his miracle. Two days before they went to where the Yankees waited. Before the Yellowlegs went back to war.

ADAM FAULCONER HAD rarely felt so useless, or so unwanted, for he realized after just a half day at McClellan's headquarters that he had nothing whatever to do. For a time those headquarters had stayed obstinately in Washington, where the Young Napoleon had insisted there were necessary arrangements that could not be made from the saddle nor by telegraph from the field, and so the blue-coated army moved slowly westward while their commander slept in the bed of his comfortable house on Fifteenth Street. A nervous silence descended on Washington when the troops departed; a silence enervated by rumors of rebel activity. Gray horsemen were reported in Pennsylvania, a barn had been burned in Ohio, the state militia was assembling to protect Philadelphia, but in all the rumor there was not one hard fact. No one actually reported seeing Lee or the redoubtable Jackson, though Northern newspapers were more than ready to print elaborate fancies in the factless vacuum. The rebels were said to be 150,000 strong, they were planning to take Baltimore, they had designs on Washington, they were marching against New York, and even Chicago was threatened. The newspapers were eagerly read by the blue army that was bivouacked not far from Washington, in the green Maryland fields, where they waited for McClellan. Meanwhile the Young Napoleon rode about the Federal capital leaving visiting cards in a score of fashionable houses,

121

each scrap of pasteboard carefully inked with the initials PPC, which had the recipients puzzled until the French ambassador explained that the letters stood for *Pour Prendre Congé* and were the polite manner of indicating that a soldier was leaving home to go on campaign.

"*Pour Prendre Congé!*" Colonel Lyman Thorne snarled at Adam. "Who the devil does he think he's impressing?"

Adam had no answer. It worried him that he was always so tongue-tied in Thorne's presence. He would have liked to have impressed the Colonel, but instead he found himself trapped into either monosyllabic answers or else saying nothing at all. This time he said nothing, but just kicked his heels gently back to coax an ounce more speed from his horse, then he leaned into the mare's neck as she rose to a snake fence.

Thorne's horse thumped down a second after Adam's. The two men were riding westward through a countryside apparently bereft of inhabitants; a countryside of neat farms and tidy orchards and well-drained fields. "Where is everybody?" Adam asked after they had cantered past another immaculate white-painted farm with a swept yard, a woodlot where the cut logs were aligned between the elm trees as neatly as soldiers in one of the Young Napoleon's beloved reviews, and a newly painted springhouse, but without any sign of a human presence.

"Indoors," Thorne answered. "Didn't you see the upstairs drapes twitch? These people aren't fools. Where would you be if two armies were close by? You put your valuables in the cellar, bury the cash in the kitchen garden, load the shotgun, dirty your daughters' faces so they don't look attractive, harness the wagon, then wait to see who comes."

"No rebels coming this way," Adam said, trying hard to make conversation with the forbidding Thorne, but even that cheerful observation met with a scornful reply.

"Damn the rebels, where are our cavalry patrols? Damn it, Faulconer, but Lee's been two days in the north and we don't know the first damn thing about what he's doing. And where are our scouts? This countryside should be thick with damn scouts. They should be tripping over each other, but McClellan won't release them. He doesn't want their precious horses to get hurt." Thorne's derision was sour and angry. "Little George will inch his way forward like a virgin edging into a barrack room," he said, "and Lee will be running wild. Did I show you Pinkerton's latest work of fiction?"

"No, sir."

The two horsemen had stopped their mounts on the crest of a long green watershed that offered a distant view westward. Thorne took out a massive pair of binoculars, wiped the lenses with the skirt of his coat, then peered at the distant view for a long time. He saw nothing to alarm him and so lowered the glasses. "Pinkerton claims that Lee has one hundred and fifty thousand men in Maryland and he reckons another sixty thousand are poised just south of the Potomac ready to mount an attack on Washington when McClellan goes to deal with Lee." Thorne spat. "Lee's no fool. He won't throw away his army in an attack on Washington's forts! He doesn't have enough men. If Lee even has sixty thousand men fit to fight I'd be surprised, but it's no good pointing out facts to frightened George, it just makes him more stubborn. Little George will believe what he wants to believe, and he wants to believe he's outnumbered because that way there's no disgrace when he doesn't fight. Hell, they should give me the army for a week. There'd be no rebellion at the end of that week, I can promise you."

The Colonel fell silent as he unfolded a map. Adam

desperately wanted to know why the army did not give Thorne a fighting command, but he did not like to ask the question, but then the Colonel answered it anyway. "I'm not one of the elect, Faulconer. I wasn't in Mexico, I wasn't at West Point, I didn't spend my peacetime nights flattering other uniformed fools with damnfool stories about slaughtering Comanches. I was brought into the peacetime army to build barracks, so I'm not supposed to understand soldiering. I'm not part of the mystical brotherhood. Have you ever seen Little George talk about soldiering? He weeps! Goes misty at the eyes!" Thorne hooted his derision. "Damn the weeping until you've given someone something to weep about. You can't win a war without taking casualties, lots of casualties, blood from one end of the country to the other. After that you can weep. But don't give me all this podsnap about sacred bonds, brotherhood, honor, and duty. We have a duty to win, that's all."

"Yes, sir," Adam said dully. He was not sure he liked what the Colonel was saying, for Adam had an idea that war was somehow mystical. He knew all war was a bad thing, of course, a terrible thing even, but when it was touched by honor and patriotism it was subtly transformed into nobility and Adam did not want to think of it as mere uniformed butchery.

He took the glasses that the Colonel offered and dutifully trained them westward. He was wondering why the older man had so suddenly appeared at the army's headquarters to suggest this long ride into Maryland, but Adam, lonely himself, had no idea of the Colonel's loneliness, nor of the Colonel's fears. Thorne, watching his army led by fools, feared that it would be thrown away before it could win the war and he feared that nothing he could do would prevent that tragedy, but still he must do what he could. "One man," he said suddenly.

"Sir?" Adam lowered the glasses.

"One man can make a difference, Faulconer."

"Yes, sir," Adam said, cringing at the inadequacy of his answer and wanting to ask Thorne more about the strange spy who had given Thorne Adam's name. How was Adam supposed to contact the man? Or the man Adam? Adam had already asked Thorne these questions and received an honest answer; that Thorne did not know, but Adam would have liked to probe the matter further in search of some clue that would tell him how he might prove useful in this campaign.

Thorne took back the field glasses. "I reckon that's Damascus," he said, pointing to a small group of houses clustered atop a low ridge some four or five miles away, "and if the rebels were advancing on Washington, which they're not, they'd be there." Thorne folded the stiff map and shoved it into a pocket. "Let's take a late lunch in Damascus, Faulconer. Maybe we'll be struck by enlightenment on the road."

The horses trotted down the long green slope to where a herd of cows was standing belly deep in a gentle creek. Ahead of Adam now was a long stretch of valuable bottomland, well watered, lush, studded with stands of trees and cut by a tangle of small streams. Doubtless the land had once been all swamp, but generations of hard work had drained the wetland, tamed it, and made it useful, and Adam, looking at the results of that honest labor, was almost overcome by love for his country. That love was real for Adam, real enough to have driven him from his native Virginia to fight for the greater entity of the United States. Other countries might boast grander ceremonies than America, they might boast mighty castles, and possess splendid cathedrals and vast-halled palaces, but nowhere, Adam fervently believed, displayed the virtue of modest, hard, honest labor like America. This was a plain man's country and Adam wanted it to be nothing more, for nothing, he believed, was worth more than simple, painstaking achievement.

"Daydreaming, Faulconer?" Thorne growled, and Adam jerked his head up to see that three horsemen had appeared from a stand of timber a mile ahead. Three horsemen in gray. "Our friends have their cavalry scouts afield, I see," the Colonel said dryly, curbing his horse, "so it seems we won't be eating in Damascus after all." He took out his field glasses and inspected the rebel trio. "Down at heels, that's for sure, but I'll warrant their carbines are well looked after." He edged the glasses up to stare at the ridge on which Damascus stood. He was wondering if he was wrong and that Lee was advancing on Washington, in which case he expected to see some evidence of gun batteries on the high ground, but he saw nothing. "It's just a patrol," he said dismissively, "nothing more. Lee's not headed this way." He turned his horse. "No point in being captured, Faulconer, let's retire."

But Adam had kicked his horse forward. The Colonel turned back. "Faulconer!" he snapped, but Adam ignored Thorne. Instead he kicked his heels again and the mare tossed her head and lifted her hooves as she began to canter.

The three rebels unslung their carbines, but did not take aim on the lone horseman who rode toward them. The Northerner did not have a saber drawn, nor was he holding any weapon, he was simply riding in a straight line toward his enemies. For a few seconds Thorne wondered if Faulconer was defecting back to the South, then the young man swerved his horse, leapt a brook, and cantered at an angle to the rebel scouts, who suddenly understood his purpose. They whooped like hunters seeing the fox in open ground and kicked back their heels. It was a race, pure and simple. Adam was challenging them, and the three rebels accepted the challenge by racing to catch him. It was a country game as old as time, only this day the prize was survival and the penalty imprisonment. Adam held his horse back, watching over his shoulder as the three pursuing horses lurched into the full gallop. He teased them by continuing to curb his good mare, and only when the closest man was within thirty or forty paces did he let go the curb rein and so give the mare her head.

She flew. She was no ordinary horse, but one of the prize beasts from Washington Faulconer's stud at Faulconer Court House in Faulconer County, Virginia. This was a mare with Arab blood, but crossed with a hardy American strain and Adam trusted his father's horse-breeding far more than he trusted his political judgment. He whooped himself, echoing the wild cries his pursuers made. This, at last, was war! A challenge, a race, a contest, something to stir the blood and add piquancy to days of boredom. The mare leapt a stream, gathered herself, took three or four paces, jumped a fence, then settled into a thumping gallop across a stretch of land newly plowed for winter wheat. The furrows made the going hard, but the mare seemed not to notice.

Thorne, watching the race as he rode eastward in parallel to the young men, saw at last some quality in Adam above the stolid, worried demeanor that the young Virginian usually displayed. But what Thorne saw he was not sure he liked. Adam, he thought, would seek sensation to test himself, not to amuse himself, not to taste wickedness, but simply to put himself through the crucible of his own expectations. Adam, he thought, might very well kill himself to prove that he was a good man.

But not now. Now he was humiliating a trio of Jeb Stuart's vaunted horsemen. The chase across the plowed field had widened the gap between Adam and his pursuers, so once again he slowed down and the three rebels, seeing the deliberate curbing, became even more determined to catch their mocking enemy. They could see his horse was tired and whitened by sweat and they believed that another half mile would surely bring it to a panting stop and so they raked back with sharp spurs and whooped their hunting call.

Adam slowed even more. Then, picking his path, he suddenly kicked his heels and put the mare toward a wider stream that meandered through steeply cut banks. Rushes fringed the stream, disguising where the banks ended and the stream began, but Adam, who had ridden since the day he could first straddle a pony, showed no hesitation. He did not ride hard at the wide stream, but instead let the mare look at it, pick her own pace, and then he touched her flanks to let her know what was expected of her. To Thorne, watching from afar, it seemed as if the mare was going far too slowly to clear the water, but suddenly she gathered herself and soared effortlessly across the wide run. Adam let her run out her jump on the far bank, then he turned her round and stopped to watch his pursuers.

Two of the rebels swerved aside rather than attempt the water jump. The third man, braver than his companions, kicked back his heels and attempted the jump at a gallop. His horse took off from the same spot where Adam's mare had started her jump, but the rebel's beast crashed down short to plunge into a stiff stand of reeds. The horse's front legs folded and its shoulder thumped with bone-cracking force into the hidden bank. The rider was thrown clear, sprawling in the stream and cursing as his injured horse struggled to its feet. The beast stumbled again, then screamed from the pain of its broken shoulder.

Adam touched the brim of his hat in ironic salute, then turned away. Neither of the two surviving horsemen bothered with their carbines, though the third man, splashing in the welter of mud and water being churned by his wounded horse, drew his revolver and prayed that the half dunking he had received had not soaked the powder loaded into the cylinder's chambers. He cocked the weapon, then cursed his loss. Southern cavalrymen provided their own horses, and a good horse was worth gold. His own horse was useless now, a thing in pain, a broken-shouldered gelding of no use to anyone. He grabbed the bridle and hauled the horse's head toward him. He looked into the beast's terrified eye for a heartbeat, then aimed and fired. The sound of the single shot faded across the warm countryside as the horse, a bullet in its brain, thrashed briefly, then died. "Son of a bitch," the rebel said, watching Adam ride calmly away, "son of a god damned bitch."

The train crept forward, jerking its couplings in a metallic rattle that concertinaed down the long line of cars, then it stopped again.

It was nighttime. The engine panted for a few moments, then went silent. A trail of moon-silvered woodsmoke trickled from its huge-bellied funnel to drift across dark fields and black woods. Far off in the night a yellow light showed where some soul was still awake, but otherwise the land was swallowed by blackness shot through with mooncast shadows. Starbuck rubbed the pane of glass by his elbow and peered out, but he could see nothing beyond a window glazed gold by the flickering light of the car's lamps and so he stood and edged his way through the sleeping bodies to the platform at the car's rear, from where he could keep a wary eye on the dozen boxcars that formed the train's tail and which held the men of his Special Battalion. If any of his men wanted to desert, then this stuttering nighttime journey gave them a prize opportunity, but the land either side of the stalled train seemed empty. He looked back up the car to see that Captain Dennison was awake and playing solitaire. His face was still not cured, but the sores had dried up and in a week or two there would be no trace of the croton oil's ravages.

It was three days since Starbuck had faced Dennison at the dueling ground, three days in which the Special Battalion had scrambled to prepare itself for this journey north, a journey that had already taken them as far as Catlett's Station, where they had disembarked from the first train and then marched five miles across country to Gainesville where they had waited until this train of the Manassas Gap Railroad had appeared. The cross-country march had saved the battalion from the chaos at Manassas where Confederate engineers were still trying to patch together the junction recaptured from the Yankees the previous month. "Consider yourself lucky," Holborrow had told Starbuck, "that they're sending you by train." The truth, Starbuck knew, was that the authorities did not believe the battalion would survive the long march north. They reckoned the men would either straggle disastrously or else desert in droves, and so the battalion was being carried in comparative luxury to where they must fight. North to Manassas, west now across the Blue Ridge Mountains, and in the morning they would face a two-day march north along the Valley Turnpike to Winchester, which had become Lee's depot for the campaign across the Potomac.

Dennison scooped the cards up, yawned, then shuffled them with practiced fingers. Starbuck, unseen, watched him. Dennison, he had discovered, had been raised by an uncle who had punished the boy because his parents had died impoverished. The result was a vast pride in Dennison, but that knowledge had not increased Starbuck's sympathy for the Captain. Dennison was an enemy pure and simple. He had been humbled by Starbuck and he would choose to take his revenge when he could. Probably, Starbuck reflected, in battle, and the thought of facing Yankee shells and bullets immediately made Starbuck shudder. The cowardice was debilitating him, sapping his confidence.

The locomotive suddenly roared. The firebox was momentarily opened so that the furnace glare blazed across the fields, then the light snapped off as the train crashed and juddered forward. Matthew Potter swayed down the crowded car and pushed open the door. "I don't think," he said, "that we've traveled faster than ten miles an hour since we left Richmond. Not once."

"It's the rails," Starbuck said. "Old, misaligned, half-loose iron rails." He spat into the darkness. "And you can bet the Yankees ain't coming toward us on broken-down rails."

Potter laughed, then offered Starbuck a lit cigar. "Do I hear an echo of Northern superiority?"

"They can build railroads up there, that's for sure. We just have to pray they don't start making soldiers half as good as ours." Starbuck drew on the cigar. "I thought you were sleeping."

"Can't," Potter said. "It must be the effect of sobriety." He half smiled. He had not taken a drop of drink in three days. "Can't say as how I feel any better," he said, "but I guess I've felt worse."

131

"Your wife's all right?" Starbuck asked.

"She seemed so, thanks to you," Potter said. Starbuck had inveigled Delaney into paying the Potters' arrears of rent, then he had arranged for Martha Potter to stay with Julia Gordon's parents in Richmond. Julia herself now lived at the Chimborazo Hospital where she was a nurse and Starbuck had only seen her for a few moments, but those moments had been enough to confuse him. Julia's grave intelligence made him feel shallow, gauche, and tongue-tied, and he wondered why he could summon the courage to cross a rain-soaked cornfield into the maws of Yankee guns, but could not raise the nerve to tell Julia he was besotted by her. "You're looking miserable, Major," Potter said.

"Martha will be happy enough with the Gordons," Starbuck said, ignoring the Lieutenant's comment. "The mother can be overpowering, but the Reverend Gordon is a decent man."

"But if she stays too long in that house," Potter said grimly, "I'll find myself married to a born-again Christian."

"Is that so bad?"

"Hell, it ain't exactly the quality that attracted me to Martha," Potter said with his lopsided grin. He leaned on the platform's balustrade and stared at the passing countryside. Small red sparks whirled in the locomotive's smoke trail, some sinking to the ground to lie like fallen fireflies that vanished behind as the train labored up the eastern flank of the Blue Ridge. "Poor Martha," Potter said softly.

"Why?" Starbuck asked. "She's got what she wanted, ain't she? Got a husband, got away from home."

"She got me, Major, she got me. Life's short straw." Potter shrugged. Much of the Lieutenant's charm, Starbuck had discovered, lay in just such frank admissions of unworthiness. His good looks and bad ways attracted women's compassion like moths to a candle flame, and Starbuck had watched, amazed, as both Sally and Julia had made a fuss over him. But it was not just women who tried to protect Potter, even men seemed taken by him. The Special Battalion was united in little except resentment, but they had combined in an extraordinary surge of protective affection for Matthew Potter. They were amused by his fallibility, envious, even, of a man who could spend three days drunk, and they had made the Georgian the battalion's unofficial mascot. Starbuck had thought the Lieutenant would prove a liability, but so far he was the best thing that had happened to the despised Yellowlegs, because Potter entertained by simply existing.

But they would need more than one charming rogue to unite them. Starbuck had done his best in the two days before this journey began. He had persuaded Colonel Holborrow to produce boots, ammunition, canteens, and even the battalion's arrears of pay. He had marched the men up and down the Brook Turnpike and had rewarded them with cider from Broome's Tavern after one particularly grueling march, though he doubted that either the reward or the experience would matter much when they joined Jackson's hard-marching troops. He had made them load their antiquated muskets with buck and ball, an antiquated charge of shot that fired a musket ball with a scatter of buckshot, then he had purloined two dozen of Camp Lee's shabbiest tents to use as a target. The first volley had riddled the tents' ridges with holes but left the lower canvas almost unmarked, and Starbuck had made the men inspect the tents. "The Yankees don't stand high as a ridge," he had told them. "You're shooting high. Aim at their balls, even their knees, but aim low." They had fired a second volley and this one had ripped the worn canvas at the right height. He could spare no more ammunition for such target practice, but just hoped the Yellowlegs remembered the lesson when the men in blue were advancing.

He had talked to the men, not telling them that they were being given a second chance, but saying instead that they were needed up north. "What happened to you at Malvern Hill," he said, "could have happened to anyone. Hell, it almost happened to me at the first battle." At Malvern Hill, he had learned, part of the battalion broke and ran after a Yankee shell had struck plumb on their Colonel's horse while he was leading them forward. The horse had been torn into bloody shreds that had blown back into the faces of the center companies, and that shock introduction to war had been enough to scare a handful of men into full retreat. The others, thinking they were being ambushed, followed. They were not the first battalion to inexplicably break into flight, but it was their misfortune to do it a long way from where the real fighting was going on and in full view of a score of other battalions. The shame clung to them still and Starbuck knew that only battle could wash it away. "The time will come," he told the battalion, "when men will be proud to say they were a Yellowleg."

Starbuck had talked to the officers and then to the sergeants. The officers had been sullen and the sergeants uncooperative. "The men ain't ready for battle," Sergeant Case insisted.

"No one's ready," Starbuck had answered, "but we've still got to fight. If we wait till we're ready, Sergeant Case, the Yankees will have conquered us."

"Ain't conquered us yet," Case answered, "and from what I hear, sir," he managed to invest the honorific with

134

a dripping scorn, "we're the ones doing the conquering. Just ain't proper to take these poor boys off to a war they ain't ready to fight."

"I thought you were supposed to have got them ready," Starbuck said, unwisely letting himself be drawn into the argument.

"We're doing our job, sir," Case said, carefully enrolling the other sergeants onto his side of the argument, "but as any regular soldier will tell you, sir, a good sergeant's work can be undone in a minute by a glory-boy." He offered Starbuck a feral grin. "Glory-boy, sir. Young officer wanting to be famous, sir, and expecting the lads to die for his fame. Bloody shame, sir."

"We go tomorrow," Starbuck had said, ignoring Case. "The men will cook three days of rations and draw ammunition tonight." He had walked away, ignoring Case's snort of derision. Starbuck knew he had handled the confrontation badly. Another enemy, he thought wearily, another damned enemy.

"So what's happening?" Potter now asked as the train swayed up the incline.

"Wish I knew."

"But we're going to fight?"

"I reckon."

"But we don't know where."

Starbuck shook his head. "Get to Winchester and fetch new orders. That's what I'm told."

Potter drew on his cigar. "You reckon the men are ready to fight?" he asked.

"Do you?" Starbuck turned the question back.

"No."

"Nor me," Starbuck admitted. "But if we'd waited all winter they wouldn't be any more ready. It ain't their training that's wrong, it's their morale."

135

"Shoot Sergeant Case, that'll cheer them up," Potter suggested.

"Give them a battle," Starbuck said. "Give them a victory." Though how he was to do that with his present officers and sergeants, he did not know. Even to get the men as far as a battlefield, Starbuck thought, would be some kind of miracle. "You were at Shiloh, right?" he asked Potter.

"I was," Potter said, "but I have to confess it was mostly a blur. I wasn't exactly drunk, but sober don't describe it either. But I do remember an exhilaration, which is odd, don't you think? But George Washington said the same, do you remember? When he wrote how he was elated by the sound of bullets? Is it, you think, because we seek sensation? Like being a gambler?"

"I reckon I've wagered enough," Starbuck said grimly.

"Ah," Potter said, understanding. "I only had the one battle."

"Manassas twice," Starbuck said bleakly, "God knows how many times in the defense of Richmond, Leesburg, the fight at Cedar Mountain. Some brawl in the rain a few days back," he shrugged. "Enough."

"But more to come," Potter said.

"Yes." Starbuck spat a shred of tobacco under the train wheels. "And still there are some sons of bitches who think I can't be trusted because I'm a Yankee."

"So why are you fighting for the South?" Potter asked.

"That, Potter," Starbuck said, "is a question I don't need to answer."

The two men fell silent as the train wheels screeched on a curve. The stink of a hot axle-box's grease soured the woodsmoke aroma of the locomotive. They had climbed high enough now for the eastern land to lie revealed beneath the moon. A scatter of tiny lights showed faraway villages or farms, while the livid glow of small grass fires betrayed the double-curving path the train had followed up the gentle slope. "You ever done any skirmishing?" Starbuck asked suddenly.

"No."

"Reckon you could handle it?" Starbuck asked.

Potter, faced with a serious question, seemed nonplussed. "Why me?" he finally asked.

"Because the captain in charge of skirmishers has to be an independent son of a bitch who ain't afraid to take risks, that's why."

"A captain?" Potter asked.

"You heard me."

Potter drew on his cigar. "Sure," he said, "I guess."

"You get your own company," Starbuck said. "Forty men. You get the thirty rifles, too." He had been thinking about this all day and finally decided to take the plunge. None of the four existing captains struck him as men willing to take on responsibility, but Potter had an impudent nature that might fit him for the skirmish line. "You know what skirmishers do?"

"Crudely," Potter said.

"You go out ahead of the battalion. Spread out, use cover, and shoot the damn Yankee skirmishers. You fight those sons of bitches hard to push them back so you can start killing their main battle line before the rest of us arrive. Win the skirmisher's battle, Potter, and you're halfway to winning the real thing." He paused to suck smoke into his lungs. "We won't announce it till we've done a day's real marching. Let's see which men can take the pace and which can't. There's no point in putting weaklings into the skirmish line."

"I assume," Potter said, "that you were a skirmisher?"

137

"For a time, yes."

"Then I shall be honored."

"Damn the honor," Starbuck said. "Just stay sober and shoot straight."

"Yes, sir." Potter grinned. "Martha will be pleased to be a captain's wife."

"So don't disappoint her."

"I fear my darling Martha is doomed to disappointment. She believes it is possible, even essential, for all of us to be Sunday school good. Honesty is the best policy, she tells me, a stitch in time saves nine, never a borrower nor a lender be, be honest as the day is long, do unto others, and all that noble stuff, but I'm not sure any of that's possible if you have a thirst and a little imagination." He tossed the stub of his cigar off the platform. "Do you ever wish the war would last forever?"

"No."

"I do. Someone to feed me, to clothe me, to pick me up every time my wings fold. You know what I'm frightened of, Starbuck? I'm frightened of peace, when there'll be no army to be my refuge. There'll just be people expecting me to make a living. Now that's hard, that's hard, that's real cruel, that is. What the hell will I do?"

"Work," Starbuck said.

Potter laughed. "And what will you do, Major Starbuck?" he asked knowingly.

Hell if I know, Starbuck thought, hell if I know. "Work," he said grimly.

"Stern Major Starbuck," Potter said, but Starbuck had gone back into the car. Potter shook his head and watched the passing night and thought of all the trains clanking and banging and thrusting through this night carrying their loads of blue-coated troops to meet this train that rattled and screeched and shuddered its lonely way north.

138

All mad, he thought, all mad. As flies to wanton boys. He could have wept.

If there was one thing that terrified Belvedere Delaney it was the fear of being discovered and captured, for he knew only too well what his fate would be. The cell in a Richmond prison, the merciless questions, the trial before scornful men, and the vengeful crowd staring white-faced at the high scaffold where he would stand with a rope about his neck. He had heard that men pissed themselves when they were hung, and that if the executioner bungled the job, and the executioner usually did bungle it, then death was agonizingly slow. The onlookers would jeer while he pissed himself and as the rope bit into his neck. The very thought made his bowels feel liquid.

He was no hero. He had never thought of himself as a hero, but merely as a quick-witted, amoral, genial sort of fellow. It amused him to make money, just as it amused him to be generous. Every man thought Delaney a friend, and Delaney took care to keep it that way. He disliked rancor, reserving his enmities for his private thoughts, and if he did wish to hurt someone he would do it so secretly that the victim would never suspect that Delaney had engineered the misfortune. It was thus that Delaney had betrayed Starbuck during the North's spring campaign to capture Richmond, and Starbuck had come as close as a whisker to a Northern scaffold, and Delaney would have genuinely regretted that fate, but he had never once regretted his part in so nearly causing it. Delaney had been pleased when Starbuck returned, delighted even, for he liked Starbuck, but he would still betray him tomorrow if he thought there was profit in the treachery. Delaney did not feel badly about such a contradiction; he did not even perceive it as a contradiction, merely as fate. Some

Englishman had just written a book that was upsetting all the preachers because it implied that man, like all other species, had not originated in a divine moment of creation, but was muckily descended from God knows what primitive things with tails and claws and bloody teeth. Delaney could not recall the author's name, but one phrase from his book had lodged in Delaney's mind: the survival of the fittest. Well, Delaney would survive.

And survival was his own responsibility, which was why Belvedere Delaney took such exquisite care not to betray his own treachery. Colonel Thorne knew he was a Northern spy, and maybe Thorne had confided in one or two others, though Delaney had asked him not to, but other than Thorne the only human being who knew Delaney's true loyalty was his manservant, George. Delaney was punctilious in describing George as a manservant, he never called him a slave, though he was one, and he treated George with a grave courtesy. "We make each other comfortable," Delaney liked to say, and George, hearing the description, would concur with a smile. When visitors came to Delaney's exquisite apartment on Richmond's Grace Street the servant would behave like any other, though when Delaney and George were alone it seemed they were more like companions than master and slave, and some shrewd folk had scented that closeness and were amused by it. It was simply another part of Delaney's eccentricities and they supposed that master and slave would grow old together and that, if Delaney died first, George would inherit much of his master's wealth along with his own freedom. George had even taken Delaney as his surname.

On the occasions when Delaney had cause to send news to Thorne it had always been George who took the risks. It was George who carried the messages to the man in

Richmond who passed them on northward, but George could not carry the messages now. George was as uncomfortable as his master at being among the rebel army, and George had no skills that could take him through a soldier's picket line. George could dress a salad, roast a duck, or whip up an exquisite custard. He could reduce a sauce to perfection, had a nose for fine wine, and could play with equal facility upon a flute or violin. He could take a coat made at Richmond's finest tailors and, with a few hours' work, so remake it that a man would swear it came from Paris or London. George had a connoisseur's eye for fine porcelain and many a time he had returned to Delaney's apartment with news of a fine piece of Meissen or Limoges being sold by a family impoverished by the war and which would fill a gap in his master's collection, but George Delaney was no man for hiding in thickets like a sharpshooter or riding across country like one of Jeb Stuart's cavaliers.

And those, Delaney knew, were the skills he would need if he was ever to send any useful intelligence to Thorne. Weeks before, when Thorne had despaired of the North's ability to spy on its foe and had demanded that Delaney somehow inveigle himself into Lee's headquarters, Delaney had foreseen the problem. George lacked the skills to carry the messages, while Delaney lacked both the skills and the nerve, and so Delaney had suggested that Adam Faulconer should be the courier, yet even Delaney had not yet devised any means of actually contacting Adam. It was all so very frustrating.

As Delaney had journeyed north he had not let the problem worry him. He very much doubted whether he would discover any intelligence worth passing on to Thorne; indeed the whole expedition, to both Delaney and to George, was a desperate inconvenience, but

Delaney knew he needed to show willingness if he was ever to garner the rewards of his secret allegiance, and so the lawyer had resigned himself to a few weeks of discomfort after which he could return home, soak in a hot bath, sip cognac, and smoke one of his carefully hoarded French cigarettes before sending a message to Thorne in the old safe manner. That message would regret his silence of the past few weeks and explain that he had discovered nothing worth passing along.

Only now he had discovered something. Indeed, within minutes of arriving at Lee's headquarters, Delaney knew he held the fate of North and South in his hand. Damn it, but Thorne had been right all along. There was a place in Lee's headquarters for a spy, and Delaney was that spy, and Delaney now knew everything that Robert Lee planned and Delaney might as well have been on the far side of the moon for all the ability either he or George possessed to send that information to the Northern army.

Delaney had caught up with Lee's men at Frederick, a fine town that lay among wide Maryland fields. Nine streets ran east and west, six north and south, a concentration sufficient to persuade the inhabitants that their town should properly be called Frederick City, a name that was proudly painted above the depot of the spur line that ran north from the Baltimore and Ohio Railroad. The spur had carried the region's fat harvest of wheat and oats east to Baltimore and south to Washington, leaving only the corn waiting for harvest, though now much of that crop had been stripped by hungry rebels. "I'd rather find shoes than corn," Colonel Chilton said querulously. Chilton was a Virginian and, like any senior officer who had been stationed in Richmond, was well known to Delaney. Chilton, a fussy man in his middle forties, was now Lee's chief of staff, a position he had gained through his punctilious diligence rather than from any flair for soldiering. "So Richmond sends us a lawyer instead of shoes," he greeted Delaney's arrival.

"Alas," Delaney said, spreading his hands. "I would it were otherwise. How are you, sir?"

"Well enough, I suppose, considering the heat," Chilton said grudgingly, "and you, Delaney? Never expected to see a fellow like you in the field."

Delaney took off his hat, ducked into Chilton's tent, and accepted the offer of a chair. The shade of the canvas offered small respite from the heat wave that had made his journey a hell of dust and sweat. "I'm well," he answered and then, asked to explain his presence, launched himself into his well-rehearsed rigmarole about the War Department being concerned about the legal repercussions of actions that, if undertaken on Confederate soil, might be considered felonious, but that, done to the enemy, fell into an unknown category. "It is *terra incognita*, as we lawyers would say," Delaney finished lamely. He fanned his face with his hat brim. "You wouldn't, I suppose, have any lemonade?"

"Water in the jug," Chilton gestured at a battered enamel pot, "sweet enough to drink without boiling. Not like Mexico!" Chilton liked to remind people that he had served in that victorious war. "And I can assure you, Delaney, that this headquarters knows quite well how to treat enemy civilians. We're not barbarians, despite what those damned newspapers in the North say of us. Carter!" he shouted toward an adjacent tent. "Bring me Order One-ninety-one."

A sweating clerk with ink-stained hands came to the tent with the required order, which Chilton scanned quickly, then thrust into Delaney's hands. "There, read it for yourself," the Chief of Staff said. "I'll be back in a few moments."

Delaney, left alone in the tent, almost did not bother to read beyond the first paragraph of the order, which was headed "Special Orders, No. 191. Hdqrs. Army of Northern Virginia. September 9, 1862." In pencil, next to the heading, a clerk had written "Gen. D. H. Hill." The first paragraph, which Delaney idly scanned, was a prohibition against soldiers going into the town of Frederick without written permission from their divisional commander. A provost guard was stationed in the town to enforce the order, which was designed to allay the inhabitants' fears about being overrun and looted by a rapacious horde of half-starving, ill-dressed soldiers. The paragraph entirely met the manufactured concerns that justified Delaney's presence in the army. "And quite right, too," Delaney said to no one in particular, though in truth he would not have cared if the soldiery had dismantled Frederick City shingle by shingle.

He poured himself a mug of warm water, drank, grimaced at the taste, then, for lack of anything else to read, went back to the order. The second paragraph arranged that local farm vehicles be commandeered to transport the army's sick to Winchester. "Poor bastards," Delaney said, trying to imagine the rigors of a fever-racked journey in a dung-stinking farm wagon. He fanned himself with the order, wondering where in hell Chilton had vanished. He leaned forward to look out of the tent and saw George standing stiffly beside the horses, but no sign of Chilton.

He leaned back and read paragraph three. "The army will resume its march tomorrow," the paragraph began, and suddenly Delaney went chill as his eyes scanned the rest of the closely written page. The order might have begun with commonplace arrangements for policing the army and providing transport for its wounded, but it ended with a complete description of everything Robert Lee planned to do in the next few days. Everything. Every destination of every division in all the army.

"Sweet Jesus," Delaney said, and was overcome by a rush of terror as he thought what would follow his capture. One part of him wanted to thrust the order away and pretend he had never seen it, while another yearned after the glory that would surely be his if he could just smuggle this paper across the lines.

General Jackson will recross the river and, by Friday morning, take possession of the Baltimore and Ohio Railroad. He would occupy Martinsburg and cut off the road by which the Federal garrison at Harper's Ferry might retreat.

General Longstreet was ordered to advance to Boonsborough, wherever in hell that might be. General McLaws would follow Longstreet, but then branch off to help capture Harper's Ferry. General Walker was to cooperate with Jackson and McLaws by cutting off another road to Harper's Ferry, and once that Northern garrison was taken, the three generals were to join the rest of the army at Boonsborough or Hagerstown. Hagerstown? Delaney's geography was shaky, but he was fairly certain Hagerstown was a Maryland town close to the Pennsylvania border while Harper's Ferry was in Virginia! Which surely meant one part of Lee's army was going north, the other south, and so leaving the two parts vulnerable to separate attacks.

Delaney's hands felt almost nerveless. The paper fluttered. He closed his eyes. Maybe, he told himself, he did not understand these things. He was no soldier. Perhaps it made sense to split an army? But it wasn't his responsibility to decide if it made sense, but merely to send this news to the Northern army. Copy it, you fool, he told himself, but just as he opened his eyes to search Chilton's table for a pen or pencil, he heard footsteps outside the tent.

"Delaney!" a cheerful voice called.

Delaney ducked out of the tent to see that Chilton had returned with General Lee himself. For a moment the usually suave Delaney was lost in confusion. The order was still in his hand, and that flustered him, then he remembered he had been given it by Chilton and so no guilt could be attached to its possession. "Good to see you, General," Delaney finally managed to greet Lee.

"You'll forgive me if I don't shake hands?" Lee said, holding up his splinted and bandaged hands as explanation. "I had an altercation with Traveller. Well on the mend, now. And the other good news is that McClellan is back in command of the Federals."

"I heard as much," Delaney acknowledged.

"Which means our foes will dawdle," Lee said with satisfaction. "McClellan is a man of undoubted virtues, but decisionmaking is not one of them. Chilton tells me you're here to make sure we behave ourselves?"

Delaney smiled. "I'm truly here, General, because I wanted to see some action." He told the lie smoothly. "Otherwise," he continued, brushing his gray coat, "it would seem to me that this uniform is not properly earned."

Lee returned the smile. "Witness your action, Delaney, by all means, but don't get too close to McClellan's men, for I should be sorry to lose you. You'll dine tonight?" He turned as the clerk who had brought the copy of Order 191 to Chilton's tent reappeared with a sheaf of envelopes that he hesitantly held toward Colonel Chilton. "That's the order?" Lee asked Chilton.

"Seven copies," the clerk confirmed, "and Colonel

Chilton's original is in that gentleman's possession," he indicated Delaney, who guiltily flourished the original copy.

"Eight copies in all?" Lee frowned and took the envelopes from the clerk and, as swiftly as his awkward bandages allowed, leafed through them to read the addressees' names. "Do we need one for Daniel Hill?" Lee asked, flourishing the empty envelope addressed to General D. H. Hill that was evidently waiting for the original copy of the order in Delaney's hand. "Jackson will surely copy Hill the relevant parts?" Lee said.

"Best to be sure, General," Chilton said soothingly, retrieving the envelopes from the General and the single copy from Delaney. He folded the order and slipped it inside the envelope.

"You know best," Lee said. "So, Delaney, what news from Richmond?"

Delaney retailed some government gossip while Chilton placed the last copy of Order 191 in General Hill's envelope, which he laid with the others at the edge of a table just inside his tent. Lee, in affable mood, was telling Delaney his hopes for the next few days. "I'd have liked to march north into Pennsylvania, but for some reason the Federals have left their garrison in Harper's Ferry. That's a nuisance. It means we have to snap them up before we march north, but the delay can't be long and I doubt McClellan will summon the nerve to interfere. And once we've cleared Harper's Ferry we'll be free to make a nuisance of ourselves. We'll cut some Pennsylvania rail roads, Delaney, while McClellan makes up his mind what to do about us. In the end he'll have to fight and when he does I pray we can so mangle him that Lincoln will sue for peace. There's no other point in coming north, except to make peace." The General made this last pronouncement gravely for, like many other Southerners, he worried about the propriety of invading the United States. The legitimacy of the Confederacy's war depended on being the aggrieved party. They proclaimed that they merely defended their land against an external aggressor, and many men questioned their right to carry that defense outside their border.

Lee stayed a moment or two longer with Delaney, then turned away. "Colonel Chilton? A word?"

Chilton had been summoning the dispatch riders, but now followed Lee across to the General's tent. Delaney was again left alone and the bowel-loosening terror almost swamped him as he looked at the pile of orders awaiting dispatch. General Hill's envelope was uppermost on the pile. Dear God, Delaney thought, but dare he do it? And if he did, how would he ever send the stolen order across the lines? His hand was shaking, then an idea struck him and he ducked into Chilton's tent and sorted through the piles of paper on the trestle desk. He found a copy of Lee's proclamation to the people of Maryland and that, he reckoned, would have to serve his purpose. He folded the proclamation twice, hesitated, looked into the innocent sunlight, then snatched up the envelope with Hill's name. It was still unsealed. He took out the order, inserted the proclamation, then pushed the stolen paper deep into a pocket of his jacket. His heart was thumping terribly as he placed the still unsealed envelope back on the pile and then stepped out into the sunlight.

"You look feverish, Delaney," Chilton said, returning to his tent.

"It will pass, I'm sure." Delaney sounded weak. He was amazed he could even stand upright. He thought of the gallows' raw pine beams oozing turpentine and dangling with a noose of rough-haired hemp. "The heat of the journey," he explained, "brought on a stomach fever, nothing else."

"Tell your man to add your baggage to ours. I'll give you a tent, then get some rest. I'll send you some vitriol for your stomach if it's still troubling you. You're dining tonight with us?" Chilton spoke about these domestic arrangements as he gummed a wafer over the unsealed envelope's flap. He had not looked inside the envelope and so had not detected Delaney's substitution. "Signatures, gentlemen," he reminded the junior officers who would now carry the orders to their destinations. "Make sure they're all signed for. On your way, now!"

The staff officers rode away. Delaney wondered if Hill would think it odd to receive Lee's proclamation, for surely he would already have received his own copy of the document that tried to justify the South's invasion of the North. "Our army has come among you," the proclamation said, "and is prepared to assist you with the power of its arms in regaining the rights of which you have been despoiled." But Delaney, if he was not caught, and if he could just devise a way of reaching Thorne or Adam Faulconer, would despoil the South of its victory. There would be no peace, no truce, no Southern triumph; just Northern victory, complete, crushing, and implacable.

If only Delaney knew how to achieve it.

STARBUCK NEVER DID LEARN the Colonel's name. He was a tall, wispy-haired man in his late fifties who was plainly overwhelmed by the responsibilities that had been thrust on him. "The town," he told Starbuck, "isn't fit to be a depot. Isn't fit, you hear me? The Yankees have been here more than once and what they didn't steal our own skulkers took. You need boots?"

"No."

"You can't have any. General Lee demands boots. What boots?" He gestured about his cluttered office that had once been a dry goods store as if to demonstrate the obvious absence of any footwear. "You don't need any?" The Colonel suddenly understood Starbuck's reply.

"No, sir."

"Do you have any to spare?" the Colonel asked eagerly.

"Not a pair, sir. But I do need axes, tents, wagons. Especially a wagon." The battalion's only transport was a handcart that had proved a brute on the short marches the Yellowlegs had so far completed. The cart carried the precious rifles and as much spare ammunition as could be piled on top, but Starbuck doubted whether the rickety vehicle would last another ten miles.

"No good asking me for wagons," the Colonel said. "You can try commandeering from the local farms, but I doubt you'll have any luck. Too many troops have been through this place. They've stripped it bare." The Colonel was in charge of the town of Winchester, which lay at the northern end of the Shenandoah Valley and was now the supply base for Lee's army across the Potomac. Starbuck's battalion had abandoned its train at Strasburg and marched north through a glorious summer dawn. Now, as the sun's heat grew stifling, the exhausted men waited in Winchester's main street as Starbuck reported for his orders. "I don't have any orders," the Colonel said as he finished searching among his disordered papers. "None for you, anyway. Who do you say you are?"

"Starbuck, sir, Special Battalion."

"Special?" the Colonel, who had introduced himself to Starbuck, but so quickly that Starbuck had never caught his name, sounded surprised. "Special," he said again in a puzzled tone, then he remembered. "You're the Yellowlegs!" He shuddered slightly, as though Starbuck might be contagious. "Then I do have orders for you, indeed I do. But aren't you called Maitland?"

"Starbuck, sir."

"Orders are addressed to Maitland," the Colonel said, feverishly searching again among the papers on the shop's counter. All the doors and windows were propped open, but the ventilation scarcely alleviated the day's oppressive heat. The Colonel was sweating as he searched. "Is Maitland coming?" he asked.

"I replaced Maitland," Starbuck said patiently.

"Someone has to get the short straw, I suppose," the Colonel said. "Can't say I envy you. It's bad enough taking willing men to war, let alone a bunch of skulkers. How many did you lose between here and Strasburg?"

"Not one."

"No?" The Colonel drew the word out to show his incredulity.

"I marched at the back," Starbuck said, and touched the Adams revolver at his side.

"Quite right, quite right," the Colonel said and went back to his search.

Starbuck had shaded the truth. Some men had dropped out, and those men he had collected and forced back onto the road, though by the time they had finished the short march the stragglers were near beat and had feet with blisters so bad that blood was seeping out of the ill-sewn shoes they had been issued at Camp Lee. Most of the shoes, Starbuck guessed, would not last a week, which meant they would need to take some off the Yankees. Other men had fallen out of the column with diarrhea, yet despite their sickness and frail feet, all the men were now present in Winchester, but still the march had been a bad augury. The battalion was simply unfit.

"You know what's happening here?" the Colonel asked.

"No, sir."

"We're about to throttle the Yankees out of Harper's Ferry. After that, God only knows. You need ammunition?"

"Yes, sir."

"We do have that, but no wagons." The Colonel scribbled on a chit of paper that he gave to Starbuck. "Authorization to draw cartridges. You'll find them stored in a barn at the top end of Main Street, but if you ain't got a wagon, Major, you'll be hard put to carry a proper supply, and I can't find you a wagon." He gave Starbuck another piece of paper. "That's a War Department form entitling a civilian to be paid for any wagon you commandeer, but I doubt you'll find one. Too many other regiments have plowed this town. Ah, and you should go to the Taylor Hotel, Major."

"Taylor Hotel?"

"Down the street, just a few steps. Place with a big porch and not much paint. Not much left to eat there either, but it's still the most comfortable place in town. Your fellow's waiting there."

Starbuck, completely confused, shook his head. "My fellow?"

"Officer! Didn't you know? Fellow called Captain Tumlin. A good one, too! First-class fellow. Got captured at New Orleans and has been in Yankee jails ever since, but he managed to escape and reach our lines. Capital fellow! Richmond assigned him to your battalion for the duration of the campaign, so I kept him here. Seemed pointless to send him all the way to Richmond while you were coming here. He's even got some men for you! Skulkers and coffee-chasers, of course, every last one of them, but you must be used to that kind of scum. I shall be sorry to lose Billy Tumlin. He's an amusing fellow, capital company. Here we are." He found Starbuck's orders and tossed them up the counter. "I hope to God you're not staying in the town," he added anxiously. "I'm hard put to feed the men I've got without feeding more."

Starbuck slit open the orders and scanned them. He smiled, cracking the sweaty dust that was caked onto his face. "Good," he said, then, in response to the Colonel's raised eyebrow, explained his pleasure. "We're assigned to Swynyard's Brigade."

The name meant nothing to the Colonel. "You're leaving today, I trust?" the Colonel inquired anxiously.

"We're either to wait here or at Charlestown, whichever's convenient, for more orders."

"You'll want to be in Charlestown then," the Colonel said emphatically. "That's a very pleasant town. A long day's march from here, but you'll have to make it sooner or later."

"We will?"

"You will if you're going north. Charlestown is just this side of Harper's Ferry. Get there early, Major, and you'll

153

have first pick of the bivouacs before the rest of the army arrives. And first pick of the girls. If there are any girls left, of course, which there might not be. Place has been picked over by both sides, but it's still very fair, very fair."

"Any Yankees there?"

The Colonel pursed his lips and shrugged. "Maybe a few. Doubtless the Harper's Ferry garrison scavenge for corn thereabouts."

In other words, Starbuck thought, the very pleasant Charlestown was Yankee-haunted, stripped clean of supplies, and half deserted. "We'll march this morning," Starbuck said, much to the Colonel's relief. "You can give us someone to show us the way out of town?"

"No need, my dear fellow. Straight up the road. Straight up. Can't miss your way."

Starbuck pocketed the orders and went out to the sidewalk and called Potter to him. "You're a rogue, Potter."

"Yes, sir."

"So be a rogue now and find a wagon. Any wagon. You're allowed to commandeer civilian vehicles, but you must sign for it so the owner can get reimbursement from Richmond, understand?"

"Yes, sir."

"Then you collect ammunition and follow us north. Take a dozen of your men to load and haul." He gave Potter the two pieces of paper. "Lucifer!"

"Major?" The boy ran up to Starbuck.

"Captain Potter is on a looting expedition, and you're good at that so you can help him. I want a wagon, anything on wheels that we can fill with cartridges. If the townspeople see soldiers combing the streets they'll hide anything valuable, but they won't notice you, so go and spy on them."

"Yes, Major," Lucifer grinned and ran off.

"Dennison!" Starbuck shouted. Dennison was the

154

senior captain and thus, whether Starbuck liked it or not, the second in command of the battalion. "Get 'em up, get 'em moving," Starbuck said. "Straight up the road. Just keep going and I'll catch up with you." There was no point in waiting. The men might be tired, but the more they marched the fitter they would be, and the longer they rested in Winchester the more reluctant they would ever be to leave the town's dubious comforts.

"You staying to enjoy the town, Major?" Dennison asked cattily.

"I'm staying to collect some more men. I'll be ten minutes behind you. Now move."

The men climbed reluctantly to their feet. It was promising to be another day of terrible heat, no day for a march, but Starbuck had no intention of traveling all day. He planned to take a few miles off the journey, then find a field in which the battalion could have an afternoon of rest, then finish the journey in the next day's cool dawn.

He walked down the sidewalk and found the Taylor Hotel, which proved to be three impressive storys of pillared balconies dominating the street. Captain Tumlin's room was on the third floor and, because the Captain was nowhere to be found in the public rooms, Starbuck climbed the wooden stairs and knocked on the room's door.

"Go away," a voice said. Starbuck turned the handle and found the door locked. "And don't come back!" the voice added.

"Tumlin!"

"Go away!" the man called. "I'm at my prayers."

A woman giggled. "Tumlin!" Starbuck shouted again.

"I'll meet you downstairs. Give me a half hour!" Tumlin answered.

The door's lock splintered at a simple push and Starbuck stepped inside to see a plump, sweating man rolling out of a disordered bed to reach for his holstered revolver. The man checked as he saw Starbuck's uniform. "Who the hell are you?" Tumlin asked.

"Your new commanding officer, Billy," Starbuck said, then tipped his hat to the girl who was clawing the grubby sheet to cover her breasts. She was a pretty black girl with a fine head of curls and sad, dark eyes. "Morning, ma'am," Starbuck said, "sure is a hot one."

"You're who?" Billy Blythe asked as he settled back under the sheet.

"Your new commanding officer, Billy," Starbuck said again. He walked to the louvered doors that opened onto the hotel's top balcony and pushed them open. From the balcony he could see the battalion forming its ranks, ready to march away, but the job was being done with pathetic slowness. Dozens of men were resting in the shade of verandahs and the sergeants were doing nothing to stir them. "Sergeant Case!" Starbuck shouted. "Show me how a proper soldier gets a battalion moving. Snap to it! The name's Starbuck," he called over his shoulder to Tumlin, "Major Nathaniel Starbuck."

"Jesus," Billy Blythe said. "You the son of the Reverend Starbuck?"

"Sure am. That worry you?"

"Hell, no," Billy Blythe said. "Just seems strange, you being a Yankee and all."

"No stranger than a man being in bed on a fine morning when there are Yankees to be killed," Starbuck said cheerfully. The street beneath him was at last showing some signs of vigor, so he turned back into the room. "Now get the hell up, Billy. I hear you've got some men for me. Where are they?"

Billy Blythe flapped a hand. "In camp, Major."

"Then get your boots on, Billy, and let's go fetch them.

You know where I might find a wagon in this town?"

"Lucky if you can find a wheelbarrow," Tumlin said. "Hell, there ain't nothing here but bad soldiers and good women." He slapped the black girl's rump.

Starbuck saw some cigars on the washstand and helped himself to one. "You don't mind?"

"Hell, no, help yourself," Billy Blythe said. "There's a flint and steel on the mantel." He waited until Starbuck's back was turned, then swung himself out from under the yellowing bedsheet.

Starbuck turned. "Billy," he said reprovingly. "You go to bed dressed?" The pinkly naked Tumlin had a pouch belted round his stomach. "That's no way to treat a lady," Starbuck added.

"Just keeping it safe, Major," Tumlin said, scrambling into a pair of long underpants. He blushed, felt in the pouch, and took out two silver coins. "You'll forgive me, Major?" he asked and tossed the coins onto the bed. "Sorry about the interruption, honey."

The girl snatched the money as Starbuck lowered himself into a cane chair and put his dusty boots up on the washstand. "You were in a Yankee jail, I hear?" he asked Tumlin.

"Most of this year," Blythe said.

"They fed you well," Starbuck said as Tumlin buttoned a shirt round his plump belly, which was distended by the money pouch.

"I was four times this size when I got took," Blythe said.

"Where were you held?" Starbuck asked.

"Union, Massachusetts."

"Union?" Starbuck asked. "Where the hell's Union?"

"Out west," Blythe said. He had met Starbuck's father and knew the family came from Boston, so placing his mythical town of Union in the west of the state seemed a safe bet.

157

"In the Berkshires?" Starbuck asked.

"I guess," Blythe said, sitting on the bed to tug on his boots. "What are they? Hills? Not that we saw any hills, Major. Just big walls."

"So how many men have you got for me, Billy?"

"A dozen."

"Stragglers?"

"Lost sheep, Major," Blythe said, offering Starbuck a lazy grin, "just little lost sheep looking for a shepherd. Hell, I'm looking for a comb."

"Here," Starbuck saw the comb on the washstand and tossed it across the room. "So you escaped?"

Blythe winced as the comb caught in a tangle of his long hair. "Walked south, Major."

"Then you'll have good hard feet, Billy, all ready for some marching."

"And where the hell are we marching, Major?" Blythe asked.

"My guess," Starbuck said, "is Harper's Ferry. And once we've bagged the Yankees there, over the river and keep going north till the Yankees beg us to stop."

Blythe pulled on his gray coat. "Hell, Major," he grumbled, "you have one hell of a way of making yourself known to your officers."

"Coat's too small for you, Billy," Starbuck said with a grin. "When were you made a Captain?"

Blythe paused to think as he buckled on his revolver. "Last year, Major. November, I guess, why?"

"Because that makes you senior to my other captains, which means you're my second in command. If I'm killed, Billy, my heroes are all yours. You ready?"

Blythe collected his few belongings and stuffed them in a bag. "Ready enough," he said.

Starbuck stood, walked to the door, and tipped his hat

again to the girl. "Sorry to have disturbed you, ma'am. Come on, Billy. Let's go."

They caught up with the battalion three miles north of town. Starbuck marched the tired men another two miles, then swerved aside into a stretch of pastureland that edged a wood and a stream and had plainly been used many times before as a bivouac. The grass was stained where tents had stood too long, scorch marks showed where campfires had burned, while the margins of the woodland were nothing but ragged stumps where troops had cut their firewood. The railroad that led north from Winchester was a half mile away, its steel rails torn up and carried away by one side or the other while the turnpike that ran parallel to the ruined rail line had been deeply rutted by the marching and countermarching of the armies that had fought for possession of the Shenandoah Valley ever since the war's beginning. The pasture was a much-abused place, but it was still pleasant enough and just far enough from Winchester to deter any man who might have been tempted back to the town's taverns.

Captain Potter had no need of the taverns. He had brought the ammunition to the encampment, but after that he had somehow found himself a jug of whiskey and by late afternoon he was wildly drunk. Starbuck was drawing up lists of the new companies, which now numbered five. He had begun to choose men for Potter's skirmishing company and was writing their names when he became aware of a surge of raucous laughter. At first he thought it a good omen, maybe an upwelling of spirit among the resting men, but then Captain Dennison stooped under the crude cotton awning that served Starbuck as a tent. Dennison was picking his teeth with a wood splinter. "Nice desk, Major," he said.

"It serves," Starbuck said. He was using a tree stump as a crude writing desk.

"You might want to redo those lists," Dennison said with amusement, "'cos I reckon you just lost yourself a captain."

"Meaning what?"

"Potter boy's drunk. Drunk as a skunk. Hell, drunk as ten skunks." Dennison spat a shred of food. "Looks like he can't be trusted after all."

Starbuck swore, picked up his jacket and belt, and ducked outside.

Potter was playing the fool. A group of men who still had some energy after the day's marching had started a game of baseball and Potter had insisted on being allowed to take part. Now, swaying slightly, he faced the pitcher and kept demanding that the ball be thrown at perfect hitting height. "Groin height!" he shouted, and the fielders egged him on by pretending not to know what he meant. Potter unbuttoned his pants to expose himself. "That's the groin! There! See?"

The pitcher, hardly able to throw for laughing, tossed an underhand lob that went wide. Potter swung madly, staggered, and recovered. "Try it closer, closer." He paused, stooped to pick up his stone jug, and took a swig. He saw Starbuck as he lowered the jug. "Captain Ahab, sir!"

"Are you drunk?" Starbuck said when he was close to Potter.

Potter grinned, shrugged and thought about the question, but could not come up with anything witty. "I guess," he said.

"Button yourself, Captain."

Potter shook his head, not in refusal, but in perplexity. "Just a bit of horseplay, Captain Ahab."

"Button yourself," Starbuck said quietly.

"You're going all stern on me, ain't you? Just like my father—" Potter stopped abruptly as Starbuck hit him in the belly. The younger man folded over, retching just as he had when Starbuck had first found him in the Hells.

"Stand up straight," Starbuck said, kicking over the stone bottle, "and button yourself."

"Let him play!" a voice shouted sullenly. It was Sergeant Case. "Nothing wrong with a game," the Sergeant insisted. "Let him play." A few men muttered their support. Starbuck, they reckoned, was spoiling their day's one small moment of enjoyment.

"Good Sergeant Case," Potter said, cuffing spittle away from his chin. "My supplier of whiskey." He stooped to the fallen bottle, but Starbuck kicked it away before crossing to face Case.

"You gave Potter the whiskey?"

Case hesitated, then nodded. "Ain't against the law, Major."

"It's against my law," Starbuck said, "and you knew it."

Case rocked back and forward on his heels. He had drunk some of the whiskey himself, and maybe that gave him the courage to convert his hostility toward Starbuck into open defiance. He spat close to Starbuck's boots. "Your law?" he jeered. "What law is that, Major?"

"The rules of this battalion, Case."

"This battalion, Major," Case exploded in fury, "is the sorriest damn collection of bloody bastards ever put under a flag. This ain't a battalion, Major, it's a rabble of skulkers who weren't wanted in any proper regiment. This ain't a battalion, Major! This ain't nothing! We ain't got nothing. No wagons, no axes, no tents, no doctor, no nothing! We weren't sent here to fight, Major, but to get ourselves killed."

There were louder murmurs of agreement. Men who

had been resting had come to see the confrontation, so that nearly all of the battalion was now grouped around the makeshift playing diamond.

"A month ago," Starbuck raised his voice, "I was in a battalion that got raided by Yankees. They killed half our officers, burned our wagons, destroyed all our spare ammunition, but we still fought a week later and won. This battalion can do the same."

"The hell it can," Case said. His fellow sergeants had come to his support, a phalanx of tough, grim-faced men who stared with blank hatred at Starbuck. "The hell it can," Case said again. "It might be good for guarding prisoners, or fetching and carrying supplies, but it ain't any good for fighting."

Starbuck turned slowly, looking at the worried faces of the men. "I think they can fight, Sergeant." He turned all the way round to face Case again. "But can you?"

"I've been there," Case said curtly, "and I know what it takes for men to fight. Not this!" He waved a scornful hand at the battalion. "No proper officer would take this rabble to war."

Starbuck stepped closer to Case. "Do I take that to mean that you won't lead them into battle, Sergeant?"

Case sensed he might have gone too far, but he was unwilling to back down in the face of his supporters. "Lead them into battle?" He scoffed Starbuck by crudely imitating his Boston accent. "Sounds like a fine Yankee phrase to me, Major."

"I asked you a question, Case."

"I ain't afraid to fight!" Case blustered and, by refusing to answer the question, implicitly backed away from the confrontation.

Starbuck could have let Case off the hook, but chose not to. "I asked you a question," he said again.

"Hell," Case said, cornered, "these men ain't fit to fight!"

"They're fit enough," Starbuck said, "it's you that ain't fit." He could have left it there, but sheer devilment made him rack the tension higher. "Take your stripes off," he said.

Case, faced with losing his rank, accepted the showdown. "You take 'em, Major," he said, "if you can." His fellow sergeants greeted the defiance with hand-clapping.

Starbuck turned away and walked to the vacated pitcher's spot. From the very first he had worried about imposing his authority on this despised battalion, and he had never done it. He had assumed that if he led they would follow, not because he inspired them, but because men usually do what is expected of them. In time, he had hoped, battle would wipe out the regiment's past history and unite it in purpose, but instead the crisis had come now, which meant that the solution could not wait for battle, but would have to be imposed now. He would exhaust the formal route first, but he knew it was doomed even as he turned back to the group of sergeants who slowly ended their clapping as he stared at them. "Sergeant Webber? Cowper?" he said. "Arrest Case."

The two sergeants spat, but neither made any other movement.

"Captain Dennison?" Starbuck turned.

"Ain't my business," Dennison said. "Finish what you started, Starbuck, ain't that what you once told me?"

Starbuck nodded. "When I've finished here," he raised his voice, "every company will elect new sergeants. Case!" he snapped. "Bring me your coat."

Case, driven to mutiny, brazened out the moment. "Come and get it, Major."

There was a moment's silence as the men watched Starbuck; then he took off his coat and revolver. He was

163

apprehensive, though he took care not to show it. Case was a tall man, probably stronger than Starbuck, and probably no stranger to casual violence—any man who had survived fourteen years in a European army had to be tough—while Starbuck had been reared in the gentler world of respectable Boston, which eschewed violence as a means of resolving argument. Respectable Boston believed in reason leavened by Godliness, while Starbuck's career now depended on beating down a bullying thug who had probably not lost a fight in a dozen years, but he was also a thug who was more than slightly drunk and that, Starbuck reckoned, should help him. "The trouble with you, Case," he said as he walked slowly toward the taller man, "is that you've spent too long wearing a red coat. You ain't a fusilier now, you're a rebel, and if you don't like the way we do things then you ought to get the hell out of here and go back to Queen Victoria's petticoats. You probably ain't man enough to fight Yankees." He was hoping to provoke Case into a rushed attack, but the big man had the sense to hold his ground and let Starbuck come to him. Starbuck broke into a jog, then aimed a massive kick at Case's groin, but a heartbeat later he jarred his left foot forward to stop his forward momentum.

Case half turned away from the kick and flicked out a hard punch with his left hand, only Starbuck did not run onto the punch, but instead rammed his right boot forward into Case's knee. It was a brutally hard kick and Starbuck recoiled from it, safe out of Case's reach. Starbuck had hoped to do more damage, but the big man's quick left hand had stalled him.

Case stumbled as pain buckled his leg. The pain made him grimace, but he forced himself upright. "Yankee," he spat at Starbuck.

Starbuck knew this had to be quick. If the fight dragged

on then his authority would be abraded with every blow exchanged. Victory had to be swift and total, and that meant taking some punishment. Case's tactics were obvious. He intended to stand like a rock and let Starbuck come to him, and every time Starbuck was in range he would inflict pain until Starbuck could take no more. So take the pain, Starbuck told himself, and put the son of a bitch down.

He walked forward with his eyes on Case's hard eyes. He saw the right hand coming and half raised his left hand to block the blow, but his head still rang as the fist crashed home on the side of his skull. Starbuck kept going forward, forcing himself into the stink of Case's unwashed wool uniform and the stench of tobacco and whiskey on the big man's breath, and the big man smelled victory as he reached to grab Starbuck's hair and pulled his head down onto his left fist.

Then Case gagged, choked, and his eyes widened as he tried to breathe.

Starbuck had hit the Sergeant in the Adam's apple. He had rammed his right hand up and forward, knuckles outward, and as much by luck as judgment had slammed the blow under the Sergeant's jutting beard to land dead on the inviting target of Case's unnaturally long neck. It was a wicked blow, taught him long before by Captain Truslow, who knew every nasty trick in the devil's book.

Case was staggering now, his hands at his throat where a terrible pain was threatening to cut off his airway. Starbuck, his own head ringing from the Sergeant's blow, stepped back to watch the big man totter, then stepped forward again and gave Case's left knee another hard kick. The big man buckled. Starbuck waited again. He waited until Case was half down, then he brought his knee up into the man's face. Blood splashed out of the broken nose as Starbuck grabbed Case's hair and rammed his head back onto the knee. He let go of the greasy hair and this time Case dropped to all fours and Starbuck kicked him in the belly, then put his foot on Case's back and pushed him down into the grass. The breath rasped and rattled in Case's throat. He twitched as he tried to subdue the gagging pain, but nothing could stop the pitiful whimpering that sounded between each desperate attempt to breathe. Starbuck spat on him, then looked up at the other sergeants. "All of you," he said, "take your stripes off. Now!"

None dared oppose him, not with Case retching into the grass. His face had gone red, the breath was hoarse in his constricted throat, and his eyes were wide with terror. Starbuck turned away. "Captain Dennison!"

"Sir?" Dennison was white-faced, appalled.

"Get a knife, Captain," Starbuck said calmly, "and cut Case's stripes off."

Dennison obeyed while Starbuck retrieved his coat and revolver. "Anyone else here think they know better than me how to run this battalion?" he shouted at the men.

Someone began clapping. It was Caton Rothwell, and his applause spread among the many men who had hated their sergeants. Starbuck waved the clapping to silence, then looked at Captain Potter. "You come to me when you're sober, Potter," he said, then walked away. He felt that he must be shaking, but when he looked at his bruised right hand it seemed quite still. He ducked into his makeshift tent, then suddenly the tension flowed out of him and he shuddered like a man with fever.

Lucifer, without being asked, brought him a mug of coffee. "There's some of Captain Potter's whiskey in it," he told Starbuck. "I rescued it from the bottle." He stared at Starbuck's left ear that was throbbing painfully. "He hit you hard."

"I hit him harder."

"Man won't like you for it."

"He didn't like me anyway."

Lucifer watched Starbuck warily. "He'll be wanting you."

"Meaning?"

Lucifer shrugged and touched his Colt revolver that Starbuck had restored. "Meaning," the boy said, "you should take care of him properly."

"Let the Yankees do it," Starbuck said dismissively.

"Hell, they can't do nothing proper! You want me to do it?"

"I want you to get me supper," Starbuck said. His ear was hurting and he had work to do, even more work now that his new company lists had to be rewritten to accommodate the names of the newly chosen sergeants. Some of the old sergeants were reelected, and Starbuck suspected threats might have been used to ensure those choices, but Case's name was not on the list. The last company to report was E, the half-formed company of skirmishers, and Caton Rothwell brought that list written in clumsy letters on the back of a tobacco wrapper. Rothwell's own name was at the top of the page. Starbuck was seated outside his tent, close enough to a fire for the flames to illuminate the page that he first read and then handed to Billy Tumlin, who had come to share a late-night mug of coffee. "Good," Starbuck said to Rothwell when he saw Rothwell's name on the list. "Don't make the mistake I did."

"Which was what?" Rothwell asked.

"Being too easy on the men."

Rothwell looked surprised. "Hell, I don't reckon you're easy," he said. "Case don't, either."

"How is he?" Starbuck asked.

"He can walk in the morning."

"Make sure the son of a bitch does."

"Where are we going tomorrow?" Rothwell asked.

"North past Charlestown," Starbuck said.

"Past Charlestown?" Billy Blythe asked, accenting *past*. "I kind of hoped we'd find billets there."

"We're joining Old Jack's men to attack Harper's Ferry," Starbuck said, "and they won't be lollygagging in Charlestown, so nor will we. You want some coffee?" he asked Rothwell.

Rothwell hesitated, then nodded. "Kind of you, Major."

Starbuck shouted for Lucifer, then gestured Rothwell to sit. "When I first met you, Sergeant," he said, using Rothwell's new rank for the first time, "you told me that your wife was in trouble, which was why you walked away from your old regiment. What was the trouble?"

It was a blunt question and Rothwell met it with a hostile stare. "Ain't none of your business, Major," he finally said.

"It is my business if it happens again," Starbuck answered just as curtly. His curiosity was not prompted by prurience, but rather because he suspected that Rothwell could be a leader in the battalion and he needed reassurance about the man's dependability. "And it is if I need new officers, and Yankee bullets have a way of creating vacancies."

Rothwell considered Starbuck's words, then shrugged. "Won't happen again," he said grimly, and seemed content to leave it at that, but a moment later he spat into the fire. "Not unless the Yankees rape her again," he added bitterly.

Tumlin, sitting next to Starbuck, hissed in evident disapproval.

Starbuck, embarrassed by the answer, did not know what to say and so said nothing.

"A Southron did it," Rothwell said, "but he was riding

168

with the Northern cavalry." Now that he was launched on the story his reluctance to tell it had disappeared. He probed inside his top pocket to bring out a square of oilcloth that was tied with string. He carefully unknotted the string, then just as carefully unfolded the waterproof cloth to reveal another scrap of paper. He handled the paper as though it were a relic, which to him it was. "Bunch of Yankee cavalry raiders came to the farm, Major," he told Starbuck, "and left her this. The Southron took my Becky to the barn that day, but he was stopped. He burned the barn though, and the next week he came back and burned the house and took my Becky out to the orchard. Beat her bloody." There were glints in the corner of Rothwell's eyes. He sniffed and held the paper out to Starbuck. "This man," he said bleakly.

The paper was an official US government form, printed in Washington, that promised payment for supplies taken by US forces from Southern householders. The payment, which would be made at the war's end, was dependent on the family being able to prove that none of its members had carried arms against the US government. The paper, in brief, was a license for Northerners to steal whatever they liked, and this paper carried a penciled signature that Starbuck read aloud. "William Blythe," he read, "Captain, US Army."

Tumlin did not move, did not speak, did not even seem to breathe.

Starbuck carefully folded the form and handed it back to Rothwell. "I know about Blythe," he said.

"You do, Major?" Rothwell asked with surprise.

"I was with the Faulconer Legion when cavalry attacked us. Blythe trapped some of our officers in a tavern and shot them down like dogs. Women too. You say he's a Southerner?"

"Speaks like one."

Tumlin let out a long sigh. "Reckon there are bad apples in every basket," he said, and his voice was so shaken that Starbuck looked at him with surprise. Somehow Tumlin had not struck Starbuck as a man easily moved by tales of hardship and Starbuck reckoned it was to Tumlin's credit that he had taken Rothwell's story so hard. Tumlin sighed. "Reckon I wouldn't want to be Mister Blythe if you got your hands on him, Sergeant," he said.

"I reckon not," Rothwell said. He blinked. "Farm belonged to my father," he went on, "but he weren't there when this happened. He's going to rebuild, he says, but how, I don't know." He stared into the fire that whirled a stream of sparks into the air. "Nothing left there now," Rothwell said, "just ashes. And my Becky's real hurt. And the children are scared it'll happen again." He carefully retied the string, then put the package back in his pocket. "Kind of hard," he said to himself.

"And you were arrested," Starbuck asked, "for trying to be with her?"

Rothwell nodded. "My Major wouldn't give me furlough. Said no one gets furlough before the Yankees are beat, but hell, we'd just whipped the bastards at Manassas so I reckoned I'd take my own furlough. Ain't sorry I did, either." He swallowed the lukewarm coffee, then glanced at Starbuck. "You arresting Case?" he asked.

"He's already in a punishment battalion," Starbuck said, "what else can they do to him?"

"They can shoot the son of a bitch," Rothwell said.

"We'll let the Yankees do it," Starbuck said, "and save the government the price of a bullet."

Rothwell was unhappy. "I reckon he ain't a safe man to keep around, Major."

Starbuck agreed, but was unsure what else he could do.

If he was to have Case arrested then he would need to send the man under escort to Winchester and he could not spare an officer to lead such a party, nor the time to write up the paperwork for a court-martial. He could hardly have Case shot on his own authority, for he had invited the fight, and so the best course seemed to let things lie, but to tread warily.

"I'll keep an eye on him," Tumlin promised.

Rothwell stood. "Grateful for the coffee, Major."

Starbuck watched him walk away, then shook his head. "Poor man."

"Poor woman," Blythe said, then let out a long sigh. "I suspect that Mister Blythe will be long gone," he added.

"Maybe," Starbuck said. "But I was fond of one of the girls who died in that tavern and when this war is over, Billy, I might just go looking for Mister Blythe. Give me something to do in the piping time of peace. But for now, what the hell do I do with Potter?"

"Nothing," Blythe said.

"Nothing? Hell, I make him up to captain and he rewards me by getting blind drunk."

Blythe stretched out a cramped leg. Then he leaned forward and snatched a burning stick from the fire and used it to light a pair of cigars. He handed one to Starbuck. "I guess I'm going to have to tell you the truth, Major."

"What truth?"

Blythe waved his cigar toward the flickering camp fires. "These men here, they ain't an ordinary battalion any more than you're an ordinary major. They don't know much about you, but what they do know, they like. I don't say they like you, because they don't even know you, but they sure as hell are intrigued by you. You're a Yankee for a start, and you ain't inclined to follow the rules. You

171

make your own rules and you fight your own fights. They like that. They don't want you to be ordinary."

"What the hell has this got to do with Potter?" Starbuck interrupted.

"Because men going into battle," Blythe went on as though Starbuck had never spoken, "don't want their leaders to be ordinary. Men have to believe in something, Major, and when God chooses to stay in heaven they're forced to believe in their officers instead. In you," he prodded the cigar toward Starbuck, "and if you show you're just an ordinary officer then, hell, they'll lose their faith."

"Tumlin," Starbuck said, "you're babbling."

"No, sir, I am not. I'm telling you that an ordinary officer would fall back on army regulations. An ordinary officer would humiliate Potter and that, sir, would be a mistake. Hell, give Potter a scare, put the fear of God in the bastard, but don't bust him back to lieutenant. The men like him."

"Let him off?" Starbuck asked dubiously. "That's weakness."

"Hell, Major, no one thinks you're weak after what you did to Case. Besides, Potter did you real proud with the wagon."

"He did that, right enough." Or rather Lucifer had done the battalion proud for, on his exploration of Winchester's side streets, the boy had glimpsed a magnificent hearse parked inside a shed. The shed had been locked tight by the time Potter's detail arrived and the owner swore there was nothing inside but baled hay, but Potter had forced the lock and revealed the black-painted vehicle with its etched glass windows, velvet curtains, and high black plumes in their silver holders. He had filled the hearse with ammunition, then, lacking horses, his men had dragged the quaint vehicle northward. "He sure did us proud," Starbuck admitted again, then pulled on his cigar. In truth he did not want to punish Potter, but he feared to send the battalion a signal of lenience. "I'll give him hell," he said after a while, "but if the bastard does it again I'll break him down to cookboy. You want to go find the son of a bitch and send him to me?"

"I'll do that," Tumlin said and shambled into the night.

Starbuck prepared himself for Potter's tongue-lashing. In truth, he thought, it had not been a bad day. Not a good day, but not bad either. The battalion had lost no one to straggling, he had faced down his enemies, but he had not made those enemies into friends. Perhaps that would never happen, but if it did, he thought, it would be in the fierce crucible of battle. And the sooner, the better, Starbuck thought, then he remembered the cornfield at Chantilly and recalled his gut-loosening fear. Oh God, he thought, let me not be a coward.

Late that night Starbuck toured the picket line that was not set against the incursion of enemies, but against the possibility of his own men deserting, then, wrapped in his dirty blanket, he slept.

Lucifer sat nearby. The boy was tired, but he was determined not to sleep. Instead he sat just outside the glow of the dying fire and he watched the makeshift tent where Starbuck slept and he watched the fire-dotted field where the battalion rested, and every now and then he would caress the long barrel of the Colt revolver that lay across his knees. Lucifer liked Starbuck, and if Starbuck would take no precautions, then Lucifer would guard him against the demons. For that, Lucifer knew, was what they were; white demons, bad as they came, just waiting to take revenge.

IT WAS PROBABLY the worst day of Delaney's life. At any moment he expected to hear that one of the precious copies of Special Order 191 had gone missing and then he would have to face the rigors of a full-scale inquiry, but to his astonishment no one seemed to notice that a copy had been purloined. The army rested in blissful, blind ignorance. Much of it left Frederick City on the morning after Delaney stole the order. They marched in the early dawn to encircle the trapped Federal garrison at Harper's Ferry, while the rest of Lee's men prepared for their own departure the next day. Cavalry patrols went eastward and reported that the Northern army was only a day's march from Frederick City, but was showing no eagerness to advance. George McClellan was behaving true to his old form, creeping timidly forward and fearing every imaginary threat while posing none himself. "Though he's not a man I'd care to attack, not if he knew I was coming," Lee said generously at lunch. The general's broken hands had been rebandaged with lighter splints and he was constantly flexing his fingers with a look of astonished gratitude that their use was partly restored. "McClellan would make a very good defensive general," he said, clumsily spooning beans to his mouth.

"There's a distinction?" Delaney asked.

"Oh, indeed." Lee cuffed spilled beans off his beard. "An attacker has to take more risks. Imagine playing chess,

Delaney, where you don't have to make a single move until your opponent has developed his attack. You should win every time."

"Should?"

"A good attacker disguises his blows."

"As you are now, General?"

Lee smiled. "Poor McClellan will be getting reports from here, there, and everywhere. He won't know where we are or what we're doing. He'll know we're besieging Harper's Ferry, of course, because he'll hear the guns, but I doubt if McClellan will raise a finger to help those poor men. Ah, Chilton! You look harassed."

Delaney felt a surge of fear, but Colonel Chilton's harassment arose from a lack of varnish rather than the loss of Special Order 191.

"Varnish?" Lee asked, finally abandoning his attempt to manipulate fork and spoon with hampered fingers. "Are we trying to smarten this army? A hopeless task, I should have thought."

"News from the north, sir. Parrott guns." Chilton collapsed into a camp chair and fanned his face with his hat brim.

"You've lost me, Chilton," Lee said. "Varnish? Parrott guns?"

"The tubes of the twenty pounders are liable to explode, sir. One of our fellows in the north knows an inspector in the factory and he claims they reckon it's because of friction inside the shell caused by the sudden acceleration upon firing. That friction ignites the shell and causes it to explode inside the tube. The factory's solution is to empty the shells of their explosive and varnish the interior walls before refilling them. Worth a try, I'd say, only we can't find any varnish."

"Grease?" Delaney suggested, "or wax?"

175

"We could try that," Chilton said grudgingly. "But wouldn't wax melt?"

"Try grease," Lee said, "but eat first. The beans are excellent." The General wiped sweat off his forehead. The heat was again stupefying.

Delaney might have suggested a solution for exploding Parrott guns, but he had still not devised a method of passing the stolen order back to McClellan's army. During the night, as he had tossed sleeplessly on the hard ground, he had imagined riding desperately eastward until he met a Yankee cavalry patrol, but he knew his horsemanship was not up to such cross-country work. Besides, any rebel cavalry seeing him would be bound to be curious and that curiosity could well lead to the gallows' steps. Now, desperate to rid himself of the incriminating document, he had hit upon one last pathetic idea. "I thought, if you wouldn't mind," he said to Lee, "that I might look at the town before we leave?"

"By all means," Lee said. "Chilton will write you a pass."

"No danger of the Yankees arriving today?" Delaney asked anxiously.

"My dear Delaney!" Lee laughed. "None whatsoever, not with McClellan in command. We'll leave tomorrow, but I doubt he'll be here for at least another three days."

"There's nothing to see in the town," Chilton observed sourly, resenting that he was required to write Delaney a pass.

"One of my mother's cousins was a minister there for a time," Delaney said, inventing a reason for his curiosity, "and I have a notion he might be buried there."

"Your mother's cousins?" Lee said, frowning as he tried to remember Delaney's family tree. "So he was a Mattingley?"

176

"Charles Mattingley," Delaney said, and there was indeed a Reverend Charles Mattingley who had been a cousin of Delaney's mother, though so far as Delaney knew the Reverend Charles was still alive and ministering to heathen tribes in Africa. "Thomas's second son," he added.

"I never knew that branch of the family," Lee said. "They moved to Maryland, aren't I right?"

"Creagerstown, General. Thomas was a physician there for many years."

"And his son's dead, eh? Poor fellow, he can't have been very old. But it's odd, Delaney, to think of you being related to a minister?"

"Charles was an Episcopalian, General," Delaney said reprovingly. "It hardly counts."

Lee, an Episcopalian himself, laughed, then fumbled open the lid of his pocket watch. "I must be at work," he announced. "Enjoy your afternoon, Delaney."

"Thank you, sir."

An hour later, equipped with the pass that would take him past the provosts guarding the stores in Frederick, Delaney walked into town. In his pocket was the copy of Special Order 191 and he felt sure that the provosts would stop him, search him, and then march him at gunpoint on the journey that would end at a Richmond gallows, but the men guarding the town merely touched their hats as he showed them Chilton's pass.

The town had a deserted air. The presence of the rebel army had stopped all traffic on the rail spur and had inhibited the country folk from coming to do their marketing in Frederick City. The shops, protected by the cordon of provosts, were open, but few people were in the streets. One or two houses flew the rebel flag, but the gesture seemed desultory, a mere formality, and Delaney guessed that when McClellan's army reached the town it would suddenly be gaudy with stars and stripes. The people of Maryland did not seem overgrateful for being liberated by the Southerners. Some were enthusiastic, but only a handful of young men had volunteered to join Lee's army.

Delaney strolled past a carpenter's shop sandwiched between two churches. A bearded man was turning chair legs in the shop and he looked up as the rebel officer passed, but did not return Delaney's greeting. A cripple, probably a man wounded in one of the war's early battles, sat on a porch taking in the sun. He ignored Delaney, which suggested he had fought for the North. A black woman, probably a slave, came toward Delaney with a bundle of laundry on her head, but turned aside into an alley rather than confront him. A solemn little girl watched him from behind a window, but ducked out of sight when he smiled at her. A pair of cows were being driven down the street, probably to give milk that would be sold to the rebel army, and Delaney called a cheerful greeting to the girl who herded them, but she just nodded curtly and hurried on, probably fearful that he would try to take the cows from her. The stifling heat seemed to condense the town's aroma of sweet hay and animal ordure into a rank stink that offended Delaney's nostrils. He stepped around some fresh cow dung and it occurred to him, with the astonishment that comes from a moment of self-revelation, that the reason he was betraying his country was simply to escape from the constriction of small church-haunted towns like Frederick City with their suspicious populations and their glorification of simple virtues and honest toil. Richmond was a rung above such places, but Richmond stank of tobacco, Washington was a rung higher still, but Washington stank of ambition, while New York and Boston were higher yet, but the one stank of vulgar money and the other reeked of Protestant virtue and Delaney wanted none of them. His reward for treachery, he decided, would be an ambassadorship: a permanent and salaried post in Rome or Paris or Athens, all of them cities that stank of jaded tastes and languid nights. He touched the pocket in which he had the Special Order concealed. It was his passport to paradise.

He found the post office on Main Street. The idea of employing the US mail to deliver the stolen order amused Delaney. There was something obvious, yet also quixotic, in the idea that appealed to his sense of mischief. He doubted whether Thorne would approve, for the vital news in the order was already a day old and it would probably be two or three days staler by the time it reached the US army, but Delaney had no other idea how to send his message.

The postmaster had a cubbyhole office at the back of the building that had the usual wooden counter, a wall of pigeonholes for letters awaiting collection, and two long tables where the mail was sorted. "Not again," the postmaster groaned when he saw Delaney.

"Again?" Delaney asked, puzzled.

"We had a Captain Gage in here this morning," the postmaster protested, "and another fellow yesterday. What was his name, Lucy?" He shouted to one of the women seated at a sorting table.

"Pearce!" she called back.

"A Major Pearce," the postmaster said accusingly to Delaney. The postmaster was a big-bellied, truculent man with a red beard. He was also a Northern sympathizer, or at least he had defiantly kept a stars and stripes hanging on his cubbyhole wall. "But they're all there," he added, gesturing at a pile of mail in a basket on his desk, "so help yourself. But nothing's come in since Captain Gage checked."

Delaney took the mail from the basket and suddenly understood what the postmaster was saying. All of the letters were addressed to places in the north, and all were from Confederate soldiers. Someone, he assumed the provosts, was making certain that no one was trying to send information to the Yankees and so they had opened and read the letters before initialing the envelopes to show that the contents had been checked. "I wasn't here to read the mail," Delaney said, but opened one of the letters anyway. It was from a Sergeant Malone and addressed to his sister in New Jersey. Betty had given birth to another son, but the child had died at a month old. Mother was as well as could be expected. Cousin John had been wounded at Manassas, but not seriously. "'These are sad times,'" Delaney read aloud, "'but we remember you in our prayers.'" He shrugged, slipped the letter back in its envelope, then dropped the pile back into the basket. "Would you," he asked the postmaster, "have an envelope you could donate to the army?"

The postmaster hesitated, then decided there was little point in being obstructive. He opened a drawer and handed Delaney an envelope. Delaney, making no attempt to hide what he did, took the copy of Special Order 191 from his pocket and slipped it inside the envelope, then folded the flap inside. "May I?" he asked and reached over the desk for the postmaster's pen. He dipped it in the inkwell, drained the excess ink from the nib, then wrote Captain Adam Faulconer, US Army, Gen. McClellan's Hdqtrs., in block letters. "It's nothing that needs bother Captain Gage or Major Pearce," he said to the postmaster, then borrowed a pencil and, very carefully, copied Gage's initials. "There," he said, the job done. "I suppose you'll charge me for a stamp now?"

The postmaster looked at the addressee's name, then

at the forged initials, and finally up into Delaney's face. He said nothing.

"He's an old friend," Delaney explained airily, "and this might be my last chance to write to him." There was a risk that the postmaster was not a Northern supporter at all, but that was a risk Delaney had to run, just as he had to risk that the provosts did not check the basket of mail a third time.

"You're all leaving then?" the postmaster asked.

"By tomorrow," Delaney said, "the army will be gone."

"Where?"

"Over the hills and far away," Delaney said lightly. Sweat trickled down his cheeks. "But I imagine," he went on, "that the Federals will be here soon?"

"Like as not," the postmaster said with a shrug. He weighed the letter in his hand, then ostentatiously put it in the drawer rather than with the other mail from the Confederate army. "It'll be delivered," he promised, "but I don't know when."

"I'm obliged to you," Delaney said.

Once outside the Post Office Delaney had to lean against the wall. He was shaking like a man with the fever. Dear God, he thought, but he had no stomach for this kind of thing. He felt a sudden need to vomit, but managed to hold it back. Sweat poured off him. He had been a fool! He had been unable to resist flamboyance. He had deliberately tried to impress a man he thought was a Northern sympathizer, but he knew the risk had been stupid and the thought of the hangman's noose made him gag again.

"Are you unwell, Major?"

Delaney looked up and saw an elderly minister in Geneva bands watching him with a sympathetic, but wary, look. Doubtless he feared Delaney was drunk. "It's the heat," Delaney said, "nothing but the heat."

"It is warm," the minister agreed, sounding relieved that it was not liquor that had caused Delaney's distress. "Do you need help? A cup of water, maybe?"

"No, thank you. I shall manage just fine." Delaney suddenly looked up as a rumble of thunder sounded in the distance. There were no threatening clouds in sight, but the sound of the far-off storm was unmistakable. "Maybe the rain will break the heat," he said to the minister.

"Rain?" The minister frowned. "That isn't thunder," he said, realizing what Delaney had meant. "Those are guns, Major, those are guns." He stared west down main street to where the green fields and heavy trees and lines of rebel tents showed. "Harper's Ferry," the minister said, "it must be Harper's Ferry. God help all those poor men."

"Amen," Delaney said, "amen." For the fighting had begun.

The guns slammed back on their trails, spewing smoke sixty feet ahead of their muzzles and scattering flaming scraps of wadding onto the grass where small fires flickered from the previous shots. The sound of the guns was huge, so huge that it was more than just a sound, but a physical sensation as though the very earth was being buffeted in space. The shells screamed across the valley to leave little smoke trails from their burning fuses, then exploded in gouts of dirty gray-white smoke above the farther ridge. The smoke trails twisted in the wind, became feathery and tenuous, then another battery fired and the grass in front of the muzzles flicked flat again as another set of smoke trails whipped across the sky. Cannon barrels hissed as the wet swabs were thrust down the muzzles. On the far ridge a Yankee battery returned the fire, but the

Northern guns were outnumbered and the rebel guns were well laid and their fuses well timed, and so the Northern gunners died man by man as the shell fragments hissed among them.

The Northern guns pulled back across the ridge, leaving its defense to infantry alone. The Southern cannon changed their aim, scattering shells among the trees, bushes, and rocks of the ridge. Some cannon were firing percussion-fused shells that plunged into the ground to gout wagonloads of dirt and leaves, others used case shot that banged apart in the air to spit musket bullets down on the Yankee defenders.

"Skirmishers?" Lieutenant Colonel Griffin Swynyard galloped his horse toward Starbuck. "Skirmishers?" he called again.

"They're out there, Colonel," Starbuck said. The Yellowlegs were on the far right-hand flank of Swynyard's Brigade, and immediately to the left of the Legion, and Starbuck had taken good care that his skirmishing company had gone forward before Maitland threw the Legion's skirmishers down onto the valley floor. Starbuck had picked his skirmishers carefully, drawing them from the men who had held up best on the marches north from the railhead. Most of his men had taken those marches hard, limping slower and slower on bloody, blistered feet as the battalion crawled painfully to reach this valley north of Charlestown just as the first of Jackson's infantry swung in from their long march that had taken them west from Frederick City to loop clean about Harper's Ferry to this ground that lay south of the besieged Federal garrison.

That garrison was attempting to defend the high ground about the river town, but so far their defense was half-hearted. The Yankee cannon had given up the fight quickly; now it was the infantry's turn to be tested.

Starbuck's detached company of skirmishers was already in action, the smoke of their rifles blowing in small gray puffs across the valley floor. The answering puffs were well up the further slope, and Starbuck was mentally urging Potter to press harder, though in fairness his skirmishers were doing well. They were far ahead of the Legion's skirmishers. The sound of that skirmishers' battle came as a series of intermittent cracks that were only audible in the intervals between the cannon fire. Swynyard was using field glasses to watch the rebel shells fall on the far ridge. All Starbuck could see there was an erratic and broken cordon of blue-coated infantry beneath their bright flags. The line was not continuous. It was interrupted by the gaps between regiments or where bushes or rocky outcrops interfered with the line's alignment, and sometimes the defending line vanished altogether where the Yankees sheltered in dips of the ground or behind boulders. "I don't see any rifle pits, Nate," Swynyard said.

"For small mercies, God, thank you," Starbuck answered.

Swynyard grimaced, but did not protest Starbuck's blasphemy. Instead he pointed to the left-hand end of the Yankee line. "Reckon you could take that ground?" he asked. "Say everything from the end of the crest to where the guns were?"

"I guess," Starbuck answered. In truth he had no idea how the Yellowlegs would behave in battle. Nor did he know how he would behave in this first battle since the terror had overwhelmed him in the rainswept fight near the mansion of Chantilly. He could feel that terror hovering near again. It gave him a curiously disembodied sensation, as though his spirit were merely watching his body and marveling that it could react so calmly to Swynyard's orders.

184

"Wait for the line to advance," Swynyard said, then he turned his horse and rode toward Lieutenant Colonel Maitland, who was mounted behind the Legion's center company.

Starbuck walked to the center of his own line where Captain Billy Tumlin stood with the color party. The color was a four-foot-square flag issued from the State Armory and it looked a sorry thing compared with the thirty-six-square feet of colored silk that flew above the Legion. Starbuck told Tumlin what the orders were, then walked out ahead of the battalion.

Starbuck's job was to reassure his men. They had been dubbed failures by the army, then issued with antique guns, and now he had to persuade them to be winners. "They ain't got cannon!" he shouted, "just muskets." Almost certainly the Yankees were all armed with rifles, but this was no time for literal truths. "They're frightened as hell," he went on. "They'll probably break just as soon as you get within shouting distance, but if you hesitate, they'll rally. Not one of you will be killed crossing the valley. Remember that! They don't have cannon! We're going to walk across and when I give the order you charge the bastards! Hold your fire until then. No point in wasting a musket shot at long range. Hold your fire, wait for the order to charge, then scream at them! The faster they run, the more equipment they'll leave behind, and the more you kill, the more boots we get. Now fix bayonets!"

He turned to stare across the ground over which they would advance. The land dropped steeply away to the left where a small stream tumbled toward the Potomac. Harper's Ferry lay where that river was joined by the smaller Shenandoah, and the confluence was surrounded by three high spurs of land that overlooked the small town. Jackson's troops now commanded the approaches to all three spurs, and all three were under pressure. Push the Yankees off the high ground and the garrison in the town, which had been swollen by other Northern troops driven to shelter by Jackson's advance, would be dominated by rebel artillery. Local people had slipped through the Northern lines to tell the rebels that close to twenty thousand Yankees were trapped there, and even allowing for exaggeration, that meant that the town must be crammed with food, weapons, and supplies; all the things the Special Battalion lacked.

Starbuck turned back to look at the battalion that now stood with fixed bayonets. It was a tiny battalion, but no smaller than many others that had been shrunken by war. The Legion was larger, but still Starbuck reckoned that the Legion was down to half the number of men who had marched to Manassas for the war's first battle. Captain Truslow strolled out from the Legion with a rifle on his shoulder, which, like Starbuck's, carried no badges of rank. "Your boys, eh?" Truslow said, nodding at the battalion.

"My boys," Starbuck agreed.

"Any good?"

"About to find out."

"Maitland's no damned use," Truslow said, spitting a stream of tobacco juice, "and he don't like me neither."

"Can't think why."

Truslow grinned. "He reckons I ain't born to it. How was Richmond?"

"Hot," Starbuck said, knowing that was not the answer Truslow wanted. "And I did see Sally," he added.

"Reckoned you might. How is she?" The question was gruff.

"Living in luxury. Making money, learning to speak French, winding the world round her little finger."

Truslow grimaced. "Never did understand her. Always

186

reckoned I should have had a son, not a daughter."

"She ain't that much different from you," Starbuck said, "just one hell of a lot prettier. She sends her love."

Truslow grunted, then glanced at Starbuck's left ear. "Someone thump you?"

"Tall man, third from the right, rear rank," Starbuck said, jerking his head toward Captain Dennison's Company A, which lay at the right of his line. "He reckoned he ought to run the battalion instead of me."

Truslow grinned. "You put him down?"

"I thought of what you would do to him, then did it."

"The hell you did. He's still alive, ain't he?"

Starbuck laughed. "And probably praying for a chance to put a bullet in my back."

"Captain Truslow!" Colonel Maitland, mounted on his horse and with a drawn sword resting on his shoulder, trotted out from the Legion's ranks. "To your company, if you please."

Truslow spat. "Never reckoned I'd say it to you," he said to Starbuck, "but you'd sure be welcome if you come back."

"I'm working on it," Starbuck said.

Truslow shambled back toward the Legion, ignoring Maitland, who trotted past him to raise a hand in greeting to Starbuck. "So you got them here?" Maitland said, gesturing at the Special Battalion.

"You ever thought I wouldn't?"

Maitland ignored the question. Instead he turned and watched the skirmishers at work. "No problems here?" he asked.

The question had been asked lightly, but Starbuck sensed the nervousness behind the elegant Colonel's words. This was Maitland's first proper battle, though it

187

hardly counted as a battle to Starbuck. The enemy guns were gone, the waiting Yankee infantry was probably taut as a cocked revolver's leaf spring, and all this action promised to be was a simple advance with a few casualties as the price of the ground gained. What lay beyond the crest was another matter, but there should be no problems here. "Should be easy," Starbuck said. A bullet whistled overhead and Maitland gave an involuntary wince that he hoped Starbuck had not noticed. "You know what he was aiming at, Colonel?" Starbuck asked.

"Us, I assume."

"You," Starbuck said. "Man on a horse with a sword. There's a bastard up on that ridge with a long-barreled sharpshooting rifle. Right now he's pushing the loader back onto the muzzle and reckoning he'll do better next time."

Maitland gave a wan smile, but did not move. Instead he glanced at Billy Tumlin, then back to Starbuck. "I'm glad you got Tumlin."

"You know him?"

"My lads rescued him. I'd have liked to keep him for the Legion, but Swynyard insisted we do things by the book."

"I like him well enough," Starbuck said, "and my need of good officers is greater than yours, Colonel."

"You really think so?" Maitland asked pointedly.

"That sharpshooter, Colonel," Starbuck said, "is tapping the bullet through the loader now. Got a breech charged with real good powder, a nice measured amount, and he's reckoning on giving you four feet of correction for the wind and to fire a wee bit lower than last time. So tell me, do you want to be buried here or is there a Maitland family plot?"

"I think Hollywood Cemetery would be more appropriate," Maitland said lightly, though he looked uncomfortable. "Discretion, you're advising, is the better part of valor?" he asked.

"Seems to work that way."

"Then I'll bid you good day, Starbuck," the Colonel touched his hat, "don't want to expose you to sharpshooters!" He turned his horse away.

Starbuck unhitched his own rifle, from which he had finally blown out the damp powder by dint of working a wire through the nipple and trickling a tiny amount of dry powder into the clotted charge that had finally, reluctantly, exploded when he fired the gun. He loaded it, then pushed a percussion cap onto the cone, hoping it was not one of the bad caps that had suddenly started emerging from the Richmond factories. Rumor said that the Negro workers were deliberately sabotaging the army, and certainly there had been a spate of bad caps filled with anything except fulminate of mercury. He lowered the hammer onto the cap, slung the rifle again, and walked back toward the battalion.

Lieutenant Coffman, who had been appointed as an aide to Swynyard, ran down the back of the brigade's line. His pouches and scabbard flapped as he ran, while he held his hat on with one hand and carried a rifle in the other. "We're to advance!" he shouted at Colonel Maitland, then ran on toward Starbuck.

Starbuck waved to show that he had heard. "Battalion! Forward! Get them moving!" he shouted. With the Legion he would probably have gone ahead of the companies, but today he planned to follow his men into the fight, not out of fear, but simply to make certain they did advance. "Forward!" he shouted again, and he heard Dennison, Peel, and Cartwright echo the call. Billy Tumlin, revolver drawn, walked behind the right-hand companies. Tumlin had no company of his own, but Starbuck had given him supervision of those two right-hand companies, as well as asking him to look after the adjutant's responsibilities, for which Potter was signally inept. "Drive 'em on, Billy!" Starbuck shouted, then moved to his own place behind Lippincott's and Peel's companies. "Forward now! Smartly!"

The four-line companies walked forward willingly enough. The rebel artillery fired over their heads, the shells sounding like great barrels rolling across the sky. Some of the men were made nervous by that sound and by the percussive blasts of the guns themselves, but Starbuck shouted at them to hurry as they instinctively crouched beneath the huge noise. "They're on your side!" he shouted, "now keep going! Sergeants! Look to the line! Look to the line!" Some men were hurrying, either out of eagerness or else a desire to get the advance over, and their haste was making the battalion ragged.

The Legion had not started forward yet, or rather some companies had advanced when Starbuck's men began walking, but Maitland had called them back into alignment and now he fussily dressed the ranks while on either side of his regiment the other battalions of Swynyard's Brigade advanced down the gentle slope. The battle flags lifted in the small breeze. The day was ragged with explosions, punctured by the hammer of cannons, splintered by rifles, and filled now by the sound of hundreds of feet swishing through the grass. A skirmisher limped back toward the Special Battalion, another lay dead with a bullet in his brain and with his arms outflung like a man crucified. Someone, probably one of the skirmishers armed with an old Richmond Musket, had already taken the man's rifle.

The Legion started forward at last. Starbuck's right-hand company, under Dennison, was lagging, maybe in the hope that the Legion would catch up and support them. "Keep 'em up, Billy!" Starbuck shouted, "chivvy them!"

Billy Blythe lumbered over to Dennison's company and waved his arms impressively. This morning's action was not to Blythe's liking. He was happy enough to shelter in the Special Battalion until the tide of war took him close enough to the Yankee lines, but he had no wish to fight, and no wish whatsoever to fight as an infantryman, but he knew he would have to keep up the pretense for a good while yet. There was no point in jumping over to these Yankees in Harper's Ferry for they were surrounded and doomed. He must wait till the battalion was across the river and so nearer to McClellan's main force. Until then he had decided he would do as much as was needed and no more. "Keep them moving, Tom!" he called to Dennison, but did not push the men himself.

Dennison called for the company to speed up, but without any conviction in his voice, and though the company did pick up its heels, some of the men, led by Case, deliberately dawdled. Starbuck himself ran over. "Move!" he shouted. "Move! Faster!"

Case slowed even more.

Starbuck dragged out the revolver and put a bullet into the turf behind Case's heels. "Move!" he shouted, "move!" He fired a second bullet, this one well wide of anyone. He had not looked at Case, nor at any other man as he fired, for he had not wanted another confrontation, just to keep the company moving, and the two revolver shots had the happy effect of moving the laggards on like startled rabbits. "Keep them going, Billy!" Starbuck snarled. "Captain Dennison! Move them!"

Billy Blythe was too shocked to respond. He stumbled

on, chivvying Dennison's company with his arms, suddenly more frightened of Starbuck than of the Yankees waiting on the ridge. The sheer force of Starbuck's anger had startled him, but he recognized it as genuine power. Starbuck was one of those men who could shift whole battalions by his personality and it was Starbuck's anger and resolve that was keeping the Yellowlegs moving across the valley under the rippling thunder of rebel shells that arched above their heads. Starbuck, Billy Blythe reflected, was the kind of man who got other men killed. Or got killed himself. "What's your name, Case?" Blythe fell into step beside Case who, to show his independence, had again started to lag a few paces behind the rest of A Company.

"Sounds like you already know it, Captain," Case said in a voice that was still hoarse from the terrible blow Starbuck had landed on his throat.

"I meant your Christian name, Sergeant," Blythe said, deliberately restoring Case's lost rank.

Case hesitated, then decided that Captain Tumlin's friendly tone deserved an answer. "Robert," he admitted.

"Hell, I got a brother called Bobby," Blythe lied. "Real nice fellow. Maybe a bit too fond of his liquor, but Lord, can our Bobby tell tales." He saw the sidelong look of resentful hatred that Case gave Starbuck. "You shoot him now, Sergeant," Blythe said quietly, "and there'll be a hundred witnesses and before you can spit on his grave you'll be standing under the guns of a firing squad. Just ain't the sensible thing to do, Bobby. Besides, you think he ain't got his eye on you? Just keep moving, Sergeant, keep it brisk. Look like we're trying to win the war, will you? That way he forgets you." Case said nothing, but he did hurry his pace fractionally. A rebel shell that had been fired too low screeched just overhead, making some of

192

the men duck. The shell exploded among the battalion's skirmish line, making Captain Potter scurry long-legged for a patch of bushes. The battalion laughed. "Starbuck's pet clown," Billy Blythe said softly.

Case gave Blythe a long, hard look as it dawned on him that the battalion's second in command might really be an ally. "If Starbuck dies," Case broke his silence, "you get command, Captain."

"I sure do thank you for pointing that out to me, Bobby," Blythe said, "and if that ever did happen, why, I'd be looking for experienced men to be my officers. No glory boys, ain't that the phrase? Just good experienced men. Proper soldiers. Know what I mean? Jesus!" This final imprecation was startled from Blythe by the sudden thunder of Yankee cannons. Enemy shells screamed into the valley to explode among the advancing infantry in eruptions of dirt, smoke, flame, and flesh.

The Yankees had kept some concealed artillery on the crest and now the gunners had hauled aside the screen of branches that had masked the cannon and opened fire on the advancing infantry. Their opening salvo was of shells, but they reloaded with canister so that every shot was now like a giant blast of buckshot fanning out from the muzzle. The canister broke apart at the cannon's mouth to spread its charge of musket balls and Blythe, appalled, saw the grass ahead of the brigade flick as though a huge, invisible broom was whipping toward the attackers. There was a pattering noise like hard rain, then a sudden scream of wind as the cloud of musket balls slashed through the ranks. Men fell, spun, retched, or staggered. One man near Blythe had a rib sticking through the weave of his butternut coat. The man stared at the splintered white bone with a look of utter incomprehension, then bubbling pale blood welled at the rent in his coat and slopped down his belly. More blood flooded his gullet, he fell to his knees, tried to speak, then collapsed onto his face.

Blythe and Case found shelter behind a boulder, where they shared a cigar as the canister rattled and sighed and slapped the air around them. Dennison's company had scattered in confusion. A few kept going forward, others lay flat, but most ran panicking toward their left where the battalion's remaining companies offered an illusion of shelter. Case hunched down beside Blythe. "This is nothing to Sevastopol," he said. "The damned Ivans shelled us day and night, day and night. Never let up for a minute."

"Experienced men, that's who I'll be looking for," Blythe said, handing the cigar back to his companion.

Case grimaced. "So what do we do about Starbuck?" he asked.

"Just wait on the good Lord, Bobby, wait on the Lord and He will provide. Don't the good book say that?"

"Is that what you're doing?"

"I'm biding my time, Bobby, but that time will come. I don't see no point in being too eager in battle. Hell, we need heroes, but some of us have to live to go home at war's end. Otherwise the Yankees will be plowing our wives and we'll be rotting in our graves."

Case peered about the boulder, looking at Starbuck's distant figure. "Can't do much without a rifle."

"Rifles will be found. Hell, I don't want to command no battalion without rifles," Blythe laughed. He was lining up his allies and doing what he loved to do. He was surviving and thriving, and he reckoned he was good at that because he took a long view of life, and dying in battle was no part of that view. He would survive.

The crash of the enemy guns stunned Starbuck into silence. He had promised his men there would be no cannon and that they could walk through the valley without fear of slaughter, but now the enemy gunners were swabbing, reloading, and ramming another volley of canister. The fear roared in Starbuck, weakening his legs and threatening to make him whimper like a whipped child. He kept going forward, not out of bravery, but because he seemed incapable of changing his direction or pace. He wanted to shout at Potter to take his skirmishers up the slope toward the gunners, but no sound would come, and so he stumbled blindly on with his mind groping for a prayer that he could not articulate. The terror was unmanning him, and that thought jarred him and he wondered if he could ever face a terror like it again. His foot slipped in a crusted patch of cow dung and vomit rimmed his throat. He fought it down, gasping for air, and he was sure that the men of the Special Battalion, whom he was leading into a murderous cannon fire just as he had led the Legion into a Yankee artillery trap at Chantilly, were despising him. He looked to his right and was astonished to see a vast gap in the brigade's line. The Legion was missing, though beyond the gap he could see the kinked line of attacking men sweeping across the smoke-smeared pasture beneath the red and blue flags. Dennison's company had vanished and half of Cartwright's was gone, but the rest of the battalion was still going forward, though no longer in neat ranks. The men had spread into the gap left by Dennison's company and some part of Starbuck's scrambled thoughts recognized that the scattering would protect them from the canister.

Another storm of missiles flicked at the ground and snatched men back like puppets caught on whiplashed strings. The Yankee gunners were doing well, aiming their canister just short of the advancing rebels so that the massed musket balls bounced up into their faces. The taste of vomit was sour in Starbuck's throat, but somehow he was managing to say the Twenty-Third Psalm to himself, and the realization that he was falling back on the faith of his father both surprised him and gave him a steadying moment. He saw that the battalion had crossed the floor of the valley and was beginning to climb its farther slope. The Northern infantry had almost disappeared, not by retreating, but by taking cover among the rocks and bushes on the crest. Below them the Yankee skirmishers were hurrying back up the slope between the smoke bursts of the rebel shells, then suddenly the crest itself was crowned by smoke as the defending infantry opened fire. The sound rippled across the valley, a splintering crackle that came an instant after the smoke appeared. The bullets whistled overhead, though a few thumped into bodies with a dull sound like a butcher's cleaver falling. Blood misted as men fell backward. "Keep moving!" someone shouted behind Starbuck. "Keep moving! Go on! Go on!" Starbuck was in the broken ranks now, pushing on ahead, his body behaving like a leader even if his mind was still reeling between terror and the need to keep his left-hand companies moving up the slope.

Confederate artillery at last targeted the Yankee guns and shellbursts cracked in the hot air above the sweating gunners. "Come on!" Starbuck screamed, amazed he could speak at all, "come on!" Every nerve in his body was screaming for him to turn and run, to find a hole and shelter for the rest of his life while the world went mad about him, but the shreds of pride and stubbornness kept him going and even made him go faster. He turned to shout encouragement to his stark-faced, clumsy men encumbered by bedrolls and packs and pouches and scabbards so that they lumbered forward with open mouths. "Come on!" he called, anger in his voice, though the anger was only at himself. The battalion was still two hundred yards from the crest, too far to order the charge, but he sensed that if he did not keep the battalion moving now, then it would go to ground and refuse to advance ever again. The Yellowlegs had already achieved far more than they had in their first battle, but to wipe the stain off their reputation they needed to keep going to victory. Rebel shells were screaming close overhead, their explosions punching the eardrums and throwing up fountains of dirt and smoke along the crest. The Yankee rifle fire had become ragged as men fired whenever they were loaded and Starbuck, seeing how sporadic were the bursts of muzzle smoke, realized that there was little more than a heavy skirmish line left on the crest. The Yankees were not going to fight for this ridgeline, but just inflict some casualties before slipping away and that thought gave him encouragement. Maybe he would not die in this cow-dunged pasture, but maybe he would give the despised battalion the victory it so badly needed, and he shouted again for his men to keep going forward, only this time the shout turned into a rebel yell and suddenly the remaining attackers were shrilling the sound with him as they broke into a clumsy run.

The canister fire had stopped. Starbuck was aware of only the sounds he was making himself. The thump of boots, the harsh scrape of breath, the desperate yelping of the war cry, the clank of his tin mug against the cartridge box, the slapping of the revolver holster against the back of his thigh. Something was burning on the crest, pumping a thick smoke into the air. Another rebel shell burst, its blast bending a bush sideways and shredding leaves among the smoke. Potter's men were in the ranks now and Potter himself was running close to Starbuck and screaming like a wild man. Starbuck blundered through a scorched, smoking patch where a shell had exploded. A Yankee skirmisher lay beyond, his head back, his hands curled, and his guts spilt into the churned dirt. Men were at last visible on the crest. They stood, aimed, fired, then dropped to reload. A bullet whistled its eerie minie sound near Starbuck, and he began to scream like Potter, a feral, terrible noise that came from the battle-mix of terror and glee. All he wanted to do now was punish the bastards who had so nearly unmanned him. He wanted to kill and kill.

"Come on!" he shouted, drawing out the last word as at last the attackers reached the gentle crest. Colonel Swynyard had been wrong and there were rifle pits along the ridge, but the Yankees were already abandoning them and going back to their next defense line, which lay on a farther ridge. The Yankee cannon were being dragged by horses back to that ridge where more guns waited and more infantry, but Starbuck had no orders to attack that far ridge. His job had been to push the Northern forces off this ridge and it was done, and he was running into clear air, blessed air, air untouched by bullets or shells, though he knew it would only be seconds before the far guns opened fire.

"Kill them!" he shouted, then leaped into a vacated rifle pit and leveled his rifle across the pile of soil at its rear. He aimed at a retreating Yankee and pulled the trigger. The hammer dropped onto a useless percussion cap and he swore, broke a fingernail levering the cap away, put another in its place, and tried again. The rifle hammered into his shoulder and its cloud of smoke hid his target. Potter was beside him, laughing. The rest of the battalion, those who had stayed the course, were in the other abandoned rifle pits and firing at the Yankee infantry as they hurried away.

The far Yankee cannon opened fire. The shells flashed overhead and thumped behind as Swynyard's Brigade went to ground on the captured ridge. Starbuck reloaded the rifle then turned to see where his men were. He could see the color sticking up from a rifle pit, he could see a scatter of wounded men crawling slowly on the slope beyond, and he could see the Legion still climbing the hill. He turned to look north and was amazed to see the land drop away to where, between the shoulders of two humped hills, he could glimpse a silver river sliding eastward. Beyond the river, in Maryland, there was smoke on the hills where other Confederate troops were tightening Jackson's grim ring about Harper's Ferry.

"Sweet Jesus, but I enjoyed that," Potter said.

Starbuck meant to tell him that he should have taken his skirmishers up against the gunners, but instead he vomited. He emptied his belly into the floor of the rifle pit. "Jesus," he said when he had finished heaving. "Jesus."

"Here," Potter handed him a canteen, "it's only water."

Starbuck rinsed out his mouth, spat, then drank. "I'm sorry," he said to Potter.

"Something you ate," Potter suggested tactfully.

"Fear," Starbuck said harshly.

A shell banged into the turf a few yards ahead of their pit. It did not explode, but instead tumbled end over end to embed itself in the spoil thrown up by the Yankee diggers. "I think we might seek other quarters," Potter said, eyeing the shell. The air above the metal shimmered from the heat of the missile's passage.

"Go on," Starbuck said. "I'll join you." Once alone he squatted in the pit, pants about his ankles, and voided his body. He was sweating and shaking. The ground thumped softly from the fall of the shells. The sky above the pit

199

was laced with smoke, but suddenly the fear drained away and Starbuck stood and clumsily pulled up his pants, belted them, then buttoned his fraying jacket and rebuckled his revolver belt and straightened his bedroll. He climbed out of the pit and, with shouldered rifle, walked among the other pits to congratulate his men. He told them they had done well, told them he was proud of them, and then he walked back down the slope to watch his stragglers climb sheepishly toward the crest. Captain Dennison was pretending to be busy as he chivvied the laggards, but he took care to avoid Starbuck, though Captain Tumlin walked eagerly across the slope with his hand outstretched.

"Hell, Starbuck, if you ain't the bravest man I ever saw then my name's not Tumlin," Blythe said.

Starbuck ignored both the outstretched hand and the compliment. "What happened to your companies?" he asked coldly.

Tumlin seemed unconcerned by Starbuck's brusqueness. "I managed to keep most of Cartwright's boys moving, but A Company?" He spat. "They're mules, Starbuck, mules. I got up here once, went back for the bastards and still they weren't moving. Did my best. Hell, Starbuck, I know you're disappointed, but I did my God honest best."

"I'm sure." Starbuck was convinced of Tumlin's sincerity. "Sorry, Billy."

"You look kind of washed up, Starbuck."

"Something I ate, Billy, nothing worse." Starbuck found a broken cigar in his pouch and lit the largest remnant. "You want to make me a list of the casualties, Billy?" he asked, then walked back to the crest as the Yankee cannon fire increased in intensity, but the shells were no longer aimed at the captured ridge, but toward a second rebel attack that was coming from their left flank. Swynyard's men had cleared the ridge to prevent its defending Yankees from flanking that second attack, which was the real assault intended to take the high ground that formed the southern skyline of Harper's Ferry. The sound of the battle thumped and snapped, filling the air with gray-white smoke.

Starbuck pulled the bayonet off his rifle as he watched the Legion climb the last few yards. Maitland had deliberately held them back from the canister fire, and the men knew it, and while they were doubtless grateful to have been spared the last stuttering fire of the Yankees' melting resistance, they also looked ashamed. The despised Yellowlegs had outperformed them, and Starbuck's men called jeering greetings to the arriving Legion. Starbuck did not try to stop them, though he knew that Dennison's company did not deserve the reward of a little pride. "Captain Dennison!" Starbuck shouted.

Dennison slouched along the crest where his men were spreading into empty rifle pits. Dennison expected a reprimand, but instead Starbuck pointed across the crest to the rifle pit he had vacated. "Your men can form the picket line," he said. "Skirmish order a hundred paces down the hill. You can stay up here," he pointed toward the rifle pit that he and Potter had vacated. "Make that rifle pit your headquarters."

"Yes, sir."

"Don't worry about the shell. It's dead. Go on, hurry. Jump in before some bastard sharpshooter starts practicing on you."

"Yes, sir," Dennison said, then shouted at his men to follow him to the forward slope of the hill. Starbuck watched as Dennison jumped into the pit, then he turned away.

"What are you laughing at, Nate?" Colonel Swynyard,

201

his horse abandoned for the battle's duration, came striding along the hill.

"Just a petty revenge, sir." He was ashamed of it now, but he could not undo the juvenile prank. "Nothing to worry you," he added.

"Your lads did well," Swynyard said, "real well, and I guess they'll prove just as sound when we have to fight a proper battle. Well done, Nate, well done." He paused. "You know why the Legion was slow?"

"No, sir."

"Then I'd better find out," he said grimly and paced toward Maitland.

And Starbuck tipped back his hat and wiped the sweat off his face. His battalion had fought its first proper fight. The Yellowlegs had not run away and life seemed suddenly sweet.

ADAM FAULCONER HAD once opposed the war. Before it began, when debate had raged like prairie fire across America, he had been passionate in his quest for peace, but that passion had been overwhelmed by the bitterness of his country's division. Adam had then returned home to fight for his native state, but he could find no allegiance there. His love stayed with a *United* States and so, risking breaking his family's heart, he had crossed the lines and replaced his gray coat with a blue.

He had not regained his passion in the North. Instead he had found a dull anger that served as a replacement for what he now perceived had been youthful fervor touched with youthful ignorance. One man, Lyman Thorne had told Adam, can make a difference, and Adam wanted to be that man. He wanted the war to end, but he wanted it to end with complete Northern victory. The man who had once opposed war now embraced it like a lover, for war would be God's punishment on the South. And the Southerners, Adam believed, had to be punished, not because they were at the heart of American slavery, but because they had broken the Union and so defiled what Adam knew to be God's country. The South was the enemy of God, and Adam His self-appointed champion.

But a champion who felt useless. True, Colonel Thorne had given him a task and it was a task that could make the difference Adam craved, but Thorne had been unable to give Adam any guidance as to how that task might be completed. He was living by hope, not by plans, and felt nothing but frustration.

The frustration was made worse by General McClellan's sluggishness. News arrived on Thursday afternoon that the rebel army had finally abandoned Frederick City to march westward, but McClellan merely filed the report and instead spoke about the need to preserve Washington. The withdrawal from Frederick could be a ruse, he claimed, a device to suck the 100,000 men of the Federal army away from Washington while a second army of rebels poured across the lower Potomac to engulf the capital. Or else, McClellan feared, the rebel withdrawal might be merely a bait to draw the Northern army out of its camps and onto a battlefield of Lee's choosing, and Lee, McClellan now believed, possessed 200,000 fighting men; 200,000 wolf-colored demons who attacked with fearful shrill cries and a desperate ferocity. McClellan would not risk that ferocity, nor uncover Washington. He would be steady.

And so, while the rebels vanished beyond the barrier of mountains that lay west of Frederick City, McClellan's army inched its way forward. There was no pursuit of the rebels and even the news that the fifteen thousand men at Harper's Ferry were under siege did not provoke the Young Napoleon into haste. Harper's Ferry must look after itself while McClellan, fearing every rumor, tried to protect his army against all eventualities. The army, he decreed, would advance on a broad front, but there was to be no unseemly haste. Caution ruled.

Adam had no say in the matter. Adam was an unwanted major attached to McClellan's headquarters and Adam's opinion was of no interest to anyone, least of all to Allan Pinkerton, who commanded McClellan's Secret Service Bureau. Adam attempted to influence Pinkerton, and through Pinkerton, McClellan, by arguing with Pinkerton's chief of staff, who was a friend of Adam's and the older brother of Adam's erstwhile friend, Nate Starbuck. James Starbuck was utterly unlike Nate. He was a Boston lawyer, honest, careful, and conscientious, and his cautious nature only reinforced Pinkerton's inflated estimates of the rebels' numbers. Adam, arguing with James at supper on the Thursday evening when they had first heard about the rebels leaving Frederick City, protested that Lee could not possibly muster 200,000 men, not even 100,000. "Maybe sixty or seventy thousand," Adam said, "but probably no more than fifty."

James laughed at the figure. "We are meticulous, Adam, meticulous. Give us credit for that. We have hundreds of reports! I know, I collate them. I compare them."

"Reports from who?" Adam demanded.

"You know I can't say," James said reprovingly. He paused to extract a scrap of chicken bone from between his teeth then laid the bone chip carefully on the edge of his plate. "But the contrabands tell the same tale, the exact same tale. I interviewed two more today." The contrabands were escaped slaves who were brought to Pinkerton's tents and quizzed about the rebel forces. They all told the same story; thousands upon thousands of rebels, endless marching columns and vast guns crushing the dusty roads beneath their iron-rimmed wheels. "Even if we allow for some small exaggeration," James said with a flourish of his fork, "we must still credit Lee with a hundred and seventy thousand. And that's far more men than we have!"

Adam sighed. He had ridden with the rebel army as late as the spring campaign and knew there could never be 170,000 men in gray coats. "How many were bivouacked at Frederick City?" he asked.

James looked owlishly solemn. "At least a hundred thousand. We have direct reports from the town."

Adam suspected the townspeople's reports were about as much use as the rumors printed in the newspapers. "What does our cavalry say?" he asked.

James frowned and probed his cheek with a forefinger before extracting another sliver of bone. "Very skeletal, this chicken," he said disapprovingly.

"Maybe it's rabbit," Adam said. "So what did the cavalry say?"

James peered at his food in the candlelight. "Don't think it's rabbit. Rabbits don't possess wishbones, do they? I'm sure they don't. And I don't think our cavalry were ordered as far as Frederick City today. In fact, I'm sure they weren't. Maybe the problem is that our cooks can't joint chickens properly? I found one kitchen fellow attacking a carcass with a cleaver! Can you credit that? With a cleaver! No attempt to joint the bird, just hacking it apart. Never seen such behavior. Wasn't even plucked properly either. I told him, do as your mother does, I said, run the skin over a candle flame and that will get rid of the feather-gristle, but I don't think he listened."

"So why don't you and I go to Frederick City," Adam ignored the culinary problems, "tomorrow morning. At dawn."

James blinked at Adam. "For what purpose?"

"Because if a hundred thousand men were encamped at Frederick," Adam said, "they'll have left traces. Firemarks. Say ten men to a campfire? So if we count the scorched patches in the fields we'll have a shrewd idea of Lee's numbers."

James laughed gently. "My dear Adam, do you have any idea how long it would take two men to count ten thousand burned patches of grass?" He shook his head. "I appreciate your interest, I surely do, but I don't think we need, if you'll forgive my bluntness, amateur help in the Secret Service. Mind you, if you can help us with some signaling problems, we would be grateful. You're something of an expert on telegraphy, aren't you? Our fellows seem unable to grasp the equipment. They probably send their messages with cleavers!" He snorted with amusement at the thought.

But Adam had no time for heavy-fisted telegraphers, but only to indulge his dull anger at the slowness of the North's army and the plodding obtuseness of its Secret Service. He decided he would ride to Frederick City himself in the dawn, not to count fire patches, but to talk to the people in the town who might give him some indication of Lee's numbers. Civilians, Adam knew, usually overestimated numbers of troops, but maybe there was someone in the town who could give him some facts that the US Cavalry had not found time to seek out themselves.

He saddled his horse before the dawn and was well through the picket line by the time the sun blazed up behind to cast the horse and rider's shadow long across the verge of the white dusty road. He breakfasted as he rode, eating bread and honey and drinking cold tea as his path wended north eastward in parallel with the unfinished railbed of the Metropolitan Rail Road. He felt redundant and useless. In truth he had small purpose for visiting Frederick, for he knew that whatever he discovered, if he found anything at all, would be discounted by Pinkerton's staff, who were busy constructing their own elaborate picture of the rebel army, but Adam was filling in time because any activity was better than another indolent day in McClellan's camp.

The countryside was curiously silent. It was the absence of cocks crowing that was strange, but that, Adam knew, was because rebel foragers must have combed these gentle farms for their supplies. It would be a hungry winter in Maryland.

He watered his horse at Middlebrook, then rode on past the bottomland where he had outgalloped the rebel patrol. His spirits, which had been depressed by the futility of his assignment, began to rise with the sun as he rode through the good country. Haystacks stood neatly in well-tended fields and woodlots were stacked high, though doubtless the advancing army would soon make short work of all that hard labor. It was an image of peace and it warmed Adam's soul that now soared into a sunlit daydream of the war's ending. He doubted he could go back to Virginia, and doubted that he even wanted to return. Instead, he thought, he would go to New England and study for the ministry. He had a vision of a shingled town built about a steepling white church amidst the heavy woods; a place of honesty and hard work, a place where a man could study and preach and minister and write. He saw a study heavy with books, and maybe with his father's ivory-hilted saber, which Adam had captured and now wore at his side, hanging above the fireplace. The saber had been a gift to Adam's great-grandfather from Lafayette, and its blade was handsomely inscribed. "To my friend Cornelius Faulconer," the inscription read in French, "who joined me in the fight for liberty, Lafayette," and Adam imagined his own great-grandchildren treasuring the weapon as a memento of two wars in which virtue had triumphed over evil. He envisioned a kitchen with a heavy black range, steaming pots, drying herbs, and heaped bowls of fruit picked from his own yard. He thought of Julia Gordon in Richmond, and wondered if at the war's ending she would acknowledge the South's sins and come north to share his imagined haven in the deep, pious silence of the New England woods.

These thoughts carried him through Clarkstown,

Hyattstown, and Urbana, until at last he crossed the Baltimore and Ohio. The rebels had prized up the rails and uprooted the ties to leave a scar across the good land, but Adam knew the North's engineers would soon repair the track and have the cars running east and west again. Ahead of Adam now was Frederick City, but all around him was nothing but deserted fields dotted with the pale marks where tents had stood and the dark smears where fires had burned. The rebels had vanished.

It was late morning when he entered the town. "Hey! Soldier!" a woman called, spotting Adam's blue coat. "Where are the rest of you?"

"They're coming, ma'am," Adam answered, courteously touching the brim of his hat.

"Lee's boys are gone, all gone," the woman said, then plunged her washing down the scrub board. "Thought you'd be here sooner."

The townsfolk greeted Adam happily. There were more Northern sympathizers than rebel adherents in the town, and the appearance of a single Yankee soldier was sufficient to prompt a display of Stars and Stripes. The flags were hung from upper story windows or hoisted on makeshift poles. Men came to shake Adam's hand and some pressed gifts on him; cigars or flasks of whiskey. Adam tried to refuse the gifts, but was embarrassed by his own apparent ingratitude and so he pretended to drink from one flask, then thrust a handful of the cigars into a coat pocket. He dismounted at Main Street. A dozen people were all talking at once to him, telling him how the rebels had gone, telling him how large their army had been, but admitting that the Southern forces had not laid the town waste. They had expected to be pillaged, but the rebels had behaved themselves, even if they had insisted on paying for their supplies with Confederate money that was next to worthless. The townsfolk wanted to know when McClellan's army would arrive and when the rebel invasion would be whipped back out of the rest of Maryland. Adam, as he tried to cope with this blizzard of talk, noticed how some people crossed the street to avoid him and others even spat as he passed. The loyalties of Frederick, despite the display of Northern flags, was plainly confused.

Adam wanted to find the mayor or a selectman, but instead he was pressed to go into a nearby tavern and celebrate his one-man liberation of the town. Adam shook his head. He was close to the post office and he decided that the postmaster, being a federal official, might be a source of some authoritative information, and so he tied his horse's reins to a hitching post, took Thorne's gold from the saddlebag to protect it from thieves and, shaking off the importunate crowd, edged into the office. "Sweet Lord above," a woman greeted his appearance, "so you got here."

"Only me, I'm afraid," Adam said, and asked if the postmaster was available.

"Jack!" the woman called, then gestured at the empty tables. "No business this last week," she explained. "Guess we'll be catching up soon enough."

"I guess," Adam said, then greeted the postmaster, a big, redbearded man who emerged from a small office at the back of the building. Some townsfolk had crowded into the post office behind Adam and, to lose their ebullient company, Adam followed the postmaster to the tiny office.

The man proved less than helpful. "I can tell you there was a mighty number of the rogues," he told Adam, "but how many?" He shrugged. "Thousands. Thousands and thousands. What did you say your name was?"

"Major Adam Faulconer."

The postmaster stared at Adam with a look close to suspicion. "You're a major? Not a captain?"

It seemed an odd question, but Adam confirmed his rank. "I was promoted a week ago," he explained. He had hung Thorne's bag of gold coins from his belt and the dull chink of the coins embarrassed him.

The postmaster seemed not to notice the sound of the money. "What's your posting, Major?" he asked.

"I'm at General McClellan's headquarters."

"Then I guess you knew to come here, Major," the postmaster said mysteriously, and unlocked a desk drawer out of which he took a stiff brown envelope that, to Adam's astonishment, had his name written on it. The handwriting was in capital letters and was unfamiliar to Adam, but he felt a tremor of excitement as he pulled the envelope open and unfolded the single sheet of paper.

The excitement turned to astonishment, almost to disbelief, as he read the Special Order. At first, scanning the opening two paragraphs, he wondered why anyone should have bothered to send him what seemed nothing more than a set of routine housekeeping instructions, but then he came to the third paragraph and, barely able to contain his excitement, he saw that he had been given all of the rebels' dispositions. He had in his hand the whole strategy of the rebel army, the positions of every last division in Lee's forces. The paper was gold, pure unalloyed gold, for Robert Lee had scattered his army. Part was at Harper's Ferry, parts were moving north toward Pennsylvania, and others were presumably guarding the road between. Adam read the order twice and suddenly knew he was not serving his country in vain. Even McClellan, given this paper, would surely realize the opportunity. The Young Napoleon could fight each part of Lee's army separately, defeating them one after the other until the rebellion, at least in Virginia and its neighboring states, would be utterly destroyed. "Who gave this to you?" Adam asked the postmaster.

"Didn't give his name."

"But he was a rebel officer?"

"He was," the postmaster paused. "I reckoned it was important, because the fellow kind of acted strange. So I kept it separate from the other letters."

Suppose it was a trap? Adam stared at the signature, R. H. Chilton. He knew Chilton, though not well. Was this a lure? But that was not his decision to make. "What did the man look like?" he asked the postmaster.

The man shrugged. "Small," he said, "plumpish. A bit, how would you say? Delicate? Like he wasn't supposed to be a soldier."

"Did he have a beard?"

"None."

Delaney? Adam thought. Belvedere Delaney? Not that the identity of Thorne's spy mattered now, all that mattered was that this precious piece of paper should get back safe to McClellan. "Thank you," Adam said fervently, then he picked up the discarded envelope, but in his haste he tore it as he tried to put the order back inside. "Use this," the postmaster gave him a larger envelope, which Adam used to hide the order. He went to put the envelope in his pocket, but found it filled with cigars.

"Have these, please," Adam said, spilling the cigars on the desk.

"Not all of them!" the postmaster protested Adam's generosity.

"I've more than enough," Adam said. He did not smoke, but Lyman Thorne enjoyed his cigars, so Adam put the last three into the envelope before shaking the postmaster's hand. "Thank you again," he said fervently.

He hurried back to the street where he thrust the curious onlookers aside and pulled himself into the saddle. He transferred the gold back to its saddlebag and pushed his horse through the crowd until at last he broke free of them and could spur down the street toward the rail depot. A butcher in a bloodied apron came out of a shed as Adam trotted past. "You want to be careful, soldier!" the butcher shouted. "There were some bushwhackers west of the town not long ago."

Adam reined in. "Rebels?" he asked.

"Weren't wearing blue," the butcher said.

"I thought the rebels were gone?"

"These are bastards from over the river. Come to pick up some plunder, like as not. But they were well to the west when I saw them, but they'll be circling round to the south to look at the rail depot. You go out that road," the man pointed due east, "and you'll be well clear of them. After ten or twelve miles you'll come to Ridgeville and you can turn south there."

"Thank you," Adam said, then he turned the horse, kicked his heels back, and urged the horse into a trot. He had a long journey ahead and he had to save his mare's strength and so he curbed his instinct to spur her into a canter. He touched his pocket, scarce daring to believe what was hidden there. Delaney? Was Delaney the traitor? And Adam was shocked at himself for having used the word "traitor," even in his thoughts, for whoever had sent the order was no traitor to the United States. But was it Delaney? Somehow Adam could not imagine the foppish, clever lawyer as a spy, but he could think of no one else who fitted both the postmaster's description of the rebel officer and Colonel Thorne's portrait of his reluctant agent. Delaney, the sly Richmond lawyer with the glib tongue, skin-deep smile, and watchful eyes.

Adam's astonishment took him past a schoolhouse, then by an empty livery stable and a Negro chapel. He splashed through a ford and spurred up the far bank onto

213

a long stretch of road that left the town behind to run between fields blotched with the scars left by rebel camps. He passed a small orchard that had been stripped bare by soldiers and it was just past that orchard, where the road bent leftward and began to run gently down toward the Linganore Run, that he saw the rebel horsemen.

He reined in. The five men were a quarter mile away, motionless, and watching him almost as if they had been expecting him. Two of the horsemen were on the road, one was well to the north, while the others were in the pasture south of the road. For a few seconds the six men all watched each other without moving, then Adam wrenched his mare's head around and spurred her back toward the town.

He had thought of trying to outrun the handful of rebels, but his horse had covered too many miles on a hot day to be capable of a lung-stretching gallop across miles of country. A McClellan-like caution was the best plan and so he kicked his heels to urge the mare back past the plundered orchard.

Adam felt a tremor run through the mare, then she stumbled, and he had to lean to his right to help her keep her balance. For a second he thought she must have put a foot into a hole, but then the sound of the shot arrived. He kicked his heels back again and the mare tried to respond, but a bullet had hamstrung one of her back legs and there was no more she could do for him. She tried one last gallant pace, then buckled and whinnied aloud with the pain. Her blood splashed bright on the dusty road.

Adam kicked his feet free of the stirrups. The dying echo of the single carbine shot crackled about the hot countryside, fading into the heat haze that cloaked the day. He glanced behind and saw the five rebels spurring toward him. He pulled the gold free, then scrambled away from the thrashing horse. He ran into the trees and drew his revolver. Sweat stung his eyes. The horse was crying pitifully, her hooves banging on the road as she fought against the pain in her leg.

Adam steadied himself against the trunk of an apple tree and leveled the revolver. The enemy was still two hundred yards away, a hopelessly long shot for a revolver, but he might be as lucky as they had been with their one fateful shot and so he emptied the cylinder chamber by chamber, aiming at the two closest men who were advancing on the road itself. His view of the enemy was blocked by the smoke of his shots and he had no idea where his bullets were going. He fired his last round, then ran back into the orchard where he crouched, panting, as he reloaded the gun. He was hurrying, and so he fumbled with the cartridges before forcing himself to be methodical. Fear battered him, but he kept it at bay by reminding himself of the stolen order in his pocket. He had to survive.

He pushed percussion caps onto the revolver's cones, then peered eastward. The two horsemen on the road had paused, reluctant to ride closer to his fire, but the other three men had vanished and Adam suddenly realized they must be riding north and south to outflank him. He would be trapped in the orchard and hunted down like a cornered fox.

He ran to the orchard's western edge. The town did not look so far away and there were stands of trees, a straggling hedge, and the remnants of a haystack to give him cover. He looked left and right and could see no enemy and so, committing his safety to God, he ran into the sunlight.

He aimed for the haystack that had been pulled apart by rebels seeking bedding, but there was enough hay left to offer hiding while he gathered his breath for the next stretch back to Frederick. Would any townsfolk hear the gunfire and come to his aid? He ran hard, expecting to hear the whistle of a bullet at any second, then threw himself into the warm, scented hay where he dragged great breaths of humid air into his lungs.

Two rebel horsemen appeared to the south a second or two after Adam had taken cover. The two rebels paused, staring at the orchard, and Adam was tempted to keep running, but knew they would spot him as soon as he left the broken stack. He twisted in his nest of hay to look north, but he could see no enemy there, but then a rumble of hooves made him look south again to see a whole troop of enemy horsemen spurring toward the orchard. The sound of the shots had not brought the townsfolk, but a whole pack of rebel soldiers instead.

They were not Jeb Stuart's cavalry. These men, as the butcher had said, were bushwhackers. They were from the northern counties of Virginia, farmers by day and fighters by night, only on this day they had given up farming to come north and see what pickings could be gleaned from the abandoned rebel camps and to ambush any Northern cavalry patrols probing west toward Lee's army. Their uniforms were the same coats they wore when they wrestled with a plow or gelded a calf, their weapons were hunting rifles and ox-killing pistols, while their hatred of Yankees had been intensified by the frequent Federal invasions of their farmland. They had been robbed, they had been insulted, they had been impoverished, and now, with the fervor of starving dogs seeking carrion, they sought revenge.

Adam checked the percussion caps on his revolver, then looked up to see the newly arrived troop trotting toward the orchard. Dust from the hay clung to the grease on Adam's gun while the smell of the dry grass reminded him of childhood games with his sister Anna, then, with a shameful pang, an unwanted memory came to his mind of the time when he had glimpsed his father clamber off a haystack, carrying his clothes on his arm, then turn to give a hand to Bessie. She had been a house slave then. A year later his father had freed all his slaves, making them servants instead, but for years Adam had been frightened of Bessie because of what he had seen. He had been confused at the time, but later he was tormented by the memories of her lissome, gleaming black body and the bright sound of her laughter as she had jumped down beside his father and pulled her pale blue dress over her head. Adam hated slavery.

But the men who hunted him now, he knew, were no slaveowners. They had barely enough money to own a horse, let alone a Negro, and they did not fight to preserve slavery, but to defend their land, and in that defense they were grim and unforgiving. He wriggled deeper into the hay, pulling great clumps of it over his body, but keeping a loophole free through which he could watch his pursuers.

The rebels had surrounded the orchard and now the majority of them dismounted, hitched their horses to tree trunks, and walked into the apple grove with rifles leveled. Adam's horse was still whinnying with pain, but a sudden shot brought silence. None of the mounted rebels who had stayed outside the orchard was looking toward the haystack and that lack of vigilance persuaded Adam to twist round and look for an escape route. There was a patch of dead ground a hundred paces away, and beyond it, in a field of long grass, a surviving rail fence offered a hint of cover that might let him work his way back to the town, where he would be much safer than in this warm but treacherous refuge. When the rebels discovered that he had escaped from the orchard they were bound to search the haystack and Adam did not want to be found hiding like a child and so he crawled to the haystack's edge, looked back once to check that he was unobserved, then burst out of the hay and ran in a low crouch toward the dead ground.

His saber scabbard tangled in his legs, making him sprawl noisily onto the grass. He unbuckled the saber's belt, let it fall away, then ran on. He heard the shout almost at once and ran as fast as he could. He should have twisted and turned like a beast trying to escape pursuing dogs, but he ran straight toward the dead ground and so gave the rebel who had first spotted him an easy target.

The rebel fired and the bullet slammed into Adam's right buttock. The sledgehammer force of the shot twisted Adam round and threw him forward so that he slid on his back into the shallow valley where he was momentarily hidden. There was blood on the grass, pain in his hip, and tears in his eyes. He gritted his teeth and forced himself upright. The pain was terrible, like a poisoned mist that clouded his thoughts, but he retained enough sense to know that he must save the stolen order. He limped north, intent on reaching the rail fence even though he knew it offered him no salvation now, but he was convinced that if he could just reach the fence he would somehow survive. He forced himself on, though every time he put his weight on his right leg he gave an involuntary cry of agony. Behind him he could hear the whooping calls and galloping hooves of the rebels.

He was trapped. He dropped the bag of gold from his belt, hoping that the loss of its weight would give him speed, but the pain was getting worse and, in a moment of clarity, he knew there was no chance of escape now. The hooves were getting louder. He had seconds, just seconds, to decide what to do, but all that was left was sheer despair and so he staggered up the hollow's far lip, where he plucked the envelope with its cigars and the Special Order from his pocket, then skimmed it into the long grass. A bullet stung the air near him as he twisted back toward the lower ground. The envelope had fallen in the meadow's long grass and Adam could only pray that the rebels had not seen him discard it and would not find it. McClellan's army must come to these fields in time and maybe the order would be discovered. Or maybe not, but Adam had done what he could and now, he knew, he must suffer capture.

He struggled another dozen paces eastward, then collapsed. His pants' right leg was soaked in blood. He lifted the revolver, waiting for his enemies to appear, and he felt a terrible regret for all he had missed in his life. He had never taken a girl into a haystack. He had been dutiful, so very dutiful, and now he could have wept for all his uncommitted sins, and that thought made him close his eyes and utter a prayer for forgiveness.

His eyes were still closed as the rebels gathered about him. They were wiry, hard-faced men who smelled of tobacco, manure, horses, and leather. They slid out of their saddles and one man plucked the revolver from Adam's nerveless fingers. The gun had been his father's and was an English-made Adams, a beautifully engineered weapon with ivory grips, and the rebel who had taken it gave a yelp of triumph as he recognized the gun's quality.

"Got ourselves a Yankee major," a second man said, peering at Adam's badges. "A real major."

Someone kicked Adam's right leg to see if he was conscious. Adam cried aloud in pain and opened his eyes to see a ring of bearded, suntanned faces. One of the men stooped and began searching Adam's pockets, pulling his coat roughly and jarring pain through Adam's side with each tug. "A doctor, please," Adam managed to say.

"Sorry son of a bitch, ain't he?" a man said, then laughed.

Another man had found the gold and that caused new whoops of excitement, and then a third man brought the wondrous saber from the field where Adam had discarded the blade. The leader of the rebels, a thin, clean-shaven man, took the saber and slid it from the scabbard. He read the inscription and, though he knew no French, he could recognize the names. "Faulconer," he said aloud, then, with wonder in his voice, "Lafayette! Son of a bitch." The man wore a black hilted saber at his side, a weapon as crude as a butcher's blade, and now he replaced it with Adam's belt and scabbard before looking again at the inscription on the French made blade. "Faulconer. That's a Virginia name."

"His name's Faulconer," the man who had searched Adam said. He had found the letter from the Inspector General's Department in Washington that appointed Adam to McClellan's army. The letter stated he was inspecting signal arrangements and it was the piece of paper designed by Colonel Thorne to explain Adam's presence in the Federal Headquarters. Now it only served to make things worse.

"What the hell's a signal inspector doing in Frederick?" the rebel leader asked.

"And carrying gold," another man added.

The leader squatted at Adam's feet and pushed the saber's tip into the underside of Adam's chin. "Are you a Virginian, Major?"

Adam stared up at the blue sky.

"I asked you a question, boy," the leader said, giving the saber a prod.

"An American," Adam said. He was feeling faint. He could sense the blood flowing out of his wound, seeping into the ground and making him delirious, but the pain was magically subsiding. He was warm, almost comfortable. "I'm an American," he managed to say.

"Hell, we're all Americans," the rebels' leader said. "But are you a Virginian?"

Adam said nothing. He was thinking of Bessie, who had looked so black and slim and beautiful as she had pulled the blue dress over her smiling face. He thought of Julia Gordon in Richmond. He thought of the dream in New England; the preacher's house, the books, the kitchen, the sound of children laughing in a tree-shaded yard.

"Son of a bitch is crying," one of the rebels crowed.

"So would you if your ass had been shot off," another man said, provoking a gust of laughter.

"Hell of a shot, Sam," a third man said admiringly, "must have been forty rods if it was an inch."

"Fifty at least," Sam said.

The saber pricked at Adam's chin. "What were you doing here, Major?"

"No damn good," one of the rebels answered for Adam, then laughed.

"Son of a bitch," the rebel leader said, then stood and sheathed the lovely saber. He pulled out his revolver and aimed it at Adam's head. "I don't have all day, Major, and nor do you, and I ain't got the patience to wait on you seeing sense. So talk now, you son of a bitch. Just what were you doing here?"

Adam closed his eyes. In heaven, he was telling himself, there would be no tears and no pain and no regrets. No tangle of crossed allegiances. No war. No slavery. There would just be joy and peace and endless calm happiness. He smiled. Such happiness in heaven, he thought, such warm, dreamy happiness.

"He ain't going to talk," a man said.

"He's Faulconer's son," a new voice intervened. "You remember? The son of a bitch deserted in the spring."

"Faulconers never were any damned good," a voice growled, "nigger-loving rich bastards."

The rebel leader fired. The sound of the shot crackled along the hollow and faded as the bullet thumped with a terrible force into the dirt beside Adam's head. "What's your name?" the leader demanded.

Adam opened his eyes. "Faulconer," he said proudly, "and I'm a Virginian."

"So what were you doing here, you bastard?" the rebel asked.

"Dreaming of heaven," Adam said and would say no more.

"You're a traitor, you son of a bitch," the leader said when he realized Adam was determined to stay silent. He fired a second bullet, and this one slammed into Adam's head, making it jerk up once as the bullet drove a fist-sized chunk out of the back of his skull. The head flopped back, blood on the fair hair and with its eyes open, then was still.

The rebel holstered the revolver. "Leave the son of a bitch where he is."

A fly crawled onto one of Adam's eyeballs, then flew down to the wound in his open mouth. The rebels walked away. They had made a good haul: gold, a fine saddle and bridle, a saber and a revolver. They did not find the envelope.

When the Virginian horsemen had gone back south a group of men came from the town to investigate what the shooting had been about. They discovered Adam's body. One of them sent for two slaves and a handcart on which the corpse was wheeled into the town, where there was a discussion about what to do with it. Some wanted to wait until McClellan's army reached Frederick City and then hand the body over, but the Episcopalian minister insisted that no one knew whether the Northern army would even

222

come to the town and that by the time anyone did arrive the corpse would surely be stinking and so a hole was dug in the graveyard where Adam, uncoffined, but in the uniform of the country he had loved, was buried with prayers. The postmaster remembered the dead officer's name, though not how to spell it, and "Adam Falconer" was burned into the wooden cross that marked the heap of soil.

While out in the pasture, close to the hollow and near to some scars of old rebel campfires, the envelope lay unnoticed in the grass.

Billy Blythe stood next to Captain Thomas Dennison and watched Starbuck. Neither man said a word, neither had to. They were both experiencing the same mix of envy and dislike, though in Dennison the dislike was nearer to hatred.

Starbuck was oblivious of their scrutiny. He was stripped to the waist, sheened with sweat, and hauling on a ten-pounder Parrott gun that needed to be taken to the final crest overlooking Harper's Ferry. The route up the hill was too steep for horses or oxen, and so the gun had to be manhandled to the summit and the Yellowlegs had drawn the duty. A dozen other guns were being similarly dragged uphill and so far the Special Battalion had made the best time, but even with fifty men hauling on ropes and another half-dozen heaving at the gun's wheels, their efforts were now blocked by a deep cleft in the rocks, and by a screen of tough undergrowth. "Son of a bitch," Sergeant Rothwell cursed the heavy weapon, then chocked its wheels with rocks so that the gun would not roll back down the last few precious yards gained. There were only fifty paces to go, but those yards could prove to be the most difficult of the climb, and could also cost them the first place in the unofficial race to reach the crest.

Starbuck smeared sweat out of his eyes then pulled free his bayonet and tried to saw through the base of one of the tangling shrubs. "Cut them down," he explained to the men around him, "and fill the gap," he gestured at the fissure in the rock just beyond the clump of bushes, but when he stooped back to the bush he found that the bayonet would not do the job. The tough, fibrous trunk took a clean initial cut, then just stubbornly resisted the steel.

"We need saws and axes," Rothwell said.

Captain Potter, who had been offering encouragement rather than muscle, jerked his head northward. "There are some Georgian boys with saws over there," he said.

Starbuck straightened up, winced at a sudden pain in his back, and wiped the bayonet clean against his pants. He sheathed the weapon. "Lucifer!" The boy clambered up the slope. "Mister Potter knows where there are some saws that need stealing," Starbuck said.

"So much for the Sixth Commandment," Potter said, raising a laugh among the exhausted men.

"Go," Starbuck said, "both of you."

Potter and Lucifer hurried away on their larcenous expedition while Starbuck went back down the slope to help the men hauling the gun's limber. Halfway down he met Captain Peel, who was climbing up with two dozen full canteens of water for the gun's hauliers. "Reckoned you'd be thirsty," Peel panted.

"Well done. Thank you," Starbuck said, pleasantly surprised. Peel, of the four original captains, was proving by far the most useful. He had transferred his allegiance from Dennison to Starbuck and if he was a weak ally, he was still a welcome one. Cartwright and Lippincott did their duties, but without enthusiasm, while Dennison was downright sullen. Billy Tumlin alone seemed able to talk sense into Dennison and for that Starbuck was grateful.

Billy Blythe was talking to Dennison now. The two men had found a private hollow just below the crest and settled there to smoke cigars. "I lost my ma and pa, just like you," Billy Blythe told Dennison. In truth his father had not been lost so much as never found after impregnating Blythe's mother, who was still very much alive but very far from her son's thoughts. "Hard being an orphan," Blythe said.

Dennison, grateful for the sympathy, but still sullen, shrugged.

"Reckon it was harder for you, Tom, than for me," Blythe said generously.

Dennison gave a slight nod, then sucked on the cigar. From far away came the muted thud of big guns bruising the air. He guessed it was a Federal battery shelling the rebels on the hills north of the trapped garrison. "I survived," he said grimly.

"Oh, sure, we survive," Blythe agreed energetically, "but it's more than that, Tom. What people like Starbuck never see is that we orphans are harder than most. Tougher. Got to be. I mean you and I didn't have proper homes, did we? Not like Starbuck. Or maybe he does see. Maybe he does understand that we're tougher, which is why he's jealous."

"Jealous?" Dennison asked. He had never thought Starbuck jealous of him. Scornful, maybe, but never jealous.

"Stands out a mile," Blythe said seriously. "That's why he holds you down, Tom." Blythe paused to pluck a shred of tobacco from his mouth. "Hell, he knows you ought to have been the battalion commander. The thing about these men," here Blythe jerked his cigar toward the men crowded about the stalled cannon, "is that they need discipline. Real hard discipline. Starbuck plays up to them, wants them to like him. He's easy on them. Hell, you or I would have whipped the rank off Potter the moment he got drunk, but not Starbuck. He went easy on him. Soft. But being soft with this sort of battalion won't work, not in battle. You know that and I know that."

Dennison nodded agreement. "Starbuck let Rothwell off the horse. The day he arrived at Camp Lee. Soft, you're right," he said.

"Rothwell!" Blythe said. "Now there's a dangerous man." He fell silent, apparently thinking. "Don't help, not being soft on men like Rothwell," he went on. "Not that I'm the right fellow to bring discipline. I know that. I'm too easygoing. I can see what's wrong, but I ain't got the nature to do anything about it, but then I ain't aiming to stay on here anyway."

"You're not?" Dennison inquired a little too eagerly.

"Hell, no. I'm fixing to go back to Louisiana. That's my patch, Tom, not Virginia. I didn't ask to be put here, I wanted to go home where I belong, and just as soon as this campaign's done I aim to be going south. Five weeks? Six, maybe? Then Billy Tumlin goes home. I'd rather be fighting Yankees in Louisiana than up here, and besides, a Virginia regiment ought to be led by a Virginian, don't you reckon?"

"Yes," Dennison, a Virginian, said fervently.

"And Starbuck, he ain't no Virginian," Blythe went on. "Hell, he ain't even a Southron. What's the point of fighting a war to be rid of the Northerners if you get a Northerner giving you orders?" Blythe shook his head. "Don't make no sense, leastwise none I can see."

"I thought you liked Starbuck," Dennison said resentfully.

"Hell, Tom, there ain't no profit in being an open enemy, not of no man! Besides, it ain't in my nature to act disgruntled, but that don't stop me seeing what's plain as a boil on a whore's backside. If I was Swynyard, and thank the Holy Lord I ain't, I'd take Starbuck away from this battalion and put you in charge." In truth Blythe despised Dennison for a boastful coward, and found it hard even to sit close to the man whose face was a cluster of scabrous patches left over from his sores, but cowardice, as Blythe well knew, was no barrier to a man's ambitions and he saw a desperate ambition in Dennison. "You should be in command," he went on, "with Bobby Case as your second. Then you should all go back to Camp Lee and put in some proper training. That's how to make this battalion into a fine fighting regiment, not Starbuck's way." Blythe shook his head as though in despair.

"Case is a good man," Dennison said. In truth he was terrified of Case and had been somewhat astonished when Tumlin called him Bobby, but Dennison did understand that Case was now a natural ally in the private war against Starbuck.

"You won't find a better man than Case," Blythe agreed vigorously, "salt of the earth. And he respects you, Tom. Told me so." Blythe sniffed as though he had been profoundly moved by Case's confidence. "And I'll tell you something else," Blythe went on. "We shouldn't be here," he waved his cigar in a gesture intended to embrace the whole siege of Harper's Ferry. "The battalion ain't ready to fight. It ain't equipped proper and it ain't trained proper." He spoke emphatically, and Dennison nodded eager agreement. "What this battalion needs," Blythe said, "is a good few months' training. The responsible thing to do, Tom, is to survive this campaign. Do no more than you have to, then take the battalion in hand for a winter's training. I won't be here to help you, because I'll have gone south, but you and Bobby Case can get the job done. But to do it, Tom, you have to survive, and Starbuck's mighty careless with men's lives in battle. You saw that yesterday. Maitland and you had the sense to hold back, you had the sense to spare your men, but not Starbuck. He was waltzing up that hill like a preacher smelling a free ride in a brothel! He gets men killed, Starbuck does, and that ain't the way to win wars. You know that and I know that."

"So what are you suggesting?" Dennison asked, scratching at one of the flaky scabs on his face.

Good God, Blythe thought, what was he supposed to do? Paint a target on Starbuck's back and put a gun in Dennison's hands? "Hell, I ain't suggesting nothing," he said, "except that maybe you and Bobby Case should be running this battalion. Once I've gone south, Tom, it won't make no difference to me, but it hurts, it hurts real bad, to see talent being held back. It ain't in my nature to say nothing when I see that, and you and Bobby are being held back."

A burst of cheering made both men turn to see that Captain Potter and Lucifer had returned with a pair of bucksaws that were swiftly put to work. A squad of outraged Georgians were following the thieves, intent on retrieving the saws, and Starbuck's men were working fast to rip down the bushes before the confrontation.

"That goddamn slave of Starbuck's," Dennison said softly, "he watches all the time. Stays awake at night, watching."

"Hell, down south we know how to treat uppity

niggers," Blythe said scornfully, "specially niggers with guns. He wouldn't last a day down south."

A burst of laughter sounded. Potter, with a face of utter innocence, was claiming that he thought the bucksaws had been discarded. He launched into an elaborate story of just chancing upon the two saws, and while he talked the Yellowlegs ripped the blades to and fro and hurled the sawn bushes up into the small ravine.

The Georgian captain demanded the saws' immediate return. Starbuck, sweat and dirt on his chest, introduced himself. He agreed that theft was a serious matter. "You can identify the saws?" he asked the Georgian.

"Hell, we saw the nigger snatch them!"

"Lucifer!" Starbuck called. "Did you take this gentleman's saws?"

Lucifer shook his head. "Captain Potter said they were lost, sir. Said I should take care of them." Another two bushes were cut through and the men scrambled up to the next tangle of brush and began work again.

"The saws were lying on our coats!" the Georgian protested.

"I think the proper procedure would be a full inquiry," Starbuck said. "If you'd like to make a report to your brigade commander," he told the Georgian, "I'll warn mine that the paperwork is coming. Captain Potter? You can write a detailed report on the circumstances under which you encountered the saws?"

"How many copies, sir?" Potter asked.

"Three at least," Starbuck said.

The Georgian shook his head. "Hell, mister," he said to Starbuck, "my boys can just take the saws now. Kind of spare you the ink. Come on, boys." He led his dozen men toward the saws, but a score of Starbuck's men offered to defend them and the Georgians checked at the odds.

Potter patted the stalled gun. "Shall we load with canister, sir?" he asked Starbuck.

Starbuck grinned, then turned to see that the last of the bushes were being cut down. He waited till the saws had done their work, then collected them. "Thank you for the loan," he told the Georgian Captain, holding out the saws. "Appreciate it."

The Georgian laughed, took the saws, and walked away while Starbuck's men stooped to the gun traces and began hauling. The heavy gun creaked and rocked as it gathered way, then it bounced up over the sawn stumps and crashed over the makeshift bridge that filled the ravine. Starbuck ran alongside the gun, cheering the men on. The gunners ran with him, eager to site the weapon and so begin the bombardment that would doom the trapped garrison of Harper's Ferry. A cheer announced the gun's emplacement, the first gun to be sited above the doomed town. The limber still had to arrive, but Starbuck's men had won the race. And in two days, Starbuck reckoned, they ought to be inside the town and with any luck there would be a rich haul of axes, spades, boots, saws, ammunition, rifles; all the things his Special Battalion needed. And after that they would go north and then, Starbuck knew, he would have to face the Yankees in battle. And maybe, he dared to hope, this would be the last battle, for that was the hope of this rebel campaign. Go north, show the Yankees that the South could not be beaten, and then make peace. That was the dream, the reason to cross the Potomac; the hope that the slaughter would end.

THE NORTHERN ARMY groped cautiously into the deserted Maryland farmlands, where General McClellan left nothing to chance. He watched his flanks, secured his communications, and advanced his forward units at the pathetic pace of ten miles a day. Pinkerton, head of the army's Secret Service, assured McClellan that he faced at least 200,000 well-armed rebels, and McClellan imagined that horrid horde waiting to ambush him like Apaches falling on an army supply train. The White House urged McClellan on while the War Department sent him contrary dispatches declaring that the further he went from the capital the more likely it was that the rebels would swarm over the river to assault the city. McClellan just inched forward, always ready to spring back if danger threatened.

Colonel Thorne had abandoned his Washington office. He could not stand the oppressive heat in the capital, where the only news from the army was grudging while every rumor of Lee's apparent ambitions was only too readily reported by the press. Philadelphia was expecting a siege; the city fathers of Baltimore had forbidden the sale of alcohol to protect the nerves of their fearful citizens; while the British Ambassador, a genial aristocrat, was reported to be packing his bags in preparation for a declaration of war against the United States. "All nonsense, Thorne," Lord Lyons told the Colonel at a White House reception. "No point in going to war with you," he added lightly, "at least not until Bobby Lee's won the thing for us. We might come in then, of course, to pick up the pieces and get some revenge for Yorktown."

"It might come to that, Ambassador," Thorne had answered gloomily.

Lyons, hearing the Colonel's despair, patted his arm. "It won't, Thorne, and you know it won't. Not while you've got that man," he nodded across the crowded room at the President of whom Lyons was famously fond. "I admit that some in Britain are not unhappy to see you embarrassed, Thorne," the Ambassador went on, "but I don't think we wish to risk embarrassment ourselves. Believe me, I'm packing no portmanteaus. Pay a call on us, see for yourself."

But Thorne had no patience for Washington's diplomatic niceties, not while the fate of the Republic was being decided in Maryland and so, with the President's permission, he packed his saddlebags and rode west to join McClellan's headquarters where, seeking Adam, he found that his protégé had disappeared. Allen Pinkerton's Chief of Staff, James Starbuck, whom Thorne had encountered earlier in the war, declared that Adam had ridden toward Frederick City two days before. "If he did," McClellan, who was visiting Pinkerton's quarters, had overheard the comment, "then he deserved what he got."

"Which is what, pray?" Thorne asked.

"Capture, I suppose. The man had no business there. I thought he was here to advise our signal people?"

"He was," Thorne lied, and knowing that McClellan knew he lied.

"Then he should have been working with the telegraphers, not exercising his horse. Unless, of course, he was here for another purpose?"

Thorne stared into the general's young, fresh face, which was set in the perpetual scowl of a man always trying to look older and more severe than his inmost fears made him feel. "What purpose might that have been, General?" Thorne asked spitefully.

"You'd know, Thorne, you'd know," McClellan snapped. He knew full well that Thorne had the President's confidence, and he feared, justifiably enough, that the white-haired Colonel was feeding Lincoln with a constant stream of unofficial news. No wonder the fool in the White House had no idea how to win the war! If the ape would just let McClellan be slow and systematic then the Union would be saved, but no, he was forever prodding and urging McClellan to go faster. And what did Lincoln know of war? My God, the man was a railroad lawyer, not a soldier. McClellan let these resentments brood in his mind as he listened to the distant grumbling of the heavy guns at Harper's Ferry.

A stirring of the thick, warm air caused that grumbling sound to swell into a sudden staccato. Thorne wondered why McClellan did not launch an army corps toward the beleaguered garrison to rescue the thousands of Northern soldiers and their tons of precious supplies from the rebels, but such an ambitious lunge was beyond the Young Napoleon's thinking. "You wouldn't mind, I suppose," Thorne asked, "if I rode toward Frederick City?"

"Your choice, Colonel, your choice, but I can't spare men to protect you. Besides, I confidently expect to camp there tonight, but if you care to ride ahead, it's your risk. Now, if you'll excuse me, I have a war to prosecute."

Thorne did ride ahead of the advancing army, but in the event he arrived much later than McClellan's vanguard. The Colonel's horse threw a shoe and by the time he had discovered a blacksmith and had the shoe nailed back onto the hoof, the Federal army was already moving into the scarred fields that had held the rebel army just a few days before. Axes sounded in the woods as men cut firewood, and everywhere drab tents unfolded in long lines. Latrines were dug, horses led to water, and pickets set to watch the empty fields.

Thorne rode into the town that was filled with curious Northern soldiers who were disappointed not to hear tales of rebel rapine and pillage. Stars and Stripes flew from windows, rooftops, and balconies, but Thorne cynically suspected that just as many rebel flags had greeted the arrival of Lee's army. Barrels of water and lemonade were placed on the sidewalk to slake the soldiers' thirst, while women handed round trays of cookies. One enterprising shopkeeper was doing a brisk trade in Confederate flags; crude things that Thorne guessed had been run up on a sewing machine, but the soldiers were eager enough to buy the souvenirs that would be dirtied, shot at, then sent home as battle trophies. Even the despised Confederate paper money, which had no real value outside the South, was being bought as keepsakes. Four young women in widely hooped skirts and fringed shawls, carrying paper parasols, walked brazenly down the center of Main Street. They were no local girls, that much was obvious, for their pinchbeck sophistication was far too flashy for Frederick City's tastes. Thorne guessed they were four of the hundreds of Washington whores who had followed the army west and were said to have their own transport, tents, and cookhouses.

A tall, white-haired preacher frowned at the sight of the girls, and Thorne, deciding that the preacher looked like a man of sense, approached, introduced himself and, without any real hope of learning anything useful, asked about Adam.

It took the preacher only a few moments and a half dozen questions to identify the missing officer. He hauled off his wide-brimmed hat and gave Thorne the terrible news. "Buried in my own churchyard, Colonel." The minister led Thorne to the graveyard, and to the mound of freshly turned earth with its makeshift wooden cross on which Adam's name had been misspelled. Someone, Thorne was glad to see, had put flowers on the grave. "You poor bastard," Thorne said too softly for the preacher to hear, "you poor innocent bastard."

So that, he thought despairingly, was that, and he rode dejectedly back to the growing Federal encampment. The desperate throw had failed. Thorne had always known it was a reckless and ramshackle chance, but he had deceived himself into believing that somehow it might work. Yet how was Adam ever to have reached Delaney? It had been a waste of a good man and, when Thorne reached the camp and found where his servant had erected his tent, he forced himself to endure the penance of writing to Adam's father. He did not know if Adam's mother still lived, and so he addressed the letter to General Washington Faulconer and assured him that his son had died a hero. "It will doubtless grieve you that he perished while fighting for his country rather than for his native state, but Almighty God saw fit to repose that patriotism in his heart and God's ways are ever inscrutable." The stilted words were hopelessly inadequate, but what words could ever suffice to tell a father of his son's death? Thorne told the General where Adam's body lay, then finished the letter with his sincere regrets. A drop of sweat smeared his signature, but he blotted it dry, sealed the letter, then pushed it to one side. Damn, he thought. The one chance to goad McClellan into a semblance of energetic soldiering had passed. Thorne had played and lost.

Except he had not lost. Two Indiana soldiers, a sergeant and a corporal, had finished pitching their tents and had wandered north out of their camp lines, across a dip in the pastureland, to a cleaner stretch of grass that was unsoiled by rebel litter. They planned to make a fire and boil some coffee away from the predatory gaze of their comrades and so they walked toward a rail fence that had miraculously remained unbroken during the rebels' stay. Rails made good firewood, and the coffee would help pass the long hot afternoon, but just before they reached the fence Corporal Barton Mitchell saw an envelope lying in the grass. It had a curiously bulky look and so he picked it up and shook out the contents. "Bless me, Johnny," he said as the three cigars appeared. He sniffed one. "Damn good too. You want one?"

Sergeant Bloss took the offered cigar, and with it the sheet of paper that had served to wrap the precious find. As he nipped the cigar's end with his teeth he glanced at the paper and, after a few seconds, frowned. There were names here he recognized—Jackson, Longstreet, and Stuart—while at its foot the paper was signed by command of General R. E. Lee.

The coffee was forgotten. Instead the two men took the paper to their company commander, who passed it up the chain of command until at last a prewar colleague of Colonel Chilton's recognized the handwriting. It seemed the order was genuine and it was hurried to General McClellan's tent.

Thorne heard the excitement and, pulling on his blue coat, ducked out of his tent and strode across to where a throng of people was gathered about the General's headquarters. Many in the crowd were civilians come to gape at the Federal general who, convinced that the order was the real copper-bottomed thing, was exultant. McClellan saw Thorne and brandished the paper triumphantly. "Here's a paper with which I can whip Bobby Lee, Thorne! And if I can't I'll go home tomorrow!"

Thorne, astonished at this sudden enthusiasm on McClellan's part, could only gape.

"Tomorrow we'll pitch into his center!" McClellan boasted, "and in two days we'll have him trapped!"

Thorne managed to secure the order. His astonishment grew as he read it, for here were written all Lee's dispositions and those dispositions revealed the enemy commander to be a consummate gambler. Lee must have known that McClellan's army was marching westward, but such was his contempt for his enemy that he had divided his army into five parts, then scattered them across western Maryland and northern Virginia. Most of the Confederate forces were besieging Harper's Ferry, others had gone north to prepare for the invasion of Pennsylvania, while smaller forces barred the hills that faced McClellan's troops. It was true that the order was now four days old, but the constant mutter of the distant guns confirmed that the rebels were still swarming about Harper's Ferry and that sound suggested that the dispositions detailed in the order were still in place, which meant that if McClellan really did march quickly then there was a genuine chance that the Northern army could be placed between the scattered units of Lee's army. Then they would be destroyed, one by one, slaughter by slaughter, surrender by surrender, page after page of history being made.

"Rebellion's end, Thorne," McClellan said as he retrieved the paper.

"Indeed, sir," Thorne said, and felt a pang of distaste for the short general whose hair was so carefully waved and whose mustaches so gleamingly brushed. A gelded cockerel, he thought, and was ashamed that he should so resent this gift of utter victory being given to such a creature.

"You don't doubt the order's genuine?" McClellan inquired, unable to hide his nagging anxiety that the order might be a ruse, though the circumstances of its finding suggested gross carelessness rather than sly design. "Pittman vouches for the handwriting," the General went on. "It's Chilton's penmanship, right enough, or so Pittman says."

"I trust Colonel Pittman's memory on the point, sir," Thorne admitted.

"Then we've won!" McClellan crowed. The ape in the White House might take the credit for preserving the Union, but George Brinton McClellan was content that the voters at the next presidential election would know who was truly to thank. McClellan in '64! And '68, by God, and maybe forever once the voters realized that only one man in the country had the nerve, prudence, and wisdom to steer America! McClellan luxuriated in that vision for a moment, then clapped his hands. "Marching orders!" he announced, then shooed his visitors away so that he could work in peace.

Thorne found Colonel Pittman, and from Colonel Pittman he traced the order's discovery back to Sergeant Bloss and Corporal Mitchell. From them he learned where the envelope had been found, and after that he rode into Frederick City and found a man who had helped retrieve Adam's body. To Thorne's delight he discovered that the body had been found only yards from where the envelope had lain, and that circumstance convinced Thorne that the copy of Special Order 191 was genuine, and not a subtle trap laid by an outnumbered enemy. "So it wasn't in vain," he told Adam in his grave. "You did well, Faulconer, you did well." He solemnly saluted the grave, then said a prayer of thanks. God, it seemed, had not abandoned His country. And well done, Delaney, Thorne added silently. The Richmond lawyer had earned a reward.

For already the first Federal troops were preparing to march with new haste and sudden purpose; preparing to march west to where Lee's betrayed army was spread so carelessly across the summer-heated land. The Young Napoleon had been offered victory and now, with uncharacteristic verve, he sprang to take it.

At dawn Harper's Ferry was shrouded in a mist that flowed like twin white rivers from the Shenandoah and the Potomac valleys to meld softly above the town. The mist flowed in utter silence, but it was an ominous silence, for by now the rebel troops commanded all the high ground about the river town and their great guns had been dragged forward to the crests so that their cold, dew-beaded barrels were pointing down to what lay hidden by the soft white vapor. The gunners had loaded and rammed their pieces, and their most distant cannon was scarcely a mile from the mist-concealed Federal defenses, a mere six and a half seconds of flight for the nineteen-pound shells that were nestled inside the barrels against the two-pound charges of coarse powder that would explode when Jackson gave the signal. There were guns to the north of the town, guns to the south, and guns to the west. A ring of guns, all silent now, all waiting for that shroud of mist to lift from the doomed town.

General Thomas Jackson paced the rocky crest of the Bolivar Heights west of the town from where he scowled at the valley mist as though it were a devilish device planted to thwart his victory. His cadet cap was pulled low over his brooding eyes, but those eyes missed nothing as he walked up and down, up and down, sometimes dragging a cheap watch from his pocket and peering at its slow-moving hands. The gunners tried not to catch his gaze. Instead they busied themselves with unnecessary tasks like greasing already lubricated elevating screws or straightening the friction primers that came bent from the factory so that they would not accidentally ignite and cause an explosion. Shirt-sleeved infantry carried ammunition up the hill trails and stacked their loads beside the waiting guns.

Most of the rebel infantry would be spectators of this battle and the hills were crowded with lines of gray and butternut uniforms waiting for Old Jack's firework display. Starbuck's battalion was close to a mixed battery of ten- and twenty-pounder Parrott guns, their trails all burned with the initials USA, evidence that Jackson had equipped his batteries with cannon taken from the Yankees. Captain Billy Blythe carried a cup of coffee as he joined Starbuck. "That's Old Jack?" he asked, nodding at the shabby, bearded figure who stumped in his huge square-toed boots up and down beside the guns.

"That's Jackson," Starbuck confirmed.

"Queer-looking fellow," Blythe said.

"Frightening as hell," Starbuck said.

"Specially to Yankees, eh?" Blythe said, then sipped at the coffee that was bitterly sour. He could not wait to get back to the North where the coffee was rich and fragrant, and not this adulterated dirt that the rebels drank. "You met him?"

"I met him." Starbuck was never particularly communicative in the morning and spoke curtly.

Blythe did not mind. "You reckon he'd say howdy?" he asked Starbuck.

"No."

"Hell, Starbuck, I'd like to shake the man's hand."

"Shake mine instead," Starbuck said, but instead of offering it he stole Tumlin's coffee and sipped it. "And if you swear in front of him, Tumlin, you'll wish you'd never met him."

"Keep the coffee, Starbuck," Blythe said magnanimously, "ain't nothing but goober pea shit anyhow. Mom-

240

ing, General!" he called aloud as Jackson's pacing brought the General close to Starbuck's men. "Fine one for a victory, sir!"

Jackson looked astonished at being addressed and stared at Blythe as though surprised to see a soldier on the hill, but he said nothing. Blythe, unfazed by this cold response, strode forward as if the General was his oldest friend. "Prayers are being answered, sir," Blythe said vigorously, "and the enemy will be crushed in the very nest where John Brown defied our legitimate aspirations."

"Amen," Jackson said, "amen. And you are, sir?"

"Tumlin, General," Blythe said, "Captain Billy Tumlin, and proud to meet you, sir. I prayed for you these many months and am grateful that the Lord has seen fit to hear me."

"'Vengeance is mine, saith the Lord,'" Jackson said, turning to look at the mist through which the topmost part of the town and the pinnacle of a church in the lower quarter was now showing. The vapor was thinning, promising to lay bare the Yankee defenses. "You're saved in the Lord, Captain?" Jackson asked Blythe.

"Praise His name, yes," Blythe lied glibly.

"I didn't hear," Jackson snapped and cupped a hand to his ear. Years of artillery work had deadened the General's hearing.

"Praise His name, yes!" Blythe shouted.

"We are a Godly nation, Captain, and a righteous army," Jackson growled. "We cannot be defeated. Fight with that assurance in your heart."

"I shall, sir, and amen," Blythe responded, then held out his hand, which the General, with some surprise at the gesture, finally clasped. "God bless you, sir," Blythe said as he shook Jackson's hand, then he turned and walked back to Starbuck. "See?" Blythe chuckled. "Easy as feeding crumbs to a bird."

"So what did you say to him?"

"I told him I was one of God's anointed, told him I prayed for him daily, and offered him God's blessing."

"You ain't a saved Christian, Billy Tumlin," Starbuck said sourly. "You're nothing but a miserable sinner."

"We have all sinned, Starbuck," Blythe said earnestly, "and fallen short of the glory of God."

"Don't preach to me, for Christ's sake, I've had my bellyful of preaching."

Blythe laughed. He was pleased with himself for having shaken the great Jackson's hand, and the tale would be a good boast in the comfortable days after he had crossed the lines. He was pleased, too, for having fooled Jackson into thinking he was with a fellow Christian. Be all things to all men, that was Billy Blythe's belief, but make sure you profit from the deceptions. "So what happens now?" he asked Starbuck.

"What do you think? We shoot the hell out of those poor sons of bitches, they surrender, then we go and shoot the hell out of the rest of the sorry bastards." Starbuck checked suddenly, arrested by the distant sound of gunfire. It was very distant, much too muted and far away to be the guns on Harper's Ferry's farther side. The same distant grumbling had trembled across the sky the previous evening, just before the sun had set in a blaze of western scarlet, and Starbuck had climbed to the ridge top to see a small billow of whiteness on the far northeastern skyline. That far whiteness, which had been touched pink by the dying day, could have been an errant wisp of cloud, except that the noise had betrayed what it truly was—gunfire. A skirmish or battle was being waged deep inside Maryland. Starbuck shuddered and was glad he was here and not there.

The last mist shredded from the valleys to reveal the small town of Harper's Ferry huddled at the point between the merging rivers. The fame of the place had somehow persuaded Starbuck that it would prove a large town, almost the size of Richmond maybe, but in truth it was a tiny place. It must have once been a pleasant, tree-shaded village built on a spur of hill that dropped to the banks of the Potomac and Shenandoah rivers, though now many of the buildings were charred ruins out of which brick chimney stacks reared gaunt. An undamaged church flew a flag that, when Starbuck borrowed a gunner's binoculars, he saw to be the British flag. "I thought those bastards were on our side," he told the gunner officer.

"Who cares? Kill 'em anyway," the gunner laughed, reveling in the wealth of targets that the lifting mist had revealed. There were federal earthworks on the edge of the town and naked batteries waiting to be shelled. The two rivers were edged by a sprawl of industrial buildings that had once been the Federal Arsenal and a rifle factory but which were now nothing but scorched roofless walls, while the massive bridge that had once carried the Ohio and Baltimore's rails over the Potomac had been reduced to a series of stone piers like the stepping stones of a giant. The only passage across the wide Potomac now was a pontoon bridge erected by Northern engineers, but as Starbuck watched a great fountain of water exploded out of the river beside the bridge, making the pontoons tug on their chains. A few seconds later there came the sound of the rebel gun that had fired the shell from the distant hills.

Jackson looked startled, for he had not yet ordered his signalers to wigwag the order to begin the bombardment, but someone in the rebel lines on the north side of the Potomac had tired of waiting and suddenly all the guns on all the hills about the town crashed back on their trails and pumped smoke and shells toward the trapped garrison. The watching infantry cheered as the wispy smoke trails of the shells' burning fuses arced down to the battered town where the Yankees waited.

And where they now died. The rebel gunners worked like fiends to sponge out, reload, and ram their guns, and shell after shell screamed down the slopes to explode in gusting swathes of smoke, flame, and dirt. The Yankee earthworks outside the town seemed to disappear in blasts of smoke, and when the smoke drifted clear the watching rebels could see their enemies running back toward the town's war-scarred buildings. A few Yankee guns tried to answer the destructive barrage, but the Northern batteries were swiftly battered into silence by the rebel artillery. To the watchers on the hills it seemed as though the river town was being turned into a pit of hell. Flames leaped up from burning limbers, smoke drifted thick, and huge trees shivered like saplings as the shells blasted the leaves away. Sweat poured down the gunners' faces and bare chests. Each recoil slammed the guns violently back so that their trails gouged deep troughs in the dirt. The wet sponges that extinguished any trace of red-hot explosive remaining in a barrel after each shot hissed and steamed as they were rammed down to the breach, then, the second that the sponge was withdrawn to be thrust into a bucket of dirty water, the loader would shove the next round into the muzzle to be rammed hard down while the rest of the team maneuvered the gun back to its proper aim. "Ready!" the gunner would shout and the team would duck aside with hands over their ears as the command to fire was shouted. The gunner yanked the lanyard that scraped the friction primer over its incendiary tube and a heartbeat later the gun would crash back behind its billow of smoke and another shell, its fuse smoking, screamed toward the town.

"I was there once," Billy Blythe said to Starbuck.

"You were?"

"Saw Mister Brown hung," Blythe said contentedly. "Smug son of a bitch."

"What were you doing there?"

"Buying horses," Blythe said. "That was my trade, see? And once in a while we came north to find a nag or two. Stayed at Wager's Hotel." He stared at the town and shook his head. "Burned to a cinder, by the look of things. A pity. I was hoping to renew my acquaintance with a girl there. Sweet as honey, she was, only a lot cheaper," he laughed. "Hell, she and I were watching out of a bedroom window when they hung that smug son of a bitch. Hung him higher than an angel. Kicked like a mule, he did, and all the time I was making that sweet little honey moan for pleasure."

Starbuck felt a flicker of distaste for his second in command. "I met John Brown," he said.

"You did?"

"He came to Boston wanting funds," Starbuck explained, "but he didn't get none from us." At the time he had been puzzled that his father had refused to help the famous abolitionist, but now, looking back, he wondered if the Reverend Elial Starbuck had been jealous of the stern, ravaged-faced Brown. The two men had been very alike. Had his father feared such a formidable rival in the abolition movement? But Brown was dead now, and in the wake of his hopeless rebellion there was a plague of death across America. "He told me I'd be a warrior against the slavocracy," Starbuck recalled the meeting in his father's parlor, "guess he got that wrong."

"You're fighting to keep the slaves, is that it?" Blythe asked.

"Hell, no. I'm fighting because I've nothing better to do."

"Slaves won't be freed anyway," Blythe said confidently.

"They won't?"

"Not this side of heaven, and if God's got any sense,

not there neither. Hell, who's going to pay the lazy sons of bitches wages?"

"Maybe they're only lazy because they don't get wages," Starbuck said.

"Sound like your pa, Major."

Starbuck bit back an angry retort. He was surprised at his sudden suspicions of Billy Tumlin and wondered if he was being unfair to the man, but he sensed that Tumlin's glibness concealed a sly dishonesty. Billy Tumlin lied too easily, and Starbuck had seen proof of that when Tumlin talked with Jackson, and now he wondered how many other lies Tumlin had told. There was something that did not ring true about Tumlin, and Starbuck found himself wondering why a man who had ostensibly escaped from a Yankee prison was so well fed and so handsomely equipped with a money belt. "I'm going to get myself a map in Harper's Ferry," he said just after the nearest gun had thumped back on its trail.

"A map?" Blythe asked.

"I want to see where Union is in Massachusetts, Tumlin. You kind of piqued my interest. I thought I knew half the back towns in Massachusetts on account of going with my father when he preached upcountry, but I sure as hell don't remember a Union. Where was it near?"

"Hell, it weren't near nowhere!" Blythe was suddenly defensive. "It was a prison, remember. Maybe the Yankees made the name up?"

"I guess that must be it," Starbuck said, content that he had unsettled his second in command, but as Tumlin moved away to find more congenial company Starbuck found himself wondering how many enemies he could afford to make in the Special Battalion. Case would kill him as soon as give him the time of day, and Starbuck suspected Dennison would do the same if he could ever summon up the courage. He could not depend on Cartwright or Lippincott, who did their duty, but with a singular lack of enthusiasm. Potter was a friend, and Caton Rothwell too, but Starbuck's enemies far outnumbered his friends. He had experienced the same divide of loyalties in the Legion and Starbuck, reflecting on the schisms, feared it was because of his personality. He envied men like Colonel Elijah Hudson, the North Carolinian whose battalion had fought alongside the Legion at Manassas and whose men seemed united in affection for him. Or Pecker Bird, still recovering from his wound, who had inspired nothing but loyalty during his time as the Legion's commander. Then Starbuck noticed Old Mad Jack pacing up and down beside the busy guns. The General, as he so often did, was holding his left hand in the air as though he was testifying to God's goodness, though in truth he only held the hand in the odd position because otherwise, he believed, the blood would puddle around an ancient wound. Starbuck watched the General and thought that there was a man who made enemies as well as friends.

Jackson chose that moment to glance up and catch Starbuck's eye. For a moment the two stared at each other with the uncomfortable sensation of recognition, but with nothing to say either, then Jackson made a growling sound as he lowered his left hand. "Have you found your Savior yet, Mister Starbuck?" he called, evidently recalling his last conversation with Starbuck.

"No, General."

Jackson veered toward Starbuck, trailing a gaggle of staff officers behind him. "But you are searching?" he inquired earnestly.

"I'm thinking about something else right now, General," Starbuck said. "I was kind of wondering why a soldier makes enemies of his own side just by doing his duty."

Jackson blinked at Starbuck, then frowned at the dirt beside his ungainly boots. He was plainly considering the question, and giving it hard thought, for he remained staring at the ground for what seemed like a full minute. One of his aides called to him, but the General flapped an irritated hand to show that he did not want to be disturbed, and when the aide called again he simply ignored the importunate man. Finally his fierce eyes looked up at Starbuck. "Most men are weak, Major, and the reaction of the weak to the strong is usually envy. Your job is to make them strong, but you cannot do that alone. Do you have a chaplain in your battalion?"

Starbuck wondered if the General assumed he was still in command of the Legion. "No, sir."

"Sir!" the aide called from beside the guns.

Again Jackson ignored the man. "Sheep need shepherds, Major," he told Starbuck, "and greater strength comes from a man's faith than from his sinews. I am, God knows, the weakest of mortals!" This was proclaimed in the energetic voice of a man sure of his own soul, "but God has given me duties and granted me the strength to perform them."

"Sir! Please!" the aide stepped closer to Jackson.

Jackson, in a surprising gesture, touched Starbuck's arm. "Remember, Major," he said, "'They that wait upon the Lord shall renew their strength; they shall mount up with wings as eagles; they shall run, and not be weary; and they shall walk, and not faint.' Isaiah."

"Chapter forty," Starbuck said, "verse thirty-one."

Jackson smiled. "I shall pray for you, Major," the General said, then turned to his aide and his smile vanished. "What is it?"

The aide was carrying a pair of field glasses that he offered to the General. "The enemy, sir," he said, pointing down toward the beleaguered town, "is surrendering."

"Cease fire! Cease fire!" It was the nearest battery commander who, lacking any orders, had decided to end the bombardment on his own authority.

Jackson seized the field glasses, but even without their aid it was possible to see two Yankees walking with a white flag between the patches of smoke that drifted from the exploded shells. The Yankees were holding a grubby white flag hoisted on a pole. "It was a pitiful defense," Jackson growled angrily. "They should be ashamed of themselves." He hurried away, shouting for his horse to be fetched.

"Cease fire!" another gun commander shouted. The rebel guns on the farther hills had still not seen the white flag and they went on firing until the signalers managed to wigwag their flags with the message about the enemy surrender, and so a silence gradually fell across the smoke-veiled, explosive-torn valley, though it was not a total silence, for out of the distant, heat-hazed north, from across the river and the faraway hills, came the sound of other guns. Someone was fighting hard, but who, or where or why, no one in Harper's Ferry knew.

Belvedere Delaney was seeing his first battle and finding it far more terrifying than anything he could have imagined or feared. He had ridden to the range of hills that barred the Yankees' approach from the east and had arrived in time to witness McClellan's attack on the southernmost of the two passes that had been guarded by pitifully small numbers of rebel troops. Prudence would have dictated that the passes be more heavily manned, but Lee had gambled on McClellan's usual supine performance and so had stripped the defenders bare to add to the men assaulting Harper's Ferry.

But McClellan was no longer supine. McClellan knew

his opponent's mind and now he lunged to break the rebel army.

To Delaney, watching from a high vantage point north of the pass, it seemed as though waves of blue-clad troops were washing up the wide valley like ocean waves running toward a beach. The foam of the breaking surf was the rill of smoke caused by exploding Yankee shells that crashed and flamed along the rebel defenses, while behind the smoke the long lines of blue infantry came remorselessly forward. Delaney was too far away to smell the blood or see the heavy coils of men's guts spewed across the summer grass, but the noise alone carried a violence that was almost unbearable. The crash of the guns was percussive, deafening, disorientating, and, worst of all, unending. How any man could live under that barrage was beyond Delaney's comprehension, yet live they did, and the occasional splintering crack of rifle volleys told him that some rebel units still fought back against the onrush of Yankees.

The Yankee tide did not come forward smoothly, indeed, to Delaney, it often seemed inexplicably slow. He would watch a line of infantry advance under its flags and then, for no apparent reason, the line would stop and the men settle down. Another line would jerk forward while busy horsemen galloped in what seemed aimless errands between the advancing lines. Only the big guns never stopped, filling the shallow pass with smoke and noise and terror.

Behind the pass, stretching out toward the gentler farmland of eastern Maryland, a mass of Federal troops was gathering. McClellan's army was crowding behind the attack ready to stream through the pass and ram their guns and rifles between Lee's scattered troops. To the west, behind the rebel lines, there was no such show of strength, only country roads carrying wagons of wounded back toward the unseen Potomac.

"I guess our message got through," Delaney said to George.

George, a handsome, light-skinned Negro, nodded. "Something stirred them," he agreed in an amused tone.

Delaney, recalling his terror at being found out, felt an immense relief. He unstoppered a silver flask and drank from it, then handed the flask to George. "A toast to Northern victory, George."

"To victory," George said, and tipped the flask to his lips. He savored the wine, then smiled. "You brought some of the '49 hock."

"Only one bottle."

"A pity it isn't chilled," George said reprovingly.

"When Richmond falls," Delaney said, "we shall bathe in chilled hock."

"You might, not me."

Delaney laughed. Rome, he was thinking, Rome was the place to go, or if Rome was pitching it too high, then perhaps Athens or Naples. He would be an ambassador for freedom in a place of suntouched beauty and decadent luxury. He would uniform George in a curled wig and a gilt-encrusted coat, and dine to the sound of a string quartet playing beneath heavy-scented flowers. By day he would lecture the natives on the arts of government and by night be lectured by them on the arts of decadence.

Beneath him, struggling to make that dream come true, the blue lines suddenly surged forward. The rebels were breaking. Men who had fought and beaten Yankees on fields across Virginia were now tasting defeat. Their defenses were shredding and breaking. Small groups of men ran westward, some shrugging off equipment so they could run faster, while others were left dead or wounded on the shell-torn turf as the victorious Yankees swept across the captured positions. The surviving rebel guns were being limbered up and whipped away, their encampments were abandoned, and everywhere the Stars and Stripes came forward. "Time to go, George," Delaney said, watching the rout.

"But to where? Richmond?"

"Back to Lee, I think. I should like to be a witness of the bitter end," Delaney said. He thought there might well be a book in it. A tragedy, probably, for though Lee was his country's enemy, he was a good man, but Delaney doubted whether goodness was the quality that won wars; only might, hard resolve, and low treachery could do that.

Delaney turned his horse and cantered west. He had betrayed the Confederacy to McClellan and now prayed he would be a witness to its destruction.

The Federal general who formally surrendered the Harper's Ferry garrison was splendidly uniformed in gold-braided blue with a shining scabbard hanging from his belt, while Jackson, accepting the great prize, was in a filthy homespun coat, shabby boots, and with his battered cadet cap crammed over uncut, dirty hair. Jackson, even in victory, looked grim, though he did allow himself a smile when Starbuck's hearse came into view. The vehicle was being pulled by the skirmishers of Potter's company, while Potter himself was riding on the box from where he cracked an imaginary whip. The Yankee General, still at Jackson's side, wondered for the hundredth time why McClellan had not come to the garrison's rescue and then, at the sight of the hearse, was overcome with mortification as he realized the utter shame of being defeated by such ragamuffin troops. None of the victorious rebels was better dressed than their general, and most were worse; indeed some of Jackson's men limped into the town on bare feet while the beaten Yankees were outfitted with the best products of the industrial north.

Colonel Swynyard came hurrying down the column in search of Starbuck. "You can jettison your death-cart, Nate!" the Colonel called. "The town's crammed with wagons. New wagons, fine wagons. I've left young Coffman guarding a pair for you. Told him to shoot any rogue who dared lay a finger on them. And I daresay we can give most of your fellows rifles now, there must be thousands here! And food. It's like Manassas Junction all over again."

For once again Jackson had captured a major Federal supply base, and once again his hungry, footsore, ill-dressed troops were given run of the North's largesse. Whoops of joy greeted each opened crate. Tinned meat was prized open with bayonets and real coffee set to boil on fires made from splintered crates that had carried brand-new rifles. Jackson's commissary officers did their best to see that the most needy units received the pick of the plunder, but the chaos was too great and the first arrivals grabbed most of the choice pickings. Starbuck's men were early enough to find some rifles, boots, food, and ammunition, but not enough for every man, yet Starbuck was able to give two of his four musket-carrying companies brand-new Springfield rifles still coated in their factory grease. The rifle locks were inscribed 1862 and were handsomely engraved with an American Eagle and "US Springfield." The hearse and one of the two wagons were loaded up with cartridges for the new rifles.

Swynyard frowned at the hearse. "Are you sure you want to keep it?" he asked Starbuck.

"The men like it. It makes them feel special."

"I suppose it would," Swynyard said, then raised his head to listen to the far off sound of gunfire. "We're marching in the morning," he said grimly. "No rest for the wicked."

"What's happening?"

"Yankees are attacking," Swynyard said vaguely, then shrugged as if to say that he knew no more. "Lee wants us all together again. It'll be hard marching, Nate. Tell your fellows they have to suffer the blisters and keep going. Just keep going." The Colonel had a map that he unfolded to show Starbuck the route they would take. "We go up the southern bank of the Potomac," he said, tracing the westward road with a nail-bitten finger, "to a ford here, near Shepherdstown, then we march east as far as here." He tapped the map.

Starbuck peered at the rendezvous, which was a town situated at a road junction just a few miles inside Maryland. "Sharpsburg," he said. The map showed a small town positioned on a wide strip of land formed by the Potomac River and one of its tributaries, Antietam Creek. "Sharpsburg," Starbuck said again. "Never heard of it."

"You're sleeping there tomorrow night," Swynyard said, "God willing."

"My men's feet willing, more likely," Starbuck said. He lit one of the captured cigars that Lucifer had discovered along with a haul of new underwear, shirts, sugar, and coffee. "Did we get any horses for the wagons?" he asked.

"A few, none of them good." The Colonel folded his map. "Early start, Nate. Get some sleep."

Getting sleep was easier said than done, for the men did not want to sleep. They had won a victory and the ease of that victory was cause for celebration and the Yankee supplies had yielded enough liquor to make that celebration rousing. Others, like Starbuck, wanted to look at the sights. They marveled at the captured cannons that were lined wheel to wheel in the armory yard and that would now take their place in the Confederate battle line, then they explored the engine house where John Brown had been surrounded with his hostages. The little firefighter's building had a handsome cupola, reminding Starbuck of the widow's walks on the houses beside the sea in Massachusetts, though this cupola, like the engine house's brickwork, was pitted by the scars made by the bullets of the US Marines who, under Colonel Robert Lee's command, had forced John Brown's surrender. Some rebels were all in favor of pulling the engine house down in case it became a Yankee shrine, but no one had the energy for the demolition and so the building remained intact. Starbuck climbed to the church flying the British flag to discover it was a Catholic building that had sheltered its parishioners beneath a neutral flag. A nearby church had been shelled to destruction, but the Catholic congregation had escaped the bombardment.

The Yankee prisoners marched disconsolately out of the town, going to the heights where they would bivouac before being sent south to the prison camps. Harper's Ferry was left to its new owners who, as night fell, lit cooking fires that flickered low as men rolled themselves in blankets and slept on ground still littered with fragments of shell casing. Starbuck had made his quarters in an abandoned railroad box wagon, but he could not sleep and so he pulled on his boots and, careful not to wake Lucifer who, after nights of watching Starbuck, had at last fallen fast asleep, slipped out of the wagon and walked between his sleeping men toward the bank of the Shenandoah.

He was bone tired, but he could not sleep, for the same fears that had prompted his morning conversation with Jackson were nagging at him. He felt presentiments of failure and suspected they sprang from within himself. He had failed to unite the Special Battalion, just as he had failed with the Legion. No battalion, he told himself, could fight well if it was riven with jealousies and hatred, but discerning the problem did not help him find a solution. It was true that he had made some allies in the battalion, but they numbered fewer than half of the total, and many of the rest were bitter enemies. He thought about Elijah Hudson and Pecker Bird and Robert Lee and decided that their popularity sprang from character, and if character was lacking, he chided himself, leadership was a hopeless ambition. Griffin Swynyard had changed his character through the grace of God and that had made all the difference; a once-hated major had become an admired colonel. Starbuck picked up a piece of rubble and tossed it into the river that here flowed fast and white over rocky outcrops to its junction with the Potomac.

So was God the answer? Was there nothing he could do for himself? Starbuck, gloomier than ever, suspected that the ambition in his own soul was the flaw that revealed itself to his men. That and the cowardice that he saw in himself. Or perhaps Maitland was right, and some men were born to lead. Starbuck swore softly. He had a vision of a perfect battalion, one that operated as smoothly as the newly greased mechanism of the captured Springfield rifles. A machine that worked.

Jackson had said that only God could give a man strength, and only strength could make a battalion work together. A battalion was composed of men with different fears and suspicions and ambitions, and the trick of it was to swamp those desires with a greater desire: the desire to work together toward victory. In a day or two, Starbuck feared, the Yellowlegs would face a real Yankee army, the same army that had made the northern horizon vague with smoke these last two days, and how would they fight then? Of the officers Potter alone was loyal, and Potter, God knew, was a weak reed. Starbuck closed his eyes. A part of him yearned for the grace of God to drench him with strength, but whenever he was tempted to yield to his Maker's will another temptation intervened, and this was a more beguiling temptation. It consisted of memories of firelit bodies, not dead and twisted and lice-ridden and scarred and filthy, but bodies on sheets. Sally pushing her hair back from her face. The girl who had died under Blythe's bullets at the tavern. He remembered her crouching by the fire, her red hair falling down her naked back, laughing as she toasted a scrap of bread on which she had melted a scrap of cheese taken from a mousetrap. Heaven, Starbuck liked to think, lay in those moments and he was unwilling to call them hell. His father had always said that being a Christian was not easy, but it had taken these last two years to show Starbuck how desperately hard it really was. He did not want to abandon sin, yet he feared that he would fail as a soldier if he did not. He wondered if he should pray. Maybe a prayer by this hurrying river would hurtle its way through the smoky air to the ear of God, who alone could give a man the strength to overcome temptation.

A stone slid on stone to Starbuck's right. He opened his eyes and saw a shadow flicker among the rubble and stunted trees on the riverbank. "Who's there?" he called.

No one answered. He decided it must have been a rat, or else one of the rake-thin cats that lived wild in the ruined armory. The lights of the town showed through trees, but they revealed nothing on this broken riverbank where weeds grew thick among fallen stones. He turned back to the water. Maybe, he thought, he should pray. Maybe he should claw and crawl his way back to God, but where would that journey end? On the Yankee side? On his knees to his father?

A click sounded and he knew it was a gun being cocked. For a second he froze, hardly daring to believe what he suspected, then he threw himself backward just as a gun flamed and banged to his right. The shot screamed over his head and a billow of smoke gusted across the water. He scrambled into a half-choked culvert that was brimming with scummy water and he dragged the Adams revolver from his holster. He heard footsteps, but could see no one. A sentry was shouting, demanding to know who had fired and why, then Starbuck saw a shape silhouetted against the tree-shrouded lights of the town and he leveled the revolver. Then a second man sprang up and he changed his aim, but both were running away, bent double, unrecognizable, scuttling toward the rusted tracks of the Baltimore and Ohio rails. He fired once, but over their heads for if he had aimed and missed then the bullet could have struck home among the encamped soldiers. More men were running toward the river, shouting warnings and questions.

Starbuck dragged himself out of the filthy water. A sentry saw him and dropped to one knee with his rifle leveled. "Who are you?" he shouted.

"Major Starbuck. Swynyard's Brigade," Starbuck holstered the revolver and brushed stinking water off his pants. "Put the gun down, lad."

An officer arrived demanding to know who had fired and why. Starbuck gestured at the river. "Thought I saw a man swimming. I reckoned it was an escaping Yankee."

The officer stared at the moon-glossed river that foamed over the rocks. "I can't see anyone."

"So I was dreaming," Starbuck said. "Now I'm going to bed."

He walked away. He heard the word "drunk" being used, but he did not care. He knew what he had seen, but he had not known whom he had seen. Two men, his men, he guessed, and somewhere in the battalion they were still loose and waiting for their chance.

Them and a hundred thousand Yankees. Across the river. Marching toward a town no one had ever heard of. Called Sharpsburg.

PART TWO

THE CREEK WELLED from a mossy spring in a low pass of the South Mountains, then flowed west and south through a rocky landscape of thin soil and old trees. Little disturbed the stream's flow in its first few miles, for there were no settlements in that part of Pennsylvania, but just east of Waynesborough the creek flowed into farmland and became muddied with the feet of cattle. There were still no bridges, for the stream was shallow enough to be forded even during the winter spate, and so it flowed on across the border into Maryland where, deepened and broadened by other streams, it reached its first bridge at Hagerstown. Fish lay in the bridge's shadow, and in summer children played in the waist-deep water.

Past Hagerstown the creek ran southward, flowing deeper and stronger as more tributaries joined, but still it was little more than a stream. In places it ran shallow over rocks, foaming and swirling through the flickering shadows of the woods before it swung in great serpent loops between lush green fields. Deer drank from the creek, men fished from it, and cattle stood in its summer pools to cool themselves.

The Beaver Creek joined the stream five miles south of Hagerstown and now the creek was almost a river. It could still be forded by horsemen, but the local folk had built handsome stone bridges to keep their feet dry. The creek flowed on, still looping, but hurrying now to its confluence with the Potomac River, where the creek was swallowed into the massive flow of water running to the eastern sea.

Some four miles north of where the creek joined the Potomac River there was a spot where a shelving bank of shingle edged the water beneath a stand of great elms. It was a pretty place, cool in summer and a favorite spot for children who liked to run into the river down the shingle bank or else swing on a rope hung from an elm bough above the water, but on a couple of Sunday mornings every summer there was no playing at the place, for on those days a procession would walk up the Smoketown Road, skirt the East Woods, then follow a track across the Miller farmland that led to the creek's steep, wooded slope. There might be fifty people in the procession, rarely more, and they walked in a solemn silence that would only be broken when someone started a hymn. Then they would all join in, their voices strong as they wended between cornfields and woods toward the water. The men would be in their suits, all of them ill-cut from a dark, thick cloth, but the discomfort of the formal clothes was a tribute to the day. The women were shawled and bonneted while the children were held firmly by the hand so that no unseemly behavior would mar the occasion. At the head of the procession strode a preacher in a wide-brimmed black hat.

Once at the river the preacher would wade into the creek and pray to the God of Abraham and of Isaac and of Jacob that He would bless this day, and bless these good people, then one by one those souls who had come to be baptized in the presence of their neighbors would walk into the water and the preacher would fold their hands on their breast, place another hand at their back, and then, with a joyous shout of blessing because a soul was being received into the heavenly host, he would thrust them backward into the creek so that the water flowed over their heads. He would hold them there for a second, then haul them upright as the congregation on the bank called loud praises for God's mercy to miserable sinners. Almost always the newly baptized men and women wept for happiness as they waded out of the creek to join the dark-suited congregation singing for them.

They sang in German. Many of the local settlers had come from Germany and they worshipped in a small, whitewashed church that had no spire, no porch, no pulpit, no decoration of any kind, though in tribute to the hard winters there was a black-bellied iron stove standing between the well-made pews. From the outside the church looked more like a humble house than a shrine, though inside it was surprisingly spacious and would be filled with light on sunny days. The Germans were Baptists, though their English-speaking neighbors good-naturedly described them as Dunkers, because of their custom of baptism by full immersion. On the Sabbath the Germans might worship in one place and the English-speakers in another, but during the week the Poffenbergers and Millers, Kennedys and Hoffmans, Middlekaufs and Pipers were good enough neighbors and hard-working farmers, and all agreed that they shared good land. Limestone might break the rich fields here and there, but a blessed living could be made from these farms so long as a family worked diligently, trusted in God, and had patience. That was why they had come to America, to thrive and live in peace beside a Maryland creek that flowed from a low pass in the South Mountains down to the wide Potomac River.

The creek was called the Antietam and the Dunker church lay just north of a village called Sharpsburg, and hardly a soul in America outside of Washington County, Maryland, had ever heard of either.

But then the armies came.

The rebels came first. Dirty, tired, ragged men with bleeding feet, boils on their skin, and lice in their beards. They marched south down the Hagerstown Pike raising a cloud of dust behind their gunwheels and shabby boots. Some had no boots at all, but walked barefoot. More rebels limped in from the east, crossing the creek on the handsome stone bridges. These rebels from the east wore bandages and had red-rimmed eyes and faces stained with black powder. They had fought to delay the Yankees at the passes in the hills and they had lost, and now they came to join Robert Lee's army at Sharpsburg.

It was a tiny army. Seventeen thousand men spread into the pastures and woodlots north of the village and the farmers could only watch as their precious rail fences were dismantled to make firewood or shelters. The army's guns, with their blackened muzzles and dirt-stained wheels, were lined on the high ground above the creek. The guns faced east.

The Yankees came next; sixty thousand blue-coated troops who crossed the Red Hill on the creek's eastern bank and then stopped. Just stopped.

The rebel guns had opened fire, bouncing their solid shot off the farmland and up over the first Northern troops to show on the river's far bank. General McClellan, told that the enemy had formed a fighting line on the creek's far bank, ordered the halt. He knew that thought must be taken, plans made, and fears understood, and so the Northern troops scattered into encampments and the rebel guns, seeing that their enemy was making no attempt to cross the creek, ceased their firing.

The gunsmoke drifted over the creek's valley and was touched pink by the setting sun. General Robert Lee watched the stalled enemy across the river, then turned to walk back toward the Hagerstown Pike where an ambulance waited to carry him to the army's headquarters just west of Sharpsburg. The General's hands were still bandaged and that made riding difficult, and so he walked while one of his aides led Traveller by the reins. Lee seemed curiously diminished out of the saddle. On horseback he looked like a tall man, but on foot he was revealed as only of average height. The ambulance was waiting beside the whitewashed Dunker church, which looked bright against the dark woods behind. The church's pews were being chopped for firewood by a battalion of Georgians who were billeted about the small house of worship.

The General had hardly spoken as he walked back from the gunline, but now he saw Major Delaney sitting slumped beside the pike that ran in front of the church. Lee smiled. "So you're alive, Major?"

"Happily, sir." Delaney struggled to his feet.

"And you have seen what you came to see, yes?"

"Fighting," Delaney said grimly.

"Rather more than I hoped you'd see," Lee said ruefully. "It seems McClellan has greater energy than I credited him with." Lee gestured to the ambulance. "Hardly a conquering general's carriage, Major, but you're welcome to share it back to headquarters. I assume you'll pitch camp with us again?"

"If I may, General."

"Unless you'd rather go home?" Lee suggested charitably. He might need every man he could muster to fight McClellan, but he could hardly imagine this pale, tired lawyer being of any great help.

"Are we to fight?" Delaney asked, climbing into the

ambulance and leaving George to lead his two horses behind the slow-moving vehicle.

"Oh, I think so," Lee answered mildly. "I rather think we must." He leaned back against the ambulance's side and looked momentarily weary, then he frowned at his bandaged hands as though frustrated by the limitations they forced on him. "At least," he said ruefully, "it stops me biting my nails." The ambulance swayed and rocked on the dry road. It was a Yankee vehicle, captured at Manassas, and highly sprung to relieve the pain of its wounded occupants, but even the best springs could not smooth out the ruts of the Hagerstown Pike as it dropped into Sharpsburg. "You know what Frederick the Great once said?" Lee asked suddenly, his thoughts reverting to the trial that lay ahead. "That the unforgivable crime in war is not making the wrong decision, but making no decision. And I think we have to fight here."

"Why?" Delaney asked, then hastily added, "I'm curious, sir," in case the General thought he was challenging his decision.

Lee shrugged. "We invaded the North, Delaney. Are we to slink away with nothing accomplished?"

"We captured Harper's Ferry, sir," Delaney pointed out.

"So we did, so we did, but we set out to do a great deal more. We came north, Delaney, to inflict hurt on the enemy and that we still have to do. I had planned to inflict that pain well north of here, but I confess General McClellan has surprised me, so now I must hurt him here rather than on the Susquehanna. But here or there, what matters is to hurt him so badly that the North cannot invade us again, and Europe will see that we can defend ourselves and are thus worthy of their support. Hurt them once, Delaney, and there's a chance we'll not have to inflict pain again, but if we just slip away then McClellan

266

will follow and we shall have to fight him on our own soil. And poor Virginia has suffered enough, God knows." The General spoke softly, rehearsing his arguments out loud, and always conscious that Belvedere Delaney carried weight in Richmond's political circles. If things went badly in the next few hours then it would be as well to have a man like Delaney retailing the General's motives to the Confederacy's leaders.

"McClellan outnumbers us," Delaney said, unable to hide his nervousness.

"He does indeed, but he always has," Lee answered dryly, "though this time, I confess, his preponderance is significant. We guess he has eighty thousand men. We have less than twenty." He paused, smiling at the outrageous imbalance. "But Jackson's men are marching toward us. We might line up thirty thousand against him."

"Thirty?" Delaney was appalled at the odds.

Lee chuckled. "Poor Delaney. You really would be happier in Richmond, I think? It would do you no dishonor to leave us. Your work here is surely done?"

Better than you know, Delaney thought, but answered instead with a quotation from Shakespeare. "'The fewer men, the greater share of honor.'"

Lee smiled, recognizing Shakespeare's line from *Henry V*. "A few men beat a great army in that battle," he said, "and I do know one thing about these men," he gestured with a bandaged hand at his ragged troops in their bivouacs. "They are the best fighting men, Delaney, that this poor world has ever seen. They make me feel humble. Wars might be won by strategy, but battles are won by morale, and if you and I, my friend, should live to be a hundred we shall never see troops as good as these. McClellan is nervous of them, very nervous, and tomorrow he has to attack them and he will do it gingerly. And if he is as cautious as I expect, then we shall have a chance to tear his army into pieces."

Delaney shuddered at the thought of battle. "He hasn't been cautious these last few days, sir," he said warningly.

Lee nodded. "He got wind of our dispositions. We don't know how, but some sympathizers at Frederick sent us a message telling us that McClellan was boasting that he had us in the bag. Well, so he did, but it's one thing to have a bag and it's quite another to stuff the wildcat inside the bag. Believe me, Delaney, his caution will return. It already has returned! If I was across that river I wouldn't be bivouacking now. I'd be pushing brigades over the valley, I'd be thrusting hard, I'd be fighting, but McClellan is waiting, and every hour that he waits brings Jackson's men closer to us."

But even when Jackson's men came, Delaney thought, Lee's army would be less than half the size of McClellan's. The rebellion was surely doomed and Delaney, rejoicing in that thought and in the part he had played in the destruction, still felt a regret for Lee. The General was a good man, a very good and honorable man, but Lee had no ambassadorships in his pocket and so Delaney prayed that on the morrow he would watch the Confederacy die in the ripe fields beside the Antietam.

Tuesday, September 17, dawned hot and sultry. The Confederate pickets, warned of an enemy attack, stared across the river through a heavy fog that slowly lightened as the sun rose above the Red Hill. The pickets feared the blast of cannons loaded with canister and the splashing of men carrying bayonets and loaded rifles through the river's fords, but no such attack came. McClellan, if he did but know it, had succeeded in the dearest wish of all fighting generals: He had trapped his enemy's army while it was split into two parts, and if McClellan had lunged across the stream he could have destroyed Lee's small army, then marched against Jackson's scattered men as they hurried north from Harper's Ferry.

But McClellan did not move. He waited.

The sun burned the last of the fog from the creek and nervous rebel pickets stared across the water at green leaves from which the smoke of campfires drifted gently. Confederate cavalry reconnoitered the Antietam's banks north and south of Lee's position, but no Northern troops were attempting the crossing, nor, astonishingly, were any Northern cavalry making similar patrols in the drowsy, heavy countryside. There were Yankee troops marching, but those men formed the tail of McClellan's huge army as it crossed the hills toward the Antietam's eastern bank. The sixty thousand Yankees became seventy-five thousand and still McClellan did not advance. He waited.

He waited just two and a half miles east of the Dunker church, on the Yankee bank of the Antietam, in the Pry family farmhouse. The farm had a substantial house, ample barns, and well-drained fields that sloped from the Red Hill down to the creek's banks. Most of the fields were stubble now, though some were tall with corn that was almost ready to be harvested. One meadow was stacked with hay, a second had a fine crop of clover, while the higher fields had just been plowed for the planting of winter wheat. Yankees were bivouacked in all the meadows and had torn down the haystacks to make their mattresses. Some played baseball, some wrote home, others lay reading in whatever shade they could discover on this hot, humid day. Once in a while a man would peer through the trees at the distant line of rebel guns crowning the western skyline, but until they received orders to attack they were content to rest. Little Mac would see them right. The newspapers might call McClellan the Young Napoleon, but to the Northern soldiers he was always Little Mac and the one thing they knew and loved in Little Mac was that he would never risk their lives unnecessarily. They trusted him, and so they were content to wait.

Colonel Thorne was not content. At dawn he was riding his horse down the Antietam toward the Potomac, and by the time the fog had lifted he had marked a half dozen crossing places on his map. He had attempted to cross one ford and been repelled by an alarmed shout from a gray-clad picket who had hastily cocked his rifle and fired a wild shot that whipped over Thorne's head. Further upstream he had watched a stone bridge and tried to count the number of rebels dug into their rifle pits on its far side. He saw them go down to the creek to fill their canteens, watched them wash, and listened to their laughter.

Now, as the morning dragged somnolently onward, he discovered General McClellan comfortably ensconced in the Pry house. Telegraphers were running wire up the hill to a signal station on the Red Hill's summit from where messages would be semaphored by relay stations until another telegraph station could send McClellan's news to Washington. One message already waited to be sent and Thorne, discovering the telegraphers setting up their equipment in the Pry's parlor, picked it up. "This morning a heavy fog has thus far prevented us doing more than ascertain that some of the enemy are still there," the message read. "Do not know in what force. Will attack as soon as situation of the enemy develops." Thorne snorted as he dropped the message. You don't wait for the enemy, he thought. My God, but Adam Faulconer had died to put the Northern army into this place and all

McClellan needed to do was order his troops forward. Those troops were in high enough spirits. They had chased the rebels off the mountain passes and rumors were whipping through the Northern ranks that Lee was wounded, maybe dead, and so were Jackson and Longstreet. The troops were willing enough to fight, but McClellan was waiting for the situation of the enemy to develop, whatever that meant. Thorne strode out of the parlor to discover the General sitting in one of a number of well-upholstered armchairs that had been placed on the lawn to give a view of the ground across the river. A telescope stood on a tripod beside the General, while in front of the armchairs, on the lawn, which sloped steeply downhill, a barricade had been erected from fence rails and tree branches. The barricade suggested that McClellan believed he might have to make his last stand here on the farmhouse lawn, firing his revolver from the comfort of an armchair while his defeated troops streamed past on either side.

"I have been south," Thorne said abruptly. McClellan, chatting with Pinkerton, who occupied the armchair next to his, had pointedly ignored the Colonel's arrival and so Thorne simply butted in.

"South where?" McClellan finally asked.

"South down the creek, sir. There are fords there, and none of them properly guarded by the rebels. One had a picket, but only a handful of men. The best crossing is at Snaveley's Ford." Thorne held out his notebook in which he had penciled a crude map. "Cross there, sir, and within a mile we'll have cut off Lee's retreat."

McClellan nodded, but otherwise seemed to take no notice of Thorne's words.

"For God's sake, sir," Thorne said, "attack now! Lee can't have twenty thousand men under arms."

"Nonsense." McClellan was goaded into the argument.

"Believe that, Colonel, and you'll believe anything." He laughed and his aides sniggered dutifully.

"Sir," Thorne deliberately made his voice respectful. "We know when Harper's Ferry surrendered, sir, and we know that Jackson's troops cannot have reached Sharpsburg yet. No troops can cover that distance that fast, but if we wait till this evening, sir, they'll be here. Then Lee will have forty or fifty thousand men waiting for us."

"General Lee," McClellan said icily, "has eighty thousand men already. Eighty thousand!" His voice rose in indignation. "And if this benighted government saw fit to provide me with the men necessary to prosecute a successful war I would already have attacked, but I cannot attack until I know, with utter certainty, the enemy's dispositions!"

"The enemy's disposition, sir, is desperate!" Thorne insisted. "They're tired, they're hungry, they're outnumbered, and in three hours, sir, you can have a victory as complete as any in history."

McClellan shook his head in anger, then glanced at Allan Pinkerton, who slouched low in his flower-printed armchair. He wore an ill-fitting jacket and had a hard, round hat on his blunt head. "Colonel Thorne believes we outnumber the enemy, Major Pinkerton," McClellan gave the chief of his secret service his honorary rank, "is that your determination?"

"Wish it was, chief!" Pinkerton took a stubby pipe out of his mouth, then went on in his broad Scottish accent and with a tone of utter confidence. "There are many more of them than of us, that I'll wager. We had a laddie ride the creek bank yesterday, what was his name? Custer! That's the fellow. Hordes of them, he says, just hordes! A good lad, young Custer."

"You see, Thorne?" McClellan asked, vindicated.

Thorne pointed west and southward to where a smear of hazy whiteness was smudged across the midday sky. "Sir," he appealed. "You see that white cloud? It's dust, sir, dust, and it marks where Jackson's leading men are hurrying to reinforce Lee, but they're ten miles off yet, sir, and so I beg you, sir, I beg you, just go now! Attack!"

"War is always a simple matter to amateurs," McClellan said, his voice dripping with scorn. "Lee would not be standing against us with twenty thousand men, Colonel, though I've no doubt he'd like us to think he has so few. It's called setting a trap, Colonel Thorne, but I'm too old a dog to fall for that one." McClellan's staff officers laughed at this evident shaft of wit. The General smiled. "You heard Major Pinkerton's evaluation, Colonel," he said, "do you doubt him?"

Thorne's opinion of Pinkerton was unpronounceable, but he made one more effort to hammer sense into his opponents. "This man who rode the lines yesterday," he demanded of Pinkerton. "Did he cross the river?"

"Now how could he do that?" Pinkerton asked, tamping down the tobacco in his pipe. "There are eighty thousand rebels across that river, Colonel, and young Custer's too canny a lad to commit suicide," the Scotsman laughed.

"Eighty thousand," McClellan repeated the figure, then pointed to the cloud of dust, "and that dust tells us that more are coming." He stretched his legs to prop his boots on the strange, fortress-like barricade and, for a time, with his head sunk on his chest, he frowned toward the distant plateau that was edged by the rebel gunline. "By tomorrow, gentlemen," he announced after a long silence, "we shall doubtless face a hundred thousand enemies, but we shall do our duty. America expects no more of us."

It does expect more, Thorne thought savagely. America

expects victory. It expects its sons to be spared slaughter in the coming years, it expects an undivided Union and to have Washington's gutters awash in beer while the victory parade marches past, but all McClellan prayed for was survival, and Thorne, appalled at the man's obduracy, could do nothing more. He had tried, and in the cause for which he pleaded Adam Faulconer had died, but McClellan commanded the army and the battle would be fought in the Young Napoleon's own good time.

And so the Yankees waited.

Nothing could have prevented straggling. For a time Starbuck had snarled at his limping, bleeding, struggling men, but one by one they dropped back in helpless weakness. The road's verges were littered with other stragglers who had dropped out of battalions further up the road, while here and there a brave soul hobbled on using his rifle as a crutch and with his feet leaving bloody footprints on the road's dust.

Starbuck's battalion at least had boots, but the boots were ill-made and were coming apart at the seams. Their real problem was plain weakness. They were unfit, and the handful of marches they had made in the last few weeks were no preparation for this hot, hard road where Jackson's staff officers goaded the troops on. Most of the other battalions were suffering from a lack of food. The army had outrun its supplies, and though the men had gorged on the Yankee delicacies captured at Harper's Ferry, that rich food had only made them ill. Now they were back on a diet of apples and corn snatched from the unharvested fields, and even the men who kept up the grueling pace were plagued by diarrhea. The column pounded on between lines of exhausted, sick men and the ever-present stench of feces.

Colonel Swynyard finally gave up trying to prevent straggling in his brigade. "It's no good, Nate," he said, "let them be." Swynyard was leading his horse. He could have ridden, as Lieutenant Colonel Maitland of the Legion rode, but he preferred to rest his horse's back and to set an example to his men.

Starbuck grudgingly let the sickest men fall out, but he would not allow any of the officers to leave the column. Billy Blythe was the worst affected. He was sweating in his tight coat and stumbling glassy-eyed, but whenever he veered toward the grass verge Starbuck would shove him onward. "You're an officer, Billy," he said, "so set an example." Blythe viciously spat out the efficacious word, but he was more frightened of Starbuck than of his weakness and so he limped on. "I thought you walked all the way south from Massachusetts," Starbuck added.

"I did."

"Hell, this is a stroll compared with that. Keep going."

Sergeant Case displayed no weakness. He marched steadily, untiringly, with Billy Blythe's bedroll over his own. When, each hour, the column halted for a ten minute rest, Sergeant Case would find water and bring it to Blythe. Starbuck watched the two and wondered if it had been they who had tried to kill him in the Harper's Ferry night, but now, under the unrelenting sun, that murder attempt seemed like a bad dream. He wondered if he had been mistaken. Maybe the shot had merely been some man's attempt to clear his musket of fouled powder, or perhaps a drunk had loosed a bullet into the night. He had seen two men running away, but that proved nothing.

Potter's company led the battalion. They lost no one to straggling, but nor should they for they were the cream of the Special Battalion. Potter marched happily enough, singing with his men, telling stories and jokes, and sometimes helping to haul the hearse with its precious load of ammunition. More ammunition was carried on the wagon, but the draft horses taken at Harper's Ferry were proving fatally weak. The wagon fell farther and farther behind, causing chaos as gun teams and battalions tried to pass it on the road.

"I assume," Potter said to Starbuck, "that there is a purpose to this exertion?"

"If Old Jack marches like this," Starbuck said, "you can be sure he's going to battle."

"You like him, don't you?" Potter observed with amusement.

"Old Jack? Yes, I do." Starbuck was faintly surprised at the admission.

"You emulate him."

"Me?" Starbuck was surprised. "Never," he said dismissively.

"Not in the matter of God," Potter allowed, "nor, perhaps, in his eccentricities, but otherwise? Yes, you do. Single-minded Starbuck, not yielding an inch, tougher than boot leather. You despise weakness."

"This ain't a time to be weak."

"I can think of no better time," Potter said dryly. "The weak are liable to fall out and be spared the slaughter. It's you strong ones who'll march gallantly into the Yankee guns. Don't worry, Starbuck, I'll be with you, but I have to tell you there's a jug of whiskey in my pack in case things get too bad."

Starbuck smiled. "Only one?"

"Alas, only one, but it's marvelous what one bottle will achieve."

"Just keep some for me."

"A sip, maybe." Potter walked on, following the hearse

with its dusty plumes. "I am astonished at my forbearance," he said after a while. "I have a whole jug and I haven't unstoppered it."

"So you are strong."

"Temporarily, maybe."

"Jackson says that strength comes from God," Starbuck said.

"He would, wouldn't he?" Potter said, casting a sidelong look at his Major. "Do I detect a soul in trouble?"

Starbuck glanced to his right to see a stretch of the Potomac showing between heavy trees. The march was taking them northward along the Potomac's southern bank, but soon, he knew, they must cross the river and thus pass into the North. "I was just thinking about God last night," he said evasively. He wondered if he should mention the murderous attempt on his life, but decided it would all sound too fanciful. "Hell," he said after a while, "when you're going into battle you're bound to think about God, aren't you?"

Potter smiled. "Has anyone determined whether Christians survive battle in greater numbers than unbelievers? I should like to know. Hell, if getting saved is my ticket to survival then you can lead me to the mercy seat right now."

"It ain't living or dying," Starbuck said, trying to ignore the burning pain in his leg muscles and the ache of the boils on his back and the harsh taste of the dust in his throat. "It's what happens after death."

"That's hardly a reason to be converted," Potter said. "I spent enough time in my father's church not to want to spend eternity with the same people," he shuddered. "Good people, yes, but oh so disapproving! I think I'll take my chances at the other destination." He laughed, then checked his amusement as a rumbling noise bruised the sky. "They've begun proceedings without us?" he suggested chidingly.

"That's not gunfire," Starbuck said, "just thunder. Summer thunder." There were clouds in the east and maybe by evening there would be a hard rain that might break the sweltering humidity that was making the march so hard.

A half hour later they turned and forded the Potomac River. A strong battery of Confederate artillery guarded the ford's Virginia bank, evidence that this was Lee's only way of escape if disaster struck the Confederate army. The water came up to their waists so that men had to hoist their cartridge pouches and cap boxes clear of the stream. Once on the far bank, in Yankee territory at last, they crossed the bridge over the Chesapeake and Ohio Canal and began walking toward a small village just four miles eastward. "Sharpsburg," Swynyard told Starbuck, "and this," he gestured at the road up which they trudged, "is our only line of retreat. If the Yankees whip us, Nate, we'll be running for our lives down this road and if they cut us off from the ford we'll be done for."

"They won't whip us," Starbuck said grimly. Rebel encampments stretched untidily on either side of the road; evidence that the column was at last nearing its destination. This was the army's rear area, the place where the transport wagons and artillery parks were sited, the place where the field hospitals readied their scalpels and probes and bandages. The village of Sharpsburg itself was a small grid of neat frame houses with whitewashed porches and carefully watered yards that had been stripped bare of vegetables and fruit. Some civilians put out barrels of water for the marching column, but claimed they had no food to give. "We're starving ourselves, boys," a pregnant woman explained.

"Get your victuals off the Yankees, lads," an old man, evidently a Southern supporter, shouted, "and God bless you!"

They turned left off the village's main street onto the Hagerstown Pike, which climbed steeply toward the higher ground. A staff officer galloped down the column, found Swynyard, and directed him northward along the pike that ran straight between fields rich with clover. They passed the Dunker church, taking it for a roadside cottage, and there they turned right onto the Smoketown Road and walked the last half mile to reach a shady wood of tall elms and heavy oak. The wood stretched to the north, while south of the road was a plowed field newly sown with winter wheat. A family's graveyard was set in the field's center, and it was there that Swynyard established his headquarters. His brigade, thinned by straggling and worn out by a summer's campaigning, collapsed in the plowed field and in two fields of stubble that lay to the east. The ground here fell gently away toward the creek and Starbuck, throwing down his bedroll in the shade of the trees just across the road from the plowed field, could see Yankee guns on distant pastures across the river.

But there was no time now to reconnoiter the ground. What was left of the battalion had to be shown where to bivouac, then a working party had to go to the springhouse of the nearby farm to find water. A few stragglers limped in and a handful of others arrived on wagons that had been sent back down the road to collect the weary. Starbuck ordered a sullen Captain Dennison down to the town to find any other stragglers and direct them up to the high ground.

Swynyard summoned his battalion commanders to the small graveyard. He showed them where the brigade's small reserve store of ammunition was being stored, then walked the officers eastward to the rebel gunline, which overlooked the deep, wooded valley of the creek. Lee had evidently decided against defending the creek's bank, but would instead let the Northern army cross the water and then climb the steep slope into the face of his guns, rifles, and muskets. "With God's help, gentlemen," Swynyard said, "we shoot them down here."

It was an open stretch of fields, a place where men would stand in the smoke and trade volleys with a horde of Yankees coming up from the woods. Maitland had his expensive field glasses trained across the valley to a plowed field where a battery of Northern guns was being sited. "Parrott guns, by the look of them," he said, "and aimed right at us."

"Near on two miles away," John Miles, the commander of the small 13th Florida regiment opined. "Maybe the sons of bitches will lose us in the smoke."

"Hell, they'll fire at the smoke," Haxall, the Arkansas man, observed.

"Our guns will deal with them," Swynyard said, cutting the pessimism short.

Maitland had turned his attention to the group of farm buildings that stood below the graveyard on the rebel held slope. "Can we turn that farm into a fortress?" he asked Swynyard. "Our Hougoumont," he added.

"Our what?" Haxall asked.

"The château of Hougoumont," Maitland answered with his insufferable air of superiority. "A fortified farm that Wellington held all day against Napoleon's men. At Waterloo," he added condescendingly.

"He also fortified the farm at Mont St Jean," Swynyard said, unexpectedly trumping Maitland's knowledge of military history, "and he lost it because the French surrounded it and the poor men inside ran out of ammunition. And tomorrow the Yankees will be all round that farm. It's too far forward."

"So we just ignore it?" Maitland asked, reluctant to give up the thought of a solid stone wall between himself and the Yankee rifles.

"Yankees won't ignore it," Starbuck put in. "They'll fill the place with sharpshooters."

"So we burn it," Swynyard decided. "Miles? Your men can fire the buildings tonight?"

"Reckon they'd enjoy that, Colonel."

"Then do it," Swynyard said, then briefly sketched the brigade's dispositions. The big Virginia regiment would hold the right of the brigade line, then would come the smaller units from Florida and Arkansas, with Maitland's men of the Faulconer Legion on the left. "You're in reserve, Nate," Swynyard told Starbuck. "Keep your men in the woods. That might give them some cover from the Yankee guns."

"I thought our guns were going to silence their guns?" Maitland observed cattily.

Swynyard ignored the comment. "It'll be a plug-ugly infantry fight, gentlemen," he said grimly. "We'll have plenty of artillery, though, and the enemy's coming uphill. The side that stands longest and shoots best will win, and that's going to be us." He dismissed the officers, but put an arm into Starbuck's arm and led him northward toward the woods. "The Legion's got good men," he told Starbuck, "but I don't trust Maitland. He's yellow. Thinks his white skin is too precious to be punctured by a bullet. That's why your men are right beside his. If Maitland starts to go back, Nate, step in."

"Step in?" Starbuck asked. "He outranks me."

"Just step in. Hold the Legion for me till I can get rid of Maitland. May not happen, Nate. Or maybe the good

281

Lord will see fit to take me home tomorrow, in which case Maitland takes over the whole brigade, and God help these men if he does." Swynyard stopped and stared down the long slope. "Just have to shoot them down, Nate, just shoot them down." He said it sadly, imagining the blue masses that would swarm up the hill next morning.

But Swynyard was wrong. The Yankees might well be planning to cross the river and climb the hill, but first they intended a flank attack and late that afternoon, as Starbuck's men were mauling the trees and raiding the remnants of rail fences for their camp fires, a mass of Northern troops crossed the creek by a bridge that lay well north of the rebel positions. The Yankees climbed to the higher ground and kept marching westward until they reached the Hagerstown Pike and there they camped. Rebel pickets fired at the Yankees, and every now and then the sound of rifles crackled angry and loud as Northern skirmishers tried to drive the Confederates away, but neither side made any attempt to attack the other's main body. General Lee watched the Federal troops making their camp to his north and their presence told him what to expect in the morning. The Yankees would march south in what promised to be a massive attack straight down the Hagerstown Pike.

But that assault, Lee knew, would be only one attack. Others would come across the creek, and maybe other Yankees would try to curl around his southern flank. So be it. He did not have the men to guard every river crossing, only to hold the high ground around the village and the Dunker church. But at least his army was growing. Two-thirds of Jackson's men had come from Harper's Ferry and the remaining third, once they had finished sending the Federal prisoners south to the camps, would hurry toward him next day. He would start the battle with less than thirty thousand men and he knew that more than twice that number were readying themselves to attack him, but if McClellan was not fought here then he would have to be fought in Virginia. It was better here, Lee decided, where the Yankees would have to climb the hills from the creek into the face of his guns.

But the Yankees encamped to the north would have no hills to climb, for they were already on the high ground. Those men would attack down the line of the pike where two long stands of timber, the West Woods and the East Woods, formed a natural funnel some six or seven hundred yards wide. The funnel was a swathe of farmland that led into the heart of Lee's position. Not that the Yankees could be seen yet from that heart, for, though they were camped in the woods that grew at the northern lip of the funnel, a thirty-acre cornfield stood between them and the rebel line. The corn stretched across the funnel and was near to harvest and so stood as tall as a paraded regiment. The stalks whispered together in the small evening breeze; a screen to hide two enemies from each other, and in the morning, Lee guessed, a place where the attacking Federals would meet his hard-bitten troops.

"So you're not my reserve after all, Nate," Swynyard said when news of the Yankee flanking march arrived. The Yellowlegs were camped at the base of the East Woods and that meant they guarded one lip of the funnel and so could expect to fight the Yankees in the dawn. "I can change you over," Swynyard volunteered.

"They'll fight," Starbuck said of his men. Besides, it was dusk, and to change the position now would mean confusion among men too tired to change bivouacs. "You ain't expecting an attack up the slope now?" he asked, indicating the farmland where the battalion commanders had met and where the farm buildings now blazed from the work of Miles's incendiarists.

"Maybe they'll come both ways," Swynyard said. "If McClellan's got any sense, that's what they'll do. And that'll mean hard work, Nate. But those boys," he waved a hand northward to indicate the Yankees who were camped higher on the turnpike, "are closest, so worry about them first." He dragged his hand with the missing fingers through his tangled beard. "Earn our pay tomorrow, that's for sure. Your boys are all right?"

"They'll fight," Starbuck said, ignoring his doubts about Tumlin and Dennison.

"Tell them I'm holding prayers in half an hour," Swynyard said. "I'll invite you, even though I know you won't come."

"I might," Starbuck said unexpectedly.

Swynyard was tempted to make a joke of Starbuck's answer, then he saw that maybe his prayers for Starbuck's soul were being answered and so he bit back his jest. "I'd like it if you did, Nate," he said instead.

But Starbuck did not come to the Colonel's prayer meeting. Instead he walked to the very right-hand end of his short line where Captain Dennison's A Company was bivouacked. Starbuck was nervous that the gesture he was about to make would be construed as weakness, but the bad blood inside the Special Battalion needed to be lanced and so he looked for Private Case and, finding the big man, jerked his head toward the trees. "I want you," he said.

Case glanced at his companions, shrugged, then ostentatiously picked up his rifle and checked that it was primed. He followed Starbuck into the trees, taking care to keep a half dozen paces behind. Starbuck remembered the shot in the Harper's Ferry night, but that was not why he had summoned Case because Case would never admit to having been one of the two men. Instead, on the eve of battle, Starbuck wanted to make peace.

Starbuck stopped when they were out of earshot of the rest of the battalion. "So what," he asked, "would the Royal Fusiliers be doing different?" Case seemed bemused by the question and did not answer. Starbuck looked into the ugly face and was amazed again by the flat brutality of Case's eyes. "Even in the Royal Fusiliers," Starbuck said, "sergeants don't get away with defying their officers. What the hell did you expect me to do? Let you keep your stripes?" Again Case did not answer. He just turned his head and spat a thin stream of tobacco juice onto a hump of limestone.

"Tomorrow," Starbuck went on, but feeling as though he was wading through a lake of molasses, "we're going to fight, and if A Company fights as feebly as it did the other day, you're all going to die." That got Case's attention. The feral gaze shifted from some distant point among the trees to stare into Starbuck's eyes. "You know how to fight, Case, so make damn sure the rest of the company fights like you. Do that, and you get your stripes back. Understand?"

Case paused, then nodded. He shifted the tobacco from one cheek to another, spat again, but still did not speak. Starbuck was about to launch himself into an earnest peroration about men not being able to serve two masters, about the need for discipline, about the value of experienced men like Case to a battalion like the Yellowlegs, but he managed to check the words before he even began. He had said all he needed to say and Case had heard all he needed to hear and the rest was up to Case himself, but at least, Starbuck thought, he had given the tall man something to look forward to beyond mere revenge.

"When tomorrow's over, Case," he said, "you can go to another regiment if that's what you want, and you can go as a sergeant, but tomorrow you fight with us. You understand me?"

Case paused. "You through?" he finally asked.

"I'm through."

Case turned and walked away. Starbuck watched him go, then walked east until he came to the edge of the wood and could stare across the valley. Distant fires flickered in far woods. Somewhere behind him, on the plateau, a gun fired. There was a pause, then a Yankee cannon answered. A battery of rebel artillery, poised on a hill to the turnpike's west, had seen the Northern gunners emplacing a battery and so had opened fire. The two sides dueled as the night fell, and fought on into the darkness so that their gunflashes lit the farmland in sudden bursts of unnatural light that spewed their powdery glare across green fields and cast black shadows among the heavy trees. To the east, on the slope that fell down to the creek, the burning farm buildings churned thick smoke and bright sparks into the night air. The cannon fire died slowly and finally ceased altogether, but then, in the echoing silence, it began to rain. Starbuck, rolled at last in his blanket beneath the trees, heard the drops pattering on the green leaves and tried to sleep, but sleep would not come. He had marched to Sharpsburg and he was more frightened than he had ever been in all his life. Because tomorrow he must fight.

"IT'S REAL COFFEE," Lucifer said, shaking Starbuck awake, "from Harper's Ferry."

Starbuck swore, tried not to believe what was happening, then swore again when he realized it was happening. It was not yet dawn. The mist in the trees was mixed with the acrid smoke of half-dead fires. The leaves dripped. The Yankees were coming today.

"You're shivering," Lucifer said. "You got a fever."

"I don't."

"Like a baby. Shivering." Lucifer prodded the nearest embers with a stick, trying to stir life into the fire's remnants. "Yankees didn't have fires," he said, then grinned. "They're hiding from us. Reckon they're more frightened of us than we are of them."

"They're on your side," Starbuck said gracelessly.

"I'm on my side," Lucifer insisted angrily, "and no one damn else is."

"Except me," Starbuck said, trying to mollify the boy. He sipped the coffee. "Did you stay awake all night?"

"I stayed awake," Lucifer said, "till I was sure they was asleep."

Starbuck did not ask who "they" were. "There's nothing to worry about," he said instead. He hoped that was true. He hoped he had defused Case's smoldering anger. He hoped he would survive this day.

"You don't worry 'cos I do," Lucifer said. "Did I hear

Captain Tumlin tell you he saw John Brown hung in Harper's Ferry?"

Starbuck had to think to remember the conversation, then recalled Tumlin talking about watching with his whore from an upper window of Wager's Hotel. "Yes," he said bleakly, trying to imbue the syllable with disapproval for Lucifer having eavesdropped. "So?"

"So," Lucifer said, "Mister Brown wasn't ever hung in Harper's Ferry. He was hung in Charlestown. Everybody knows that."

"I didn't."

"Your Captain Tumlin," Lucifer said sourly, "don't know shit from a sugarcone."

Starbuck sat up and pushed the clammy folds of the blanket away. He was shivering, but he guessed it was just the damp. That and apprehension. He heard twigs snapping in the woods, but there was a strong picket line to the north so the sound had to be his own men stirring. He wondered how long it was till dawn. The mist was thick as gunsmoke. Everything was damp—the wood, the ground, his clothes. His rifle was beaded with dew. The day was chill now, but it promised to be burning hot, a day of rank humidity, a day when the spent powder would choke the rifle barrels like soot clogging a chimney.

"Shit from a sugarcone," Lucifer said again, trying to provoke a response.

Starbuck sighed. "We're a makeshift battalion, Lucifer. We get the dregs." He snapped one of his laces as he tied his boots. He swore, wondering if the small accident was a bad omen. He fiddled out the broken lace and, in the dark, rethreaded what was left and tied a knot. Then he stood up, every bone and muscle aching. Fires were coming to life in the fields and wood, the flames dulled and misted by the fog. Men coughed, spat, grumbled, and pissed. A horse whinnied, then there was a clatter as a man blundered into a stand of arms. "What's for breakfast?" he asked Lucifer.

"Hardtack and half an apple."

"Give me half of the half."

He strapped on his belt, then checked that the cartridge pouch was full, the cap box filled, and the revolver loaded. For hundreds of years, he thought, men had woken thus to a day of battle. They had tested their spear points, felt their sword edges, made certain musket flints were tight, then prayed to their gods that they would live. And hundreds of years from now, Starbuck supposed, soldiers would still wake in a gray dark and go through the same motions with whatever unimaginable means of death they carried. He hefted his rifle, checked the percussion cap, then slung it on his shoulder. "To work," he said to Lucifer. "Earn our pay."

"What pay?" Lucifer asked.

"I owe you," Starbuck said.

"So I ain't a slave?"

"You're free as a bird, Lucifer. You want to fly away, then you fly. But I'd miss you. But if you stay today," Starbuck added, knowing full well that Lucifer would stay, "then you keep out of harm's way. This ain't your fight."

"White men only, eh?"

"Fools only, Lucifer. Fools only," Starbuck said, then walked slowly through the dark wood, feeling his way where the feeble light of reviving fires did not show a path. He talked to waking men, stirred the laggards, and organized a work party to fill the battalion's canteens. Biting bullets off cartridges filled the mouth with salty gunpowder so that an hour into a fight men were parched and water was worth its weight in gold. He sent another party to bring up spare ammunition from the graveyard so that the battalion could have its own reserve supply at the wood's edge. It was there, where the wood bordered the road, that he stopped to listen to an unseen band of men who softly sang a hymn among the dark mist-shrouded trees. "'Jesus, my strength, my hope,'" they sang, "'On thee I cast my care; With humble confidence look up, And know thou hear'st my prayer.'" The familiar words were strangely comforting, but someone else had also been listening and started to sing another hymn in a voice much louder than those of the men who had gathered for their morning prayers.

"'Hark how the watchmen cry!'" Captain Potter sang in a remarkably good clear tenor voice, "'Attend the trumpet's sound. Stand to your arms, the foe is nigh, The powers of hell surround.'"

Starbuck discovered Potter among the trees. "Let them be," he chided Potter gently for disturbing the prayers.

"I just thought my choice more appropriate than theirs," Potter said. He was in a feverishly excited mood, so much so that for an instant Starbuck wondered if the stone bottle of whiskey had been emptied, but there was no smell of liquor on Potter's breath as, more quietly, he sang the hymn's last quatrain. "'By all hell's host withstood, We all hell's host o'erthrow, And conquering them through Jesus' blood, We on to conquer go.'" He laughed. "Funny, isn't it? The Yankees are probably singing that as well. Both of us clamoring to Jesus. He must be confused."

"How are your pickets?" Starbuck asked.

"Awake. Watching for the host of hell. I came to fetch them a bucket of coffee. I guess proceedings won't begin till light?"

"I guess not."

"And then," Potter said with unholy relish, "we can

expect something very nasty. Is it true they outnumber us?"

"So far as we know, yes." Starbuck felt a trembling that seemed to begin in his heart and flicker down his arms and legs. "Maybe by two to one," he added, trying to sound laconic as though he faced battle every day. And what day was it? A Wednesday. There was nothing special about Wednesdays at home. Not like Sundays that were given to God and solemnity, or Mondays that were his mother's washday and when the whole Boston house would be busy with servants and steam. Wednesdays were just Wednesdays, a half marker between Sundays. His father would be saying prayers with the servants. Did anyone in the house wonder where the second son was today?

There was a glimmer of lightening in the fog that lay to the east. "'*Per me si va ne la città dolente*,'" Potter said suddenly and unexpectedly, "'*per me si va ne l'etterno dolore, Per me si va la perduta gente*.'"

Starbuck gaped at him. "What the hell?" he asked.

"'Through me you enter the city of sorrows,'" Potter translated dramatically, "'through me you come into eternal pain, through me you join the lost people.' Dante," he added, "the words inscribed above the Gates of Hell."

"I thought it said 'Abandon all hope, all ye who enter here'?" Starbuck said.

"That, too," Potter said.

"When the hell did you learn Italian?"

"I didn't. I just read Dante. There was a time, Starbuck, when I fancied myself a poet, so I read all the poetry I could. Then I discovered a quicker way to Elysium."

"Why in God's name did you study medicine?"

"My father believed I should be useful," Potter said. "He believes in usefulness. Saint Paul was a tentmaker, so Matthew Potter must have a trade, and poetry, my father believed, was not a trade. Poetry, he declared, is not useful unless you're a psalmist, in which case you're dead. He thought I should be a doctor and write uplifting hymns in between killing my unsuspecting patients."

"You'd make a good doctor," Starbuck said.

Potter laughed. "Now you sound like my mother. I must find that coffee."

"Matthew," Starbuck stopped Potter as he walked away. "Look after yourself today."

Potter smiled. "I have a conviction that I shall live, Starbuck. I can't explain it, but somehow I feel charmed. But thank you. And may you survive too." He walked away.

Beyond the fog the sun was lightening the eastern sky, turning the dark to gray. There was no wind, not a breath, just a still, silent sky heavy with the sullen gray wolf-light, the light before dawn, before battle.

Starbuck flinched, then closed his eyes as he tried to compose a prayer to fit the day, but nothing came. He thought of his younger brothers and sisters safe in their Boston beds, then went to form his men into line.

Because it was a windless, lovely dawn beside the Antietam.

Gunners begin most battles. The infantry will win or lose the fight, but the gunners start the killing and even before the fog had lifted the Yankee gunners across the Antietam began their bombardment. They had positioned their guns the previous evening and now, with nothing to guide their aim but the tops of trees protruding through the fog, the gunners opened fire.

Shells screamed eerily through the vapor. The Federal guns that had been brought across the river joined the cacophony, banging their missiles over the cornfield into the whitened vacancy where the rebels waited. The rebel guns answered, aiming blind at first, but as the fog thinned they were able to fire at the diffused glare of muzzle flames that made livid patches in the mist whenever an enemy gun fired.

Shells plowed the fields newly sown with winter wheat. Dirt vomited up from each impact and for once, Starbuck noted, it was brown dirt rather than the redder Virginian soil. The smoke of each explosion hung motionless in the windless air. A loose gun horse galloped across the field behind Starbuck's battalion. It had been struck by a shell fragment and blood was gleaming on its left hindquarter. The horse caught sight of the waiting infantry and stopped, eyes white, red flank shivering. A gunner finally caught the gelding's bridle and, patting the beast's neck, led it back toward the battery. Each time the rebel guns fired the fog shuddered.

Starbuck paced slowly behind his men. Some were lying down, some were crouching, and some kneeling. The Yankee guns to the north were firing shells that rumbled overhead. Some of the shells whistled. Once, looking up, Starbuck saw a tiny trail of fuse-smoke in the fog, a streak of white vapor thicker than the whiteness about it. The gray light had turned white. It was thinning out.

The gunners worked as though they believed they could win the battle by themselves. The shells plunged and cracked into the high rebel ground and the noise ricocheted about the plateau. One man in Starbuck's battalion was telling his beads. "Jesus, Mary, and Joseph," he prayed, "Jesus, Mary, and Joseph." He said the names again and again, and each time a shell exploded he would twitch. One shell struck high in a nearby tree and the crash of the explosion was followed by a slow, awful creaking as a branch slowly tore away. "Jesus, Mary, and Joseph," the man wailed desperately.

"Where are you from?" Starbuck asked the man.

The soldier looked up at Starbuck. His eyes were empty and scared.

"Where are you from, soldier?"

"Richmond, sir." He had an Irish accent. "Venable Street."

"And before that?"

"Derry."

"What was your trade, lad?"

"Saddler, sir."

"I'm glad you're a soldier now."

"You are?"

"I thought the Irish were the best fighters in the world?"

The man blinked at Starbuck, then smiled. "They are, sir. Had lots of practice."

"Then I'm glad you're here. What's your name?"

"Connolly, sir. John Connolly."

"Then pray hard, John Connolly, and shoot low."

"I will that, sir."

Starbuck's battalion, a tiny regiment, was at the southern edge of the pastureland, a hundred paces behind the cornfield. His two left-hand companies were in the open, facing the corn, while his right companies were huddled in the East Woods. Potter's skirmishers were higher up the wood, waiting for the Yankees. The rest of Swynyard's Brigade was bent back at right angles, lining the wood's edge and then strung across the plowed field toward the family graveyard.

Swynyard joined Starbuck. "A quarter to six," he announced, "or thereabouts. My watch stopped in the night." He glanced to the left. "They look good," he said of the neighboring brigade.

"Georgians," Starbuck said. He had introduced himself to the colonel of the battalion next to him and the man had been cordial, but Starbuck had seen the flicker of worry when the Georgian colonel had learned that the Yellowlegs were guarding his right flank.

Swynyard turned and stared southward across the pasture toward the Smoketown Road, which was just becoming visible in the thinning fog. "Lots of troops ready to back us up," he said.

"Lots?" Starbuck answered wryly, knowing that Swynyard was merely trying to reassure him.

"There are some, anyway," Swynyard admitted wryly. A new battery of rebel guns was being positioned in the pasture, its muzzles pointed ominously northward in a sign that Lee expected the first Yankee attack to come straight down the funnel between the woods. Straight across the cornfield. Straight at the waiting men who crouched beyond the corn. Some Georgian skirmishers were already up among the stalks that stood high as a standing man.

Swynyard dragged his maimed hand through his straggling beard, a gesture that betrayed his nervousness. He was worried about the eastern flank, the long slope that fell with ever-increasing steepness toward the creek. His fear was that the Yankees would embroil his brigade in a fight at the funnel's mouth, then attack up that slope to smash in behind his men. And once the Yankees were up on the high ground about the Smoketown Road there was nothing to stop them carving Lee's army into fragments, but so far there were no signs of Yankee activity on the creek itself. There were no reports of men trying to cross the river, no sounds of guns being dragged down to the fords and bridges, and no glimpses of blue-coated troops filing down the farm tracks toward the Antietam's eastern bank.

A new barrage of guns sounded. These were the rebel guns positioned on the hill to the west of the turnpike and they were firing slantwise across the funnel's northern mouth. "I suspect," Swynyard said, "that our erstwhile brethren are stirring."

"God help us," Starbuck blurted out.

Swynyard put a hand on Starbuck's shoulder. "He does, Nate, He does." The hand on Starbuck's shoulder suddenly convulsed as the sound of rifles crackled through the morning. The skirmishers were engaged. "Not long now," Swynyard said in the unconvincing tone of a dentist trying to soothe a nervous patient. "Not long." His hand convulsed again. "Last night," he said quietly, "I had to fight the temptation for a drink. It was as bad as those first few nights. I just wanted a mouthful of whiskey."

"But you didn't?"

"No. God saw to that." Swynyard took his hand away. "And this morning," he went on, "Maitland searched the Legion's packs. Confiscated their liquor."

"He did what?" Starbuck asked, laughing.

"Took every last drop he found. Says he won't have them fighting drunk."

"So long as they fight," Starbuck said, "why does it matter?" The neighboring battalion was fixing bayonets and some of Starbuck's men followed suit, but he shouted at them to put the blades away. "You'll need to kill a few with bullets first," he called to them. He could not see any enemy because the tall corn hid everything to the north. The field was a screen to hide a nightmare. He could hear gunfire in the woods and guessed that Potter had opened fire.

The neighboring battalion stood ready to give fire. "Get 'em up, Nate," Swynyard said.

"Stand!" Starbuck shouted and the two left-hand companies struggled to their feet. They were thin companies, still missing many of their stragglers, but the remaining men looked confident enough as they waited. The battalion's battle flag was at the center of the two companies, where it hung lifeless in the still air. "I wish I could see the bastards," Starbuck growled. His stomach was churning and the muscles of his right leg involuntarily twitching. He had been constipated for two days, but was suddenly scared that his bowels would void. He had been spared the worst of the cannon fire, for the East Woods served to hide his men from the Yankee guns across the creek and the guns to the north were firing overhead, but still the fear was sapping him. Somewhere ahead of him, somewhere beyond the mist-shrouded stalks of tall corn, there was a Yankee infantry attack coming and he could not see it, though now, dimly, he could hear the sound of boots and drums and men shouting. He looked for the enemy's flags, but could not see them and he guessed this opening attack had not yet reached the cornfield. The skirmishers' rifles cracked and every now and then a rifle bullet would flick a corncob aside and whistle just over the battalion's head. One such bullet came close to Swynyard, startling the Colonel.

"Ahab," Swynyard said.

"Sir?" Starbuck asked, thinking that Swynyard had joined in Potter's fancy about Captain Ahab, the *Pequod*, and Moby Dick.

"He was slain, remember, by a bow drawn at a venture. I always think it would be a pity to be killed by an unaimed bullet, but I suppose it's how most men die in battle."

"King Ahab," Starbuck said, realizing what Swynyard meant. "I don't suppose there's much difference between an aimed and an unaimed bullet." He was forcing himself to sound calm.

"So long as it's quick," Swynyard said, then gasped with surprise.

New Yankee guns had opened fire. The gunners had seen the rebel skirmishers in the corn and now, before their own infantry marched into the tall stalks, the gunners tried to weed the crop of enemy riflemen. The artillery was loaded with canister that scythed through the corn. Barrel after barrel fired, and patch by patch the corn was blasted aside. Each shot bent great swathes of corn that tossed as though they were caught in a hurricane. The bullets flicked up from the hard ground to twitch skirmishers aside and some kept going right through the crop to thud into the infantry waiting in the pasture. Two of Starbuck's men reeled backward, one with brains welling out from a shattered patch of skull. The other man screamed, clutching his belly. "There's a doctor in the graveyard," Swynyard said.

"Peel!" Starbuck shouted. "Get these men back!" He would use men from the two right-hand companies to take the casualties back to the graveyard. "Make certain your men come back here!" he called to Peel, then he cupped his hands and shouted at the two left-hand companies to kneel again. The corn was thrashing and whipping, and patches of it were being slung high into the mist that looked thicker to the north, but that thickness was just gunsmoke clogging the air. More canister slapped and slashed the corn, the bullets whistling as they ricocheted on overhead. The surviving rebel skirmishers were retreating. One man crawled on bloody hands through the stalks, another limped, a third collapsed at the field's edge. Still more canister poured into the bloody field, the worst of the fire going into the center, and so sparing Starbuck's companies the full force of the cannonade. Two rebel howitzers were lobbing shells over the corn, trying to find the enemy batteries, while the rebel cannon on the western hill scorched shells down into the pasture where the Yankees advanced. It was still an artillery fight, a complicated mesh of trajectories under which the infantry moved forward to death.

Then, as suddenly as it had begun, the Yankee canister ended.

The corn was still. The day almost seemed silent. Scores of guns were firing, and men were shouting, but it seemed silent. The corn stood thick in patches and lay crushed in swathes. Small flames flickered among the fallen stalks where the wadding from the skirmishers' rifles had started fires. And, at last, there were flags visible above the standing corn. Tall flags hanging limp from staffs that bobbed up and down as the color bearers marched through the cornfield.

Some of Starbuck's men aimed their rifles. "Wait!" he called. "Wait!"

The Yankees were at last visible through the remnants of standing corn.

They were a dark line in the cornfield's mist. They were a horde of men advancing beneath their brilliant flags. They were death in blue. There were thousands of them, a mass of men, a drum-driven multitude with bayonets on their rifles.

"Two brigades, I'd guess," Swynyard said calmly.

"Wait!" Starbuck called to his men again. The Yankee attack was wide enough to overlap the cornfield, which meant that the eastern end of the blue line was now in the woods. "Tumlin!" he shouted.

"Starbuck?" Tumlin appeared at the wood's edge. The trees above him had been made ragged by Yankee shells that had stripped some branches of leaves and ripped other branches away.

"Take Dennison's company and support Potter!"

Starbuck shouted. "The sons of bitches are coming through the trees!" Tumlin ducked out of sight without acknowledging the order and Starbuck knew he should go and make certain Dennison's company did move up through the wood, but the sight of the Yankees coming through the shattered cornfield was holding him rooted to the pastureland. The nervousness had ebbed, displaced by the need to hold his men taut.

"Coffman," Swynyard called the young Lieutenant. "Tell Colonel Maitland to advance in support here. He knows what to do. Go on, lad." Coffman ran.

"I'll put Truslow's company into the woods," Swynyard said, sensing Starbuck's nervousness about the battalion's right flank. A crash of exploding shells drowned the Colonel's next words. Some rebel staff officers had ridden to the Smoketown Road, from where they were staring north through big field glasses, and the Yankee gunners across the Antietam were doing their best to kill the mounted men. The salvo of shells gouged the road and its verges with craters. Smoke screened the horsemen. Somewhere a bugle was playing, its notes brazen and rousing. The Yankee drummers were rattling away.

Rebel guns fired from the woods to the west of the cornfield. They used solid shot that plowed into the Yankee lines. A flag went down, and was immediately snatched up. Starbuck had found one of the limestone ribs that hunched its way through the soil and was standing on it for a better view. He could hear hard and solid rifle fire in the woods, but none of his men was running out of the trees, so the fight there had to be under control. Truslow's company from the Legion came running up the edge of the wood and Swynyard went to divert them into the trees. If Truslow was there, Starbuck knew, then he could forget the wood.

"Wait!" Starbuck called to his men. The Yankees were at the center of the cornfield now and it was their turn to be hit by canister. The strike of the bundled shot cut down swathes of corn and drove up spurts of dust from the dry ground. Huge gaps were being torn from the Yankee ranks, but every time the dreadful scythe cut down a handful of men there were others who jumped over the fallen bodies to fill the hole. The Yankees had fixed bayonets. Their flags hung as limp as the rebel battle flags. One brave man waved his banner to and fro so that the Stars and Stripes made a fine show, but his gallantry was rewarded with a blast of canister that snatched him and the flag backward. The flag flew over the heads of the advancing men. Starbuck could hear the boots trampling the corn. He could hear the Northern sergeants shouting harshly at their men to stay in line, to close up, to keep marching. He could hear the drummer boys frantically trying to win the war with the speed of their sticks.

"Aim low!" he told his men. "Aim low. Don't waste your shots! But wait! Wait!" He wanted the first volley to be a killer.

The misted air was full of noise. Shells rumbled overhead, bullets whistled, the boots splintered the corn. Rifles cracked in the woods. The rebel line looked a perilously thin thing to withstand the Yankee hammer blow. "Wait!" Starbuck called, "wait!" Yankee skirmishers were deep in the corn, sniping at his men. A corporal came out of the line with a bloody shoulder, another man choked on his own blood.

The Yankees were two hundred paces away. They looked fresh, well-clothed, and confident. Starbuck could see their mouths open as they shouted their war cries, but he could hear nothing. He stared at them and he suddenly thought that this was how the makers of America had seen the Redcoats. The rebels then had been just as ragged, and the enemy just as well armed and smartly uniformed, and his fear was abruptly swamped by a fierce desire to shatter this overweening enemy. "Fire!" he shouted, "and kill the bastards!" He screamed the last three words and his two companies opened fire a second before the rest of the rebel line fired to blanket the pasture with rifle smoke. "Kill them!" Starbuck was shouting as he walked up and down behind the line. "Kill them!" He pushed through the files and fired his own rifle, then immediately dropped the butt to the ground to begin reloading. His pulse was racing, the fire was in his veins, the madness of battle was beginning its magic. Perfect hate casts away fear. He rammed the bullet down.

"Fire!" Captain Cartwright encouraged his men. It was a straight infantry fight now. The Yankee gunners were unsighted and so the blue-coated riflemen had to fight and kill and endure the bullets coming back. The rebel guns drenched the attackers in canister, blasting new gaps in the surviving corn. A spray of blood misted the air and somewhere a man screamed terribly until his screams were cut short by the meaty thump of a bullet burying itself in flesh. Starbuck smelled the horrid stink of burned powder, he heard the whistle of a minie bullet whip past his ear, then the rifle was back in his shoulder, and he aimed low into the corn and fired.

The gunsmoke was hanging in the still air like a layer of fog. Some men, in order to see beneath the smoke, lay down to aim. Starbuck ducked and could see Yankee legs among the corn. He fired, then backed out through the files to see how his men were faring.

The Yellowlegs were sticking to the fight. They were ramming their bullets, priming the guns, pulling their triggers, but some were falling. Some were dead. The noise was obliterating sense; it was a deafening sky of fire, a numbing rattle laced with screams. More men fell. Starbuck's line was thinning, but suddenly Davies's company from the Legion was pushing into their ranks to add their fire. Davies grinned at Starbuck. "Christ," he said in awe.

"Fire!" Starbuck shouted. Survival now depended simply on outfiring the enemy. "Captain Peel!" He ran toward the trees to summon the last of his shrinking battalion. "Peel! Bring your men!" Peel's company still had the old-fashioned Richmond muskets that were loaded with buck and ball and Starbuck reckoned the smoothbore volleys might work a wicked slaughter in this close-range battle. "Into line! Anywhere!" He pushed men helter-skelter into the ranks, no longer caring whether the companies kept their cohesion. "And fire! Fire! Just kill them!" He screamed the words as he emptied his revolver chamber by chamber into the shroud of smoke. "Kill them!"

Bullets whipped back from the Yankees. Stabs of flame showed where they fired, and Starbuck saw that the flame lances were getting closer as the attackers advanced, their progress fed by the rear ranks, who moved up to take the place of the dead. The rebels were backing away, not in panicked retreat, but step by step, keeping their line, firing and firing at the blue horde that slowly, inexorably, like men wading against an outflowing tide, was forcing its way to the cornfield's southern edge. It was there that they stopped, not because the rebel fire grew worse, but simply because the field's margin served as a natural boundary. Behind them was the illusory cover of what corn remained standing, while ahead of the cornfield were open pastures and rebel batteries, and the Yankee officers could not persuade their men to march into that smoky, death-swept vacancy. The rebel line had also checked, aligned now on its guns, and there the two sides stayed and traded shot for shot and death for death. The wounded hobbled back from their line, but the rebels could spare no men now to carry the injured back to the surgeons. The rebel wounded must bleed to death or else crawl on hands and knees beneath the bruising noise of the big guns.

The Georgians were bringing in reinforcements, and then Colonel Swynyard appeared behind Starbuck with the big 65th Virginia battalion. "Nate! Nate!" Swynyard was only yards away, but the noise of the battle was so great that he needed to shout. "They're firing on the graveyard!" He pointed to the East Woods, meaning that Yankees had somehow reached the trees' southern end and were threatening Swynyard's reserve of ammunition. "Find out what's happening for me!"

Swynyard feared his right flank was about to be turned, but for the moment he would hold on in the pasture where he was tumbling his battalions into the tiny space where the firefight was hottest and where he would fight his brigade as though it were one single battalion. Starbuck, running to his right, sensed that this dawn slaughter was horrendous. He could not ever remember a battle swelling into horror so fast, nor ever seeing so many wounded or dead, yet miraculously his despised battalion had stood the fire and was still standing it and still giving back as good as they got. "Well done!" he shouted at them, "well done!" No one heard him. They were deafened by the blistering noise.

He ran into the trees. A score of wounded rebels had taken shelter beneath the closest trees, and some men, even though unwounded, had joined them there, but Starbuck had no time to stir those laggards back to their duty. Instead he ran northward in the cover of the trunks to where he could hear his skirmishers fighting. They were very close by, evidence that the Yankees had indeed pushed them hard back. Truslow's men were among Potter's skirmishers, who in turn were mixed up with a company of Georgian skirmishers who had retreated to the trees rather than risk the canister that had been cutting the corn short, and now they all fought together. Starbuck saw Truslow reloading his rifle behind an elm tree that was scarred by bullet strikes. He dropped beside him. "What's happening?"

"Bastards ran us back," Truslow said grimly. "Reckon they've reached the road on that side of the wood." He jerked his beard eastward. He was suggesting that the rebels now only held the southwestern corner of the trees. "Sons of bitches have breech loaders," Truslow added, explaining why the Yankees had been so successful.

Breech-loading rifles were much quicker and easier to load, especially when a man was lying down or crouching behind cover, and so the Yankee skirmishers were pouring a much heavier fire than the rebels could maintain, but now the fight had stalled in the corner of the wood where thick brush, scattered stacks of cordwood, and the limestone outcrops gave the rebels enough shelter to frustrate the withering Yankee fire.

"Seen Potter?" Starbuck asked Truslow.

"Who's he?"

"Thin fellow, floppy hair."

"Over to the right," Truslow jerked his chin. "Be careful going through here. Sons of bitches are good shots." A bullet whipped a chunk of bark off the elm. "Like Gaines's Mill," Truslow said.

"That was a hellhole."

"So's this. Be careful."

Starbuck gathered himself for the dash across the wood. He could hear the heavy firing from the cornfield, but that fight seemed distant now. Instead he had entered a different version of hell, one where a man could not see his enemy, but only spot the gouts of rifle smoke that marked where the Yankee sharpshooters lurked. It was dark under the trees, a darkness caused by the remnants of fog and the thickness of powder smoke. Starbuck wondered what time it was. He reckoned the Yankees had attacked at six o'clock and somehow it felt like midday already, though he doubted if even a quarter of an hour had passed since he had first glimpsed that blue mass marching steadily toward the cornfield. "Give my love to Sally if anything happens," he said to Truslow, then he sprinted away from the elm, dodging and darting among the trees. His appearance provoked an instant fusillade from the Yankees. Bullets lashed about him, thumping into trees like ax blows, whistling in the air, flicking through leaves, then a shot seared across his back. He knew he had been hit, yet he was still running and he guessed the wound was nothing but a near miss that had laid open his skin. He saw Potter behind a stack of cordwood and dived to join him. A Yankee jeered his plunge for safety.

"I'm almost tempted to pray," Potter said.

"Your prayers are answered," Starbuck said, "I'm here. What's happening?"

"We're holding," Potter said laconically.

"Where's Dennison?"

"Dennison? Haven't seen him."

"I sent him to reinforce you. Tumlin?"

"No sign of him," Potter said. Every few seconds the stack of wood was thumped by a Yankee bullet, and every thump would hammer a log a half inch out of alignment. "They're Pennsylvanians," Potter said. "Call themselves the Bucktails."

"How the hell do you know that?" Starbuck asked. He had rammed his rifle into a space between the logs and, without bothering to aim, fired toward the hidden skirmishers.

"We got one of them. Stupid man got too far ahead and Case pulled him down."

"Case? So Dennison's company is here?"

"Private Case is," Potter said, jerking his head west to show where Case was crouching behind a fallen tree. A dead Yankee was beside him and Case had taken the man's breech-loading rifle and was using it to fire steadily into the brush where puffs of smoke betrayed Yankee positions. "The fellow had a deer's tail pinned to the back of his hat," Potter went on. "Full of fleas, it was. He's dead now. It's difficult to live with a slit throat, it seems."

"Where's Sergeant Rothwell?"

"Sent him back for ammunition."

"What's happening out there?" Starbuck jerked his head toward the east, where the Smoketown Road angled through the trees.

"God only knows," Potter said.

Starbuck peered eastward, but could see nothing beyond the trees. He knew some of the Pennsylvanians had got past this point and were now firing toward the graveyard from the southern edge of the wood. For a second he thought about trying to lead an attack that would cut those men off from their companions, then he abandoned that idea. The Yankees were too thick on the ground and too good to be taken that lightly. A Yankee counterattack would destroy his skirmishers and open the brigade's flank to the fire of the Pennsylvania breech-loaders.

"There's blood on your back," Potter said.

"Bullet scrape. Nothing serious."

"Looks impressive." Potter had made a loophole in the

cordwood and fired through it. The shot was answered by a half dozen bullets that made the whole log pile quiver. "The bastards can fire three bullets to our one," Potter said. "They're using Sharps rifles."

"I heard. Can you hold?"

"So long as the Yankees don't reinforce."

"Then hold on." Starbuck patted Potter's back, then dashed to his left. His appearance provoked a flurry of shots, but Starbuck had already dropped behind the dead tree where Private Case had found refuge. Case glanced at Starbuck, then peered back toward the enemy. The dead Yankee's throat was cut almost to the spine so that his head lolled back in a mess of fly-encrusted blood.

"Where's Captain Dennison?" Starbuck asked.

Case did not answer. Instead he aimed, fired, then levered down the trigger guard to expose the breech of the Sharps rifle. A puff of smoke curled from the open breech as he pushed a stiff linen-wrapped cartridge into the barrel. He pulled up the trigger guard and Starbuck noted how a built-in shear sliced the back off the cartridge to expose the powder to the firing nipple. Case put a new percussion cap on the nipple and aimed again.

"Where's Dennison?" Starbuck asked.

"Ain't seen him," Case said brusquely.

"You came up here with him?" Starbuck asked.

"I came because there were Yankees to be killed," Case said, as loquacious suddenly as he had ever been with Starbuck. He fired again and his shot was rewarded with a yelp of pain that turned into a wail of agony that echoed through the wood. Case grinned. "I do so like killing Yankees." He turned his flat, hard eyes on Starbuck. "Just love killing Yankees."

Starbuck wondered if that was a threat, then decided it was simple bravado. Case was doing his duty, which suggested that the awkward conversation in the dusk had done its work. "Then just keep killing them," Starbuck said, then waited until a sudden rattle of shots suggested that the nearest Yankees might be reloading before he sprinted back through the trees. He ran for three or four seconds, then twisted sideways and dropped behind a tree just a heart's beat before a rattle of shots whipped the air where he had been running. He crawled a few yards and rolled into cover, waited a few seconds, then ran back to the wood's edge.

The firefight in the pasture still raged, though now both sides were lying down rather than standing up to the killing volleys. Swynyard was crouching, an anxious look on his face. "Pray it's good news," he greeted Starbuck.

Starbuck shook his head. "Bastards have taken most of the wood. We've only got this corner. But they ain't there in force. Just skirmishers." A shell dropped just behind the two men, struck a limestone outcrop and, instead of exploding, bounced up to tumble through the air. It made a weird screeching noise that faded quickly away. "What's happening here?" Starbuck asked.

"Stalemate," Swynyard said. "They ain't coming forward, we ain't going forward, so we're just killing each other. The last man alive wins."

"That bad, eh?" Starbuck asked, trying to sound light-hearted.

"But it's going to get worse," Swynyard promised, "it's going to get one whole lot worse."

When the sun rose above the Red Hill it offered a slanting light to give the watchers at the Pry Farm a marvelous view of the battle, or at least of the battle's smoke. To General McClellan, ensconced in his armchair, it seemed as though the woods on the creek's far side were alight, so much smoke was hanging in and above the trees. That smoke, of course, denoted that the enemy was dying, but the General was still in an irritable mood, for none of his aides had thought to cover the armchairs in the night and consequently the upholstery was damp from the dew that now had seeped through his pants. He decided to make no complaint, mainly because a small crowd of civilians had gathered beside the house to stare at him in admiration, but he petulantly refused the first cup of coffee because it was too weak. The second was better, and came in a fine bone china cup and saucer. "A table would be useful," the General observed.

A side table was fetched from the house and somehow balanced on the sloping lawn behind the barricade. The General sipped the coffee, placed it on the table, then put an eye to the telescope that was conveniently mounted on its tripod beside him. "All goes well," he announced loudly enough for his civilian admirers to hear, "Hooker is driving them." A shadow fell over the telescope and he looked up to see that Colonel Thorne had come to stand behind his chair. "Still here, Thorne?" McClellan asked testily.

"Apparently, sir."

"Then doubtless you heard me. All goes well."

Thorne could not tell, for the attack of Hooker's corps was hidden by trees and smoke. The noise told him that a considerable battle was being fought, for both artillery and musketry sounded hard and fast across the creek's valley, but no one could tell from the noise what was happening on the ground. All Thorne knew for sure was that the First Corps, under General Hooker, with thirty-six guns and over eight thousand men, was attempting to drive down the Hagerstown Pike toward the heart of the rebel position. That much was fine, but what Thorne did not understand was why McClellan had not launched his other troops across the Antietam. The rebels would have their hands full containing Hooker, and now was the time to hit them in the flank. If McClellan threw everything he had against the rebels then the battle would surely be over by lunchtime. The Confederates would be broken and fleeing to the Potomac where, piling up against the single ford that was their retreat, they would be easy pickings for the Northern cavalry.

"What of the other attacks, sir?" Thorne asked, gazing at the battle through a pair of field glasses.

McClellan chose not to hear the question. "Fine china," he said, inspecting the coffee cup that was prettily painted with pansies and forget-me-nots. "They live well here," he spoke to an aide and sounded grudging, as though a rural farmer had no right to possess such good china.

"The purpose of good government, sir, is to provide its citizens with a prosperous existence," Thorne snarled, then turned his glasses northward to where another corps of the Northern army was waiting beside the Hagerstown Pike while Hooker's men attacked. Two whole corps had crossed the river the day before, but only one was driving south. "Is Mansfield to back up Hooker?" he asked.

"Mansfield will do his duty," McClellan snapped, "as will you, Colonel Thorne, if you have any duty other than to bother me with questions that are none of your concern."

Thorne backed away from the reproof. He had done what he could to spur McClellan, and to do more was to risk arrest for insubordination. He paused beside the ever-growing crowd of local people who had come to cheer the North to victory and to observe the great Northern hero, McClellan, and, so far as Thorne could judge, Hooker's attack did seem to be deserving applause, but he still feared for the day. It was not defeat that Thorne feared, for the North outnumbered the South far too heavily to risk defeat, but he did fear a stalemate that would allow Lee to survive and fight another day. McClellan should be swamping the rebels with attacks, drowning them in fire and crushing them with his vast army, but all the signs suggested that the Young Napoleon would be cautious. So cautious that he was here, in his armchair, rather than in his saddle and close to the fighting. Lee, Thorne knew, would be close to where the dying was happening. Thorne had known Lee before the war and he admired the man, and Lee, Thorne knew, would not be admiring the china before a gallery of awestruck spectators.

But Lee was the enemy this day, and an enemy who needed to be destroyed if the Union was to be preserved. Thorne took out his notebook. He knew that whatever happened today, McClellan would paint it a victory and McClellan's supporters in the Northern press and in the Congress would demand that their hero should keep command of the army, but only total victory would justify McClellan keeping command, and Thorne was already seeing that happy outcome slip from the Young Napoleon's nerveless grasp. If Lee did survive to fight another day then Thorne was determined that the North would have a new general, a new hero, to do what should be done this day. Thorne wrote his notes, McClellan worried about a surprise rebel attack that would wrong foot his army, and across the creek men died.

The Confederate reinforcements swelled the defenders' fire, while the Yankees at the edge of the cornfield died. Their fire slackened and the rebels, scenting an advantage, began to advance in small groups. The Yankees retreated, yielding the cornfield's edge, and that prompted a sudden shrill outbreak of the rebel yell and the Georgian Brigade was charging into the corn with fixed bayonets. The surviving Yankees broke and ran. Swynyard held his men back, shouting at them to align themselves on the wood instead. "Bayonets!" he shouted. "Forward!"

The Georgians stormed into the cornfield. A few wounded Yankees tried to hold them off with rifle fire, but those brave men were killed with bayonets, and still the Georgians advanced through corn that had been cut down by canister, trampled by boots, scorched by shell fire, and dampened by blood. Beyond the ragged corn the Georgians could see a pasture thick with the retreating enemy and they gave the rebel yell as they hurried forward to chase the Yankees even further.

Then the Yankee gunners saw the rebels in the corn and the canister started again; great gouts of death fanning over the broken field to spin men down and douse the corn in yet more blood. The Pennsylvanians in the trees took the Georgians in the flank with fast rifle fire and the rebel counterattack stalled. For a moment the men stood there, dying, achieving nothing, then they too pulled back from the wrecked corn.

Starbuck found the remains of his three companies close to the wood. Potter's company was still fighting among the trees, while Captain Dennison's men had vanished. Cartwright was shaking with excitement, while Captain Peel was white-faced. "Lippincott's dead," he told Starbuck.

"Lippincott? Christ, I never even knew his first name," Starbuck said.

"It was Daniel," Peel said earnestly.

"Where's Dennison?"

"Don't know, sir," Peel said.

"I don't even know your name," Starbuck said.

"Nathaniel, sir, like you." Peel seemed embarrassed by the admission, almost as if he thought he was being presumptuous.

"Then well done, Nate," Starbuck said, then he turned as Lieutenant Coffman arrived with an order from Colonel Swynyard. Starbuck's men, along with the big 65th Virginia, were to attack into the trees to rescue the brigade's skirmishers from the deadly Pennsylvanian Bucktails. It took a few minutes to align the three Yellowleg companies; then, without waiting for the larger Virginian regiment, Starbuck ordered them into the trees. "Charge!" he shouted. "Come on!" He was screaming the rebel yell, wanting to put the fear of God into the enemy, but when the Yellowlegs charged past the skirmish line they discovered the Yankees were gone. The Bucktails had fired so fast that they had exhausted their ammunition and were already slipping back out of the wood. They left their dead behind, each corpse with a buck's tail on its hat. Swynyard's attack, denied its prey, slowed and stopped.

"Back where you started from!" Colonel Swynyard called. "Back to your positions! Back! Captain Truslow! Here!"

He put Truslow in charge of the wood, giving him every skirmisher in the brigade as his force. The Pennsylvanians would probably return, resupplied with their unique cartridges. Truslow had found one of the Sharps rifles and was exploring its mechanism. "Clever," Truslow said sourly, reluctant to praise anything Northern.

"Accurate, too," Starbuck said, looking at his own dead skirmishers. Sergeant Rothwell was alive, and so was Potter, but too many good men had died. Case was alive, leading a small coterie of his cronies. Case, like a couple

314

of his friends, had pinned a dead Pennsylvanian's buck's tail to his own hat to show he had killed one of the feared skirmishers and Starbuck liked the gesture. "Case!" he shouted.

Case turned his gaze on Starbuck, saying nothing.

"You're a sergeant."

A flicker of a smile showed on the grim face, then Case turned away. "He don't like you," Truslow said.

"He's the one I fought."

"The one you should have killed," Truslow said.

"He's a good soldier."

"Good soldiers make bad enemies," Truslow observed, then spat tobacco juice.

The brigade formed again where it had started the day, though now its ranks had been thinned by death. Men from Haxall's Arkansas regiment helped the wounded back to the graveyard, while others brought water from the springhouse of the burned farm. Starbuck sent a dozen men to loot the cartridge pouches of the dead and distribute the ammunition. Lucifer brought Starbuck a full canteen of water. "Mister Tumlin," Lucifer said gleefully, "is in the graveyard."

"Dead?" Starbuck asked savagely.

"Hiding behind the wall."

"Dennison?"

"Him too," Lucifer grinned.

"Sons of bitches," Starbuck said. He turned to run over to the graveyard, but just then a bugle sounded and the Yankee artillery began to fire again and Starbuck turned back.

The second Northern attack was coming.

In Harper's Ferry the noise of battle was like distant thunder, but a thunder that never ended. Vagaries of wind would sometimes dull the sound to a grumble, or else magnify it so that the ominous crack of individual guns could be heard.

The captured Federal garrison had been marched away to captivity and now the last rebel soldiers prepared to leave the small, ransacked town. The troops were General Hill's Light Division, three thousand of Jackson's best men, and they had seventeen miles to march to reach the source of the bruising noise that filled the sky.

It promised to be a hot day, a searing hot day, a day when marching would be hell, but nothing to the hell that waited for them at their journey's end. General Hill wore his red shirt, a sign he expected to fight.

The Light Division began its march, while ten miles north, but blocked from them by the wide Potomac River, their comrades pushed new powder into blackened rifle barrels and a new mass of Yankees, more numerous than the first, came down the turnpike.

And the battle was scarcely a half hour old.

BILLY BLYTHE RECKONED he had miscalculated. He had only ever seen one battle and that had been fought close to the Bull Run, where the hills were smaller and steeper than this high plateau between the Antietam and the Potomac, and at Manassas there had been far more woods, which had provided easy places for a man to hide while the battle's tide washed extravagantly past. He had planned on doing just that this day—slipping away in the confusion and finding some deep place in the green trees where no one would find him until the killing was over.

Instead he discovered himself on a high, bare place cut by fences and lanes, and where the only woods were either firmly in rebel hands or else were the scenes of savage fighting. And that meant there was nowhere to hide and nowhere to run, and so Billy Blythe sheltered behind the graveyard's low stone wall and wondered just how he was ever going to abandon the rebel army and join the Northern troops. He made what preparation he could. For a time he had busied himself among the wounded, though it was no act of mercy that had motivated him, but rather the need to discover a well-bloodied gray coat that he could exchange for his tight jacket. Then, wearing the blood-damp coat so that he looked like one of the wounded himself, he settled down to wait.

"You hurt?" Dennison saw Tumlin lying against the wall.

"Nothing that'll kill me, Tom," Blythe answered.

Dennison reloaded the rifle he had borrowed from one of the wounded. Every few moments he would peer over the stone wall's coping and fire a shot at the Yankee skirmishers who edged the East Woods. He had fled from those woods earlier, driven out by the terrifying fire of the Pennsylvanian rifles and now, with half of his company, he sheltered behind the graveyard wall. The other half of his company was lost. Dennison knew he should not be here, that he should have stayed with Starbuck's battalion, but he had been drowned by terror in the opening minutes because he had never imagined that battle could be so overwhelmingly violent. At Gaines's Mill, where the Yellowlegs had earned their derisory nickname, Dennison had never come close to the real battle, but somehow he had imagined that combat would prove to be a more decorous business, something like the prints of the Revolutionary War that hung on his uncle's walls. In those prints the two opposing lines always stood upright with noble expressions of grim resolve, the dead had the good manners to lie face down so that their wounds were hidden, while the wounded were relegated to the edges of the pictures where they expired palely and gracefully in the arms of their comrades. That had been Dennison's expectation, but in the first few shattering moments of this bloody day beside the Antietam he had discovered that the reality of battle was a gut-loosening slaughter in which a man's wits were banished by noise and where the wounded died with their bellies slit open, their brains splattered on turf, and their voices screaming helplessly as they thrashed in agony. And all the while the noise banged on and on, and the bullets hissed and whistled, and the terrible shells crashed incessantly.

A doctor, his hands, sleeves, and shirtfront drenched

in blood, saw Billy Blythe's coat and stepped over the recumbent bodies toward him. "You need help, soldier?"

"I'll be back on my feet right soon, doctor," Blythe answered. "Bleeding's stopped and I'll be back in the line when I've got my breath. You look after the others, sir."

"You're a brave man," the doctor said, and moved on to find another casualty.

Blythe grinned, then lit a cigar. "Reckon you're doing the right thing, Tom," he said to Dennison.

"I am?" Dennison had knelt ready to fire another shot, but just then a bullet struck the wall's top and ricocheted on into one of the trees that shaded the graves, and Dennison slumped back down beside Blythe.

"Keeping your men in reserve," Blythe said. "That shows you've got your wits about you. I admire that."

Dennison shuddered as a shell exploded nearby to rattle the stone wall's far side with scraps of metal. "We can't stay here all day," he said, some small part of him recognizing that there was a duty to fulfill on the field.

Blythe twisted round and raised his head above the wall. "You could take your men back to the woods now," he said. A few moments before those woods had been edged with Yankees firing at the graveyard, but those marksmen seemed to have disappeared and, for the moment at least, the nearer edge of the trees seemed deserted, but another Yankee attack was coming, which suggested that the southern edge of the trees would once again become a battleground. Which meant that Blythe would wait. If the rebels regained a firm hold of the trees then he might go back and find a place to hide, but till then he would let the stone wall shelter him.

Dennison snatched a look at the shattered branches and riven trunks of the East Woods, which looked as though a giant ax-man had gone berserk among its trees, then ducked back. "Maybe I'll keep my men in reserve," he said.

"Good decision, Tom," Blythe said. "But I doubt Starbuck would agree. Starbuck just wants your men dead. Hell, he don't care." Dennison looked scared at the mention of Starbuck and Blythe shook his head. "Reckon you'll have to deal with Mister Starbuck if the Yankees don't oblige you. And that means dealing with his lackeys too. Like Sergeant Rothwell. Perhaps Bobby Case can help you?"

"I ain't seen Case," Dennison said. "Maybe he's dead."

"You'd better pray not. You're going to need friends, Tom, otherwise Starbuck will have you on a court-martial. I know you're doing the right thing, and you know it too, but will Starbuck know? You'd better make sure, Tom. I'd hate to see a good man like you sacrificed by a Yankee bastard like Starbuck. I reckon you'd best find Bobby Case and talk to him. Do your duty by the battalion and your country."

Dennison looked shocked at the thought of being court-martialed for cowardice. "Deal with Starbuck?" he asked faintly.

"Unless you want a few bad years in prison. Of course, they could just shoot you, but most court-martials end in prison, don't they? You and some niggers chained together picking cotton or breaking up rocks?" Blythe was making it up as he went along, but he could see his words were getting through to Dennison's dulled senses. "My name ain't Billy Tumlin," Blythe went on, "if you don't have an urgent need to take care of Starbuck. Starbuck and Rothwell."

"Starbuck and Rothwell?" Dennison asked.

"And Potter, too," Blythe said. "And that damned nigger boy. Get your enemies out of the way, Tom, then you can soar! You can be a great soldier. My, I envy you.

I won't be here to see it on account of being back home in Louisiana, but I'll watch your career. Upon my soul, I will."

"You reckon Case will help me?" Dennison asked nervously. He was afraid of Case. There was something very dangerous in Case's big, brooding presence and unreadable eyes. "You sure he'll help?"

"I know he will," Blythe said firmly. It had been Case who had helped Blythe during the night in Harper's Ferry, but that attack on Starbuck had been both opportunistic and clumsy. Things would be much easier now, for what was one pair of deaths among so much carnage? "I told Bobby you'd make him into an officer," Blythe said. "I reckon Bobby Case deserves to be an officer, don't you?"

"I reckon," Dennison agreed vigorously.

"So find him, Tom, and do your duty. Hell, you don't want to see Starbuck throw a whole battalion away, do you?"

Dennison settled back to think about matters while Blythe leaned contentedly against the wall and drew on his cigar. It was as easy, Blythe reckoned, as stealing from a country church poor-box. He would have his inconvenient enemies killed, then he would somehow cross the lines to his reward in the North. He touched his Federal commission, which was still hidden in his pants pocket, then waited.

To Starbuck it was like a nightmare from which he had awoken, only to find the nightmare was real. The rebel line had hurled one attack back, but now another identical assault tramped stolidly down the funnel between the East and West Woods. It was like Ezekiel's valley of dead bones on which the sinews were stretched, the flesh placed, and the skin wrapped before the breath of God animated the dry bones into a great army. And now, in this waking nightmare, that army advanced on Starbuck and he wondered, in the name of God, just how many more warriors the Yankees could produce.

The new attack again filled the space between the West and East Woods. It came beneath flags, accompanied by drums, trampling over the blood and horror of what was left of the first attack. Yankee skirmishers ran forward, dropped to their knees in the remnants of the corn, and opened fire.

The rebel guns, charged with canister, roared at the advancing line. Starbuck saw one skirmisher lifted from the ground by the strike of the canister and flung backward like a rag doll hurled by a petulant child. The man sprawled back to earth, then, amazingly, picked himself up, found his rifle, and limped away. A rebel skirmisher shot him in the back and the man pitched forward onto his knees, hesitated, then fell flat.

"Wait!" Swynyard was loping along the back of his line. His men were lying down and, at a casual glance, they looked like a solid brigade, but Swynyard knew that too many of the prone men were already dead. They had been killed in the first attack, and too many of the living would soon share their fate. Swynyard looked behind but could see no more reinforcements. "We hold them here, boys," he called aloud. "Hold them here. Wait till you see their belt buckles. Don't waste bullets. Hold hard, boys, hold hard."

More Yankees were pushing through the East Woods. The rebels had nothing there but Truslow's heavy skirmish line, and after trading a handful of shots, that line pulled back rather than be overrun. Starbuck saw Potter emerge from the trees and ran over to join him. "What's happening?"

"Thousands of the sons of bitches," Potter said breathlessly. His eyes were bright, his face drawn, and his breath hoarse.

"Brigade attack," Truslow, who had followed Potter from the trees, offered more usefully. He put his men at the end of Swynyard's line where they crouched, waiting for the storm to break.

The rebel gunners had seen the gray skirmishers come out of the East Woods and, reckoning that there were Yankees to be killed, switched some of their fire onto the trees. Shells hammered into the timber where great elms swayed as if caught in a hurricane. Branches splintered down with the iron shards of shell fragments, leaf scraps blew like rain. More shells poured into the woods while the other rebel guns cracked their loads of canister at the Yankees in the cornfield, who were at last in range of the waiting rifles.

"Fire!" Swynyard called.

The rifles began their work, but every downed Yankee was replaced by more men from the rear ranks. The edge of the wood was infested by Yankees, who hid behind trees and shot at the rebels in the open pasture. The Northern skirmishers targeted the rebel gunners, trying to suppress the deadly canister, and minute by minute their bullets did their work. The Northern line came forward in small groups, knelt, opened fire, then darted forward again. The sound of the Northern volleys was like shredding calico or like a canebrake burning. There was no beginning and no end to the rifles' noise, just a continuous splintering horror that filled the air with whistling lead. The rebels began to glance behind, wondering where salvation lay in this open-air hell. The smoke stretched in another thin cloud above the cornfield.

Starbuck crouched among the men of Cartwright's

company and fought as a rifleman. There was nothing else to do. There were no useful commands to shout, no reserves to fetch, nothing to do but fight. The fear that had haunted him for a month was still there, but at bay now, lurking like a beast in the shadows. He was too busy to be aware of it. For him, as for the others who still survived in the rebel line, the battle had become a tiny patch of earth circumscribed by smoke, blood, and burning grass. He had no conception of time, nor of what happened elsewhere. He heard the shells boom overhead and the unending thunder of the guns all around, and he knew that the foul-smelling air all about him was thick with bullets, but all his concentration was now on loading and firing. He picked his targets, watching one group of Yankees trying to work their way down the edge of the East Woods. He would choose one man, watch him, wait till the man checked to load his rifle, then fire. He saw an officer, shot at him, then dropped the rifle butt onto the ground as he pulled a cartridge from the bottom of his pouch. An enemy bullet hit the rifle's stock, almost snatching it from his grasp and driving great splinters from its butt. He swore, rammed the bullet home, brought the broken stock up to his shoulder, primed the cone, and saw the officer was still alive, still shouting his troops forward, and so he fired again. His shoulder was tender from the rifle's recoil and his fingernail was bleeding from picking the hot shattered caps from the cone. The rifle's barrel was almost too hot to touch. The man next to him was dead, shot through one eye, and Starbuck rifled the man's pouch to find six cartridges.

Truslow was hit in the thigh. He cursed, clapped a hand on the bleeding wound, then scrabbled in his pouch for a tin of moss and spider's web that he had kept for this moment. He ripped his pants leg apart, gritted his teeth, then stuffed the mixture into the entry and exit wounds. He rammed the moss and web in, suffering the pain, then picked up his rifle and looked for the son of a bitch who had shot at him. Robert Decker was crawling among the dead, rescuing cartridges, which he tossed to the living. Potter was firing and loading, firing and loading, always keeping his front toward the enemy so that no bullet struck the precious bottle of whiskey in his pack.

The Yankee line seemed to thicken rather than thin. More blue-coated troops were coming down the funnel to stiffen the attack, and now a Northern gun team galloped right into the cornfield and slewed about in a shower of dirt and broken stalks to position their cannon on a slight rise of ground that lay at the field's northern margin. A gun horse went down to a blast of rebel case-shot. It screamed and flailed at the air with its hooves. It thrashed its neck, spraying blood while a gunner cut it out from the rest of the panicking team that he ran back out of rifle range. Another gunner shot the wounded horse, then his companions fired their first shot—a shell that landed plumb in the center of the rebel line. The Yankee gunners were screaming at their own infantry to clear a field of fire so they could load with canister. "We can't last," Truslow growled to Starbuck.

"Jesus," Starbuck said. If Truslow sensed defeat, then disaster must be close. He knew Truslow was right, but still he did not want to admit it. The Yankees had come within an ace of breaking the fragile line, and when that line was dead or captured they would charge across the plateau's top to pierce the very center of Lee's army. The rebels were still enduring the Northern fire, but Starbuck guessed that most, like him, were simply too scared to run away. A man trying to retreat across the plateau would make himself an easy target and it seemed safer to crouch low behind barriers of the dead and keep on fighting.

The Yankee gun in the cornfield coughed a barrel of canister that churned dead and living flesh before ricocheting on into the pasture behind. A rebel gun was hand-spiked round to fire at the Yankee cannon, but a group of blue skirmishers killed the rebel gun crew. A color bearer in the Yankee lines waved a flag and Starbuck saw the arms of his home state, Massachusetts. A foolhardy Northern officer galloped a horse behind his men, encouraging them. Such men made choice targets, but the rebels were too few and too desperate to do anything now but pour a blind fire straight into the gunsmoke in hope of keeping the overwhelming Yankee mass away. More Northern canister crashed from the gun in the cornfield and more rebels died. Truslow's leg was soaked in blood. "You should see a doctor," Starbuck said. He was shaking, not with fear, but with a desperate excitement. He had one cartridge left.

Truslow gave a short efficient opinion of all doctors, then fired before dropping down behind a corpse that offered some cover as he reloaded. The corpse twitched as a bullet struck home with the meaty sound of an ax blow. Starbuck had reloaded his revolver during the pause between attacks and now fired all its chambers at the nearest group of Yankees. Truslow was right, he thought. They should retreat, but a retreat would become a rout. Better, perhaps, to lie here and let the victorious Yankees roll right over the line. He rammed his last cartridge into his rifle and peered across a corpse to find a final useful target. "Sons of bitches," he said vengefully.

Then, suddenly, there was a screaming sound, an exultant sound, a high-pitched wailing terror of a sound, and he looked to his left and saw a new rebel unit streaming across the pasture. Some of the newcomers were in gray, some in butternut, but most wore the remnants of the gaudy *zouave* uniforms with which they had begun the war. It was the Louisiana Tigers, a fearful regiment of scoundrels from New Orleans, and it charged right past the rebel line, with bayonets fixed and with their battle flag streaming in the smoke. A sudden salvo of shells burst among the regiment, but the ranks closed up and screamed relentlessly on.

"Forward!" Truslow shouted. "Come on, you bastards!"

Astonishingly, the frail rebel line rose from among the dead. The Yankees, taken by surprise, seemed to pause in sheer disbelief. It was their turn to see the dead come to savage life. "Come on!" Truslow shouted. He was limping, but nothing would stop him.

"Bayonets!" Starbuck shouted.

It seemed a terrible madness had cloaked the rebel line. It was on the verge of rout, but, spurred by the Louisiana Tigers, it charged forward instead of running back. Men were screaming the rebel yell as they ran. The Yankees in the cornfield offered one scattered volley, then began to retreat. Some, unwilling to abandon their victory, shouted at their comrades to stay in the cornfield and those men formed small groups to resist the broken rebel charge.

The rebel yell was the song of those men's death. For a few brief seconds the two sides clashed in the corn. Bayonets parried bayonets, but the rebels outnumbered the Northerners who had stayed to fight. Starbuck, unaware that he was screaming like a maniac, banged a rifle and bayonet to one side, then lunged his own blade into a face. He kicked the man as he fell, reversed his rifle, and hammered the bullet-splintered stock down into the bloody face.

A volley sounded. The Yankees had reformed north of

the cornfield and were pouring volley fire at the Louisianans. More fire came from the woods on either side of the cornfield. There were Yankees in both.

"Back! Back!" someone shouted, and the rebels ran back through the cornfield to their old position. Starbuck paused long enough to loot the cartridges from the man he had wounded, then ran after his men. Bullets whip-sawed from either side. He was aware of bodies everywhere: sprawling, broken, explosive-torn, mangled dismembered bodies—white bones and brain, blue intestines, sheets of blood. Some men lay on their own, but most were in groups where they had been cut down by canister and some, horrifically, moved slowly beneath their carapaces of fly-crawling blood. A man moaned, another called on God, a third coughed feebly. Starbuck crouched as he ran, then at last he was out of the cornfield and back in the rebel line. Potter had been wounded. A bayonet had slashed off half his left ear, which now dangled amid a blood-soaked hank of hair. "Just a scratch," he insisted, "just a scratch. The whiskey's safe."

The rebel line lay down again. Men shared canteens and doled out cartridges they found in dead men's pouches. The Yankees had regrouped, but they seemed unwilling to go back into the cornfield that had become a slaughteryard for both sides. Instead they crouched while the rebel canister whipped the air overhead and their own guns returned the fire. The lone gun on the slight knoll in the field had been abandoned, but there were other Yankee guns close behind it and those guns were firing away. Starbuck aimed at one of the gunners, then decided to save his ammunition.

He stood. The blood in the small of his back had crusted his shirt and now that crust pulled painfully away to wash a gush of warm liquid down his buttocks. His throat was arched, his eyes raw with smoke, and his bones aching with weariness. He found the Irishman who had been telling his beads before the battle and sent him back to the springhouse with a dozen canteens. "Go easy now," he told him. "Give the trees a wide berth." The Yankee sharpshooters were back at the edge of the East Woods, though the smoke that lingered in the windless air was spoiling their aim, and their fire, which would have been terrifying in another circumstance, seemed puny after the tempest of rifle fire that had preceded the Louisianan charge.

Colonel Maitland was lying face down close to the Smoketown Road. Starbuck did not recognize the man until he crouched beside him and tugged at Maitland's pouch in hopes of finding some pistol cartridges. "I'm not dead," Maitland's muffled voice protested, "I'm praying."

Starbuck touched the canteen at Maitland's belt. "You got water?"

"It is not water, Starbuck," Maitland said reprovingly, "it is cordial. Help yourself."

It was neat rum. Starbuck coughed as the raw liquor hit his powder-abraded throat, then spat the rest onto the grass.

Maitland rolled over and retrieved the canteen. "Good things are wasted on you, Starbuck," he said reprovingly. The Colonel, having confiscated the Legion's liquor, must have drunk most of it, for he was helplessly drunk. A bullet hit a nearby gun barrel with a great clang like a cracked bell struck. The gunners spiked their piece around and gave the Yankees in the East Woods a dose of canister. Maitland lay back on the grass and stared at the gunsmoke churning in the blue sky. "When you were a child," he said dreamily, "did you find summer endless?"

"And winter," Starbuck said, sitting beside the Colonel.

"Of course. You're a Yankee. Sleighbells and snow. I

once rode in a sleigh. I was only a child, but I remembe
the snow was like a cloud around us. But our winter i
slush and impassable roads." Maitland fell silent for a
moment. "I'm not sure I can stand," he finally said in a
pathetic voice.

"No need at the moment."

"I have been sick," Maitland said solemnly.

"No one knows," Starbuck said, though in fact the fron
of the Colonel's elegant uniform was thick with vomit. I
had caked in the yellow braid and lodged behind the
glittering buttons.

"The truth is," Maitland said very solemnly, "that I
cannot abide the sight of blood."

"Kind of a drawback for a soldier," Starbuck said mildly

Maitland closed his eyes for a moment. "So what's hap
pening?"

"We drove the bastards off again."

"They'll come back," Maitland said darkly.

"They'll come back." Starbuck stood and took the can
teen out of the Colonel's nerveless fingers and emptied the
rum onto the ground. "I'll get you some water, Colonel."

"I'm very much obliged to you," Maitland said, stil
staring at the sky.

Starbuck walked back to the ravaged battle line. Swyn
yard was staring across the cornfield with vacant eyes. His
right cheek was twitching as it had done when he had
been a drunkard. He looked up at Starbuck and it took
him a moment to recognize the younger man. "Can't do
that again," he said grimly. "One more attack and we're
done, Nate."

"I know, sir."

Swynyard took out his revolver and tried to reload it
but his right hand was shaking too much. He gave the
gun to Starbuck. "Would you mind, Nate?"

"Are you hit, sir?"

Swynyard shook his head. "Just dazed." He stood up slowly. "I stood too close to a shell burst, Nate, but God spared me. I wasn't touched, just dizzied." He shook his head as if to clear his thoughts. "I've sent for cartridges," he said carefully, "and water's coming. There are no more men. Haxall's hurt bad. Got a lump of iron in his belly. He won't last. I'm sorry about Haxall. I like him."

"Me, too."

"I haven't seen Maitland," Swynyard said. "Thank you, Nate," this was for loading the revolver that the Colonel now returned to its holster.

"Maitland's still here," Starbuck said.

"So he didn't run away? Good for him." The Colonel glanced up and down his line. On paper he commanded a brigade, but the men left in the firing line would hardly have constituted a regiment in the prewar army and the brigade's various battalions had become inextricably mixed as Swynyard had fed men into the battle, so that now men simply clung to their friends or nearest neighbors while officers and sergeants looked after whoever was within sight. "The textbook," Swynyard said, "would probably suggest we disentangle ourselves and get back into our proper battalions, but I think we'll forget the textbook. They'll fight just as well as they are." He meant, Starbuck suspected, that they would die just as well, and indeed, at that moment, it seemed impossible that they should do anything but die. The Yankees were quiet, but that lull would not last, for Starbuck could see more blue coats showing beyond the jagged wreckage of the corn-field. The enemy had attacked twice, and twice they had been thrown back, but now the Yankees gathered their forces for the next advance.

Starbuck sent Lucifer to Maitland with a canteen of water. The boy came back grinning. "One happy man, the Colonel," he said.

"He's not the first to get drunk on a battlefield," Starbuck said.

"Mister Tumlin," Lucifer happily reported more news, "is wearing a new coat. All bloody."

Starbuck no longer cared about Tumlin, nor Dennison. He would deal with them after the battle, if there was anything left to deal with. Now, back among the dead who sheltered the living in the shell-blackened pasture, he waited for the Yankees.

Whose drums began to sound again. Whose guns opened fire again.

For the third attack was coming.

Two miles to the south, where the Antietam Creek turned sharply westward as it ran down to the Potomac, a whole corps of the United States army waited in hiding on the creek's eastern bank. Twenty-nine battalions of hardened troops, backed by guns, were ready to cross the river and slash north toward the road that ran west from Sharpsburg. Once that road was captured then all Lee's troops north of the town would be cut off from their retreat, and this corps was the lower jaws of that terrible trap.

Some of the troops were sleeping. Others cooked breakfast. The rebels knew they were there, for the rebel artillery across the creek kept up a harassing fire, but the Northern troops were concealed by woods and reverse slopes and the rebel shells whirred overhead to explode harmlessly in woods or pastures.

No orders came to cross the creek, and for that the commanders of the battalions closest to the water were grateful. The stone bridge that crossed the creek was narrow, and the far bank was precipitous and crowded with rebel infantry who had dug rifle pits into the slope so that any attack down the road and onto the bridge would be a bloody affair.

Still farther south a group of officers worked their way through thick brush and timber to where they could see a ford. The ford offered a way of outflanking the rebels defending the stone bridge, but when the officers came in sight of the creek their hopes fell. The far bank was just as steep as the slope that lay beyond the bridge, and the ford, far from being unguarded, had a picket line of gray infantry dug into its sharp slope.

"Whose idea was this?" one man, a general, asked.

"Some damned engineer colonel," an aide answered. "Thorne, he's called."

"The bastard can cross first," the General said as he peered through field glasses at the far bank. The sound of the battle in the north filled the sky, but above its din he could just hear the sound of voices coming from over the water. The rebels here seemed light-hearted, as if they knew that on this terrible day of slaughter they had drawn a long straw.

A trampling of feet in the woods made the General draw back from the trees' edge. Two of his aides were approaching with a farmer dressed in a thick wool coat and a shovel hat. Cow dung was plastered on the man's pants.

"Mister Kroeger," one of the aides introduced the farmer, who still retained enough Old World servility to pull off his hat when he was named to the General. "Mister Kroeger," the aide explained, "says this isn't Snaveley's Ford."

"Not Snaveley's," Kroeger agreed in a German accent. "Snaveley's down there," he pointed downstream.

The General cursed. He had fetched seven battalions and half a dozen guns to the wrong place.

"How far?" he asked.

"Long ways," Kroeger said. "I use it for the cows, yes? Too steep here for cattle." He motioned with his hand to demonstrate how steep the far bank was.

The General swore again. If he had been given cavalry, he told himself, he would have scouted these lower banks of the creek, but McClellan had insisted on the army's cavalry staying close to the Pry farm. God alone knew what good they were doing there, unless McClellan fancied that they would protect him during a fighting retreat.

"Is there a road to Snaveley's Ford?" he asked.

"Just pastures," Kroeger answered.

The General cursed a third time, prompting the farmer to frown in disapproval. The General slapped at a horsefly. "Send a reconnaissance party downstream, John," he told an aide. "Perhaps Mister Kroeger will guide them?"

"You want the troops in march order, sir?" the aide asked.

"No, no. Let them have their coffee," the General frowned in thought. If this dung-encrusted farmer was right and the ford was a good long way downstream, then maybe it was too far away to let his men outflank the defenders at the bridge. "I need to talk to Burnside," he said. "There's no great hurry," he added. It was, after all, still early. Most of America would not have had their breakfasts yet, certainly not the respectable part, and McClellan had sent no orders for the lower jaw of the trap to swing shut. Indeed, McClellan had sent no orders at all, which suggested there was plenty of time for coffee.

The officers walked away from the creek, leaving the woods there in peace. North of Sharpsburg the armies fought, but in the south they brewed their coffee, read the latest letters from home, slept, and waited.

The third Union attack was not centered on the cornfield, but rather drove down the turnpike toward the West Woods. Starbuck could see its progress by the thick cloud of smoke churned up by the rebel shells that tore into the leading blue ranks, then by the ripping sound of rifle fire exploding from the northern edge of the West Woods. The sound of the battle rose to a frenzy that matched the two previous fights at the cornfield's edge, but for the moment this was someone else's fight and Starbuck rested. His eyes were smarting and his throat, despite the mouthfuls of water he had gulped down, was still dry, but his pouch was half full of cartridges again; some were gleaned from the dead and the others from the brigade's last reserves that had been fetched up from the graveyard. The Yankee gunners had manned the cannon in the cornfield again, but its canister was being soaked up by the makeshift barricades of the dead, who protected the living riflemen in the gray line. The worst threat to his men came from the big federal guns on the Antietam's far banks, but those gunners were concentrating the worst of their fire on the rebel batteries that lay close to the Dunker church.

Potter scuttled across to Starbuck and offered him a canteen. "Your man Truslow's back in the woods."

"He ain't my man. His own, maybe. Yankees are gone?"

"They're still there," Potter said, jerking his head toward the northern part of the East Woods, "but not those bastards with the Sharps rifles. They've gone." Potter lay down, sharing the corpse that protected Starbuck from the canister. Potter's ear was crudely bandaged, but blood had seeped through the knotted length of rag to crust on

335

his coat and shirt collars. "You want my men back in the woods?" he asked.

Starbuck glanced toward the woods and was rewarded by a flash of bright blue feathers. "Bluebird," he said, pointing.

"That ain't a bluebird. That's a bunting. Bluebirds have got reddish chests," Potter said. "So do we stay here?"

"Stay here," Starbuck said.

"I hear Colonel Maitland is stewed?"

"He ain't too sprightly," Starbuck admitted.

"This is my first stone-cold sober battle," Potter said proudly.

"You've still got the whiskey?"

"Safe in its stone bottle, wrapped in two shirts, a piece of canvas, and an unbound copy of Macaulay's *Essays*. It isn't a complete volume. I found it dangling in a Harper's Ferry privy and the first thirty pages had already been consumed for hygienic purposes."

"Wouldn't you rather have found his poetry?" Starbuck asked.

"In a privy? No, I think not. Besides, I already have swathes of Macaulay in my head, or what remains of my head," Potter said, touching the bloody bandage over his left ear. " 'To every man upon this earth Death cometh soon or late, And how can man die better Than facing fearful odds.' " Potter shook his head at the appropriateness of the words. "Too good for a privy, Starbuck. My father hung the works of Roman Catholic theologians in our outhouse. It was, he said, the only thing they were fit for, but the insult misfired. I damn nearly converted to popery after reading Newman's lectures. Father thought I was constipated till he found out what I was doing, and after that we used newspapers like every other Christian, but

Father always made sure that any verses of scripture were cut out before the sheets were threaded on the string."

Starbuck laughed, then a warning cry from the mix of Georgians and Louisianans who lay to his left made him peer over the corpse, on which the flies were already crawling and laying their eggs. The Yankees were in the cornfield again. He could not see them yet, but he could see a trio of banners showing over the shattered field and it would only be a few seconds before the Northern skirmishers came into sight. He pulled back his rifle's hammer and waited. The flags, two Stars and Stripes and a regimental color, were well to his left, suggesting that these attackers were staying close to the turnpike rather than spreading across the whole cornfield. Still no skirmishers appeared. He could hear a band playing somewhere in the Yankee lines, its melody diluted to a delicate threnody by the insistent percussion of shells, canister, and rifle fire. Where the hell were the Yankee skirmishers? The heads of the leading rank of attackers were in view now and Starbuck suddenly realized that there were no skirmishers coming, just a column of formed troops advancing carelessly in the open. Maybe they believed the real battle was being fought in the West Woods where the cacophony of shell fire and rifles was loudest, but they were about to discover that the battered line of rebels in the pasture was not all dead men.

"Stand up!" a voice shouted from among the Georgian survivors.

"Stand!" Starbuck took up the cry and heard Swynyard echo it.

"Fire!" Starbuck shouted, and on either side of him the ragged remnants of the rebel line stood like scarecrows from among the bloodied dead and poured a volley into the compact Yankee formation. The attacker's front file collapsed, then a roundshot ripped through the remaining ranks like a ball thumping into skittles.

Starbuck rammed a bullet home, propped the ramrod against his body, fired, and loaded again. The Yankees were spreading out, running crablike across the cornfield to match the rebel line with a line of their own. More blue uniforms were streaming up behind. God, he thought, but was there no end to the bastards? The rebel line coalesced into groups as men instinctively sought the company of others, but then, when the Yankee fire became torrid, they lay down again to fight from behind the corpses. Men lying down fired more slowly than men standing, and the slackening of rebel fire persuaded the Northern officers to shout their men forward, but the advance was checked when the rebel guns opened fire with case shot—metal balls that exploded in the air to rain down a shower of musket balls—and that deadly shower persuaded the Yankees to lie down. Truslow's company was firing at the Yankees' open flank, evidence that no Northerners had attacked down the East Woods, but then Starbuck saw Bob Decker running zigzag in the pasture, crouching low and evidently looking for someone. "Bob!" Starbuck shouted to attract his attention.

Decker ran to Starbuck and dropped beside him. "I'm looking for Swynyard, sir."

"God knows." Starbuck raised himself to peer over the corpse that sheltered him and saw a Yankee flag carrier kneeling in the corn. He fired and dropped back.

"Truslow says there are Yankees beyond the wood, sir." Decker pointed east.

Starbuck swore. Till now that open flank had been blessedly free of Yankees, but if an attack did come from the open country to the east then there was no way that the survivors in the pasture could cope with it. The

Yankees would sweep into the East Woods, then out into the pasture, and the Yankees pinned down in the cornfield would join the attack. "You find Swynyard," he ordered Decker, "and tell him I've gone to take a look."

He ran eastward. Bullets whipped past him, but the lingering smoke spoiled the Yankees' aim. Starbuck saw Potter and shouted at him to bring his company, then he was in the trees. He jumped a newly fallen branch, twisted past two rebel corpses, then ran on until he reached the Smoketown Road. He paused there, wondering if the Yankees still held the trees beyond, but he could see no movement and so he crossed the dirt track and ran on through the trees. A wounded Yankee called out for water, but Starbuck ignored the man. He headed toward the wood's edge through trunks gouged and splintered and drilled by bullets.

He dropped in the shadows at the tree line. To the east, where the land dropped away to the creek, he could see nothing, but to the north, where the Smoketown Road emerged from the trees to vanish beneath a crest neatly plowed into furrows, were Yankees. Another damned horde of Yankees. They were two wide fields away and for the moment they were not moving. Starbuck could see officers riding up and down the ranks, he could see the banners hanging in the still air, and he knew that the Yankees were being readied to attack. And all that stood between them and Lee's center were two shrunken companies of skirmishers.

"The good Lord is surely testing us today," Swynyard said, catching sight of Starbuck. The Colonel knelt beside him and stared at the waiting Yankees. Potter was behind him with a dozen men; all that remained of his company.

Starbuck felt a vast relief that Swynyard had arrived. "What do we do, sir?"

"Pray?" Swynyard shrugged. "If we bring our men here then we open up the cornfield, if we leave them there, we open up this door."

"So we pray," Starbuck said grimly.

"And send for help." Swynyard backed away. "Leave someone here to watch them, Nate, and let me know when they advance." He ran off through the woods.

Starbuck left Sergeant Rothwell to watch the Yankees, while he led Potter and his men back across the Smoketown Road to the inner edge of the East Woods, where Truslow was harassing the Yankee flank in the cornfield. "What are those sons of bitches doing?" Truslow asked, meaning the Yankees formed on the Smoketown Road.

"Dressing ranks. Getting a speech."

"Let's hope it's a long one." Truslow had torn away the pants leg from his wounded thigh and bound the injury with a bandage torn from a dead man's shirt. He spat tobacco juice, lifted his rifle, and fired. He was aiming at the cannon that still stood on the knoll in the cornfield, keeping its gunners in shelter so they could not rake the rebel line with canister. He reloaded, took aim, then turned to his right before pulling the trigger. There were shouts among the trees and Truslow was suddenly shouting at his men to fall back. The Yankees were coming through the woods again.

Starbuck saw a banner among the shredded leaves. He fired at the color bearer, then fell back with Truslow's company. "Rothwell!" he shouted through the trees, knowing he would not be heard, but knowing he had to warn the Sergeant. "Rothwell!" He did not want the Sergeant marooned in the trees and he wondered if he should run to fetch the man.

But then all hell broke loose on the cornfield's far side.

* * *

General McClellan dabbed at his lips with a napkin, then brushed crumbs of toast from his lap. He was aware of the gaze of the civilian spectators and he kept a stern look on his face so that none of those onlookers would be aware of the worries that racked him.

He was risking a trap. He knew it instinctively, even if he did not know just what form the trap would take. Lee outnumbered him, he was sure, and Lee was fighting a defensive battle and that could only mean that the enemy was disguising his intentions. Somewhere in the landscape a mass of rebels was waiting to attack, and McClellan was determined not to be caught by that surprise assault. He would hold men in reserve to counter it. He would frustrate Lee. He would preserve the army.

"Sir?" An aide stooped beside McClellan's chair. "Dan'l Webster, sir, he's unhappy."

"Unhappy?" McClellan asked. Daniel Webster was his horse.

"The civilians, sir, they're plucking his tail hairs. As souvenirs, sir. We could ask them to move, sir? Up the hill, maybe?"

"There must be a stable?"

"He's in the stable, sir."

"Then shut it!" McClellan did not want to lose his audience. He rather enjoyed their admiration. Indeed, stretching his legs once in a while, he liked to chat with them and assure them that all was well. There was no need to worry mere civilians with his concerns, or tell them that he had telegraphed Washington with an urgent request that every Northern soldier available should be hurried west toward the army. Those soldiers could not of course reach the battlefield in time to join the fight, but they might provide a rear guard behind which his army could retire if Lee's masterstroke brought chaos. The hotheads in his army, fools like Colonel Thorne, might wonder why he did not unleash the men poised to cross the river and attack the rebels' flank, but those fools did not understand the army's danger.

More men marched down to the creek where the columns waited for the order to cross. One unit sang "John Brown's Body" as they marched close to the Pry farm and McClellan scowled. He hated that song and had tried to forbid it being sung. So far as McClellan was concerned there had been nothing to admire in John Brown's foolish adventure. The man had tried to start a slave rebellion, for God's sake, and his hanging, McClellan believed, had been richly rewarded. He tried to ignore the music as he stooped to his telescope to watch the troops on the creek's far side, who were forming up for a new attack on the smoke-wreathed woods. "That's Mansfield's corps?" he asked an aide.

"Yes, sir."

"Tell them to go!"

He would let Mansfield attack and see what happened. At best they would push Lee's men back and at worst they would provoke the dreaded riposte. McClellan almost prayed for that riposte to happen, for then, at least, the fears would take solid shape and he would know just what he had to deal with. But for now he would go on attacking in the north and stay alert for the horror he knew must come.

Three miles away, in a grove of trees near Sharpsburg, Robert Lee stared at a map. He was not studying the map, indeed he was hardly aware that he was looking at it. Belvedere Delaney was among the aides who hovered nearby. The General liked Delaney and had invited him to keep him company. It was good to have someone slightly

342

irreverent, someone who offered amusement rather than advice.

A crescendo of firing sounded from the higher ground north of the town. In a moment, Lee knew, the gunsmoke would billow above the skyline to mark where the fighting had erupted so suddenly. "That's it," he said mildly.

"It?" Delaney asked.

Lee smiled. "Hood's men, Delaney, almost our last reserves. Not, to be honest, that they were reserves." Lee had ruthlessly stripped troops from the southern part of his battle line to preserve the army's northern perimeter so that now, beyond a fragile skin of troops that edged the creek, he had nothing to fight an outflanking attack from the south.

"So what do we do?" Delaney asked.

"Put our trust in McClellan, of course," Lee said with a smile, "and pray that Ambrose Hill reaches us in time."

The Light Division was marching as it had never marched before. It was still south of the Potomac and a long way from the ford at Shepherdstown, but the ever-present sound of the big guns was the summons that kept them moving. Staff officers rode up and down the long column urging the men on. Marching troops were usually given ten minutes' rest an hour, but not today. Today there could be no rest, just marching. The dust kicked up from the dry road choked men's throats, some limped on bare bleeding feet, but no one straggled. If a man dropped out he dropped like the dead, dropped out of sheer exhaustion, but most kept grimly going. They had no breath to sing, not even to speak, just to march and march and march. To where the guns were sounding and the piles of dead grew high.

GENERAL JOHN HOOD'S division burst out of the West Woods to hit the flank of the attacking Yankees like a tidal wave. Most of Hood's men were Texans, but he had battalions from Alabama, Georgia, Mississippi, and North Carolina in his ranks, and all were veterans. They stopped the Yankee advance dead on the turnpike, then spread their battle line across the pasture, where they faced north toward the cornfield. One volley was enough to decimate the Yankees advancing through the corn, then the Texans were screaming the rebel yell and plunging forward with bayonets. Some small groups of Yankees resisted and were cut down, but most just fled. The North's attack was spent, the rebel counter-attack was surging, and the survivors of the old defense line, the battered, bleeding men from Georgia, Louisiana, and Virginia, went forward with Hood's men.

The Yankee artillery by the North Woods took up the battle. They could not use canister, for the ground in front of them was littered with wounded Northerners, and so they cut their shell fuses as short as they dared and opened fire. The shells crashed into the cornfield, flinging men aside and adding a new skein of smoke to the cirrus-like canopy that hung above the trampled crop. The noise reached a new and dreadful intensity. The Northern gunners worked frantically, double-shotting some guns to belch out pairs of shells that exploded a heartbeat after

344

firing. The guns by the turnpike were unhampered by wounded men and they turned their canister on the Texans advancing on the road. One barrel load of bullets ripped up forty feet of snake fence and drove its splintered remnants into a company of rebels. Yankee infantry appeared from the North Woods to add their volley fire, and all the while the rebel cannon lobbed their long-fused shells over the flags of Hood's Division to harry the Northern gunners.

The Yankee gunners at the northern edge of the cornfield died hard. They tried to keep the fight going, but they were in easy range of the Texan skirmishers and one by one the guns were abandoned. Still the Confederates drove forward, skirting the piles of dead and dying in the cornfield, struggling through the rage of bullet and shell as though they could sweep the Yankees clear up to Hagerstown and beyond. Some officers tried to check their men, knowing they were advancing too far, but no voice could be heard in the tempest of iron and lead. The battle had become a gutter fight, rage against rage, men dying in a cornfield that had become death's kingdom.

A regiment from Mississippi pursued the broken Yankees toward the northern edge of the broken corn, sure they were chasing shattered troops to utter defeat, but the Yankees had Pennsylvanian infantry waiting at the rail fence. The blue-coated riflemen were lying down, resting their barrels on the fence's lowest rail. A standing man could see nothing but smoke, but at ground level the waiting infantry could see the legs of the attackers.

They waited. Waited till the rebels were just thirty paces off, then loosed a volley that ripped into Hood's men and silenced the screaming rebel yells in one curt blow. For an instant, an odd, mind-numbing instant, there was a silence on the battlefield as though the wings of death's angel were sweeping overhead, but then the silence passed as the Pennsylvanians stood up to reload and their ramrods clattered in hot barrels and the Northern guns jarred back on their trails to add more carnage to the slaughter in the corn. The front rank of the Confederates was a horror of writhing bodies, blood, and moans. A man snatched up the fallen banner of Mississippi and was shot down. A second man gripped the flag by its fringe and dragged it back through the corn as the Pennsylvanians fired a second volley that thumped into flesh with brutal force. The flag fell again, riddled with bullets. A third man seized the banner and raised it high, then walked backward from the blazing rifle fire until he was driven down with bullets in his belly, groin, and chest. A fourth man speared the flag on his bayonet and pulled it back to where the survivors of his battalion were forming a crude line to return the Pennsylvanian fire. The space between the two lines seemed to be a shifting mass of dirt, a heaving, crawling pile of giant maggots that blindly struggled to find safety. It was the wounded pushing the dead away and trying to rejoin their comrades.

The right flank of Hood's attack swept into the East Woods. There, protected by the battered trees from the effects of the Northern guns, the Texans drove into the Yankees, who were advancing southward. Men fought within spitting distance. For a time the two sides traded shots, neither willing to retreat and neither able to advance, but slowly the rebel fire gained the advantage as more men came from the pasture. The Yankees retreated and the retreat became hurried as the rebels pushed forward with bayonets.

Starbuck and his men were weary, bruised, wounded, and parched, but they fought among the trees with the desperation of soldiers who believed that one last effort would rid them of their enemies. Again and again the Yankees had come forward, and again and again they had been pushed back, and this time it seemed as if they could be pushed clear back out of the woods altogether. One group of Northerners turned a pile of cordwood into a miniature redoubt. Their rifle barrels spat long flames over the logpile, the tongues of fire oddly bright in the shadow of the trees. Starbuck used his revolver, firing at murderously close range into the Yankees, who suddenly abandoned the logs as a rush of screaming Texans swept up from their right. A small black dog stayed with its dead master, running back and forth and barking piteously as the rebels ran past. Starbuck unslung his rifle, paused to reload it, then ran on toward the fighting. He came to the road that ran through the woods and crouched at its edge, watching as Yankees dashed across to escape the charge. He fired, saw a man sprawl in the grass that grew down the road's center, then he sprinted over the dirt road himself. The fight seemed to be dying as the Yankees legged it out of the trees and so he squatted by a limestone knoll and began the laborious business of reloading the revolver.

Lucifer ran over the road, leading the black dog on a makeshift leash of two rifle slings. "You shouldn't be here," Starbuck said, making space for the boy behind the knoll.

"I always wanted a dog," Lucifer said proudly. "Got to find him a name."

"There are still Yankees in the wood," Starbuck said, pushing down the lever that rammed the revolver's chambers.

"I shot one," Lucifer said.

"You damn fool," Starbuck said fondly. "They're fighting for your freedom." He levered down the last chamber,

347

then upturned the gun to push on the percussion caps.

"I'd have shot more," Lucifer said, "only the gun don't work." He offered Starbuck his revolver. The trigger hung limp.

"It needs a new stop spring," Starbuck said, handing the gun back, "but you shouldn't be fighting. Hell, these bastards are trying to liberate you and you're killing the poor sons of bitches." Lucifer did not answer. Instead he frowned at his gun and twitched the trigger in hope that it would engage on some part of the mechanism. The small dog whimpered and he soothed it. It was a puppy, scarce weaned, with coarse black hair, a snub nose, and a stump of a tail. "The bastards will kill you," Starbuck warned him. "You and your dog."

"So I die," Lucifer said defiantly. "And in heaven we get to be the masters and you all are our slaves."

Starbuck grinned. "I don't reckon on seeing heaven."

"But maybe your hell is our heaven," Lucifer said with relish. "Imp," he added.

"Imp?" Starbuck asked, "imp of Satan?"

"The dog! I'm going to call him Imp," Lucifer said delightedly as he ruffled Imp's ears. "Got to get you some meat, Imp." The stumpy tail suddenly wagged as the dog licked Lucifer's face. "I always wanted a dog," Lucifer said again.

"Then keep him safe," Starbuck said, "and keep yourself safe."

"I ain't going to be killed," Lucifer said confidently.

"Every corpse here thought that," Starbuck said grimly.

Lucifer shook his head. "I ain't," he insisted. "I ate a Yankee grave."

"You did what?"

"I found a dead Yankee's grave," Lucifer admitted, "and I waited till midnight, then I ate a scrap of dirt from the

348

grave. No Yankee can kill me now. My mother taught me that."

Starbuck heard something pathetic in the last few words. "Where is your mother, Lucifer?"

The boy shrugged. "She's alive," he said reluctantly.

"Where?"

The boy jerked his head, then shrugged. "She's alive." He waggled the useless trigger. "But they sold me out. Reckoned I was worth something, see?" He touched his skin. "I ain't real black. If I'd been real black they'd never have sold me, but they reckoned I could be a house slave." He shrugged. "I ran away."

"So where is your mother?" Starbuck insisted.

"Hell, she's probably sold by now. The master never kept the niggers he'd slept with, not usually. I don't know where she is." He said the last words angrily, as if to demonstrate that he did not want to talk about the subject any more.

"And your mother taught you magic?" Starbuck asked.

"It ain't magic," Lucifer insisted, still angry. "It's a way of staying alive. And it ain't for you."

"Because I'm white?"

"Alice Whittaker," Lucifer said suddenly, not looking at Starbuck. "That's her name. Ain't he a fine puppy?"

"He's fine," Starbuck said. He wondered if he should ask more, but suspected that Lucifer had already revealed more than he wanted to. He leaned over and fondled Imp's ears and received a lick as a reward. "He's fine," he said again, "and so are you." He holstered his reloaded revolver and stood up. There was still sporadic firing higher up the wood, but he wanted to see what had happened to the formed troops who had been waiting on the Smoketown Road and so, warning Lucifer to stay where he was, he crept cautiously through the trees. He expected to find Yankee stragglers, but this part of the wood was almost empty. Two rebels limped past on their way to the doctors and a dead Pennsylvanian Bucktail lay against a tree with a look of surprise on his face, but otherwise the trees were deserted.

Sergeant Rothwell was lying down at the edge of the wood where Starbuck had left him. There was blood on his back and Starbuck's first thought was that the man was dead, then he saw an arm move. He ran to the Sergeant's side and carefully rolled him over. Rothwell moaned. His teeth were chattering, his face was yellow, and his eyes closed. There was blood on his chest. "Rothwell!" Starbuck said.

"In the back," Rothwell managed to say, then he stiffened and his body shook in a terrifying spasm. Another moan escaped his throat. "In the back," he said again, "but I never turned my back. Honest to God, I didn't turn." He was desperate to deny that his wound denoted cowardice. "Oh, Jesus, sweet Jesus," he said. He was crying from the pain. "Sweet Jesus."

"You're going to be all right," Starbuck said.

Rothwell caught hold of Starbuck's hand and gripped it hard. His breath was coming in short, shallow gasps. His teeth chattered again. "They shot me," he said.

"I'll get you back to the doctor." Starbuck looked around for help. A dozen rebels were running north through the trees, but the deafening sound of the battle in the cornfield drowned out Starbuck's shout. The men ran on.

"In the back," Rothwell said, then suddenly he screamed as the pain whipped through his body. The scream faded to a pathetic moan. He gulped in air and the breath scraped in his throat. "Becky," he said, and the tears rolled down the dirt and sweat on his face, "poor Becky."

"Becky will be fine," Starbuck said helplessly, "so will you." He used his free hand to wipe the tears away. Rothwell's body heaved in a spasm and the tears came more freely. "It hurts," he said, "it hurts." He was a strong man, but now wept like a child and each breath came harder and harder. "Oh, Becky," he finally managed to say in a voice so feeble that Starbuck scarcely heard it. Rothwell was still alive, for his fingers were pressing on Starbuck's hand. "Pray," he said, then whimpered again.

Starbuck said the Lord's prayer, but before he had reached the words "Thy kingdom come" the Sergeant died. His belly heaved up in a massive spasm and his mouth suddenly brimmed with blood that spilled down both cheeks. He shook his head, then slumped back still.

Starbuck prized the dead fingers away from his hand. He was shaking himself, terrified by the horror of Rothwell's death, and when he looked up to stare across the fields where the Yankees had been formed he could not see because of the tears in his eyes. He cuffed the tears away and saw that the Yankees were still waiting at the far side of the two wide fields. Other Northerners were retreating toward those troops, pursued by rebel bullets. For the moment the Yankees had been hurled clean out of the East Woods, but not, it seemed, out of the cornfield, for Starbuck could still hear the full fury of rifle and cannon fire still thundering and cracking on the far side of the woods.

He stood and slung his rifle. It was time to sort out the chaos, to find the survivors of his battalion and report to Swynyard. He walked through the trees and back across the Smoketown Road. A Yankee reeled in front of him— dazed, whimpering, and wearing a mask of blood through which his frightened eyes showed white. Two prisoners

351

were being prodded toward the rear by a small man with a bristly beard and a smoothbore musket. Two squirrels, killed by shellfire, hung from the rebel's belt. "Dinner!" he called cheerfully to Starbuck, then pushed the two frightened Yankees onward. The wounded and dead lay in clumps where the fighting had been fiercest and everywhere a sheen of gunsmoke hung between the trees like a hint of autumn mist. So many scraps of leaf had been blown from the trees by shells and bullets that the ground between the trunks was green as parkland. Starbuck, suddenly overcome with weariness and with despair for Rothwell's miserable death, leaned against a bullet-scarred trunk. Sweat trickled down his face.

He was feeling in his pouch, hoping to find a cigar among the handful of remaining cartridges, when a familiar figure showed among the distant trees. There were a score of rebels in sight, most of them searching the dead for plunder and ammunition, but there was something peculiarly furtive about the plumpish figure who advanced through the trees with an elaborate caution, then suddenly saw something and darted to one side and knelt on the ground.

Tumlin. God damn Billy Tumlin. Starbuck pushed away from the tree and stalked the big man. Tumlin glanced to left and right once in a while, but saw nothing to disturb him. He was stripping the blue coat from a Yankee corpse and was so intent on dragging the sleeves off the dead man's awkward arms that he did not know Starbuck was near him until the warm rifle barrel touched the back of his neck. Then he jumped in alarm.

"You got a thing about coats, Billy?" Starbuck asked.

"Coats?" Blythe managed to say as he stumbled backward against an elm trunk.

"You're wearing a new one today. Ain't as small as your

last one." Starbuck slung the rifle, then touched the blood patch on Tumlin's chest. "Got hit, Billy?"

"Nothing serious," Blythe said. He wiped sweat off his face and offered Starbuck a grin.

Starbuck did not return the smile. "So where have you been, Billy?"

Tumlin shrugged. "Saw a doctor," he said.

"He patched you up?"

"Kind of," Blythe said.

Starbuck frowned at the mess of blood on the gray coat. "Looks bad, Billy. Looks real bad. Man could die from that kind of chest shot."

Blythe gave what he hoped was a brave smile. "I'll survive."

"You sure?" Starbuck asked, then he punched the blood patch, punched it forcefully enough to push the heavy man back against the tree. Blythe winced at the blow, but he did not react like a man who had been hit on a fresh wound. "I hear you've been skulking in the graveyard, Billy," Starbuck said.

"No," Blythe said unconvincingly.

"You bastard," Starbuck said, suddenly overcome with a blinding anger, "you white-livered piece of shit." He punched Tumlin on the bloody patch again, and this time the man did not even flinch. "That ain't a wound, Billy. It ain't even your jacket." Blythe said nothing and Starbuck felt a pang of pure hatred for a man who did not do his duty. "Was John Brown wearing a coat when he was hung?" he asked.

Blythe licked his lips and glanced left and right, but there was no escape in sight. "John Brown?" he asked, confused.

"You saw him hang, didn't you?"

"Surely did," Blythe said.

"You and the whore, right? And she was leaning out the window and you were leaning on top of her, ain't that right?"

Blythe nodded nervously. "About the size of it," he said.

"So tell me about it, Billy," Starbuck said.

Blythe licked his dry lips again. He wondered if Starbuck had gone mad, but guessed he had to humor the fool whose face was so drawn and hard. "I told you," Blythe said, "we watched him swing on a gallows outside Wager's Hotel."

"In Harper's Ferry?" Starbuck asked.

Blythe nodded. "Saw it with my own eyes." He flinched as a shell crashed through the branches overhead and exploded further down the wood. Leaf scraps sifted down.

Starbuck had not moved as the shell whipped overhead. "John Brown was hung in Charlestown," he said, "and that's a fair ways from Wager's Hotel, Billy." He took out his revolver. "So what other lies have you told, Billy?"

Blythe glanced at the revolver and said nothing.

Starbuck pulled back the revolver's hammer. "Take off the coat, Billy."

"I—"

"Take it off!" Starbuck shouted and rammed the revolver's muzzle up under Blythe's plump chin.

Blythe hurriedly unbuckled his belt, let it drop, then pulled off the borrowed coat. The only blood on his shirt was the small stain that had rubbed off from the inside of the jacket.

"Drop the coat, Billy," Starbuck said, grinding the foresight of the Adams into the bulging flesh. "You don't deserve to wear that coat. You ain't a man, Billy Tumlin, you're a coward. Drop the coat." Blythe let the coat fall and Starbuck pulled the revolver back and lowered its hammer, making the gun safe. Blythe looked relieved, but then Starbuck whipped the pistol's heavy barrel across Blythe's face to open a cut on Blythe's right cheekbone. "Now you're really wounded, Billy," Starbuck said. "And get the hell out of my sight. Go on, go!"

Blythe stooped to retrieve his revolver, but Starbuck put his foot on the belt. "Without a weapon?" Blythe asked.

"Go!" Starbuck shouted again and watched the heavy man blunder away.

Starbuck picked up the revolver and walked in the other direction. "Lucifer!" He saw the boy leading his new dog. "Here! New gun for you." He tossed Tumlin's belt to the boy. "Now get out of here before a Yankee shoots you." He saw Truslow shouting at men to stop looting the dead and get themselves up to the wood's edge, then he heard something far worse. Drums and cheers. He turned and ran back to where Rothwell's body lay. Then swore.

Because the Yankees were coming again.

Billy Blythe was weeping as he worked his way back north through the woods. He was not weeping because of the cut on his face, but for shame at being humiliated by Starbuck. He imagined an exquisite revenge, but first he had to survive the horror of this battle and get back where he belonged—in the North.

He found the body he had been stripping of its jacket and, after checking that Starbuck was not in sight, he dragged the coat free. He looked for his revolver, but it was gone. He cursed, then pulled on the bloody gray coat, which still lay beside the elm tree. He bundled the blue jacket under his arm, then, touching his pants pocket to make sure his precious United States commission was still safe, went on northward. Men were running past him, going to the wood's eastern margin, where a new rattle of rifle fire was filling the trees with sound. They ignored Billy Blythe, taking him for another wounded man.

He went as far north as he dared and there discovered what he had been seeking. He found a log pile, and behind it were three Northern bodies, still warm, all of them bloody and all of them dead. Blythe crouched, peeled off the gray coat and pulled on the blue, then wriggled down beside the logs and heaved the three corpses on top of him. He knew the Yankees were attacking again, and this time, he reckoned, the rebels would not stand. Blythe believed the battle was turning, and it was time for him to turn with it. A shell whipcracked through the trees overhead, making him whimper, but then at last he was deep in the leaf mold beside the logs and protected by the warm bodies above. He lay still, feeling a dead man's blood trickle onto his back. He wished he could repay Starbuck for that blow across the face, but guessed Starbuck would not be alive to take the repayment. He hoped Starbuck's death was agonizing, and that thought consoled him as he waited under the corpses for rescue.

Billy Blythe had survived.

Belvedere Delaney was making himself useful. Lee had gone to the higher ground, but he had not invited Delaney to accompany him and so Delaney had searched for his servant, George, thinking it was time for the two of them to begin preparing for a tactful withdrawal. Delaney had discovered George carrying pails of water to the wounded men waiting for the surgeons in the garden of a house just north of the village.

These men were the fortunate wounded, the handful

that had been brought down from the fighting to the comparative peace in the rebel rear. Most of these men were victims of Yankee shells, for the men with bullet wounds were too far forward to be fetched back by the handful of ambulance wagons and those men would suffer where they lay, but these men were receiving the best care the Confederate army possessed. The worst afflicted could not be cared for at all because the surgeons' efforts were being saved for the men who stood a chance of survival. Some ether was available and the lucky few were thus anesthetized before the saws and knives slashed at their broken legs, but most men were given a slug of brandy, a leather gag to bite on, then told to play the man, be quiet, and lie still. Orderlies held them firm on the table while a surgeon in a blood-soaked apron sliced into the mangled flesh.

Delaney's first instinct was to shy away from the horror, but an overwhelming pang of pity made him stay. He carried cups of water to wounded men, then held their heads up as they sipped. One man went into spasm and bit the cup's rim so hard that the china shattered. Delaney held another man's hand as he died. He wiped sweat from the forehead of an officer with bandaged eyes who would never see again. Six or seven women from the village were helping with the wounded and one of them was defiantly wearing a small Stars and Stripes pinned to her apron as she moved among the blood and vomit and stench of the garden. George crouched beside a South Carolina sergeant and tried to staunch the blood that kept hemorrhaging from a crudely bandaged slash at his waist. The man was dying and wanted reassurance that the battle was being won, and with it the war, and George kept saying over and over in a soothing voice that the rebels were charging forward, that the Yankees were falling back, and that

357

victory was imminent. "Praise the Lord," the Sergeant said, then died.

One man pleaded with Delaney to find his wife's daguerreotype at the bottom of his cartridge pouch. Delaney pulled out the rounds and there, under them all, was the precious scrap of copper sheet wrapped in a piece of chintz. The woman looked heavy-jawed and dull-eyed, but just glimpsing her face gave the dying man peace. "You'll write her, sir?" he asked Delaney.

"I will."

"Dorcas Bridges," the man said, "Dearborn Street in Mobile. Tell her I never did stop loving her. You going to write that down, sir?"

"You're going to be all right," Delaney tried to reassure the man.

"I'm going to be just fine, sir. Before this day's through, sir, I'll be with my Lord and Savior, but Dorcas now, she's got to manage without me. You will write to her, sir?"

"I'll write." Delaney had a stub of pencil and carefully wrote Dorcas's address on a scrap of newspaper.

Delaney collected a dozen other names and addresses and promised to write to them all. He would write, too, and he would say the same thing in each letter, that their husbands or sons had died bravely and without pain. The truth was that they had all died in horrid pain. The lucky lost consciousness, but the unlucky felt the agony of their wounds right till the last. At the rear of the house, where an herb garden grew, a pile of amputated arms and legs grew higher. A small child watched the pile with wide eyes, thumb in her mouth.

While on the high ground the guns went on and on.

Starbuck found the remnants of Potter's company still miraculously clinging together. They were close to

358

Rothwell's body, lining the edge of the East Woods and firing toward the Yankees who marched south. A tatterdemalion mix of men were in the rebel line. There were Georgians, Texans, Virginians, Alabamians, and nearly all had lost touch with their officers, but were simply joining the nearest rebel line and fighting on. The noise in the wood was deafening. The Yankees had brought up new guns that were banging case shot into the trees, there were Northern skirmishers behind the limestone outcrops in the plowed fields, and all the while the fight in the cornfield was swelling into its old fury.

The Yankees were advancing in a column of companies, making themselves a tempting target for the rebel riflemen. "I wish we had cannon," Potter shouted to Starbuck, then pulled his trigger. Truslow fired steadily and grimly, each bullet thumping into the mass of blue uniforms that kept coming forward, though the closer the attack came to the trees, the more chaos was ripped into its leading ranks. Colonel Maitland had come into the woods, where he was swinging his sword and shouting drunkenly to kill the swine. Swynyard came running south through the wood and knelt beside Starbuck at the edge of the trees. He waited till Starbuck had fired. "They're in the woods again," Swynyard shouted, pointing north.

"How many?"

"Thousands!"

"Shit," Starbuck said, then poured powder into his barrel, spat in the bullet, picked up his ramrod, and shoved it down hard. His right arm was tired and his right shoulder one agonizing bruise from the gun's recoil. "Who's holding them?" he asked Swynyard.

"No one."

"Jesus," Starbuck swore again. He waited for the smoke to clear and suddenly, right in front of him, he saw a

Yankee officer on horseback. The man was white-bearded, his uniform was heavy with braid, and he was shouting desperately at the milling Northerners who were recoiling from the fire from the woods. Starbuck wondered if the man was a general, then aimed at the inviting target. At least a dozen other rebels had seen the man and there was a small fusillade of shots, and when the rifles' smoke had thinned, there was only a riderless horse.

The firing in the cornfield reached a new intensity. Swynyard tapped Starbuck's shoulder. "See what's happening, Nate. I don't want to be trapped here."

Starbuck ran through the woods. Above him was the noise of bullets and case shot whipping through the leaves, provoking a constant shower of leaf scraps. The wood's center was empty, except for the dead and dying, but as he neared the western edge the rebels became thick again. They were firing at a single regiment of Yankees, which appeared to have made a lone charge through the broken corn. The Yankees seemed confused and abandoned, for no other battalions had supported their charge, and now, surrounded by rebels, they had huddled into a mass that was inviting a grim punishment from the rebels. One of the blue-coated men waved a New York flag to encourage his comrades, then a case shot cracked into smoke just above the flag that fell instantly. The Yankees began to retreat, and the rebels, heartened by the small victory, pushed forward into the corn again. It seemed to Starbuck that every rebel in Maryland was being thrust into the fight in one last desperate attempt to hold the position. Men were running from the West Woods to thicken the line that trampled forward into the corn. Captain Peel was there with more survivors from Starbuck's battalion and Starbuck ran to join them. The ground in the cornfield felt lumpy because of the fallen cobs and because so many blasts of canister and case shot had littered the earth. A skin of smoke hung at breast height above the corn, while everywhere there was puddled blood, broken men, flies, and shattered weapons.

The rebel line advanced clear through the cornfield, but was again stopped at its northern edge. The Northerners had their own battle line waiting and that line gave a terrible volley that cracked into the rebel counterattack. Cannons belched canister, battalions fired volleys, but the insanity of battle had gripped the Southerners and instead of retreating from the overwhelming fire, they stayed and fired back into the Yankees. Starbuck scrabbled among the last few cartridges in his pouch and listened to the terrible swish of canister raking through the fallen corn and to the thump of bullets striking home. Some men knelt to fight and others lay down to see beneath the thickening smoke band.

The fight seemed to last forever, though later, counting his cartridges, Starbuck knew it could only have been a couple of minutes. He was unaware of making any sound, but he was keening a high moaning noise that was the product of pure terror. On either side of him men fell, and at every second he expected to suffer the banging impact of a bullet, but he stayed where he was, loading and firing, and he tried to blot out the noise of the screams and the bullets and the guns by singing the high unchanging note. He was working slowly, his brain fuddled by the chaos, so that he had to think about each action. The spent powder had caked in the grooves of his rifle's barrel, making it hard to force each bullet down. He had propped his ramrod against his belly to make it easier to retrieve after each shot, but it kept falling into the corn and every time he stooped to pick it up he wanted to lay down and stay down. He wanted to be anywhere in all the world except here in death's kingdom. He loaded again and saw one of his men fold slowly over, gasping for breath. Another man dragged himself back through the corn, leaving a trail of blood from a shattered leg. A Yankee drum lay discarded in the corn, its skin punctured by bullets. Little flames flickered in the corn where bullet wadding had started fires. A Georgian officer was on his knees, hands clasped at his groin as he heaved in small breaths and stared in desperate misery at the blood spilling down his thighs. The man looked up and caught Starbuck's eye. "Shoot me," he said, "for pity's sake, man, shoot me."

Then, from the northern part of the East Woods, a new volley crashed.

And the rebel line collapsed.

It had fought since dawn, but now, in the face of yet more Yankee attackers, the defense disintegrated. The collapse began with one battalion, then the panic spread to the neighboring units and suddenly a whole brigade was running. Starbuck was not aware of the panic at first. He had heard the massive volley off to his right and he was aware of screams and cheers from the edge of the woods, but he doggedly went on loading his rifle while the Georgian officer pleaded for death, but then a nearby man called out a warning and Starbuck saw Yankees running through the smoke. He snatched up his ramrod and ran with the other rebels. Some Yankees sprinted ahead, angling in front of Starbuck in their eagerness to cut off a retreating flag. He let the ramrod drop and dragged the revolver from behind his back and fired wildly into the blue coats. A rebel sergeant swung his rifle by the barrel to bring its heavy stock down on a Yankee head. Starbuck heard the impact of the rifle butt just as a bearded Yankee lunged at him with a bayonet. Starbuck stepped aside so that the blade went past him, he thrust the revolver into the man's belly, and pulled the trigger, but nothing happened. In despair, screaming, he swung his clumsy rifle so that the bullet-shattered stock slammed into the side of the Yankee's head. Starbuck could smell the man's uniform, the tobacco on his breath, then the man stumbled. Starbuck kicked him hard and ran on. He stumbled over cornstalks, canister balls, and bodies. There were cheers behind and panic in front. He expected a bullet at any second and dropped the broken rifle to gain a mite of speed.

The momentum of the Yankees' attack carried them down through the East Woods and caused more rebels to join the flight. The Northern guns on the Hagerstown Pike hurried the fugitives along with round after round of case shot. The rebels tumbled out of the yard of the burned farm, they abandoned the graveyard, they fled for the trees in the west and so abandoned the morning's hard-fought battlefield to the Yankees. Here and there groups of men retreated slowly, in ranks, firing as they went, but most of the gray-clad infantry simply ran and only slowed when they realized that there was no Yankee pursuit. The Northerners were as confused as the rebels and, though some men pushed doggedly on, more stopped in the cornfield to reload and fire at the rapidly vanishing enemy. Starbuck recognized some men from Faulconer's Legion and joined them. He plucked up a Springfield rifle from a dead Texan and checked that it worked. A handful of the Yellowlegs were still with him, and then, on the Smoketown Road, he saw Lucifer and Imp walking west with Potter's company. He joined them, then crossed the dirt ruts of the Hagerstown Pike to reach the shadows of the trees beyond.

Colonel Swynyard was shouting his own name in an attempt to rally his brigade. Handfuls of men joined him, milling in confusion among the woods just north of the Dunker church. Behind them now was a stretch of pastureland that had been turned into hell's outpost—a swathe of killing ground littered with bodies and slick with blood, a smoke-hung graveyard of the unburied dead over which Yankee battalions advanced in uncoordinated pursuit of the rebel fugitives. Shell bursts punctured the pasture, scattering dead men and hurrying the last rebels toward the West Woods.

Some of the panicking rebels had not stopped in the West Woods, but had kept going into the farmlands beyond. Rebel cavalry were dispatched to round them up and send them back to the West Woods, where officers and sergeants bellowed out unit names. Here and there the vestiges of companies formed, and shattered battalions gathered under their torn and stained colors. Other officers did not worry about rejoining their battalions, but just tugged and pushed men into makeshift companies at the wood's edge and told them to open fire on the pursuing enemy. A wagon was whipped up the Hagerstown Pike and dropped off boxes of artillery ammunition for the gun teams that had hastily deployed in front of the woods. The wagon's team was hit by a Yankee shell and dying horses screamed as gallons of their blood washed down the road's deep ruts. The ground in front of the rebel batteries was at last free of fugitives and the gunners opened fire with canister that dropped more dead among the army of corpses that lay beneath the smoke.

For a moment it seemed as though the guns would hold the Northern advance, then lines of blue troops appeared in the smoke that hazed the land east of the batteries. Gunners desperately tried to handspike the guns about to face this new threat, but then a rippling volley whipped a storm of minie bullets that clanged off cannon barrels, drove splinters from gun wheels, and threw down the gunners. In the pause while the infantry reloaded, the surviving gun captains brought up their horse teams and dragged the guns back through the trees. A Yankee cheer sounded, then a battalion charged into the vacated ground where the grass had been flattened and scorched by the cannon blasts. No one opposed them and the troops, a big Pennsylvanian regiment, found their lodgment in the West Woods. They captured the Dunker church, which was filled with wounded men, and there they stopped, for the woods around them were alive with rebel survivors who began a galling fire. The Pennsylvanian commander sent messengers to the rear with pleas for support and ammunition. Some Northern guns came to help the Pennsylvanians, but the gunners unlimbered too close to the woods and rebel sharpshooters raked them with fire. The guns pulled back, one hauled by infantry because all its horses had been shot. The abandoned wagon had caught fire and its remaining load of shells banged off one by one to vomit a filthy smoke into the white-hot sky.

General Jackson raged up and down the wood shouting at men to form in company, to find their battalions, to turn and fight. He knew this was the moment for the Yankees to strike. If one Northern corps, even one brigade, should reinforce the Pennsylvanian lodgment about the Dunker church and carry the attack straight on through the woods, then the dizzied men in gray would break. The Yankees would win the day, the rebel army would be turned into a rabble fleeing for a narrow ford, and by winter the streets of Richmond would be filled with strutting Yankees. General Lee, recognizing the same danger, was assembling a line of guns on a ridge to the west of the woods so that if the triumphant Yankees did burst through the trees, they would be met by a killing barrage that might at least slow the pursuers and give his men time to make a fighting retreat toward the Potomac.

But the Yankees were as dazed as the rebels. The swiftness of the Northern advance had left their units scattered across the field. All of the ground that lay east of the Hagerstown Pike and north of the Dunker church was in Yankee hands, and some Northern units had crossed the Pike to find a dangerous shelter in the edge of the West Woods, but the reinforcements they needed were nowhere in sight. Rebel guns in the south of the battlefield were thrashing the beaten ground with shellfire and rebel infantry was firing from the woods, and so the pursuit stalled as the Yankees, like the rebels, tried to pull order out of chaos.

The rebel panic in the West Woods subsided. Men counted their cartridges and some glanced nervously behind in an effort to spot a route away from the carnage, but as the Northern firing died away the rebels began to reform. One by one the companies were remade, the gaps in the line were mended, and the cartridges replenished.

"I borrowed poor Haxall's watch," Colonel Swynyard joined Starbuck. "He won't need it in heaven, poor man, but I'll send it to his wife."

"He's dead?" Starbuck asked.

Swynyard nodded, then shook the watch and held it to his ear. "It seems to be working," he said dubiously, then looked at the watch's face. "Almost nine o'clock," Swynyard said, and Starbuck immediately frowned and wondered why it was not getting dark. "In the morning, Nate," Swynyard said gently, "in the morning."

The day was still young.

Yankees walked through the East Woods and out into the cornfield. One man vomited at the sight of the field. The stench of the place was worse than a slaughterhouse. Men lay shattered, their blood spilled wide, their bowels open in death. Sightless eyes gazed through smoke, mouths were open and filled with flies. Rebel and Yankee lay together. The wounded called for help, some wept, some called for a merciful shot to the head. A few, pitifully few, stretcher bearers had begun work. A chaplain, overcome by the horror, fell to his knees at the edge of the trees and let tears fall onto an open Bible. Other men moved among the horror in search of plunder; they carried pliers to take gold-capped teeth and knives to cut off wedding ring fingers or else to quiet their victims' protests. A battery of guns checked at the cornfield's edge, the team's drivers unwilling to run their heavy weapons over the field of corpses, but an officer shouted at them to damn their squeamishness and so they cracked their whips and forced the guns across the bodies. Blood turned black. Steam came from the deeper blood pools. The sun was climbing, the very last mist had gone from the creek, and the day's sweltering heat was rising.

Mister Kroeger, the farmer who had undertaken to be the Yankees' guide to the Snaveley Ford, insisted on visiting his farm first. The cows needed milking, but as no orders had come from McClellan ordering an attack across the river, no one thought to hurry the farmer. The Yankee troops detailed to cross the bridge on the lower creek stared from their hiding places and wondered how in the name of a merciful God they were supposed to cross several hundred yards of open land, then cram themselves onto a bridge just twelve feet wide, all the while being raked by the rebels in the rifle pits who waited on the farther bank.

A new and heavier corps of Northern troops forded the river well to the north of the lower bridge. Their crossing was not opposed and the fresh troops began the long climb to the plateau where they would serve to reinforce the Yankees who had beaten the rebels out of the East Woods and the cornfield. Thirteen thousand men climbed the hill, their bands playing and colors flying as they drew nearer and nearer to the death-house stench that waited at the slope's summit. The long lines of advancing men paused and broke apart whenever they reached a rail fence, but once over the fence the long ranks reformed and pushed on. It would take the newcomers some fair time to reach the summit, and once there they would need to be shown where to attack, and all that while the rebels were desperately patching together the northern half of their army and so, for a while, the plateau was eerily silent. Once in a while a gun would fire or a rifle crack, but both sides were drawing breath.

One man, at least, had survived the battle and would fight in it no more. Billy Blythe waited until the sound of firing had died away and until the first excited rush of storming Yankee troops was long gone past his hiding place, and only then did he free himself from the deadweight of the men who concealed him. The woods were full of curious Yankees, but no one took any particular notice of Billy Blythe in his loose blue coat. He staggered to make himself look like one of the many wounded men waiting for help under the cover of the trees.

He found a dead rebel officer behind a rotting trunk and took the man's belt with its holstered Whitney revolver. Then, still staggering, he made his way east to the Smoketown Road, where a press of vehicles jammed the dirt track and its grass verges. Wagons were bringing new ammunition for the cannons and ambulances were lining up for the wounded. One of the ambulances was carrying the dying body of General Mansfield, who had been shot off his horse as he had tried to urge his men into the East Woods. "Can you walk back?" a sergeant shouted at Blythe.

Blythe mumbled incoherently and lurched more impressively.

"Come on, lad, up with you!" The sergeant boosted Blythe's heavy body onto the bed of an empty ammunition wagon that would trundle north to Smoketown before crossing the creek by the upper bridge.

Blythe lay in the wagon and stared at the sky. He smiled. Caton Rothwell, one of the two men who had sworn to kill him, was dead, shot in the back by Blythe himself, and Blythe had sown enough discord to be fairly sure that Starbuck would be removed before the day was through. He chuckled as he admired his own cleverness. Damn it, he thought, but there were few men to touch Billy Blythe for sheer cunning. He fingered his commission, then struggled to sit up. A Pennsylvanian Bucktail officer, wounded in the leg, sat beside him and offered him a cigar. "Hell," the Pennsylvanian said.

"Life is sure sweet," Blythe said.

The Pennsylvanian frowned at Blythe's accent. "Are you a reb?" he asked.

"A major in your army, Captain," Blythe promoted himself to celebrate his survival. "I was never a man to change allegiance to my country, certainly not on account of a pack of Sambos." He accepted the Pennsylvanian's cigar. "Hell," he went on, "I can understand fighting over land or women, but over darkies?" Blythe shook his head. "Just plain don't make sense."

The Captain leaned back on the wagon's sideboard. "Jesus," he said faintly, still shaking after his time in the cornfield.

"Praise His name," Blythe said, "praise His holy name." For Billy Blythe was safe.

Captain Dennison was safe too. He was in the West Woods, where he had found Sergeant Case. The two men were some twenty yards behind the remnants of Starbuck's battalion, where they were concealed in the muddle of disorganized and leaderless men. "Captain Tumlin didn't make it," Dennison said nervously, "leastwise I ain't seen him. And Cartwright's dead. So's Dan Lippincott."

"So the battalion's yours," Case said, and then, after a pause, "or it will be when Starbuck's dead."

Dennison shuddered. He had been scared half to death by the retreat across the open country, a retreat marked by the whistle of minie bullets and the jeers of Yankees and the thump of exploding shells.

"Yours," Case said again, "and you promised to give me back my company. As a captain."

"I did," Dennison agreed.

Case pushed a rifle into Dennison's hands. "It fires true," he said, "and it's loaded."

Dennison stared at the gun as though he had never seen such a thing before. "Swynyard might not confirm me," he said after a while.

"Bloody hell, Captain, we all have to take our chances," Case said, then levered down the trigger guard of his captured Sharps rifle to make sure a round was in the breech. It was. That meant he had three rounds in all, and after they were fired the gun would be useless. Dennison looked up at Starbuck and tentatively raised the rifle to his shoulder, but Case pushed it down. "Not now, Captain," he said scornfully. "Wait till the Yankees come again. Wait till there's plenty of noise."

Dennison nodded. "You're firing too?" he asked, needing reassurance.

"Head shot," Case said. "You go for the body," he patted the middle of Dennison's back to show where the nervous Captain should aim. "One of us will get the bastard. Now wait." Case had not been fooled by Starbuck's offer of leniency. He guessed that the Yankee bastard was scared of him and had tried to buy Case off by returning his stripes, but Robert Case was not a man to let a grudge be settled cheaply. Starbuck had humiliated him, and Case wanted his revenge. He also wanted the commission. In a month, he reckoned, he could be commander of the Yellowlegs and then, by God, he would whip the bastards into a disciplined unit. Maybe he could change their name, call them the Virginia Fusiliers, then have the bastards march into battle like they were on Aldershot's parade ground.

The two men crouched low, both waiting for the odd silence on the battlefield to end.

The first Yankee hammer blow had fallen, and under it the rebel line in the north of the battlefield had crumbled. The second blow now climbed steadily up from the middle part of the creek while the third, concealed in the hollows and trees beyond the Antietam, waited for the order that would launch them across the gently flowing stream to cut the rebels' retreat.

On the far side of the Potomac, the marching Light Division heard the sudden lull in the gunfire. Sweating men looked nervously at each other and wondered if the silence meant that the battle was already lost. "Keep going!" the staff officers shouted, "keep going!"

They had miles to march yet and a deep, wide river to cross, but they kept on toward the ominous silence and the pyre of smoke that dirtied a sky above a field of dead.

"SEVENTY-NINE MEN, SIR," Starbuck reported to Swynyard.

"The Legion's down to a hundred and four," Swynyard said bleakly. "Poor Haxall's men don't even make a company. The Sixty-fifth is a hundred and two." He folded the scrap of paper on which the totals had been penciled. "More men will come in," he said, "some are hiding, some are running." Swynyard's Brigade was shrunken small enough to be collected in a half-acre clearing of the West Woods. The Yankees holding the Dunker church were not more than two hundred paces away, but neither side had ammunition to spare and so each was treating the other gingerly. Now and then one of the rebel skirmishers who ringed the Pennsylvanians fired, but return fire was rare.

"God knows how many have died," Starbuck said bitterly.

"But your men stood and fought, Nate," Swynyard said, "which is more than the punishment battalion did at Manassas."

"Some stood and fought, sir," Starbuck said, thinking of Dennison. He had not seen the Captain and did not care if he never saw him again. With any luck, Starbuck thought, Dennison was dead or captured, and so, he hoped, was Tumlin.

"You did well," Swynyard insisted. He was watching an ammunition wagon stop on the track that led through the clearing. The wagon's rifle ammunition was for his brigade, a sign that their fighting was not done this day.

"I did nothing, sir," Starbuck answered, "except chase after my men." The battle had been chaos almost from the first. Men had become detached from their companies, they had fought with whoever they found themselves, and few officers had kept control of their companies. The rebel defense had been made by men just standing and fighting, sometimes without orders, but always with vast pride and a huge determination that had finally been eroded by one heavy attack after another.

"Charmed," Swynyard said sardonically.

"Sir?" Starbuck asked in puzzlement, then saw that Swynyard was staring at Lieutenant Colonel Maitland, who was strolling along the decimated ranks of the Legion. Maitland was grinning vacuously and spreading lavish compliments, but he was also having some trouble in keeping his footing. His men grinned, amused at the sight of their inebriated commander.

"He's drunk, isn't he?" Swynyard asked.

"He's soberer than he was," Starbuck said. "Much."

Swynyard grimaced. "I watched him in the cornfield. He was strolling through fire like it was the garden of Eden and I thought he must be the bravest man I'd ever seen, but I suppose it wasn't bravery at all. He must have drunk all that liquor he confiscated."

"I guess."

"He was telling me last night," Swynyard went on, "just how scared he was of not doing his duty. I liked him for that. Poor man. I didn't realize how scared he really was."

"If Old Jack sees how scared he is now," Starbuck said dryly, "he'll be lucky to keep his rank." He nodded to the left where Jackson was riding toward Swynyard's Brigade along the reformed line.

"Colonel Maitland!" Swynyard shouted in a voice worthy of a sergeant. "To attention, if you please! Now!"

Maitland, astonished by the peremptory order, snapped to attention. He was facing his men so only they could see the surprised look on his face. Jackson and his aides rode their horses behind the drunken Colonel and so noticed nothing. The General reined in close to Swynyard. "Well?" he asked curtly.

"They can fight, sir," Swynyard said, guessing what the curt question meant. He turned and pointed at the bullet-pocked wall of the Dunker church that was just visible through the leaves. "Yankees there, sir."

"Not for long," Jackson said. His left hand rose slowly into the air as he turned to gaze at Swynyard's ranks. "A brigade?" he asked, "or a battalion?"

"Brigade, sir."

Jackson nodded, then rode on down the line of exhausted men who he knew must soon fight again.

"Three cheers for Old Jack!" Maitland suddenly erupted and the Legion gave three rousing cheers that Jackson pointedly ignored as he spurred on toward the next brigade.

"What do you do with Maitland, sir?" Starbuck asked.

"Do?" Swynyard seemed surprised by the question. "Nothing, of course. He's doing his duty, Nate. He ain't running away. When this fight's done I'll have a word with him and suggest he might be better employed back in the War Department. But at least he'll be able to say he fought the good fight at Sharpsburg. His pride will be intact."

"And if he doesn't go?"

"Oh, he'll go," Swynyard said grimly, "believe me, Nate, he'll go. And once he's gone I'll put your boys into the Legion and give the whole lot to you."

"Thank you, sir."

Swynyard looked over Starbuck's shoulder and jerked his beard to suggest that there was someone needing Starbuck's attention. Starbuck turned and, to his astonishment, saw it was Captain Dennison who, very formally, was reporting for duty.

"Where the hell were you?" Starbuck snapped.

Dennison glanced at Swynyard, then shrugged. "Where I was told to be, sir. In the graveyard."

"Skulking?" Starbuck snarled.

"Sir!" Dennison protested. "Captain Tumlin ordered us there, sir. Said the Yankees had skirmishers attacking our wounded. So we went there, sir. Fought them, sir." He patted the black-muzzled rifle that now hung from his shoulder. "Killed a few, sir."

"Tumlin ordered you there?" Starbuck asked.

"Yes, sir."

"Son of a bitch," Starbuck said. "Where the hell is Tumlin?"

"Don't know, sir. Shall we fall in, sir?" Dennison asked innocently. A dozen men of A Company were with Dennison and none of them looked as tired, strained, or scared as the other survivors from the Yellowlegs.

"Fall in," Starbuck said. "And Captain?"

"Sir?"

"I gave Case his stripes back."

"He told me, sir."

Starbuck watched Dennison go to join the remnant of his company. Sergeant Case was there, the buck's tail still pinned to his gray hat, and, for a second, Starbuck wondered about that bullet in Caton Rothwell's back. Then he dismissed the suspicion. There had been enough stray Yankees in the woods to account for that miserable death. If it was anyone's fault, Starbuck thought, it was his for not leaving two men to watch from the wood's edge.

"What was all that about?" Swynyard asked when Dennison had fallen in.

"God knows, sir. Either he's lying, or Tumlin disobeyed me. But that bastard," Starbuck jerked his head toward Dennison, "ain't never been civil to me in the past, so the hell knows why he's starting now."

"Battle, Nate," Swynyard said. "It changes men."

A bugle sounded to the east. Starbuck turned and stared through the trees toward the horrid ground where so many had died. Till now he had been fighting an enemy who had come from the north, but the collapse of the rebel line in the cornfield meant that from now on they would be facing east. Another bugle called. "Bastards are coming again," Starbuck said.

"Then let us make ready," Swynyard said very formally.

Because the battle was still not lost, nor won, and the Yankees were coming again.

The first division of Union reinforcements came up from the creek in fine style, but when they reached the plateau there was no messenger to guide them to where they were needed. One Northern general was dead, another had gone back wounded, and so there was no one to tell the newly arrived troops where to attack. Their own general saw where the lingering gunsmoke hung thickest and pointed with his sword. "Keep going! That way! March!" A second Yankee division was climbing from the creek, but the general did not wait for it to join him. Instead he formed his men into three long lines of battle, one behind the other, and sent them through the East Woods. Once through the trees they reformed their lines and advanced

376

across the cornfield where the wounded cried out to stop men treading on them.

The attacking division would have made a fine sight if it had been maneuvering on a parade ground, but on a battlefield the serried mass of men was an invitation to the tired rebel gunners waiting beyond the turnpike. The cannons opened fire. Case shot cracked gray above the attackers' heads while solid shot whipped through rank after rank of men, one shot sufficient to kill or wound a dozen men. The Yankees pushed on, closing their ranks after each bloody strike and leaving behind them a new trail of dead and injured men.

The Pennsylvanians around the Dunker church heard the guns and prayed that someone was coming to their support. Their attack had driven a deep wedge into the center of the rebel army, but their ammunition was now desperately low. Their colonel had sent for help, but none was coming. Skirmishers probed the woods around the church, looking for other Northern troops who might have found shelter in the trees, but there were no allies within reach and one by one the Pennsylvania skirmishers were killed or wounded by rebel sharpshooters. The Northern colonel looked behind him for help while his pickets reported the noise of troops gathering in the surrounding trees.

The troops were rebels. They were fresh and unblooded this day. In the dawn they had been guarding the bridges and fords across the lower part of the creek, but no Yankee attack had materialized and so, in desperation, Lee had stripped his southern defenses of every man that could be spared. Those men had marched through Sharpsburg and up the hill to where Jackson now hurled them at the Dunker church.

The rebel yell echoed in the woods. Volleys clattered

against the church walls, thumped into trees, and ricocheted off stone. For a time the Pennsylvanians resisted the tightening ring, but they were isolated and outnumbered and finally they broke. They ran, abandoning their wounded, crossing the turnpike, and not stopping until they were out of range of the rebel rifles.

The rebels did not pursue. Jackson had freed himself of the Pennsylvanians and now he turned his men north to where the great parade ground attack had pushed across the cornfield and into the northern part of the West Woods. The attacking division had suffered horribly from the rebel guns, but enough men survived to reach the trees and sweep the rebel gunners out of their path. A handful of Confederate skirmishers fled, and suddenly the Stars and Stripes were being carried into the West Woods. "Keep going!" officers shouted, knowing their men would be tempted to stay in the shelter of the bullet-flecked trunks. "Keep going!" The three battle lines marched on westward as if they planned to push clean on down to the Potomac, but the guns Lee had placed behind the wood greeted their appearance at the tree line. Another cornfield lay beyond the wood and it was filled with rebel sharpshooters who, concealed by the standing corn, poured rifle fire into the blue ranks. The Yankees paused to reform lines that had been tangled by their advance through the trees.

The three impressive battle lines were jumbled together now, but still they faced westward, as though their general believed his object was to reach the distant Potomac. In truth the enemy lay to the south, where Jackson had collected every man he could find and was leading them through the trees against the unprotected Yankee flank. Guns hid the noise of the advancing troops. There were rebel guns firing from the western hill and Northern guns firing from higher up the Hagerstown Pike, but then, drowning even the thunder of the artillery, an almighty crash of rifle fire splintered across the sky with a sound like the very veils of heaven being ripped apart.

The second division of Yankee reinforcements had climbed from the creek. They were supposed to follow the first division, which was now isolated in the West Woods, but the second division had lagged behind and now, reaching the plateau, they could see no sign of the men they were supposed to reinforce. For a few moments they waited, their general officers seeking directions amid the chaos, but then, lacking any orders, they marched southeast toward the beckoning landmark of a white spire of a Sharpsburg church that could just be glimpsed above the trees. For a few moments the Yankees advanced across the open farmland unobserved and unhindered, but in their path was a farm lane and the lane was an attacker's nightmare. For years heavy farm wagons had broken the lane's dirt surface and, because the track ran gently downhill toward open ground, the rains had washed the debris away so that year after year, generation by generation, the lane had sunk ever deeper beneath the farmland's surface so that by now a man on foot could not see over the lane's sloping banks. The Yankees did not know it, but they were placidly advancing over sunlit pastureland toward a natural firestep that was crammed with rebels. These Confederate troops guarded the center of Lee's line and they had not fired a shot all morning, but now, at last, they pushed their rifle barrels through the long grass that grew beneath the rail fence at the bank's lip and aimed at the unsuspecting Yankees. They let those Yankees come real close, then pulled their triggers.

Starbuck heard that first slaughtering volley fired from the sunken lane. The sound told him that the battle was widening as more Yankees crossed the creek, but his fight was still in the northern part of the field where five thousand Yankees were readying themselves to continue their westward attack, unaware that Jackson was coming from their unguarded southern flank.

Swynyard's brigade advanced on the right, emerging from the trees where the woods narrowed to cross a small pasture. The Hagerstown Pike was immediately to Starbuck's right, and beyond that lay the pastureland where the rebels had resisted attack after attack from the cornfield. The pasture was rilled with bodies heaped in rows like tidelines showing where the fight had ebbed and flowed. More bodies were folded over the fences, where men had been killed as they clambered over the rails to escape the Northern advance. Starbuck's men walked past the horror in silence. They were weary and numbed, too tired to even look at the place where they had fought so long. A Yankee artillery battery stood well out of rifle range at the pasture's far side. The battery's guns were firing south, and every shot propelled a jet of flame-filled smoke that spat fifty yards from the gun's muzzle before billowing into a vaporous mist that hung in the still air. The gunners appeared not to have noticed the rebel soldiers across the turnpike, or else they had more inviting targets to the south. Starbuck watched the gunners leap aside as their huge weapons leaped back with each shot. It was, he thought, as if those gunners were fighting a quite separate battle.

The gunners were the only living Yankees in sight and it struck Starbuck as strange that so many men could be swallowed so comprehensively into so small a patch of countryside. The noise of the battle was awesome, yet here, where in a few hours thousands had died, the living seemed to have vanished.

Then, just as Starbuck was marveling at the emptiness of the landscape, a Yankee officer rode from the trees just fifty yards ahead of the brigade. He was a young man, full-bearded and straight-backed, who carried a long, shining sword blade. He curbed his horse to stare at the distant gunners, then some instinct made him look to his right and his jaw fell open as he saw the approaching rebels. He twisted in the saddle to shout a warning toward the trees, then, before calling the alarm, turned back again to make sure the Confederates were not figments of a fear-racked imagination. "Would someone please shoot that man?" Swynyard called plaintively.

The Yankee realized his danger and raked back his spurs as he hauled on the reins. His horse twisted round and leaped back toward the trees before a single rebel had time to draw a bead on the inviting target. Starbuck heard the astonished Yankee shouting a warning, then the shout was swamped by the rebel yell that, in turn, was drowned by a shattering volley of rifle fire and an eruption of screams.

"Bayonets!" Swynyard shouted, "quick, boys!"

The brigade dragged the long blades from their holsters and slotted them onto fire-blackened muzzles. The pace quickened. Colonel Swynyard was in the front now, a sword in his hand, and Starbuck felt the tiredness slough away to be replaced by a sudden and unexpected exhilaration.

"Fire!" Swynyard shouted. The Yankees had appeared. Scores of men had tumbled in disarray from the trees, only to be flanked by Swynyard's attack. "Fire!" the Colonel shouted again. Rifles flamed, then the bayonets drove forward. "Don't let them stand!" Swynyard roared. "Get them moving, boys, get them moving!"

The Yankees stood no chance. They had been attacked

on their open flank and the three battle lines crumpled. The Yankees nearest to the point of attack had no room to turn and face the rebels; the unlucky were driven down by vengeful Confederates while the fortunate fled to tangle with the battalions behind who were struggling to turn their companies through ninety degrees. The cumbersome maneuver was confused by the trees and by the rebel shells that tore through the high branches to explode shrapnel and leaves down into the confusion. The Yankees in the northernmost part of the wood stood the best chance, and some battalions there managed to turn their lines, but most of the regiments collided as they wheeled, officers shouted contradictory orders, fugitives jostled the nervous ranks, and always, everywhere, there sounded the vicious yelping of the rebel war cry. Panic prompted some Northern units to open fire on fellow Yankees. Shouted orders were lost in the din, and all the while the rebel attack swept on like a flood seeking the weakest parts of a crumbling dike. Some Northern units put up a fight, but one by one the defenders were outflanked and were forced to join the retreat. For a time some battalions in the northern part of the woods resisted the attack, but at last they too were outflanked and the whole division tumbled in panic from the trees to flee into the shelter of the North Woods.

The rebels pursued into the open ground and now the Yankee batteries by the Hagerstown Pike could join the fight and their case shot boomed and cracked into the gray ranks. Yankee skirmishers sheltered behind haystacks and farm buildings to lay a deadly fire on the rebel ranks, while out of the East Woods, which had seemed deserted not long before, new batteries of Northern guns appeared and, with the fuses of their shells cut perilously short, took the rebel charge in the flank.

Starbuck was kneeling beside the broken fence that

edged the turnpike. His battalion, which looked scarcely bigger than a company, was strung along the road where they sheltered from the Northern artillery that fired across the cornfield. Starbuck gazed in horror at the trampled corn where the bodies lay in clumps. Here and there a cornstalk survived, but for the most part the field looked as though a herd of giant hogs had rooted up a graveyard. Except that some of the bodies still lived and once in a while, in a lull of the guns' awful sound, a weak cry for help sounded from inside the corn.

The fire of the Yankee guns stopped abruptly. Starbuck frowned, guessing the cause. One or two of his men glanced at him nervously as he gingerly stood, then as he climbed onto a wobbling patch of surviving rail fence. At first he just saw a cloud of gunsmoke, a cloud so thick that the sun was like a silver dollar in the sky, then in the lower smoke he glimpsed what he feared. There was a line of Yankees advancing out of the East Woods to take the rebels in the flank. "Back to the trees!" Starbuck shouted, "form there!" This battle, he thought, was a nightmare without end. It flowed like molten lava across the plateau and his poor battalion was being swept with the flow from one crisis to another. He paused halfway across the small pasture that separated the West Woods from the pike to cut off a dead Yankee's cartridge pouch, then he joined his men. "Take your bayonets off," he told them. "We'll just have to shoot the bastards down." He was about to send a man to find Swynyard and tell him the news, but suddenly there was no need, for a rush of rebels arrived at the tree line to add their rifles to Starbuck's shrunken battalion.

The Yankees were walking to death. They were crossing the cornfield, stepping around the bodies, advancing toward the pike with its broken fences, and, once there, they were within point-blank range of the mass of rifles waiting in the shadows. "Wait!" Starbuck called as the Yankees reached the shattered fence on the far side of the road. There were not as many Northerners as he had first feared. He had thought a whole brigade might be crossing the cornfield, but now he could see only two Stars and Stripes and two state flags hanging limp in the still air. It was a pair of forlorn battalions thrown into horror. "Wait," he said, "let them get close."

The two Northern battalions, their careful lines disordered by the need to step around the dead and dying in the corn, crossed the remnants of the first rail fence, then Starbuck shouted at his men to fire. The opening volley stunned the Yankees, throwing them down in a new tideline of dead and dying. The rear ranks stepped forward and fired at the rebel rifle smoke, but the Yankees were firing at shadows in shadows and the rebels had flesh-and-blood targets. Starbuck pulled his trigger, crying aloud with the pain of the rifle's recoil as it pounded back into the raw bruise of his right shoulder. At this range it was impossible to miss; the Yankees were not even a hundred yards away and the rebel bullets were thumping into the shrinking lines, banging on rifle stocks, jetting blood from men who were thrown two paces back by the force of the bullets, yet somehow the enemy clung to their position and tried to return the dreadful fire.

Sergeant Case was at the right-hand end of Starbuck's line, though by now there were so many rebel units firing at the Yankees that it was hard to tell where one battalion began and another ended. The Sergeant wriggled back from the firing line. He had not shot once, saving his three bullets for his own purposes, but now he worked his way north until he could see Starbuck standing beside a tree. Case edged into some brush, then raised his head and watched Starbuck fire. He saw him drop the rifle's butt to reload, and Case glanced around to make sure no one was watching him and then he brought up the Sharps rifle and aimed at Starbuck's head. He had to be quick. The rifle's leaf sight was folded flat, for he was so close to his target that the heavy half-inch bullet would not drop as much as its own width in its brief flight. He put the front leaf sight on Starbuck's head, lined the rear notch, and pulled the trigger. Smoke billowed to hide him as he scrambled out of the brush and back toward the tree line.

Starbuck had lowered his head to spit the bullet into his rifle. A bullet whipped past his skull to whack the tree beside him with the force of an ax hitting timber. Splinters of bark lodged in his hair. He cursed the Yankees, brought up the gun, primed, aimed, and fired. A Northern flag-bearer whipped about as he was hit in the shoulder and his flag rippled prettily through the smoke as it fell. Someone snatched up the banner and was immediately hit by a pair of bullets that threw him back across the broken fence. The Yankees were at last going back from the galling fire. They went reluctantly, holding their ravaged ranks as they stepped rearward so that no man would show his back to the enemy.

None of the rebels pursued. They fired as the Yankees retreated, and kept firing until the two battalions had disappeared into the smoke hanging over the cornfield. The two battalions went as mysteriously as they had arrived, their contribution to the day a row of bodies by the pike's bullet-riddled fences. There was a pause after the Yankees vanished, then the shells began to come again, crackling through the high branches, exploding leaves and twigs in showers, and spitting metal fragments down to the woods' floor.

A staff officer shouted for Swynyard's brigade to form up in the wood. Swynyard himself was talking to a grim-faced General Jackson. The Colonel nodded, then ran toward his men. "The Yankees are in the church again," he explained grimly.

The brigade stumbled south through the trees, too tired to speak, too dry-mouthed to curse, going to where more Yankees waited to kill and be killed.

And it was still only morning.

Colonel Thorne watched grimly as General McClellan tried to understand the messages that arrived from across the creek. One dusty messenger spoke only of defeat, of a horde of rebels destroying General Sumner's troops in the far woods, while other aides brought urgent requests for reinforcements to exploit successful attacks. McClellan met all the messengers with the same stern face with which he had learned to hide his uncertainties.

The Young Napoleon was doing his best to understand the battle from his view across the creek. It had seemed simple enough in the dawn: His men had attacked again and again until at last the rebels had been pushed out of the nearer woods, but in the last hour everything had become confused. Like a spreading forest fire, the battle was now raging across two miles of countryside and from some places the news was all good and from others it was disastrous, and none made sense. McClellan, still fearing Lee's masterstroke that would destroy his army, was holding back his reserves, though now a sweaty, dust-covered messenger was begging him to send every man available to support General Greene, who had recaptured the Dunker church and was holding it against every counterattack. McClellan, in truth, was not too sure where the Dunker church was. General Greene's messenger was promising that a successful attack could split the rebel army in two, but McClellan doubted the optimism. He knew that General Sumner's corps was in desperate trouble to the north of the church, while to the south there was a maelstrom of fire erupting in the bare fields. That fire was sucking in every new brigade that crossed the creek. "Tell Greene he'll be supported," McClellan promised, then promptly forgot the promise as he tried to discover what was happening to the far south, where General Burnside was supposed to be across the creek by now and advancing on the rebels' single road to retreat.

But, before General Burnside could cut that retreat, he first had to cross a twelve-foot-wide stone bridge, and the bridge was guarded by rebel marksmen well dug into the steep slope on its western bank, and General Burnside's men were piling in heaps of dead as they tried to storm the crossing. Again and again they rushed the bridge, and again and again the rebel bullets turned the leading ranks into quivering heaps of bloody men who lay in the broiling sun and cried for help, for water, for any relief from their misery. "General Burnside can't get his men over the Rohrbach Bridge," a messenger admitted to General McClellan. "It's too closely defended, sir."

"Why doesn't the fool use a ford!" McClellan protested.

But no one was certain where the ford was and the General's map was no help. McClellan, in desperation, turned on Thorne. "Go, show them! Hurry, man!" That, at least, got rid of Thorne, whose baleful gaze had unsettled the General all morning. "Tell them to hurry!" he shouted after the Colonel, then he looked back to the open fields across the creek where the battle had become so inexplicably fierce. A message had arrived telling of a trench-like lane that was holding up the advance, but McClellan was not at all sure why his army was even attacking the hidden obstacle. He had not ordered any such assault. He had intended for his attacks to hit hard in the north and, once that enemy flank was turned, to harry the rebels from the south before advancing to glorious victory in the center, but somehow the Northern army had become embroiled in the center long before the enemy's flanks had collapsed. Not only embroiled, but, judging from the white smoke that boiled up from the fields, the center was fighting as hard as men had ever fought.

It was hard because the rebels were in the sunken road, and from its lip they were turning the fields of newly sown winter wheat into croplands of the dead. Thousands of men, bereft of orders when they crossed the creek, marched toward that battle and one by one the brigades went forward until the rebel fire ripped their ranks apart. One Northern battalion was defeated before it even came within sight of the rebels, let alone within reach of their rifles, for, as it was marching past a spread of farm buildings, a rebel shell tore into a line of beehives and the enraged insects turned on the nearest targets. Men scattered in frantic disarray while more shells plunged blindly into their panicked ranks. Northern guns were taking up the fight, dropping shells over the heads of their infantry at the rebels in the road, while from beyond the creek the heavy Parrott guns fired at the rebel rear to smash the wagons trying to bring ammunition to the road's defenders.

It was nearing lunchtime. In the kitchen of the Pry farm the cooks readied a cold collation for the General as telegraphers sent a message to Washington. "We are in the midst of the most terrible battle of the war," McClellan reported, "perhaps of history. Thus far it looks well, but I have great odds against me. Hurry up all the roops possible." The twenty thousand men of his reserve, who could have given him victory if he had hurried them cross the creek and sent them to the Dunker church, layed horseshoes in the meadows. Some wrote letters, ome slept. Theirs was a lazy day in hot sunlight, far from he blood and sweat and stink of the men who fought and ied across the creek.

While to the south, still far to the south, the rebel Light Division marched toward the guns.

tarbuck crouched in the woods. Sweat poured down his ace and stung his eyes. The remains of the Yellowlegs vere back at the edge of the trees near the Dunker church nd it was plain that the Yankees were also back in force bout the small building, for when Potter's skirmishers ad run forward they had been greeted by a withering blast f rifle fire that had spun one man down and persuaded the thers to seek cover. Yankee bullets whipped through the rees as more rebel battalions were brought back to make he assault on the church. To Starbuck this fight for the hurch was like a private skirmish that had little connec-ion with the storm of fire that sounded further south. If he battle did have a pattern, then he had long lost all nderstanding of it; instead it seemed like a series of des-erate, bloody, and accidental clashes that flared, ourished, and died without meaning.

This new fight for the church also promised to be bloody or, while Starbuck waited in the trees, the Yankees rought up two guns that unlimbered just across the turn-ike from the Dunker church. The horses were taken back vhile the gunners rammed their weapons, but instead of pening fire, the gun's commander ran toward the church. le was evidently seeking orders. The nearest gun was no aore than two hundred yards away and Starbuck knew that one blast of canister would be sufficient to destroy what remained of his battalion.

The idea came to him then, but he was so befuddled and tired that it took some few seconds for him to realize that the idea could work, then more seconds while he debated whether he had the energy to make the necessary effort. The temptation was to do as little as possible. His men had fought beyond the expectations of anyone in the army and no one could blame them now for letting other men do the dying and fighting, but the appeal of the idea was irresistible. He twisted and saw Lucifer crouching with his dog. "I want the officers here," he told the boy, "all except Mister Potter."

The boy darted away through the brush while Starbuck turned back to stare at the nearest gun. It was a Napoleon, the French-designed cannon that was the workhorse for both armies. Its flared muzzle could fire a twelve-pound roundshot, canister, shell, or case shot, but it was the canister that the infantry feared most. The Napoleon might not have the range and power of the big rifled cannon, but its smoothbore barrel spat canister in a regular, killing pattern where the larger rifled guns could skew the shower of lead into strange shapes that sometimes flew safely overhead. The Napoleon, so far as the infantry was concerned, was a giant shotgun mounted on massive wheels.

The Yankee gunners were relaxed, plainly unaware that enemy infantry was close. A faded Stars and Stripes hung on the limber, which stood with its lid open. A shirt-sleeved man carried ammunition and stacked it close to the gun, where another man leaned on the barrel and cleaned his fingernails with a knife. Every now and then he glanced over his right shoulder toward the east as if he expected to see reinforcements coming, but all he saw

vere his gun's horses cropping the pasture's bloodied grass
a hundred yards away. After a time he yawned, folded the
knife, and fanned his face with his hat.

Dennison and Peel joined Starbuck. These, with Potter,
were his only captains. After the battle, Starbuck thought,
here would needs be wholesale promotions, but that could
wait. Now he told the two men what he wanted, cut short
their anxieties, and sent them away. A minute later their
shrunken companies came to the tree line, where Starbuck
concealed the men in the shadows and thick brush. He
walked behind the line of men telling them what he
expected of them. "You don't fire till the gun has fired,"
he said, "then you kill the gunners. Then you charge. One
shot up your barrel, bayonets on, don't stop to reload." An
excitement touched Starbuck's voice and communicated
itself to the men who, tired as they were, grinned at him.
"They say we're no good, lads," Starbuck told them, "they
say we're the Yellowlegs. Well, we're about to give the
army a present of one gun. Maybe two. Remember, one
shot only, don't fire till the cannon's fired, then charge
like there was a score of naked whores serving that gun."

"Wish there were," a man said.

There was a sudden crashing in the timber behind Starbuck, who turned to see the drunken Colonel Maitland,
who had somehow recovered his horse and now rode with
drawn sword toward Starbuck's battalion. "I'll lead you,
boys!" Maitland shouted. "Victory all the way! Up now!
Get ready."

Starbuck grabbed the bridle before Maitland had a
chance to rouse the men to a premature attack. He dragged
the horse round, pointed it toward the heart of the woods,
and slapped its rump. Maitland somehow kept his seat as
he rode away shouting and brandishing the sword. The
noise he made was drowned by the furious sound of the

fighting further south. "Wait, lads," Starbuck calmed his men, "just wait."

Sergeant Case stared at the unsuspecting gunners. He was tempted to fire at them as soon as the attack on the Dunker church opened, and so deny Starbuck his victory by alerting the gunners to their danger, but Case only had two bullets left for his Sharps rifle and he dared not waste one. His hatred of Starbuck was being fed by what he perceived as Starbuck's unprofessionalism. Soon, Case reckoned, the battalion would be so shrunken that it would cease to exist, and what of Dennison's promise then? Case wanted to be an officer, he wanted to command the Yellowlegs, whom he planned to drill and discipline into the finest battalion in the Confederate army, but now Starbuck was threatening to thin its emaciated ranks even further. It was amateurism, the Sergeant thought, sheer bloody amateurism.

A cheer sounded in the woods, then the rebel yell erupted. Swynyard's voice shouted out of the shadows. "Go, Nate! Go!"

"Wait!" Starbuck shouted at his men. "Just wait!"

A splinter of rifle fire met the rebel charge, then a louder volley sounded as the charging rebels fired at the Yankees. The gunners had sprung to life. The barrel of the nearest gun was aimed roughly where Starbuck's skirmishers were placed and Starbuck prayed it was not charged with canister. He watched the gun captain duck aside and yank the lanyard that scraped the friction primer across the tube. The gun bucked violently back, spitting its flame and smoke toward the trees.

"Fire!" Starbuck shouted. Dimly over the crack of his rifles he heard the clatter of bullets striking the cannon. He hauled out his revolver. "Now charge!"

He ran from the trees and could see that the gunners

had been hit hard. The gun captain was on his knees, holding his belly with one hand and the gun's wheel with another. Two other men were down while the rest of the crew hesitated between reloading and looking for the danger.

The Yellowlegs charged. The gun lay beyond the junction of the turnpike and the Smoketown Road and the remnants of two sets of fences lay in their path, but the men leaped the rails and stumbled on as fast as their tired legs would carry them. It was a race now between the weary infantrymen and the hard-hit gun crew, who began trying to handspike the Napoleon round to face the attack. A wounded gunner was holding a charge of canister, ready to plunge it down the barrel, then he saw the race was lost and he just dropped the charge and fled toward the east, his suspenders flapping about his legs as he limped away.

The second gun tried to save the first, but before its gunners could charge the barrel and turn the gun, the defenders of the Dunker church gave way. They had been attacked from two sides, caught in a screaming vice of vengeful gray, and the thousand Yankees under General Greene had taken enough. They scattered and fled, and the gunners of the second Napoleon simply brought up their horses, limbered up the gun, and galloped away. Starbuck's men, still screaming their challenge, pounced on the first gun, slapping its hot barrel and shouting their victory while, just yards away, the broken Yankees streamed past, pursued by rifle fire from the woods. Starbuck's men watched them go, too tired to make an effort to interfere. A wounded gunner begged for water and one of Starbuck's men knelt beside the man and tipped a canteen to his lips. "Never knew you boys were there," the gunner said. He struggled to sit up and managed at last to prop himself against his gun's wheel. "They said it only was all our boys in the trees." He sighed, then felt in his pocket to bring out a wrapped tintype of a woman that he set on his lap. He stared at the image.

"We'll find you a doctor," Starbuck promised.

The man looked up at Starbuck briefly, then stared again at the tintype. "Too late for doctors," he said. "One of you boys put a bullet in my guts. Don't hurt much, not yet, but there isn't a doctor born who can help. If I was a dog you'd have put me down by now." He gave the portrait a gentle touch. "Prettiest girl in Fitchburg," he said softly, "and we've only been married two months." He paused, closed his eyes as a spasm of pain flickered deep in his guts, then looked up at Starbuck. "Where you boys from?" he asked.

"Virginia."

"That's her name," the gunner said, "Virginia Simmons."

Starbuck crouched beside the man. "She is pretty," he said. The photograph showed a slender, fair-haired girl with an anxious face. "And I reckon you'll see her again," he added.

"Not this side of the pearly gates," the gunner said. He had grown a wispy brown beard in an evident attempt to make himself look older. He glanced at the revolver in Starbuck's hand, then up into Starbuck's eyes. "You an officer?"

"Yes."

"You reckon there's a heaven?"

Starbuck paused, struck by the intensity of the question. "Yes," he said gently, "I know there is."

"Me, too," the gunner said.

"'I know that my Redeemer liveth,'" Starbuck quoted.

The gunner nodded, then looked back at his wife. "And

I'll be waiting for you, girl," he said, "with coffee on the boil." He smiled. "She always likes her coffee scalding hot." A tear showed in his eye. "Never knew you boys were there," he said in a weaker voice.

Some of the rebels had pursued the broken Yankees out into the pastureland, but a barrage of canister drove them back. One musket ball struck the barrel of the captured cannon and Starbuck ordered his men back to the trees. He stooped to the wounded gunner to see if the man wanted to be carried back, but the man was already dead. His lap was puddled with blood, his eyes were wide open, and a fly was crawling into his mouth. Starbuck left him.

Back at the tree line some of his men put their heads on their arms and slept. Others stared sightlessly east where the gunsmoke lay like a sea-fog, while in the corn, the pastures, and the ravaged woods, the wounded cried on unheeded.

The heat of the battle had moved south, leaving the scene of the morning's fighting full of exhausted survivors too weak to fight more. Now it was the sunken road that acted like a giant meat grinder. Battalion after battalion walked into the rebel fire, and battalion after battalion died on the open ground, and still more men came from the east to add their deaths to the day's rich toll.

But the rebels were dying as well. The road might be a defender's dream, but it had one shortcoming. It ran directly eastward from the Hagerstown Pike, then bent sharply south and east so that once the Yankees had managed to place a battery on a line directly east of the road's first stretch, they were able to enfilade the stubborn Confederate defenders. Shells plunged into the sunken road and the steep banks magnified the carnage of each explosion. The fire of the defenders grew weaker, yet still they drove back one attack after another. The Irishmen of New York nearly broke through. They had been told that the Confederates were the friends of the British and that was incentive enough to drive the green flags forward. The flags had golden Irish harps embroidered on the green and the Irishmen carried the harps further forward than any flag had yet reached, but there was no bravery sufficient to carry men through the last few murderous yards of fire. One black-bearded giant of a man screamed his war cry in Gaelic and urged his compatriots on as though he could win the war and avenge his people single-handed, but a rebel's bullet put the man down, and the charge, like so many others, was finally shredded into raw and bloody tatters by the remorseless rifle fire. The Irish made a new line of bodies, closer than any others to the lane's fiery lip, while in the lane itself, where the shells plunged to tear dead bodies into mincemeat, the rebel dead thickened.

Other men died on the lower creek, where every effort to take the Rohrbach Bridge had failed. The corpses lay like a barrier on the east bank and the very sight of so many dead served as a deterrent to the waiting Yankee battalions, who knew their turn must come to assault the deadly passage. Thorne came there too, and came with the authority of his enemy McClellan. He found General Burnside on the hill overlooking the bridge. "Where the hell are the guns?" Thorne snarled.

General Burnside, astonished at being addressed in such a peremptory fashion, sounded defensive. "Waiting to cross," he explained, gesturing toward a lane behind the hill where the guns were sheltering.

"You need them up here," Thorne insisted.

"But there are no roads," an aide protested.

"Then make a road!" Thorne shouted. "Get a thousand

men if you have to, but drag the damn things up here. Now! Two guns, twelve-pounders, canister and case shot only. And for Christ's sake, hurry!"

South of the Potomac, marching in swirls of dust under the merciless sun, the Light Division was also being chivvied and harried to keep moving, to keep moving, always to keep moving toward the sound of the killing.

While on the Pry house lawn General McClellan enjoyed his lunch.

TWO NAPOLEONS WERE fetched to the summit of the hill above the Rohrbach Bridge and their presence turned the battle for the crossing. The very first blast of canister whipped a half-dozen sharpshooters out of their hiding places in the tops of the trees on the western bank, and left others dangling lifelessly from the ropes that had held them safe to the branches. The second and third discharges of canister decimated the rebel defenders in their rifle pits.

A Pennsylvania battalion, promised a keg of whiskey if they took the bridge, charged forward. There were still enough rebels to kill the leading ranks, but the men behind leaped over their dead and stormed onto the stone roadway that arched across the creek. More Yankees followed, jostling between the balustrades as they hurried to carry their revenge to the rebels, who scrambled hurriedly out of their pits and up over the hill.

Downstream, at Snaveley's Ford, another brigade at last made the crossing to the western bank and the Yankees were finally loose in Lee's rear, but it was one thing to be across the creek and quite another to form the battalions and brigades into their columns. Guns had to be fetched over the creek, disarray had to be straightened, and the ground had to be reconnoitered. Thorne cursed McClellan for keeping the army's cavalry at headquarters where it served no purpose. If the cavalry could have been unleashed here, behind the rebel army, he could have struck panic into Lee's men, but the Northern cavalry was two miles away and General Burnside would not advance his infantry until all was ready. A handful of rebel skirmishers harried the Northerners as they laboriously marched unit after unit across the river. Thorne raged at Burnside for speed, but Burnside would not be hurried. "The day's young yet," he said, indicating the brevity of the shadows, "and there's no need for impetuosity. We shall do it properly. Besides," Burnside went on as though his next point was irrefutable, "we can't attack till the infantry is resupplied with ammunition. Their pouches are empty, Thorne, empty. Men can't fight with empty pouches."

Thorne wondered how any general could have failed to carry sufficient ammunition for a day's hard fighting, but he bit back the comment. The day was indeed young, and it needed to be, for Burnside's units were crossing the bridge at a snail's pace and, once over the river, they lingered aimlessly until staff officers arrived to direct them to their proper places. Burnside's advance, when it came, would be a slow, grinding assault instead of a lightning strike, and Thorne could only pray that Lee did not choose to retreat before the North's trap swung ponderously shut. He forced his horse up the steep hill where the rebel defenders had fought for so long and, once at the summit, he stared across an empty landscape of cornfields, shade trees, and pastureland, and, in the heat-hazed distance where it was marked by the dust kicked up by a trail of ambulances going slowly south toward the river, he could see the enemy's only route home. A rebel skirmisher fired at Thorne and the bullet whipped close beside his ear. Thorne saw the patch of smoke and reckoned the shot had been all of four hundred yards. He raised his hat in ironic salute to a well-aimed near miss, then turned his horse down from the high ground.

The sunken lane at last fell. The Yankees, capturing the road, found they could not cross the track without stepping on the bodies of its defenders, and though those defenders had failed, they had hurt their attackers so hard that the Yankees were in no fit state to advance further.

The battle, which had burned so fierce, smoldered in the afternoon. Weary men staggered about the plateau that was hung with smoke and smothered with the foul miasma of bodies beginning to rot in the hot sun. Batteries waited for new ammunition, infantry counted their cartridges, and officers counted their men. Units that had started the day five hundred strong were less than a hundred now. The dead possessed the field, while the living searched for water and peered into the eye-stinging smoke for a sign of the enemy.

The rebels were hardest hit. There were no reserves left, not one man, and so Lee made a barrier of artillery to defend Sharpsburg and its single road, which led back to the Confederacy. The guns were just in place when a weary messenger on a tired, dust-stained, and sweat-whitened horse came up the track from the town. Hill's Light Division had reached the ford. The Confederacy's last troops were crossing the river and coming north.

The rest of Lee's army waited. They knew the mauled Yankees were making ready and that soon the blue ranks would appear over the brow of the plateau and the fighting would begin again. The dead who had been searched for ammunition were searched again and the precious cartridges shared out. There was no hot water to clean out the fouled barrels of the rifles, nor any urine, for the men were parched dry by thirst and sweat. They waited.

The spring that would drive the Yankees' trap shut

was coiling itself tight as Burnside's men slowly readied themselves for the advance, but General McClellan could not shake the northern part of the battlefield from his fears. It was from that northern sector, which had been harrowed by death all morning, that he expected the great rebel counterattack that would jeopardize his army's existence. One of his generals reported imminent disaster in those northern fields, while another claimed that with one more effort the North could sweep the rebels out of the West Woods and back through Sharpsburg altogether, and so fierce was their argument that once his lunch was taken McClellan crossed the creek for the first and only time that day. He met his generals, he listened to their arguments, and then he pronounced his verdict. Caution, he declared, was best. The generals must hold their ground against the worst the rebels could throw against them, but they were to make no more attacks. The enemy, he said, must not be provoked and then, with that decided, McClellan went back to his armchair, from where he sought reassurance that his heavy reserve of men was still in place to meet the rebel attack he knew must be coming. After all, as he explained to Pinkerton, the rebels did outnumber him.

"That they do, chief, that they do," Pinkerton agreed enthusiastically. "Hordes of the scoundrels, just hordes!" The Scotsman blew his nose vigorously, then unfolded the handkerchief to inspect the result. "It's a miracle we've done as well as we have, chief," he opined, still staring at the handkerchief. "Nothing short of a miracle."

McClellan, who rather thought it was his superior generalship that had staved off disaster all day, grunted, then stooped to the telescope to watch as the troops in the center of the field at last began their advance from the sunken lane. Their job was to hold Lee's men in

Sharpsburg while Burnside cut behind them. It was a grand sight, McClellan thought. Thousands of men marched beneath their flags. Wisps of smoke drifted across the telescope's lens, giving the great attack a fine romantic flavor.

It was less romantic in the ranks. There, advancing across open fields toward the massive gun line assembled on the hill above the village, the North suffered as the smoldering battle burst again into livid flame. The cannons' long range meant the infantry had no chance of replying, but could only trudge through the smoke of the explosions and across the blood of their comrades until it was their turn to be hit. Ahead of them was the skyline above the village, but that skyline was rimmed by guns that pumped tongues of flame and billows of smoke. The shells screamed and wailed and cracked and killed, while from beyond the creek the heavy Federal guns returned the fire with big shells that rumbled in the sky to flower in bloody gouts on the rebel artillery line.

Burnside's men started forward at last. There, and only there on all the battlefield, a band played as the flags were carried up the hill to begin the grand attack that would cut the retreat of the rebel army.

For at last the Northern trap was swinging shut and the long day's killing was coming to its climax.

The Yankees in the North and East Woods were quiet, but the northern flank of the Federal advance on Sharpsburg was visible from the woods about the Dunker church and those men, like the larger mass that advanced from the captured sunken lane, were met by the horror of Lee's artillery line. Some of Starbuck's men fired their rifles at the distant enemy, but most were content to shelter in the trees and watch as the artillery explosions gouged the enemy. Their own gun, the Napoleon they had captured, stood fifty yards away. Potter had begun to carve a legend on the gun's trail, "A gift from the Yellow-legs," but the hardness of the wood had blunted his small pocket-knife and he had abandoned his efforts. "It's odd," he said to Starbuck now, "but one day this will all be in the history books."

"Odd?" Starbuck frowned as he tried to wrench his thoughts from his parched weariness to Potter's airy statement. "Why odd?"

"Because I guess I never thought of America as a place where history is made," Potter said, "at least, not since the Revolution. History belongs to the rest of the world. Crimea, Napoleon, Garibaldi, the Indian mutiny." He shrugged. "We came to America to escape history, isn't that right?"

"We're making it now," Starbuck said curtly.

"Then we'd better make sure we win," Potter said, "because history is written by the winners." He yawned. "Do I have permission to get drunk?"

"Not yet. This thing ain't over."

Potter grimaced, then stared at the cannon. "I've always wanted to fire a cannon," Potter said wistfully.

"Me too," Starbuck said.

"How difficult can it be?" Potter inquired. "Ain't nothing but an oversized rifle. A man don't need a college degree."

Starbuck gazed at the enemy, whose enthusiasm had been blunted by the day's carnage so that their advance now wavered under the rain of artillery shells. Maybe another gun, opening from their flank, would push them back. "We can try," he said, encouraged by the thought that the Yankees were far enough away for their skirmishers to be inaccurate. "A couple of shots, maybe."

"It is our gun," Potter said firmly. "We'd be sadly remiss not to check that it works before handing it over."

"True," Starbuck hesitated, once more gauging the distance between the Napoleon and the distant Yankees. "Let's try it," he decided.

Three of Potter's company volunteered to serve as crew, one of them the Irish saddler, John Connolly, who had a bloody bandage round his left arm but insisted he was fit enough to fight; then Lucifer insisted that he knew something of artillery, though Starbuck suspected the boy simply wanted to join in the excitement of firing a cannon.

No Yankee noticed them as they ran forward. The gun was still pointing toward the woods by the Dunker church, so Potter and his men lifted the tail and maneuvered the heavy barrel around while Starbuck rummaged in the limber that had already yielded three full canteens of water and a boiled ham wrapped in canvas for his hungry men. Now he pulled out a bag of powder, a case shot, and a package of fuses. The instructions on the packet told him to tear off the paper, then press against the small end of the fuse. "I thought this was supposed to be easy," Starbuck said. He had extracted one of the fuses, a simple paper tube filled with powder, but he could not relate the tube to the printed instructions.

"Give it me," Lucifer said, and he tore the fuse into halves and pushed one half into a drilled copper plug that formed part of the case shot. "Five seconds is too long," Lucifer said, judging the distance to the enemy. "Give it two and a half."

"How the hell do you know all this?" Starbuck asked.

"Just do," Lucifer said, once again hiding his past. His

g was tied to his belt by its leash of rifle slings that
most tangled Lucifer's legs as he carried the shell to
e gun. "You have to put the powder in first," he told
tarbuck.

Starbuck pushed the powder bag into the tube, then
ucifer plugged the case shot into the muzzle. A bullet
histled overhead. Starbuck guessed it was an errant shot,
ot deliberately aimed at his men.

Lucifer had taken charge now. He had found the fric-
on primer and a vent pick and, once the charge had
een rammed down the barrel, he leaned over the muzzle
nd pushed the pick hard down to pierce the canvas bag
f powder. He inserted the friction primer, attached the
nyard that had been in the dead gunner's hand, then
epped back. "Ready," he said.

"What about the elevation?" Colonel Swynyard had
en the activity about the gun and come to join the
akeshift crew. "Looks low to me," he added, gesturing
the wormed elevating screw.

Starbuck gave the screw a pair of turns, but it seemed
make little difference. Maybe a man did need a college
egree after all. "Let's just fire the damn thing," he said,
en held up a hand. "Wait." The dead gunner with his
ife's picture still on his lap had fallen behind the wheel
d Starbuck first dragged the body clear, then picked up
e tintype. It seemed sacrilegious to throw it away, so he
t the picture in his pocket, then nodded at Lucifer.
ou fire it," he said.

Fifty yards behind the gun Sergeant Case took aim. He
d found Captain Dennison and the two men were in
e brush at the wood's edge. Case had almost given up
pe of finding an opportunity to kill Starbuck, but sud-
nly Starbuck was fifty yards away and in the open while
ase and Dennison were hidden deep in brush. "Fire when

405

the nigger pulls the string," Case told the Captain. "Y
go for the bastard's body, I'll go for a head shot."

Dennison, dry mouthed, could not answer, so j
nodded. He was desperately nervous. He was about
commit murder and his hand was shaking as he rested
rifle on a small hillock. The men about the cannon h
their backs to him and he was suddenly unsure whi
was Starbuck, but then he recognized the revolver hols
Starbuck always wore at the small of his back and
aimed a few inches above it, where the gray jacket w
darkened by a smear of blood. Case, calmer th
Dennison, aimed at Starbuck's black hair. "Wait till th
fire," he warned Dennison.

Dennison nodded again, and the small movement w
enough to dislodge the sights from his target. He hurried
reaimed and had only just realized that he was sightin
the wrong man when Lucifer ducked away from the g
and yanked the lanyard.

The Napoleon crashed back, its wheels bucking s
inches up from the turf as the lunette at the end of
tail plowed hard back through the dirt. The noise w
immense, a crack to hurt the ears of anyone within fif
paces. Smoke gushed ahead, writhing with flame, a
under the cover of the noise, while the remnants of th
Yellowlegs cheered, Case and Dennison fired.

Potter pitched violently forward onto the ground.

Starbuck was turning as the bullet hit Potter and,
he turned, a mist of blood exploded from the side of h
face and then he too fell.

The shell screamed across the field. The elevation ha
been much too low and the smoking case shot ricochete
off a patch of dry ground to explode harmlessly behir
the Yankees. It killed no one.

"It's all yours," Case said, lowering the Sharps rifle. "A

ours." And soon, Case thought, it would all be his. The Virginia Fusiliers, the smartest regiment in the Confederacy.

"Thank you, Captain," Dennison managed to answer.

While to the south the great guns boomed and the Yankees closed on Sharpsburg.

Lee could only watch as disaster threatened. He stood on the low height above the town, where his guns were lined along the edge of Sharpsburg's cemetery, and he watched as a flood of Yankees filled the countryside to the east and to the south.

His men were still fighting. Their cannons were tearing huge holes in the Northern files while the gray infantry was stubbornly defending every fence, wall, and farm building, but it was the Yankees who had the advantage. There seemed so many of them. Wherever Lee looked another battalion or brigade would appear from hidden ground to join the advance on the town and toward the road that ran south toward the Confederate states. An aide checked each new appearance through a telescope and each time, just as Lee hoped that it might be one of the Light Division's battalions appearing on the flank, the aide would laconically announce, "It's Yankee, sir."

"Are you sure?" Lee asked once.

"Sir?" The aide offered the telescope.

"Can't use it," Lee said, gesturing with his bandaged hands.

The guns banged on, layering a new mist of smoke across the high ground. Some of the guns had been dismounted by the heavy Yankee counterfire, others lay canted on splintered wheels that gunners struggled to change. One of the army's few heavy Parrott guns had exploded, killing two of its crew and foully wounding another three. "Try to find out if they varnished their shells," Lee said to the aide.

"Sir?" The aide frowned in puzzlement.

"The gun crew. The Parrott," Lee explained. "Find out if they greased the shells. Not now, just when you have a moment."

"Yes, sir," the aide said and trained his telescope south again.

Belvedere Delaney climbed up through the gravestones to join the nervous band of aides who stood a few paces behind Lee. Delaney's uniform was bloody and his face sheened with sweat. Lee noted his arrival and smiled at him. "Are you wounded, Delaney?"

"Other men's blood, sir," Delaney answered. He was tired through and appalled beyond measure by what he had seen this day. He had never dreamed that such horror could exist outside of slaughterhouses. The town was filled with wounded, and every house was sheltering dying and broken men. Yet the worst moment of the day had been when Delaney had gone down into a cellar to fetch some apples that the householder was storing for the winter and now offered to the wounded troops. As Delaney had filled a pail with the fruit he had felt liquid drip on his head. It had been blood seeping through the floorboards. He had begun to weep then, and his eyes were still red.

Lee saw that the lawyer was engulfed in horror. "Thank you for all your efforts, Delaney," he said gently.

"I did nothing, sir," Delaney said, "nothing," and he suddenly felt guilty, for it was he, surely, who had precipitated this slaughter. He suddenly resented it, fearing that the memory of blood dripping through floorboards would sour his idyllic life in some foreign capital. He shook that suspicion away, then frowned and managed to blurt out what he had been sent to say. "Colonel Chilton wonders if you should withdraw, sir."

Lee laughed. "And you were the only man brave enough to convey the message? Maybe you should abandon the law, Delaney, and take up soldiering. We need brave men. But in the meantime you can tell Chilton that we haven't lost yet." Delaney flinched as the shrapnel from a Yankee shell whipped the air overhead. Lee appeared not to notice the whirring sound of the hot metal. "We haven't lost yet," he said again with a tone of wistfulness.

"No," Delaney said, not because he believed the General, but because it was not his place to point out the obvious. The Yankees were winning. Half the Southern army lay in exhaustion and the other half was being driven remorselessly back by the vast Northern assault. Colonel Chilton had readied an ambulance to hurry Lee away from the imminent disaster, but Lee, it seemed, was not willing to go.

More troops appeared in the south. Lee glanced at them, but even at this distance it was possible to see that the new men were wearing blue. He sighed, but said nothing. The aide turned the glass on the newly arrived troops who were dangerously close to the single road south. The air was hazed by the heat and obscured by filaments of smoke and the aide stared for a long time before he spoke. "Sir?" he said.

"I know, Hudson," Lee said gently. "I've seen them. They wear blue." He sounded immensely tired as if he was suddenly realizing that it was all over. He knew he should make some effort to withdraw now, to rescue what he could of his army, but he seemed consumed by a terrible lassitude. If he did not escape then he would be captured and McClellan would have him as his guest at dinner and the humiliation of such a meal seemed unbearable.

"Re-equipped at Harper's Ferry, sir," the aide said.

"I'm sorry?" Lee asked, thinking he must have misheard the aide.

Hudson's voice rose in sudden excitement. "They're our men in Yankee coats, sir. It's our banner!"

Lee smiled. "The flags look alike when there's no wind."

"It's our banner, sir!" Hudson insisted. "It is, sir!" And suddenly the splintering sound of musketry echoed across the landscape and the far-off blue-coated troops were whitened by smoke as they fired a volley at other troops, also blue-coated. New guns were unlimbering and their fire was streaking slantwise across the attacking Yankee troops. It was the Light Division, come at last, and Lee closed his eyes as though he was at prayer. "Well done, Hill," he murmured, "well, well done." He would not have to eat McClellan's humble pie. More troops appeared to the south, these in gray, and suddenly the Yankee advance, which had reached almost to the gardens at the edge of Sharpsburg, was checked.

For the Light Division had arrived.

Lucifer, pulling the lanyard that had fired the gun, saw the two shots fired from the edge of the trees. A heartbeat later he connected the two shots with the two bodies on the gun's far side. Potter was flat on his belly, Starbuck was on his knees, but with his head on the ground spilling blood. Neither man moved until Starbuck, after a hopeless effort to straighten up, collapsed.

Lucifer shouted in anger and drew his revolver. He ran toward the patches of smoke, tugging the small dog along by its leash.

Colonel Swynyard realized a second after Lucifer that the shots had been fired from the rebel side. He started after the boy and saw one man rise up out of the brush.

Lucifer had drawn his revolver and was pointing it at the man. The Colonel shouted at him. "No! No, boy! No!"

Lucifer did not care. He fired, and his bullet went wide up into the trees. He slowed to take proper aim, knowing that the man who had shot Starbuck would need twenty seconds to reload his rifle. "Murderer!" he screamed at Case and raised the revolver again.

Case dropped the trigger guard and put his last cartridge into the breech of the Sharps. He snapped the guard up and thumbed the percussion cap into place.

Lucifer fired again, but even at twenty yards a revolver was inaccurate.

"No!" Swynyard called again and ran after the boy.

Case raised the gun. He saw the look of terror dawn on Lucifer's face and that look pleased him. He was grinning as he fired.

The boy was plucked backward. The force of the heavy bullet was so great that it lifted him off the ground and tugged the small dog back with him. The dog yelped in terror as Lucifer fell back, then whined as the small body twitched. Blood was pumping out of a hole in Lucifer's skull and the twitching stopped quickly.

Swynyard stooped by the boy, but knew he was dead long before he put a hand on the small throat. He looked up at Case, who shrugged. "He was shooting at me, Colonel," Case said, "you saw him."

"Name?" Swynyard snapped, standing up.

"Case," Case said defiantly, then slung the rifle. "And there ain't no bloody law 'gainst shooting niggers, sir. Specially niggers with guns."

"There is a law, Case, about shooting your own officers," Swynyard said.

Case shook his head. "Hell, Colonel, me and the Captain were firing at a pair of bloody Yankees out in the field." He jerked his beard toward the Smoketown Road. "Out there, Colonel. I reckon they killed Starbuck. Weren't me."

A second figure stood up beside Case. Swynyard recognized Captain Dennison, who licked his lips nervously, then nodded his head to support Case's statement. "In that patch of brush, Colonel," Dennison said, pointing toward the road. "Pair of Yankee skirmishers. I reckon we killed them both."

Swynyard turned. About three hundred yards away, just beside the Smoketown Road, there was a small patch of thorns where a mess of bodies lay thick under the pall of filmy smoke that smothered the field. Not enough smoke, Swynyard reckoned, to show that a pair of Yankee skirmishers had fired from the bushes, but he felt a terrible weariness as he understood that the two men would stick by their story and it would be a hard one to disprove. He turned back to them. He would put them under arrest anyway. There had been a time, he knew, when he would have shot them down like dogs, but he obeyed a higher law now. He would do the proper thing even though he guessed it would be useless.

He opened his mouth to speak, then saw a look of utter horror show on both men's faces. They were staring past him and Swynyard turned to see what had scared them.

Starbuck was standing. The left side of his face was a horror of blood. He staggered, then spat a great gob of thick blood and scraps of broken teeth. The bullet had gone through his open mouth, scored across his tongue, torn away four teeth from his upper jaw, then ripped out through his cheek. He walked unsteadily toward the two men, then paused beside Lucifer. He knelt by the boy and Swynyard saw the tears rolling down to mix with the blood. "Nate," Swynyard said, but Starbuck shook his

head as if he did not want anything said. He stroked
Lucifer's dead face with his hand, then untied the whimpering puppy from the boy's belt. He stood and walked
toward Case and Dennison. He spoke to them, but the
wound made his words a blood-curdled mumble. He spat
again, then pointed toward the clump of bushes. "Go,"
he managed to say.

Swynyard understood. "Go and find the men you
killed," he ordered the two.

"Hell," Case said, "there's a bunch of dead Yankees
there!"

"Then bring me two warm bodies!" Swynyard snapped.
"Because if they aren't warm, Captain Dennison, I'll know
you're lying. And if you are lying, Captain Dennison, I'll
have the two of you in front of a firing squad."

"Go!" Starbuck snarled, spitting more blood.

The two men walked east. Starbuck waited till they
were gone, then turned back to the gun. Blood was pouring
down his face as he heaved on the handspike to turn the
trail the few feet necessary so that the barrel was pointing
toward the Smoketown Road.

"No, Nate," Swynyard said. "No."

Starbuck ignored the Colonel. He went to the limber
and brought back a bag of powder and a canister. Two of
Potter's men rammed the cannon while Connolly ran to
retrieve the vent pick from Lucifer's body.

Potter rolled over. He was crying. Swynyard, who had
not expected his protest to work, knelt beside him. "Is it
hurting, son?"

"Stone jug of whiskey," Potter said, "best damn whiskey
I ever saw. I was saving it, Colonel, and they bust it. God
damn bust it. Now my back's soaked in whiskey, but it's
all on the outside and I was praying so hard for it to be
on the inside."

Swynyard tried not to smile, but could not help it. "You ain't hurt?" he asked.

"Had the breath knocked clean out of me," Potter said, then sat up. He took Swynyard's offered hand and hauled himself to his feet. "Had my back to them, Colonel," he said, "and I was shot in the back."

"There are proper procedures," Swynyard said lamely.

Starbuck gave his opinion of proper procedures, an opinion so muffled by blood that it came out as a splutter of gore and bone. He bent, spat again, then straightened and cupped his hands about his shattered mouth. "Case!" he roared.

Case and Dennison had been advancing cautiously into the open, almost as scared of the distant Yankees as they were of what waited for them on their return to the battalion. Then they saw there would be no return. The cannon was fifty yards from them, and aimed straight for them. Dennison shook his head, Case began to run, and Starbuck whipped the lanyard back.

The smoke of the cannon enveloped the two men, but not until the blast of canister had turned them to red ribbons of flesh.

Starbuck did not even look to see what the canister had done. He walked back to Lucifer and cradled the dead boy in his arms. He hugged him, rocking the small body, and dripping blood onto the boy's bloody face. Swynyard knelt beside him. "You need a doctor, Nate."

"It'll wait," Starbuck managed to say. "I never knew his real Christian name," he added, speaking slowly to articulate the words through the torn-up mess inside his mouth, "so what the hell can I put on his grave?"

"That he was a brave soldier," Swynyard said.

"He was," Starbuck said, "he truly was."

The guns to the south fell silent. The silence seemed

414

unnatural, for all day long the sky had been bruised by fire, but now there was silence. Silence and a small wind that at long last stirred the smoke and carried the stench of battle east across the creek. The killing was over.

In the night the wounded cried. Some died. Flickering campfires showed where the armies rested, the small flames marking the advances the Yankees had made during the day's long fight. The North and East Woods were theirs, and all the field that lay between the creek and the high ground above the town, but the rebels had not broken, they had not fled. The Light Division, sweating from its aching march, had struck Burnside's flank and hurled his carefully composed columns back just when they had thought they had broken through to the town.

Confederate Provosts searched the town's wooden houses for men who had taken refuge from the fighting. They rousted the fugitives from cellars and attics, from cowsheds and springhouses, then marched them back to their units. A child, killed by a Yankee shell that had screamed over the ridge to plunge into Sharpsburg, lay in her best frock on a parlor table. A house burned, its stone chimney stack all that was left when the sun rose above the Red Hill on the Thursday morning. The plateau was still hung with a haze of smoke and by the stench of the dead that lay in ghastly windrows across the fire-scorched fields.

All night men had trickled back to Swynyard's Brigade so that now there were 112 men left in Faulconer's Legion and seventy eight in Starbuck's battalion. When the rising sun dazzled them they shaded their eyes and stared east from the woods close to the Dunker church and waited for the Yankees to attack. But the Yankees did not come.

415

Instead, an hour after dawn, a man rode across the field with a white flag and sought permission from the rebels to rescue the Federal wounded, who lay crying in the bloody fields. Men who had cursed and killed the day before now joined together to disentangle the dead from the dying. Yankee and rebel worked together, filling the ambulances with broken men. The first shallow graves were dug, though it seemed that all the digging in the world would prove unequal to the task of burying the dead.

Captain Truslow decided to doctor Starbuck. There were no surgeons to spare for lightly wounded men, so Truslow used a rusty pair of long-nosed pliers to take out the scraps of tooth and bone. He lay Starbuck flat and stooped over the mangled mouth. "God in his heaven," he complained when Starbuck flinched at the pain. "Worse than a girl, you are. Just lie still, for Christ's sake. Water!"

Captain Potter poured water from a bucket to swill the blood from Starbuck's open mouth. Truslow probed again, swilled out the blood once more, then kept digging and tugging until he was sure every loose scrap of bone and tooth was free. He put three crude stitches into Starbuck's cheek. "This'll take the gloss off your good looks," Truslow said happily, knotting the cotton thread.

"Women like a scar," Potter said.

"He did enough caterwauling without a scar," Truslow growled, "so God help the ladies now." He had found a small bottle of brandy on a dead Yankee and he poured the raw spirit into Starbuck's bloody mouth. "Swill it out," he said, then gave Starbuck a pad made from a folded strip torn from the bottom of a dead man's shirt. "Bite on that till it stops bleeding," he ordered.

"Yes, doctor," Starbuck mumbled.

In the afternoon Starbuck dug Lucifer's grave beneath an elm tree while Potter carved the words "A brave soldier" into the elm's trunk. Potter went to remove the revolver from Lucifer's body before they put it in the shallow grave, but Starbuck stopped him. "Leave it with him," he said. "God knows he might need it where he's going." Potter nodded, but unbuckled the pouch to take out the remaining cartridges. Inside the pouch he found a carefully wrapped oilcloth package that he took out and showed to Starbuck. Starbuck took it, untied the string, and found the piece of paper that Caton Rothwell had shown him on the night after the fight with Case. He read the signature aloud. "Billy Blythe," he mumbled. "Son of a bitch."

"Who?"

Starbuck showed him the paper. "That was Tumlin's revolver," he said, pointing to the gun that Potter had placed in Lucifer's right hand, "and this paper belonged to Sergeant Rothwell. Jesus." He stopped, realizing that Tumlin must have killed Rothwell. "Now why the hell would Tumlin take it off Rothwell's body?"

"God knows," Potter said.

"I'd like to meet Mister Tumlin again," Starbuck said. He spat blood. "God," he went on vengefully, "but I would like that." He put the paper in his pocket, then helped lift Lucifer into his grave. They covered him with soil.

"You want to say a prayer?" Potter asked.

"I already have." Starbuck picked up Imp's lead and led the dog to the wood's edge. He bit down on the pad, almost relishing the pain as he stared at the field, which was thronged with soldiers of both sides. They were exchanging stories and swapping Northern newspapers for Southern journals. Some had cloths tied about their faces to keep away the stink of the dead.

417

Potter came and stood beside Starbuck. "I never did get my whiskey," he said wistfully.

Starbuck took the bloody pad from his mouth. "When we're back south," he promised, "you and I will get drunk together."

"I guess we are going back south," Potter said.

"I guess," Starbuck said, then spat a dribble of bloody spittle. Lee's army was in no state to stay, no state to fight. It had taken one hell of a beating and, though it had given one as well, it had no choice but to retreat.

Gunners limbered up the cannon that Starbuck's men had captured and towed it away toward Sharpsburg. Swynyard had insisted that the legend Potter had begun carving on the trail be finished so that the gunners would know that the despised Yellowlegs had captured the gun, and so Truslow had burned the words into the wood with the red-hot tip of a bayonet. Swynyard now crossed to Starbuck. "How's the mouth?"

"Painful, sir."

Swynyard drew Starbuck out of Potter's earshot. "Mister Maitland," the Colonel said, "confessed to me that he can't abide the sight of blood."

Starbuck, despite the pain in his jaw, smiled. "He said as much to me," he said.

"He's squeamish." Swynyard shrugged. "Told me he once fainted when one of his slaves had a nosebleed. I guess he wanted a chance to overcome the fear, but it didn't work. He agrees with me that Richmond might be a more suitable place for him to work." The Colonel's ravaged face split in a smile. "So the Legion's yours, Nate. What's left of it. Them and the Yellowlegs."

"Thank you, sir."

Swynyard paused, staring across the field where the

living moved so slowly among the dead. "I've got some other news."

"Good, I hope."

Swynyard nodded.

"Jackson just promoted me. I'm a Brigadier General."

Starbuck smiled again, tearing at the stitches in his cheek. He ignored the pain and held out his hand. "Congratulations, General."

Swynyard had tears in his eyes. "God has been good to me, Nate, so very good. Why did I wait so long to find Him?" Starbuck made no answer and the General smiled. "I'm having a prayer meeting at sundown," he said, "but I don't suppose you'll come?"

"I don't suppose I will, General," Starbuck said.

"And after prayers," General Swynyard said, "we march."

"Home?" Starbuck asked.

"Home," Swynyard said.

Because the invasion was over.

HISTORICAL NOTE

HE BATTLE OF ANTIETAM (Sharpsburg, to souther-
ers) is famous for being the bloodiest day in all America's
istory. Close to 23,000 men died in that one day. It was,
a the proper sense of the word, a shambles.

Lee was a gambler, and his decision to fight in the fields
out Sharpsburg was one of his biggest wagers. He feared
he political consequences of a retreat without a battle,
d hoped that his opponent's natural caution would
ake McClellan fumble and yield the outnumbered rebels
famous victory. The gamble failed. Lee's pride demanded
at his army stay in place on the day after the battle, for
at, by the soldiers' terms of honor, denoted that the
attle was not lost, but the campaign was nevertheless a
ilure. The North was spared a prolonged invasion and
o European country was encouraged to join the South. By
eping his army on the field Lee could claim a technical
ictory, but on the Thursday night the rebel army slipped
way, and by Friday evening there were no rebel soldiers
ft in the United States other than the dead and the
risoners.

Lee's invasion failed, but it was hardly because of
eorge McClellan, who was presented with a marvelous
aance to end the war at Antietam. If he had attacked
wenty-four hours earlier, he would undoubtedly have
estroyed Lee's army, which was smaller than it ever would
e again until the war's very end. Yet McClellan was

421

racked by doubts and waited while Lee was reinforce
And if, when he did at last summon the courage to attac
McClellan had coordinated his assaults, he would ha
routed Lee, but instead the Northern attacks came one
a time, and Lee was able to move his shrinking forces
meet each new assault. McClellan's plan of attack h
been to engage Lee's flanks, then send the killing blc
through the center when the rebel reserves had be
depleted, but the fight never remotely resembled that pla
Instead the battle degenerated into a series of bloo
encounters over which neither side had full control.
has been called a soldier's battle, for it was the commo
soldier who fought it, and fought it with an extraordina
bravery. McClellan could have resumed the fight
Thursday and, with his huge reserve, which had not fir
a shot, he would surely have finished the business quick
enough, but he was too frightened to try. He claimed h
soldiers were tired, and Lee's army was allowed to sl
away to fight again. Lee's army had suffered grievously a
all it had to show for its efforts were the captured gu
and supplies from Harper's Ferry.

Antietam was McClellan's last battlefield comman
He himself believed he had displayed the highest milita
artistry, but President Lincoln had taken enough of th
Young Napoleon's timidity and new generals would no
take over the North's army. McClellan went on to mal
himself a political nuisance. He ran as the Democrat
candidate for president in 1864, but, fortunately for th
Union, he failed to unseat Lincoln. To his dying day th
Young Napoleon would defend his appalling leadershi
but the truth is that with McClellan's dismissal the rebe
lost one of their strongest military assets.

The story of the Lost Order is famous. No one knov
how the copy was lost, and after the war, when survivo

onducted endless autopsies on their campaigns, everyone
nvolved denied any knowledge of the order. All that we
now is that the two soldiers from the 27th Indiana regiment found the order wrapped around three cigars and
ts discovery was enough to prod McClellan out of his
ustomary caution. If the order had not been found, Lee
vould probably have reached the Susquehanna as he
lanned, but once his strategy had been revealed the
nvasion was doomed. The two soldiers who found
he order, Bloss and Mitchell, were both wounded in the
ornfield.

The fight in the cornfield and the battle for the sunken
ane were the two bloodiest episodes in the battle, with
he struggle for the Rohrbach Bridge (now named the
3urnside Bridge) coming close behind. To walk the terrain
oday is to marvel at the bravery of men who could attack
cross such open country in the face of terrible fire. The
attlefield is well preserved, though the East and West
Woods are much shrunken from their former sizes. A road,
eavily lined with regimental memorials, now runs south
f the cornfield while an observation tower stands at the
ogleg corner of the sunken lane. Anyone wanting to
now more about the campaign and battle should read
tephen Sears's *Landscape Turned Red*, a book that was
onstantly by my side during the writing of *The Bloody
Ground* and, to my mind, is the finest book on a single
Civil War battle, maybe on any nineteenth-century battle,
ver written.

Antietam was indeed a ghastly affair. The North was
adly led and its men's bravest efforts were wasted, but the
ebel retreat afforded President Lincoln the opportunity to
roclaim a victory and, in its wake, to issue his Emanci-
ation Proclamation. The war, which had been ostensibly
bout states' rights, was now firmly a moral campaign to

abolish slavery. But to proclaim the slaves free was one thing, to liberate them was another, and the road to Richmond would prove to be hard and long. Lee had been rebuffed at Antietam, but he was far from beaten. Starbuck will march again.